CADMIAN'S
⊀ CHOICE ⊁

The Fifth Book of the Corean Chronicles

L. E. Modesitt, Jr.

TOR®
fantasy

A TOM DOHERTY ASSOCIATES BOOK
NEW YORK

This is a work of fiction. All the characters, organizations, and events portrayed in this book are either products of the author's imagination or are used fictitiously.

CADMIAN'S CHOICE: THE FIFTH BOOK OF THE COREAN CHRONICLES

Copyright © 2006 by L. E. Modesitt, Jr.

Edited by David G. Hartwell

A Tor Book
Published by Tom Doherty Associates, LLC
175 Fifth Avenue
New York, NY 10010

www.tor-forge.com

Tor® is a registered trademark of Tom Doherty Associates, LLC.

ISBN-13: 978-0-7653-5467-9
ISBN-13: 0-7653-5467-5

First Edition: April 2006
First Mass Market Edition: June 2007

Printed in the United States of America

0 9 8 7 6 5 4 3 2

Praise for the Corean Chronicles

Soarer's Choice

"A thunderous, satisfying climax . . . Modesitt's panoramic, battle-filled final installment ranks among his best work." —*Publishers Weekly*, starred review

"The characters have become more fascinating with each novel; moreover, this one includes even more action than either of its predecessors . . . which contributes mightily to bringing the adventures of Dainyl, Alector of Corus, and Mykel, an officer in the native military corps, to a stunning conclusion while leaving enough unanswered questions for many more Corean stories." —*Booklist* (starred review)

Cadmian's Choice

"Vividly imagined . . . well-crafted fifth volume of [Modesitt's] Corean Chronicles." —*Publishers Weekly*

"Dedicated Modesitt fans will anxiously await the next installment." —*VOYA*

Alector's Choice

"Modesitt's fourth entry in his Corean series (after 2004's *Scepters*) contains plenty of fine world-building and intelligently developed magic. Modesitt fans, knowing what they're in for, will find reaching the end of the challenging fantasy well worth the effort." —*Publishers Weekly*

"Corus is a fascinating land, full of both new and ancient magic, and the inhabitants are possibly the most fascinating of all, with complex motivations underpinning their every action." —*Romantic Times BOOKreviews*

Scepters

"In the trilogy . . . Modesitt has portrayed Alucius's development as both man and soldier and created a world original in its details but familiar in the cussedness of its inhabitants, human and nonhuman. It's a notable achievement." —*Booklist*

Darknesses

"A superb fantasy . . . a strong epic fantasy that will have the audience wondering where the author will take them next." —*The Midwest Book Review*

Legacies

"L. E. Modesitt, Jr. uses his fabulous world-building skills to introduce a new fantasy world of ancient magic. . . . Strange creatures or supernatural beasts are glimpsed but not yet explained. . . . An intriguing study in contrasts with its elements of Talented vs. normal, female vs. male leadership, prosperity vs. poverty." —*Romantic Times BOOKreviews*

"Offers us strong characters, a brand-new world with its own subset of peoples, magical beings, and beasties."

—*SFRevu.com*

For Carol Ann

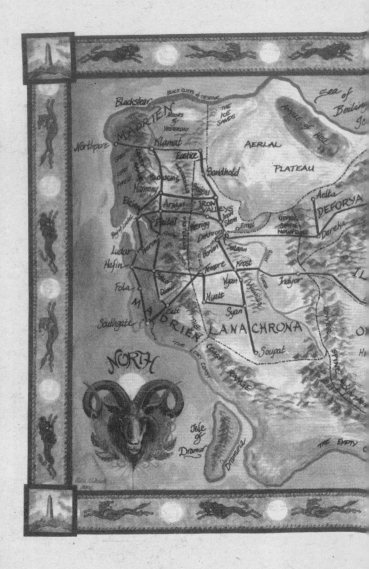

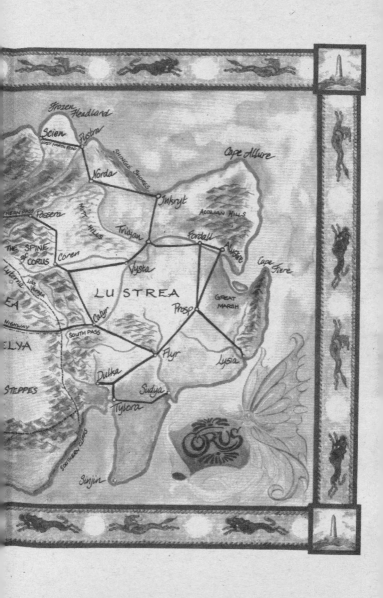

ALECTORS OF ACORUS

KHELARYT   Duarch of Elcien

    ZELYERT   High Alector of Justice
    CHEMBRYT   High Alector of Finance
    ALSERYL   High Alector of Transport

SAMIST   Duarch of Ludar

    RUVRYN   High Alector of Engineering
    JALORYT   High Alector of Trade
    ZUTHYL   High Alector of Education

BREKYLT   High Alector of the East [Alustre]

ASULET   Senior Alector—Lyterna
PAEYLT   Senior Engineer—Lyterna

SHASTYLT   Marshal of Myrmidons
DAINYL   Submarshal of Myrmidons—West [Elcien]
ALCYNA   Submarshal of Myrmidons—East [Alustre]
DHENYR   Colonel of Myrmidons—Operations [Elcien]
NORYAN   Majer of Myrmidons, deputy to Alcyna

Table Cities
[Recorders of Deeds]

Elcien [Chastyl]	Lytera [Myenfel]	Norda [Kasyst]
Ludar [Puleryt]	Tempre [Patronyl]	Prosp [Noryst]
Alustre [Zorater]	Hyalt [Rhelyn]	Blackstear [Delari]
Dereka [Jonyst]	Soupat [Nomyelt]	Faitel [Techyl]
Lysia [Sulerya]	Dulka [Deturyl]	

The young choose once, choose twice, even thrice,
and never ever seek or ask advice.
The older wiser landers ask a friend, someone wise,
but never seem to do as he'd advise.

So choose as if an unwise choice would kill,
because, when one expects it least, it will.

1

Mykel leaned forward on the ancient chair in the officers' mess, finishing rubbery egg toast a good glass before morning muster, thinking about how much more training his battalion needed, and debating whether he should extend the mounted unit maneuvers practice another week. Another ten days *might* help, if he canceled end-day passes. He shook his head. That would be too hard on both mounts and morale. He'd known that rebuilding Third Battalion would be difficult and take time, but he had his doubts about whether he'd be allowed that time.

Captain Vield walked through the doors to the mess and straight toward Mykel.

Mykel offered a pleasant smile, although he distrusted the purposeful stride of the captain, not personally, but because Vield was the colonel's adjutant. The captain's aura was a golden brown that suggested a background in the Lanachronan farming district. Mykel silently warned himself, far from the first time, not to comment on what the aura revealed. He kept reminding himself because his growing sense of the depth of life and its ties to the land was so new, and he had yet to get adjusted to it—or to know truly its extent. He'd always had an extraordinarily good sense of aim with a rifle, but the seeing of auras was all too recent. From what he'd overheard, that sort of talent was something like what the alectors were supposed to have, and the last thing he needed was to have an alector examining his abilities, not that anyone had ever suggested that. Still . . . he had the feeling that concealing the ability was for the best, especially where alectors were concerned.

"Majer, sir?"

"Yes, Captain?"

"Colonel Herolt would like a moment of your time before muster, sir. At your earliest convenience."

"I was just finishing, Captain." Mykel stood, glancing around the mess. The plastered walls had once been white, but time and decades of food preparation had turned them a light beige. Even the yearly whitewash succumbed to the underlying beige within a few weeks.

The only officer in the mess from Third Battalion was Captain Culeyt, and he was eating with one of his former comrades—an undercaptain from Fourth Battalion. Rhystan had not eaten yet, nor had any of Mykel's undercaptains.

Mykel could sense Vield's eyes following him as he left the mess. Since the campaign in Dramur, Mykel had been far more aware of others' feelings about him—or their scrutiny—as a result of the life-sensing that was a complement to his vision and not restricted to where his eyes focused. He crossed the stone-paved courtyard in the light before dawn, making his way to the regimental headquarters building.

The outer anteroom was empty, and the door to the colonel's study was ajar.

"Majer Mykel, come on in. Close the door behind you."

Colonel Herolt did not rise when Mykel stepped into the study, but merely gestured for him to take a seat. "How are you this morning? How are you coming with getting Third Battalion back into shape?"

"We're working at it, sir."

"I've noticed." Herolt paused. "I'd like to give you more time, but we don't have it." His eyes fixed on Mykel. "We've received two sets of orders from Myrmidon headquarters."

"Yes, sir." Mykel smiled politely, waiting. From the earlier conversation with the colonel when Mykel had been given command of the Third Battalion, Mykel knew that whatever mission was assigned to Third Battalion would be difficult.

"Fourth Battalion will be going to Iron Stem to maintain order there after all the difficulties. I had thought about sending you and Third Battalion, but the other requirement seems particularly suited to your capabilities, Majer. Second Battalion is returning from the grasslands, and reports permanent casualties over thirty percent. Fifth Battalion is still operating out of Northport, and Sixth Battalion is finishing up the relocation of the Squawts from north of the Vedra. That doesn't leave me—or you—much choice."

Mykel nodded, waiting. A year earlier, he would have asked for details immediately and inquired about the high casualties taken by Second Battalion. One thing he had learned was that such inquiries would not be answered, and would only irritate the colonel.

"Majer Hersiod and I will be briefed by the Marshal of Myrmidons tomorrow about Iron Stem. It's a more delicate . . . situation."

"Yes, sir." Mykel understood. He didn't like what Herolt was suggesting—that Mykel was lacking in finesse and just about everything besides battlefield and anti-insurgent tactics—but there was little enough he could or should say.

Herolt smiled again. "There are armed groups in the south similar to the Reillies, and they have been causing trouble in the hills west of Hyalt."

Hyalt? That was about as far as one could get from anywhere, even more isolated in some ways than Dramur, Mykel reflected.

"The leader and the worst of the troublemakers were handled by a Myrmidon squad several weeks ago, but the others have gone to ground and scattered throughout the region. This is similar to what you encountered in Dramur, but on a smaller scale. You should be able to handle it, while completing your retraining and rebuilding Third Battalion."

"Do we have any information on the troublemakers, sir?"

"Very little. The High Alector of Justice believes that

stronger local control is necessary in the area, and part of your deployment will require that you facilitate the rebuilding of a local Cadmian garrison there. There was only a small local garrison there. It was scarcely more than a patroller outpost, and the rebel elements wiped them out.

"Third Battalion will take a transport ship to Southgate first. There you will oversee the remainder of the training of two companies going to Hyalt. They're locally recruited Cadmians. The officers and squad leaders will come from the contingent in Southgate, but you will be in charge, Majer. You will continue training them on the ride to Hyalt. You're expected to arrive there around the first week of summer. While you are pacifying the rebels, you will supervise the rebuilding of the garrison in a larger and more permanent locale and install the local Cadmian cadre there. You're to have Third Battalion ready to ride out a week from Octdi. You'll embark from the Elcien pier. . . ."

Mykel listened as the colonel went on to outline the schedule and the details of the embarkation plan.

". . . and now you know what I do, Majer." Herolt stopped and looked at Mykel.

"Do we know to what degree the locals supported the rebels?"

"The local merchants and crafters were the ones who reported the rebel activity and who requested assistance in establishing a large local patrol force. The High Alector was reluctant to create a large locally controlled peacekeeping force, and that's why a local Cadmian garrison will be established."

Mykel kept an attentive expression in place, walling away his consternation. The ride from Southgate to Hyalt would take between two and three weeks. Spring had begun two weeks earlier, and that meant he would have less than a month to work with the new Cadmians before they began the ride to Hyalt—and that was if Third Battalion embarked on the Duarches' transport within the week. Hyalt didn't sound that different from Dramur, except that he wouldn't have to deal with a prison mine and independent local seltyrs. But then, he suspected there would be something else. There always was.

As the most junior battalion commander, he had known that he would get the least-agreeable deployments and duties, but more than half the rankers in Third Battalion were little more than recruits themselves, and three of his company commanders were junior undercaptains.

"I did mention the sort of duties that would fall to Third Battalion, Majer, did I not?"

"Yes, sir."

"Do you have any other questions?"

That was a perfunctory question, Mykel knew, because the colonel had already indicated that he had provided all he knew—or would say. Still . . . "If you obtain any additional information or briefing materials, sir, I would very much appreciate being able to study them."

"Anything we get, Majer, you'll certainly see." Herolt smiled and stood. "I'm expecting Majer Hersiod, to tell him about his assignment to Iron Stem."

With a nod, Mykel slipped out of the colonel's study and made his way to the north wing of the building and his own, far smaller study. He did not see Hersiod, and that was probably for the best. He also hadn't liked the almost casual way that the colonel had dismissed the high casualties inflicted on Second Battalion, although the grassland nomad brigands were reported to be far better horsemen than the mounted rifles. In the past, from what he recalled, the Myrmidons had dealt with them, but it was clear that had changed, and he doubted he would find out why any time soon, because Third Battalion would have left Elcien before Second Battalion returned and the colonel wasn't about to answer questions from Mykel that didn't pertain to Third Battalion. Not for the first time, Mykel wished that he had access to one of the rumored Tables of the alectors, the ones that were supposed to show what happened anywhere on Corus.

While he waited for his officers, Mykel unrolled the maps until he found the one that showed the southwestern areas of Corus, from Southgate to Soupat and north to Krost and the west to Hafin. After unrolling the map and securing the corners with lead map weights, he took out the calipers and measured the distance from Southgate to Zalt and then north to Tempre and back south to Hyalt. Six hundred twenty vingts, roughly, or more than two long weeks, at least twenty days on the road. Given that, he could understand the need for a larger permanent garrison in Hyalt, but he had to wonder why one had not been established earlier.

As always, Rhystan was the first to arrive.

"Good morning, sir." Rhystan's deference had concerned Mykel at first when he had first taken command of Third Battalion. Rhystan had been senior to him when they had both been captains, but Mykel hadn't been about to argue when the Marshal of Myrmidons and the High Alector of Justice had promoted him to majer over Rhystan. The senior captain in Third Battalion, Rhystan commanded Sixteenth Company.

"Good morning." Mykel gestured to the center chair across the desk.

"Swerkyl said that the colonel received a dispatch early this morning—well before breakfast, delivered by pteridon."

"You know things before I do." Mykel laughed easily. "Did Swerkyl know what was in it?"

"He never does. He just assumes the worst." A wry smile appeared on Rhystan's thin lips, then vanished. "How bad is it?"

"We had two choices—either go and do patrol duty in Iron Stem . . ." Mykel paused. ". . . or what we got, and that's another bunch of rebels in the hills, this time in Hyalt."

"From what I heard from Clensdyf about the Iron Valleys, the colonel was kind."

"Fourth Battalion is going to Iron Stem." Mykel stopped and gestured for Culeyt to enter the study. Behind him were the three undercaptains. He waited until all five officers in their maroon-and-gray uniforms were seated in the small study that had once been Majer Vaclyn's and was now assigned to him. In the center was Rhystan. To his right was Culeyt, who had been recently promoted from undercaptain and transferred from Fourth Battalion to take over Fourteenth Company. Loryalt, Fabrytal, and Dyarth were all undercaptains. Fabrytal was the most junior, a former senior squad leader from Fourth Battalion, but he was commanding Fifteenth Company, Mykel's former command and the only company besides Sixteenth Company that had come out of the Dramurian campaign largely intact. Fourteenth Company had been left with a core of some forty seasoned rankers, but Thirteenth and Seventeenth Companies had been effectively wiped out, necessitating their re-formation with a majority of recruits and only a handful of experienced rankers pulled from elsewhere in the regiment.

Mykel waited for a moment. "First off, I'm changing the drills for the next week. We'll be moving out to the broken-ground training area from now on. We'll be working on tactics against irregulars."

The red-haired Loryalt raised his eyebrows, but did not speak.

Rhystan saw the expression, and the faintest smile crossed his thin lips.

"I can see you have a question, Loryalt," Mykel observed.

"Ah . . . no, sir."

Mykel laughed.

So did Rhystan.

"You're wondering why we're moving onto broken-terrain training when Thirteenth, Fourteenth, and Seventeenth Companies still are not up to standards in field drills." Mykel's words were an exceedingly charitable assessment of the three companies, mainly troopers barely more than recruits with squad leaders who had mostly been rankers promoted earlier than what would have been normal. "First, the break will do your men good. Second, we've gotten orders."

"So soon?" murmured Fabrytal almost inaudibly.

"The Myrmidons smashed some rebels in Hyalt, but not all of them. We're being sent to finish the job. That includes training some local Cadmians in Southgate and on the ride from there to Hyalt. They'll be manning a new garrison in Hyalt, and in addition to running down the remaining rebels, we get to supervise building the garrison and setting up the local structure there." Mykel shook his head. "I know. They're calling it a local garrison, but they're taking recruits from Southgate. Officers and squad leaders, too."

"The hardasses, probably," suggested Rhystan.

"Almost certainly," Mykel agreed. "The colonel emphasized that Third Battalion was in charge."

"When do we leave, sir?" asked Culeyt.

"A week from Octdi, from Elcien. . . ." Mykel went on to explain the schedule. As he did, he could only hope that he and his captains could make the next two weeks as effective as possible in improving the readiness and skills of Third Battalion.

2

Submarshal Dainyl looked out through the window of his study, out across the front courtyard of Myrmidon headquarters in Elcien. For a Londi, the first day of the week, the weather had been less than promising all day, and by midafternoon a light and cold spring rain fell from low gray clouds. His right arm and left leg still ached slightly, a reminder that they had not healed fully. Through Talent, both his and Lystrana's, in another few days he would be close to being completely healed, but he was not going to be staying in Elcien so long as he would have preferred.

The rain continued to fall heavily enough that he could not see beyond the walls of the compound to the towers that flanked the Palace of the Duarch to the east. When he'd been a colonel and the operations chief, he'd had a study with a view of the rear courtyard, and the flight stage where he'd been able to see the pteridons take off and land. He still missed being a flying officer. He supposed he always would.

His eyes dropped to the stack of reports on the polished wood of the table desk before him. Colonel Dhenyr had brought them in less than half a glass before, just when Dainyl had *thought* he'd managed to get current on everything. He slowly picked up the top report and began to read. He needed to get through the stack, because he would be leaving on Tridi morning on his trip to Alustre. That gave him just two days to catch up on everything. The topmost quintal report was from Captain Fhentyl, the commanding officer of the Myrmidon Fifth Company in Dereka.

Dainyl hurried through the text, looking to see if any more skylances had vanished, but Fhentyl's report stated that all weapons and equipment were present and in working order. Dainyl nodded. The last thing he wanted to discover was that more skylances—or pteridons—had vanished. For the moment, at least, the ancients remained quiet. How long they would remain inactive was another question.

He set aside the Fifth Company report and lifted the next one—Sixth Company at Lyterna. All was satisfactory there as well. As he set that report atop the Fifth Company report, a tall figure appeared in his study doorway—Marshal Shastylt.

"Dainyl . . . if you would join me in my study." The marshal was a typical alector in general appearance, somewhat over two and a half yards in height, with shimmering jet black hair, deep-set violet eyes that dominated, a strong nose, and an alabaster complexion.

"Yes, sir." Dainyl set aside the report and rose, following his superior officer out of the study and down the corridor to the end. He did close the study door behind him after he entered. Shastylt always preferred complete privacy when addressing his subordinates. Dainyl had learned that quickly years earlier when he had been promoted from command of First Company to the head of operations.

As usual, Marshal Shastylt studied Dainyl as he entered Shastylt's spaces. The marshal's violet eyes were unblinking, his alabaster face smooth and pleasant, and a faint smile played over his lips. He seated himself and gestured for Dainyl to take one of the chairs across the table desk from him.

"Are you ready to go to Alustre on Tridi? The Highest asked about that this morning."

"Yes, sir." Dainyl kept his Talent shields tight and high, as he always did with the marshal and the High Alector of Justice. Once he had returned from resolving the rebellion in Dramur, he had hoped for more than a few weeks with Lystrana before heading to Alustre, since he and his wife had had little time together over much of the last year. Yet he knew that spring was the best time for him to be away from headquarters, since the indigens and landers usually were more occupied with their own affairs, especially those in the outlying regions where trouble seemed to brew. "After Alustre, I'll visit a few other eastern areas, unannounced, as we discussed. While I'm there, is there anything else you'd like me to look into?"

"No. Don't spend too much time in the other cities, Alustre is most important. Tyanylt had planned to visit Alustre before his untimely death and the . . . difficulties in Iron Stem and Dramur. High Alector Zelyert has always been concerned that those in Alustre might develop a different interpretation of the plans of the Archon for Acorus. Unfortunately, the Recorders of Deeds can only use the Tables to view landers and indigens or physical events. Periodic visits to alectors and frequent personal communications remain one of the few reliable keys to assuring that all alectors are working toward the same goal in the same fashion."

The skills of the Recorders had only been revealed to

Dainyl after he had become a submarshal, and he was just as glad they were unable to view alectors—or he had been until he had discovered some very real disadvantages for him personally. He nodded. "I remain concerned about the losses of pteridons—and about the loss of the Cadmian company on its relocation from Scien. Isolated losses of pteridons in high and cold areas where the ancients still have their portals—"

"We don't know that those are portals, Submarshal, not for certain."

"No, sir." Dainyl offered an agreeable smile. He wasn't about to reveal the extent of his Talent, not after years of keeping that hidden. "But I did observe the cave with the stone mirror in Dramur from a pteridon, and upon two occasions, there was an ancient present. When I landed, no one was there. There was no exit from the cave, and the mirror was placed where it would have been difficult if not impossible to climb down, and especially without being observed."

"They might have other abilities."

"That is certainly possible, sir. But when in doubt, I tend to follow the *Views of the Highest*."

"Ah, yes. Well . . . I will be spending much of the next few days with the High Alector and possibly the Duarches. Because I may not be here immediately before you depart, convey my best wishes to Submarshal Alcyna, and, should you see him, to High Alector Brekylt."

"He's been the Highest of the East for as long as I can recall."

"Twenty-some years. It may be time for a change, but that is the decision of the Archon and the Duarches. He is one of the oldest alectors outside of Lyterna."

"He must know a great deal." Dainyl briefly thought about asking, *Just as Submarshal Tyanylt was?* But the question would have served no purpose except to reveal that Dainyl knew more than Shastylt thought he did, particularly about the circumstances of Tyanylt's death . . .

and Dainyl was well aware that Shastylt already harbored suspicions about Dainyl.

"That he does. He is cautious, and he and Submarshal Alcyna have worked closely together over the past ten years."

That was all Shastylt really had to say to confirm what Dainyl suspected—and why he was being sent to Alustre so soon after having been promoted to submarshal.

"Did High Alector Brekylt ever serve as a Myrmidon?"

Shastylt laughed. "That was not one of his qualifications. He was the High Alector of Trade in Ludar. His predecessor suggested that the Duarchy in Ludar be moved to Alustre, but nothing came of that after Viorynt's Table accident, and Brekylt was appointed the High Alector of the East."

"I remember something about that." Dainyl recalled that the Highest of the East had suffered a fatal translation mishap using a Table to return to Elcien. That had occurred years ago, when Dainyl had been a junior captain in Lysia. With what Shastylt had just revealed, Dainyl doubted that the "mishap" had been coincidental in the slightest degree. "I can see why you feel communications with Alustre are most important."

"I thought you might once I mentioned the history." Shastylt's tone was dry. "Distance and time have a way of blurring matters."

"Does Alcyna have a husband? I don't recall anything about that."

"No. She has always steered clear of obvious personal commitments."

And that was doubtless how she had become a submarshal, reflected Dainyl, before he went on. But then, Shastylt had separated from his wife years before, long before she had removed herself to Sinjin, and the marshal had followed that same pattern of avoiding deep personal commitments.

"I've met Captain Josaryk before," Dainyl said. "He seems straightforward enough. What about Majer Noryan? Is there anything I should know about him?"

"He's been in command of Third Company for almost five years. He was transferred from Seventh Company in Dulka something like seven years ago. Alcyna promoted him to majer three years ago, insisting that his value merited that."

"You had some concerns about that, sir?"

"I did discuss it with the High Alector of Justice, but we decided that Alcyna had a valid point, although no one really knew much about Noryan." Shastylt's increasingly drier tone suggested to Dainyl that the decision had not been the marshal's, but that of the High Alector.

Abruptly, the marshal stood. "It's getting late, and the High Alector is expecting me to join him to brief the Duarch on the situation in Hyalt."

"You don't think we'll need to send a squad of Myrmidons back down there?" Dainyl rose quickly.

"I think the Cadmians will be sufficient." Shastylt shrugged. "If not, we can have a squad there in less than two days." He smiled. "I probably won't see you much in the next few days. I wish you well in preparing to visit Alustre."

"Yes, sir." Dainyl returned the smile, then turned and left the marshal's study.

Although he'd already briefed Colonel Dhenyr on what the operations chief would be covering for him, Dainyl still had another six quintal reports to read before he felt he could leave headquarters for the day. He was still struggling to get matters in order before he left, and wondering if two days would be enough.

3

Dainyl sat in the dim warmth of the corner of the sitting room on the main floor of the house, his half-sipped brandy on the side table that separated him from Lystrana. He shifted his weight, then settled back into the large upholstered chair that would have swallowed even the tallest of landers. Once the serving girls had left for their quarters after cleaning up the evening meal, Lystrana had blown out the wall lamps. The green carpet looked more like dark gray, even to the night-sight of an alector.

He glanced at his wife. In the dimness, the alabaster skin of her face shone below the shimmering black hair that was the mark of all alectors—except the truly ancient ones.

Lystrana smiled, warmly, but faintly. "You're worried about going to Alustre tomorrow."

"Wouldn't you be?" Dainyl laughed softly. "We've lost six pteridons in less than two seasons. With only eight companies of Myrmidons, that's a concern, especially if the ancients are planning something. All but two have been lost east of the Spine of Corus, and that's under Alcyna's jurisdiction. Do you think she and Brekylt will be pleased to see me, especially under those conditions?"

"You've never met her, have you?"

"The last time I was in Alustre was something like thirty years ago as a captain. She was a senior majer, and not interested in a former ranker who would never be more than a captain."

Lystrana laughed. "She'll have to talk to you now. You're her superior."

"Technically, we're equals." He reached out and lifted the goblet, inhaling the aroma of the Syan Amber before taking a small sip and savoring it.

"You've been designated as Shastylt's successor."

"That can always change. Tyanylt was his successor." Dainyl did not have to emphasize the irony of his words.

"They won't replace you immediately. They need you as an example."

"Ah, yes, the alector who rose through the ranks. I could almost do without that, except that you're right. It would look untoward if anything happened to me immediately, unless, of course, it could be attributed to Alcyna and Brekylt."

"You think that Zelyert and Shastylt worry about Brekylt attempting to replace them?" asked Lystrana softly.

"They're worried, and because Zelyert's recorder can't tell what alectors are doing, I'm their stalking pteridon."

"No recorder can use a Table to view Talent, except an alector standing before a Table and using it. I certainly wouldn't want them using one to watch us." Lystrana gave a mock shudder.

"For all that," Dainyl went on, "I'm not certain that it's just that they think Alcyna and Brekylt want to replace or remove them."

"What other reason could there be?"

"What if they don't want the Master Scepter to be transferred to Acorus? And Brekylt does? Or has proof that's what they intend?"

"You don't believe that . . . ?"

"I don't know, but I should have considered the possibility sooner. Zelyert has stressed the fragility of the ecology here and the slowness of lifeforce growth. He's truly concerned about that, for whatever reasons he may have, and he's hinted that lifeforce growth on Efra has been far easier and more productive than here on Acorus. He and the marshal disagreed with Tyanylt, and when I met with the Duarch, he said that Shastylt and Zelyert did not see everything, although they thought they did. Khelaryt also said that there was great danger in not transferring the Master Scepter here, because those who controlled Efra were even more calculating than those who claimed to serve him."

"If what Khelaryt says is true, that is a frightening prospect."

"I don't think the Duarch was mistaken about any of that, even if he is shadowmatched to the needs of the Archon. I think he struggles against the shadowmatch conditioning."

"Anyone with Talent so great could not help but do so, yet the Duarches have such power that some restraint is necessary." Lystrana sipped from her goblet. "There are so many currents beneath everything, and I fear they are strengthening."

"Can you tell me how? Or why?" Dainyl looked through the darkness at his wife, an alectress perhaps more powerful than he was by virtue of her position as the chief assistant to the High Alector of Finance in Elcien.

"We've talked about it, dearest, over and over. Lifeforce on Ifryn is fading rapidly. There are fewer alectors on each world than the last, and yet the lifeforce needs are higher. I've heard rumors that more senior alectors are trying the long translation from Ifryn. My highest has reported that several wild translations have translated into Table chambers across Corus."

"What does a wild translation look like?"

"Anything . . . half alector, half sandox, or part pteridon. Those are the commonest ones. The worse appear away from the Tables, anywhere on the world, and then vanish within a glass, their lifeforce spent. Those who almost make the translation appear in a Table chamber, in some monstrous form or another. They seem to be drawn by someone using the Table to travel or communicate."

"Now you tell me." He paused. "Is that why some translations fail? What about the wild translations?"

"That's one reason. Some of the creatures—they're creatures even if they were once like us—survive, and some do not, but those that do must be killed as well, because they have great strength and little intelligence."

Dainyl shook his head. "The more I learn, the more I fear."

"With each new world we transform, as Asulet told you, we lose more knowledge and technology. Here on Acorus, no one realized that the ancients still survived—"

"I wonder about that," mused Dainyl. "I know Asulet is one of the oldest, and he's close to the Duarch of Lyterna, if Lyterna had a Duarch, but he never said that. In fact, he's hinted that everyone knew there were still ancients. Now . . . they might have died out had we not worked to increase and improve the life-forms."

"You think the Archon and his advisors miscalculated?"

"Alectors must never miscalculate, according to the *Views of the Highest*. What is it?" Dainyl frowned, trying to recall the passage. "Ah, yes, we must see the universe as it is, not as we would have it be, and we certainly should not follow the irrational path of calculating based on what we wish an outcome to be."

"You're being cynical."

"A little. But Asulet was very clear in pointing out how many hundreds died establishing Lyterna. Could it not be that there weren't enough alectors with knowledge and not enough lifeforce to find and force an entry to another world? Wide as the universe is, worlds that will support us are few."

"So they avoided the ancients, calculating that they would die off in time?"

"That's my feeling, and that calculation was based on wistful thinking . . . or the irrational as declared in the *Views of the Highest*." Dainyl finished the last of the brandy and set the goblet on the side table. "Now that we've warmed Acorus and life-form mass and lifeforce are increasing once more, the ancients are recovering as well."

"There's not enough lifeforce for us both, is there?"

"You would know that far better than I, dear one," Dainyl demurred.

"Not if we must take another thousand alectors in translation from Ifryn in the next few years. Those are the numbers set forth by the Archon."

Neither mentioned that those thousand Ifrits would be the survivors—and that more than two thousand would perish attempting the long trip through the world translation tubes. Nor did they discuss the thousands of Ifrits who would never have the opportunity even to attempt the arduous Talent-journey from Ifryn to Acorus.

Dainyl shook his head.

"What is it?"

"I don't know exactly what Shastylt has in mind, and whether he's hoping Alcyna will find a way for me to suffer an accident, or for me to force her and Brekylt into unwise actions. I have no certainty about what Shastylt and Zelyert are planning, or whether they're right or the Duarch is. I have no idea whether the ancients are preparing for some sort of attack, where it might occur, and how it might take place—only that they have the ability to destroy weapons and creatures I grew up believing were invincible . . . and yet I'm supposed to project absolute certainty and confidence?"

"Isn't that what shows leadership?" Lystrana asked with a soft laugh. She rose from her chair and extended a hand in invitation.

Hand in hand, they went up the stairs to their bedchamber.

Later, as he lay beside the sleeping Lystrana in the darkness, he could sense, ever more strongly, the lifeforce of their daughter within Lystrana. Were all unborn children so strong in potential Talent? Or was he sensing what he hoped, rather than what was? What did the future hold for Kytrana? Or was that, as well, all too dependent upon what he did in the seasons and years ahead?

He looked up through the darkness at the ceiling overhead.

4

Dainyl supposed he could have requested the duty coach to take him from the house to the Hall of Justice where he would begin his translation to Alustre, but he felt that was an abuse of position. Every morning Dainyl was in Elcien, a hacker named Barodyn—an indigen, of course—drove Dainyl to Myrmidon headquarters. Lystrana had calculated that the three coppers each way were far cheaper than having a personal carriage, what with the stable and horse and driver that would have been required.

When Dainyl stepped through the gates of the front courtyard on Quattri morning, two glasses earlier than usual, in the gray of dawn, he wore the traveling uniform of a Myrmidon officer—a blue flying jacket over a shimmercloth tunic of brilliant blue, both above dark gray trousers, with a heavy dark gray belt that held his lightcutter sidearm. His collar bore the single stars of a submarshal. He carried a set of saddlebags that held a spare uniform and personal toiletries.

The morning sun had not yet climbed barely above the dwellings to the east, and possibly not even above the waters of the back bay separating the isle from the mainland, when the hacker reached back from his seat and opened the carriage door. "Good morning, Submarshal, sir."

"Good morning, Barodyn." Dainyl climbed into the coach and closed the door, settling onto the hard seat as the hacker eased the coach away from the mounting block.

The driver guided the coach through two turns and headed west on the boulevard, bordered by the public gardens of the Duarch. The main boulevard extended from east to west, down the middle of the isle from the bridge in the east to the gates at the Myrmidon compound at the west end of the isle.

As always, Dainyl spent a moment taking in the gardens, although they looked bleak in the early spring, despite the precisely trimmed hedges and stone paths. The fountains flowed, but the topiary that included a lifelike pteridon, a rearing horse, and a long hedge sculpted into the likeness of two sandoxen and a set of transport coaches looked more like a framework of sticks. There was only a hint of the greenery that would fill out the images when the warmer days of late spring finally arrived.

Ahead to his left was the Palace of the Duarch, south of the boulevard. Flanking the palace were two towers— pointed green cylinders that almost melded with the silver-green sky to the west. Across the boulevard from the palace and the towers was the Hall of Justice, whose golden eternastone glowed even before the morning light struck it.

Dainyl nodded solemnly. He might have smiled had he not been worried about the journey ahead. For him, Table travel was too new to be taken casually, especially not when Table "accidents" had been known to happen to those out of favor with the most powerful of the High Alectors.

Still, he reflected, as he often did, that Elcien was indeed a marvel, built on an island of solid stone. The stone-walled shops with their perfect tile roofs were set around market squares that held everything produced on Acorus. Vessels from across the world disgorged their goods from the wharves and docks on the southern shore into endless warehouses.

The hacker eased the coach to a halt. "Submarshal, sir?"

After he stepped out, Dainyl extended two coppers, plus an extra copper, although the trip was only half the distance of his normal morning ride.

"Thank you, sir."

As the first rays of the morning sun struck his back, carrying his gear, Dainyl marched up the wide golden marble steps of the Hall of Justice toward the goldenstone pillars that marked the outer rim of the receiving rotunda. Above the architrave connecting the pillars—thirty yards above the polished stone pavement—was a frieze depicting the aspects of justice conveyed by the Duarchy. From the cornice over the frieze angled a mansard roof of man-sized green tiles glinting metallically in the early light.

Dainyl crossed the receiving rotunda, far too early in the day for petitioners to have assembled, his boots barely clicking on the octagonal sections of polished gold and green marble. On the far side, he turned left toward a pillar behind and beyond the dais. He summoned a hint of Talent and would have vanished to the sight of those without Talent, had any been present at so early a glass. Then he reached up and turned the light-torch bracket. The solid stone moved to reveal an entry three yards high and one wide, and a set of steps beyond leading downward and lit by light-torches.

The warmer and moister air surrounded him as he stepped through the entry and the stone closed behind him. At the base of the staircase, he turned right along a stone-walled corridor until he reached a doorway on the north side.

A single alectress appeared, glanced at Dainyl, then nodded. "Submarshal. Will we expect you back shortly?"

"Several days, I would judge, at the least. The Marshal and the Highest have requested I go to Alustre."

"Have a good trip, sir." The alectress, an assistant to the High Alector of Justice, stepped back into her study.

Dainyl released the hidden Talent-lock, then opened the door, and closed it behind him, replacing the Talent-lock. He stood in a small foyer, lit by single light-torch, with a second door before him, also with a Talent-lock. A moment later, he released that lock and stepped into the Table chamber, replacing the second lock behind him as well.

The walls of the Table chamber were of white marble, and the floor was of green. Two sets of double light-torches set five yards apart in bronze brackets on each side wall provided the sole illumination. Unlike other Table chambers, the one in the Hall of Justice had no furnishings, just the Table itself. The Table itself looked like any other Table—a square polished stone pedestal in the center of the room that extended a yard above the stone floor. The stone appeared black on the side, but the top surface bore silvery shimmer that was mirror-like. Each side of the table-like pedestal was three yards in length, and because the Table extended below the floor, its actual shape was closer to a cube. Visible only through Talent was the purple glow that emanated from the Table.

After taking a firmer grip on his saddlebags, Dainyl took a long step onto the Table, then a slow and deep breath, concentrating on reaching out with his Talent to the well of darkness below and within the Table. He could feel himself dropping into . . .

. . . *a torrent of turbulent purplish blackness that buffeted him. Intense cold invaded every span of his body, sweeping through his uniform and flying jacket as if he had been unclothed. He saw nothing with his eyes, but reached out with his senses for the dark gray locator, bordered in purple, that identified Alustre. The closest locator was the bright blue of Tempre, and there was also one of crimson gold that beckoned. Dainyl used thought and Talent to press himself toward the more distant wedge of dark gray.*

After what felt like a glass, he began to sense the closeness of the locator wedge he sought, even as other locators swirled by him—wedges of amber, brilliant yellow, green, gray. . . . Well beyond, in a sense he could not have explained, stretched a distant purple-black wedge—the long translation tube back to Ifryn with a sense of distance so overpowering that Dainyl felt almost nauseated.

He continued to concentrate, focusing on the dark gray, now so near—and yet not quite so close as it seemed—before reaching with his Talent to link himself with a line of purple Talent to the dark gray locator wedge that was Alustre. With an abruptness that still nearly stunned him, he felt the dark gray hurtling toward him, even as silver loomed before him, then shattered around him.

Dainyl had to take a lurching step before he regained his Balance. He stood on a Table in another windowless chamber. His entire body shivered, and frost had appeared on his flying jacket and uniform, then vanished, melting as quickly as it had appeared.

Like the Table chamber in Lyterna, the room was empty. Unlike it, there was a set of rich black-and-silver-bordered hangings on the walls, each with a scene hold-

ing an alector. A long black chest was set against the wall
across the Table from the single entrance—a square arch,
in which a solid oak door was set. It was clear that Dainyl
had arrived in the residence and administrative center of
the High Alector of the East.

He stepped off the Table and walked to the archway.
Again, he had to release a Talent-lock before he could
open the door. Outside, in the corridor on each side of the
arch, were two alectors, both wearing black-and-silver
uniforms, rather than the blue-and-gray of Myrmidons.

The guard on the left held a lightning-edged short
sword ready, the weapon used for guard duty inside
buildings. His eyes scanned the uniform and the stars on
Dainyl's collar. Then he said, "Submarshal, sir?"

"I'm here to see Submarshal Alcyna. She is expecting
me."

"Yes, sir. There should be a duty coach at the west portico. If you go to the end of this corridor and take the stairs
there, and then turn right when you reach the main
level . . ."

"Thank you." With a smile, Dainyl departed, but used
his Talent to extend his hearing, hoping to learn something.

". . . wouldn't want to be around headquarters after he
gets there . . ."

"Why not? Submarshals and marshals come and go."

"Most of them worry about the politics, and who's
who. They wouldn't know one end of a skylance from another. He's the one Captain Josaryk was talking about.
Came all the way up from ranker . . . crushed that revolt
in Dramur . . ."

". . . brass bitch won't like that . . ."

Dainyl concealed a wince and kept walking. Although
he couldn't help wondering what the rankers who had
served under him called him behind his back, he wasn't
certain he wanted to know.

The main corridor leading to the west portico was
floored in a shimmering silver-gray marble, the octago-

nal tiles outlined with thin strips of black marble. The walls below the black marble chair railing were also silver-gray marble. Above the railing, the walls were a textured white. At intervals, silver-and-black-bordered hangings decorated the walls, with each tapestry showing a scene from somewhere in the east of Corus.

He heard several children laughing as he passed an open archway. Walking toward him was a slender alector wearing dark silver trousers, a black belt, and a black shimmersilk tunic. The man took in Dainyl's uniform and stars, then nodded politely as he passed.

Dainyl had forgotten how Alustre had affected the silver and black, as opposed to the greens and blues of the west, but the colors took on a new significance in light of Marshal Shastylt's concerns—those both voiced and unvoiced.

At the archway that separated the interior of the residence from the portico stood two alector guards, also attired in black trimmed with silver. Both barely looked at him, but Dainyl was well aware of their scrutiny as he passed and stepped out into the stiff spring breeze. Despite the fact that it was afternoon in Alustre, the air felt cooler than in Elcien, but that was because of the wind, since both had similar climates, even a continent apart.

The pavement of the portico was not marble, but white granite, unyielding underfoot, and the columns were smooth circular pillars, also of white granite, and unadorned, not even fluted.

Dainyl glanced toward the waiting area farther west, then nodded. As the Table guard had said, a duty coach was indeed waiting at the west portico, with the Myrmidon colors on the door. The driver smiled as the submarshal approached.

"Submarshal, sir. I was hoping you'd arrive on my duty." The Myrmidon ranker smiled. "Undercaptain Chelysta is a cousin. If you see her when you get back to Elcien, would you tell her that Granyn sends greetings?"

"I'll be happy to. Are you from Alustre?"

"No, sir. My parents are on the regional alector's staff in Lysia. My mother's sister is Chelysta's mother."

With slightly less than a thousand alectors on Acorus, running across relations was scarcely unheard of. What was unusual was mentioning it, and that suggested that Granyn was new to the Myrmidons. "Is this your first posting?"

"Yes, sir."

Dainyl smiled. "We'd best be going."

"Yes, sir." Granyn grinned.

Before Dainyl entered the coach, he turned and looked back at the residence. Unlike the Palaces of the Duarches in the west, which soared into the silver-green sky, the eastern residence was long and solid, only three stories showing above ground level, with two wings angling from the central rectangular core. The outer walls were of a white granite, reinforced with lifeforce, almost slab-like. The only exposed columns Dainyl had seen were those supporting the roof of the west portico, although, given the symmetry of the residence, there were doubtless columns supporting the east portico as well.

Once he was inside the coach, Dainyl considered—again—what lay ahead. The question was not whether Alcyna and Brekylt were plotting, but what they were plotting.

As he considered what he might do to tease out information, Dainyl watched as young Granyn drove them along the divided boulevard that ran from the hilltop residence overlooking Alustre itself to the ring-road that encircled the main sections of the city. Like the eastern residence itself, Alustre sprawled more than did either Elcien or Ludar, with more space between dwellings and structures—except for the warehouse and commercial area directly around the wharves. The bulk of the city lay east of the river and north of Fiere Sound. While there were piers across the river, they were far smaller, and served mainly the fishing community there.

The eastern Myrmidon headquarters were on a bluff

east of the city proper, and less than a vingt southeast of the park-like grounds surrounding the residence. The walled compound overlooked both the river and the ocean—and the Cadmian compound even farther to the south.

Granyn guided the coach to a smooth halt directly adjacent to the long mounting block serving the headquarters building, also constructed of perfectly cut and fitted white granite, with blackish green roof tiles that shimmered in the midafternoon sun.

As he swung out of the coach, his gear in hand, Dainyl looked up at the driver. "Thank you, Granyn."

"My pleasure, sir." The young alector smiled broadly.

The duty officer was waiting in the entry corridor even before Dainyl stepped into the building. "Submarshal, sir, welcome to the eastern headquarters." She was an undercaptain, and her violet-green eyes met Dainyl's evenly.

"Thank you," he replied gravely.

"Submarshal Alcyna requested that I convey you to her study immediately, sir, but would you like to leave your gear here at the duty desk? I can have it taken to the visiting senior officers' quarters for you."

"I would appreciate that." As he handed her the saddlebags, Dainyl had no doubts that they would be inspected, at least through Talent, but they held nothing beyond necessities. He also reflected that one of the disadvantages of Table travel was that he was totally on his own. Then, that explained, in a way, why the higher alectors were so Talented. No one without Talent-strength could use the Tables and survive. Was his trip to Alustre another test? He repressed a snort. Was there any doubt of that?

He followed the undercaptain down the corridor—which had a green marble floor, the same as headquarters in Elcien, and the first similarity he had noticed.

Stopping short of the open doorway at the very end of the hallway, the undercaptain gestured. "Submarshal Alcyna's study, sir."

Dainyl entered the study, a space even larger than Marshal Shastylt's spaces in Elcien. Except for a single depiction of the city of Alustre—in black ink on white paper and framed in black and silver—the walls were bare. There were no coverings on the polished and shining green marble floor. The main furnishings were the wide ebony table desk, a circular conference table, also of ebony, and an ebony bookcase two yards high and three long. The eight wooden armchairs were all finished in silver, with five set around the conference table, and three before the table desk, with a larger chair set behind the table desk.

Alcyna did rise from behind the table desk, if somewhat belatedly, after Dainyl closed the study door behind him. She was short for an alectress, barely two yards in height, with eyes as black as her hair. Her smile was perfunctory.

"Good afternoon, Alcyna."

"Good afternoon, Dainyl. I cannot say that I'm extraordinarily pleased to see you."

"I understand." Dainyl certainly did. Alcyna had to have felt that she should have been the one tapped to succeed Marshal Shastylt, but that would never happen. In all the centuries the Myrmidons had existed, no alectress had ever risen higher than submarshal, and Alcyna was only the second to hold the rank. He smiled. "And you will understand if I tell you that I was not extraordinarily pleased to have been ordered to Alustre."

He settled into a chair in front of the desk and gestured for her to seat herself behind her desk. His eyes went to the wide south window. "You have a lovely view of the sound."

Alcyna remained standing, looking at Dainyl, then pressing a Talent-probe at him, a probe that was fully as strong as any of Shastylt.

Dainyl merely smiled, letting the line of purple, invisible to any without Talent, sheet away from his shields, even as he gestured once more for her to be seated. For all the power she had displayed, he could sense that Alcyna had held back some of her strength. "I'm not here to deliver orders or bad news or anything like that."

"You have shields worthy of a High Alector, Dainyl. It's too bad you have little else, but that makes you a perfect tool for Zelyèrt and Shastylt." Alcyna finally seated herself.

"You already knew that. Otherwise . . ." He shrugged. "It would have been difficult to cover up my death in your study."

"Better and better." Alcyna laughed.

Dainyl was amazed at the warmth of her laugh, so at odds with the coldness he sensed within her.

"You have learned a great deal from Lystrana, haven't you?" noted Alcyna. "Does she wish to be the first woman to hold the Duarchy?"

"Not any more than do you." Dainyl watched her closely, with both eyes and Talent.

"Oh . . . so she wishes to advance you."

"No more than you wish to advance Brekylt, or . . . perhaps a great deal less."

"Now that we have all that out of the way," she replied brightly, "why are you here? Officially, that is?"

"I told you. Shastylt ordered me to come here and meet with you, and to see what you and the Myrmidons are doing. I also wanted to learn more about the pteridons we've lost in the last two seasons."

"Don't tell me you don't know how that happened, Dainyl." Her voice was mocking, but with a gentleness of tone that was almost disarming. Almost.

"Oh . . . I know that it had to be the ancients. What I was interested in was the circumstances surrounding each loss." As he finished speaking, he could sense both curiosity and disinterest, but he waited for her to reply.

"They were interfering. So I had a squad attack them."

"The ones lost near Scien, you mean? The ones lost over the Spine of Corus were on solo flights."

"If you had Talent other than shields, Dainyl, you would be formidable. But then, if you did, you wouldn't be Shastylt's submarshal."

"Did your squad kill the ancients?"

"In one case, yes. In the other, we think so. There aren't very many left, you know, and each one that we destroy frees more lifeforce for us. I don't know why the Duarches just didn't rid the world of them in the beginning, when they were dying out."

"I would judge they felt it was unnecessary. It still probably is." About that, Dainyl had his doubts, but wanted to see how she reacted.

Alcyna shrugged. "I wanted to see what it would take."

"And . . . was it worth it? To lose two pteridons?"

"No. Not to take out one ancient, but it was useful to learn they cannot stand up to several skylances concentrated on them at once."

As appalled as he was at Alcyna's casual spending of the lost Myrmidons and pteridons, Dainyl could at least understand her reasoning—and that she was telling the absolute truth, at least as she saw it . . . with some reservations.

"There may be hope for you yet, Dainyl. You don't even look shocked. You would have been once, you know."

Dainyl wasn't certain that represented an improvement in his character, but he nodded. "Times and circumstances change."

"I'd be happy to turn all the records of those flights over to you for your inspection."

"I'm certain that they reveal nothing that they should not."

"I imagine your records of what happened in Dramur don't, either."

"How can you say that?" Dainyl grinned. "They're absolutely accurate in what they state."

Alcyna laughed in her misleadingly warm tone. "We must have a leisurely dinner together, the three of us. Brekylt is actually in Dulka today and this evening, but I am certain he would be pleased to have dinner with us tomorrow night. I assume you will be staying for at least a day or two."

"I would be pleased to accept such an invitation. And tomorrow morning, I will take you up on the suggestion that I peruse the records of the encounters with the ancients," replied Dainyl, although he was well aware that Alcyna had not strictly tendered such an offer. "In the meantime, perhaps one of your undercaptains could provide me with a guided tour of the headquarters compound this afternoon. I would not wish to impose upon you unduly."

"You are so thoughtful." Alcyna paused. "Undercaptain Veluara would be pleased to do so, once you have inspected the senior guest quarters. I will send her there to meet you."

"I appreciate that." Dainyl recognized the undercaptain's name as a squad leader in Fourth Company, but he had seen nothing else on her.

Alcyna rose. "I'll walk over to the senior officers' quarters with you."

Dainyl stood, conscious that his left leg was still slightly sore, possibly from the chill of Table travel, and followed Alcyna.

The corridor outside her study remained vacant, and not by coincidence, Dainyl was certain, as she accompanied him back down and through the back archway and double doors.

The flight stage stood in the rear courtyard—equidistant from the back of the headquarters building, the front of the pteridon stages, and the quarters. Only half the pteridons were sunning themselves on the top of their stages, their blue crystal beaks and talons glinting in the afternoon sun.

"Is one of the companies deployed, or are you running dispatches?"

"There are two squads from Third Company temporarily flying out of Norda under Majer Noryan. From there they can cover the area south of Scien, as well as the Northern Pass. We've had reports of brigands along the pass, but so far no one has lost anything. Another squad remains at Coren until the High Alector of Justice is satisfied that situation is fully in control."

"Will it ever be, given the greed of landers?" asked Dainyl.

"Enough so that third squad can return. Possibly within a few weeks." Alcyna started up the outside steps to the upper level of the quarters building.

Dainyl followed her up the stairs and along the railed balcony to the south end of the building.

"You should find these quite comfortable, far better than the quarters of Cadmian officers in Dramur."

"I am certain I will."

An even warmth flowed toward Dainyl as Alcyna opened the quarters door.

"I had the duty staff light the stove in the sitting room," she said. "It is a brisk day, and Table travel can be somewhat . . . chilling."

"You are very thoughtful." Thoughtful—and forewarned by someone of exactly when to expect a traveling submarshal, and that notice had to have been through a Table.

"Undercaptain Veluara will be here shortly. If you discover anything that needs my attention, don't hesitate to ask me."

"From what I have already seen, Alcyna, I doubt that there will be any need to bring anything to your personal attention."

Once Alcyna departed, Dainyl walked through the quarters, taking in the sitting room with the wide window that offered a view of the flight stage, the rear of headquarters, and the greenish waters of the sound beyond the bluff. A wide table desk was set against an inside wall, with a settee and two armchairs positioned so that the heat of the black porcelain stove radiated to all three.

The bedchamber contained an enormous triple-width bed, a chest that would have swallowed without difficulty ten times what Dainyl had brought in his saddlebags.

Again, he observed that all the furniture was either black or silver, or some combination of both. He also noted that his spare uniform had been hung in the oversized armoire, and his toiletries laid out in the bathchamber. His Talent senses suggested that nothing had been altered or searched at length.

After washing up, he returned to the sitting room and settled into one of the armchairs to soak up the warmth while waiting for the undercaptain to appear.

Through the window he could see one of the Duarches' sea vessels headed southeast down the center of the sound toward the ocean. His first impressions suggested that, outwardly, everything was as it should be, and that meant that Alcyna and Brekylt had gone to great lengths to conceal whatever they had in mind.

Was he imagining that?

He shook his head.

5

Under the bright midmorning sun of Tridi—on the warmest day of early spring so far—Mykel shifted his weight in the saddle of the roan. His fingers dropped to his belt, barely brushing the hidden sheath that held the dagger of the ancients—that miniature blade that was not only older, but tougher and harder than any steel forged by men or alectors on Acorus. Mykel had done his best to dismiss the legend that it bore a curse for its possessor, and the belief that the curse and dagger could be released only when the dagger was accepted as a gift by one's worst enemy—one's worst good-hearted enemy at that.

His lips curled. He hadn't realized he'd been that hated when he'd accepted the dagger from the chandler in Jyoha. He hadn't paid for it, now that he recalled what had happened. The chandler had accepted his coins only as a gift to the hungry children of the village. Not that he had felt cursed, not any more than any Cadmian officer, at least. Besides, in a strange way, the dagger reminded him of Rachyla, although he doubted he would ever see the seltyr's green-eyed daughter again. She certainly would not wish to see him, and he doubted he would soon return to Dramur.

He shook his head, then watched from the low rise as Seventeenth Company's third squad rode along a dirt track that resembled all too many roads in the more remote areas of Corus.

"Third squad! On the guide! Firing line to the left! Firing line to the left!" The high-voiced order came from Esceld, the stolid but young squad leader.

The trooper riding guide turned left and halted at the angle that presented the best firing position for the battered straw targets set on stands a hundred yards to the south.

The squad's response was ragged at best.

"Third squad! Fire!"

Instead of a volley that should have been almost synchronized, the rifle reports were even more ragged than the line of twenty-one mounts.

"Stand easy!" ordered Esceld, looking to the older and more grizzled figure mounted to his right.

"Don't fumble with your pieces!" ordered Bhoral. "You rein up in a firing line, with your weapons ready. You fool around with your piece, and Reillies and irregulars will give you your own plot of land."

As he listened to the battalion senior squad leader address Loryalt's third squad, Mykel concealed a grin—and the exasperation beneath. After seeing the problems the undercaptain was having with Seventeenth Company, Mykel had sent Bhoral to help the undercaptain's squad leaders with training.

"Spemat! You want to die now?" continued Bhoral. "You keep that up, and I won't wait for some Reillie to plug you. That's if your mates don't get you first."

The angular redhead flushed and stiffened, but kept his

eyes on the straw targets set on the hillside to the south.

"You think any irregulars are going to wait while you figure out which end of the rifle is the stock and where the trigger is?" demanded Bhoral.

"Third squad! Column by twos! Forward!" ordered Esceld.

After a last glance at third squad, Mykel turned his mount and eased the roan toward the next hill, where Fifteenth Company and Sixteenth Company were practicing marksmanship against weighted sand-glass targets that sprang up from irregular positions. Neither company needed that much maneuvering practice, and Mykel hadn't been that pleased with the marksmanship of any of the companies in Dramur—not when it turned out that he'd accounted for almost a quarter of all the casualties inflicted on the seltyrs' troops by Fifteenth Company.

As he rode over the low hillock to the next terrain maneuvering area, Mykel heard the sound of rifles. Before he had ridden another hundred yards, the firing died away.

Rhystan turned his mount and rode to meet Mykel.

The two reined up well back of Sixteenth Company.

Mykel could hear the voice of Murthyt—the company senior squad leader.

"Remember. You get a moment when no one's firing, and you reload, even if you got a shell or two in the magazine. Might not get a chance later."

"His voice carries," Rhystan said. "Farther than mine."

"How are they doing?"

"Better than when we were preparing for Dramur, Majer." Rhystan offered a tight smile. "Some of them are actually hitting the targets consistently."

"I'm glad to hear that. Sixteenth Company will have to take the lead. I'll be counting on you especially." Mykel was stating the obvious, but he'd learned that what he'd often thought obvious wasn't always to others. "How is Fabrytal doing?"

"He'll be fine. He needs experience, but he's solid, and he's got a good senior squad leader in Chyndylt." Rhystan paused, then asked, "How bad do you think it'll be? Compared to Dramur?"

"Better and worse. The irregulars probably won't have the kind of equipment and mounts the seltyrs' companies did, but the ones that are left have survived an attack by the Myrmidons. They were good enough to wipe out the local garrison. The colonel said it was small and not very well commanded."

"I can't say I understand."

"That they didn't send a battalion with the Myrmidons? I don't, either, except that I don't think they like to mix us. Maybe they worry about the Myrmidons using the skylances on us." Mykel frowned. "I got the impression that they thought the Myrmidons had eliminated the problem."

"Without troops on the ground? It doesn't work that way. Not for long, and then we've got to pick up the pieces later, when the locals think it ought to have been solved, and the rebels or brigands are better prepared."

Mykel laughed, ruefully. "Something like that is always the problem. By the time anyone realizes it's a problem and we get sent . . ."

"Like Dramur," affirmed Rhystan. "Will we have to patrol until they start shooting the way it was there?"

"Not from what the colonel's said, and unless things change, I'll be the senior officer."

"That'll be good." Rhystan paused. "Ah . . ."

"Yes?" Mykel had a good idea what Rhystan had in mind, but he wasn't completely sure. So he waited.

"You led Fifteenth Company from the front, Majer . . ."

Mykel laughed again, with warmth and amusement. "You're being very tactful, Rhystan. I take it that you feel such tactics are not appropriate for battalion commanders?"

"No, sir. We might get stuck with another Majer Vaclyn. Or I might get stuck doing it."

"You'd do fine, but I'd rather not hand you command that way, and I hear what you're saying."

"That could be hard for you, sir, seeing as you're the best shot in the battalion."

Mykel grinned. "I didn't say I wouldn't use my rifle, Captain. I'll try not to use it from the front."

"I won't argue with that, sir." Rhystan laughed softly. "I might remind you, though."

Mykel hoped Rhystan didn't have to, because, if the captain did, one way or another matters would not be what either of them wished. He just smiled. "I'm going to check on Fifteenth Company. You don't need me looking over your shoulder. Carry on."

"Yes, sir."

Mykel eased the roan along the dirt track, thoughts swirling through his mind, the same thoughts he'd had for weeks. He'd been in the Cadmians for ten years, and he'd never seen—or heard of—as much action and unrest as had happened in the last two years. He'd never encountered an ancient before, nor had he ever heard of anyone who had. Yet less than two seasons ago, one had talked to him, insisting that he find his talent to see beyond his eyes or he would perish. That was unprecedented. So was the destruction of two pteridons by the ancients, and the fact that Myrmidon Submarshal Dainyl had avoided explaining the true cause of their destruction.

Now, in less than two weeks, Third Battalion would be headed south, to deal with another rebellion of sorts.

Just what was happening . . . and why?

6

An alector who speaks of choices has no place in the governing of a world, for the very word implies an equality between alternatives, and such choice is an illusion. Thus, the alector either deceives himself or others. If he deceives himself, he will administer badly. If he deceives others, his deception will eventually be discovered, and the anger created by such deception will undo any benefits that may have momentarily accrued.

While each alternative facing an alector may have differing advantages and disadvantages, alternatives are never equal. The task of any high alector is to determine the best of alternatives in light of the desired objective and then implement his decision in the manner most efficacious for its accomplishment.

Those who prattle about choices either lack understanding of the matter before them or seek to deceive others into believing that a true choice between equal alternatives exists. The only choice is between a good alternative and one not so good. An alector who cannot differentiate between such and make such a determination based upon what is and what will be has failed to learn enough to understand the situation before him. If one must decide between dissimilar alternatives, the overall effectiveness of each must be determined, as well as the costs, the timing, and the lifeforce expenditure gained and that required.

In the case of similar alternatives, the same process must obtain. No two pearapples are equal, nor are any two oaks, nor any two steers, nor any two alectors. Nor are any two alternatives. Each alternative has ramifications and outcomes, and those must be studied and determined, in light of what best serves the Archon and the future of all alectors.

Views of the Highest
Illustra
W.T. 1513

7

Undercaptain Veluara knocked on the door to the senior officers' quarters precisely half a glass after Alcyna had departed. As he rose from the chair, Dainyl supposed that there was some significance to the timing, and that he might find it in due course. Then again, given Alcyna's reputation, he might not. He just intended to discover what he could about what was happening in Alustre and the east, then return to Elcien, and report what he had discovered to the marshal. He had few doubts that discovering would be easier than returning, since Alcyna was the type who would want him to know how clever she was before arranging some fatal accident or incident.

Just before he opened the door, he paused. Alcyna might be far smarter than that, but, however she handled it, he doubted that he would have to worry as much on the first day or so. Too early an "accident" would have the marshal and High Alector Zelyert both after her.

Undercaptain Veluara stood tall, nearly as large and as muscular as Dainyl. She wore a flight jacket over her uniform, unfastened, and her eyes were a blackish brown, a color unusual for an alector. She also seemed to be older than the usual undercaptain, although that was not something Dainyl intended to ask or suggest. "Submarshal, sir? Submarshal Alcyna asked me to be your escort for an informal tour."

Dainyl nodded, stepping out onto the balcony and closing the quarters door behind him. "It's kind of you, and I appreciate it."

"Where would you like to begin, sir?"

"With a tour of headquarters here. I am certain everything is in order and as it should be, and I would like to report that to the marshal. I leave the order of inspection to you, Undercaptain."

"I would suggest we begin with the outbuildings, sir. Perhaps the pteridon squares?"

"That would be fine."

Dainyl followed the tall undercaptain down the steps and south across the courtyard of the headquarters compound. Despite her size, her movements were practiced and graceful.

The pteridon squares were identical to those in Elcien, each thirty yards on a side with a massive perch across the roof. The perch was oriented to face the rising sun. Even with only twenty-one pteridons in a company, the space required for each company was considerable.

As he walked down the open area that split the squares of the two companies, past the duty square, Dainyl glanced at the nearest pteridons, those of Fourth Company, presumably third squad, taking in the afternoon sunlight. Their blue crystal eyes held a darkness that had no color, and their long blue crystalline beaks were hard enough to shatter iron. Each blue leathery wing, even folded back against a pteridon's body, was more than ten yards long. The comparatively short legs ended in three crystal claws—two opposed by one, so that a pteridon could perch anywhere or grasp whatever it wanted, given that the claws were as hard as the beak.

"You're a squad leader in Fourth Company. Third squad, as I recall."

"Yes, sir." There was the faintest tone of surprise in her voice, as well as hidden amusement.

"How have you liked serving under Captain Josaryk? You were in Third Company before, weren't you?"

"Captain Josaryk and Majer Noryan are good officers, sir."

"Were you on any of the patrols where the pteridons were lost this past winter?"

Undercaptain Veluara did not reply for the briefest of moments. "That depends on what you mean, sir. We did some of the overflight patrols, but three of the four losses in the west were from Third Company after I left."

"I don't suppose you saw what happened?"

"No, sir."

About that, the undercaptain was telling the truth.

"Have you ever seen one of the ancient ones?"

"Sir? Has anyone? Have you?"

"Since they once inhabited the higher and colder areas, and there are more of those here in the east," replied Dainyl, not answering her question in a fashion similar to the way she had avoided his, "I had thought it might be more likely that you or others in Third and Fourth Company might have seen them."

"I know Major Noryan did, but he said he wasn't able to talk about it. He sent a sealed dispatch to Lyterna, though."

Dainyl did not comment, although he had never seen the report.

At the end of the pteridon squares, the undercaptain turned west. "The armory is on the lower level in the corner here."

"About the ancients," Dainyl prompted.

"Only from a distance, just once, west of Scien, when we were looking for the missing Cadmian company. That was when third squad was relieving second squad. It was just a green globe of light. I could barely make it out, and then it was gone."

From what he could tell through his Talent, Dainyl was fairly certain that she was telling what she had seen— mostly. "The old reports say that they could hover. Could you tell?"

"It looked that way."

"Has anyone found any sign of the Cadmians yet?"

"No, sir. Major Noryan thinks they were caught in a sudden early blizzard. Those can get fierce that far north. If that's what happened, we might find them when all the ice melts. The North Road won't be clear until early summer this year."

"Even though it's eternastone?"

"Yes, sir. That's one reason why the submarshal decided to close the posts at Scien. The town is mostly deserted anyway, except for the fishing crews in the summer, and a handful of indigens who like ice and cold."

"What about Pystra?"

"It's not much better, but it's east of the Frozen Headland, and the harbor's clear of ice most winters."

"Besides the problem in Coren, have you had much trouble with indigen intransigence?"

"There's always someone who tries to get around the Code, thinking that he can get a few more golds, but we do a lot of overflights, looking for patterns that would show life-form abuse or misuse." She paused. "What really happened in Dramur? I don't mean to pry, sir, but the reports we got seemed so strange."

In short, Alcyna wanted to see what Dainyl would reveal to an attractive and attentive undercaptain. "What happened there wasn't life-form abuse, or anything else that could be seen from the air. Some of the local landowners spent years amassing enough golds to bribe an engineer in the rifle manufactory. They were trying to take control of Dramur while still appearing to follow all the provisions of the Code." That was truthful enough, so far as it went. "Dramur is far enough away from any Myrmidon post that what they were doing went undetected for a time. The marshal discovered some aspects of the plan and sent for me. It took two seasons to resolve, and it won't happen again."

Veluara nodded. "You want to see the armory?"

"Every bit of it." Dainyl laughed. "Otherwise, how could I explain to the marshal?"

His words got the faintest smile from the undercaptain.

"You have not been in Alustre in recent years, have you?" asked Veluara.

"No. Not since I was a captain," replied Dainyl. "At that time, Submarshal Alcyna was a senior majer."

"You both have come far since then."

"It has been a while." Dainyl wasn't about to get into a discussion of how either he or Alcyna became submarshals, not with an undercaptain, and especially not with one as sharp and experienced as Veluara. He realized that he had best be more careful with his comments. "How did you choose the Myrmidons?"

"What other choice was there? I wasn't that interested in engineering, and I like being outside. What about you, sir?"

"After the armory," Dainyl said with a laugh.

"Yes, sir." Veluara smiled openly, leading the way toward the wide archway. The left door of the double doors was ajar. "Technical Squad Leader Vresnyl is in charge of the armory," she added in a low voice before she pulled the door open.

Inside was a small stone walled and floored foyer, with a stone counter, waist-high, in the middle of the rear wall. By the time they reached the counter, a broad-shouldered and short alector stood at the counter, waiting. Behind him was a small chamber with little besides a row of tall cabinets against the wall, all closed.

"Tech Leader Vresnyl, Submarshal, sir."

"I'm pleased to see you, Vresnyl. Weren't you in Lysia before?"

"Yes, sir." The armorer smiled. "Been here just over a year."

"How are you finding Alustre?"

"It's cooler, and that's better in the summer, and worse in the winter. Armory's a little bigger. Otherwise there's not that much different."

"Have you had any problems with skylances?" Dainyl asked.

"Like they did in Dereka, sir? No, sir. Every single one's accounted for. With proper maintenance, they'll last almost forever. We follow the rotation schedule and send them to Lyterna for inspection every three years. We've never had one fail, though. Haven't lost any, either."

"What about sidearms?" Dainyl smiled broadly as he asked, since he doubted there were more than five anywhere in the east, reserved as they were for nonflying senior officers.

"You need one, sir? If it's not working right, that'd be the first one in more than a century."

"No." Dainyl grinned. "I had to ask, though." He paused. "Would you show me through the workroom and repair spaces?"

"Yes, sir. I'd be pleased to." Vresnyl gestured to the cabinets. "Those hold the training lances, and not much else." He turned and moved toward the door on the south end of the small chamber.

Dainyl made his way around the counter and followed, with Veluara behind him.

Vresnyl stopped just inside the next small room. "Here's the crystal testing equipment for the skylances and the sidearms, and the collector that puts a basic charge in a replacement crystal. Only had to do that once or twice this past year. Sometimes happens when they've been flying in winter weather, high clouds and not much sun."

"Where do you keep the replacement crystals?" Dainyl knew where they were supposed to be.

"Those . . . there aren't that many, you know, sir. Those are kept in the usual place, in the vault and lockbox in the watch pteridon's square. After the business in Dereka, the submarshal moved all the skylances there as well. Had another pair of lockers built, one for each company. That's when the flyers are here. On deployment, the lances stay with the pteridons, like always."

Dainyl nodded and turned to Veluara. "Are they doing that for the companies in Dulka and Lysia?"

"That's what I understood, sir."

The precaution made sense, but it also concentrated the control of the fearsome weapons, and that left Dainyl uneasy, even though they were supposedly useless except when used in conjunction with a pteridon. He looked to the armorer. "Let's see what else you have."

"Yes, sir."

After that came the storeroom for gear—pteridon saddles, skylance holders, special winter flying parkas, all items that wore out more quickly than pteridons and sky-lances. Below the main storeroom was the storeroom for specialized equipment used less frequently, such as emergency crystal beacons, or the crimson armbands worn by Myrmidons for the administration of justice, the lash and mace of justice, special solutions, and the cross-form to which malefactors were fastened.

After he closed the lower storeroom, Vresnyl turned to Dainyl. "That's what we have for the Myrmidon·equipment, sir."

"How much blasting powder and other explosives do you have down below for the High Alector of Transport?"

"Well . . . sir, not so much as they've got in Dereka or the west. There's not so much of a call for it here. It's on the lowest level."

"I think we can skip that, but, if you'd show me the road-cutting equipment . . . that should wind up what I need to see."

"That's all in the lowest vault. You'll have to unlock the Talent-locks, sir."

Quietly, the three walked to the end of the corridor and then down the wide ramp that descended in a half circle.

After walking another fifty yards, Vresnyl stopped at a solid steel gate, infused and strengthened with lifeforce. He unlocked the gate and swung it open on heavy wide hinges attached to plates fused to the stone walls. A foyer of sorts—two yards deep and three wide—fronted a second door, not quite the width of the foyer itself.

The armorer looked to Dainyl.

The submarshal stepped forward and let his Talent-senses range over the octagonal lock plate. After a moment of study, he found the lock node and released it. "It's released."

Vresnyl looked at the lock, nervously, then inserted a green-tinged key, turning it. There was barely a click as the solid steel door slid to the left, recessing into the stone.

The chamber beyond was not that large, no more than

fifteen yards wide and ten deep, and lit by only a handful of light-torches, spaced along the side walls above the ten lockers on each side. The road-cutting equipment consisted of three identical four-wheeled wagons, each perhaps two yards wide and three long, spaced side by side in the bay. Each was clearly designed to be drawn by a sandox, although the wagon tongue had been unbolted and was set beside the heavy wheels. The rear of the wagon was filled with crystals in matrices linked together so that the power drawn from the crystals and the life-force of the world could be concentrated and focused through a crystalline discharge formulator that looked like a larger version of the end of a skylance, except for the tip, which was shaped into an arc of sixty degrees. The three wagons were the only equipment visible.

For several moments, Dainyl studied the nearest wagon, with both eyes and Talent, gleaning what he could.

Vresnyl shifted his weight from one booted foot to the other. Veluara was silent.

"Where are the operator suits?" asked Dainyl after a time. Because the road-cutting equipment drew lifeforce randomly, any engineer operating the equipment needed to wear the protective coveralls that contained and maintained his own lifeforce.

"In the lockers there, sir."

Dainyl walked to the nearest wall locker and opened it. Within was a single coverall, shimmering a dull gray. He closed the locker door, then turned. "We can go now."

Once Vresnyl re-locked the inner door, Dainyl concentrated and replaced the Talent-lock. Then the three stepped out into the lower corridor.

The armorer locked the outer door and looked up, in relief. "I can't say as I like going in there, sir. If they were powered up, those would suck a man dry in moments, except maybe for the Duarches."

"I understand, but the marshal was rather insistent." On what, Dainyl did not say, because he couldn't, since

Shastylt had merely conveyed the desire that his subordinate discover all that he could.

"We all have our duties," replied Vresnyl uneasily.

"So we do."

Dainyl and Veluara followed the armorer back up to the main level of the armory.

There, Dainyl turned to Vresnyl. "Thank you. I appreciate your care and diligence, and so does the marshal."

"Thank you, sir."

Neither Dainyl nor Veluara said a word until they were back in the open air of the compound courtyard.

"I've never seen the road-cutting equipment before," offered Veluara.

Neither had Dainyl, although he had read of it, and he had hoped that seeing it would provide some insight . . . into something. He felt it had, although uncharged and inert as the equipment had been, he wasn't certain yet what understanding he might have gained. "It is impressive, and foreboding."

"I don't think I'd want to operate it."

"I doubt there would be any need—not unless we get an earthquake or avalanche that blocks one of the high roads through the Spine of Corus."

"The wagons aren't very big for what they can do."

"Neither is a skylance," replied Dainyl dryly.

"There is that, sir."

"What's next?"

"The carpentry and maintenance shops are just ahead. . . ."

Dainyl nodded. It would be a long, but necessary, afternoon.

It was indeed. By the time he had walked through every building in the headquarters compound, Dainyl's leg was definitely aching, and reminding him that it had been shattered not that many weeks before. As he had suspected even before he had left his temporary quarters, everything he had seen was spotless, all the equipment was present and accounted for, and the Myrmidons he met were invariably friendly. On the technical and operational side, the eastern regions of the Myrmidons appeared well run.

When Veluara escorted him back to the quarters, the sun was hanging just above the rolling hills on the far side of Alustre and the river.

"Sir . . . Submarshal Alcyna wanted you to know that the private dining room in the mess area has been reserved for you. She regrets that she cannot join you tonight, but she has cleared her schedule for all the other evenings you will be here in Alustre."

"Thank you. I need to think for a while, but I appreciate the submarshal's concerns . . . and your guiding me through the compound." Dainyl wasn't certain that he wanted to be isolated in a private dining room, but he could also understand Alcyna's motives. Dainyl wouldn't have wanted her wandering through the mess in Elcien with his junior officers—if for very different reasons, he suspected.

After he closed the quarters door behind him, he sank into one of the armchairs.

8

Quattri morning dawned cloudy and misting, and Dainyl slept later than he would have wished ideally. He had not slept well, awakening several times, although his Talent-alarm had not been the reason. He had to hurry through washing up, dressing, and breakfast in the private dining area in order to make it to headquarters to get in his report reading before he was to depart on his late-morning tour of the eastern residence. All in all, he spent two glasses in Majer Noryan's study reading through the daily logs and reports of Third Company, all written in the majer's meticulous hand. According to the operations schedule, Noryan and two squads of Third Company were in Norda.

When Dainyl finally discovered it, the entry for the encounter with the ancients was brief:

21 Duem 1743
First squad lifted off from temporary quarters in Scien at one glass after morning muster, with Majer Noryan taking operational control. The squad flew a line abreast centered on the North Road with half-vingt spacing. Second squad lifted off a fifth of a glass later. A half glass after the flight began, Kagayn noted a green globe of light on a rocky peak to the south of the road, located at vingt-post 37 from Scien. When he investigated, a flash of green light surrounded him and his pteridon. Zuluya followed, and there was a second flash. When the light faded, both pteridons and Myrmidons had dropped from the sky, and two pyres burned on the ice. Majer Noryan ordered the remaining Myrmidons from first squad and all Myrmidons from squad two to mount a concentrated skylance attack on the peak and the globe of light. Under the concentrated power of nine skylances, the green globe exploded into shards that appeared to be frozen flame. These vanished before striking the ground. Third Company encountered no further difficulties during the road sweep, but no sign of the missing Cadmian company was discovered this day.

That was all Noryan had written, and there were no other references to the ancients or anything like them.

Dainyl frowned. He was certain that the reports he had seen two seasons earlier had indicated the pteridons had been lost in separate incidents. He continued to look through the reports, but found nothing more.

Finally, Dainyl replaced the reports and stood, convinced that he had found all he would find. Alcyna and Noryan had reported the incident, and the majer had reported what appeared to be a proper response to an attack. From his own encounters in Dramur, Dainyl was certain that Noryan was either mistaken or lying about the ancient's destruction. What bothered him more was that Alcyna had believed that the ancient had been destroyed. His own problem was simple. To charge the two with either incompetence or falsification of reports would prove nothing and create an argument about precisely how the pteridons had been lost. In addition, it might well require revealing the extent of his own Talent, and capabilities he had concealed for years. Such a revelation would immediately make him a greater and more immediate target for both Zelyert and Shastylt than Alcyna . . . and could well lead to having all three, as well as Brekylt, looking to create an unfortunate accident for one Submarshal Dainyl.

Before too long, he would doubtless have to reveal such, but now was not the time, not when there were two "official" reports—at least as he recalled. He saw no point in acting immediately, not until he rechecked the records at headquarters. With a wry smile, he left the majer's study and walked toward the duty desk to meet Undercaptain Veluara for his tour of the lower level of the eastern residence. More properly, he supposed, he was a guest or visitor, since he had no real authority except over the Myrmidons, and he would be seeing the administrative areas of the east, dealing with five of the six branches of the Duarchy: Finance, Transport, Engineering, Trade, and Education. The sixth branch, of course, was Justice, and all functions associated with it in the east were handled by Alcyna and her subordinates.

The High Alectors of Justice, Finance, and Transport were located in Elcien and reported directly to Khelaryt, the Duarch of Elcien, while the other three were in Ludar and reported to Samist, the Duarch there. Each branch had an eastern regional alector, corresponding in position to Alcyna, and each reported on a day-to-day basis to Brekylt, but any High Alector could override Brekylt if he felt it necessary.

Dainyl could not remember that ever occurring and, from what he'd observed, doubted he ever would. Either Brekylt or the high alector who disagreed would resign—or suffer an accident. He snorted. The Duarches—and especially the Archon—valued the appearance of consensus highly.

Since the morning remained somewhat chill, Dainyl had worn his flying jacket over his uniform. The sky was a clear silver-green, but the wind out of the northwest was brisk, more like late winter than spring.

Undercaptain Veluara stood waiting by the duty desk. She also wore a flying jacket, fastened almost to her neck.

"Good morning, Veluara."

"Good morning, sir. Are you ready?"

"As ready as possible."

She turned and started for the archway to the main front entrance. Dainyl followed.

Outside, young Granyn stood waiting beside the duty coach. "Where to, Submarshal, sir?" asked the Myrmidon, opening the door.

"The residence, for the administrative sections."

"West portico, sir."

Dainyl gestured for Veluara to enter the coach. A fleeting expression between confusion and consternation flickered across her features before she stepped up from the mounting block and into the coach. Dainyl followed, and Granyn closed the door, then vaulted up to the driver's bench.

"Which courier flight is the hardest?" Dainyl asked as the coach pulled away from the entrance to the headquarters building. "In the east."

"I don't know as I could pick one route, Submarshal. The ones to Norda and Passera are bitter in the winter. The longest route is the one to Sinjin in the summer.

We've never had to do that one more than once or twice a quint, though. The route to Passera runs every Quattri."

"That's a day and a half each way."

"Yes, sir. It's almost eleven hundred vingts."

"Have you ever gone through the Spine of Corus except by the passes?"

"No, sir. You'd run the risk of flying out of the lifeforce levels. Why . . ." Veluara broke off whatever she might have said.

"I was thinking about the ancients. Supposedly, they like high and cold places. Have you ever seen one?"

"Yes, sir, but only from a distance." She frowned. "Didn't I tell you that?"

"You may have." Dainyl had been concentrating with his eyes and Talent, and decided that Veluara was definitely lying about how closely she had seen an ancient. He had wondered that when he had first asked her. "You told me you weren't with the squads that had lost pteridons."

"That's right. None of Fourth Company was, and I would have recalled that."

The last words were odd, Dainyl reflected, but he smiled. "I can imagine that it would be hard to forget an ancient."

The coach turned onto the wide avenue that led to the eastern residence, and Dainyl caught a glimpse of the east wing. Unlike the Palaces of the Duarches, or Myrmidon headquarters, where only alectors were permitted, the lower level of the residence was open to any who had business there. That was a necessity, since intelligent landers were the backbone of the day-to-day administration of Corus and since the various decisions and permits were issued directly from the administrative section of the residence.

As Granyn slowed the coach at the stone circle before the west portico, Dainyl studied the residence. The west wing alone extended a good hundred yards and was at least forty yards deep. The east wing was a mirror image of the west. Surely, among all the alectors in the residence, there should be *someone* that Dainyl knew. If not, he would have to come up with another stratagem.

Once the two Myrmidons stepped from the coach on the main level of the west portico, Veluara looked to Dainyl. "I'd thought it would be easiest to begin with engineering, sir. It's closest to the portico, and there aren't many in the engineering section here. Most of the engineers in the east are at Fordall, near the manufactories. There are some at Dulka also."

Dainyl smiled politely. Everyone in Elcien referred to the manufactories as being in Alustre, yet they would have been discomfited if anyone had suggested that the manufactories in Faitel were in Elcien. It was just another manifestation of the chauvinism that pervaded the western capital cities, he suspected.

He glanced back at the mounting blocks, where another carriage had drawn up, and two landers, one white-haired, had stepped out. The younger man gesticulated angrily, then lowered his arm after several words from the older. While Dainyl wondered what the exchange had been about, he returned his attention to the undercaptain.

Veluara turned right toward the first archway. There were no guards, and she opened the golden oak door.

Dainyl stepped through the doorway and into a corridor with polished white granite floors, and lined with doors that stretched a good hundred yards. "If most of the engineers are elsewhere, what do the ones here do, then?"

"Convey the requests of the High Alector of Engineering and take requests and grant permits, I would imagine."

They passed three doorways on the left, and three on the right. The doorways on the right were closed, but those on the left were open, and in each study were two desks, with a lander at each, apparently reading reports or, in one case, studying some sort of building plans. Through his Talent, Dainyl could sense that at least one of the studies to the left held an alector.

Veluara stopped at the fourth door on the left and

opened it for Dainyl. Inside was a gray-haired lander woman, seated at a table desk in a small foyer. To her right was a closed doorway.

"Yes? Might I help you?" The assistant smiled brightly, although Dainyl sensed little warmth behind the expression.

"I'm Undercaptain Veluara, escorting Submarshal Dainyl. He's here to see the supervising engineer."

"Just a moment." The woman rose quickly, hurried to the door, opened it a crack, and spoke. "The submarshal from Elcien is here to see you, sir."

"Send him in, Selya. Send him in."

Selya opened the door and stepped back, still offering an empty smile.

Veluara followed Dainyl, closing the door behind them, then stepping forward and to the side. "Supervising Engineer Jostyl, this is Submarshal Dainyl from Myrmidon headquarters in Elcien. . . ."

"Ah, yes. High Alector Brekylt had passed the word that you might stop by." Jostyl was slightly taller than Dainyl, but far more angular and much thinner. His face was narrow, especially for an alector, and his deep-set eyes were a light violet. "Please, please sit down."

Dainyl took one of the wooden armchairs across the table desk from the engineer.

"I must say that I've seldom been visited by a Myrmidon of such rank before, and certainly not in recent years. What can I do for you?"

"I'm not certain," Dainyl offered with an open smile. "Marshal Shastylt felt that I should have a better feel for what occurred east of the Spine of Corus and meet some of the key people in Alustre."

"How key I am . . ." Jostyl shook his head.

"I understand that the majority of the engineering and manufactory activities are in Fordall. How does that affect what you do?"

"We handle the requests from towns and cities for major repairs and engineering improvements, structures like bridges and access causeways. We also inform the local regional alectors in the east . . ."

Dainyl listened as Jostyl explained, interjecting questions of his own, as appropriate.

"How many alector engineers are there in Fordall? . . .

"Is any expansion of the manufactories in Fordall planned? Especially of the facility producing rifles?"

At that question, Jostyl frowned. "None. There is absolutely no need for additional production."

Dainyl mentally marked the reaction before continuing his questions.

"Is there any thought of a high road from Sudya or Tylora to Sinjin? . . ."

As Dainyl finally stepped out of Jostyl's study and past Selya, close to a glass after they had entered, he could sense the assistant's eyes on him—as well as a combination of anger and resentment, yet he knew he had never seen the woman before he had stepped into the study.

"Education is the next section, sir," offered Veluara once they stood out in the main corridor.

"That's fine." Dainyl noted a few landers walking along the corridor, but all moved to avoid the two Myrmidons.

Veluara introduced him to the supervisor of education, and after a short conversation, because Dainyl needed less information, they walked through the section, also small, with but three alectors and twelve lander assistants. After two sections, and two glasses, they had covered roughly seventy yards of the long granite-walled corridor. Dainyl had seen less than ten alectors, and none that he knew, and learned little he had not already read or understood.

"What section is next?"

"That would be trade, sir. The rest of the west wing is for trade. The east wing is largely finance, and, of course, the supervisors and staff for the residence itself. The regional alector for transport is in Prosp for the week, I understand, but his chief assistant is here. His name is Zulanyt. . . ."

Dainyl concealed a smile. Surely, there could be only one Zulanyt. Then, Zulanyt had been several years older than Dainyl and less than perfectly friendly when they had shared tutors.

After the pleasantries had been exchanged, and before Dainyl seated himself in the small study occupied by Zulanyt—an alector shorter and broader than Dainyl— the submarshal turned to Veluara. "Undercaptain, Zulanyt and I go back a long time. We have a few things to talk over. I certainly don't want you forced to listen to us reflect. Why don't you take the coach back to headquarters, and then send Granyn back to wait for me?"

"Ah . . ." Before she said another word, Veluara realized that Dainyl's questioning suggestion was a polite order. "Yes, sir. I'll send him right back. Are you sure you won't need anything else? You haven't toured finance . . ."

"I'm sure Zulanyt can introduce me."

"I can do that," affirmed the older alector, who continued to smile pleasantly until Veluara had left the small study, closing the door as she departed.

Dainyl maintained his own smile, even as he studied Zulanyt.

"You've certainly gone farther than anyone could have possibly imagined." The smile vanished. "What do you want? You certainly didn't stop by to chat. As I remember, I was never particularly warm to you, and I can't imagine that you recall me with great kindness."

Dainyl laughed. "No. I can't say that you provided me with the warmest of recollections. But I was curious as to how you got from Elcien to Alustre."

"By sandox and coach, like any other low-level alector who isn't a Myrmidon."

"But why did you choose the eastern region?" Dainyl arched his eyebrows, thinking that Lystrana could have arched either one—and to greater effect.

"It's where bright young alectors without connections go to become noticed, especially if they don't want to become Myrmidons. Didn't you know that?" Zulanyt's voice dripped irony. "Do you know how much you'll be detested, if you aren't already?"

"Because I'm the exception, the alector with few connections who made it to second-in-command of the Myrmidons, the one the senior alectors will name to prove that it's ability that counts and not relationships and connections? I assume that's what you meant."

"You're far more cynical than you used to be."

"Aren't we all?"

"You didn't answer my question," Zulanyt pointed out. "That's definitely a trait of an alector on the way up."

"No. I'm still slow about some things. I was sent here to see what is happening. You were always quite willing to tell me—and anyone else—what we didn't wish to hear." Dainyl shrugged. "I felt it couldn't hurt to see if you still felt that way."

"You realize that High Alector Brekylt will be interested in why you stopped to see me and dismissed your escort? That undercaptain worships the stones Alcyna stands upon and is already reporting that we're talking. By tonight, Brekylt will know as well."

"Then tell them the truth, that I was prying and trying to find out if anything untoward is happening. Is it?"

"It always is, everywhere in Corus. It always has. You should have learned that by now," replied Zulanyt.

"There's a difference between a nephew or niece being preferred for an assistant's position over someone less known and whether the regional alector or eastern submarshal is concealing the reasons for the disappearance of . . . shall we say, entire companies. Or whether a Cadmian garrison is being moved because certain individuals don't care for cold weather."

"I wouldn't know anything about that."

"You're the chief assistant to the eastern regional alector for Transport. What can you tell me about the elimination of the high road coach service between Pystra and Scien?"

"There's nothing secret or untoward about that, Dainyl. There wouldn't even have been anyone in Scien in the winter for the past ten years if it hadn't been for the Cad-mian companies there. It was a terrible place to locate a town. So when your High Alector ordered the Cadmians to Norda, and everyone else left as well, what reason was there to send coaches there?"

"Did any of your drivers see the ancients?"

"Ancients?" Zulanyt's voice turned incredulous. "They died a long time ago."

"Not all of them," replied Dainyl dryly. "One of them was seen just before a company of Cadmians disappeared riding to Pystra on their way to Norda. That's why I won-dered if your drivers had seen anything. They travel the routes regularly and would be likely to notice anything that changed."

"No one ever reported anything. You're sure that there are still ancients?"

"A few have been reported by reliable sources." Dainyl paused only slightly. "Can you tell me if passages on the coaches are up or down in the past year?"

"Passages for alectors are about the same. Those for landers and indigens are down, perhaps by a fifth. Why did you ask?"

"Did the drop-off occur in the fall and winter, or ear-lier?"

"As I recall, it was in the fall and early winter, and passages have been normal for the last quint." Zulanyt looked squarely at Dainyl. "You still aren't answering my questions."

"I was curious as to whether lander passages dropped off before there was unrest along the Spine of Corus, at the same time, or afterward."

"Why would you . . . Oh."

"Exactly," replied Dainyl. "If the drop-off preceded the unrest, we could look at passages as a sign, but it sounds like people just reacted to what had happened."

Dainyl asked more questions, from the state of the roads to barge shipping to the ports, but Zulanyt had little more of interest to offer. After little more than half a glass, Zulanyt escorted Dainyl to the east wing, and to the eastern regional alector of finance, Kaparyk, then took his leave.

Kaparyk, while the image of the typical alector with his shimmering black hair, broad face, and purple eyes, greeted Dainyl with both a broad smile and a sense of warmth that required little Talent for Dainyl to sense.

"Submarshal Dainyl . . . I'm pleased to meet you. I have met Lystrana upon a number of occasions. An impressive woman, your wife."

"I was fortunate."

"She has that rare ability to hold almost all the accounts in her head, and the rarer capability of knowing what they mean." Kaparyk laughed. "Once the staff saw what she could do, there haven't been nearly as many problems with the accounts, either. She's the best chief assistant to the High Alector of Finance that I've known."

"How long have you been in your position?"

"Twenty-five years and a quint."

"You have seen a few."

"Five. The last one. . . ." Kaparyk shook his head. "He got dizzy and fell off a pteridon on the way to somewhere—Arwyn, as I recall. Poor fellow, it was probably better that way. He'd made a terrible mess of the audit of the engineering accounts. Took your wife a quint to set it right."

The "unfortunate" assistant hadn't made a mess, Dainyl recalled. He'd tried to conceal the theft of certain engineering equipment that had been under his wife's supervision. When she had disappeared, her successor discovered the discrepancies. Then Davalt had had his "accident."

"But enough of that," Kaparyk went on. "What can I do for you?"

"I don't know. Not in a definite way, that is." Dainyl quickly explained his tour and concluded, "So I'm introducing myself and asking if there's anything I should know that would benefit the Myrmidons and the High Alector of Justice in carrying out our duties."

Kaparyk's eyes twinkled. "I imagine you know that already, from Lystrana."

Dainyl shrugged. "Certainly about finance, but she wouldn't see what you do here in Alustre on matters impacting finance indirectly that might also affect the Myrmidons."

"I can't imagine any of that being very useful. There are more Cadmians in Norda, Dulka, and Lysia, and none left at Scien, and that's probably a good thing. The winters at Scien meant that the maintenance and supply costs there were a third again that of any other Cadmian compound of equivalent size."

"There are still more at Lysia," offered Dainyl.

"Seems strange to me," said Kaparyk. "Do you know why there are more forces there?"

"It was ordered long before I became submarshal." Earlier, Dainyl had checked the records to see if he could discover why there were two full battalions of Cadmians in Lysia, as well as a Myrmidon company, when Lysia was a relatively isolated seaport, serving an area with little history of unrest and no particularly remarkable resources. He had found nothing, except spare directives ordering various unit transfers. In that light, the continued buildup in Lysia worried at him, but Kaparyk had effectively admitted he didn't know why. Was it because it was isolated enough that Brekylt could build a power base there?

Dainyl asked a handful of other questions, all answered easily by the eastern regional alector of finance.

"Oh," interjected Kaparyk, "I almost forgot. You might mention to Lystrana that chief engineer Rensyl in Fordall has adopted the same accounting systems as Azerdyl once used, in dealing with the transport and road maintenance accounts of the eastern region."

Noting the slightest emphasis on the words "accounting systems," Dainyl replied, "I'll be sure to pass that along.

Is this something likely to be of interest to the marshal?"

"It's rather complex, and I'm certain that your talented wife will be able to explain it far better than I ever could."

Dainyl feared that Lystrana could indeed, and that Kaparyk had doubtless survived by such indirection. "Then I will let her." He smiled.

Kaparyk had little else to offer, and after leaving the finance alector's ample study, Dainyl walked to the nearest archway and then created his Talent-based sightshield, the ability he was not supposed to have, before making his way to the staircase that led down to the Table chamber. While he kept the sightshield around him, he also walked along the side of the corridor.

The staircase and the lower hallway leading to the Table were so deserted he scarcely needed the sightshield—not until he reached the pair of guards stationed outside. Neither of the two young alectors looked in his direction. Nor did either say anything for a time.

"Quiet morning."

"Always quiet here."

Dainyl waited, listening, but neither spoke. Finally, he dropped the sightshield and cleared his throat.

Both alectors stiffened.

"Sir! We didn't see you."

"That was obvious," Dainyl replied dryly.

"Ah . . . sir?"

Dainyl stepped forward and released the Talent-lock on the outer doorway, then opened the door and stepped into the foyer, closing the door behind him.

He remained in the foyer, extending his Talent-senses back into the corridor in order to listen.

"That's the other submarshal?"

"He's the one."

"Swear he wasn't here, and then he was."

"They're like that. You don't want to cross them."

"What do you do if one's after the other?"

There was a low laugh. "Do as little as you can, and stay out of the way."

"Josaryk's wagering on this one."

"Majer Noryan is backing the other one."

"That's because—"

"Enough. Shouldn't be talking about it. Not really."

The guards were silent, and Dainyl released the second Talent-lock and stepped into the Table chamber. For a time, he stood there, just letting his senses range over the Table, trying to get a feeling of how the Table felt. Lystrana had told him that the Tables could also be used for communications, and Asulet had suggested that they had other purposes as well.

Dainyl could sense a node of *something* within the Table, and he probed slightly with his Talent. Abruptly, a purple glow appeared above the black surface of the Table.

Dainyl leaned forward. Was someone about to arrive? From Elcien?

A vague and indistinct image appeared, seemingly within the Table, of gray walls. He squinted—and found himself viewing the outer walls of the Myrmidon headquarters in Elcien. But, while he could see a carriage pass by the front gates, he did not see any Myrmidons, not a one, nor any pteridons.

The glow above the Table intensified, and a rush of chill air cascaded over Dainyl as an ugly pink-purple mist expanded above the middle of the Table. He stepped back, his hand dropping to the lightcutter at his side. Absently, he noted that the image of headquarters had vanished.

With another wave of chill air, a . . . creature—that was the only word for it—appeared on the Table, a composite of alector and pteridon, alector from the mid-chest down, and pteridon above that, with crooked and truncated wings that barely fit within the chamber. Without warning, it lurched toward Dainyl, blue crystal beak jabbing downward.

Dainyl yanked out the lightcutter and fired, throwing up Talent-shields in front of himself. The lightcutter beam shimmered and reflected off the pteridon-like head of the creature. It slashed forward with its beak, striking his Talent-shields. The impact hurled Dainyl back into the stone wall.

The creature whirled, looking for others. In that moment, Dainyl used the lightcutter beam to aim for the middle of the chest—the human part of the monster.

A sharp hiss followed, and the monster collapsed in a heap.

Holding the lightcutter ready, Dainyl looked at the corpse, a twisted figure with the head and winged shoulders and beak of a miniature pteridon. Beneath the head was an alector's body in the green trousers and purple tunic usually worn by senior fieldmasters.

He waited several moments, but the hideous form did not move, and Dainyl sensed no lifeforce. He extended a Talent-probe. Nothing, and the dead creature was not disintegrating, either, the way alectors usually did.

Now what? If he hadn't made his presence known to the guards, he could have raised Talent illusions and just left. But then, if he hadn't been trying to work with the Table, the wild translation wouldn't have focused on him. Could he use the Table to cart the dead alector to a Table less frequently used?

He climbed up onto the Table and grasped the shoulders of the repulsive form that had once been an alector, then concentrated. The Table turned to black mist beneath him, and he plummeted down . . .

. . . *into chill darkness. The lifeless form of the wild translation was a leaden weight, not on his arms, but his mind, and he searched for the purple-edged green locator that was Norda. After endless instant moments, he could sense the purple and green. He extended a Talent-probe. Instead of the rushing sense he had felt before, the green locator crept toward him, slowly, ever more slowly, but the silver-green barrier finally loomed closer and closer, and then shattered around him.*

Dainyl staggered several steps, and dropped the wild translation onto the Table. Ice had coated its form, although a misty fog immediately began to rise in the warmer air of the Table chamber.

A figure in green by the door to the chamber began to turn toward the Table.

Dainyl concentrated and dropped back into the blackness.

He plunged downward into and beneath the Table. His entire body shuddered, as though it had been coated with ice that pressed in upon him. For an endless moment, he did nothing, wondering what he was doing in the chill, trying to sort out the confusion, even as his legs and hands lost their sensation.

The dark gray locator, bordered in purple, that was what he sought, and his thoughts reached for that locator wedge.

In time, seemingly forever, gray-silver sprayed away from him, and . . .

. . . he stood back on the Table in the chamber in Alustre, his lungs gasping for air, his entire frame shivering as he climbed down from the Table and leaned against it, trying to catch his breath and warm up. For a time, misty fog enshrouded his entire form before dispersing. Slowly, he began to regain his strength, but decided to wait before leaving the chamber.

He still did not understand why the wild translation had not immediately turned to dust—or fire. His eyes traveled across the stone walls of the windowless chamber, unmarred except for the brackets for the light-torches and hangings. Abruptly, he looked at one light-torch bracket, somehow different, although it appeared the same as did the others to his eyes.

Straightening, Dainyl slowly walked to the bracket, realizing, as he did, that it was a concealed lock, its Talent so muted that it was not obvious until he stood next to it. There was a concealed door within the Table chamber.

Should he try it?

He could feel a ragged grin cross his face. If . . . if anyone were inside, after dealing with the wild translation and two trips between Tables, he was scarcely in the best condition to take on another challenge. Investigating the hidden door would have to wait, but he would check all the Table chambers he used in the future to see if they had such doors.

He squared his shoulders and walked to the foyer door, opening it, and then re-setting the Talent lock behind him. He opened the outer door.

Both guards stiffened.

"That didn't take long, sir."

Dainyl offered a smile. "Sometimes, it doesn't." He closed the door and replaced the second Talent-lock. "I hope the rest of your duty won't be too long."

As he walked away, he extended his Talent-senses, listening.

". . . couldn't have traveled too far . . ."

". . . some of them use it for other things, they say . . ."

"Best you keep that to yourself . . ."

Dainyl kept walking down the corridor toward the steps. He needed to eat, and get some rest before his evening meal with Brekylt and Alcyna. The effort required by his brief Table transits underscored why it was better not to use the Tables too frequently—not until he was more adept, anyway.

As he climbed the steps, trying not to breathe hard, he couldn't help wondering about the wild translation. Had he caused it by attempting to investigate the Table, or had he just drawn it to him? What about the hidden chamber? Why did the recorders need hidden chambers within largely hidden chambers?

9

Just before sunset, Dainyl made his way from his quarters and across the paved courtyard. To his right, a single pteridon angled in from the south, flared gracefully, and settled onto the stone flight stage, where the Myrmidon flyer dismounted and handed a dispatch case to the waiting duty messenger.

Dainyl followed the messenger into the rear entrance to the headquarters building.

"The weekly report from Fordall, sir," the messenger announced, handing the dispatch case to the undercaptain at the duty desk.

The junior officer saw Dainyl behind the Myrmidon messenger and rose to his feet. "Submarshal, sir. The duty coach is waiting for you. Submarshal Alcyna will meet you at the residence. She is traveling from her house just outside Alustre."

"Thank you." Dainyl nodded and made his way out to the front and the coach. The driver was not Granyn, but a woman, a junior Myrmidon ranker.

"Submarshal, sir. The residence?"

"That's correct." Dainyl paused. "Did you come from Transport, driving sandoxen coaches?"

"Yes, sir."

"What routes? I drove the Hafin-to-Krost leg, and sometimes the Tempre-Syan square." He laughed. "That was a few years back."

"The Northern Pass run from Dereka to Passera. Seven years." Her voice was pleasant, but Dainyl could sense a faint anger and resentment behind the words.

"Sometimes, it takes a while," he replied. "For me, I drove for almost eleven years."

"Sir . . . eleven years?"

"A little more than ten and a half," he admitted with a smile. "I never thought they'd take me for the Myrmidons."

The driver looked at him for a long moment before her eyes shifted to his star insignia. Then she laughed. "Guess I shouldn't complain."

"I didn't get your name," Dainyl said.

"Olyssa, sir."

"How long have you been here at headquarters?"

"Just a year, sir. Well . . . four quints, actually."

"I'd judge it'll be another three quints before there will be an opening for a flyer here in Alustre, but you never know what might come up. You're next in line after Granyn?"

"Yes, sir."

"How do you like it here?"

"Much better than being a sandoxen driver, sir, and I've been helping Vresnyl in the armory."

"With all the changes in the handling of skylances, you mean?"

"Yes, sir, and learning about crystal replacements and testing."

"Did you help with the testing of the lances used against the ancient?"

"Oh, no, sir. The submarshal and Vresnyl did that."

"I suppose they had to replace some of the crystals."

"Yes, sir, but I don't know how many. Vresnyl keeps those under lock, and he said that I wasn't supposed to say much about it, except to my superiors."

Dainyl suspected that, at the time, no one had thought he might be visiting. "That's wise of you both." He smiled. "I suppose we should be getting to the residence."

"Yes, sir."

Dainyl stepped from the mounting block into the coach, closing the door behind himself. As the coach passed out through the compound gates, he nodded. His inquiry had been a thrust in the dark, but Olyssa's answers confirmed that more than a few details were not being reported to the marshal. Alcyna had mentioned sending a report to Lyterna about the ancients, and when Dainyl had been in Lyterna in late winter, Asulet had told him that too many of the senior alectors were interested in power rather than understanding and that High Alector Zelyert played "little games." Was Alcyna using the reports about the ancients to turn Asulet against Zelyert and Shastylt? Or merely fomenting unrest?

Dainyl snorted. That wasn't the question. Rather the

question was exactly how she had done so. He also worried about the finagling in accounts suggested by Kaparyk, particularly since there was no reason for an alector to amass golds other than to fund some sort of covert operation.

This time, the duty coach slowed to a halt under the central portico of the residence, actually a raised entry on the second level on the front of the structure that allowed Brekylt and his guests and visitors to avoid the administrative and government studies and functionaries on the main level.

Dainyl opened the door and slipped out of the coach.

"I'll be back in two glasses, Submarshal, and wait until you're ready to depart," Olyssa said immediately.

"That won't be a problem?" While Dainyl knew it was the ranker's duty, he didn't want to appear too callous or accepting.

"No, sir. I'd just be waiting at headquarters, otherwise."

"I'll see you then."

When Dainyl turned and stepped off the mounting block, a young alectress moved forward from where she stood beside one of the unfluted stone columns flanking the covered colonnade that led to the receiving rotunda. She wore the black-trimmed silver tunic and black trousers that signified she was attached to the residence staff—or to Brekylt's personal retinue.

"Submarshal Dainyl, High Alector Brekylt sent me to escort you, since you haven't been to the private quarters of the residence before." She inclined her head slightly.

"Thank you." Dainyl had no doubts that he would have an escort no matter how familiar he became with the residence and its private quarters. He followed the alectress along the colonnade, through a vaulted archway and past two lander guards in black and silver, one of whom opened the right half of the double doors. Once inside, she headed straight back through a high-ceilinged entry hall, black marble columns spaced at four-yard intervals along the white walls. The floor of the entry hall was composed of black octagons set in white granite.

Beyond the entry, the corridor narrowed to a width of a mere six yards, and the stone floor was white granite. At the end of the corridor was another set of golden oak double doors, guarded by a young alector in the black and silver. He nodded to Dainyl's escort, then said, as he opened the right-hand door, "Welcome, Submarshal. The High Alector is expecting you."

Dainyl's escort stepped back, and he walked through the door alone, Talent-senses alert. The foyer beyond was empty, and Dainyl faced archways to the left and right.

"To the right," called a voice.

Dainyl stepped through the archway, and followed another corridor to the first open doorway on the left. Beyond was a study, the inner wall lined with shelves of books. The outer wall held shelves as well, but between them were floor-to-ceiling windows, and in the center of the outer wall was a set of open double doors.

Alcyna and Brekylt rose from the pair of armchairs set before the table desk.

Brekylt was but a shade shorter than Dainyl, and slender. His wide expressive mouth offered a smile, and he Talent-projected warmth and friendliness. "Submarshal Dainyl, I've heard only good things about you. It's good to see you here in Alustre."

Behind that projection, well shielded, but not from Dainyl, was a sense of coolness and calculation. Dainyl smiled in response, inclining his head. "I'm pleased to have the chance to visit Alustre again, and to see you. I'm also grateful for the dinner invitation."

"I'm the one who is pleased," replied the High Alector. "It has been some time since the submarshal of the west has dined with us. Tyanylt never did, you know. Neither did Weylt."

"I hadn't known," said Dainyl with a soft laugh, "but I'm more than happy to break that precedent."

"So are we." Brekylt smiled again. "There are only the

three of us. I had thought it would be more pleasant—and more intimate—to enjoy the balcony overlooking the conservatory gardens."

"Brekylt has plants from all over Acorus in the garden—only the most beautiful and the most fragrant, of course," added Alcyna.

"The gardens must be very special, then," Dainyl replied.

"Nothing like them anywhere on Corus, not even in Lyterna." Brekylt turned and walked through the open doors of the study and out onto a balcony within the glass-roofed conservatory and overlooking the gardens below. The light of the almost-setting sun turned the white-granite walls and pillars orangish red, and the scent of flowers filled the warm moist air.

Dainyl followed Alcyna, stopping well short of the stone half wall at the edge of the balcony. To his right, five yards away, was a table, set with three places, in full formality. The silver gleamed, as did the crystal goblets. Dainyl concentrated on Brekylt. "It's pleasant here."

"One of the great privileges of being the High Alector of the East." Brekylt lifted an amber long-necked bottle and filled three of the four wine glasses set on a side table. The vintage was so clear that the glass would have appeared empty, except for the slight silver sheen to the wine. "You must try the Argentium Grande." He gestured for Dainyl and Alcyna each to take a glass.

Dainyl inclined his head to Alcyna.

"Thank you, Dainyl. You are so aware of the proprieties." She took the middle glass.

Dainyl took the leftmost one. He lifted it, then inhaled, using the gesture and his Talent sense to check the wine, but he sensed nothing untoward. "It has a wonderful aroma."

"It's from Elcadya," replied Brekylt, holding his glass. "Every bit as good as anything out of the Vyan Hills, and better at times." He sipped the wine.

"Elcadya?"

"The vineyard region some fifty vingts to the north of Flyr." Brekylt set down his wine on the side table and picked up the empty glass, tapping the rim with his forefinger. A clear tone filled the balcony. "The crystal goblets come from just north of Vysta . . ."

Dainyl laughed and added, "And they're every bit as good as those from Krost, if not better at times."

Alcyna laughed as well. "I think he understands your point, Brekylt."

"I'm certain he does." The High Alector of the East set down the empty goblet and lifted his wine, not drinking any. "But does he know why matters have turned as they have?"

"No . . . I don't," Dainyl admitted. "I have the feeling I'm about to learn, though." He took a sip of the Argentium—as good as Brekylt had suggested. "You're right about the wine."

"He's right about many things." Alcyna's tone was dry.

"I imagine so. One doesn't become and remain the Highest of the East without great knowledge."

Brekylt moved to the balcony wall, where he gestured at the gardens below.

"They're beautiful," Dainyl said.

"They are indeed. Like Acorus itself, they require much care, much planning, and careful pruning—but not too much. Do you see the jaelithum there, with the silver blossoms?"

"It's especially pleasing."

"It is. It wasn't supposed to be there. The original jaelithum was planted in the far corner. No matter what the gardeners did, it failed to thrive. It finally died. The one there planted itself, and I told them to let it grow. Everyone has remarked on its beauty and fragrance."

"Some plants are suited for some locales, and some are not," Dainyl observed, as he knew he had been led to conclude.

"Exactly. All worlds are like that, and Acorus is no exception. There are sand and lime near Vysta and the sloping hills with right exposure to sun in Elcadya."

"But those exist in Krost and the Vyan Hills as well," pointed out Dainyl.

"They do indeed, but does either Duarch remark upon the vintages of Elcadya or the crystal of Vysta?"

"I couldn't tell you." Dainyl laughed ruefully. "I've not dined at their tables. You would know better than I."

"They do not," murmured Alcyna, who had moved to the balcony wall, at Dainyl's right, so that he stood between the two, "especially not Khelaryt."

"Life is like the gardens here," Brekylt said genially. "Some plants and trees you can place anywhere, and others will grow only in certain places. One cannot decree that the jaelithum must only grow in the corner. One must work with what is, not insist that it all follow a plan laid down years before. After all, to build lifeforce, we must be gardeners as well as administrators."

"And, according to the *Views of the Highest*," Dainyl couldn't resist adding, "we must not see choices where there are none."

"Exactly." Brekylt swallowed the last of his wine. "Enough of gardens and lifeforce. We should eat before what we have planned spoils, and you must tell us all about our acquaintances . . . and how they fare . . ."

Dainyl understood that message as well. No matter what he tried, Brekylt and Alcyna weren't about to tell him more than they already had. For all their overt courtesy, they both had made what they had conveyed to Dainyl very clear, so obvious that it could not have been missed. Whether that meant that they felt he was naïve about matters, not that bright, or whether it was all designed to mislead him—he didn't know. Not yet.

He might as well enjoy the dinner . . . and listen not just to what was said, but how it was said.

10

A light rain fell outside the mess, turning the predawn grayness of Quinti into a misty gloom. Inside, Mykel sat at a table along the wall, slowly eating his egg toast.

Fabrytal sat across from him, finishing his own breakfast. "Chyndylt's a good senior squad leader. After another deployment, he might make a good undercaptain."

"I'd thought he might," replied Mykel, refraining from pointing out that he'd made the observation to Fabrytal several weeks earlier. "But it's better not to say anything to him at all. When you think he's ready, make the recommendation to me. That way, if the colonel doesn't want to accept it—or wants to delay it because there aren't any officer slots available—Chyndylt doesn't get angry or resentful. There's no sense in creating a problem when you don't have to."

"I can see that, sir." Fabrytal paused. "What's it like in Dramur? Majer Dohark must have liked it to accept the post there."

"It's like every place else, Fabrytal. It has good points and bad. Majer Dohark said he was tired of the cold, and liked the idea of being in charge of a post."

"How many companies?"

"Two—but he has orders to expand to a full battalion. The two companies weren't enough to cover much more than Dramuria and the guano mine. That was one reason why the growers on the west side of the island thought they could do what they wanted. . . ." Mykel laughed. "I can fill you in on that on the ship to Southgate. I imagine you have a few things to do right now."

"I do need to check with Chyndylt before muster. By your leave, sir."

Mykel nodded, and after the undercaptain had left, took another bite of egg toast that was cooler than he liked and firm, just short of being rubbery.

"So . . . they've decided that you have a talent for butchery, Mykel."

Mykel looked up to see Hersiod sitting down at the end of the adjoining table. While Mykel hadn't avoided the older major over the past weeks, he hadn't gone out of his way to seek him out, either. "Butchery? That's not a good idea, as you've pointed out."

"I understand you do it so well, though. How many nearly defenseless companies did you destroy in Dramur? Something like ten? Was that it?" Hersiod's voice was light.

Mykel could sense the other's anger, not from the tone of voice, but rather as though it were a color, or a smell. It wasn't either, but related in some fashion to his growing ability to see people's auras. "Well . . ." He drew out the word, trying to reply with a bantering tone himself. "They had very new rifles and a lot of ammunition, and they were trying to kill us. They kept attacking, and they wanted a fight. So I figured I'd oblige them, but I didn't see much point in losing men I didn't have to." He shrugged. "You're headed to Iron Stem, I heard. Did the colonel tell you how long you'll be there?" Mykel took a swallow of the slightly watered hot cider, concentrating on Hersiod.

"It might be better if you concentrated on your own battalion, Mykel. What we're doing won't help you." Hersiod's smile was anything but warm. "But then, you're being sent to do what you do so well. Butchering . . . I beg your pardon . . . *disciplining* those who have not seen the error of their ways."

Mykel smiled in return. "Discipline is important. You've often made that point." Mykel could sense a certain hardness . . . an intransigence within Hersiod . . . something, like the anger concealed by Hersiod, that carried a color Mykel could sense with his growing talent, could almost see—the faintest pinkish purple.

At the same time, the older major's words and attitude reminded Mykel of Majer Vaclyn just before Vaclyn had snapped and attacked Mykel. Did being in command of a battalion do that to some men after a time? Or were they always that way?

"I'm so glad my words have made an impact upon you, Mykel." Hersiod lifted his mug, as if in a toast, and sipped the steaming cider.

Mykel lifted his mug, empty as it was, in response. "I can't imagine them not making an impact, coming as they do from a senior majer." His words, even and polite, were true enough, in more than one way. He knew he should just have nodded and agreed, but he'd always had trouble in making himself agree to what he perceived as outright falsehoods and blatant inaccuracies, even when agreement would have made his own way far smoother.

The sense of anger in Hersiod darkened. "We are only Cadmians, Mykel. We are not alectors. We serve at their pleasure. You are a majer at their pleasure. You could be nothing as quickly. You might keep that in mind."

"That has been made extremely clear to me." Mykel didn't have to evade or equivocate to say that.

An expression of surprise flashed across Hersiod's features, then vanished as if it had never been. "That is very good to know."

Mykel rose from his table. "I hope your day and your training go well." He nodded and turned.

Hersiod did not offer a reply.

Mykel left the mess and started across the courtyard through the mist that had replaced the rain, heading to meet his captains and undercaptains. Something . . . something about Hersiod, about Fourth Battalion, about their being assigned to Iron Stem, reminded Mykel of Majer Vaclyn, something more than stubbornness and intransigence. But what?

As he neared the Third Battalion barracks, the certainty that there was a connection nagged at Mykel, but he could not identify what it was, no matter how he struggled to remember and recall.

11

By Sexdi night, Dainyl had reviewed every record in the eastern Myrmidon headquarters even halfway pertinent to his concerns, observed the majority of pteridons and their squares, and had three more meals with Alcyna—two more than he had desired or needed, especially since he had learned little more than the fact that Alcyna was quite talented in revealing nothing that she had not already told Dainyl. He'd seen nothing that referred to engineering or to road building or maintenance, but had not expected that he would. He had discovered that, periodically, she transferred Myrmidons from company to company, far more often than Tyanylt or he had done in the west, and most of the transfers were not for reasons related to promotions. They couldn't be. Promotions were infrequent.

His sleep was less than untroubled, despite the various precautions he had taken, including a Talent-alarm on the door to his bedchamber, and he awoke early on Septi morning. After a quick breakfast, he packed his gear, pulled on his flying jacket, slung the saddlebags over his shoulder, and walked down the steps to the courtyard, and through the wind that swirled warm and chill air together toward the headquarters building. He glanced to the south, where gray clouds were building, suggesting that the warm rains of mid-spring were indeed on their way.

Someone must have seen him carrying his gear, because, by the time he reached the duty desk inside headquarters to request the coach, Alcyna was walking toward him.

"You're leaving, Dainyl?"

He shrugged. "What can I say? You are remarkably able. Your records and accounts are a marvel, and you maintain order and discipline without excessive force or overmanagement. I did note that you tend to transfer Myrmidons more than in the west."

"That's because squads can get too cliquish without regular rotations."

There was more there, but Dainyl didn't have any way to press. "I'll report that as well. Those kinds of insights just show your attention to detail, and are the sorts of things that I'll be pleased to report to the marshal."

"I do hope that you found your tour instructive." Her smile was polite.

"With your example, how could it not be?" His smile was warmer than hers, if not by much.

"Do give my warmest regards to Marshal Shastylt, and enjoy the spring in Elcien."

"It's cooler there, and it will be a while."

"The coach is standing by." Her words were the equivalent of a dismissal.

"Thank you. I hope I can be as hospitable to you when you come to Elcien." Dainyl inclined his head, then turned and walked out to the coach, where Granyn waited.

"To the residence, sir?"

"The west portico, Granyn." Dainyl swung up into the coach and closed the door behind himself.

As he rode toward the residence, Dainyl considered how little he had learned—and how much less he trusted either Brekylt or Alcyna. Brekylt's remarks about gardening might well have been an indirect invitation for Dainyl to join them in whatever they planned—or at least an opening to explore such—but Dainyl knew all too well that following that path would have been too dangerous. He could conceal what he felt well enough, but he had never been able to counterfeit interest in what he disliked, distrusted, or detested, and Alcyna and Brekylt were all too skilled at reading people. He had no doubts that his shortcomings along those lines were why he was indeed the submarshal and why the Highest and Marshal

Shastylt had sent him to Alustre. His next stop would be Norda, unannounced, to see what else he could discover.

When he exited the coach at the west portico of the residence, he turned to the driver. "The best to you, Granyn. I hope it's not too long before you're flying."

"Thank you, sir."

Dainyl smiled, nodded, turned, and walked briskly to the rear corridor and the steps down to the lower level and the Table chamber.

The two alector guards stiffened as Dainyl approached, but neither spoke as he released the Talent-locks and opened the outer door to the foyer leading to the Table chamber. After closing the outer door, he paused, using his Talent to listen, but neither guard said a word. Their silence suggested that they'd been alerted about something. With that in mind, he released the Talent-lock on the inner door, then eased it open and stepped inside.

The Table chamber was empty. At least, the part he saw was. He looked at the wall holding the light-torch bracket with the hidden Talent-lock, but whatever was behind the wall was shielded from him by the stone itself. After a moment, his saddlebags over one shoulder, he turned back toward the Table, over which seemed to hang a Talent-mist.

As he moved closer to the Table, a pair of long purplish arms formed from the mist, rising from the silver surface and reaching toward Dainyl. What they were, Dainyl had no idea, but they exuded menace.

He stepped back.

The arms thickened and lengthened, separating as if to encircle him.

He unholstered the lightcutter at his belt and fired at one arm. The blue fire seared through the right arm, but the arm was unchanged. The surface of the stone on the far side of the chamber took on a glazed appearance.

Dainyl raised full Talent-shields, and the arms stopped,

halted by the barriers as Dainyl stood behind his shields.

He had no doubt that he could have stepped up onto the Table—and perhaps even translated—but he didn't think shields were that effective in a translation tube. He didn't want to prove that. He also didn't like the idea of someone using the Table against a submarshal and getting away with it.

Still . . . he could feel the increasing pressure exerted by the arms—clearly drawing strength from the Table or through it—and he was beginning to sweat with the effort of maintaining shields.

He cast his Talent-senses around the chamber, realizing that the hidden door was in fact open, that it was concealed by the same Talent-cloak as the lock, and that he had not probed deeply enough. The thinnest line of purple talent ran from the Table to the doorway.

Dainyl turned toward that doorway, sensing someone behind the Talent-illusion.

The illusion vanished, and in the open stone doorway stood an angular alector, clad in green and black, the colors of a Recorder of Deeds, although Dainyl had never met one.

A line of Talent-fire, as hot as anything from a lightcutter, flared toward Dainyl, sheeting around his shields, but rocking him back a half step. He took a half step forward, then another.

More Talent-fire surged from the Recorder of Deeds, and again Dainyl's shields held, but his broad forehead was dripping sweat, and the corners of his eyes stung from where the sweat had run into them.

Dainyl doubted he could match the other alector in projecting Talent-force, and trying to do so would only weaken his own shields. But one didn't have to always use projected Talent to stop a Talent-wielder. He took two more steps. Another blast of Talent slammed at Dainyl, but another two steps brought him to where he could almost have reached out and touched the recorder. He did not.

Instead, he concentrated on bringing his own shields

forward so that, instead of forming a circle around Dainyl, they formed one around the recorder, a wall that Dainyl began to contract.

The recorder suddenly realized what Dainyl had done, and tried to step back, but found himself encircled, his own shields being squeezed back around him by the greater power of Dainyl's.

The sweat streamed down Dainyl's face, but he concentrated on contracting the shields around the other alector, ever more tightly. The recorder's hands and arms came up, trying to push back against the encircling force, to no avail. His mouth opened, but the scream was soundless, lost behind two sets of shields. His face slowly turned dark crimson.

CRUMPT! Dainyl felt himself being hurled back across the room, his back slamming into the stone wall.

His vision turned black for a long moment, but he struggled through the darkness, somehow reaching out and steadying himself against the wall with his "good" left arm. When he could see clearly again, all that remained of the Recorder of Deeds was fast-vanishing dust, and his lifeforce-treated shimmersilk raiment, crumpled in the opening to the hidden chambers.

Dainyl's left leg ached, with shivers of pain running up and down it. He could tell he hadn't rebroken it, but he hadn't done it much good, either. Absently, he noted that the purple mist and arms had vanished.

"Zorater!" The call came from the hidden chambers.

Dainyl was tired, but he certainly didn't want to stay in Alustre, not after what had just occurred, not when his ability to hold shields was diminished. He scooped up the saddlebags that he had dropped along the way and scrambled to the Table and onto it, wincing as he did, concentrating on dropping into the blackness below. . . .

The chill jolted his overheated and tired frame, so much that for a long, if timeless, moment, the black chill of the translation tube enfolded him. Where should he go? He'd intended on traveling to Norda. Should he? Returning to

Elcien might raise too many questions. At the moment, no one would really know what happened, but if he appeared in Elcien the marshal might well ask too many questions. No. Better to carry on what he had planned . . . somehow.

He cast his Talent-line out, seeking the green locator wedge, bordered in purple, that was Norda. The Talent-line and the locator wedge touched, and Dainyl could sense himself closer, but the chill surrounding him seemed more intense than on his last journey. Because he'd been overheated, or because he was tired?

He concentrated on the greenness of Norda, sensing it grow ever nearer. Then, just as he felt he was about to reach the Table . . . a line of golden green appeared, as if beside him . . . and then vanished . . . or retreated, he thought, before vanishing. At that moment, the barrier sprayed away from him. . . .

He stood on yet another Table.

Two alectors stood before the opening to the hidden chamber—did all Table chambers have them? One began to form a Talent probe, one with flame.

Dainyl projected a shield that slammed into the alector's hand, throwing him into the stone wall behind him.

The recorder beside the fallen alector raised a hand in greeting. "Submarshal! We didn't expect you. My assistant was too hasty. He was worried about a wild translation. We've had a number of them recently, and one only a few days ago, although it arrived dead, but it has been disconcerting. I apologize for his carelessness."

The stunned alector shook his head. "My apologies, sir . . . I am so sorry. I thought . . . I was worried about a wild translation."

He was sorry, Dainyl sensed, but not for mistaking Dainyl, but for failing to catch the submarshal off-guard.

"Sometimes mistakes happen," Dainyl replied. "You're fortunate I sensed it in time." He smiled coldly. "Most fortunate."

The alector swallowed.

"I'm Kasyst, Submarshal Dainyl. How could we help you?"

"I'm here to see Majer Noryan and the Myrmidons."

"Yes, sir. They're actually billeted in the adjoining compound, sir. It's but a hundred yards. I would offer a coach, but we don't have one."

"I'll manage." Dainyl kept his shields in place as he moved toward the archway leading to a foyer from the chamber. Unlike the other Table chambers he had visited, there seemed to be only one actual door.

As he passed through the archway from the Table chamber, he could hear Kasyst's low words to his assistant.

". . . causal use of power . . . one of *them* could turn you into dust . . ."

". . . Myrmidon officer . . . not a High Alector . . ."

"A submarshal, and might as well be a High Alector."

Dainyl didn't exactly feel like a High Alector, although Asulet had said something along those lines. In any case, he needed to find Majer Noryan. He wasn't looking forward to the meeting. Not the way matters had been going so far. He also wondered what the golden green had been, almost the same shade and feeling as the ancient soarer he had encountered in Dramur. Were they trying to attack through the Table grid? Or did their mirror portals work in the same fashion as did a Table?

12

Dainyl had slung his saddlebags over his shoulder and walked up the long narrow steps to a door on the ground level of the regional administration building. The door was Talent-locked and shielded. Dainyl shielded himself as he emerged in a back hallway, but the corridor was both empty and unguarded. After rebuilding the Talent-lock, he made his way to the nearest exit, a single oak door that opened onto a redstone-paved courtyard.

Despite the bright sunlight of early morning—the local time was two glasses earlier than in Alustre, Dainyl reminded himself—the wind was winterlike and gusting when he began to cross the courtyard, and he was glad for the flight jacket.

He was still a good thirty yards from the first pteridon square—there were only a handful, since Norda held only a Cadmian battalion on a regular basis and seldom hosted Myrmidons for long—when a Myrmidon ranker came hurrying toward him, then abruptly stopped.

"Submarshal?"

"Submarshal Dainyl from Elcien."

"Yes, sir. You're here to see Majer Noryan?"

Dainyl nodded.

"He's in the Cadmian headquarters, sir. It's this way. Good thing you're so early. He's going to take second squad on a recon run along the north road."

Dainyl followed the ranker to a study at one end of the one-story redstone structure. Inside, Noryan stood with two undercaptains. He had obviously commandeered the largest study in the building, and from the smaller lander-sized furnishings, had doubtless displaced the Cadmian majer who commanded the Eighth Battalion, Mounted Rifles.

"Greetings, Majer," offered Dainyl.

Noryan was huge, even for an alector, almost as large physically as Khelaryt, the Duarch of Elcien, close to three yards in height with shoulders to match, and a square head set on a thick neck. He turned and blinked as his eyes took in the stars on Dainyl's collar. "Submarshal, sir. I can't say that we expected you this morning."

"I'm making a number of unannounced visits, pursuant to the marshal's orders." Dainyl's words represented only a slight extension of the marshal's instructions.

"We'd heard that you would be in Alustre, sir, but no one mentioned . . ."

"They weren't told." Dainyl smiled. "I understand you'll be taking a squad on a recon flight shortly."

"That was the plan, sir."

"Still searching for the missing Cadmian company?"

"Yes, sir. We're also looking for other signs."

"Then I'll take only a part of a glass of your time, and you can get on with your recon."

Noryan glanced to the two undercaptains. "Carloya, have second squad hold for me. Veltuk . . . go ahead with the northwest run as we discussed."

"Yes, sir."

The two inclined their heads politely, and murmured, "Submarshal, sir," as they eased past Dainyl.

Dainyl closed the door after they left.

"How might I help you, sir?" Noryan's smile offered an expression somewhere between politeness and worry.

Dainyl was impressed by the other's shields, because he detected very little other emotion. "We've had a number of incidents with the ancients, Majer, and yours was the most recent. Your report was brief and to the point, a good Myrmidon report, but I thought it might be worthwhile to hear if, on reflection, you might have recalled something else."

"There wasn't much else to recall, sir. The old creature took out two of my rankers. We didn't even attack them. We were looking for those missing Cadmians. Kagayan saw something, and he turned toward it. Zuluya was flying wing on him and followed. The creature hit them both with something. None of us saw anything but a flash of green. Next thing I knew, both pteridons and riders were pyres on the ice below the cliff."

"Did they have their skylances at the ready?"

"Always do here in the north. The indigens here have rifles. They'll shoot at anything that moves—or they would if they didn't know we'd flame them on the spot."

"I take it that the sudden appearance—or reappearance—of the ancients at this time was as much a surprise to you as it was to Submarshal Alcyna, although I understand she had a strategy."

Noryan laughed, ruefully. "The submarshal . . . she was the one who'd given me standing orders on how to deal with the ancients if they ever showed up. I'd told her that they were orders I'd never need."

Dainyl's Talent told him that the majer was telling the truth as he'd seen it . . . and that Noryan was letting Dainyl see that. But Alcyna had given Noryan standing orders about the ancients? Not orders on the spot? "I imagine many of us had thought that. The submarshal was more perceptive. Do you recall when she first talked to you about them?"

"Had to have been sometime last harvest, maybe earlier. She didn't emphasize it that much. She just said that there had been some strange sightings, and there might be an ancient or two left. She suggested that they were powerful and that one skylance, or even two, might not do much to stop them." Noryan shrugged.

"What happened after your squads all fired?"

"Just what I reported, sir. There was a flare of green light. It looked like shards of green glass flying everywhere for a moment, but we never found anything. There was a circle of melted rock on the bluff. No one's seen any of the creatures since. I'm just guessing, but there probably aren't too many of them left anywhere on Corus."

"There never were very many," suggested Dainyl. "Was there any sort of structure near where they attacked? A shelter or a cave?"

"We did close flybys—the snow's too deep to land safely there. We didn't see a sign of anything, and there wasn't anything there last harvest before the snows began."

"I assume that the 'other signs' you're looking for on the recon are signs of the ancients."

"Yes, sir. Or any tracks by locals that might link them to the ancients."

Dainyl had wondered that himself when the ancient appearances had begun in Dramur. "Has there been any sign of any indigens nearby where the ancients appeared?"

"No sign of anyone . . ."

At the end of another quarter glass, Dainyl knew no more than he had after the first few questions he'd asked. He smiled. "I've taken enough of your time."

"I wish I could have told you more, but that's what happened."

"You can't offer more than what you know." Dainyl stepped back and opened the door. "By the way," he asked from the half-open door of the study, "who is the majer in command of the Cadmian battalion?"

"Ferank. He's using one of the studies on the other side of the hall."

"Thank you. The best on your recon. I hope you have some success in finding out what happened to the Cadmians."

"We may not ever know. The locals say that people have been vanishing here for centuries. They won't go into the higher hills, won't even travel some of the lower ones except in groups." Noryan laughed. "There's nothing there, except maybe an old building or two. The weather's bad enough to account for all of the disappearances. They find bodies and bones every spring, sometimes even in the summer. You can get snow and hail in the high hills in midsummer." He moved away from where he stood beside the undersized desk. "I'd best be getting out to the squad."

"I won't keep you longer."

Once Noryan had departed, Dainyl located Ferank two doors away on the other side of the hall. In appearance, the Cadmian majer was far different from Noryan. The lander was rail-thin, blond, with watery blue eyes, and bolted to his feet at Dainyl's appearance in the doorway.

"Submarshal, sir, what can I do for you?"

"I was just passing through, Majer, and wanted to get your thoughts about a few things." As he closed the door and moved into the chamber, Dainyl remained standing.

If he tried to sit in one of the low chairs set before the table desk in the small study, he'd be uncomfortable in moments.

"Yes, sir. About what, sir?"

"I'd be interested in hearing what you know about the missing mounted rifle company."

"I've been reporting all I know, sir." Ferank's brows wrinkled in puzzlement.

"I'm certain you did, but I'd like to hear it in your words directly from you."

"Well . . . sir, you know that we've kept two companies in Scien. It's been that way since the time I entered service. They say that the winters have been getting warmer, but I was born there, and I never saw that. They seemed as cold as ever. Whatever the reason, late this past fall we got orders from the colonel in Alustre—that's Colonel Ubarak—to consolidate the whole battalion here in Norda. I ordered Thirty-third Company here immediately, with Thirty-fourth Company to follow the next week.

"Thirty-fourth Company left Scien on Londi. No one ever saw them again, and the early winter storm didn't hit until Septi. They should have been in Pystra by Quinti. By Sexdi at the latest. I had no word, and when one of Majer Noryan's squads stopped here to overnight I asked about a possible recon to see what happened. They couldn't do one then because of some trouble in Coren. I sent back scouts, but they found no traces. When the Myrmidons could fly over the road, they didn't find anything either."

"Nothing?"

"Not a trace, sir. Not a scrap of equipment, not a trace of flesh or bone. The road between Scien and Pystra is pretty barren, too. There's not much in the way of trees, except scrub. Even the hills are low, except for the one set of ridges where I heard they lost some pteridons. After that, it snowed so much that the whole highway's buried. It usually is earlier than it was this year."

"Is there any record of companies or squads being lost along the north road before?"

"No, sir. Not in any of the records we have, and they go back almost a century. I checked."

That fact did not reassure Dainyl in the slightest. "Have any steps been taken to replace the company?"

"We've recruited about half of those we need locally, and we're supposed to get some veterans to leaven the company within the next two weeks. It's hard because we have to keep the hill folk in line in the summers, and the people around Norda have relatives among them."

"What's the problem with the hill folk?"

"The usual. They want to timber too much of the land, and there aren't enough trees here anyway. They don't want to build with stone or brick—it's too much work. Lately, they've been using mesh nets in fishing the lakes, and overfishing. They complain that the Code of the Duarches has rules that are too strict and unsuited to the north. If the district patrollers go out alone, they get shot at. So we have to make sweeps and send the ones we pick up to the road camps. They're no good at the nature camps; they kill more trees than they plant . . ."

Dainyl listened patiently.

After leaving the majer, Dainyl spent the remainder of the day walking through the Cadmian compound, talking to both rankers and squad leaders. He doubted he'd learned too much from it, except that there was more resentment about the Code of the Duarches in the east than was ever reported to the marshal, or, at least, than he had seen in any reports.

It was past sunset when he returned to the Table chamber, and the chamber itself was empty. The door to the hidden chambers was closed, but he would leave that aspect of matters . . . for the moment.

13

After using the Table from Norda to reach the one in the Hall of Justice in Elcien, Dainyl made his way from the Table chamber up and out of the hall. He stepped out into an afternoon far warmer than it had been in Norda. He was still bemused by the fact that when he traveled by Table, he crossed Corus faster than did the sun. He had left Norda after sunset and arrived in Elcien by mid-afternoon.

After hailing a hacker on the boulevard, he took the coach to Myrmidon headquarters. There he dropped his gear in his study and knocked on the marshal's door before stepping inside, since his Talent-sense revealed that no one was with Shastylt.

The marshal looked up, a momentary expression of annoyance crossing his face. "You've returned early, far sooner than might be wise."

Dainyl looked tiredly at Shastylt. "I'm far from done, but I'd like it reported . . . or let it be known . . . that I'm here."

"You do look a bit worn. I hope that the duties of your position don't prove overtaxing, the way they did with Tyanylt."

Dainyl smiled politely. "Normally, it wouldn't be any problem at all, but my arm and leg are not quite fully healed. I have run into a wild translation on one Table and an inadvertent assassination attempt in Norda, because the assistant to the recorder feared I might be a wild translation. In addition to that, I had to deal with . . . I have no idea what to call it when a Recorder of Deeds gets possessed by something through the Table. There wasn't much I could do except let events take their course."

"Yes . . . I did receive a report from the High Alector of Justice . . . something about the Recorder of Deeds in

Alustre having apparently died around the time of your departure. Most unfortunate, I fear."

"From my point of view, it could have been even more unfortunate . . ."

"You look like you've survived well enough." Shastylt's smile was perfunctory. "What have you learned?"

"That you have every right to be concerned, and that there's no proof at all of anything."

The marshal frowned. "That seems to be contradictory."

"Brekylt made an interesting comment. We were standing over his gardens the other night, and they are magnificent. He observed that one must often work with what is, rather than base actions on a plan developed centuries before. He concluded by noting that we had to be gardeners as well as administrators. After that, he would only talk pleasantries."

"Ah . . . I understand. Everything is so precisely as it should be."

"And Brekylt has put out the word, if quietly, that younger and more able alectors without contacts who do not wish to be Myrmidons will be rewarded for their ability if they chose to serve in the east."

For the briefest moment, Dainyl could sense surprise from Shastylt, although the marshal's facial expression changed not in the slightest. "That is not surprising."

"Not in itself," Dainyl agreed pleasantly. "Also, Alcyna has been transferring Myrmidons from company to company, and not just subsequent to promotions."

"To reduce loyalty to the company and increase loyalty to her, no doubt."

"I thought that might well be the reason." Dainyl was far from sure it was the only reason, but he saw no point in saying that because he didn't know what else the other submarshal had in mind.

"You had said you were not finished. What do you plan?"

"After catching up on various reports, a good night's

sleep, another day here, and then, at the beginning of next week, some more unannounced inspections and tours in the east. While everything is controlled from Alustre, nothing will be discovered there."

"You intend to travel by Table from Elcien on a regular basis, instead of going from Table to Table in the east?"

"I intend to alternate. For the moment, that would seem far more effective." Dainyl laughed. "I need to check some matters here for a day or so. When I return to the east, I will be rising very early."

"So you will. How long will you pursue such a course?"

"Until I learn what you need to know, sir." Dainyl paused. "Submarshal Alcyna issued standing orders to Majer Noryan on how to deal with the ancients several months before there were encounters with any ancients."

Shastylt did not bother to conceal his surprise. "You're sure of that?"

"She indicated she had issued orders, and Noryan confirmed the timing. Oh . . . you might know this, but she also has been sending reports on the ancients directly to Lyterna."

"Do you know to whom?"

"She did not say, and there was no record of those reports in any of the files. I did not press."

"That was wise. I should have you visit more places. Do keep me posted, Submarshal."

Dainyl understood the dismissal. "That I will, sir." He inclined his head, stepped out of the study, closing the door behind himself.

As he walked back to his own study, he reflected on Shastylt's reaction. The marshal clearly had known that Alcyna was sending reports to someone in Lyterna, yet he had not known that she had been aware of the danger posed by the ancients before any of the attacks on Myrmidons and pteridons. He also had not known about Brekylt's efforts to recruit alectors personally loyal to him and not necessarily to the Duarches. More important, Shastylt continued to conceal his own agenda—and that of High Alector Zelyert.

Dainyl did not bother to close the door to his own study. Even after only five days, reports were stacked on Dainyl's table desk. For a long moment, he just looked at them. Then he turned and walked to the archives, where he began to search through the older reports, searching for the Fourth Company reports filed about the loss of pteridons in Scien. In less than a quarter glass he had found them—and they read exactly as had those he had read in Alustre.

Was his memory failing him? He distinctly remembered that there had been two separate reports of losses.

He continued to search, but found nothing that supported his recollections. Then he checked the writing of the report, but it was the same as all the others in the Fourth Company file, and it matched what Majer Noryan had said. That suggested the first reports had been wrong in some fashion—and had been replaced with the correct ones after the fact. Was that because someone knew Dainyl would be inspecting in the east? Had Alcyna originally wanted to conceal her strategies for dealing with the ancients?

Dainyl shook his head. How could he prove that Alcyna—or Brekylt—had managed to replace false reports with accurate ones? And since the reports had been his direct responsibility at the time, even mentioning a substitution that he could not prove would do him little good and much harm. No one was about to listen to the fact that he'd been sent to Dramur during that time.

Finally, he turned and walked back to his study, still convinced the original reports had been replaced. But by whom?

Back in his study, his eyes fell on the stack of reports. It looked taller than when he had left. Slowly, he sat down and began to read. The majority of the reports, he just glanced through and set aside. He was looking for any information dealing with either past areas of difficulty, areas where signs indicated emerging troubles, or anything dealing with the ancient soarers. The report on Dramur was favorable. Majer Dohark of the Cadmians appeared to have matters well in hand there. The Fourth Cadmian Battalion, Mounted Rifles, was on its way to Iron Stem, suggesting that problem was still not fully under control. No more skylances had vanished from Dereka.

While Dainyl looked for any information on Hyalt, the only reference was in the report from the Cadmian headquarters. Third Battalion, under the command of a Majer Mykel, was being dispatched to complete the pacification of the area and the training and rebuilding of a local garrison.

Dainyl smiled uneasily. Based on what Mykel had accomplished in Dramur, the majer was doubtless the most qualified for the assignment, but the majer was far from conventional in his tactics and approach. Given the fact that the Hyalt situation had been created by a wild lander Talent, and that Mykel possessed latent Talent, Dainyl reminded himself to follow the Cadmian effort in Hyalt closely as it developed . . . assuming he could, with Shastylt's preoccupation with what was happening in Alustre.

Even though he forced himself to read through the reports, what Dainyl really wanted to do was to go home to Lystrana. He needed to discuss what he had discovered with her. He also looked forward to having an uninterrupted night's sleep.

14

Almost immediately after dinner, one where Dainyl and Lystrana discussed the weather and other pleasantries, they made their way up to their bedchamber, leaving the two serving girls to clean up. Dainyl made certain that the door was closed before he removed his boots, tunic, and trousers, and stretched out on the long bed. "It feels so good to take the weight off that leg."

"You have more on your mind than that." With a smile, she added, "And more than me, and that's unusual when you've been gone."

"I'm worried."

"You're always worried these days."

"Let me tell you what happened, first. . . ." Dainyl recounted his visit, event by event, including the matter of the altered reports—and the wild translation that had not disintegrated.

"The translation—that happens sometimes," said Lystrana. "I've heard of that. Despite their appearance, it's as if the translation changes them from alectors into landers . . . or something else related to them."

"I wonder how that happens."

"I don't know. Asulet might."

Dainyl nodded. If he ever saw the senior alector again in person, he could ask—if he remembered.

"What do *you* think about the reports?" she asked.

"The Third Company reports had to have been changed recently," he pointed out, "when someone let Alcyna know I'd be coming east." He stopped. He was so tired, but he should have seen the obvious. "Dhenyr. He's the only one in headquarters who knew what I'd be doing. He either did it, or told someone who did."

"Someone had to use a Table, if the reports are written in the same hand."

Dainyl liked that not at all. "Then . . . that means a high alector or someone like you, a chief assistant."

Lystrana nodded.

There was little enough he could do about that, except watch. He had held back one matter until the last. ". . . Oh, I also met with Kaparyk in Alustre. He had nothing but compliments about you. He did say to tell you that Chief Engineer Rensyl in Fordall has adopted the same accounting systems as Azerdyl once used, in dealing with transport and road maintenance accounts of the eastern region."

Lystrana stiffened. "Did he say it that way?"

"Exactly. He also did not answer when I asked him if this might be of interest to the marshal. He said, instead, that it was complex and that you could explain it far better than he could. That suggested to me that some sort of military equipment is being fabricated under the rubric of road construction."

"Azerdyl led the abortive eastern rebellion two centuries back. He was the head alector of finance in the east, and the High Alector of the East was under his personal shadowmatch."

"But Kaparyk used the words 'accounting systems.'"

"That suggests that Rensyl is using them under Brekylt's direction." She frowned. "You're right to be worried."

"Some aspects are clear enough, but others . . . I can't see where they're coming from." Dainyl stifled a yawn.

"You're tired. It's been a long day, and you've traveled the Tables as well."

"I am tired," he admitted, "but too worried to sleep yet. Not well, anyway. Then there's Shastylt. He *knows* Alcyna and Brekylt are plotting something, and yet he's not doing anything."

"Oh . . . but he is."

Dainyl laughed softly. "What am I doing? Upsetting matters enough to provoke them into premature action or forcing them to postpone their plans? Or worse yet, setting myself up as a target, thereby providing Zelyert and Shastylt—through my death—with a rationale and a means to guide both Duarches?"

"What do you think?"

"The third. Shastylt's reactions don't make sense otherwise."

"Unless that's what he wants you to think," Lystrana offered, settling herself onto the corner of the overlarge bed.

"Why would he make it so obvious? What deeper motive could he have?"

"What about setting up Zelyert? Then he can advise the Duarches—and he still would have direct control over the Myrmidons, especially with Alcyna gone."

"So . . . that's his way of warning me without actually saying so, because he doesn't want to take anyone into his confidences? He figures that I'll be loyal out of necessity, if I survive. If I don't, I can't reveal anything along the way."

"He also knows you'll be honest and loyal out of personal integrity."

"Isn't that what the *Views of the Highest* says? That we won't survive without integrity or some such?"

Lystrana laughed ironically. "Shastylt should reread it."

Dainyl shook his head. The higher he rose in the Myrmidons, the more complex—and the more deadly—the plots and intrigues became. "You didn't seem to think it was military equipment that Rensyl was hiding in the transport accounts. What else could it be?"

"Road-building equipment. That's under the Myrmidon control and guarded by Alcyna."

Dainyl only had to think briefly about the road-building equipment he had viewed in Alustre before nodding. "Will it bring down a pteridon?"

"It might. It also might be sufficiently powerful to destroy an ancient."

"You're suggesting that Brekylt is worried about the ancients, and that he feels the Duarches aren't taking the potential threat seriously enough?"

"Are they?"

"Not from what I've seen." Dainyl looked at Lystrana, seeing for the first time the circles under her eyes. "You're tired, too."

"Carrying a child, even this early, is tiring. She presses for more lifeforce."

"I'm sorry."

"That's the way it is, dearest."

If he hadn't been so exhausted, with pains shooting through both his right arm and left leg, and seeing Lystrana so drained, Dainyl would have laughed, if ruefully.

The High Alector of Justice was afraid that transferring the Master Scepter to Acorus would not only destroy the world before its time, but reduce his power and influence. The High Alector of the East and Alcyna wanted the Master Scepter transferred, but only after removing Zelyert and Shastylt, in order to gain influence, and they well might be building weapons to use against the ancients, presumably because they feared that ancients might block the transfer of the Master Scepter. The Duarch of Elcien wanted the transfer because he feared worse if the Master Scepter went to Efra instead of Acorus. And no one talked about any of it, or why it was better for it to be transferred to one world rather than the other.

But then, according to the *Views of the Highest*, there was only one best alternative.

Dainyl slowly rose to get ready for bed—and sleep too long delayed.

15

On Octdi morning, just after dawn, Mykel stood on the wide goldenstone pier that held the *Duarches' Honor*. With a length of more than two hundred yards and a main deck that rose a good fifteen yards above the pier, the vessel towered over Mykel and the men and mounts of Third Battalion as they waited to board. The greenish gray metal of her hull plates gleamed dully in the light of a sun that had barely risen and struggled to shine through hazy clouds. As with all of the great ships of the Duarchy, there were no masts and no sails, and no coal was taken aboard. So the propulsion system could not be one of the rare steam engines such as those used in the manufactories of Faitel, the city of artisans and engineers where Mykel had grown up.

Mykel glanced to his right at the long ramp that angled from the pier into a hatchway several decks below the main deck, and then at Undercaptain Dyarth, who stood holding his own mount, waiting to lead the troopers and mounts of Thirteenth Company up the ramp.

The faintest halo of yellow-brown surrounded the mount, that aura that enfolded all living things—or the larger living creatures—but was visible only to Mykel and the soarers, and perhaps a few others. Dyarth's aura was stronger than his mount's, an orangish yellow. As Mykel had quietly concentrated on sensing such auras over the past few weeks and become more adept, he had come to realize that the auras of most people—at least all those he had encountered—seemed to contain some shades of brown, but there was a wide variation, while the more limited auras of other creatures seemed very similar. All horses seemed orangish yellow. He hadn't been able to sense auras for small creatures, but he had no idea whether that was because creatures below a certain size had none or that he could not discern them.

From behind Dyarth, Mykel could hear the low murmurs of the rankers.

". . . rather ride than take a ship . . ."

". . . easier on the mounts this way . . . say it's only two and a half, three days by sea. Take us more like a week just to ride to Southgate."

"Something happens on land . . . know where you are. Something happens at sea, and where are you?"

"That kind of thinking, be glad you're not a Myrmidon."

Several rankers laughed.

"What's the farthest you've had to carry a battalion?" Mykel asked the deck mate who stood beside him, a gray-haired and wiry man close to the age of Mykel's own father.

"Maybe twenty years back, we took a whole battalion to Lysia. For some reason, the High Alector of Justice replaced all the Cadmians there. I was just a fresh deckhand then."

Three quick chimes rang out from the deck above.

"You can start 'em up the ramp, Majer. Keep a good two yards between each horse. No more than two on the ramp at once."

"Thank you." Mykel turned to Dyarth. "Thirteenth Company, forward. Two yards between each mount. Only two on the ramp at once. Pass it back."

"Yes, sir. Thirteenth Company! Forward! Two yards between . . ."

Bhoral followed Undercaptain Dyarth.

"Everyone forms up on the forward deck after the mounts are stabled," Mykel said as Bhoral passed him.

"Yes, sir."

Mykel could have gone ahead and left Bhoral to bring up the rear, but he could get a good look at each and every trooper as they passed by him, and if his odd talent told him something he didn't already know about the troopers in his battalion, so much the better.

By the time Thirteenth Company and almost half of Fourteenth had passed him, his senses confirmed that, as the troopers were of differing sizes and shapes, so were their auras. He looked past a young ranker and stiffened inside. The man who was next in line did not meet Mykel's eyes, and his aura held streaks of an ugly red.

Mykel struggled mentally to recall the name of the trooper—Sacyrt. The ranker had been transferred from Second Battalion, and, although Mykel could not have proved it, the color of his aura suggested a troublemaker. "Sacyrt?"

"Yes, sir." Surprise and wariness colored the ranker's voice.

"You're being transferred to Seventeenth Company. I trust you'll find it a better fit. I expect the best from every man."

"Yes, sir."

As the older ranker led his mount past Mykel, he heard murmurs.

". . . picked Sacyrt out . . ."

". . . just hope he doesn't pick any of us out . . . don't want a majer watching you . . ."

Mykel hoped Sacyrt felt the same way, but trouble-makers usually thought that different rules applied to them. He concentrated on the men as his own former company—Fifteenth Company, led by Fabrytal—started up the ramp.

By the time the last troopers and mounts—except his own—had walked up the ramp and into the ship, Mykel had a dull headache. He rubbed his forehead, took a deep breath, then untied the roan from a cleat attached to the nearest bollard. His saddlebags bulged, partly from the ammunition belt he had tucked in at the last moment.

He stepped onto the railed ramp. The surface had been coated with lacquer and then dusted with sand, so that hooves had more purchase than on bare or painted wood.

"Easy, big fellow," he murmured to the roan, trying to project reassurance. The railing on the ramp was sturdy, but not enough to take the weight of a spooked mount, and just before the ramp entered the ship, man and mount would be some ten yards above a very hard stone pier.

Once inside the ship, where all the bulkheads and decks seemed to be of the same greenish-tinted steel, another crewman stood waiting. His eyes took in Mykel's collar insignia. "Majer, your horse's stall is forward. Straight to the next passageway. Then turn forward—that's to your right—and go as far as you can. Your stall will be the first one on the right."

"Thank you."

As he led the roan inboard and then forward, Mykel was reminded once more that the ship had been built to carry horses—or alectors. The overheads in the main passageways were close to three yards in height.

The stalls were narrow, each one barely half the width of one in the stables in headquarters, but that was as much for the protection of the mount in heavy seas as to save space. Still, it would take very heavy seas to make footing unsteady on the *Duarches' Honor*.

After stabling the roan, Mykel made his way forward and up two decks, carrying his saddlebags and gear. Unlike the last trip, he rated a stateroom to himself, even if it had little more than space enough for two bunks, one atop the other, and two doorless lockers barely able to hold an officer's travel gear. Mykel left the saddlebags and hurried forward to the open section of the main deck forward of the superstructure.

Bhoral and most of the Third Battalion were already there.

"Seventeenth Company's last squads are still coming in," announced Bhoral.

"We can wait a few moments, but I'll need to report to the captain." Mykel glanced aft and up at the open forward bridge where there stood two alectors—the captain and his executive officer, two of the three alectors on a Duarchy ship. The other was the chief engineer.

"You been on many of these ships?" Mykel's only other shipboard travel had been to and from Dramur, but Bhoral had spent twenty years in the Cadmians.

"Not many," replied the senior squad leader. "This is the fourth. There aren't that many ships. Ten, I think. Ship this size and this fast, you don't need many."

Mykel glanced past Bhoral. "Here come our lagging squads."

The rankers and squad leaders of the fourth and fifth squads from Seventeenth Company eased into place.

"Third Battalion, report!" ordered Bhoral.

"Thirteenth Company, all present and accounted for. . . ."

"Fourteenth Company, all present. . . ."

When the muster was completed, Mykel stepped forward. "The rules here are simple. We'll muster twice a day, before breakfast, and before supper. From lights out to morning call, you stay in your bunking spaces or the shipboard latrines . . . if you can stand them. . . ."

That got a slight laugh.

"All other times, we have the freedom of the main

deck, the mess deck, and the stable deck. Don't go anywhere else. We'll be on the ship until Decdi. That's all
for now."

"Dismissed!" ordered Bhoral.

Mykel turned and moved quickly back to the ladder up
to the ship's bridge. When he reached the lower bridge,
he found himself facing a ship's officer, a man with graying brown hair and a single silver diamond insignia affixed to his collar.

"Majer, I'm Cylison, the navigator's mate. The exec
asked me to take your report. He and the captain will be
occupied for the next few glasses."

"I'd like to report that Third Cadmian Battalion,
Mounted Rifles, is ready for departure."

"I'll convey that to the exec and captain." Cylison
smiled. "You're fairly new to battalion command, aren't
you?"

"Is it that obvious?" Mykel laughed ruefully.

"Not by the embarkation. That was as smooth as any
I've seen, but you're the youngest majer I've encountered
in fifteen years. You came hurrying up to report, and you
were surprised to see me. You're all told to report embarkation to the captain, but that means he needs to be informed, not that you'll normally see him or the exec. If
the captain needs you, you'll know."

Mykel nodded, trying not to be thrown off by the fact
that the navigator's aura also bore faint tinges of purplish
pink, something he'd seen before only with Majer Hersiod, but the navigator didn't seem at all intransigent the
way Hersiod had.

"We should be porting in Southgate around the second
glass past midday on Decdi, but that could change if we
run into high seas. That sometimes happens this time of
year, but the reports from the Myrmidons indicate seas
are calm as far south as Hafin." Cylison smiled warmly.
"How did you get to be a majer so young . . . if you don't
mind my asking?"

"Third Battalion was the one assigned to the Dramu-

ran . . . problem." Mykel still wasn't certain what to call
the last campaign, and the most generally used term was
the word "problem." "After the majers in charge were
killed, the senior captain took over running the compound in Dramur, and I ended up commanding the remaining companies of Third Battalion. The submarshal
of Myrmidons appreciated what we did. The senior captain was immediately promoted to majer in charge of all
Cadmian operations on Dramur, and I ended up with
Third Battalion." Mykel shrugged. "How did you—"

"I'm sorry to have to break this off, Majer, but the captain will be needing me—and your report. Best of luck in
Southgate, in case I don't see you before we port." With
that, Cylison turned and hurried up the ladder to the upper bridge.

Mykel managed to keep a pleasant expression on his
face as he came back down the ladder and forward to a
spot on the main deck, a good thirty yards aft of the bow
on the starboard side of the ship. Once there, he looked
back at the bridge, where he saw the two alectors, but not
the navigator. Neither looked in his direction.

The ship *hummed*, or so it seemed, as Mykel watched
the last of the heavy lines be unfastened from the man-
high bollards on the dock and then reeled in by the deck
crew. Mykel sensed *something*, not exactly like an aura,
nor like the ancient soarer who had confronted him in
Dramur, but similar and yet different. There was the same
sense of purpleness that had tinged the navigator, except
it was far stronger, and that was despite the fact that it was
located somewhere aft and far below him. Was that what
propelled the vessel? But how? Did it touch or affect all
those who crewed the ship? Had Hersiod returned from
his last deployment by ship? Offhand, Mykel didn't
know, but he thought not.

Rhystan eased up to the railing beside Mykel. "Could I
join you, Majer?"

"Please."

After several moments, Rhystan broke the conversational silence. "Couldn't tell this ship from the last one, except for the name. Even the alectors up there—" He gestured back toward the bridge. "—look like every other alector."

"They even call all the ships something of the Duarches," Mykel added. *"Duarches' Honor, Duarches' Legacy, Duarches' Valor . . ."*

"Majer . . . what do you think about Hyalt?" Rhystan's words were cautious.

"There's more that we haven't been told," Mykel replied.

"You said that they sent the Myrmidons there first?"

"According to the colonel, the Myrmidons used their skylances and smashed the heart of the irregulars. Now we're supposed to run down the rest and build a stronger local garrison."

"There isn't any more?"

"I'm sure there is. I asked, but never got any more information. So I even dug up histories of the place, and I've got a stash of maps with my gear."

"Sounds like another mess, sir, Dramur all over again."

There was the slightest lurch, and then a dull *thrumming* vibrated through the *Duarches' Honor* as the vessel eased away from the pier.

"Let's hope that's enough, sir."

"You've been through it once before," Mykel pointed out. "That will help. And if you see anything I should know, don't wait to tell me."

"I won't." Rhystan paused. "That's all I had for now, sir."

"I'm here if you need me."

Rhystan nodded, then stepped away.

Once Rhystan had left, Mykel glanced aft, back toward Elcien. Even after two voyages, he was still amazed at how quickly the huge vessel had built up speed. Less than a quarter of a glass had passed, and they were several vingts west of the western tip of the isle that held Elcien.

Rhystan's remarks—and what he sensed about the ship

itself with his new talent—bothered him. Perhaps his younger brother Viencet had been right after all, that there was far more behind the alectors, and that they had made a concerted effort to hide it.

He glanced aft, in the direction of the unknown force that he was convinced propelled the ship, a force that Mykel had just recently learned to sense. That suggested that the alectors—or some of them—could also sense it. Yet they kept it hidden, and, the Cadmians, even the officers, were limited to where they could go on board the ship, and the engine spaces were sealed.

That suggested to Mykel that his "talent" was something that possibly many alectors had, and that few landers or others did. Should he conceal what he could see? How?

He looked out across the dark green waters of the Bay of Ludel.

16

On Octdi, Dainyl had slept later than he should have and had not arrived at headquarters until nearly a glass after morning muster. That had been the first time he'd *ever* been so tardy. Even so, he had been exhausted, and not really fit for more than catching up on reports, and getting briefed by Colonel Dhenyr. After Dhenyr left, Dainyl found himself wondering how Alcyna had suborned the colonel—if she had—since Dhenyr hadn't been stationed in the east for close to ten years.

For all that, Dainyl paid close attention to the colonel. Fortunately, little of major consequence had occurred in Dainyl's absence. The marshal had been nowhere to be seen, not during all of Octdi, for which Dainyl was more than grateful.

After another night's decent sleep, Dainyl had spent

the half-day of duty on Novdi at headquarters, checking Cadmian deployment schedules and Myrmidon duty rotations against the accounting ledgers. As always, the maintenance requirements for Lysia seemed high, and he mentally reaffirmed his decision to visit Lysia after Prosp and Dulka. He'd decided to visit Prosp and Dulka first, because not much of import seemed to have happened there, although the resupply levels seemed higher than they should have been in Dulka. He wanted his unannounced inspections to seem as innocuous as possible in the beginning. Also, he'd have more background information before tackling Lysia.

The remainder of Novdi and all of Decdi, he spent with Lystrana—happily, trying to avoid thinking about the political currents that swirled through Elcien, Ludar, and Alustre, with ripples that might affect all of Corus.

Londi morning found Dainyl at the Hall of Justice, less than half a glass after dawn. As he walked along the stone-walled and subterranean corridor toward the Table chair, a door opened ahead of him on his left.

"Dainyl . . . there you are." High Alector Zelyert's voice was deep, rumbling, with an overtone of warmth that was not matched by the emotions behind his shields. "Shastylt said you would be here early. I would like a few words with you before you depart."

Dainyl inclined his head, leaving his personal shields firmly in place. "As you desire, sir." He followed Zelyert into the small and spare chamber that was the High Alector's private study.

The High Alector of Justice stood a quarter of a head taller than Dainyl, and his flawless alabaster skin was even paler than that of the submarshal, especially in contrast to his shimmering black hair and deep violet eyes. As usual, at least when Dainyl had seen him, Zelyert wore a tunic of brilliant green, trimmed in a deep purple, with matching purple trousers.

Dainyl closed the door and stood waiting.

Zelyert did not seat himself. "I will be brief. Marshal

Shastylt relayed your concerns about the fashion in which the lesser submarshal has handled the ancients and about the recruiting practices of the High Alector of the East. You were right to be circumspect . . . and cautious. There may be reasons for these actions that are in fact perfectly acceptable and in accord with the Code and the greater purposes of the Archon. Or they may be as you suspect."

"Highest . . . sir . . . I do not assume to know enough to claim a suspicion, only that what I perceived appeared to merit your attention and that of the marshal."

Zelyert laughed, a sound at variance with the earlier warmth in his words. "I can see why Shastylt holds you in such esteem, Dainyl. You prefer to let the facts speak as they will."

"I have observed that what one sees often is a reflection of where one stands, sir, and that more than one pair of eyes are often necessary to see what is."

"You sound like the mystic Dulachamyt, now, and a fighting commander cannot afford to rely on mysticism."

"I stand corrected." Dainyl maintained a pleasant smile and an equally pleasant tone of voice.

"You do indeed, and I am pleased that you remain wise enough to understand that. What do you hope to discover on these journeys?"

"Whatever may be at variance with what I was told in Alustre. If nothing appears at variance, then I will report that."

"Whatever you discover, you and the marshal will report officially that nothing is at variance. Leave it to us to report any discrepancies to the Duarches personally. If there are significant discrepancies, others besides the High Alector of the East may well be involved, and it would not be wise to provide advance warning to them."

"Yes, sir. I can see that."

"Good. I thought you would. Have a productive journey. We look forward to hearing what you discover."

"It may take trips to a number of Tables, sir, and as long as a week, if not longer."

"Take the time necessary, Dainyl. What you discover, one way or another, is of great import." Zelyert smiled, then gestured toward the door. "I will not keep you longer."

"Highest . . ." murmured Dainyl, inclining his head before turning and departing.

Dainyl made his way to the Table chamber, making certain that he replaced each Talent-lock that he passed. Before he stepped onto the Table, he slowly studied the entire chamber, seeking out, with Talent and all other senses, any possible hint of another hidden chamber. So far as he could tell, there was none. Was that because there were so many other adjoining chambers within the Hall of Justice, and all were hidden? Or was the use of Talent and architecture merely more clever?

His conversation with Zelyert had been disturbing, for all its superficial pleasantness, particularly the points about Shastylt and Zelyert reporting privately anything Dainyl might find out. Dainyl had strong doubts that, if facts came to light suggesting less than honorable behavior by those he served, they would ever reach the ear of the Duarch. Nor would other information. And if Dainyl even revealed such to the marshal, Shastylt would certainly attempt to handle him as he had Tyanylt. Yet, at the moment, all Dainyl had were suspicions, without a single fact to support them—and he might well be wrong.

Finally, he stepped up onto the Table, concentrating, falling through the stone and into the depths beneath. . . .

The darkness beneath the Table was slightly less dark than he recalled, but more chill. In the distance that could have been yards, or vingts, or hundreds or thousands of vingts from him, he could sense the directional wedges of the fourteen Tables, although the bright blue of Tempre and the brilliant yellow of Ludar were the clearest and strongest.

Because he did not wish to arrive in Prosp any more tired than necessary, he immediately concentrated on the silver locator that marked that Table and linked to it with a thin line of purple Talent. As he felt himself ever closer to that Table, although there was no physical sense of motion, once again, briefly, if time even existed within the translation tubes, he thought he sensed a flash or a line of golden green. Then he was at the thin wall of silver, with insubstantial shards shattering away from him and vanishing.

He took only a single step on the silvery and polished surface of the Table, making sure that his shields were firmly in place even before taking in the Table chamber around him.

The space was empty, but, as in Alustre, black and silver-trimmed hangings of scenes in the east ornamented the walls. Directly before Dainyl was a vista of the Great Marsh, with the volcanoes of Cape Fiere rising above the sea of rushes.

He could sense immediately the special light-torch bracket, touched with Talent, that marked the entrance to the hidden chambers beyond. His hand on his sidearm, he stepped off the Table, still alert for any possible attack, either from the Table, a wild Talent, or an overenthusiastic Recorder of Deeds or assistant. No one appeared, nor did he sense anyone.

Stopping short of the door to the chamber's entry foyer, he released the Talent-lock, and cast out his senses. There was no one in the foyer. Beyond the outer door in the corridor, however, there were two guards, Cadmians rather than Myrmidons. That made sense because there were no Myrmidons stationed anywhere near Prosp, and only two companies of local Cadmians. The rich and agricultural lands that stretched away from Prosp had never seen much unrest, doubtless because there were few places for rebels to hide and no reason to rebel.

Dainyl had chosen Prosp because he had hoped the setting and situation would favor less plotting and guile, and thus, more directness. He put his hand on the door and opened it, stepping out.

Both Cadmians had been leaning against the limestone wall. They scrambled erect.

"Sir! We didn't know . . . we didn't expect . . ."

"I would have hoped not," replied Dainyl pleasantly. "I'm looking for your commander."

"The overcaptain, sir?"

Dainyl nodded.

"He'll be across the courtyard in the headquarters building."

"Then I'll find him." Still leaving his shields up, Dainyl turned, walked down the corridor, and headed up the stone steps to the ground-floor level of the building.

". . . hope that's not trouble . . ."

". . . Myrmidons . . . always trouble . . . those stars . . . that's a marshal, I think, and that's big trouble . . ."

Not for the two Cadmians, Dainyl thought, and probably not for the overcaptain, but he needed to find out more before deciding.

Someone saw him crossing the sun-flooded courtyard, almost warm enough to be pleasant without the flying jacket he wore, because the overcaptain was waiting for him just beyond the entry foyer to the small, single-story headquarters building.

"Overcaptain Morash, sir. At your service, whatever that might require."

"Just a few questions, Overcaptain. If you'd lead the way to your study . . ."

"Yes, sir. This way."

After he closed the study door, Dainyl remained standing, not wanting to cramp himself in the undersized chairs.

"What can I do for you, sir? We don't see submarshals here." The bulky and graying overcaptain chuckled. "Matter of fact, I haven't seen Colonel Ubarak ever, or his predecessor, either. We just get dispatches, and not many of those."

"You make it sound as though there's little need for your companies here," Dainyl suggested.

"Now, I wouldn't be saying that, sir. No, sir. Folk here are just like folk everywhere. At times, if we weren't here, they might do what they shouldn't. Sometimes, they need protection, too. Last fall we had to take to the field against some hill folk that had come from northeast of Flyr. Must have been close to fifty of them, armed with good rifles, too. They burned Ceantor's villa, and looted his strongroom. Took one of his daughters, too." Morash shook his head. "Sad business, that."

"What happened?"

"What could we do? They broke the Code. We surrounded them. None of them would surrender. We killed nearly all of them, except for the ones who were wounded and couldn't fight. Some of them died anyway. The justicer sent the rest of them to the quarries south of Catyr for life. They killed the girl. Couldn't believe we wouldn't just let them walk in and take what they wanted."

Even though the quarry laborers were well fed and not mistreated, the work was grueling, Dainyl knew, and few lasted more than five or ten years. "How often does something like that happen?"

"I'd have to check the records to be really accurate, Submarshal, but as I recall, it takes a couple of years for the hill folk to forget. Say every three-four years. If we weren't here, though, they'd be long gone before one of the battalion outposts could send anyone. Our road patrols do a good job of keeping the brigandage down, too."

Dainyl had his own ideas about why, but he asked, "Just by patrolling the roads?"

Morash smiled. "It's simple enough. There are only a few places where goods and coins are concentrated, and that's in the towns and in the strongrooms of the growers and the factors or when people travel the high roads. The growers and factors guard their golds well. We guard the marketplaces and the roads." He shrugged. "We can't do much about all of the petty theft, cutpurses, and that, but most of them get caught in time and sent to the labor camps or quarries."

"I suppose you don't get many dispatches directly from the Myrmidons or the High Alector of the East?"

"Not many. In fact, I can only recall one in the past year, and that was a reminder to keep the pteridon squares ready. That happened after the troubles out west in Coren."

"You don't seem to have problems like that."

"No. But it's a different place. Here, every grower and every holder has his own lands. If he doesn't work them right, he suffers. If he has a problem that's not his making, and he works hard, others will help him. Out there, folks see lands and trees that look empty, and for just a little extra effort, they can pick up quite a few more golds."

"If they overlog the slopes, the rains wash off more soil, and the rivers flood, and everyone suffers," Dainyl pointed out.

"You know that, Submarshal, and I can figure it out, but the ones that suffer are downstream and out of sight, and people have trouble giving up coins for people they don't know and might never see."

Dainyl nodded. He knew what the overcaptain said was true, but it was a facet of lander thought that had always given him difficulty. How could they *not* see, especially when it was something taught in every school?

In the end, Dainyl only spent three glasses in Prosp, inspecting the one company in the compound and making a brief scrutiny of equipment and dispatch orders.

After eating a hearty if plain meal at the small mess serving the handful of Cadmian officers, he made his way back to the Table chamber, pondering the general order from Brekylt about the pteridon squares. It might have just been a reminder, but it also might have been a step in making sure Myrmidon companies could be moved quickly.

This time, the Recorder of Deeds for Prosp was waiting in the Table chamber. He was a comparatively young alector, Dainyl sensed, but he reeked of raw Talent. He bowed to Dainyl. "Submarshal, we had no word that you would be traveling to Prosp. For this reason, we regret that we were not here when you arrived."

Dainyl kept his Talent-shields in place as he replied. "Even a Recorder of Deeds cannot be everywhere."

"We would wish to be of service, Submarshal, but we cannot do so if we do not know when you will arrive."

"You are forgiven," Dainyl said with a smile, managing to keep the expression in place, even as he wished he had not delivered the gentle rebuke. He couldn't very well say that he didn't want the Table guardians knowing when he would be arriving or where he was headed.

"Sir?" The recorder radiated displeasure.

Dainyl wanted to crush him for his youthful arrogance. Instead, he said, "I act at the request of the High Alector of Justice and under the command of the Duarch, and cannot offer explanations or schedules. If you wish, seek an explanation from them."

This time, the recorder paled.

Dainyl stepped onto the Table, maintaining his shields even as he dropped through the silver-dark surface into the chill blackness below.

17

The spring sun that beat down on Mykel as he rode away from the harbor was as hot as it was in midsummer in Elcien, if not even hotter. Beside Mykel rode Captain Muerwyn, their guide and escort, as well as a company commander stationed at the Cadmian compound just northeast of Southgate itself.

"It's only about half a vingt to the inner ring," repeated Muerwyn. "We'll take it until it intersects the northeast road out to the compound."

Mykel turned in the saddle and looked back. So far as he could tell, Third Battalion continued to ride in good order. He turned his attention to the buildings on each side of the harbor boulevard. None were more than two stories in height, and the exterior walls were finished with white stucco. All followed the same plan he had seen in Dramuria, with few exterior windows and a central courtyard, although some of those courtyards were less than five yards on a side. From the depth of the few barred windows, Mykel judged that the thick walls themselves were either of brick or stone. The roofs, like those in Dramuria, were tiled, but the tile was a pale sandy red. The difference that stood out was that the walls of the houses and buildings in Dramuria had been of dressed gray stone, while every structure in Southgate was white, and the walls clearly had been continually washed in white over the years, so much so that Mykel found himself blinking from the intensity of the reflected light.

"This is the trade quarter?" he asked.

"Mostly, sir. There are some artisans and crafters. Mainly potters and stoneworkers."

That also figured. There were no metals or coal nearby, and the area was too hot for sheep and too dry for cotton, and the nearest large forests were more than a hundred vingts to the north or east.

Mykel looked at the boulevard ahead, flanked by somewhat larger structures, although none were any taller than those he had already passed. A sign caught his eye— STYLEN AND SONS, FACTORS IN CLOTH. Rachyla had come from Stylan Estate in Dramur. Was the similarity a coincidence? He snorted softly. Although he'd been told that some wealthy seltyr families from Dramur had close ties to Southgate—and often interests in businesses there— Mykel doubted that Rachyla would have admitted being related to a mere cloth factor, even if it were so. An ironic smile crossed his lips at the thought.

He couldn't help but wonder how she was doing, since her father's estate had gone to a male cousin. Seltyr women could not inherit, a custom that bothered Mykel. His own sister Sesalia would certainly inherit from their parents—although it was unlikely that there would be that much for any of the three of them. Viencet would be the neediest, unless matters changed dramatically.

Mykel forced his attention back to the boulevard ahead. According to the maps he had studied, the center of Southgate was bounded by a ring road, and within the ring lived the more powerful and wealthy of the lander factors who controlled the trade and commerce of the city. Southgate was far more independent than any city except Dramuria, without any regional alector or Myrmidons. The closest administrative centers were in Ludar and Tempre.

Third Battalion had ridden less than half a vingt along the boulevard from the harbor before they neared the inner ring, arcing away from the boulevard in both directions. The pavement was smooth gray granite, and it was, unlike the other streets, a good thirty yards in width. The outer edge was bordered by a granite wall two yards high, except where other boulevards or streets entered the ring road. Mykel looked both east and west, but he saw no riders on the inner ring and only a single carriage heading on to his right, roughly southward. There was no one on foot.

"There's not much traffic on the inner ring," he observed.

"It's reserved for horses and carriages," Muerwyn replied. "Those on foot must use the outer lane." He pointed.

Mykel's eyes followed the captain's gesture. A narrower lane ran outside the low wall, one with scattered pedestrians and peddlers.

"We'll go left and pick up the boulevard on the northeast side of the ring," Muerwyn said, turning his mount.

Mykel looked to his right, across the expanse of the ring road at a villa, the walls surrounding it a good four yards high. At each corner where the walls joined was a stone tower. The walls did not form a square or a rectangle, but a trapezoid. The side of the wall nearest him was roughly a half-vingt long. He looked ahead, still to his right, but farther along the ring road. There was another walled and apparently palatial villa, one of a number set in a circle inside the inner ring. Those walls were also white, glaring white.

"There seem to be quite a number of those villas," offered Mykel.

"Thirteen, in all. The wall lengths are identical, but the villas within differ. Or so I've heard. They're not terribly interested in inviting Cadmians to dine with them."

"Where did all such wealthy landers come from?"

"Where do they come from anywhere?" replied Captain Muerwyn.

That wasn't exactly a helpful answer, reflected Mykel. "Are most factors, or do their coins come from other sources?"

"I'd guess that half are factors, and perhaps a third own estates to the northwest. The lands to the northeast are not that fertile and better suited to grazing."

"And the others?"

"I couldn't say, sir. I'm from Dimor, myself."

Mykel studied the walls, some sort of white granite, but not eternastone, at least not any that he knew. He hadn't realized at first just how large each villa was, but he had ridden close to half a vingt paralleling just one wall. A quick estimate suggested that each trapezoid was roughly a half-vingt across the outer and larger side, a vingt in depth, and something like two fifths of a vingt across the shorter base.

Once past the first villa, Mykel glanced down the avenue toward the center of the area bounded by the inner ring road.

"All the villas face the square," explained the captain.

Mykel said nothing, continuing to study the ring road and the villas. At the next intersection, he turned in the saddle for a better look. From what he could glimpse, there were no gates in the side walls, or those closest to the ring road. That meant any gate had to be on the wall that faced whatever might be in the center of the area bounded by the ring road.

There was a central circular area with steles of white

stone, but before he could see more, his mount carried him past the road, and the walls of the next villa blocked his view of whatever lay down the radial road to the center of Southgate. "What's down there?"

"The city center. It's just a circular square with some columns. No markets, no taverns, or inns. Certainly, no pleasure houses." Muerwyn gave a barking laugh.

Mykel turned in the saddle once more to look back, but the battalion remained in good riding order. He said nothing while they covered more than two vingts along the inner ring, instead studying what he could of Southgate. The more he saw, the more uneasy he felt, and it was not just the glaring whiteness of all the structures, yet he could sense nothing he could put a finger on.

The buildings outside the inner ring continued to resemble those he had seen earlier, resembling those in Dramuria, except for the whiteness of the walls. He felt as though they were little older, or perhaps even newer than those on Dramur. "Is Southgate a newer city?"

"Newer?" Muerwyn looked puzzled. "It has been here for centuries. How could it be new?"

"From what I can see, Southgate has no eternastone. There are no green towers within sight."

"Eternastone is for roads, not buildings."

That alone told Mykel that Muerwyn had not traveled far, but he asked anyway. "You've spent all your time with the Cadmians in Southgate?"

"No, sir. I started in Dimor, and then was posted to Zalt, before I was transferred to the compound here."

Muerwyn might as well have spent all his time in Southgate, Mykel thought.

"There's the northeast road ahead, the one with the pillars on each side," announced the captain. "The compound is a little less than two vingts from here."

The vanguard escort troopers turned onto the northeast road, and Mykel and Third Battalion followed. The dwellings and shops bordering the road became progressively smaller as the Cadmians rode on, but their plastered outer walls remained a shimmering white.

Even when Mykel could see the walls of the Cadmian compound—also white—and the half-vingt of open ground that separated the meaner inns and taverns from the compound itself, the pavement of the road remained granite . . . and not eternastone.

Southgate was not at all what he had expected, not in the slightest, and far more disturbing than Dramuria had been, although Mykel could not have said exactly why. He hoped he was mistaken.

18

As he dropped into the darkness, Dainyl immediately began to search for the maroon and blue locator vector wedge that was Dulka. Just when he had located it and begun to extend a Talent line to link to the Dulkan Table, he felt himself wrenched, grasped by shoulder and leg.

How could that be?

Purpleness flooded over his left side, like the arms from the Table in Alustre.

Although he could not turn physically in the translation tube, he extended his Talent senses. From what he could tell, the arms flowed from the silver locator that was Prosp. What was the young recorder trying to do? Trap him in the chill? Keep him there until his thoughts congealed in the cold?

What had he done to break clear of the arms in Alustre? He'd suffocated the recorder there with his shields. That wasn't likely to work here.

Could he even form a shield in the tube? Dainyl visualized his Talent coating his garments on his left side, then expanding. Even in the chill of the blackness, he could feel heat building inside his body, as if trapped by his own shields. He kept pressing, expanding the shields against the grip of the purple arms he could sense and feel but not see.

Slowly, ever so slowly, he could sense his shields expanding.

Abruptly, the arms released.

Dainyl Talent-linked to the maroon and blue locator wedge, then found it flashing toward him.

In moments, he shattered the silvered barrier.

Dainyl managed not to stagger as he stood on the Table in the empty chamber. He studied the chamber, noting that while it, too, had a hidden chamber, that chamber door was closed. At one end of the chamber was a statue of a single figure, close to three yards in height. From what Dainyl could recall from his one meeting with the Duarch of Elcien, the statue was an accurate representation of Khelaryt. The stone figure held a silver scepter topped with glittering blue stones arranged to simulate a flame. A dozen light-torches illuminated the chamber, many more than in any other Table chamber Dainyl had visited thus far, and in their light, the gem-flame sparkled.

The decorative hangings on the side walls contained no scenes, but only angular and unfamiliar designs. Between the two hangings to Dainyl's left was an archway and a stonewalled corridor beyond that appeared to end at a wall. His Talent revealed no one near.

After stepping down from the Table, he stood for a time beside it, letting his body readjust from the combination of internal heat and external chill.

Should he have reemerged in Prosp? Confronted the young recorder? No . . . he might have emerged into a lightcutter beam with weakened shields—or his shields might not have worked for the moment of emergence, and he didn't want to chance that unless he had no other options. Should he have gone back to Elcien? In retrospect, perhaps that would have been wisest, but he hadn't made that decision, and immediately attempting another Table journey now before trying to recover seemed unwise.

Finally, he wiped his forehead and walked into the corridor, realizing as he neared the apparent end that it was only a screen wall, with passages on each side around the central screen. Both the screen wall and the lower archway before it had been finished with blue ceramic tile, except for a single course at the edge, done in maroon.

His Talent-senses revealed a large hall beyond the screen wall, with a platform overlooking it. He could sense but a single person beyond the wall. Still, he held his shields as he stepped around the wall and onto the platform. The amphitheatre beyond was dimly lighted by a handful of light-torches. Their illumination was almost swallowed by the size of the cavern that had to have been carved from the stone by some version of the road-building equipment Dainyl had inspected in Alustre. Or did similar equipment still exist in Dulka?

He extended the slightest Talent probe. The entire amphitheatre filled with a purplish light. Dainyl could feel the abrupt amplification of his Talent, but not why. In that light, he saw a young alector, who stood on the platform, holding a bucket and a brush, gaping at Dainyl.

"You're one of the recorder's assistants?" asked Dainyl.

"Ah . . . yes, sir. Yes, sir. He's not here. I don't know where he is, sir."

"I'm not looking for him. I'm Submarshal Dainyl, and I haven't been to Dulka before. I was looking for Majer Faerylt."

"The Myrmidon commander, sir? Oh, no! That was my fault. I should have left the screen in the regular position. Fa—" He broke off what he might have said. "This way, sir. This way." The young alector set down bucket and brush and hurried past Dainyl and around the screen.

Dainyl followed.

Once Dainyl stood on the Table side of the screen wall, the younger alector reached up and turned one of the light-torch brackets.

The screen wall that Dainyl had thought fixed slid forward and to the left, while a section of the wall flanking where the screen wall had been pivoted, revealing a corridor leading to a set of steps—and also concealing any trace of the large cavernous amphitheatre.

"At the top of the staircase, sir, through the door, turn right and follow the hallway. It comes out on the main level of the small tower in the northwest corner of the Myrmidon compound."

"And if I went left?" asked Dainyl with a smile.

"You would end up in the administration building—that's where Regional Alector Kelbryt and his assistants are."

"Are you from Dulka?"

"Yes, sir. My mother's the trade assistant to Alector Kelbryt."

"And your father is the Recorder of Deeds?"

The youth swallowed. "Yes, sir."

"I won't tell him about the screen wall. If I run across him, I'll just say you gave me directions." Dainyl smiled warmly. "It would help to know your name, though."

"Zudet, sir."

"You'd like to follow your father as recorder?"

"I couldn't be a recorder here, sir. You can't be a recorder in the place closest to where you're born."

"Can't be . . . or shouldn't be?" asked Dainyl. "Because the ties to the nearest Table are the strongest?"

"Yes, sir." Zudet's tone was quietly resigned.

"Thank you, Zudet." Dainyl turned and headed up the stairs. As Zudet had not mentioned, there was a Talent-lock on the door, but he released the lock before opening the door and stepping through, replacing the lock after he closed the door behind him.

He made it to the main level of the tower and ten yards into the redstone-paved courtyard before a Myrmidon ranker spotted him—and his insignia.

"Submarshal in the compound!" The ranker, clearly older, from the lines running from his eyes and the darkness behind them, hastened up to Dainyl and stiffened to attention. "Sir! At your service."

"I'm looking for Majer Faerylt."

"I don't believe he's in headquarters at the moment, sir, but the duty squad leader would know for certain. This way, if you would, sir."

Dainyl followed the Myrmidon across the courtyard. He could see the lower mountains to the west and north, rising high enough in the distance to be seen above the walls, even from inside the compound. The Myrmidon buildings were all redstone, and the pteridon squares to the south were in good order, with most of the pteridons present, not surprisingly, late in the afternoon. One squad appeared to have landed recently and was racking gear. The compound appeared extensive enough to hold two full companies, rather than the one that had always been stationed there.

"Submarshal in headquarters!" announced the ranker as Dainyl stepped through the doorway into the corridor leading to the duty desk.

An undercaptain bolted upright and waited as Dainyl approached.

"Undercaptain Weltak, sir. At your command, sir." Weltak was worried.

That Dainyl could tell even without Talent-sensing. "I'm Submarshal Dainyl, from headquarters in Elcien."

Somewhere down the corridor was the faintest muttered "Frig!"

"Submarshal . . . sir!" The undercaptain stiffened. "There was nothing in the order book that . . . no one mentioned that you would be coming to Dulka."

"There is a point to unannounced visits and inspections, Undercaptain," Dainyl said dryly. He was rapidly tiring of the unspoken presumption that his unanticipated arrival was somehow unfair or unprecedented. But then, it might well be unprecedented, and that was not a good thing, from his perspective. "Where is Majer Faerylt?"

"He's with Regional Alector Kelbryt, sir. That's where he said that he'd be."

"Fine. I'll need an escort there."

Weltak stood, immobile. Dainyl could sense the conflict.

"I can take you, sir." Another undercaptain appeared, wearing his flying jacket. "Sledaryk, sir. We just landed a bit ago."

"I saw you racking your gear. Are the skylances all going in the duty square?"

"Yes, sir. Since this winter. That was when we got the orders to change procedures."

Dainyl nodded in acknowledgment. As he recalled, Faerylt had reported a single skylance lost two seasons earlier, but he saw no reason to mention it.

"You came up from the tower, sir?" asked Sledaryk.

"Yes. Is that the quickest way to the RA?"

"Yes, sir."

"Then we'll go that way."

Dainyl let the undercaptain lead the way, back across the courtyard, into the corner tower, and down and then into the lower level of the adjoining structure. There they took the redstone steps up to the second level and halfway along a corridor before stepping through an archway into an anteroom.

An alector stood and moved forward as Dainyl entered behind Sledaryk. "Myrmidons are not—"

"Not what?" asked Dainyl pleasantly. "Submarshal Dainyl. I'm here from Elcien to see Kelbryt and Faerylt."

"The RA is in conference, sir."

"With Majer Faerylt, no doubt." Dainyl was being highhanded. He hoped—and feared—that the suspicions that fueled his behavior were correct. "Since I'm here to see them both, I'm certain they won't mind." He stepped toward the closed door, strengthening his shields as he did.

"I'll announce you, sir." The assistant turned and rapped on the door. "Submarshal Dainyl from Elcien is here to see you." He waited a moment, and then opened the door, gesturing for Dainyl to enter.

The chamber beyond was long and narrow, with a se-

ries of floor-to-ceiling windows. All the walls were paneled in a dark cherry, and the window casements were in-
set in the stone walls, also framed in cherry. The five
windows themselves were each less than a yard wide,
spaced slightly more than a yard apart, extending the
length of the outer wall. Against the inner wall were two
bookcases, whose shelves held more small art objects
than books. The windows provided a sweeping but interrupted vista of the mountains.

Two men, one in green and one in the silver-gray and
blue of a Myrmidon officer, stood facing Dainyl. Neither
spoke.

Dainyl strengthened his shields.

The door closed with a near-inaudible *clunk*.

Purpled Talent-bolts flew toward Dainyl.

His shields held, but the intensity of the joint attack
against his shields unbalanced him, and he staggered
back against the heavy door for a moment. Then he
straightened, widening his stance.

Both the other alectors began to move toward Dainyl,
keeping well away from each other.

"He has shields, but not much more," murmured Kelbryt.

Another set of Talent-bolts splattered away from
Dainyl.

From the way they moved, Dainyl understood that they
intended to batter at him, probably physically, and even
with Faerylt's lightcutter, as soon as they got closer to
him. At close range the impact of Talent and weapons on
his shields would be even greater.

Dainyl needed to act, and Faerylt was clearly the less
Talented alector.

Still holding his shields, Dainyl drew the lightcutter
and fired at Faerylt's face. The momentary shock was
enough for the majer to hesitate, his shields flickering. In
that moment, Dainyl fired again—Talent-boosting the
lightcutter's beam through the majer's less than effective
shields.

Faerylt went down, his face a charred mess.

Dainyl turned to Kelbryt, who lunged toward the sub-marshal.

Dainyl wrapped his own shields around Kelbryt, contracting them, so that nothing escaped—not sound, not energy.

For a time, only the heavy sound of Dainyl's breathing filled the chamber.

A heavy thud followed as the dead form of Kelbryt dropped forward onto the stone floor with an impact that reverberated through the stone.

Dainyl took several steps and rested against the table desk, his lightcutter trained on the door to the chamber. No one entered.

As he tried to regain some modicum of strength, he considered what had happened. Kelbryt . . . the name was familiar, yet he'd never met the regional alector, not that he knew. Zudet had to have told his father that Dainyl had arrived, and the recorder must have warned the RA. If not that, then they had already planned for his arrival. Dainyl didn't care for either alternative. He also had to ask himself what he was missing. While he had no doubts that Brekylt and Alcyna were scheming to grab power in some fashion or another, he had yet to find any concrete evidence of such a plot—except the attacks.

Was he looking in the right place? Could Shastylt have sent him out, and set up the attacks?

Dainyl nodded. That was also possible.

What about the recorders? In escaping the attacks from them through the Tables, had he discovered a power about the Tables that they did not wish discovered? Could it be the strange underground chamber that amplified Talent? Both were possible, but, if so, that also suggested that the Recorder of Deeds in Dulka was either allied with the plotters or had deceived them into thinking someone else had ordered Dainyl's removal.

From his meeting with the Duarch of Elcien, he was more than certain that Khelaryt was not behind the attacks, but Shastylt could be. Zelyert could be, and, of course, Alcyna and Brekylt.

Dainyl waited until both bodies had vanished into dust. By then he was breathing normally, but dull aches suffused his body, reminding him that he was still not fully recovered from the injuries suffered in Dramur. He also felt very exposed. After what had just happened, he had few choices but to barge ahead, a tactic counter to the quiet, behind-the-scenes expertise that had gotten him to where he'd been selected as Operations Director for the Myrmidons. He smiled wryly. Now . . . remaining behind the scenes was more than a little unlikely.

He held the lightcutter at the ready as he stepped forward and opened the outer door.

The assistant who had opened the door turned pale as he saw Dainyl. "Submarshal? Sir?"

"Apparently, I intruded upon an argument of some sort. Majer Faerylt was attacking the regional alector with both his sidearm and Talent. I wasn't able to stop the majer except by killing him, and he had already murdered the regional alector." Dainyl really didn't care if the assistant knew the truth. His cool voice became harder and colder. "That is exactly what you will report to High Alector Brekylt, as well as to the High Alector of Justice. Is that absolutely clear?"

"Yes, sir."

"If there are any more arguments or disturbances here in Dulka, I will hold you directly and personally responsible—immediately."

"Yes, sir." The man's eyes lowered, and he swallowed.

Sledaryk stood by the outer door, waiting.

"Back to Myrmidon headquarters, Undercaptain."

"Yes, sir!"

Beneath the formality of Sledaryk's response, Dainyl detected a vague sense of satisfaction.

They had made it all the way back to the corner tower and had started across the Myrmidon compound before the undercaptain spoke again.

"What happened, sir?"

"You heard, Sledaryk. That's what happened. Majer Faerylt apparently thought he was far better than he was, and far more important." The last sentence was certainly true enough. "I want to speak to all the officers. Immediately, and I don't care where they are."

"Yes, sir."

While Sledaryk passed the word, Dainyl seated himself in the commander's study, behind the desk that had once been Majer Faerylt's, his eyes taking in everything in the chamber in turn. There were no personal artifacts, not that he could see. Not a one. He might have missed a small item that had personal significance to the late majer, but it was clear that Faerylt had not been a sentimental or overtly prideful officer—and that suggested arrogance to Dainyl.

"Sir?" offered Sledaryk from the study door. "Everyone's here."

"Come in." Dainyl stood, waiting, surveying the four junior officers as they entered the study and stood facing him. Finally, he spoke. "For the record, I am Submarshal Dainyl. I've been conducting unannounced inspection tours all across Corus. When I went to meet Majer Faerylt and the RA, I discovered the majer had murdered Alector Kelbryt, and I was forced to kill him in order to stop him from doing the same to me."

None of the four looked surprised.

Dainyl waited, once more, before speaking. "I've met Sledaryk and Weltak. I don't recall meeting any of you before. If I have, please excuse me. Matters have been rather . . . intense here." He looked at the female undercaptain.

"Lyzetta, sir. I'm the junior undercaptain. Klynd is the senior undercaptain."

Dainyl shifted his gaze to the officer beside her. "Is that correct, Klynd?"

The man looked squarely at Dainyl. "Yes, sir."

"Then, for the moment, you're the acting commander

of Seventh Company. Once we're done here, choose someone to act as squad leader in your place."

"Yes, sir."

Dainyl surveyed the four, slowly, both with his eyes and his Talent-senses. "What is so important to keep from a submarshal that both a majer would attack me and an RA?" He sensed surprise from Lyzetta and Weltak, but none of the four spoke. After a moment, he went on. "I can see that acting Captain Klynd and Undercaptain Sledaryk are not surprised and have some thoughts along those lines. Now . . . we can draw this out, and I'll find out, and be even more displeased, or you two can explain and make the process far less painful."

Sledaryk paled, while Klynd moistened his lips.

They exchanged glances, and Sledaryk nodded to his senior.

"It's like this, Submarshal," Klynd began. "When the High Alector of the East assigned his son as the regional alector three years ago, that's when Submarshal Alcyna promoted Faerylt to majer. With the new RA and the majer being close, we started getting more supplies. Not a lot more, but before that, we got what we needed. The majer said we'd be needing reserves. Sure enough, the summer before last, the RA hired the locals to begin building a new compound for us. It's almost finished. Looks like there's room for more than two companies. Last year, they added to the Cadmian compound out on the high road and transferred another two companies of Cadmians here."

"Do you know where the Cadmians came from?" Dainyl didn't recall any such transfer crossing his desk. He could have checked if he'd been at headquarters, but that would have to wait.

"No, sir. No one said."

"Why did you think this was strange? Did you think the majer was hiding something?"

"I don't know, sir," Klynd replied. "The thing is that in thirty years, we never got extra supplies, not unless we had extra flights or something. Certainly, no one said anything about a new compound. Then, the High Alector of the East visited two times a year ago, and three times last year. I've never seen one before. It could be because his son was the RA, but the two of them met with the majer every time. The majer and the RA spent lots of time together. Usually, company commanders only meet occasionally with RAs or High Alectors. After that, there was the trouble in Coren last winter. Sixth Company out of Lyterna was the one first assigned to overfly that. We heard that before Captain Elysara could even get a squad airborne, the Highest of the East went to someone in Lyterna, and next thing we knew, the marshal changed the orders, and we were on the way. Sixth Company could have gotten there a day earlier."

"Even in winter?"

"You don't have to fly over the Spine. You take the midvale valley and pick up the river heading east. Unless there's a storm, it's an easy flight."

Dainyl hadn't known that, but every company had local knowledge. "You were the ones who discovered the timbering against the Code?"

"Wasn't that much, sir—a patch maybe a quarter vingt on a side. Understood they killed some patrollers over it."

"Was there any evidence of earlier timbering?"

Klynd shrugged. "Might have been, but not anytime recently. There were two or three patches where the tree growth looked younger, but I'm not a forester."

Dainyl was getting an even more unsettled feeling. He turned to Sledaryk. "Were you in charge of the overflights at Catyr last winter?"

Sledaryk frowned. "Yes, sir."

"The initial reports indicated overlogging, followed by rains, a mud dam, more rains, and a flood. Is that correct?"

"Pretty much, sir."

Dainyl could tell that the undercaptain wasn't telling everything. "Captain Klynd has suggested he could find just a small bit of overlogging. The area at Catyr had to be much larger for there to be that much flooding. How did you miss the logging?"

"We were never assigned to fly near Catyr. Not for the last two years, maybe longer. Not a single squad, sir. You can check the flight logs, sir. We weren't told not to fly there, but no one got assigned there."

Dainyl managed to keep his expression pleasant. *What* had been going on in Dulka? More important, what had been behind it all? "Was there anywhere else you would have expected to patrol where you didn't?" His eyes went from one junior officer to the next.

"No, sir."

"No, sir . . ."

In the end, even after another glass of questioning and discussion, Dainyl had discovered little more than had been revealed in the responses to his first questions. The squad leaders just didn't know any more.

He'd be staying in Dulka for the night, perhaps longer. He was too tired to chance another Table translation, not when recorders could apparently attack him during such a trip, brief as it was. He'd also definitely need to set Talent alarms to ensure his sleep wasn't interrupted fatally. He just hoped he could eat and get some rest before something else went wrong. He had no doubts that it would. He just didn't know when.

19

Midafternoon on Londi had come and gone before Mykel had Third Battalion settled in the Cadmian compound outside of Southgate on the northeast road. Since he had not seen the post commander yet, he crossed the paved courtyard, trying to ignore the fine reddish sandy soil drifted into corners everywhere. Although he blotted his forehead, the sweat there was more from his own hurrying to ensure everything was in order than from the heat of the day. That might well change by the time late spring arrived. Mykel didn't want to consider still being in Southgate by full summer. He headed for the small headquarters building set twenty yards inside the south gate, a gate with hinges that shined only where casually visible, and with rust elsewhere else. Mykel doubted it had been tested or closed in years.

The door to the headquarters was ajar, and a patina of fine sandy dust had drifted across the gray tiles of the foyer. Beyond the second archway was an open hall, with two desks, one vacant. At the other sat a senior squad leader who did not look up until Mykel was less than two yards from him.

"Majer Mykel to see the post commander."

The senior squad leader rose, not quite languidly, eventually assuming a pose approximating attention. "Yes, sir. Overcaptain Sturyk has been expecting you, sir. This way, sir." His steps toward the commander's study were as leisurely as his bearing.

The study door was open, and Mykel stepped inside, immediately closing it, and ignoring the momentary frown on the overcaptain's face. Sturyk had whitish blond hair, threaded with silver. His narrow face was tanned, and his bearing distinguished. He was doubtless at least fifteen years older than Mykel. He rose even more slowly than had the senior squad leader.

"Majer . . . you are Majer Mykel, sir?"

Mykel could sense the older officer's consternation at discovering his superior was more than a decade younger. Even Sturyk's lifeforce thread had contracted slightly. "The same, Overcaptain."

Sturyk offered a smile, belatedly. "You must excuse me, Majer. When I heard Third Battalion was being sent here, I had assumed I would see Majer Vaclyn. How is he?"

Mykel returned Sturyk's smile with one he hoped was sympathetic, gesturing for the other officer to resume his seat. "The strain of the campaign in Dramur took a heavy toll on the majer. He began to think everyone was his enemy, and in the end, he even attacked a senior alector."

Mykel settled into the chair across the desk from Sturyk.

"Oh, dear. He was such a perfectionist. I can see where that could happen."

Vaclyn had been a perfectionist about the wrong things, but Mykel wasn't about to get into that. "I ended up with the field command there, and was confirmed as the commander of Third Battalion by the Submarshal of Myrmidons and by Colonel Herolt."

"For such experience, you wear your years well, Majer."

"I entered service young, Overcaptain, and I've seen my share of action." Mykel smiled more professionally. "Since I didn't see you when we arrived, I thought I would find you and let you know the details of my mission and the requirements that it will place on you and the Cadmians here."

"I've already made the adjoining study available for you, sir. It's the same size as this one. They're the largest in headquarters, and the visiting barracks and stables were made ready last week."

"I saw that, and we appreciate that. What about the two companies of trainees?"

"The last of them arrived on Novdi. They're quartered in the trainee barracks in the southwest corner."

"What can you tell me about them?"

Sturyk shrugged. "Recruits are hard to get in Southgate. Cadmian duty is regarded as barely a step above being a deckhand on the most decrepit of fishing boats or being a day laborer in the granite quarries to the north. Half are minor malefactors—petty theft and the like—and the other half are desperate in one way or the other. You've got two or three decent squad leaders, and a fresh captain and a barely promoted undercaptain. Both of them are honest and originally came from the Hyalt region, but not from Hyalt itself. They were detached from other companies and sent here."

Mykel hadn't expected any better. He did hope that

the two officers were not only honest, but competent. "We only have a month before we ride out, and that means a full training schedule Londi through Novdi, starting tomorrow—"

"Ah . . . Majer . . ."

"Yes?" replied Mykel.

"We . . . ah . . . there are no duties on Novdi, except for the duty squads, of course. That has always been the policy in Southgate."

Mykel understood, in yet another way, why he had been sent. He was likely to have problems in getting Sturyk's active cooperation without some form of coercion. The compound commander had a routine, and it doubtless worked well for the garrison and policing duties generally assigned.

"Overcaptain, I'm certain your policies have worked well for the situation here, but I've been tasked with a difficult situation that requires whipping less than raw recruits into a semblance of Cadmians, and that will require nine days a week, perhaps all ten."

"The policy here has been longstanding, Majer. I'm sure you understand the difficulties involved in changing—"

"I'm not ordering a direct change in your policies," Mykel replied politely, "only in those areas where Third Battalion requires support."

"Majer . . ." Sturyk shrugged helplessly.

"Having all of Novdi in a nonduty status may be the longstanding Southgate policy," said Mykel evenly, "but that is not what is set forth in the regulations. At the very least, Novdi morning is a duty period, and we will be using Novdi, perhaps even Decdi, as necessary, in order to have these men ready in the time required by Colonel Herolt and by the Marshal of Myrmidons."

"That timetable, sir, I fear, is unrealistic."

"It may well be, Overcaptain Sturyk." Mykel smiled pleasantly. "Would you like to write up a report and submit it to me stating why the timetable is unrealistic?"

Sturyk's petulant frown vanished as he swallowed. "I think not, sir."

"Then I will report to Colonel Herolt that you believe we can meet the timetable, if we use Novdis for training. I'd like a brief note from you agreeing with me."

Sturyk swallowed again. "Sir . . . that is coercion."

"Overcaptain . . . you cannot have it both ways. I'm perfectly willing to put your objections on the record, and if I fail, then you will be proven correct." Mykel smiled. "If you are not willing to object, then I would like your agreement on record."

"Yes, sir."

Mykel could sense the palpable dislike emanating from Sturyk. He wished he had learned to be more politic, but he doubted that anything besides veiled force would ever have moved Sturyk. Mykel had tried not to sound like Majer Vaclyn, but feared he had anyway. Was that what happened when officers became battalion commanders? That they were placed in positions where they had to make demands that seemed unreasonable to junior officers? He smiled again. "After all, Overcaptain, we'll only be here a month, and, I'm sure that Colonel Herolt will be pleased to learn just how cooperative and supportive you have been."

"I'm certain we can work things out, sir." The dislike behind Sturyk's professional smile was replaced by a sense of calculation and caution, feelings that were obvious to Mykel, yet he knew that he would not have seen and sensed them a year earlier, certainly not nearly so directly and clearly.

As he left the study, heading out to find the officers of the trainee companies, he wondered if there were some way he could not only sense what others felt, but offer them reassurance . . . or confidence, in the case of his own officers.

There was still so much yet to learn, and he feared he would learn too much of it by making mistakes. His fingers dropped to his belt, just above the concealed dagger—was he becoming a true dagger of the ancients, as likely to slash himself as others? Or had he been sent because Colonel Herolt knew all too well the limitations of Overcaptain Sturyk?

20

Dainyl crossed the Myrmidon courtyard in the darkness of early evening on Duadi. He'd indicated he would be leaving on Tridi. Leaving earlier seemed wiser, especially since he had no real evidence that would suggest misdeeds by Alcyna or Brekylt—or even what they might be attempting. After a day and a half of talking to Myrmidons and checking the records and logs of Seventh Company, what he had discovered was only what could be inferred by what had *not* been ordered or undertaken.

There was indeed a new Myrmidon compound that was almost completed, and it certainly had enough space for two companies. It was also well to the north of the present compound and away from the hillier ground—supposedly to allow easier takeoffs and landings. Yet it was not noticeably larger than the present compound, and the current Myrmidon post was far more convenient to the Table and in excellent repair. The current post was higher in the hills and had walls that could be defended. So why were Brekylt and Alcyna building a new compound?

The flight patterns were less clear, but still suggestive. Seventh Company had conducted routine patrols of the river and the port at Tylora, and occasionally even overflown Sinjin. Parts of the southeastern High Steppes had been watched for grass fires or other lifeforce damage. Following reports of scattered brigandage, various squads had periodically patrolled the high roads to Flyr and even the road from Tylora to Sudya. On two occasions, they had even found brigands. But over a period of four years, according to the logs and records, there had been no surveillance or monitoring flights to the north along the eastern flank of the mountains that comprised the Spine of Corus. Likewise there had been no written orders from Alcyna—or anyone else—directing the scope of Seventh Company flight operations.

Dainyl paused before the door concealing the stairs down to the Table chamber, studying it carefully before releasing the Talent-lock. Even so, he felt more Talent, just beyond the door, and linked to the door itself. Rather than open the door immediately, he extended his Talent-senses beyond. The finest film of Talent lay on the other side, a web linked to the door and across the corridor—obviously an alarm of some sort. Whatever was happening in the east involved many of the recorders, if not all of them—or the recorders were opposed to Dainyl for reasons of their own, perhaps because he had killed the recorder who had tried to murder him or because he had learned too much about what they could do with the Tables.

He studied the web for a time, noting that single strands ran from the web and the door, melding into a larger strand that ran along the top of the corridor and down the steps. Using his own Talent, he created miniature shields, very delicately, to immobilize the unseen—but clearly sensed—purple threads leading to that telltale strand. Only then did he gently use his Talent to rearrange the web so that he could open the door and step through.

Leaving the miniature shields in place, he made his way down the steps and then to the right toward the Table chamber. He found no more Talent-webs, but in the dimness of the Table chamber, in addition to the Talent-purple glow of the Table itself, he could sense that the Table was somehow more energized.

He took a deep breath, then stepped onto the Table and concentrated, dropping into . . .

. . . *the chill darkness of the translation tube. "Above" him he could sense the formation of the purple arms, but he linked immediately with the brilliant white locator of Elcien. Again, he had the illusion of the locator hurtling through the darkness at him until the silver-white barrier shattered.*

Dainyl stood on the Table in Elcien, breathing heavily, mist forming on his flight jacket and then dispersing. He stepped off the Table, alert for any manifestation from it, but he could sense none, and, after releasing the first Talent-lock, he stepped from the chamber into the foyer beyond. He had no sooner emerged from the foyer and re-placed the second Talent-lock, when High Alector Zel-yert appeared in the outer corridor.

"Sir," offered Dainyl, slightly surprised at seeing Zel-yert so late in the day, although it was before sunset.

"Dainyl . . . Shastylt thought you might be returning before the end-days, if only for a brief respite."

"Yes, sir. I had planned to travel out again in the morn-ing." Dainyl had no desire to talk to Zelyert, but prudence was more than called for.

"I will take but a few moments of your time." Zelyert gestured toward his private study and turned, expecting Dainyl to follow.

He did, closing the study door behind him.

The High Alector of Justice seated himself. "Shastylt has not reported on your activities. . . ."

Seating himself, Dainyl replied, "That is doubtless be-cause I have not completed my investigations and have not made a report to him, sir."

"What have you discovered?"

"There were no overflights of the Catyr area—the one that was overlogged and flooded this winter—for close to four years. There were no orders not to fly there, just or-ders to fly everywhere else."

Zelyert nodded. "You think this has some link to Brekylt?"

"When I arrived at Dulka, I went to pay my respects to the regional alector. You may have already heard what occurred."

"There was a report that the Myrmidon majer there attacked the RA, and that you arrived only at the end. It's too bad you weren't a bit sooner, Submarshal." Zelyert's tone was mild.

"That was the official report, and the way it should remain," Dainyl replied. "I might add that the RA was Brekylt's son, and that the majer and he were very close friends. I might also add that Brekylt has paid a number of visits to Dulka in the past years, more than to any other Myrmidon post, and that Dulka has been receiving supplies slightly in excess of its needs on a continuing basis since Kelbryt had become the regional alector. The Cadmian compound was enlarged, and there is a new Myrmidon compound nearly completed, but it is farther from the Table and in a less defensible position."

"At times, we do need new compounds," Zelyert said mildly. "I was told that the winds around the old compound were erratic and dangerous."

"Yes, sir."

"I take it that they both attacked you," Zelyert said. "How did you prevail?"

"My shields were stronger than their Talent. Call it a test of endurance. In the end, I used the lightcutter."

"Brekylt won't believe the report, you know?"

"I'm certain he won't. But I doubt he'll want attention called to the irregularities in a region administered by his son."

Zelyert laughed, softly. "You're correct there, but he is a deadly enemy. He will be after you."

As if he were not already, thought Dainyl. "Wasn't that the point of sending me, sir? The diligent, not-that-bright submarshal with heavy shields and not too much else?"

Zelyert's second laugh was louder, and contained a greater sense of amusement. "Your Talent may not be what it could be, Dainyl, but the diligent exterior masks an observant interior. Do you wish to continue this . . . investigation?"

"I cannot see much of an alternative, sir. There's little enough evidence of what Brekylt intends—or even what his intentions are. I believe they're harmful to the Myrmidons and the Duarchy, but there's no real proof of that. Even if I stopped now, he'd remain an enemy. The only way out of the mess is through it."

"Spoken like a true Myrmidon." Zelyert rose. "I look forward to seeing what comes of your efforts." He paused. "I'm certain you know this, but I would suggest you not place any great trust in any officers in the east."

Dainyl stood. "Yes, sir." He meant to place no great trust in any senior Myrmidon officers or High Alectors anywhere.

21

The greatest fault of those an alector governs is their failure to see themselves as they are. An alector cannot allow himself the luxury of self-deception, whatever the possible rationale or cause. Most alectors understand this, and it is reinforced by our codes and our institutions, and those who do not are less worthy than the steers whose lives we direct, for we should know better.

Yet true self-knowledge is rare indeed among steers, for their actions and their self-identity are inseparably intertwined. A steer will rationalize himself into believing an action that is against his own self-interest is for his good and the good of others in order to maintain his self-image. He will avoid actions to improve himself and his self-image, merely to maintain the image he holds of himself.

For this reason, an alector who must administer activities and programs that affect the well-being of the self-deluding masses—comprising flawed alectors and the vast majority of steers—cannot ever assume that those masses will understand what is truly in their self-interest. Therefore, do not ever rely upon those who are governed to understand the rationale for the decisions that must be made and implemented.

At the same time, a conscientious alector must resist the temptation to behave arrogantly, to declare by word or action that there is no reason to explain one's decisions and actions. For there are those few who do understand. Also, despite their self-delusion, all but the most ignorant of the masses can appreciate the effort and the thought behind a well-presented explanation, even one with which they do not agree.

Arrogance is always the downfall of those in power, even of alectors, and even the most self-deluded of the masses will rejoice to see an arrogant administrator brought low. . . .

Views of the Highest
Illustra
W.T. 1513

22

Dainyl had not even attempted to return to Myrmidon headquarters on Tridi evening, but went straight home. He and Lystrana had enjoyed dinner and then retired to their chambers. While they had discussed Dainyl's adventures, neither could add much insight to what he had experienced, and, eventually, they slept.

Quattri morning, well before dawn, found Dainyl standing before the Table in the Hall of Justice. He'd actu-

ally enjoyed the long walk from his house to the Hall, and
was glad he'd arrived before the Highest had appeared.

He smiled wryly, then stepped onto the Table, wearing
his flying jacket, but carrying nothing. He concentrated,
letting himself drop downward . . .

. . . *into the darkness, seeking the orange-yellow locator of Lysia, his senses alert for any trace of the purplish
arms or anything else untoward.*

*In the endless yet equally close distance, he could per-
ceive the orange-yellow, but the locator seemed to be
tinged with certain overshades of . . . pinkish purple,
overlaid with silver. None of the other locators had such
overshades, he realized, but as he focused on the locator
wedge that was Lysia, the overshades vanished.*

He extended a line of Talent toward the locator.

*As he did, he sensed, seemingly flanking him, but out-
side the deep-purpled darkness of the translation tube,
blackness—pure blackness—within which flashed an
globe of amber-golden-green.*

*For a moment, he just tried to sense the greenish Tal-
ent, for it had to be something of the ancient soarers,
their system of portals and mirrors, but the green vanished, although the deeper blackness did not. But had the
green vanished? Or was that deeper blackness shaded
with green?*

*He felt colder, chill, and dropped his explorations of
whatever he might have sensed, concentrating on Talent-
linking with the Table at Lysia.*

*The yellow-orange rushed toward him, and he flashed
through the silver barrier, unseen shards spraying out
from him.*

A single step sufficed for him to gain his balance on
the Table. His entire uniform was covered with a thin
layer of frost, one that did not turn to mist or sublime
away immediately, so that he was cloaked in a personal
fog for several moments.

His Talent-senses indicated that the chamber was
empty, but his hand still sought the butt of his sidearm,

even as he reinforced his shields. The doorway to the hidden chamber that adjoined most of the Table chambers slid open. Dainyl stepped forward and off the Table.

The recorder who stood in the opening of the usually hidden doorway smiled, an expression both humorous and ironic. "Rather an impressive entrance, Submarshal, if chilling." The doorway closed behind her, leaving the two alectors alone in the chamber.

"Just chilling," replied Dainyl. A female recorder? He hadn't realized that there were any.

"Your shields are also impressive. You will pardon me if I do not attempt to test them." The recorder was slender, a good head shorter than Dainyl, and wore dark green trousers and tunic, unadorned, although the tunic was short-sleeved. Her boots were black, and her eyes were green, unusual for an alector.

"I'd prefer that you didn't," Dainyl replied.

"A rather unfortunate series of events has occurred following a number of your translations, Submarshal."

Dainyl shrugged. "That may be. The results were not of my choosing. I would have preferred totally uneventful translations." He continued to study the recorder.

"Asulet suggested the same." The recorder grinned. "By the way, I'm Sulerya. I'm his daughter."

Dainyl was not surprised that the senior alector in Lyterna had placed his daughter well, but Asulet had never mentioned her. "Might I ask why you seem more cordial than your peers?"

"Isn't it obvious? I was the first, and for a time, the only female recorder. Total nepotism. My father insisted on it. Since he doesn't insist often, and since he is, in fact, effectively the duarch of Lyterna, no one wanted to cross him."

Sulerya's words and feelings rang totally true to Dainyl.

His shields still up, he decided to press. "You know that Brekylt and Alcyna are sending messages to others in Lyterna?"

"It's no secret there that Paeylt wishes to make changes my father opposes. That's one reason why he has been unable to rest for the past three centuries."

Dainyl had no idea who Paeylt was.

"Why can't your father . . . deal with Paeylt?"

"He controls the engineering facilities there. Father holds the environmental facilities and support services. No one else has the expertise of either. It is a delicate balance. Failure of either would destroy Lyterna, and the destruction of Lyterna would create a downward spiral in lifeforce all across Acorus."

"So they are locked in a stalemate, and Paeylt is younger and will use time to force your father?"

"That is his hope."

"What do you—and your father—expect of me?"

"Father was quite explicit." Sulerya offered a rueful smile. "He told me not to harm you, to answer your questions honestly, but not to oppose actively the other recorders or the Highest of the East."

"He's playing a deep game." *And one that might just be hard on a certain submarshal*, Dainyl reflected silently.

"It's the only game that offers hope."

"Can you explain why?"

"Yes."

"Then would you, since you're supposed to answer my questions honestly?"

"Perhaps we should adjourn to my private study?"

"The hidden one?"

She nodded.

"Who knows about those, besides the recorders and their assistants?"

"The High Alectors—mostly. The marshal. Some of your predecessors did. Tyanylt did not."

The stone doorway reopened, and Dainyl followed Sulcrya through, noting carefully the Talent-mechanism. Sulerya's Talent was as deft as her father's as she closed the hidden entrance.

Her study was smaller even than the space Dainyl had

occupied as a colonel, and held but a black chest, set against one wall, a writing table, and three wooden chairs. The single wall hanging was a pen and ink drawing of a seaport—Lysia. She closed the study door, took one chair, and waited for Dainyl to seat himself.

"In return for answers," Sulerya began, "Father and I ask one stipulation."

"What might that be?" asked Dainyl warily.

"That you report nothing you learn from us until you can verify it from your own observations."

Dainyl paused. "There must be a reason for that, beyond protecting you two. I doubt Asulet needs protection, and I'd wager you've found ways to protect yourself."

"It's to protect you."

Dainyl needed to think about that for a moment. "It's also another form of assurance for you and your father. I become another player, and that expands the complexity, and keeps Zelyert, the Duarches, and Brekylt and Alcyna from acting even more precipitously." He laughed softly. "That's assuming I survive. Realistically, I don't have a choice."

"That's true."

"I'll abide by the stipulation."

"Father said you would. He said you're one of the last truly honorable Myrmidons."

Not only was that assessment frightening, but Dainyl also recognized the direct play on his own sense of honor. "An appeal to my vanity as well."

"Of course . . . and your honor, of which there is too little in these desperate days."

"Let's start there," Dainyl said. "Why are these desperate days?"

"You know as well as anyone. There's not enough lifeforce mass to support all those who wish to translate here from Ifryn. Zelyert is trying to create situations that depict Acorus as far less desirable. What he doesn't understand is that such depictions will only assure that the least honorable and most desperate Ifrits on Ifryn will attempt the long translation here. The others will use their influence and position to translate to Efra."

That, unfortunately, made sense to Dainyl. "Surely he sees that."

"I'm certain he does, but he sees no alternative. The mass of hangers-on around the Archon are Talent-rich and poor in all practical skills. If the Master Scepter is located here and too many of them followed, they could swallow all the excess lifeforce on Acorus and turn all alectors into beings with lifespans shorter than those of the indigens. The Duarch of Elcien has worked to persuade the Archon to send more alectors with technical abilities before those on Ifryn perceive how short time is there. He has had some success, especially in obtaining Table and translation engineers, and a handful of biologists and life-form specialists."

"Where does Brekylt fit into this? He opposes Zelyert, but is he backing the Duarch of Elcien?"

"No. His patron is the Duarch of Ludar, and both he and Samist believe that the Master Scepter should come to Acorus—without the Archon and his hangers-on. They have not said so, but their plans have. They have also persuaded the Archon to translate a number of ambitious younger engineers. They have gone to Alustre—Fordall, in practice. There are others, as well, but we cannot track them once they leave the Table chambers, and the recorders where they have appeared have not been helpful."

"The engineers and the recorders—they seek total control of the Tables and translation tubes?"

Sulerya smiled. "Shastylt underestimates you."

"I'm not sure about that. I'm wondering if he's setting me up against Zelyert to clear his own path to being High Alector. Then he could either dispose of me, or make me marshal, as suits his needs."

"He could be. That would be incredibly foolish."

"Are you the only recorder not supporting Brekylt and the Duarch of Ludar?"

"No. Chastyl in Elcien is Zelyert's creature. That's why you never see him. Then there's Delari. She's the recorder in Blackstear, and, of course, Myenfel in Lyterna is loyal to Father. Except for Lysia, all the other recorders east of the Spine strongly support Brekylt. Ludar belongs to Samist, and so do Hyalt and Faitel. Jonyst in Dereka stands alone, but he would not oppose Father, and he is honorable. The others cooperate with those backing Brekylt and Samist, but their support is tacit or coerced through various measures."

"Such as?"

"Patronyl in Tempre would prefer to support Father, but not Khelaryt, and his family resides in Alustre. Nomyelt in Soupat has an un-Talented son who is a squad leader in the palace guard at Ludar. That sort of thing."

Dainyl mentally counted. Three recorders backed Asulet; one backed Zelyert; seven backed Brekylt and Samist, two others went along with them, while one was independent, whatever that might mean. "How many supporters have the Duarch of Elcien and your father lost to the recorders recently?"

"Not that many. Most Table travelers have strong shields."

Dainyl decided to let the mention of the attacks inside the translation tubes wait for a bit. "Just who is Paeylt? Beyond opposing your father?"

"He's the head engineer in Lyterna. He designed and laid out the larger cities, except Southgate. Father had Arylan plan Southgate as an indigen and lander port, and Dramuria, of course."

"Of course?" Dainyl wanted to shake his head.

"He felt that there ought to be areas where the landers and indigens had more freedom. He wanted to see if that resulted in faster and more efficient lifeforce growth, but they had to be isolated, so that, if they became too destructive of lifeforce, they could be controlled."

"Did it?"

Sulerya shrugged. "It worked in Dramur, but not in Southgate."

"What about the western isles?"

"That was tried. Putting Tables there would have stressed the world too much. The lack of Tables and the distance meant there was no oversight and supervision. Predictably, the indigens destroyed the ecology within a few hundred years. When the Archon found out, he was less than pleased. The survivors were either destroyed or relocated. The isles were reseeded with unsentient fauna and supporting flora."

"You obviously control the Table here, but what about the Myrmidons?"

"Captain Sevasya is Khelaryt's daughter. He insisted she command here, and she's one of the oldest Myrmidon captains. Alcyna and Brekylt have not involved her. Instead, they transfer the Myrmidons most loyal to the Duarch of Elcien here, as well as the occasional trouble-maker."

Dainyl had known all along that there was far more than he knew taking place, but he now realized just how ignorant he had been. How much more should he trust Sulerya? Did he have any real choice if he wanted to survive? "How does a recorder create the purple Talent-arms? Through the Table?"

"Yes. It takes experience and practice."

"I've been attacked by them three times—twice in the translation tubes."

She frowned. "That's not good."

"No, it wasn't," Dainyl said dryly.

"That's not what I meant. Feeding that kind of energy back into the links and the grid could set up a nasty energy feedback system. Conceivably, it could funnel life-force right out of the whole world, or destabilize the grid. It could also destroy the user."

That meant someone wanted Dainyl dead very badly—or one of the junior recorders was far too eager to do

Brekylt's bidding . . . if not both. *Unless it wasn't a recorder*, reflected Dainyl. "Could it be someone else using a Table?"

"Any highly Talented alector could use a Table for that—given enough practice and experience—but who else would have the access and experience?" She paused. "It could be that Brekylt has suborned an assistant to one of the older recorders."

"Without warning them of the dangers?"

Sulerya laughed. "Brekylt has never been known for undue concerns for his followers, despite his seeming warmth."

That certainly fit with what Dainyl had observed. "Could that destroy the tubes? Especially the long links to Ifryn? Without excessive loss of lifeforce?"

Sulerya cocked her head, as if thinking. Finally, she replied. "It's possible, but cutting the links, without moving the Master Scepter here, would sever the lifelinks of every alector as matters now stand."

Dainyl nodded. "You're on speaking terms with the other recorders, aren't you? Or message terms, anyway?"

"You want me to point out that these attacks have been made and the dangers?"

"I don't see how it could hurt. If it doesn't reduce the attempts, we're no worse off, and the fact that you've been told about them indicates that at least some of the victims have escaped, which might suggest ineffectual tactics with high risks for everyone."

"I can try." She smiled. "I'll walk over to the Myrmidon headquarters with you. Sevasya should be there this morning. She'll be glad to see you."

If she were, thought Dainyl, she'd be among the few of the Myrmidon commanders in the east who was.

They both rose, and Dainyl followed her from her study through the Table chamber and out through unguarded doors. The corridor to the staircase had been cut through solid stone, unlike most of the other Table chambers. Beyond the doorway at the top of the steps was a walled courtyard. The warmth of the sunlight was more than welcome, but the air was moist, and he suspected that, even for him, Lysia in summer might be too damp.

"What's Captain Sevasya like?" asked Dainyl as he and Sulerya crossed the paved compound courtyard. His eyes took in the immaculate pteridon squares, and the cleanliness of the walls and windows. "Her reports are always precise, but they don't convey much beyond great and quiet competence."

"You obviously have not met her," replied Sulerya.

"No. My service has been in the west."

"I'll let you decide for yourself, Submarshal."

"You're just like your father," Dainyl replied with a laugh. "He only said what he wanted and not a word more."

"That may be." Sulerya grinned. "I am glad you're not like your mother."

Dainyl didn't bother to conceal the wince. "You've met her?"

"Once. That was a number of years ago, long before you joined the Myrmidons."

Dainyl decided not to say more for the moment. His mother had always had a way of making an impression, not always one useful to Dainyl.

The duty officer bolted upright as the two entered the small, one-story stone structure. "Submarshal, sir! Recorder."

"We're here to see the captain, Ghedyn," offered the recorder.

"Yes, sirs," replied the Myrmidon. "She's in her study."

Sulerya turned left and led Dainyl to the second doorway. It was open.

"Sevasya . . . one of your superiors arrived while I was on duty." A mischievous smile followed Sulerya's words. "So I escorted him here. I'm certain you two have Myrmidonish business to discuss, and I will leave you in his capable hands."

Dainyl—not totally pleased with that introduction—stepped into the study with a smile, still holding his shields.

Before he could speak, Sulerya added, "If I'm not in the chamber when you return, Dainyl, wait a moment. I may have more information for you." With that, she closed the study door, leaving the two Myrmidons alone.

Captain Sevasya was broad shouldered, and taller than Dainyl—one of the few alectors or alectresses of such height besides the Duarch Khelaryt. She also radiated Talent, much as her father did, even as her black eyes appraised him.

"Submarshal Dainyl, how good to see you." She smiled, exuding warmth—but with cool confidence behind it.

"It's good to see you, Captain. It's especially refreshing to arrive here welcomed."

"Are you here because you support Asulet, or my father?" She delivered the question, bluntly phrased, with the same warmth.

"I'm not certain whom I should support, except that it won't be Brekylt or Alcyna," he replied dryly.

"You sound somewhat skeptical, Submarshal."

"There are times for that, especially when dealing with the Duarch's daughter."

"And when little is as it once seemed?" Sevasya's eyebrows arched.

"I'm not sure the past was ever what anyone thought."

"How might I help you?"

"Any information you have on actions Brekylt and Alcyna have taken against the Marshal, the Highest of Justice, or your father would be useful." Dainyl took the chair across from her table desk.

Sevasya sat as well, an amused smile still in place. "Isn't that the problem, sir? I can point to no single action that would confirm that they have planned any adverse actions against any of their superiors. Oh . . . there are individuals who have suffered mishaps, and those who have died. There have been unusual transfers of personnel. In no case is there any link to the Highest of the East that could not be supported as a justifiable act in the course of duty."

Dainyl waited, a pleasant smile upon his face.

"There's no doubt that they plan some sort of treachery, as you well know. But to remove them—or for them to suffer a mishap—without some form of proof would have large numbers of faithful alectors in the east rising against the Duarchy—or whoever was perceived as its agent. Right now, you are the one suspected of being that agent."

That wasn't exactly a surprise to Dainyl, but her words still sent a chill through him. "What do you suggest I do, then, Captain?"

"Finish your inspection tour, and wait until an opportunity arises. It will, because Brekylt will have to act in order to gain whatever power or control he desires. It won't happen immediately, however. If you do nothing upon your return to Elcien, except to issue a report extolling the state of readiness in the east, that will confound them."

"What about visiting Dereka . . . and those insignificant other difficulties facing me?" Dainyl offered the question dryly.

Sevasya laughed. "Submarshal, sir, I am quite certain you will manage, as you have all along. Visiting Dereka should pose no problems, now that Colonel Dhenyr serves in Elcien as your replacement."

"Do you think he had anything to do with removing firelances, say, in order to weaken Fifth Company?"

"I doubt he had anything to do with that. With other matters, yes, but handling firelances under those conditions would require Talent and initiative, and he was selected for lack of such." Sevasya's voice was both warm and ironic. "Especially after his predecessor showed that lack of obvious Talent did not necessarily preclude initiative and effectiveness."

"Dereka is the closest Myrmidon company to Lyterna," mused Dainyl.

"It is, and I'm very fond of both Captain Elysara and Captain Fhentyl. You might find the visit to Dereka enjoyable, even informative, sir."

That answered another question, even as it raised a third. "Why?"

"I'm certain I couldn't say, sir, but it is the oldest city on Acorus."

In short, Dainyl should go, and the Duarch's daughter, whether she was technically under his command or not, wasn't about to say why . . . or much more about anything.

He stood. "I would very much appreciate it if you would give me a tour of Eighth Company."

"I'd be delighted, Submarshal, and everyone will be pleased to meet you."

Those words were genuine, and heartfelt, and that disturbed Dainyl as well, although he could not have said exactly why.

With a smile, he opened the study door and stepped into the corridor, waiting for the captain.

23

Slightly past midmorning on Quinti, Mykel reined up next to Bhoral as the third squad of the First Hyalt Company wheeled into a firing line, a very ragged firing line. Some of the troopers seemed uncomfortable, if not unsteady, in the saddle. Most had never been on a mount a week earlier, and that meant extra time in teaching them about horses. Mykel couldn't begrudge that. He'd needed that instruction years back.

For a time, he watched as the squad continued to practice standard mounted maneuvers. Then he turned to the battalion senior squad leader. "They're improving. It's slow, but even as soon as it is, I can see some improvement. You're getting results, especially with what you have to work with."

Bhoral gave a faint smile. "They're beginning to realize that they can do something, and that they'll get regular rations and pay. A good lot of 'em never have."

That was true of all too many of the locally raised Cadmian forces, Mykel had come to realize, and why he and Third Battalion were in Southgate. "How are matters working out with getting supplies?"

"After the first day or so, all of a sudden, we stopped having problems. Couldn't say why, but I'm not complaining."

"Good. Still . . . be as pleasant as possible."

"I've laid that on heavy with the squad leaders. They know." Bhoral gave a creased smile. "Hope you don't mind that I told 'em what you said to the officers."

"No. It holds true for all of us." All Mykel had said to his officers was that no one was to treat anyone in the compound with disrespect. If they had a problem, they were to bring it to him. He'd only had to go to the over-captain once, and that was to explain the need for extra fodder and water because of the longer use of the mounts. Fodder was a problem because the area around Southgate wasn't all that fertile, not compared with other areas supporting Cadmian mounted companies.

"I'm going to see how the combat squad-on-squad drills are going." Mykel nodded to Bhoral and then eased the roan around the north edge of the main drill field to the east side. There, Fourteenth Company's squads were taking on the squads of Second Hyalt Company, using rattan sabres.

Again, Mykel reined up, this time beside Captain Culeyt. Once more, he watched for a time, before saying anything.

"What do you think?"

"Sir . . . half of them still think a sabre's an axe."

"Many of us did at one time," Mykel said with a laugh. "They're looking better. It'll help your men, too."

"The recruits aren't any threat."

"No," Mykel replied, "but when your men have to explain what they're doing, and then keep doing it, it reinforces their skills." He grinned. "But . . . to make sure they don't get sloppy, tell them that they'll be running a drill with the rattan sabres against Sixteenth Company the day after tomorrow."

"Sir? Sixteenth Company?"

"You're the one who just said that the Hyaltans were no threat."

"Yes, sir." Culeyt shook his head.

Mykel continued his rounds of observation for another two glasses, before riding back to the compound, where he unsaddled the roan and brushed him out before he walked back to the headquarters building.

He settled behind the battered wooden table desk in the study provided for his use—he didn't really think of it as his—and began to write. He'd decided to make more changes in the training schedule, based on what he'd observed, deciding to beef up the individual weapons training. Some of the unit maneuvering training could be incorporated into the ride to Hyalt, but doing that with weapons would have been far more difficult—and time-consuming.

Less than half a glass later, he looked up to a knock on the half-open door. "Yes?"

"Overcaptain Sturyk would ask a moment of your time, Majer." The squad leader was far more precise and respectful than he had been when Mykel had first introduced himself. "If you would not mind?"

"That would be fine."

Mykel had barely set down the pen before Sturyk appeared, and he stood. "Overcaptain."

"Majer. You've been so involved with your training that I thought I had best catch you when I could, sir. If this is convenient?"

"This is fine." Mykel gestured toward the chairs in front of the table.

"Oh, no, sir. This will only take a moment." Sturyk paused. "Before that . . . It's said that you acquired . . . a certain appellation . . . as a result of your efforts in Dramur, Majer, sir. I would not wish to pry . . ."

Was that why there had suddenly been such a change in attitude and so much cooperation? Mykel offered a smile he hoped was ironic, or wry, or self-deprecating. "I've been told that I did acquire a name—one having to do with ancient knives that cut the user as deeply as the one attacked. It wasn't something I sought."

"That explains much. There have only been a handful of men called daggers of the ancients." Sturyk shook his head. "I do not envy you, Majer. Both the ancients and the alectors will try to break you." The overcaptain forced a smile. "That was not why I requested a moment of your time." He extended an envelope. "I must explain. That is an invitation. Every spring, just before summer, the Council of Southgate holds a ball, a dance, if you will. As a matter of courtesy, the commander of the compound and any senior officers in residence are always invited."

A ball was the last thing Mykel felt like attending. He tried not to show that feeling as he took the envelope, of heavy parchment, and sealed in deep blue wax. He did not open it.

"I realize that you're working hard, sir, but I fear . . ."

"They pay for the compound's expenses, don't they?"

"Yes, sir."

Mykel could see the relief on Sturyk's face. "I'll be there, but I'll have to be in uniform."

The overcaptain chuckled. "That's what they want. It will be formal, and everyone will say a few words about how much they appreciate your coming, but it's as much to show that they're on speaking terms with the Cadmians as anything else. This year . . . they'll appreciate it more, because you're not married, and that means you can talk and dance with their eligible daughters."

"I doubt they'd want a Cadmian for a husband," Mykel pointed out, thinking of Rachyla.

"Of course not, but they'll feel very wicked in having met you, especially . . ." Sturyk's words trailed off.

"Does everyone in Southgate know?"

"No, sir. Only a few, but, by the time of the ball . . ."

Mykel wanted to groan. He couldn't dance, except a few folk dances his sister had taught him years before, and he was going to be on exhibit as the dangerous "dagger of the ancients." How many other aspects of command were there that he had no idea of and had yet to face?

"It should be very interesting." He managed a smile.

"It's likely to be very long, sir. My wife dreads it, but it is one of the responsibilities that accompany command here." Sturyk managed a long-suffering smile.

That expression was convincing enough that Mykel actually believed Sturyk's words. Had Mykel not been in Dramur—and experienced the condescension and near-contempt of the seltyrs there—he might not have.

"That's all, sir." Sturyk nodded. "By your leave?"

"Thank you."

Mykel did not open the envelope until he stood alone in the study. Then he broke the seal and extracted the heavy card, reading it slowly. "The Council of Southgate requests the honor of the presence of Majer Mykel, Commanding, Third Cadmian Battalion, Mounted Rifles . . ."

He shook his head. At least, he had almost four weeks before he had to worry about that. A ball, for the Duarches' sake!

24

Dainyl returned to headquarters late on Quattri. Sulerya had provided no more information and had told him that finding out what she had in mind would take longer than she had thought. When he reached El-cien, Dainyl saw neither the marshal nor Lystrana that night. She had left a note at their home explaining that she'd be spending the night in Ludar because she and the High Alector of Finance had an early-morning meeting with the Duarch of Ludar to apprise him of some "irregularities" in the engineering accounts in the east.

Had she tracked down proof of what Rensyl was doing? Was the eastern engineer actually fabricating weapons based on road-building equipment? When Dainyl and Lystrana had last talked, he had not known of the possible involvement of the Duarch of Ludar with Brekylt. He hoped his wife would be safe while she accompanied her Highest.

He slept uneasily.

As a result, he was up early and in his study at Myrmidon headquarters well before morning muster—and that was after a quick inspection of the compound and First Company.

Just after he finished with fourth squad, he recalled something and turned back to Undercaptain Chelysta. "I forgot to mention that I ran across one of your cousins last week."

"Sir?"

"Granyn. He's a junior ranker at Myrmidon headquarters in Alustre. He's a driver, waiting for a place as a flyer. He said to send his greetings."

Chelysta shook her head. "That imp. I've only seen him once—that was when he was barely walking. He was always getting into things."

"He might get into Third Company under Majer Noryan."

"Majer Noryan?" Chelysta shook her head. "I never thought he'd make majer. Thin as a rail and not much taller than me. He was a translation orphan, you know. Didn't have many friends. More at home with horses. Came from a tiny place where his foster mother was the only alectress around. I didn't even hear he'd joined until later." Chelysta shook her head. "And Granyn . . . that's hard to believe."

"Your cousin has that air, still, but he works hard. Anyway, I promised I'd let you know." Dainyl smiled. "How are things going?"

"Some of the dispatch runs have been tight until first squad got replacement pteridons from Sixth Company in Lyterna. Captain Elysara sent word that there weren't any more spares at Lyterna—or anywhere else. Can't believe we lost two of them."

"It happens. Not often, but it does," Dainyl replied.

"But how, sir?"

How was he going to answer that without revealing the role of the ancients? He offered a rueful smile. "You know that pteridons can only fly so high before they reach an altitude where there's no lifeforce?"

"Yes, sir."

"There are places, usually in the mountains, where there's no lifeforce, and sometimes no one knows that they're there. Under certain conditions"—like an ancient being present and unfriendly—"a pteridon and rider can't escape."

The undercaptain winced. "I suppose we're lucky that there aren't too many places like that." She paused. "Is there any way to tell?"

"The only way I know is that the few I know about were near ruins of the ancients in the mountains."

"No one ever mentioned that."

"There aren't many," Dainyl said. "Do you have dispatch duty tomorrow?"

"No, sir. Not until Octdi."

"I hope you get good weather." He nodded and then turned.

As he walked back to his study, he considered what Chelysta had said. Noryan was certainly not rail thin and short. Could there be two with the same name? He spent a quarter glass going through all the rosters, but there was only one with that name, and he came from the area near Lysia. Chelysta must have been talking about when he'd been a youth.

The issue of spare pteridons was another matter. According to the Myrmidon records, before the recent losses there had been ten additional pteridons in the cavern squares at Lyterna. Why had Elysara indicated there were no more replacements? Was she saving them to keep them from going to the east in the future? Or was that a decision by Asulet? Dainyl had no doubts that the elder alector's decisions would weigh heavily with the Myrmidon captain in Lyterna, possibly even outweigh anything except direct intervention by the Duarch of Elcien.

Dainyl settled into his study and took out several sheets of paper, jotting down thoughts and phrases for the report on his eastern inspection tour. He wasn't about to attempt even a rough draft until after he spoke with the marshal.

He'd worked for close to a glass when Colonel Dhenyr appeared in his doorway.

"Sir?"

"Come in, Colonel. What can I do for you?"

"It's about the Iron Stem flights. The marshal ordered a recon on Septi. He wants third squad to do it, but they're scheduled for dispatch duty then . . ."

"You'll have to adjust the dispatch schedule. Have fourth squad take their duty and run a three-squad rotation until third squad returns." Dainyl paused. "That'll be down to a two-squad rotation for the first part of next week, with second squad doing a sweep of the Vedra." He studied the colonel, even as he wondered why Dhenyr had even asked him. That was the sort of adjustment Dainyl had made routinely when he had been operations chief. "You'll get used to making those adjustments. Just don't accept a request from the Duarch's assistants without checking with me or the marshal." Dainyl had learned that one the hard way.

"Yes, sir. Thank you, sir."

Once Dhenyr had left, Dainyl leaned back in his chair, setting the pen aside. The colonel's Talent-shields were adequate, but not impressive. His organizational skills were modest, to say the least. He could be charming, and his record showed that he had been a good flyer and flight commander, but those were scarcely abilities that merited promotion to colonel—except that the Duarch of Elcien would not have wished Sevasya moved from Lysia, although Dainyl did not know why, nor would Asulet have wanted Captain Elysara transferred from Lyterna. Ghasylt and Fhentyl weren't senior enough, and Majer Keharyl in Ludar owed his allegiance to Samist. The other company commanders were all in the east, and loyal to Alcyna, and, presumably, Brekylt. So Dhenyr had to be the choice. Yet Sevasya had suggested that there were other reasons as well, without detailing them. That was another reason why Dainyl wanted to go to Dereka.

"Dainyl!" The marshal marched into the study, closing the door behind him.

Dainyl stood. "Sir."

"What do you plan to do, now that you've finished your inspection tour of the east?" asked Shastylt.

"I thought I'd write a brief message commending all the Myrmidon companies in the east for their cooperation, their readiness, and their dedication to the Duarchy, and saying that such readiness reflected most favorably upon all Myrmidons, from the newest rankers to the submarshal of the east."

"Excellent!" Shastylt laughed.

"After that, sometime in the next few days, I'll be going to Dereka. I know there's probably nothing I can do about it, but they did lose five skylances there, and a handful of alectors vanished."

The marshal frowned.

"Besides, Asulet told me that it was an ancient city before we rebuilt it. I'm still concerned about the ancients and any links to the skylances."

"Submarshal Alcyna has a strategy for dealing with them. Didn't you tell me that?" Shastylt's tone was gently ironic.

"You'll pardon me, sir, if I'm skeptical about a strategy

that costs two pteridons and two alectors for every ancient destroyed. There just might be more than a few hundred ancients hiding up on the Aerlal Plateau—or in the
heights of the Spine of Corus."

"And you'll find an answer by going to Dereka, Submarshal?"

"Probably not, but if I visit every Myrmidon outpost
that can be reached by Table, neither Brekylt nor Alcyna
can bring a complaint to the Duarches that I singled out
the east for inspections. In practice, I don't have to visit
Ludar, so that just leaves the Myrmidon companies in
Dereka and Lyterna, and I can claim I've already been to
Lyterna. In addition, we are not faced with an immediate
crisis, and this is a good time to remind all of them that
headquarters does issue the orders and to let them put a
face with a name." Dainyl smiled politely. "Besides, they
won't put mere suspicions on paper, and I might learn
something more."

"There is that."

"If you have objections, sir . . ."

Shastylt waved a large hand, dismissing the idea.
"No . . . no. You're right. Now is a good time to make
those visits. I'd hope you could make them as brief as
possible. We may be facing some other difficulties before
long."

"Iron Stem?"

"The Cadmian battalion commander has reported a
number of disappearances around Iron Stem. In some
cases, his scouts have vanished. Their footprints just
ended, he claims."

"You scheduled recon for the area."

"I don't know what it will show, but . . ."

"It's close to the Aerlal Plateau," Dainyl said. "Do you
think it could be the ancients?"

"It's probably the Squawts. They're all over the area and
even more devious than the indigen Reillies. Either way,
the recon should provide information for the Cadmians."

"If it's not Iron Stem . . . are you thinking about Brekylt?"

"The Highest reported that certain resources have been diverted to the engineering manufactories in Fordall. This has been going on for a time, and it was handled in a very sophisticated manner."

"What are they manufacturing that they don't want known?" Dainyl knew very well, but decided to avoid that issue. "Is that where the seltyrs of Dramur got their rifles?"

"It could be." Shastylt paused. "Or Brekylt could be building something more formidable."

"I'll leave for Dereka tomorrow," Dainyl said.

"Do that." Shastylt started to leave, then turned back. "As before, no written reports about anything involving the east."

"Yes, sir."

Dainyl looked at the empty open doorway for several moments after the marshal left. Then he reseated himself and began to draft his report to Alcyna and the Myrmidon company commanders of the east.

25

Dainyl eventually made his way home on Quinti, where he paced around the lower level and then the foyer—until he heard the door open. He whirled, stepped forward, and wrapped his arms around his wife—tightly.

"I'm so glad to see you." He held on to her for a time.

"Careful . . . there are two of us. . . ." Lystrana stepped back, smiling. "That was quite a welcome."

He nodded, not wanting to say more at the moment. "You didn't have any trouble in Ludar?"

"We can talk about it later. I'm hungry . . . and not so

hungry. Some cheese might be good. Some warm bread, if we have any."

"Zistele just took some out of the oven."

"Good." Lystrana covered her mouth. "Kytrana is making . . . some things more difficult. Your mother stopped by the other day. She said uneasy digestion means a strong child."

"That sounds like her." Dainyl gave a wry smile, taking Lystrana's cape and hanging it on one of the wall pegs beside the door. "Everything that's difficult bodes for a better future."

They walked toward the sunroom, filled with the late afternoon light. Dainyl eased out a chair for Lystrana.

"I'm not delicate. I'm just carrying a child."

"I didn't say a word."

She laughed. "You didn't have to."

Zistele slipped the basket of bread and a small platter of cheese onto the table. "Supper will be ready in half a glass, alectress."

"Thank you."

As was their custom, Dainyl's and Lystrana's conversation before, during, and after the evening meal dealt with matters other than matters of the Myrmidons and Duarchy.

"Your mother said you were a greedy little boar from the time you were born."

"I had to be. She didn't like feeding me," countered Dainyl.

Lystrana sighed softly, and Dainyl could sense the melancholy.

"You're thinking about your mother?"

She nodded. "I just wish . . ."

"I know." Dainyl didn't need to say more. Lystrana's mother had stepped into a Table twenty-two years earlier, and never emerged. Her father had never truly recovered, and had retreated to Lyterna. He'd only lived another four years after his wife's death.

"She would have been so happy."

"I'm sure she would have been."

Later, before they retired to their bedchamber, Lystrana poured half a goblet of the Vyan Grande brandy into a goblet for Dainyl, but less than a fingerful of brandy for herself.

"Is that . . . ?"

"I'm being careful. A little doesn't hurt, even helps."

They walked upstairs without speaking.

After closing the door, Dainyl sat on the chair beside the shuttered window, holding his goblet.

Lystrana propped herself up on the wide bed. "Why don't you start?"

"Me?"

"You."

"I think some of the recorders are watching the Tables for me, but the translation wasn't a problem." He paused. "I thought I sensed a green flash, like the ancients. Have you ever felt anything like that?"

"I can't say I have. Can you tell me any more about what it's like?"

"It's . . . just amber-green . . . for a moment. In any case, when I got to Lysia, the recorder there was quite welcoming. It didn't make much sense, until she informed me that she was Asulet's daughter. Likewise, Captain Sevasya is the younger daughter of the Duarch of Elcien . . ." Dainyl rushed on to inform Lystrana of what he had discovered and what had occurred until he had returned. "Then, when I read your note, I have to say that I was more than a little worried. Today, I spent some time with Shastylt and wrote out my report on my tour. I tried not to worry too much."

"It might be a good thing that I didn't know what you found out when we met with Samist," mused Lystrana. "Once I knew what to look for with Rensyl's accounts, the patterns were obvious. I just pointed them out to my Highest, and he insisted we both brief the Duarch of Ludar, rather than the High Alector of Engineering."

"I'm glad he insisted on that. There have been far too many strange things happening with the engineers lately. The thousands of rifles secretly fabricated for the seltyrs on Dramur, Paeylt's efforts to undermine Asulet, and this business with Rensyl. Did you sense any reaction from Samist?"

"He's very conflicted, like you said Khelaryt was when you met him. It was almost as though he wanted to hear and understand . . . and didn't. My Highest—have you ever met Chembryt?—tried to get the Duarch to see the problem."

"I haven't met any of the High Alectors personally, except in passing at receptions. You think that Samist is fighting the shadowmatch conditioning?"

"I think it's more than that. We've been forced to allocate more golds for supplies to several of the regional administrative centers—Hyalt, Tempre, and Dulka are the ones requiring more these days. They all have different reasons. In Tempre, the RA—that's Fahylt—has documented Squawts crossing the Vedra and buying up more grain and fruit, increasing prices at a time of local drought. In Hyalt, Rhelyn claims that he's having to purchase supplies from Salcer and Krost, with higher transport costs, because neither Hyalt or Tempre can supply him fully. Kelbryt claimed that he had to spend extra golds on helping pay for the remediation of the floods north of Dulka."

"Those were in Catyr, some four hundred vingts north of Dulka," Dainyl pointed out. "Kelbryt had something else in mind. Otherwise, why would he and Faerlyt have attacked me before I said a word?"

"I didn't know that, but even chief assistants to the High Alector of Finance can't speak out too often," Lystrana replied. "That's particularly true when the Duarch is being curt, as if he didn't want to talk about the extra outlays. Especially after we'd already pointed out the problems in the east."

"That may be true of both Duarches. They don't like to

hear about problems," reflected Dainyl. "I'm more inclined to think along the lines Asulet suggested, but I'm
not even sure I agree totally with him."

"What do *you* think?"

What did he think? Dainyl did not speak for a time. Finally, he replied. "I think Zelyert and Asulet are right about
the lifeforce constraints. Asulet is certainly correct about
how much knowledge we lose with each new world translation, but his real interest is lifeforce creation. Alcyna is
accurate in the dangers presented by the ancients, and
Brekylt is right about the dangers of holding too closely to
a rigid plan. Khelaryt distrusts both the Archon and those
on Efra, but he is compelled to obey the Archon. I'm not
certain that Shastylt is interested in anything but power, although he'll use Zelyert's words to the greatest effect."

Lystrana nodded. "That's a good summary."

Dainyl understood what she meant. He really hadn't
offered his own thoughts, except as judgments on others.
"I don't know what to think. Acorus won't survive long if
the Master Scepter is transferred here. That's clear. It
should be clear to most of the High Alectors."

"What if it is?" questioned Lystrana.

Dainyl nodded slowly. "The internal personal conflicts
of the Duarches would make sense, and so would all the
plotting. Even the Efrans would prefer it, because—"

"The political second-raters and hangers-on would
come here. That would allow the High Alectors from Ifryn
and Efra to build Efra without so much lifeforce drain."

"But they would need to make sure that lifeforce
progress continued here and that they could retransfer
the Master Scepter in generations to come," Dainyl
pointed out.

"We've been getting Table engineers," replied
Lystrana. "And lifeforce specialists."

"Even the ancients must suspect something."

"They wouldn't have to. In any fashion one considers
it, we're a threat to them."

Dainyl looked past Lystrana, at the shuttered window

on the far side of the bedchamber. "All the disruptions fomented indirectly by Zelyert haven't changed anything."

"Do you think they were meant to?"

"No," he admitted.

The silence stretched out between the two of them.

After a time, Dainyl spoke. "You asked what I thought." He gave a twisted smile. "I think most of those involved know the problem. Each has his or her own solution and plans, and not a single one trusts another. No one's words can be totally trusted, even when they're true, because the truth can be used as much to deceive as a lie, and it's more effective. All we can do is look for acts and signals." He looked at his wife. "Am I wrong?"

She shook her head slowly.

26

Early on Sexdi, just after dawn, Dainyl stepped onto the Table in the Hall of Justice. He wanted to visit Dereka before Shastylt decided it was a poor idea—or sent Dainyl somewhere else. He let his Talent link to the darkness below and within the Table, and felt himself dropping . . .

. . . *into the chill of the translation tube. Immediately, he concentrated on locating the crimson-gold directional wedge that was Dereka.*

Again, for a moment, he thought he sensed the faintest purplish pink shading to the locator for Dereka, but when he extended a Talent line to link with the Table there, he no longer sensed the faint purplish overshades. Nor did he sense anything like the purplish arms.

With no sense of delay, Dainyl felt himself sliding through the silvered barrier, which seemed to melt away, rather than shatter into shards.

He stood on another Table, in a chamber with but a single wall hanging facing him, a rendering of a green eternastone tower set against a beige background, and bordered in crimson. The light-torches on the walls were at full illumination, revealing that the bare stone walls, unlike those of any other Table chamber he had visited, were of gold eternastone. The main doorway from the chamber was closed by a heavy door of golden wood, but Dainyl didn't think it was oak.

In the open doorway to the hidden chambers stood another recorder. His shimmering black hair bore faint traces of silver, a sign of great age, if not so great as that of Asulet. He had to be the oldest alector Dainyl had met outside the confines of Lyterna, both from his hair and from the dark purple of his Talent. His smile was warm, welcoming, and without the calculation Dainyl had sensed behind other projections of warmth.

"Submarshal, Recorder Sulerya said that you might be paying us a visit. I'm Jonyst."

"The most independent of recorders, I understand." Dainyl stepped off the Table.

"I have been called that, just as some have called you the most independent of submarshals. Welcome to Dereka."

"Thank you. I'm hoping for a better look at the city than in my past visits. Those were all too long ago, and I really never left the Myrmidon compound."

"Few Myrmidons do. It takes a special alector to feel at home in Dereka."

"Is that because some of the city holds a sense of the ancients?"

"It holds more than that. Much of this building they built. Not the interior walls, but the outer walls and the internal structural walls. When the first engineers realized that the only place to put the Table was here . . ." The recorder shook his head. "We have ten times the space we need, but none of the first regional alectors wanted their people here."

"What do you do with it all, then?"

"The transport staff has the top floor, and everyone working for me has a capacious study, even the driver. It's a waste in some ways, but . . . the exterior maintenance is almost nothing."

"You've never seen any sign of the ancients? Has anyone?"

"I'm convinced that the few survivors must visit unseen. I've occasionally sensed Talent of a type neither we nor even the wild Talents of landers possess."

Dainyl could sense the shading of the truth. "Occasionally?" His tone was both dry and suggestive.

Jonyst paused, looking at Dainyl. Then he nodded. "That's right. You ran into an ancient in Dramur, didn't you?"

How had the recorder known that? "I did."

"It's more than occasional, but not all that often. I tell everyone it's occasional, though. You understand why, I trust."

Dainyl did. "The alectors who like Dereka are those who have less Talent or who are less Talent-receptive?"

"That's generally so—except for the regional alector and his senior assistants. The building where they work is built partly on a dead zone. There are a number in this area. They thought that would discourage any ancients. It did. It also ages alectors far more quickly. So the term for a regional alector here is only five years. It's said that Samist once sent someone who schemed against him here for fifteen years. The fellow died a year after he left."

"I can't say that I'd heard that."

"Few have. It was a good hundred years back."

"The Duarch Samist generally appoints the RA here?" asked Dainyl.

"Samist appoints the RA here. Khelaryt does Lysia. Samist appointed Yadaryst last year. He's a cousin of some sort, translated from Ifryn maybe ten years back."

Dainyl nodded.

"In the end, it probably won't matter. Besides, no one really wants to think about Dereka."

"Why not? Because it's linked to the ancients? And because of strange occurrences here?"

"There are strange occurrences everywhere."

"It's the only place where large numbers of skylances have vanished. Could that have been the work of the ancients? Or is there another explanation?"

Jonyst fingered his square chin. "It had to be a wild lander Talent or an ancient. Wild alector Talents don't last long here."

"What about the five alectors who disappeared without a trace? Do you think the ancients had anything to do with them?"

"It's possible."

"You don't think so, I take it?"

"All five had recently been translated from Ifryn. They were traveling across Corus taking lifeforce measurements for the Archon. These days, that could be a dangerous occupation."

"It could, depending on what they discovered."

Jonyst looked intently at Dainyl. "What do you think their measurements showed?"

"From what I've seen, total lifeforce on Acorus is behind what was planned and expected."

"Just so. Like it was any great surprise." Jonyst snorted, then abruptly turned and walked to the formal exit door. He released the first Talent-lock and opened the door. Dainyl followed, careful to close the door and replace the Talent-seal before following Jonyst up the stone stairs. The recorder opened the door at the top, then closed it behind Dainyl, replacing the second Talent-lock.

The two stood in a small foyer that opened into a larger chamber beyond, one with wide windows. The windows, overlooking a boulevard, had extraordinarily low sills set in walls paneled in the same golden wood as the doors, although Dainyl could sense the eternastone walls behind the wood. The room was a library of sorts, he realized, although all the bookcases were set on the inside walls. There were two circular tables, each surrounded by five comfortable chairs.

"I haven't seen a recorder's chambers like these before."

"You won't either. As I told you, they're not all that practical." Jonyst laughed softly. His laugh ended abruptly. "We'll send you off in the carriage. The Myrmidon compound is south of here, and it's not a short walk."

"That I do recall."

"I like your wife. I trust her. She's got good judgment. Don't make me change my mind."

Dainyl managed not to start, although he did blink. "I trust her judgment explicitly."

"So I'd heard. Will you be here long?"

"I'd only planned to be here today."

"That's long enough." Jonyst turned again. "We'll have to go the long way to get down to the carriage."

Dainyl had to hurry to catch up to the shorter and older recorder. The building had ramps, one of the few in Corus that did, rather than stairs, and the lower ramp led to a low foyer, whose ceiling was less than half a yard above Dainyl's head.

"Out through here."

Under a portico, clearly added later, waited a carriage.

"Guersa . . . take the submarshal where he needs to go, and wait for him."

"Yes, sir." The driver, a blonde lander, nodded.

"Thank you for the carriage," Dainyl said politely.

"It's the least we can do, Submarshal. I'll see you later today. Give my best to young Fhentyl." Jonyst nodded and moved back.

"That I will." As he stepped into the carriage, Dainyl glanced back north along the boulevard. In the late-midmorning light, he saw yet another gold eternastone building and, beyond it, the green eternastone tower that marked the major cities of the Duarchy, and a few other locales of import.

"The Myrmidons, sir?" asked the driver.

"That's right."

Dainyl sat back in the leather-covered seat, thinking. Sulerya *had* said Jonyst was independent. The recorder had as much as told Dainyl not to hang around Dereka, and Dainyl didn't think the warning had much to do with the ancients.

Samist controlled most of the appointments in Dereka, while Khelaryt controlled those in Lysia. Those were exceptions to the rule, because usually the RA appointments were alternated between the Duarches, and the High Alectors of the six branches appointed their own people to their regional administrations. Why were Lysia and Dereka different? Dainyl had no idea; he hoped Lystrana did.

The Myrmidon compound was almost a full vingt south of any buildings in Dereka, and its gray stone walls appeared somehow out of place, as did the feeder aqueduct that supplied water. The Cadmian compound was north of the city, Dainyl recalled. Of the eight cities that held both Myrmidon and Cadmian contingents, in half they were geographically separated, and in half they were located adjacent to each other. Was that chance—or plan?

Dainyl had no idea, nor did he know if that happened to be relevant to anything.

Guersa brought the carriage to a halt by the gates. "Only you can enter, sir." Her explanation was apologetic. "I'll be waiting here until you're ready to return."

"Thank you. It's likely to be at least a glass. It's more likely to be two. If you'd like to rest somewhere or get a bite to eat . . ."

"You're sure, sir?"

"I'm certain."

"I'll be back in a glass, sir."

Dainyl turned and walked toward the gates. They were unguarded, as were all Myrmidon gates. The duty messenger saw him and bolted into the headquarters building.

The few moments it took Dainyl to cross the granite-paved front courtyard and enter the building were enough to alert the post, because a tall alector wearing the uniform of a Myrmidon captain stood in the front foyer waiting for Dainyl.

"Submarshal Dainyl . . . I had heard you were touring the companies. I didn't expect you here so soon." Captain Fhentyl was one of the youngest Myrmidon captains Dainyl had met. That was obvious, not from his physical appearance, which was impressive, given that he was as tall as Majer Noryan, and muscular, but in a tapered fashion, rather than being bulky and blocklike as Noryan was. Rather his lifeforce and Talent bore the brighter purple of youth. Dainyl concealed a frown. By comparison, Noryan's lifeforce had seemed not just older, but much older, yet Chelysta had spoken as if Noryan were close to her age.

"I won't be here that long," Dainyl offered, "but I haven't visited Dereka in many years."

"We're pleased to see you. If we had known, sir, we could have provided a more impressive welcome."

Dainyl laughed. "I've never felt the formal receptions and inspections were worth the effort put into them— either for the officer being greeted or the units that had to provide them." He paused. "I will inspect, but that will tell me more than prearranged pageantry."

"Yes, sir. Right now?"

"This very moment, but don't call a formal muster. I'll inspect as things are. We'll begin with the pteridon squares."

"Very good, sir." Fhentyl turned toward the rear door from headquarters.

Dainyl followed the captain.

The pteridons were in good order, as they always were. So was their equipment.

The pteridon squares were a good yard shorter than any Dainyl had seen before. After looking over the last square, he stopped and addressed Fhentyl. "The height of the squares . . . ?"

Fhentyl laughed. "Every officer who hasn't been stationed here asks. This is the oldest Myrmidon compound. When they built the later ones, they raised the squares a yard and a third. It was either a point of pride or a tradition, but even when the compound was enlarged, they didn't raise the squares."

That was another story Dainyl hadn't heard.

"Where do you store the skylances when a squad isn't flying?"

"We've gone to storing them all in lockers in the duty pteridon's square. We haven't lost any more, not since . . ."

"You took over?"

"I doubt if it happened to be that, sir."

"You were an undercaptain then. What do you know about the missing skylances?"

Fhentyl flushed. "Not much, sir. They were here, and then they were gone. We checked everything, even took apart some of the stonework. After the last ones disappeared, Majer Dhenyr had the recorder question every Myrmidon. I don't know as he had much choice. The regional alector found out . . ."

"Was Majer Dhenyr close to the RA?"

"Close? That'd be hard to say. He went over there maybe once every two weeks to brief him. He never looked happy when he came back. Not that I saw anyway."

"Have you briefed Yadaryst?"

"No, sir. If he asks, I will, but I'd not be one to ask for trouble." Fhentyl flushed slightly.

"I take it that the RA is known to be a hard alector?"

"Yes, sir."

Dainyl decided not to press on the matter of the RA. "What do you think happened to cause the skylances to disappear?"

Fhentyl glanced northward, back toward Dereka. "I don't like to say things like this . . . but what else could it be? A pteridon will kill anyone who intrudes who's not a Myrmidon. I know—maybe I'm not supposed to—that

an ancient can destroy a pteridon. Seems to me that anything that could do that could take a skylance."

"That makes sense, except for one thing. If they worried about the skylances as weapons, why would they
take a handful and leave the others?"

"Maybe to make a point, sir?"

Dainyl frowned. "Then . . . why did they do so secretly?"

Fhentyl shrugged helplessly. "I couldn't say, sir. It
couldn't be to copy them, because they don't work except
with a pteridon."

Dainyl stiffened inside. He'd need to check the dates,
but Fhentyl's suggestion had triggered another possibility. Maybe the ancients had another motive. "No one's
lost any since the last one turned up missing here."

"No, sir." Fhentyl flushed. "I mean, you'd know more
than I would, sir."

"We'll have to think about it. Now . . . you can show
me the armory."

"Yes, sir."

Even as quickly as they were moving, Dainyl could see
that Guersa would have plenty of time for a meal—and
still a long wait.

27

Because Dainyl had a little time, after he
finished his inspection of the Myrmidon compound, he
had Guersa give him a brief tour around Dereka.

As they drove up the boulevard, the driver pointed to
her left—due west. "That's the engineers' complex.
Everyone else under the RA is in the main building.
Well . . . except for the transport people in our building."

Dainyl studied the walled enclosure surrounding a

paved courtyard and several two-story structures within. "Why do the engineers have a separate place?"

"It was always that way, they say. It could be because they had to widen the roads. It was a real effort to put the road through the Upper Spine Mountains. All the land around it is dead. Almost nothing grows there. Then, they had to repair the aqueduct . . . well . . . reassemble the section the cliff fell on, and build the extension down to the Myrmidon compound. There's no water—even from wells—anywhere near Dereka."

That didn't seem to justify a separate establishment—especially since the High Alector of Engineering served Samist, and the RA was appointed by the Duarch of Ludar. But then, reflected Dainyl, half of the other regional administrative heads were not.

Farther northward, the driver pointed to her right at a massive structure surrounded by goldenstone walls. "That's the building where the RA and the other administrators work."

To Dainyl's eye, the building looked more like a palace, except for the modest extension to the rear, barely visible.

The rest of Dereka was laid out in much the same fashion as any other Duarchial city, with wide streets coming off the two main boulevards, and dwellings and shops all constructed of stone. The roofs were of split dark slate, rather than tile. From what Dainyl could see on his brief tour, the most visible remnants of the ancients were the three golden eternastone buildings, the aqueduct, and several walls, and those had clearly been modified and rebuilt.

He paused. The ancients' structures were their form of eternastone. What had been strong enough to adapt and modify them? Or were they far, far older than they appeared, and their strength had waned?

Guersa eased the carriage to a halt outside the building that held the Table. "Here you are, sir."

"Thank you. I appreciated the tour—and your waiting for me."

"That's what drivers are for, sir."

"Thank you, anyway." Dainyl offered a parting smile before heading inside.

Jonyst met Dainyl in the low-ceilinged foyer, barely a glass before sunset. "How did your day go, Submarshal?" The recorder's eyes and mouth held the hint of a smile.

"Generally as expected. I thank you for the loan of your driver and carriage. Guersa made matters much easier."

"I'm glad that we could help." Jonyst started up the ramp.

"I do appreciate it." Dainyl followed, not saying more until they were back in the library room that overlooked the boulevard.

"Fhentyl told me that Majer Dhenyr had you interview all the Myrmidons after the last skylance vanished—and that none of them could have been involved."

"I'd doubt it. There's always the possibility of Talent-tampering, but that leaves signs as well. I didn't detect anything like that." The recorder cleared his throat. "An extremely Talented alector might have been able to do it."

Dainyl laughed, softly. "I'd wager that you've never run across any that Talented."

"There's always a first time for anything, Submarshal. That's a good thought to keep in mind. There are more than a few alectors who died because they saw something and didn't believe it could happen."

"I can see that."

"I imagine you can. That's one reason why you're a submarshal and still alive."

Dainyl mentally noted the order in which Jonyst had mentioned the two items.

"How is your wife these days?"

"We're expecting a daughter," Dainyl said. "So far

they're both doing well. Lystrana has to watch what she eats, though."

"Good to hear. Daughter will need the best from both of you. Good shields, especially."

"They said we'll be getting more translations from Ifryn."

"We already are. Not all of them approved. More wild translations than I've seen in years."

"How are they getting access to Tables on Ifryn?"

Jonyst shrugged. "How does anyone?"

"Corrupt recorders or High Alectors," suggested Dainyl. "Or stealth and Talent?"

"All three, but generally the second. When life is at stake . . ."

"You expect to see more wild translations, then?"

Jonyst nodded slowly. "I'd be certain of it." Then he offered a smile. "Shouldn't trouble you or Lystrana. We need to get you back to Elcien." He turned toward the foyer outside the top of the staircase down to the Table chamber, releasing the Talent-lock on the door as he did. Without looking back, he headed down the stairs.

Dainyl glanced around the library a last time, sensing the serenity of the chamber, then started downward, after closing the door and replacing the Talent-lock.

Jonyst had left the door open at the base of the steps and stood beside the Table.

Dainyl joined him. "I just realized that I haven't seen any of your assistants."

"You won't. I keep them busy. Whelyne is the only one who could take my place, and one of us is always here. You might see her, but not me. The other way around, also."

Dainyl concentrated on recalling the assistant's name—Whelyne. He noted that the concealed doorway to the hidden chambers was closed—and that without his Talent, he would have had absolutely no chance of discovering that those chambers even existed. "The hidden chambers for recorders were planned from the beginning, I take it?"

"Old as I am, Submarshal, I wasn't around then. The first Tables were placed in a hurry, with crude enclosures over pits in the ground. They were as cold as the tubes themselves. Paeylt claimed that some of the chill came because the Tables absorbed the ambient cold. Dereka was among the last because they had to cut into the stone. But you're partly right. Dereka was also the first besides Lyterna that was provided a more finished area. That was also before my time. We've done what we could since then."

"Thank you." Dainyl moved toward the Table.

"Give my greetings and best wishes to Lystrana."

"I will."

Dainyl stepped up onto the Table, then concentrated on the darkness beneath. For just a moment, he could sense an aura of purpled pink all around him, but that vanished as he dropped . . .

. . . *into the chill darkness of the translation tube.*

While the purpled pink had vanished, Dainyl felt, as if from the corners of his eyes, although he could properly see nothing, only sense through his Talent, vague lines of amber-green.

Knowing he couldn't afford to linger in the darkness, he focused on the white locator that was Elcien, linking. It flashed toward him.

The silvered white of the barrier sprayed away from him.

He stood in the Table chamber in Elcien.

By the doorway was a figure in the green garb of a recorder. The recorder did not speak, but watched as Dainyl stepped off the Table.

Dainyl searched his memory for the recorder's name, finally saying, "You must be Chastyl."

"At your service, Submarshal."

At *his* service? An odd response, given that the recorders officially answered to no one except the

Duarches or the Archon. "I'm glad to meet you. In all the times I've used the Table, I haven't seen you." Dainyl smiled. "I suspect you've been well aware of my uses, though."

Chastyl stiffened, ever so slightly, before replying. "We recorders do our best to keep the Tables functioning, and that includes monitoring their use."

"I'm glad you do. I'd hate to make these trips by pteridon." Dainyl inclined his head to the recorder. "Thank you, and a good day to you." The Talent-lock on the inner door had not been replaced, and he eased past the recorder, still keeping his shields in place, and into the foyer.

Because of the difference in time, it was still late mid-afternoon in Elcien, and that meant Dainyl needed to check in at headquarters. He could at least catch up on dispatches and any occurrences and not be surprised on Septi morning.

28

After a long week of dealing with training—both his own battalion and the two new companies—and two late nights writing up the required reports to Colonel Herolt, Mykel decided that he had to get away from the compound. Immediately after a late breakfast on Decdi, late being a glass after sunrise, he saddled one of the spare mounts and rode out, heading back down the northeast high road toward Southgate. He felt slightly guilty because, while he had given his officers and rankers the day off, they were limited to the area within two vingts of the compound—at the discretion of their officers. That included a handful of taverns and shops, but Mykel intended to explore somewhat farther—the center of Southgate, in fact. Why he felt it necessary, he would have been hard-pressed to explain.

As he left the compound, on the short stretch of stone paving that connected the Cadmian outpost to the wider high road, he looked to the northeast. He could just make out the subtle change in the road surface, a vingt or so farther out, where the granite paving of the road leaving Southgate was replaced by eternastone stretching as far as he could see to the northeast. Heat waves danced above the surface of the stone.

In places like Elcien, Ludar, and Faitel, the eternal paving ran without interruption through the town. The same was true in smaller towns like Arwyn and Harmony, or small cities like Klamat. Yet, from what he had seen, there were no roads or buildings of eternastone in Southgate.

Why was Southgate different?

He turned his mount southwest on the high road, smiling wryly, because he doubted that anyone could tell him. The fingers of his left hand swept by his belt, not actually touching the leather, but close enough that he could feel, in a way he still had trouble describing, the miniature dagger of the ancients concealed in its special slot.

From his actions, Overcaptain Sturyk had clearly displayed both fear, respect, and pity for Mykel—and all three emotions seemed linked to Mykel's unasked-for appellation as a dagger of the ancients. Yet Mykel had the feeling that the emotions associated with the term were limited to Dramur and Southgate.

Mykel reached the outskirts of Southgate, less than half a vingt from the compound. The first structure was a tavern, as usual near Cadmian outposts, but the door to the Overflowing Beaker was closed, and the windows were still shuttered. Beyond that was a two-story narrow house, narrow in front, with a deep covered porch. The main section of the house extended a good twenty yards back from the highway.

Two women wearing little more than shifts lounged on battered wooden rocking chairs on the porch. Mykel

could feel their eyes on him, but neither spoke, either between themselves or to Mykel, as he rode past the
house—certainly a brothel in fact, if not in name,

For another half vingt, he rode past various establish-
ments designed to separate Cadmians from their coins.
Those farther from the compound and closer to the main
sections of Southgate seemed less disreputable and
merged with more traditional shops, such as a copper-
smith's, a cooperage, and a fuller's, although the fullering shop appeared more dingy than the ones Mykel had
known in Faitel, despite its whitewashed stuccoed plaster outer walls. He saw but a handful of people, mostly
older women, out on the stone sidewalks that bordered
the high road.

Farther from the Cadmian compound, the shops gave
way to small dwellings, all with few windows looking out
on the high road, and all built around central courtyards.
The courtyards looked so small that Mykel wondered
how they could offer much respite from the summer heat,
but perhaps the brilliant white stucco reflected enough of
the sun to help. Still, early in the day as it was, he could
feel sweat beginning to ooze down his back, and it was
still spring.

He rode slowly, letting his eyes range across the houses
and occasional shops. Neat and clean as they were, there
was something within Southgate that did not feel right to
Mykel. Try as he might, though, he couldn't put a finger
on why he felt that way or what had created that feeling.

As on the ride from the port, the closer he rode to the
inner ring and the center of Southgate, the fewer people
he saw, and most of those he did see were on horseback
or in carriages and far better attired, generally in white.
The few exceptions were young women, uniformly
dressed in light gray tunics and trousers, with matching
gray head scarves that covered their hair and the lower
part of their faces. They carried baskets, filled with all
manner of items, from laundry to produce, even small
glazed tiles in string bags in one case.

He slowed the mount as he neared the inner ring. When he looked at the center of Southgate, with morning sun reflecting off the brilliant white walls surrounding the huge central villas—also brilliant white—Mykel had to squint, so intense was the light.

He crossed the inner ring at a measured walk and continued to ride southwest along the paved road that led between the walls that surrounded two of the villas. The road narrowed to a width of ten yards. The space from the edge of the road to the base of the walls measured perhaps fifteen yards and was covered in white gravel. Not a single bit of vegetation appeared to mar the whiteness. The sides of the crenelations on the top of the walls showed no interior stone, just a white surface.

As he neared the end of the walls of the two villas, he could see a second granite boulevard, one that curved around a central park in the center of which was some sort of white stone plaza. The street he traversed ended at the boulevard, and he eased to his right and onto the boulevard. The park to his left was edged with a low granite wall, no more than a yard and a half high. Beyond the wall was an expanse of grass, broken by curving stone walks, and hedges no higher than the enclosing wall. The park—if it were such—was empty.

Mykel kept riding. Shortly, on his right, he passed one of the gates to the enclosed villas. The gates were of iron, but had been painted white with so many coats of paint that they shimmered. Behind the closed gates he could only see a stone drive leading to a covered portico.

Ahead, he saw another street entering from the right, again running in the open space between the walls of two villas. This street continued into the park. Mykel turned his mount down it, toward the center of the parklike area. Once more, the park was separated from the street by the same low granite wall.

The street ended in yet another boulevard, if it could be called that, which circled what appeared to be a raised circular platform of brilliant white granite a hundred yards or so across. Directly in front of Mykel was a stele of white stone set ten yards out into the gray granite of the innermost circular boulevard.

Mykel reined up and surveyed the area. Four streets ran through the park, each radiating out from the white stone—or the stelae set at the four cardinal points of the compass. There were no decorations or statutes rising from the circle of whiteness—just the circle itself.

After a moment, Mykel urged his mount the few yards toward the stele before him so that he could make out what had been carved upon it.

When he was less than a yard from the stele, he eased his mount to a halt and began to study the series of scenes sculpted into the stone. The bottom row depicted men at work—raising a wall, constructing a ship, plowing a field, presumably set outside Southgate. The three images above that showed men riding, hunting, and fighting another force. There was a single wider image above those—it showed thirteen men seated at a table, each holding a scepter. Mykel looked more closely. Standing directly in the center, back of the seated men, was a sculpted figure of an alector—although the stone did not convey the purple eyes or the jet black hair. The alector stood behind the center seltyr, the only one who sat on something resembling a throne. The alector was not threatening, not carrying a weapon, just there.

Mykel frowned. Except for the images on the stele, there was no sign of alectors in the construction of Southgate, even in the high roads. He flicked the reins, riding around the innermost boulevard, so that he could see the three other stelae, but all carried the same images.

Slowly, he rode out of the park—or memorial . . . or ceremonial plaza—turning his mount back toward the Cadmian compound. As he rode around the boulevard that circumscribed the central plaza, he noted that all the gates to the villas opened onto that boulevard and each gate was set directly in the middle of the wall facing the plaza.

As he guided his mount back up the street between two sets of walls, he realized something else. He'd sensed nothing living in the plaza, except the stunted grass and short hedge.

29

The next week passed slowly, and Dainyl finally caught up on the back reports. He also received a polite note from Alcyna the following Septi, a good ten days after he had toured Dereka, expressing appreciation for the unexpected objectiveness in his report. He had pushed aside his irritation and showed the note to Shastylt.

"Better and better." That had been the marshal's only real comment—without elucidation.

While Dainyl felt he should have been pleased that matters were going so well, the quiet worried him as much as adverse reports from across Corus would have. Quiet or not, worries or not, he and Lystrana had enjoyed the warmth of the late spring end-days.

On Londi, he had made an informal inspection of First Company after the morning muster. He had returned to his study and reviewed the latest entries in the master accounting ledgers, but found nothing that suggested irregularities. He had not expected he would.

There was a cough, and Dainyl looked up. Colonel Dhenyr stood in the open doorway, and Dainyl nodded for him to come in.

"Sir, here are the latest reports from the Cadmians." The colonel handed over a shcaf of papers.

"Anything interesting there?"

"Their Fourth Battalion . . . you should probably read it yourself, sir."

Dainyl always read the reports in the entirety—

sometimes quickly, but he read them—and Dhenyr's implication that he did not generated more irritation. Even though he told himself he had asked the colonel, he found he was still irritated. "Thank you. I will."

Rather than immediately seek out the Fourth Battalion section, Dainyl lifted the thick report, looking at the first page of summary regimental report from the Cadmian headquarters in Elcien, which began with Second Battalion. So far as Dainyl had been able to discern, there had never been a First Battalion, and the lowest denominated Cadmian company was Eighth Company in Second Battalion. In a way, that might have made sense, if the lowest numbered company had been ninth company, since there were eight Myrmidon companies. He pushed away that minor puzzle and began to read the summary from Colonel Herolt.

. . . Second Battalion, Overcaptain Wekeryt, commanding [acting], is undergoing rebuilding and retraining after returning in midspring after a year and a half deployment to Ongelya. Second Battalion was successful in destroying the loose confederation of grassland nomad brigands, but fatalities and permanently disabling casualties exceeded thirty percent. Second Battalion will be ready for deployment in early harvest . . .

Dealing with the grassland nomads had been a Myrmidon duty. Sending a battalion of mounted rifles was asking for high casualties. The fact that the numbers had not been higher suggested a fair degree of competence by whoever had been commanding the battalion or poorer tactics by the nomads, or some combination of both.

Dainyl kept reading.

. . . Third Battalion, Majer Mykel commanding, is currently deployed to the Southgate Cadmian compound. Third Battalion is engaged in training two companies, composed largely of recruits raised in the southwest area surrounding Southgate . . . scheduled to ride to Hyalt, conducting additional training on route, to establish a replacement compound and to complete pacification of the Hyalt area, as per the orders of the Marshal of Myrmidons. No discrepancies or casualties reported to date on this deployment.

Dainyl couldn't help but wonder how Majer Mykel would fare in Hyalt. Then he frowned. The casualty levels for Third Battalion in Dramur had been far greater than the thirty percent listed for Second Battalion, yet Third Battalion had been sent out only a month after returning to Elcien. Then, who else could have been sent?

. . . Fourth Battalion, Majer Hersiod, commanding, is currently deployed to Iron Stem, based out of the Cadmian compound. The battalion is providing support to the local Cadmian forces in maintaining order at the iron and coal mines, and the iron works. Battalion patrols are also providing security against large local predators. Casualties reported to date are moderate . . .

Fifth Battalion, Majer Druvyr, commanding, remains deployed to Northport, with companies rotating duties along the northwest high road, with garrisons in Klamat and Eastice . . . engaged in maintaining order between longtime settlers and Reillies recently relocated north of the high road . . . Casualties light, no recent fatalities . . .

Sixth Battalion, Majer Juasyn, commanding, returned from a year's deployment in the Vedra triangle north of Tempre the second week of spring . . . patrol actions against Squawt brigands and settlements established in violation of the Code were successful, as detailed in the commander's report. The surviving Squawts, primarily women, children, and elderly men, were relocated to the Semal area . . . No new casualties reported . . .

Dainyl turned to the detailed reports of the battalion commanders, making his way through them as well. When he had finished the last of them, he walked to the doorway of the marshal's study.

"Ah . . . Dainyl . . . what can I do for you?" Unlike so many times in recent weeks, the marshal was cheerful and smiling.

Dainyl stepped into the study. "I must have missed something, sir. I was reading the reports from Cadmian headquarters, and I came across the report from their Second Battalion . . ."

"Oh . . . yes. That. What about it?"

"In the past, from what I recall, it was judged more effective to use Myrmidons against the nomads."

" 'Effective' is the key word, Dainyl. Myrmidons are indeed more effective. Unfortunately, it requires days and days of overflights, and heavy use of skylances, which, in turn, result in grassfires. The grasslands are suffering a severe drought at present . . ."

Dainyl understood all too well. "The lifeforce loss?"

"I'm gratified that you grasped that so quickly. Your predecessor never did understand, poor alector."

"I knew there had to be a reason, but since the deployment decision was made before I became submarshal . . ." Dainyl paused. "There was one other thing. The majer in charge of the Fourth Battalion reported rather large wolves of what appeared to be a new breed. Is that something we should inquire about with Asulet or someone in Lyterna?"

"I'd heard something about that. How big are they?"

"They're reported to be close to three yards in length,

not counting the tail, and it takes several rifle shots to bring one down. They also have large crystal fangs." Dainyl almost missed the slight stiffening of the marshal at his last words. "The fangs seemed unusual."

"I'd appreciate it if you'd send an inquiry to Lyterna. Regular dispatch should suffice. It may just be a species that the life-form masters thought had died out, and, for some reason, has found a predatory niche, but it wouldn't do to overlook it. Asulet will want to know, one way or the other."

"I'll take care of that. I'm sorry to have bothered you about the shift in tactics with the nomads, but I appreciate the clarification."

"What were their casualties?" Shastylt's tone was close to indifferent.

Dainyl could sense the buried concern.

"Over thirty percent."

"It could have been far worse." Shastylt nodded. "That's better than I feared. Thank you."

Dainyl nodded and stepped back.

"Close the door, if you would."

After leaving the marshal's study, Dainyl returned to his own desk, closing his own door as well. He needed to write the dispatch to Asulet, and to have Dhenyr draft a short letter acknowledging receipt of the reports.

Was the lifeforce issue that critical? Basically, the marshal—and the Duarches—were sacrificing landers and indigens to conserve the world's lifeforce, and they were counting on the higher birth rates and the greater promiscuity of the indigens to compensate for the troopers lost dealing with problems handled previously by Myrmidons. In turn, that implied an almost desperate need for more lifeforce, more quickly than originally planned.

In addition, despite his apparent indifference, Shastylt had been worried by the "new" predator. The crystal fangs suggested at least a partial reliance on lifeforce for sustenance. To Dainyl, that translated not into a new predator, but an old one, perhaps one dating back to the time of the ancients. Were the predators making a comeback because Acorus was returning to a warmer climate? Or was something else at work?

Slowly, he took out several sheets of paper. He'd need to be careful—very careful—in the way he phrased the notification to Asulet because it was also clear that Shastylt had not wanted to be the one telling the elder alector.

30

Beware of the alector, or especially of the steer, who declares that, because ethical standards, or values, or morals are expressed and codified by the Archon, they are merely the product of our society and, furthermore, that each region of a world, if left to itself, would have expressed its own standards and values, and such values and standards would have validity equal to those set forth in the Code. This argument contains within it two assumptions. One is correct, but the second is false.

The first underlying assumption is that the environment in which individuals are raised affects their beliefs and values. This is true, and that truth forms the rationale and necessity for a uniform system of education and understanding for all alectors so that regional influences can be recognized and balanced.

The second assumption is that, since differing geographies and other regional factors give rise to differences in beliefs and practices, each region's standards can only be judged in the context in which they arose. By extension, logic then requires the presumption that value systems arising out of differences in climate and locale are equal in their validity, and that no value system is intrinsically superior or inferior to another. Early history has shown, all too clearly, that this assumption is demonstrably and egregiously false. When two sets of values conflict, or are compared, one set will prove superior. . . .

Unfortunately, often which set of values is "superior" has been determined by which possessor of values had the greater might and power, rather than upon the ethical considerations of each. To avoid this, the early Archons investigated the structural basis of laws and values . . .

The bases of any ethical or administrative standard must rest in fact upon three determinations. The first determination is whether such a standard is correct. Such correctness must be determined by asking whether the standard provides the greatest good for the greatest number in all conceivable circumstances at all times, and conversely, and of equal importance, that it provides the least harm in all times and circumstances, even unto those who are powerless.

The second determination is whether the standard can be implemented both so that it applies practically and yet falls with equal force upon all, regardless of their beliefs, their wealth or lack thereof, or their physical characteristics.

The third determination is that the total number of standards shall be the absolute minimum necessary for the maintenance of order.

In oversimplistic terms, a law must be fair; it must be practical; and it must be able to be implemented. The same is true of values. They must be fair; they must be practical; they must be limited in scope to what is necessary for consensus; and they must be understood and accepted by the vast majority of individuals.

While these principles are indeed the basis for sensible governing, they are far from accepted as widely as they should be. As noted earlier, there is a desire, particularly by steers, to insist that the world or the universe in which a world exists must have been created, and that such creation requires a supra-intelligent creator, a deity, if you will. From this flows the assumption that the wisdom of such a deity, as revealed by a prophet, is the basis of the standards and values of the believers in that deity, and that any belief system revealed by a deity is superior to any codified by mere mortals. Yet such believers continue to ignore the fact that the prophet who revealed the wishes or commandments of the deity has always been in fact a mortal . . .

Views of the Highest
Illustra
W.T. 1513

31

More than a week had passed since Dainyl had sent off his inquiry to Asulet. He had not received a response, and so far as he knew, neither had Shastylt. Little else of note had occurred. The past twenty-five days had been as uneventful as any he could recall in his years at Myrmidon headquarters. Even the weather in Elcien had been warm and mild, and on the previous Decdi, he and Lystrana had spent the afternoon in the Duarch's Park, just strolling along the stone walks, talking, and enjoying the spring flowers, the sunlight, and each other.

As he sat in his Myrmidon study right after morning muster on Tridi, he could not but feel that, behind all the quiet, something was building. Yet he could find absolutely no concrete evidence of any sort that would support his feeling.

"Sir?"

Dainyl looked up. Hasekyt—the duty orderly—stood in his doorway.

"Yes?"

"The marshal would like to see you, sir."

Dainyl rose immediately. When Shastylt summoned anyone through an intermediary, trouble followed. Tyanylt's untimely death was a perfect example.

Stopping short of the half-open doorway to Shastylt's study, Dainyl reinforced his shields, then entered.

Before Dainyl had taken two steps into the study, Shastylt burst out laughing. "You're the most observant submarshal in decades, but I'm not angry with you. Close the door and sit down."

Dainyl did, but only relaxed his shields marginally.

"Asulet sent a response to your inquiry about the new predator. It's singularly unhelpful. He states that it's a matter that needs to be discussed in Lyterna—at our convenience—and that he'd be happy to see either of us."

"That doesn't sound good." Dainyl had the feeling he was understating matters, but wanted to hear what the marshal felt.

Shastylt snorted. "The last time he sent a message like that was years back, just before the Vedra flooded and wiped out good portions of Dekhron and Salaan."

"When do you want me to leave?"

"Half a glass ago. Matters are quiet here, but they won't stay that way, and I'd like you to find out what he'll tell you and get back as soon as you can."

"Yes, sir."

Less than a quarter of a glass later, Dainyl was in the duty coach headed for the Hall of Justice. He had grabbed his flying jacket, although the day was warm enough that he would not be needing it, except for the Table translation. Once at the Hall, largely deserted so early in the morning, he made his way into the underground warren beneath the public spaces.

One of Zelyert's assistants peered at him quickly, then nodded and returned to her small study as Dainyl removed the Talent-lock on the outer foyer door. The inner chamber was empty when he entered it and stepped onto the square blackish silver surface of the Table.

He concentrated . . .

. . . letting the blackness rise around him, trying to center his attention on the pink locator wedge that was Lyterna.

Yet almost immediately, he could sense the heavy pink-ish purpleness—and then the purpled arms reaching for him. There was not a single set of arms, but two; they seemed to block the translation tube in all directions.

Dainyl reinforced his shields, feeling the heat build within his body, even as the chill from outside tried to leach away strength and volition.

He began to search . . . what about the amber green lines? Dainyl had sensed them before, if briefly. As the purple arms drew nearer, he cast out a Talent-probe, try-ing to visualize it as amber-green, rather than purple. He stretched, seeking the amber-green somewhere beyond the translation tube, a tube that felt endless in all directions, for all that he knew and sensed that it was not.

The purpled arms drew closer, forming a web contract-ing around him.

A hint of that amber-green he sought appeared some-where above, and he grasped for it with all the Talent-strength he possessed. His body convulsed, as if dozens of bullets had struck him simultaneously. Then all his be-ing felt as though he were being twisted into convoluted segments, then stretched the entire length of the transla-tion tube.

For a moment, the briefest of instants . . . he was sur-rounded by golden green . . . and a single winged ancient, even more hazily present than when he had last beheld one of them, studied him with fine greenish Talent-probes.

He thought he sensed a thought . . . .

You have not changed enough. . . .

Dainyl debated not answering, then forced a thought at the ancient. **How should I change?**

You must become of the world, not separate from it.

How did one become of the world, besides living and working—and loving—in it?

Before Dainyl could formulate another thought, he was back in the darkness and chill of the translation tube . . . hurtling toward the pink locator wedge of Lyterna. All too soon the silvered pink barrier appeared and he found

*himself flung through it. Silver shattered, and lines of
pain ripped down his arms.*

He rolled across the table as though he'd been pitched
like a ball through the tube, barely getting his arms out in
time to stop himself from falling off the Table.

The man who stood and gaped at him openmouthed
was clearly not the recorder, but one of his assistants.
Dainyl could sense the residue of purpleness, suggesting
that the younger alector had been at least partly involved
in trying to trap Dainyl in the translation tube.

Dainyl quickly regained his feet and strengthened his
shields. "Which of Myenfel's assistants are you?" After
he spoke, he realized he did not feel quite so cold as
usual. Bruised, but not cold.

"Ah . . ." There was a pause, then a reluctant admis-
sion. "Choranyt, sir."

"Choranyt." Dainyl nodded. "I'm here to see Asulet,
at his request. Do you know where he might be at the
moment?"

"No, sir. I really don't. He might be . . . where he usually is?"

"The museum . . . or his . . . ?" Dainyl realized he'd
never know what to call the area where Asulet worked.

"Yes, sir."

"I'll find him." The submarshal left the Table chamber,
trying to recall the directions back to the museum.

In time, a good quarter of a glass, he found himself
standing before the recessed niche that held a pteridon,
its lifeforce held in abeyance.

Then he heard steps coming from his left, and he
turned, his shields at full strength.

"I must admit I did not expect so prompt a response to
my dispatch," offered the silver-haired Asulet.

"We thought it best to come immediately."

"We? Or you?"

"The marshal did not dispute my suggestion."

"If he's wise, he won't," replied Asulet. "How was your
journey? Sulerya said that you've had some difficulties."

"I had a rather undignified arrival," admitted Dainyl. "I rolled out of the translation tube."

The silver-haired alector raised his eyebrows, but said nothing, waiting.

"Someone tried to trap me when I translated from El-cien here. There were two sets of those purple arms, one in front of me, and one behind. When I arrived on the Table here, one of Myenfel's assistants was in the Table chamber. He'd been using the Table for something."

"Which assistant?"

"Choranyt."

"I'd expect something like that from him. How did you manage to evade the trap?"

"I'm not exactly sure," replied Dainyl. "Except I dodged the arms by slipping outside the tube."

"That can be extraordinarily dangerous. Most alectors who try that end up as wild translations."

"I had the feeling that, if I didn't do something, I'd end up dead."

"That was their intent."

"Whose intent?"

"Paeylt's and Brekylt's. I assume that Sulerya told you about Paeylt."

"Not much, except that he opposes you and has his own supporters here in Lyterna and elsewhere, and seems to be allied with Brekylt and Alcyna."

"That's all you need to know at the moment." Asulet turned. "If you would come this way?"

Dainyl followed the elder alector through several narrow redstone-walled corridors and through two more concealed stone doorways until they stood in another open space, this one also with niches in the walls.

Asulet gestured to the blue-tinted niche. "Observe."

Dainyl stepped forward and studied the creature frozen in life and time. For just an instant, he thought it might be a huge black-coated shaggy dog, with a body three yards in length. But the creature's entire posture screamed that it was a hunter. The smaller teeth in the large jaw were razor-sharp, and the long crystal fangs exuded menace. So did the greenish yellow eyes. The long legs and large paws suggested a creature at home in winter chill.

"That's your predator."

"You captured this one?"

Asulet shook his head. "Majer Hersiod had a carcass sent to us as soon as they felled one. It arrived in rather poor condition, but the identification was easy enough to make. It's an ice-wolf. This one has been here since . . . for a very long time."

"Then they're native? From the time of the ancients?"

"No. Not exactly. Several of them appeared in the early years, but they died off from starvation. None has been seen in more than a thousand years."

"Maybe there were just too few to be noticed," suggested Dainyl.

"They're not normal predators. They prey on lifeforce."

"You're suggesting that the ancients created or bred them?"

"Or preserved them until they could survive," added Asulet.

"We're seeing more ancients. We've lost pteridons for the first time, and now these . . . creatures." Dainyl didn't like the implications, not at all. "What can we do, besides kill them?"

"For the moment, that seems the best course. But I thought you—and Shastylt and Zelyert—should know. Especially Zelyert."

"Do Brekylt and Alcyna know?"

"They will. There's really no way to keep it quiet for long. Sooner or later one of the creatures will be observed in the colder and higher reaches of the east."

"You think it came from the Aerlal Plateau?"

"Where else is high and cold near Iron Stem?"

"Why now?"

"I do not know. I could speculate, but speculating where the ancients are concerned has always been fraught with danger and inaccuracy. So I will not."

"Is there anything else you would suggest?"

"Don't get close to one."

"Are they as dangerous as an ancient?"

"Oh, no. They can be killed by standard weapons. They're a far greater danger to livestock and herders . . . or landers or indigens traveling isolated areas alone."

Dainyl almost repeated a variation of his question about why the creatures had reappeared after such a long absence, but another look at Asulet convinced him that the elder alector would only say what he had said, and would not take well to repeated questioning, especially from someone junior to him.

"Is there any other information I should know . . . or that you would care to pass on, sir?" Dainyl finally asked.

"Not at the moment, Submarshal. I will escort you back to the Table." Asulet smiled. "It will save both of us time."

"I'm sure it will." Dainyl offered a sheepish grin. "But I wasn't about to trust Choranyt."

"A wise decision."

Dainyl lost track of the passages and concealed doors that Asulet took before they reached the main corridor outside the Table chamber.

There, the elder alector opened the door, releasing the Talent-locks, and led Dainyl inside. Dainyl strengthened his shield.

"Excellent," murmured Asulet.

Choranyt looked at the two. His face paled.

"Have a good trip, Submarshal." Asulet's tone was formal.

Dainyl stepped onto the Table, focusing on the darkness beneath.

He dropped swiftly into the chill blackness, immediately seeking the brilliant white locator that was Elcien, and extending a Talent-probe.

No purple arms appeared, but for a moment, somewhere "behind" him, he sensed a momentary black and purple flash.

Then he was sliding though the silvered white barrier at Elcien.

He stood alone in the Table chamber, and only the briefest hint of frost-fog lifted off his flying jacket. As he stepped off the Table, his Talent indicated that no one else was around.

Still he made his way to the private study of the High Alector immediately, recalling Asulet's slight emphasis on the High Alector's name, but the study was empty. When he turned to leave, one of the younger assistants stood in the anteroom doorway.

"I was looking for the Highest."

"He left earlier, Submarshal. He will be in Soupat until early this afternoon."

"Soupat?"

"Yes, sir. He didn't say why."

"Thank you."

With that, Dainyl left the Hall of Justice and finally managed to hail a hacker to take him to Myrmidon headquarters.

He had barely turned down the corridor to his own study when Undercaptain Yuasylt—the duty officer—called to him.

"Submarshal, sir. The marshal was looking for you."

"Thank you." Dainyl walked past his own study to the marshal's. "I just got back."

Shastylt nodded, saying nothing. He did not rise.

Dainyl walked into the study and closed the door. He remained standing.

"Well . . . did he have anything useful to tell us?"

"The predator is one that dates back to the time of the ancients. It feeds on lifeforce . . ." Dainyl summarized the rest of what Asulet had told him, not that it took long, since Asulet had been brief to the point of being cryptic.

Shastylt frowned. Then he pulled at his chin. "Asulet was telling the truth?"

"Yes, sir. He was worried, and he didn't want the word

spread. He said Brekylt and Alcyna would find out, sooner or later."

"Did he tell you why this was happening now? Does he have any ideas?"

"He might have ideas, but he declined to share them. Politely, but firmly."

"The ancients are behind this. Do you think that Brekylt has worked out some sort of alliance with them?"

Dainyl didn't know what to say. The idea was preposterous, given his experiences with them. But he certainly couldn't share that knowledge with the marshal. After a moment, he replied. "Brekylt would seek an alliance with anyone or anything that furthered his ambitions. From the reports I've studied, and what little I've seen, and from what Asulet has told me, the ancients see us all as enemies. Besides, how would they even communicate?" Dainyl felt much safer phrasing the last concept as a question, rather than stating it as a fact.

"There is that . . . but those two are inventive."

"I would agree with that, but Alcyna directed her Myrmidons to attack them, and the rankers were telling the truth about the attacks. I can't see the ancients allowing that."

Shastylt pursed his narrow lips before replying. "No. They would not." After a time, he focused his eyes directly on Dainyl. "What do you think about it?"

"I think the ancients are planning something. We have not seen them in hundreds of years, not really, and now, within two seasons, they've destroyed six pteridons, and now there's a lifeforce predator that no one's seen in a thousand years. That's not coincidence. It also suggests that they know the time for the transfer of the Master Scepter is near, or at least that more alectors will be coming to Acorus."

"More alectors have already been translating here. They could have noticed that," mused the marshal. "I want you to watch for any other signs . . . anywhere. Don't report them. Just tell me."

"Yes, sir."

Dainyl returned to his own study, closing the door. He needed time to think. First, somehow he needed to get word about the giant ice-wolf predator to Zelyert in a way that wasn't obvious to Shastylt, and before long. He also wanted to think about what the ancients had said about him not changing enough. Had he changed at all? How? Was that good?

He couldn't help but recall the near-casual way that the small soaring creature had used her power to hurl him back into the translation tube. Yet, if they had the kind of power that he had seen and experienced, why hadn't they just attacked? Or was it because there still were so few of them? He wished he knew more—or how to find out more without putting himself at the mercy of creatures who had shown themselves to be powerful and dangerous.

His eyes drifted to the window and the clear silver green sky beyond. Not even a sign of a storm, but he knew that the times and the weather could change quickly.

32

The hired carriage drove through the open gates of one of the villas in the center of Southgate, carrying Mykel, Overcaptain Sturyk, and the overcaptain's wife, a brunette a good fifteen years younger than Sturyk, Mykel judged.

Mykel wore his better uniform, clean and with everything polished, but without his sabre. He had been persuaded to accompany the couple in a rented carriage, because Sturyk had insisted, telling Mykel, "Arriving on horseback is just not acceptable, sir."

Mykel hadn't felt like arguing about that. If his taking a carriage made Sturyk more comfortable and resulted in better relations between the Cadmians and the factors

and high landers of Southgate, then that was a small price
to pay.

"This is Seltyr Elbaryk's place," offered the overcaptain. "Every year the ball is in a different villa. If I'm
commander long enough, Sheranyne and I might get to
see them all."

"Are all those who own the villas seltyrs? I thought
some were factors."

"Oh . . . that's the rank title. Some are factors. Some
own lands. Several have ships, and some of those probably smuggle goods."

"The same title is used in Dramur, but all of the seltyrs
there are large landholders," offered Mykel.

"Most of the seltyrs here have family or trade ties to
Dramur. They're a close-knit bunch."

The carriage came to a halt under a covered, but open
portico.

Mykel stepped out of the carriage, onto the mounting
block. He would have held the door for Sheranyne—the
overcaptain's wife—except that a footman in spotless light
gray already had opened the carriage door and held it.

"Welcome to Villa Elbaryk."

"Thank you." Mykel nodded and glanced westward,
where the sky still held a faint shade of silver from the
earlier sunset. Only Asterta was visible in the early-evening sky, a small green disc high in the eastern sky.

"The ballroom is straight ahead through the main entry
and then up the grand staircase to the left."

The three walked abreast, Mykel to the left of Sheranyne, Sturyk to the right. Mounted on every white granite pillar was a brass lamp polished to a fine luster, with
light radiating through glass panels showing neither
smudges nor soot. The walkway was covered with a thick
black-carpeted runner, fringed with white and gold. The
spring evening was warm, with a hint of flowers, but also
with a touch of dustiness in the air.

The main entry was a vaulted stone enclosure, windowless, that soared a good three stories, lit by an enor-

mous crystal chandelier. Mykel wondered if the oil for
each miniature lamp was fed down through a tube in the
heavy links of the twined brass chains supporting the
chandelier, or if each lamp had its own reservoir to be
filled.

"Impressive, is it not?" asked Sturyk.

"Rather," murmured Mykel. The villa was more like a
palace, like something he would have imagined for one of
the Duarches.

Two couples walked up the staircase ahead of them.
The staircase circled up and around the side of the entry,
its carpeted steps each a good five yards wide. One of the
women half-turned to say something to the younger
woman behind her. While her gown was cut low enough
to reveal that she was shapely and extremely well en-
dowed, it covered her shoulders and upper arms. The
younger woman's gown left her arms and shoulders bare,
although she wore a filmy silver shawl over them.

Mykel suspected that either woman's gown cost more
than several years of his pay as a majer, and he didn't
want to speculate about the worth of the jeweled choker
worn by the older woman. "The couple ahead . . . a seltyr
and his wife?"

"Oh, no. That's Orefyt. He's a cloth factor, one of the
larger ones, but certainly not so wealthy as a seltyr.
Everyone does wear their best to the ball."

"If they are not seltyrs," added Sheranyne, "their very
best."

At the top of the grand staircase was another foyer,
only larger than any officer's mess Mykel had ever seen,
and on the far side was an archway hung in deep green
velvet, trimmed with silver. At one side stood a tall man
in a formal gray shimmersilk tunic who announced, "Ser
Orefyt, Madame Orefyt, his daughter and son."

Did formality in Southgate require everything be
linked to the man?

Mykel tried not to be obvious as he squared his shoulders, but he felt as though he headed into a skirmish—

without weapons. As the three of them stepped through the archway, the functionary in gray shimmersilk tunic bowed, then declaimed, his deep bass audible above the strings of the quintet playing on a dais in the left-hand corner of the chamber, "Majer Mykel, Overcaptain Sturyk, Madame Sturyk."

Mykel could sense the eyes upon him, even though he did not see anyone looking directly at them, and the mass of so many auras and their lifeforce pressed at him.

The ballroom was a good thirty-five yards across, with a domed ceiling that rose some ten yards above the center of the chamber. The archways to the adjoining anterooms were set off by double columns. The walls and the inside of the dome were silver-white, the effect dimmed by the low light from the brass lamps set in wall sconces and by the heavy dark green velvet hangings trimmed in silver. The floor was comprised of alternating green and silver tiles in the shape of diamonds. About fifty couples were dancing, each pair careful to remain clear of others, moving not quite sedately to the music.

Mykel let himself be guided by Sturyk toward a short line of four people. Both men wore tunics and trousers of brilliant white shimmersilk, with white boots polished to a reflective shine, unlike the others in the ballroom, who seemed to be wearing all variety of color. The wives of the two men wore shimmersilk gowns of deep green, and stood a half pace back, partly behind their husbands' shoulders.

Sturyk halted before the first man. "Seltyr Benjyr, my wife Sheranyne." Then he half-turned. "My superior, Majer Mykel, commander of the Third Battalion."

Mykel bowed slightly. "I am honored." Before he finished his words, he noted that Sturyk and his wife had nodded to the second couple and passed on, leaving him alone with the four in the receiving line.

"No, Majer," replied the seltyr, a black-haired and almond-skinned man almost as tall as Mykel, "I am the one honored. We seldom see high-ranking Cadmians here in Southgate, and it has been years since one has been able to attend our ball." With a nod slightly more than polite, he nodded to the next man. "Seltyr Elbaryk, this is the distinguished, and, I might add, deadly, Majer Mykel."

"We have heard much of you, Majer. It is indeed a pleasure to see you in the flesh. May you enjoy the ball and the hospitality of my home."

"I am certain I will, and I thank you."

As Mykel stepped away, he could not help but hear the words between the two.

"He is young for a dagger . . ."

"But far sharper . . . best to let him go his way, for that will serve us best."

Mykel was more than certain he had been meant to hear the last words.

Sturyk and Sheranyne stood, slightly apart from the others, their attire far less ostentatious than that of those around them.

"I take it that Seltyr Benjyr is the first among equals?" asked Mykel.

"They don't even pretend they're equal," replied Sturyk. "He is the Seltyr of Seltyrs. No one questions him. You should be complimented. He spent more time with you than many of the wealthier factors."

"I hope that's favorable notice." Mykel laughed. He wasn't about to explain why he'd received the attention.

"Better that than being ignored. Now all you have to do is enjoy yourself. The younger women with the bare shoulders and shawls are the ones who are not married."

"They'd be very flattered if you asked them to dance," suggested Sheranyne. "But ask their parent or escort, not them."

Mykel thought he understood why. "I'm not good at dancing."

"It doesn't matter," replied Sheranyne with a gentle laugh. "Some will like you for yourself, and the others will use you to make their suitors jealous. The parents of every eligible girl you ask to dance will be grateful as well."

"Because it grants them attention and because they can't possibly marry a Cadmian officer?"

"It's unlikely," replied Sheranyne, with a mischievous smile, "but it has happened."

Mykel felt like swallowing both boots. He bowed. "I beg your pardon, Madame."

She laughed, good-naturedly, half-turning to Sturyk. "You see, dearest. He understood with only a smile."

Sturyk laughed as well.

To cover his embarrassment, Mykel gazed across the ballroom for a moment. He tried to shut out the welter of personal auras, the feel of so many people, and just look at the dancers and those standing around the edge of the ballroom.

"There are refreshments in the adjoining salons," said Sturyk, "but it's considered poor manners to retreat there immediately upon arriving, and particularly without having danced at least for a time. I can see several of those I know observing us."

Mykel permitted himself a wry smile as he looked back at the overcaptain. As soon as Sturyk had mentioned refreshments, Mykel had thought about slipping away.

"If you will excuse us." Sturyk and his wife eased out among the dancers.

Mykel envied the grace with which they moved. He scanned the dancers, and those standing at the edge of the dance floor. After a time, he found his gaze being drawn to the far side of the ballroom, to a black-haired woman in a plain, but flattering, pale green shimmersilk gown. She wore a shawl. He realized that she was the only young woman he had seen without a male escort or a parent beside her. There was something . . .

Mykel stiffened, standing stock-still. The woman was Rachyla. He would have known her anywhere. What was she doing in Southgate? How could she have gotten to Southgate so quickly? He feared he already knew why.

Finally, he walked toward her, stepping around the edge of the dance floor, avoiding the couples moving to the music in a step he did not know or even recall seeing.

She watched him, neither overtly encouraging nor discouraging him. As he drew nearer, he could sense her aura—almost totally black, shot through with faint traces of green, unlike any other he had seen. Was that because she was a seltyr's daughter? No . . . none of seltyrs had felt that way.

"Lady Rachyla." He bowed slightly as he stopped a yard short of her. "I cannot say how surprised I am to see you here."

"Then, I suggest you do not try." She laughed, in the ironic and musical way that Mykel could only recall for the instant afterward. "I see you are a majer now. I had not expected to see you, either, but then I heard that you would be here, and I found that I was not surprised."

"Unlike me."

"It is good to see you surprised, Majer. I saw that so seldom."

"How did you come to Southgate?"

"By ship, of course. Is there any other way from Dramur?" Her deep green eyes fixed on him.

"I meant . . ."

"I know what you meant, Majer. Have you come to ask me to dance? To make the obligatory appearance and flatter your ego that you may choose any of the women, and none will refuse you?"

"I know little of dancing, and I can see that you have changed little."

"I have changed more than you know, Majer, and so have you. You were not afraid to take a dagger of danger . . . yet you fear to dance with a woman who has nothing?"

Mykel smiled. "I did not say I feared to dance. I said I did not know much about it, and your feet may suffer."

Rachyla shook her head, then held out a hand. "Let us dance."

Mykel stepped forward and took her hand. He held her lightly, if firmly, trying to follow the steps of the others and to keep his boots away from her slippered feet, as the small orchestra played an unfamiliar air. He couldn't help wondering how he had ended up dancing with the daughter of a seltyr of Dramur in Southgate.

"For a man with two right feet, you do not dance badly."

"I just follow your lead."

"Would that more had."

"You have relatives here?" Mykel finally offered, barely avoiding stumbling—and another couple.

"You did not know? Elbaryk is a cousin. His mother and mine were sisters. He must bear a certain . . . responsibility."

"So . . . your maternal cousin must assist you, while your paternal cousin takes everything your father left?"

"Few would state it so directly."

"Including finding a husband?"

"Majer . . . who would wish a wife with no property? Of those who would, who would I, or my cousin, find acceptable?"

"I would not close off that possibility. I recall your telling me something like that once."

She laughed, once. "You would use my own words."

"Better than mine," he returned.

After a silence, she spoke again, her voice low. "You would not have killed my father that day."

"No. I would have had him imprisoned."

"You are too honorable to be a Cadmian, Majer. It will destroy you—or you will destroy all that you now support."

Mykel didn't have an answer to her comment.

"It is said you are going to Hyalt."

"Yes."

"And you will kill more who rebel against the evil ones?"

"Only if they shoot at us."

"How can they not when you are the tool of the Duarches? Can you not see that?"

"I can be honorable and see what can be done."

Rachyla laughed, yet it was not a mocking expression, but one more of ironic sadness.

The music stopped with a flourish.

Mykel inclined his head to Rachyla. "Thank you, Lady Rachyla. Might I have—"

"If you have the slightest regard for me, Majer, do not ask me to dance again," she murmured.

Mykel concealed a wince.

"Not until you have danced for at least several glasses with others. And do not call me 'Lady,'" she added in an even lower voice. She inclined her head to him. "Thank you, Majer." Her thank-you was louder and clear to those nearby.

Mykel bowed again. "My thanks and gratitude to you. Might I escort you . . ."

"My cousin's wife is there by the double column."

Mykel offered his arm. Rachyla took it, but with the tips of her gloved fingers barely resting on the forearm of his uniform tunic. They walked to the edge of the dance floor

Madame Elbaryk smiled politely as Mykel bowed once more, both to her and to Rachyla. Then he stepped back and turned.

"Mykel?"

He looked to his left and saw the overcaptain and his wife at the edge of the dance floor, less than three yards away. He joined them, not looking back, much as he would have liked to.

"That didn't take you long," observed Sturyk. "Is she some relative of Elbaryk's?"

"His cousin," Mykel replied.

"She dances well," added Sheranyne.

"She had to. I don't dance well at all." Mykel managed a smile.

The orchestra began to play again.

"I suppose I should find another young woman," Mykel said.

"They'll love you for it."

"Sturyk!"

"We should dance, dear."

Mykel turned and surveyed those standing beyond the dancers, but his thoughts kept going back to Rachyla. Without looking in her direction, he tried to see if he could sense the darkness of her aura, but there were so many auras that his head began to ache. He had to close his eyes for a moment.

When he opened them, he resigned himself to following Sturyk's—and Rachyla's—suggestions. After several moments, he picked out a thin-faced and brown-haired young woman who stood disconsolately, almost alone, clearly accompanied by a younger brother or cousin. She was neither beautiful nor unattractive.

He eased up to the pair, then smiled, looking to the youth. "Might I have a dance with the young woman?"

She smiled, but her eyes warned her escort against declining.

"You might, Captain," replied the youth, not quite sneering.

"Majer," corrected Mykel. "Thank you." He turned to the young woman. "You will excuse me if I am not an accomplished dancer."

"I can manage that, Majer. I'm Quesalya."

They stepped out onto the dance floor.

"Where are you from?" she asked after several moments.

"I was raised in Faitel, but I'm currently stationed in Elcien, permanently, that is. Is your escort your brother?"

"Yes. Carlosyn wishes he didn't have to be here."

"He seemed less than pleased," suggested Mykel. "Do you live in Southgate itself?"

"We live to the northwest. Father's warehouses are in Southgate. Have you been a Cadmian for a long time?"

"Close to eleven years, all told."

"That's a long time . . ."

Quesalya was not quite the dancer that Rachyla was, but she was skilled enough that Mykel could read her movements and keep from stepping on her toes or careering into other dancers. When he escorted her back to her brother, she gave him a wide smile. "Thank you, Majer."

"It was my pleasure." He bowed. As he slipped away, Mykel felt that he had made someone happy, or less unhappy.

After that, he asked close to a score of young women to dance, choosing those who seemed to have been forgotten or who looked neglected. All the time, he felt as though he were being watched, and by more than a few people. He kept his eyes open for Rachyla, but without letting his gaze linger on her. He never saw her on the dance floor.

After a time, he slipped away, sampled the refreshments, but contented himself with a glass of a pale white wine before returning to the ballroom, where he danced with several more unmarried women.

He could see that people were beginning to slip away, decided to approach Rachyla once more. She stood well away from Madame Elbaryk.

"A last dance?" He bowed.

"If you insist, Majer."

Was there the faintest hint of a smile in her eyes? Mykel wasn't sure, but he found that, as on Dramur, he wasn't that certain about anything concerning Rachyla.

Neither said anything for several moments.

"I watched you," Rachyla said.

"A few people did," he replied dryly.

"People will say that you chose your partners to make yourself and the Cadmians look good."

"I imagine they will."

"You did not dance with them for those reasons, I think."

"What do you think?"

"You ask a mere woman?"

"I asked you." Mykel put only the slightest emphasis on the "you."

"You are a dagger of the ancients. You are honest. You would be kind. Your blade has three sharp edges, and you will cut yourself more deeply than anyone else. Yet they will die, and you will suffer every death."

"That doesn't sound very promising." He offered a low chuckle, one he didn't feel.

"You were the one who asked."

"I did. That's true. Did Madame Elbaryk say anything about my asking you to dance?"

"She said you were handsome and dangerous."

Mykel decided to gamble. "And she also said that you were like your mother, too?"

Rachyla stiffened, almost stumbling. "How did . . . you were never . . ." Then she smiled and shook her head. "You are truly the dagger . . ."

"Was I right?"

"You know you were."

Mykel had the feeling that, while he might not have liked Rachyla's mother, he would have respected her, and that was very unlike the feelings he had for the male seltyrs of either Dramur or Southgate.

"You do not care much for my cousin."

"How can you say that? Before tonight, I never met him, and we exchanged only a few words." Mykel was all too conscious of how close she was . . . and still . . . as Dohark had once said, how dangerous.

"To me, it is as obvious as the uniform you wear, Majer."

"How about to your cousin?"

"Were you not a dagger of the ancients, you would be beneath notice."

"That's good to know. I suppose that means that I should not come calling upon you."

"That would not be wise. It also would not be possible."

"Oh?"

Rachyla did not reply. Several long moments passed before she said, "Sometimes, late on Novdi afternoons, just before sunset, I'm allowed to walk in the memorial park to meditate."

"I've been studying the stelae there. If we happened to meet, would that be taken amiss?"

"Not if it did not happen often." Her eyes did not meet his.

Yet, Mykel could sense she was neither lying nor leading him on.

"Then, it will not happen often."

"That would be for the best."

Shortly, the music died away, and once more Mykel had to escort Rachyla back to Madame Elbaryk. This time, the seltyr's wife's smile was less than perfunctory.

Mykel made a point of dancing with several more young women, including a second dance with three others, including Quesalya.

It was late when he rejoined the overcaptain and his wife and they made their way out of the ballroom and down to the portico—and the waiting hired carriage, far plainer than those others lined up outside.

Mykel glanced heavenward. Asterta was now in the western sky. Selena, a mere crescent, hung just above the eastern horizon. He'd danced with Rachyla under the warrior moon goddess, but did that mean anything? He doubted it.

Neither Sturyk nor Sheranyne said much until the carriage was well away from the villa of Seltyr Elbaryk and headed around the inner ring road to the northeast.

"I thought you said that you couldn't dance, Majer?" Sheranyne's words were a mischievous accusation.

"I can't. I just followed what everyone seemed to be doing, and tried not to step on anyone's toes."

"That's dancing," said Sturyk.

"You made several of those girls very happy."

"I did?"

"At least one will receive an offer of marriage because you asked her to dance."

That did surprise Mykel.

"You are a handsome man," she went on, "and there are worse fates than to be married to a Cadmian. Far worse. Some of the reluctant suitors know that as well." She grinned. "Of course, it didn't hurt to mention that you are unmarried."

Mykel laughed. "She must have been a friend of yours."

"She is, but we won't tell."

Mykel was certain he didn't want to know.

He also knew that, on the next Novdi, he would be at the memorial park.

33

On Quinti, Dainyl was in the Hall of Justice immediately after morning muster. When he had left Myrmidon headquarters, Shastylt had been closeted in his study, preparing for a meeting with the High Alector of Justice later in the day. Even after three seasons as acting submarshal and submarshal, Dainyl found that the marshal seldom if ever revealed the subject of the meetings, and never the substance.

None of Zelyert's assistants more than nodded, after ascertaining his identity, and Dainyl stepped onto the Table, shields in place, with some trepidation. He concentrated, then dropped . . .

. . . *into the chill darkness, although it did not seem as dark as it once had.*

He immediately concentrated on finding the purple-rimmed black locator that was Blackstear. It was more difficult to discern, but Dainyl still took what seemed but a moment to fix upon it.

Even as he Talent-linked to the locator, he was searching for signs of the purple arms and traces of the golden green translation tubes—if they were indeed such.

Blackstear flashed toward him.

For a moment he sensed several instances of the golden greenness, but they seemed more like indistinct globes set in an amorphous black mist. Was there some of that mist surrounding the purple chill of the translation tube?

He was still trying to determine that when he burst though the silvered-black barrier.

He'd been so intent on what he'd tried to sense in translation that he had to take two quick steps to catch his balance and re-form his shields. Only a hint of fog and mist rose from his uniform and flying jacket, but part of that had to be because the Table chamber was far cooler than most, close to uncomfortably chill.

A tall and angular woman in the green usually worn by the recorders stood beside a black wooden chest, shoulder-high. She smiled, an expression of amusement and warmth. "Greetings, Submarshal. I wondered how long it would be before I saw you."

Dainyl stepped off the Table, keeping his shields in place, although he doubted the recorder had any unfriendly intent. "You're Delari?"

"The very same. You're Dainyl. By the way, give my best to Lystrana. I haven't seen her in years. That's not surprising. There's little of interest to her Highest here. In fact, there's little of interest to anyone here."

"Yet there's a Table here." He paused, recalling some of what he had gathered from Asulet and others. "Only because it must be for grid stability?"

"That's the sole reason." Delari motioned toward the hidden doorway that opened with her gesture. "Would you care to join me for some cider or ale? The cider's hot."

"I wouldn't want to intrude . . ."

Delari laughed. "Submarshal . . . you can't be here for any other reason than to see me. There are no Myrmidons here, and the nearest Cadmians are more than two hundred vingts south. Sulerya said you'd be here sooner or later."

Dainyl shook his head. "What can I say?"

"How about that you'd be delighted to join me?"

"I would indeed." Dainyl found himself warming to her cheerful, but no-nonsense warmth, especially since his Talent-senses detected nothing but what she presented. In the cool chamber, the warm cider sounded like a good idea.

"That's better. After we talk, I'll show you what there is to see of Blackstear, mostly snow and evergreens."

Dainyl followed her back to a small chamber with a circular table and three chairs.

"Take any chair. They're all the same."

As he seated himself, she poured him a mug of steaming cider from a heavy covered pitcher. Then she sat down across the table from him. "How can I help you?"

"Unofficially, I'm trying to find out what you know about Brekylt and Alcyna, and to what degree some recorders are backing them . . . and why?"

"Sulerya told you all that."

"Has anything changed?"

"Not much." She gave a crooked smile. "Did you know that Choranyt suffered a Table mishap?"

Dainyl had to think for a moment. "Myenfel's assistant? What happened?"

"Myenfel doesn't think recorders should get involved with much besides the proper use of the Tables. He informed the other recorders that Choranyt was attempting to manipulate energies within the translation tubes, and that resulted in his unfortunate death."

"I see. How do you think the recorders in Norda and Alustre took that message?"

"Everyone said that they would instruct their assistants—once more—about the dangers."

Dainyl nodded. "The effect of the warning might last a few weeks."

"Unless you make more unannounced translations to the east. Otherwise, everything will remain quiet, except

for the increasing number of translations from Ifryn—
and the associated wild translations."

"Do the majority of them go to Lyterna?"

"No . . . I've noticed more headed to Dulka and Hyalt,
although they can show up at any Table, even here. Some
have enough skill to arrive at Ludar or Elcien."

"Is Blackstear's lack of . . . strategic value why you're
recorder?"

"You are direct."

"Sometimes I can't find the indirect way to ask the
question."

Delari sipped her cider before replying. "Lysia and
Blackstear form the most distant points on the grid, and
that's true in terms of geography and energy lines, which
are not always the same in terms of distance. Asulet felt
that we would provide more stability, especially in the
times approaching. There was little argument about my
becoming recorder in Blackstear. People would prefer
not to be here. I have but one assistant."

"Why do you think some of the recorders support
Brekylt?"

"Why does anyone do anything? Because they feel it
will benefit them."

"As a recorder, you must have some feel for the lifeforces of Acorus. How do you feel about the Master
Scepter being relocated here, rather than on Efra?"

Delari took a long, deep breath. "From anyone but you
or Asulet, I would not entertain that question."

The opening to her answer chilled Dainyl. He didn't
know why, but it did.

"I fear that Acorus cannot sustain the Master Scepter
long enough to rebuild what must be rebuilt. Yet . . . the
Archon must know this. Certainly, the lifeforce masters
on Ifryn should. I suspect that the professed indecision is
to encourage Ifrits there to choose to translate without
knowing the final decision. That would leave those who
merely wish to drink the pleasures of the Archon's court
waiting until it is too late for safe translations."

"Too late?"

"Oh, yes. There's a usage factor, and it's especially critical for the long translations between worlds. If there is too little use, the tubes cool and contract, and only the strongest can safely translate. If there is too much, then they expand and the walls become thinner, and wild translations are more likely. At the end of the translations from Inefra to Ifryn, when the Archon and scepter had left Inefra, and the Tables were open to any who would try, the tube actually spewed alectors into the darkness, into the deep of the voids between stars."

Dainyl nodded slowly. He had no doubts that the Archon would do what he thought necessary to reduce those who could contribute little to building Acorus or Efra.

"You aren't surprised. Did you know that?" asked Delari.

"No, I didn't, but it doesn't surprise me. From what I can tell, more lifeforce is required with each world."

"Not exactly. You were born here, weren't you?"

"Yes. So was Lystrana."

"Those of us born here draw less lifeforce. Those born on Ifryn draw more. Those born on Inefra, not that there will be that many, will draw four times what those born on Ifryn do, and those born on Ifryn will draw four times more than you or I or Lystrana will."

"You think that the Archon is trying to reduce the numbers translating here or to Efra?"

"I don't know. It would be wise, for the sake of the world, but how does one tell his supporters that there is no room for those who are not productive, not if we are to have a future as a people?"

How productive was he, mused Dainyl. Was keeping order all that productive? "Why are you telling me this?"

"You need to know, and you cannot afford to tell anyone besides Lystrana, and I trust her."

Dainyl finished the cider. "That was good. It is chill here."

"It is always chill here." Delari laughed briefly.

"What else should I know?"

She shrugged. "What do you want to know?"

"There is one other thing. . . . Have you seen any signs of activities by the ancients?"

"You think that . . ." Delari broke off her sentence.

"As more alectors are translating, we've had more sightings of ancients, and they've destroyed at least one pteridon." Dainyl felt safe saying that. Word was out in enough places that Delari could have heard about one lost pteridon from anyone. "Also some skylances are missing, taken in the night right before a pteridon."

Dainyl could feel her Talent reading him.

"You're not telling me everything."

"No, but what I've said is true, and you could have heard it anywhere."

"I don't know about that here in Blackstear."

Dainyl waited.

"I've sensed flashes of what seemed to be amber-green Talent, to the east, possibly in the heights of the Black Cliffs. There are reports that more livestock is missing, and some of the Reillies have said hunters have disappeared just west of the Ice Sands. Whether the disappearances are the weather . . . or murders . . . or the ancients . . . how could you tell?"

"Their Talent is amber-green."

"You really think something is about to happen?"

"Both the marshal and the Highest are worried. So are Brekylt and Alcyna. She even issued orders on how her Myrmidons should deal with any ancients they might encounter."

"That . . . that would not be good."

"Why not?"

"I can't say. I mean . . . I don't know, except that one of the first recorders in Dereka, before Jonyst, supposedly encountered an ancient, and all that was left of either was a crater in solid rock and a Talent-dead area around it."

"No one ever mentioned that."

"I'm not surprised."

When he thought about it, neither was Dainyl.

Delari stood. "Let's go up above. You at least need to take a quick look at Blackstear, such as it is." She pulled a heavy jacket off a wall peg, so bulky that it made Dainyl's flying jacket look thin.

Dainyl followed her up a long set of wide stone steps and then back along a stone-walled corridor. Light flooded in from high clerestory windows, but the air remained chill.

"Here's the north portico. You can get the best view from here." Delari opened the heavy oak door.

As soon as he stepped out onto the portico, despite the sunlight, Dainyl understood why Blackstear wasn't a popular destination. The Table building stood on a low hill, with the portico facing north. A narrow stone road wound down from the building toward the river to the northwest. Only two piers and a single warehouse stood in the small harbor where river and ocean met. Less than a score of dwellings and shops clustered behind the pier warehouse. To the east of the Table building a forest of evergreens stretched into the distance. The ground under the evergreens was covered with snow that looked to be waist-deep. Directly north of the portico stretched a vingt or so of open tundra, showing heaps of snow in places. Beyond that, Dainyl could see the iron gray waters of the ocean, and farther to the north, a line of white he supposed was ice. A bitter but light wind blew out of the northeast.

Despite the heavy flying jacket, he shivered. "How long have you been here?"

"Twenty years." She grinned. "I do use the Table a lot to visit Sulerya. The warmth in Lysia helps, and the translation tubes aren't any colder than Blackstear in the winter."

"There really isn't much here."

"There wouldn't be anything if the grid stability didn't require a Table here."

Dainyl could see that.

After a few moments more, he turned. "I've seen enough."

"You don't want to visit the harbor?"

He didn't miss the glint in her eyes. "No, thank you. Blackstear is worth a short visit, if only to remind one of how much we take for granted . . . but I don't need to see the harbor to gain that appreciation."

After Delari closed and sealed the door, Dainyl followed her back down to the Table chamber.

He was back in Myrmidon headquarters in Elcien by the first glass of the afternoon. Once more, he looked for Zelyert, but the High Alector of Justice was not in, and Dainyl hurried back to headquarters.

He had only just settled behind his desk and picked up the first of yet another stack of reports when the marshal stood in his doorway.

"Sir?"

"You were gone this morning." Shastylt glared.

"You were busy, sir. I took a quick trip to Blackstear."

"Why did you go to Blackstear? Just to see it?"

"I haven't been there. That's true, but I went to see if the recorder or her assistants had noted any actions by the ancients."

"In Blackstear?" Despite Shastylt's dubious tone, the marshal closed the study door.

"The ancients like cold areas—and high ones. The land is much higher leading up to the Black Cliffs. And it's cold. We can't check places like the Aerlal Plateau, but I thought it was worth a glass or two to talk to the recorder there."

"What did you discover?"

"There are people and livestock missing. Some of the Reillies are complaining. There's unexplained Talent use."

Shastylt frowned, then nodded. "It is a ley node, and high there."

Dainyl had no idea what he meant by a ley node and waited for his superior to continue.

Shastylt did not and looked at Dainyl.

"Do you still think they're concentrated somewhere on the Aerlal Plateau?" Dainyl finally asked.

"There, or high in the Spine of Corus."

"If they do have a redoubt or something up in the Aerlal Plateau," asked Dainyl, "how could we even bring an attack against them?"

"For the moment, we would have to wait, and attack when they enter our lands. As the lifemass on Acorus grows and the air warms, we can employ the road-building wagons and cut a highway from the south, from, say, Deforya, one by which we can send the Cadmians against them."

"I have my doubts that rifles would be effective." That was as much as Dainyl could say without revealing his own experiences.

"We would have to equip them with some variation of lightcutters, and the casualties would be high. More troubling is the strategy that it appears they are developing."

Dainyl had an idea, but decided against saying it outright. "Using attacks against Myrmidons and pteridons to require us to draw more on the lifewebs?"

"Exactly. If we are required to draw on the lifeweb for shields, that will reduce the lifeforce available before it can be built into a higher and self-sustaining capacity."

Left unsaid was the point that too little lifeforce would certainly mean that the Master Scepter would have to be transferred to Efra, rather than Acorus.

"Did you find out anything else?"

"No, sir." Dainyl smiled wryly. "Except how cold it is in Blackstear."

"Have we had any more reports from the Cadmians about Iron Stem or Hyalt?"

"One more predator in Iron Stem. It killed some herders, but the Cadmians took care of it. Third Battalion is still training the new troops in Southgate."

"If anything happens, let me know. I'm off to the Hall of Justice." Shastylt turned, opened the door, and departed leaving Dainyl to his reports—before he began reviewing Dhenyr's first attempt at a logistics projection for the coming seasons.

34

In the dimness of dawn, Mykel walked to the mirror in his quarters. He had not slept all that well, thinking as he had about Rachyla—and about what she had said. Had he changed that much in the season since he had last seen her? Had she? Or had his emerging ability to sense the auras of people merely revealed more of who and what she was?

He'd never heard of a "dagger of the ancients" before going to Dramur, much less encountered one of the ancient soarers. He'd never heard of anyone who had met one. He had a better idea what the soarer had meant by developing his talent, but no real guidance on how he should. The sole advice on that had come from Rachyla, who had told him that the alectors would destroy him if they ever discovered he was a dagger of the ancients. He'd half-dismissed that at first. Now, especially after traveling on the alectors' ship and sensing what lay within it, he had the definite feeling she'd been right, although he couldn't have explained why in any logical fashion.

He also could not help but wonder how a dagger of the ancients had found its way to Rachyla's grandsire. From what she had hinted, it had been his undoing in some fashion, and she felt the dagger would do the same to Mykel.

Standing in the cool morning air, he looked at himself—a taller-than-average lander, with a broad forehead under short and fine blond hair, light green eyes, moderately wide shoulders, and short-fingered hands with large palms. His chest still showed a pinkish scar where he'd been shot, a wound that should have been fatal, but had not been.

Did the mirror show or reflect auras?

He tried to sense what his own aura might be, but the mirror revealed nothing. The only impression he felt was one of darkness surrounding himself. Did he have an aura as black as Rachyla's? Or was he imagining things?

Finally, he shrugged. He certainly had no way to tell what his aura was like, not that was reliable, anyway.

He finished dressing, and stepped outside onto the balcony of the senior officers' quarters. There, for a quarter glass, he stood in the long shadows of sunrise, watching as rankers crossed the paved courtyard, trying to sense their auras. While he had noted auras in passing, he had not taken the time to just watch before. He had difficulty in discerning any aura at all if a ranker was much more than twenty yards away, although there were some few whose auras were clear from twice that distance. He had watched for only a short time before he realized that people with black auras had to be rare. He sensed not a single one anywhere close to as dark as Rachyla's, and only one ranker whose aura betrayed even a trace of black. None showed the flashes of green.

He also suspected that auras indicated something about the lands where people were born, because the majority of rankers from the Southgate Cadmians had auras centered in "color" around a tannish yellow, while the majority of those from Third Battalion bore shades of browns, ranging from reddish brown to golden brown. He still had not sensed any more of the pinkish purple shade shown by the navigator's mate—or by Hersiod. Could that coloration result from being close to the alectors? Certainly the mate was, but why would Hersiod show such coloration? Or could that have been a result from the time he and Colonel Herolt had been briefed by the Myrmidon officer? Yet the colonel hadn't carried the pinkish overshade.

Although he would have liked to confirm more of what he had observed, he needed to eat and prepare for the long day ahead. He walked down the narrow steps to the courtyard and hurried toward the officers' small mess.

Two local Cadmians stiffened as he approached.

"Carry on." Mykel smiled.

"Yes, sir."

Behind him, he caught a few words.

". . . Crelyot saw him on the range . . . never missed . . ."

". . . doesn't put up with sowshit . . ."

". . . Delast overheard . . . majer's lived through wounds'd kill an alector . . ."

How had that gotten around? Mykel had never said anything, but some of the rankers from Fifteenth Company might have. He frowned. Was his hearing better—or was he just more aware?

When Mykel entered the mess, Rhystan looked up from where he sat at one of the three tables. Loryalt, Dyarth, and Fabrytal were seated in the corner table. All three avoided looking at Mykel as he walked toward Rhystan.

"You mind if I join you?" Mykel knew Rhystan wouldn't and couldn't object, but he still felt he should ask.

"No, sir."

Mykel sat down on the other side of the small table. Within moments, the Cadmian orderly had set a platter and a mug before him. Mykel's eyes dropped to the platter—fried goat, some slices of a soft white cheese, slices of quince that had been preserved in something acidic, and overtoasted bread.

"It gets to you, doesn't it?"

Mykel laughed. "I manage not to think about it until I get here."

". . . don't know how he can . . ." The murmur was from Loryalt, but Mykel ignored it.

"How was that ball the other night?" asked Rhystan.

"I was as out of place as a Squawt at a Reillie wedding." Mykel took a swallow of the cider, except that it was cider cut with the same fruit juice he hadn't recognized from the first—and had decided not to ask about. Still, it was better than ale in the morning. "I think the least costly gown worn by any of the women would have taken more than a year's pay. Make that two years' pay. I had to dance with some of the unmarried women—that's what the custom is . . ."

"A great trial, I'm sure."

"Dancing wasn't, I'll admit. But you have to ask their parent or their escort. One little snot—he was the brother of the young woman—called me an undercaptain." Mykel had almost said "captain," but decided the exaggeration was more politic. "Another young woman said that one dance was enough."

Rhystan shook his head. "I was already getting the feeling that they don't like Cadmians."

"Oh . . . they like us well enough, just so long as we stay in our compounds and only appear when called. Like well-trained guards." Mykel took a bite of the goat. He still didn't like it, but that was what there was to eat.

"That's always the way it is. Worse here than Dramur, I think."

"Yes and no." Mykel paused. "In Dramur, no one wanted us around. I'm not so sure that they looked down on us so much. Here, we're welcome to spend blood and sweat to protect them, but not to get too close."

"It could be." Rhystan sounded doubtful.

Mykel looked to Loryalt. "How is Sacyrt fitting in with Seventeenth Company?"

"Sacyrt? Oh . . . the one from Second Battalion that you tranferred from Fourteenth Company. He's a cold one, but he's been keeping in line. Keeps to himself, Clastyn says."

"That's probably for the best." Mykel still worried about the ranker—his dark aura had held such reddish ugly streaks—but he couldn't do much except suggest that the undercaptain and his squad leaders keep an eye on the man.

Loryalt frowned, but didn't reply.

After a moment, Rhystan spoke. "It's too hot here. Be glad when we head out. Are you still looking at next Tridi?"

"If we don't get rain or worse."

"Rain? What's that?" Rhystan snorted.

"It's what falls from the clouds in the winter here. That's what they tell me." Mykel had to force himself to eat the soft and slimy cheese. "You're scheduled for drills against the First Hyalt this morning. Bhoral's worried that some of the troublemakers there are getting too high an opinion of themselves."

"They probably are. Their last drills were against Thirteenth Company. You want us to press them?"

Mykel nodded. "Fifteenth Company will do the same against Second Hyalt."

"I suppose tomorrow, we'll go against Thirteenth?" Rhystan raised his eyebrows.

"Seventeenth. Fifteenth will go against Thirteenth."

Mykel could sense the unease among the undercaptains, and that was good, because some of them had inflated ideas of how well their men were performing.

Rhystan, his back to the undercaptains, grinned at Mykel.

35

Just past midday on Novdi, less than a glass after he had returned from Myrmidon headquarters, Dainyl looked out the sunroom windows at the gray skies and drizzle. Novdi was usually only a half day of duty, and matters had been so quiet that he'd felt perfectly justified in leaving sharply at noon, especially since Lystrana had worked late the night before and dropped into bed exhausted—both from a last-moment review of shipbuilding accounts and from an overactive unborn daughter's antics of the night before. Since Shastylt had left headquarters by midmorning, there was no point in staying any longer than normal.

He turned as he sensed Lystrana's approach. "I'd hoped it would be warm and sunny."

"I know. So had I."

Dainyl glanced back at the clouds.

"Jeluyne's exhibition is this afternoon in the lower hall of the Duarch's Palace," Lystrana ventured. "It's the last day. The quartet will be playing, too. After that we could have something to eat at Eanthyro's. We could give the girls the rest of today off, and all of tomorrow."

"Are these her paintings of Elcien and Ludar?" asked Dainyl warily. Jeluyne was an older alectress who was a friend of his mother.

"They're supposedly quite good. Khelaryt has selected one for his permanent gallery."

"I'm sure that they're excellent. She's an outstanding artist."

"If we see your mother there, we won't have to call on her so soon."

Dainyl could sense the humor behind his wife's words. "We might as well. I haven't been to many of the recent social events, and it would be nice to eat out."

"I'll tell the girls, and I'll be ready in less than a quarter glass." Lystrana smiled and hurried off.

It was more like half a glass later, at a time when there was a lull in the rain, when Dainyl stepped outside and put up the banner indicating the desire for a carriage. Zistele and Sentya had already left, hurrying off to the eastern market square, the one favored by the younger landers and indigens. Dainyl and Lystrana stood in the foyer, the door ajar so that they could watch for a carriage.

Since they were going to the Duarch's Palace, if not for a formal event, Dainyl wore his blue and gray dress uniform. Lystrana wore gray shimmersilk trousers with a blue shirt and a dark gray vest, both slightly looser than

Dainyl knew she would have preferred, although her childbearing status was not yet that visible.

"It's too quiet," he mused.

"You've been saying that for days."

"I have, and I know that Brekylt hasn't stopped whatever he's plotting."

"Probably not." Lystrana paused. "Oh, I didn't have a chance to tell you last night. We got a dispatch yesterday that Rensyl suffered a fatal fall from a pteridon when he was being taken from Fordall to Alustre. His creative accounting is being remedied. One other engineer was involved. He was executed, and a team of experienced engineers have translated from Ifryn to replace and enhance the expertise of the engineering force in the east."

"Convenient." Dainyl paused. "Engineers from Ifryn, not from Ludar or Faitel?"

"I thought that was interesting."

"It suggests that Brekylt has the support of someone highly placed there."

"The Archon wouldn't go against the Duarches. I can't see that."

"But he might go around them," suggested Dainyl. "Or, if it's his idea, he could have told Samist. If not, who knows who it could be? What did your Highest say?"

"He didn't say anything, but he's worried. He went and saw Khelaryt, but he didn't look any happier when he returned. He did say that Zestafyn had already been sent to Ludar. I'd prepared some material about it, and I think he sent it with Zestafyn. That was one of the reasons I was late getting home."

"Khelaryt's worried, then."

"Concerned, anyway."

At that moment, a covered carriage pulled up outside. Dainyl hurried out through the drizzle that had resumed and held the carriage door for Lystrana. He looked up at the gray-haired hacker. "The Duarch's Palace. The north entrance."

"North entrance, yes, sir."

The hoofs of the carriage horse were louder in the rain, and neither Dainyl nor Lystrana said anything on the ride. When they stepped out of the carriage, they were the only ones entering the palace, but that might have just been chance. They made their way under the covered portico and through the lower archway, past the Duarch's guards, and into the lower great hall of the palace.

More than a score of alectors moved among the paintings, and Dainyl thought he saw his mother, but she disappeared behind a small group discussing one of the larger works.

The hall was floored with the traditional octagonal tiles of green marble, linked by smaller diamond tiles of gold marble, as were all of the large formal chambers. The hangings on the side walls, between the goldenstone columns, were of dark green velvet, trimmed in gold. Upon the small dais at the south end of the hall were seated four musicians, playing something Dainyl half-recognized and should have known. He frowned, trying to recall what it was.

"It's Ghestalyn's 'Translation Variations,' " murmured Lystrana.

"Thank you."

"We might as well start here," she suggested.

Each painting was set upon its own easel, and separated from the others by several yards. Dainyl paused before the first on the east side of the hall, a view of the Duarch's Palace from out in the bay, clearly just at sunset. The walls shimmered with an unworldly glow, and Jeluyne had caught that transitory orange twilight illumination that lasted but for moments, but promised a glorious future.

"Not bad," he murmured. He couldn't have even done a single brushstroke, but no alector would admit such in public.

"I like this one," said Lystrana from before the second easel.

Dainyl slipped beside her and murmured in her ear. "I like you better."

Lystrana flushed ever so slightly, then shook her head. "What do you think of the painting?"

Dainyl studied the image of an oceangoing vessel, spray flying from the bow, with rocky cliffs set behind the ship, probably Ludyn Point. "It's well done, but I think she does buildings better."

They moved on down the row of paintings.

"I haven't seen Kylana, and she's usually here every chance she gets," mused Lystrana. "She always wants to be seen."

"Preferably with those in power," murmured Dainyl. "Or those who can tell her the latest intrigues on Ifryn."

"Some information on that wouldn't hurt," Lystrana replied in an even lower voice.

"True."

Most of the images were ones recognizable to either Lystrana or Dainyl, if not both, until they reached the third painting in the second row. The painting showed a market square, filled with landers and indigens. Just to one side of the center was a lander patroller, wearing the double-scepter badge of the Duarchy, his finger pointing accusingly at a smashed squash or gourd on the stone sidewalk before the small produce stand. The seller was an indigen woman who was backed up against her small cart, listening. Behind them both, a sly-looking man was lifting the seller's coin box. None of the others in the square seemed to notice either the dispute between the patroller and the woman—or the ongoing theft.

"Clever," said Dainyl. "I suppose that must be the eastern market square."

"It could be any market square," replied his wife.

"Lystrana!" called a voice Dainyl recognized all too well. "And Dainyl."

The two turned to see Dainyl's mother moving toward them. Alyra wore the dark silver gray that she usually affected, with a shimmering silver vest.

"It's so good to see the two of you out." Alyra immediately faced Lystrana. "How are you feeling?"

"I'm fine. At times, Kytrana makes me uncomfortable, but I understand that's to be expected."

"Oh, it is. Dainyl left me uncomfortable more than sometimes." Alyra frowned, slightly. "I'm glad to hear that, but that wasn't exactly what I meant. Didn't you hear? Your colleague Zestafyn was attacked by a wild translation last night just as he was about to translate from Ludar back to Elcien."

Dainyl could sense Lystrana's shock, although his wife only nodded somberly as she asked, "Last night? Just last night? How is he?"

Alyra shook her head. "It was one of the dangerous ones. There was a Talent explosion."

"Oh . . . oh . . . I didn't know. Poor Kylana."

"Indeed . . . poor child. She was so distraught she must have found a lightcutter and turned it on herself. Such a terrible tragedy. So truly awful."

Dainyl swallowed silently. His mother scarcely knew Kylana and had cared less for her posturing. What Alyra was conveying was not sympathy or gossip, but a warning.

"She was so devoted to Zestafyn," Lystrana replied, "but I never would have expected anything like that."

"So unexpected. Such a tragedy. One moment, you're doing what you're supposed to be doing, carrying out your duties . . . and the next moment . . ." Alyra shook her head. "I suppose anything can happen anymore, even to the most faithful administrators and Myrmidons. But . . . we shouldn't dwell on what we can't change." She smiled brightly. "I'm so glad to see you here. How are you finding the exhibit? Isn't Jeluyne marvelous? I so admire her use of color and her choice of subjects."

"This one is certainly different," Dainyl said.

"One can't ignore the landers and indigens. They have their place. I do prefer the one of the Duarch's Palace, myself . . ."

Dainyl had never heard his mother prattle so. She was more than worried.

He definitely needed to get to see Zelyert, and not just

about the growing number of icewolves. The High Alector might well know that, but Dainyl doubted he knew about why Zestafyn had been killed. Equally important, Dainyl also needed to discover what Zelyert knew.

And . . . he and Lystrana needed to maintain their personal shields far more than they had.

36

Late in the afternoon on Novdi, Mykel rode at a measured pace southwest along the high road, heading back toward the center of Southgate. Despite his earlier worries, the training was going well, and he'd had no problem in letting the rankers and officers knock off two glasses earlier.

He yawned, then stretched in the saddle. He had to admit that he was tired. In addition to trying to keep track of each company's progress and needs, at night, he'd been studying maps and whatever he could find about the Hyalt area. He'd talked to those senior rankers and squad leaders—both in his battalion and among Sturyk's troops—who had any knowledge of the roads, the trade, or the area. He knew more than when he'd begun, but not much.

He'd also spent more time trying to get a handle on his talent, studying the auras of various Cadmians, seeing if the auras indicated how they might act or react, and their self-possession. He had some ideas, but how accurate they were he wouldn't know until Third Battalion saw action, and he was in no hurry for that to happen.

The road and the side streets were far busier on Novdi afternoon than they had been on the previous times he'd ridden out from the compound. Several times he had to rein up or slow down to avoid carts, wagons, or peddlers on foot. He tried to listen as he rode, and occasionally caught fragments of conversations, some with meaning and some baffling.

". . . no need fullering . . . sweat it up . . ."

". . . Merysa took in more coins after the ball . . . than all week . . . young swells can't barely touch women . . . fancy like that . . . looks that good herself . . . best one in the house . . ."

". . . might well as chisel cork . . ."

". . . fodder's up again . . . another copper a quint . . . suppose have to mix in fish meal . . ."

For all the traffic in the outer areas, the center of Southgate was as subdued and quiet as it had been the last Decdi he had been here. Mykel saw no one in the park, but he was earlier than an hour before sunset.

There were no hitching posts as such, but he did find a section of railing not far from the stele he judged to be closest to the villa of Seltyr Elbaryk. He tied his mount there and walked back to the stele. He *had* wanted to study the relief carvings.

For a moment, he just looked at the images in the stone. From their appearance, they had been done recently, but they felt old. Still, the stele didn't have the feel he had begun to notice with the eternal stone of the high roads. The other aspect of the stele was that there were absolutely no words inscribed in the stone beneath or above the relief.

Mykel glanced around, but saw no one in the nearer section of the memorial park. He slowly walked along the stone wall to the next stele. It was identical to the first. He continued to the third, and then the fourth. All were identical.

Having established that, Mykel looked more closely at the carving itself, trying to discern differences between the figures of the seltyrs.

Almost half a glass later, he sensed that someone was coming. He did not turn immediately, but it had to be Rachyla. Her aura was unmistakable. Someone was with her, and from what he could sense, it appeared to be a much older woman.

He continued to look at the stele, although he no longer studied it, but just waited, feeling as though he stood on the edge of a precipice.

"Majer?" Her voice bore a surprise Mykel knew she did not feel.

He turned. "Rachyla . . . what are you doing here?"

"What are *you* doing here?"

"Taking some time away from the compound. The park and the stelae had interested me, and I thought I'd look at them more closely. What about you?"

"I am taking a walk to where I can meditate." Rachyla turned to the graying woman. "This is my aunt Herisha. She is my mother's youngest sister."

Although Rachyla had not said, Mykel gathered the impression from Herisha's gray garments and withdrawn demeanor that she was not the aunt who was the mother of the current seltyr.

"And have you found anything startling in your perusal?" Her tone was not quite mocking.

"There's a certain oddness about the image. Some things are obvious, though. The number of seltyrs matches the number in Southgate, and the number of villas around the memorial park. That would stand to reason, but behind them is an alector, and that is a much larger figure. Yet there never has been an alector in Southgate. There is no regional administrator, and there are no Myrmidons."

"Perhaps the carving is a warning that, seen or not, there is an alector behind the seltyrs of Southgate."

"That is possible."

"Would you mind, niece, if I went over to the bench and rested?" asked Herisha.

"I should have suggested it," Rachyla said, "although I will not be long. The majer is most courteous . . . for a Cadmian officer."

Herisha nodded and turned, limping her way to a stone bench some twenty some yards away, close enough that the older woman could see everything, but hear little.

"It's hard for her to walk long distances," observed Mykel.

"She likes to leave the villa as much as I do, and I would not deprive her."

"You are both prisoners."

"I have been a prisoner before, Majer. Have you forgotten?"

"No. I never will."

"Neither will I." Surprisingly to Mykel, her tone was matter-of-fact, neither hard nor cutting.

"How did you come to be here?"

"My cousin Alarynt offered me the choice of dying in my bed or 'visiting' Elbaryk. I don't have to spell out my choice, do I?"

"He couldn't marry you off?"

"No. If I had sons to another seltyr, even to a junior son, they would have a claim on Stylan."

Mykel should have guessed that.

"Besides, Alarynt is small-minded and vicious in a devious fashion. By returning me to Elbaryk, he places a burden on him. If anything happens to me, Elbaryk will be accused of not honoring his own mother and the women under his care. Those things do matter to him, unlike Alarynt."

The more Mykel learned of the seltyrs, the less he cared for them and their customs, and, somehow, the more he cared for Rachyla.

"Do not pity me, Majer." Those words were cold.

"I have admired you. I admire you more, the more I learn."

"Such a desirable fate, to be admired by a Cadmian officer and a dagger of the ancients."

"And respected, unlike some others who claim they care."

Rachyla half-turned. "There are no images of the daggers of the ancients." She made it as a flat statement. "Not anywhere."

Mykel understood her change of subject, he feared. "Why might that be?"

"Memorials are for those who do great deeds. The few daggers who survived tried nothing of import, and those who attempted more were all discovered by the evil ones and killed."

"Your history is so cheerful," Mykel said dryly. "Do you know any that is more encouraging?"

"For a Cadmian and a dagger of the ancients? I think not."

"You have such promising futures for us both," he said gently.

"I cannot change what will be, Majer. You must understand that."

Mykel thought she had given the slightest emphasis to the word "I," but he was not certain.

Rachyla stepped back. "I must meditate. Herisha must be able to report that I did. Good afternoon, Majer."

"Good afternoon, Lady Rachyla."

"I am not a Lady of Dramur."

"You are, and you always will be." Mykel bowed ever so slightly. *To me, if to no one else.*

She turned and walked swiftly toward her chaperone, not ever looking back. Mykel watched her for a time, then finally walked back to where he had tied his mount. He had to believe that he would see her again, yet Third Battalion would be riding out well before the next Novdi.

He mounted slowly, looking toward the memorial park, but Rachyla was nowhere to be seen.

37

In the end, Dainyl just appeared at the Hall of Justice early on Londi, prepared to wait for Zelyert. He did not have to, because the High Alector of Justice was there and motioned him into his private study.

"And where are you headed today, Dainyl?"

"Just to see you, sir."

"Oh?"

"Some information has come to my attention. I never know what you may know, sir," Dainyl began, "but there are several matters which, by themselves, would seem insignificant—"

"Dainyl . . . things are bad enough without your sounding like Shastylt. Just tell me."

"The icewolves have reappeared in the Iron Stem area, and they're lifeforce predators. Asulet won't speculate, but I'm judging he believes the ancients are using them for some purpose to weaken us. Second, the Duarch's head of intelligence discovered that one of Brekylt's chief engineers was diverting significant resources to constructing some sort of equipment in Fordall. It might be military equipment, perhaps forbidden equipment. On his return from reporting to the High Alector of Engineering and possibly the Duarch of Ludar, he suffered a Table translation mishap in Ludar with enough power to create a Talent explosion. His wife immediately—apparently— killed herself with a lightcutter that was never issued to him or her. Third, even before Zestafyn was killed, the chief engineer who had been diverting resources died in a pteridon mishap while being transported to Alustre, and a number of experienced engineers were translated from Ifryn to Alustre to replace him and the others involved in the transgression."

Dainyl could sense that Zelyert was not all that surprised by the icewolves, or by Zestafyn's death. The other occurrences did create a reaction, almost hidden, but not quite.

"Does Shastylt know of these?"

"He knows about the ice-wolves. He was the one who dispatched me to Lyterna to talk to Asulet. They kill by taking lifeforce, but rifles are effective against them."

"And the other matters?" pressed Zelyert.

"They are not properly within Myrmidon jurisdiction, and I thought you should know."

The High Alector of Justice nodded slowly. "You do not trust your own marshal."

"He is very preoccupied these days, sir."

"You are standing over the translation tube to oblivion, figuratively, of course." Zelyert's deep voice was mild.

"Perhaps, sir, but I thought such a translation would be less likely once the information was in your possession, since—"

"Since someone wanted to keep it from me? Nonsense. Young Zestafyn doubtless wanted to strike some sort of bargain with those around Samist. He always has been playing both sides."

Those words rang untrue, both in sound and to Dainyl's Talent-senses, but he just nodded slowly.

"Even if he were not, that is the way in which it must be handled. Personal venality must be the cover for now."

Dainyl doubted that would convince many, but he wasn't about to argue.

"It won't convince those that know," Zelyert continued, "but what it will do is suggest that we are not strong enough to open the matter to the Duarches or the Archon." His eyes narrowed. "What else have you discovered?"

"That the ancients have increased activities in the north, not all that far from Blackstear."

"They would have to reappear now. Why do you think that is so?"

"I would judge that they can sense changes in lifeforce and Talent and the increased usage of the Tables for long translations."

Zelyert stood. "That will do for now. You can send me a dispatch on any future developments that affect the Myrmidons or Cadmians."

Dainyl rose as well. "Yes, sir."

Dainyl was fortunate to find a carriage outside the Hall of Justice and arrived at Myrmidon headquarters a quarter glass after morning muster, not that his presence was usually required, but he'd always felt that senior officers who worked shorter glasses undermined their own authority and credibility.

Unfortunately, the calm lasted only until midmorning, when the marshal summoned him, this time through the duty messenger.

"Why were you in the Hall of Justice?" asked Shastylt before Dainyl had even closed the door to the marshal's study. The senior alector's voice was silky.

"Because the Highest wanted to know about the icewolves and how they had affected the Cadmians. He also wanted to know if we had seen any more activity by the ancients."

"I suppose you had to tell him?"

"Could I have really said no to him?"

"At times, you would do better to avoid him . . . if you understand what I mean."

Dainyl did, unhappily. "I have spent little time in the hall now that my investigations of the east and Dereka have been completed."

"That's for the best." Shastylt paused. "Do we have any newer reports from either Southgate or Iron Stem?"

"We do, but nothing has changed. The Cadmians in Iron Stem report killing another of the icewolves, but matters with the iron works and mines are quiet. The Cadmians will be leaving Southgate on Tridi to ride to Hyalt with the new Hyalt companies. Third Battalion will be conducting more training en route. Also, from our Myrmidons, the recent reports show that we've lost no more pteridons or skylances."

"What is Alcyna planning?"

"She's only reporting that everything is normal— except that, even with the melting snow, Third Company has had no success in locating the missing Cadmian company."

"Will they find them, Submarshal?"

"I would doubt it, sir."

"So would I." Shastylt looked up. "That will be all."

"Yes, sir."

With each passing week, Dainyl liked less and less the balancing act he was attempting between Shastylt and Zelyert, especially since he trusted neither. Shastylt he trusted least, because he felt the marshal's ambition was far more personal, while whatever Zelyert was attempting had at least some rationale of a higher purpose.

But then, he reflected, either would remove him if it suited the purpose at hand, and Zelyert was more to be respected than Shastylt.

38

Mykel stood beside the roan in the stable, ensuring that the materials he would present to the Hyalt council were secure. There was a proclamation, a work authorization for the new compound, and a letter of credit with no specified limit, although Mykel had been informed that he had best have good reasons if he drew more than two hundred golds a month. There was also a set of plans, based on those of the compound at Southgate, if a smaller version. He fastened the saddlebag tight, and then checked the saddle girths before leading the gelding out of the stall.

After walking his mount out of the stable into the early-morning light and mounting, Mykel glanced around the compound. Third Battalion was forming up for the ride to Hyalt in good order, far more quickly than they had a month before, not that Mykel had emphasized the in-post formations nearly so much as weapons practice, combat tactics, and field maneuvers. But there was a definite carryover. The two Hyalt companies were slower, but better than he had expected, if not yet so sharp as he had hoped they would be.

He turned the roan, checking the compound, checking the various companies. Some of the local Cadmians were watching as well. The dirt and dust he had noted when he arrived had vanished, and the local Cadmians appeared sharper. He wasn't certain why, since he'd never said a word to Overcaptain Sturyk. Was it the power of example?

He almost snorted. More likely the power of fear.

Beyond the southwest corner of the compound lay Southgate, and in the center of the city were the villas of the seltyrs—and Rachyla. He kept thinking about her—and that was foolish. He certainly didn't understand her. She'd volunteered where and when he could find her, and then she'd made it very clear that her situation—and her inclination—precluded any future between them. Mykel wasn't interested in merely bedding her, and he couldn't marry her, because she wasn't about to marry a mere Cadmian. Nor would her cousin want her to marry anyone. In any case, a Cadmian officer had no business even thinking about marriage until he was senior enough and settled enough to be a compound or a regimental commander.

Mykel felt a crooked smile cross his lips. Telling himself that was all very good, but he wasn't doing very well at listening to himself.

Overcaptain Sturyk walked from the headquarters building toward Mykel, who waited for the older officer.

Sturyk stopped several yards from Mykel and looked up. "I see you're ready to move out."

"Less than a quarter glass, I'd say."

"I just wanted to wish you well, Majer."

"Thank you. You've provided solid support for Third Battalion, and I conveyed that to Colonel Herolt in my last dispatch report."

Sturyk smiled. "I appreciated the copy, sir."

"Sometimes a record helps, as I'm certain you've found."

"Yes, sir. Do you know when you'll be returning? Or how long you'll stay on the return?"

Mykel shook his head. "That all depends on our success in Hyalt and how long it takes. How we return to Elcien—

that's up to the colonel or the marshal. They may order us somewhere else, rather than back through Southgate."

"You're welcome here, anytime. The best of fortune, Majer."

"Thank you. And to you." Mykel could see that the battalion was formed up, and he rode the score of yards into position to receive the muster report from Bhoral.

"Third Battalion, all present and ready to ride, sir. First and Second Hyalt Companies, present and ready to ride."

"Thank you." He nodded to Bhoral. "Let's go."

"Battalion . . . forward, by companies . . ."

Mykel eased the roan forward. Thirteenth Company would lead for the first glass, and he'd ride with Undercaptain Dyarth.

The sound of hoofs on stone, the occasional squeaking of the supply wagons, and occasional commands were the loudest sounds that marked Third Battalion's departure from the compound. Mykel did not actually join up with Thirteenth Company until just outside the gates.

"Good morning, Dyarth." Mykel moved his mount in on the left of the junior officer.

"Good morning, sir. Looks like it's going to be a hot ride."

"It probably will be until we get past Zalt. After that the land is higher, and we might get rains in the Coast Range. That'll be a while, though." Even on the high roads, and carrying their own rations, it would take at least five days to reach the way station at Zalt. A full week beyond Zalt lay Tempre, and then another five days to Hyalt. All that assumed good weather and no troubles with brigands or the supply wagons.

Mykel doubted that everything would be trouble-free, although he'd had the wagons inspected and had insisted on spare draft horses

Neither officer spoke, except for orders to the company and battalion, until they were on the high road. The sun was still low in the eastern sky, and Mykel was glad that they were headed northeast, rather than due east and directly into the sun.

"Sir?" ventured Dyarth. "Southgate . . . the people there . . . they were pleasant enough, but not like in Arwyn or Harmony or even up in Klamat."

"Are you suggesting that they were more interested in our rankers' coin than in their person?" Mykel asked.

"It did seem that way. Was Dramur like that?"

"Worse, I'd say. People shot at us there."

"More than the Reillies or Squawts?"

"Yes. Majer Vacyln lost two entire companies to those kinds of attacks." Mykel wasn't about to take responsibility for those casualties, not when the late majer had ignored his advice.

"What do you think about Hyalt?"

"I don't know. I've tried to get more information, but no one seems to have much." That bothered Mykel as much as anything.

Less than a glass to the northeast of the last dwellings that could be properly said to be part of Southgate itself, rather than cots or huts—or estate villas overlooking the grasslands—the road began to slope downward on a gentle but definite grade into a wide and shallow valley. The grass that grew, while showing spring green, was definitely sparse. There were no cots or huts in the valley, and Mykel did not see any goats or sheep—or cattle.

"Poor land," observed Dyarth. "Leastwise, they're not overgrazing it."

"I imagine the alectors would have something to say if they did."

"That's true."

Half a glass later, Mykel looked back. From where he rode, it appeared as if the higher ground on which Southgate had been built might once have been an island or a peninsula, but he hadn't looked at the area around the harbor that closely. Certainly, the lower terrain through which Third Battalion rode was less fertile than the higher ground, and the opposite was usually the case. He could recall his cousins talking about how bottomland was so much richer—and how often the alectors restricted what they could do with it.

He glanced at the high road ahead, stretching endlessly ahead, straight as a rifle barrel.

39

Mykel blotted away the dampness from his forehead, then shifted his weight in the saddle as the roan carried him southward on the high road. Beside him rode Rhystan, since Sixteenth Company was riding van for the rest of the morning. According to the last vingt-post, Hyalt was another five vingts ahead. Mykel's eyes took in the terrain on both sides of the road, land covered with grass, thick and with the teal shade of new growth. To his left, grasslands stretched to the eastern horizon. To his right, the grasslands rose slowly to a hillcrest less than half a vingt away, then dropped, only to rise into a slightly higher rolling hill farther west. Perhaps three vingts west of the road, the grasslands ended, replaced with wooded hills that, in turn, were replaced by the low mountains that formed the eastern edge of the Coast Range. From what Mykel could see, the trees were low evergreens, mixed pines and junipers.

In the few road cuts, Mykel had noted that the soil was thin with reddish sand beneath. That explained why he and Third Battalion had seen only scattered flocks of cattle on the grasslands. Farming or heavier grazing would have ruined the grassy plains.

He turned and looked back over his shoulder at the riders—and the supply wagons that followed the column. Over the three weeks it had taken to ride from Southgate—with rest stops for men and mounts—Mykel had worked in as much training as possible. The two new companies now looked like Cadmians when they rode.

At the sound of fast-moving hoofs on the road, Mykel turned. He kept riding, waiting as one of the scouts rode swiftly toward the battalion.

"Sir? Wagons ahead! Carrying something pretty heavy."

Ahead in the distance, Mykel saw three heavy wagons, each drawn by six dray horses, and all were heading northward. He could insist that the wagons give way, but heavy as they were, and with the sandy soil beyond the shoulders of the road, there was a good chance that they might get mired or break a wheel. He also didn't like riding past them in single file or narrow formation.

Mykel turned in the saddle, looking at Toralt, the duty messenger. "Pass the word. At my command, we'll ride, fast trot, to the hillock on the right up ahead. Form up in battle formation facing the road. Same company order as now."

"Ride to the hillock, fast trot, form up in battle formation, same company order. Yes, sir." Toralt turned his mount out of formation and headed toward the rear.

"More practice, sir?" asked Rhystan.

"Mostly. I doubt that irregulars would use wagons—or even know we were on the way—but you never know when you're first arriving somewhere."

Less than a tenth of a glass later, Toralt rode back and reported. "Sir! All the officers stand ready."

"Battalion! Forward!"

"Sixteenth Company . . . forward!"

"Thirteenth Company . . ."

Before long, the entire force was formed into a line of battle on the hillock on the west side of the high road.

"Rifles ready!"

The command echoed across the battalion.

The wagons were close enough that Mykel knew they posed no threat, but he wanted the younger Cadmians in particular to get the feel of waiting . . . and waiting . . .

with rifles ready. He'd seen too many inexperienced
troopers fire too soon because they were impatient.

Slowly, the wagons crept northward on the high road,
nearing the battalion. Each wagon carried a driver and a
guard with a rifle up front, with four mounted guards in
front and two riding behind. While the wagons didn't
creak or sag, the measured pace of the team and the faint
crunching of sandy soil that had drifted across the enternastone in places and was being flattened by the heavy
iron tires of the wagons were more than enough to tell
Mykel that they carried ingots of some sort. The sign on
the black-painted side of each wagon was simple: MINZT
AND SONS, TEAMSTERS.

Mykel could sense the unease on the part of the teamsters and even the armed guards, who kept looking back
at the Cadmians long after the wagons had passed the formation on the rise overlooking the high road.

Once Third Battalion was back on the road, Rhystan
looked at Mykel. "They didn't do badly."

"No. We'll see how they do against irregulars—if there
are any."

The captain gestured out at the grasslands to the east.
"Doesn't look like there's much here. How do they live?"

"There's some dryland nut trees to the south, and
there's a tin mine to the southwest, and a copper mine to
the west. They've got cattle here as well. Some of them
are sent north and butchered in Tempre or shipped down-
river to Faitel and Elcien." He grinned. "That's what the
books and everyone I talked to told me, anyway. They've
got some clay too, and there's a china works. Hyalt's
smaller than Dramuria, they say."

"Why would they have irregulars out here, then?"

"There's always someone who's not happy with the
way things are. Hyalt's far enough away from places that
people think matter that no one pays much attention. If
someone starts yelling about the Duarches or the Cadmians in Faitcl, how long is it before they get carted away?"

"A glass, if they're lucky," replied Rhystan.

"No one paid any attention here, not until it was too late."

"You think that's the whole story?"

Mykel laughed. "It never is. We found that out in Dramur. I just hope what we don't know isn't as bad as it was there."

"That makes two of us, Majer."

For all his explanations to Rhystan, and even with his concerns, Mykel still felt uneasy.

40

Dainyl stood at the window of his study, looking out into the early afternoon. The sun poured down from a cloudless silver-green sky, and the faintest breeze of early summer wafted through the partly open window. For the last month, nothing untoward had occurred. No pteridons or skylances were missing. No Myrmidon casualties or accidents. No wild Talents had been reported. Iron Stem remained calm, and the Fourth Cadmian Battalion had managed to contain the handful of icewolves that had appeared, although local Iron Valley herders had complained about a handful of dead sheep and cattle. The Third Cadmian Battalion was close to arriving in Hyalt. Neither Shastylt nor Zelyert had tasked him with any new or thankless tasks. Matters were calm. As Submarshal of Myrmidons, Dainyl should have been pleased.

He was not.

There were far too many aspects of events that hinted at troubles to come, yet about which Dainyl could do nothing—not without incurring the wrath and displeasure of the marshal, the High Alector of Justice, and the

Duarch of Elcien—because there was almost nothing in the way of hard proof about any of his suspicions. The hints were there.

Some were in the small stack of reports on the corner of his desk. There was the report that Seventh Myrmidon Company had moved to its new compound in Dulka, and another from Seventh Company reporting that Undercaptain Sledaryk had been transferred to Lysia when Undercaptain Hasya had requested a stipend after fifty years of service. Alcyna had promoted Undercaptain Veluara to captain and transferred her to take command of Seventh Company, rather than promoting Undercaptain Klynd to replace the late Majer Faerylt.

Others were scattered bits of information, like Majer Noryan's past, the "replaced" report about the pteridons lost to the ancients, the resource diversions by the eastern engineers, and the mysterious deaths associated with its discovery.

The shadow of a pteridon crossed the outer courtyard—an incoming dispatch flight, not that there would be anything but routine messages, if recent dispatches were any indication.

Dainyl was surprised, less than a quarter of a glass later, when the duty messenger rapped on his study door. "A dispatch for you, Submarshal."

"Thank you." Dainyl stood and took the envelope.

After the messenger departed, he checked it. The Talent-seal was unbroken, and when he opened the envelope, he found that the message inside was brief.

Submarshal Dainyl—
At your convenience, since you were deputed to handle the matter, I would like to request your presence in Lyterna to discuss additional developments regarding the ice-wolves and similar predators. These may have a significant impact on Cadmian and Myrmidon operations.

The signature was that of Asulet, underneath the title of Alector of Lifeforce.

Dainyl made his way to Shastylt's study, since the marshal was in, and his presence was never something Dainyl could count upon.

The marshal did not rise from behind his desk. "You have that worried look, Dainyl. I should say that you look more worried than usual, since you never look unworried anymore."

"Isn't that my task, sir, to worry about the routine matters so that you can concentrate upon the others?" Dainyl extended the envelope. "This just arrived with the dispatches."

Shastylt took it, read it quickly, and handed it back. "Is there anything happening now that Dhenyr can't handle?"

"No, sir. Everything else is quiet. For now."

"You worry too much, Dainyl." Shastylt chuckled. "Wait to worry until we actually have problems we can address. Just take the duty coach and use the Table this afternoon. Asulet will be there. He never goes anywhere."

Behind the marshal's banter, deep behind, Dainyl could sense more than a little worry. "Does he ever leave Lyterna?"

"He hasn't in years, or if he has, no one knows about it. There are sections of Lyterna that no one knows about but him." There was a brief pause. "Find out what he has to say and then let me know. If I'm not here when you get back, I'll be here in the morning."

"Yes, sir." Dainyl nodded and departed.

Less than half a glass later, he walked down the subterranean corridor beneath the Hall of Justice toward the Table chamber. Outside of a single assistant, he saw no one in the hidden warrens. Nor did he sense anyone else.

The Table chamber was also empty, and he stepped up onto the Table, his shields ready for anything—he hoped—as he concentrated and dropped through the Table and . . .

. . . into the chill purple darkness. He immediately concentrated on finding the pink locator wedge that was Lyterna and Talent-linking to it. As he felt the distant Table moving toward him, he continued to be alert for any signs of trouble—and for amber-green flashes in the deeper blackness beyond the translation tube.

He thought he sensed one such flash before the silvered-pink barrier at Lyterna shattered into its insubstantial and vanishing Talent-shards.

Standing on the dark Table, he strengthened his shields. He had not worn his flying jacket, not with the warmth of the day in Elcien, and the frost boiled off the shimmersilk of his uniform tunic as he stepped off the Table in Elcien,

Myenfel was the one who waited for Dainyl. "I trust you had no difficulties, Submarshal."

"None at all, thank you. I appreciate your concern."

Myenfel only nodded in response, then gestured. A gray-haired and frail-looking alector appeared. "Eshart will take you to Asulet. It's likely to be quicker that way."

"Thank you."

Myenfel offered a brief smile, then nodded to the gray-haired alector.

Eshart said not a word, but immediately headed out of the Table chamber and down the long light-torch-lit corridor, then up a narrow staircase, and along the main gallery east of the so-called Council Hall, and past the grand pteridon mural of a scene that never was. It was a scene Dainyl also hoped he never would see—and hadn't thought at all possible until the events of the past season.

Another series of twists and turns and a narrow hallway—almost a tunnel—brought Dainyl out in a wider corridor he recognized, since, to his left, he could see the niches that held the ancient examples of Acorus—and the sparc pteridons—preserved in time against a future need. Eshart turned right and then stopped at the first door—open.

"Come in, Dainyl." Asulet's voice issued from within the chamber. "Please close the door."

Dainyl stepped into the room, closing the door, and found himself in a study paneled in wood of a deep golden shade—or was it oak that had aged centuries? He took a moment to survey the chamber, since he'd never been in Asulet's study before. Bookshelves comprised one entire wall, and every space was full. A line of wooden cases was stacked against the back wall, under a painting of Dereka—or a Dereka that was meant to have been, because the image held twin green towers. The wide table desk was also of ancient oak, as were the two wooden armchairs before it, and the upholstered chair behind it. As with all chambers within the underground structure, there were the light-torches, the air ducts and returns—and no windows.

Asulet stood at the corner of the desk. "Are you finished cataloguing all that I have here, Dainyl?"

"I doubt that I ever could, sir. Even if I could, I wouldn't understand a fraction of it."

"At least you know that. Sit down."

Dainyl waited until Asulet eased his gaunt frame into the chair behind the desk before taking a seat.

"You arrived quickly, as usual."

"Matters are quiet. I doubt that they will remain so, but Shastylt says that I worry too much."

"As if he does not." Asulet leaned forward. "There are two matters I would like to discuss with you, Dainyl. The first one deals with the predators. The icewolves feed on lifeforce, as you know. What you may not know is that there was another lifeforce predator, far more deadly, that also feeds on lifeforce. Its rough form is that of an indigen. Although it appears slightly smaller, it is quite strong, and its skin is rock-hard and tannish. It may sparkle in the light at times—"

"Do you have one preserved here?"

"No. They are more intelligent, and very rare. We were

never able to capture one. One fieldmaster insisted that he saw one sink into the ground instantly, but no one else saw that happen, and there are no other records that support the claim. There are enough records and other evidence to support the existence of this predator. Like us, when they die, nothing long remains, but even without lifeforce-treated shimmersilk, their skin is almost impervious."

"You think they may be reappearing also?"

"I think a few have always been around, but with the reappearance of the icewolves, there may be more of them."

"Why would they be more of a problem than the ice-wolves? Or can't they be killed with standard weapons?"

"It's difficult to stop them with a standard Cadmian rifle. A skylance or a lightcutter will suffice—if one gets a direct blast. I'd suggested rifles of larger caliber in the beginning, but the engineers insisted that was unnecessary. The Duarches also didn't want rifles with excessive power in widespread usage, and they didn't want to create the idea that weapons used by indigens could come with larger barrels and cartridges. They felt a single rifle model would discourage firearms . . . invention."

And cannon, Dainyl thought. "So the Cadmians should be warned and told that only concentrated fire is effective?"

"I would suggest waiting until there are reports of such creatures—if there are. They may not reappear. I thought you and the marshal should know about the possibility."

"Thank you. If they should reappear, we'll have some idea of how to respond."

"I would hope so. The second matter is a report from Sulerya. The number of translations—and wild translations—has increased to a level that we would not expect for several years, yet there are no reports of these translations. My own measurements show a greater life-force drain."

"The wild translations . . . isn't there quite a range? I heard about one—after it was killed, it didn't disintegrate. The body just remained there like a lander's. How could something like that happen?"

Asulet fingered his chin. "That has happened once or twice. My best judgment is that the alector panicked and tried to become part of Acorus while still in translation."

"Is that possible? Becoming part of Acorus?"

"Oh, yes. Even you or I could do it, if we didn't try it in a translation tube, but it wouldn't be a very good idea. It takes an enormous amount of Talent, and, in the end, we'd be more like Talented landers—smaller, weaker, and possibly even less intelligent."

"You speak with authority. I assume someone tried it, then?"

"Poor Turbryt did. So long ago that you don't want to know. He couldn't figure a way to change back, and he was desperate enough to try the long translation." Asulet shook his head. "He ended up as a wild translation on Ifryn, and . . ."

Dainyl winced. After a moment of silence, he spoke quickly. "All the successful translations from Ifryn are going to Alustre or other Tables in the east? Besides Lysia?"

"That appears to be the case, but not entirely. There are also more going to Hyalt."

"They're not being reported to the Duarches?"

"I could not say, but it appears unlikely that Khelaryt knows about them. Zelyert would not, and I would not be amiss to his knowing, but do not seek him out. He likes to feel that he is the one discovering and controlling."

That made sense and fit with what Dainyl had observed.

"Oh, Dainyl . . . I might add that you've become more Talented. It won't be long before Zelyert notices, if he hasn't already. Shastylt probably won't notice, because he tends to shut out things that don't accord with his views, and he doesn't think people ever change."

"What do you suggest I do?"

"Whatever you can—like all of us. That's all I had." Asulet's smile was both warm and wintry. "I assume you can find your way back to the Table."

Dainyl smiled. "I think so. Give my best to Sulerya, if you see her."

"That I will, and my best wishes to Lystrana."

Dainyl rose, bowed slightly, and departed. It seemed strange that he had traveled halfway across Corus for such a short conversation—except that what Asulet had said was not something that either he or Dainyl would have wanted in writing.

As he walked back, he saw only two older menial alectors in the corridors, and the Table chamber was empty.

Once in the chamber, without hesitation, he stepped onto the Table and concentrated.

In the darkness of the translation tube, he could sense a web of purple "ahead" . . . somehow linked to Elcien or the tube pathway between the two. It felt as though it were looking for him, or that whatever lay behind it was doing so.

Could he translate somewhere else—Blackstear—and then make a second translation? What if he did? Would that stop the webmaker? Or would he find yet another web "before" him?

He certainly didn't want to try what he had done the last time. Getting involved with the ancients was dangerous and likely to get more so. Yet he had to do something. The chill was seeping into him.

He extended a line of Talent.

The weblike barrier strained toward him, colder even than the chill darkness around him, drawing him toward it. He could sense that it was designed to suck out his very lifeforce.

Another one appeared "behind" him.

The ancients had said that he could change. He didn't want to change, especially after what Asulet had just told him, but the ancient's words implied he might be able to do some things as they did. What if he changed just his Talent-force?

Trying to focus his thoughts and Talent in the enervating chill, he concentrated on replicating the sense of

*greenish Talent he'd seen from the ancients. A line of
yellow appeared.*

*Dainyl needed more green, and he concentrated on
amber and green. What resulted was something amber-
greenish lying over purple pink. He could barely think—
but he thrust it forward, trying to create a link to the
blackness and green outside the purple darkness of the
translation tube.*

*Brilliant purple-pinkness coruscated all around him,
and, if he could have, he would have closed his eyes, but
the brilliance seared through him, blinding even his
Talent-senses.*

*His teeth wanted to chatter, and his body to spasm with
the frigidity around him, but when he could again sense
what lay around him, the webs had vanished.*

*A series of green points flashed around him, and then
vanished.*

*His Talent-link with Elcien was shaky, but he firmed it
up and then flashed through the white-silver barrier.*

His legs shook, and he half-staggered off the Table,
then leaned against it, gasping and shuddering.

The entire Table chamber darkened, as if the light-
torches had dimmed. Dainyl glanced at them, but the
darkness hadn't come from them. Another wave of darkness dimmed the chamber, lasting longer than the first.

Sulerya had said that using Talent energies in the tubes
between Tables was dangerous. Had his defenses caused
what was happening?

A third and briefer wave of darkness emanated from
the Table. Dainyl waited a time, but there was no more
darkness. Finally, he straightened and made his way from
the chamber through the outer foyer and into the outer
corridor. He replaced the outer Talent-lock and turned,
more than ready to head back to headquarters, although
he felt more like going home and sleeping.

"Traveling again, Submarshal? Where?" Zelyert stood
several yards down the corridor, smiling, although there
was little warmth in the expression.

"Lyterna. Asulet had some information—"

"He's always interesting. You can spare a moment, can't you?" Zelyert motioned for Dainyl to follow him.

Since the Highest's question was a command, Dainyl entered the small private study, careful to close the door behind him. Since Zelyert remained standing, so did Dainyl. Tired as he was, he was careful to maintain full shields.

"What did he officially tell you?" asked the High Alector of Justice.

"He fears that there is another of the lifeforce predators loose. It's likely to become more of a problem."

"Oh . . . the sander things. I've read the reports on them. They could be a problem for the Cadmians. Their rifles don't have enough impact power to break their outer skin. Does he really think they'll reappear?"

"He thinks that the icewolves are the first step."

Zelyert nodded. "He's usually right about those things."

"You've had more experience with him, sir, but it seems that way to me."

"Why did he really want you there?"

Dainyl didn't even debate denying that Asulet had another reason. "He's worried. He's gotten information that large numbers of wild translations are taking place. Based on that, he thinks that other successful translations from Ifryn are taking place. The alectors who are making the translations aren't arriving in the places where he or you could track them, though."

"I thought it might be something like that. Did he tell you not to tell me?"

"No, sir."

"He's learned something, at least. What do you intend to do about it?"

"I don't know that it's something that is my task, sir, but I haven't had time to consider it. I don't think translating to Alustre would tell me anything."

"It wouldn't, and it would be futile, and dangerous, not to mention that it doesn't have anything to do with your duties. For the time being, Dainyl, I suggest you deal with Myrmidon and Cadmian matters."

"I have been, sir."

"I know, and I suggest it remain that way, and that it be clear to everyone that you are doing so."

"Yes, sir."

"And Dainyl?"

"Yes, sir?"

"You're very wise not to try to deceive me."

"I wouldn't even think it, sir."

"That's the mark of a good marshal . . . or submarshal." Zelyert smiled. "That's all I wanted to know."

Dainyl made his way out and up through the concealed stairs and though the Hall of Justice. He still had to report on the sander creatures to Shastylt, and he wasn't at all happy with Zelyert's parting words.

41

"**Not exactly the best spot** for a compound," observed Culeyt.

Mykel and the captain had reined up on the low rise overlooking a rubble-strewn set of buildings and a wall roughly fifty yards square. Rather, the outside dimensions were fifty yards. One section of buildings had collapsed. The remainder had clearly been pillaged, with no windows, no glass, no doors. Over the too-low wall, Mykel could see dirt-covered paving stones in the center of the small garrison. Less than fifty yards separated the ruined garrison from the two-yard-high weathered brick walls of the loading yard of an abandoned factor's warehouse. What remained of the warehouse was little enough—

stone cornerposts, a few charred timbers, and shattered roof tiles. By comparison, the compound buildings had fared relatively better.

"No. You could heap up earthworks here or even timber barricades and fire down. They didn't expect anyone to attack them. Not when they built it, anyway. It's more like an overgrown town patroller station."

"Looks like someone looted it," added Bhoral, from where he had reined up behind the two officers.

"I'm certain they did. We'll camp here until we get things squared away, but this is no place for a real compound." Mykel turned his mount. "Captain, Fourteenth Company will accompany me. Bhoral, pass the word that the others are to do what they can here for temporary quarters. Sixteenth Company will stand by, ready to ride, until I get back. I'll tell Captain Rhystan myself."

Mykel rode farther up the hillside to the low crest. From there he could survey Hyalt and some of the surrounding area. The town lay east of the rise on which the garrison had been built, with the high road dividing it so that a third lay west of the road, and two-thirds to the east. The larger dwellings in the town were situated on a raised flat stretch of land slightly to the northeast of the town square. At the south end of the town, the road turned eastward, just north of the narrow creek that wound to the southeast. From the maps, he knew that that stretch of road connected Hyalt and Syan, some two hundred and fifty vingts east.

He turned in the saddle, looking out over the hills to the west, covered with a mixture of grass and junipers, with occasional low pines. He frowned as he noted, farther to the west, a redstone structure apparently carved into the side of a bluff. A single freestanding redstone building was situated out from the bluff, and a low stone wall set off both structures from the surrounding rolling grasslands. A stone road ran from there toward Hyalt.

After a moment, he nodded. That had to be where the

regional alector was located, but he wondered why the compound was set so far from the town itself. Then he shrugged. That was probably for the best. He wasn't certain he wanted to be close to any alectors.

At that thought, his fingers brushed his belt, and he could sense the faint green force emanating from the concealed dagger of the ancients.

He rode down the slope toward Sixteenth Company and Rhystan.

"You find it, sir?" asked Rhystan.

"Find what?" Mykel grinned.

"Whatever it was." Rhystan grinned back.

"The alectors' local headquarters are out to the west. Part of it's tunneled into a cliff. Seems odd. Everywhere else, they're close to the center of things."

"Everything about this place seems strange."

"I'm taking Fourteenth Company with me to pay a visit to the council head. You're in charge. Sixteenth Company is on standby, in case someone's unfriendly. The others are to do what they can to make the garrison temporarily usable. We'll need to find a better site for a permanent compound."

"Much better." Rhystan shook his head. "There's no good way to defend this with just a company. It's better than being in the open, but not much."

"That's why we need to get working on building a new compound first—and why I need you to be on guard."

"We'll be here." Rhystan nodded.

As Mykel rode back toward Culeyt, he heard Rhystan's voice.

"Sixteenth Company! Listen up! . . ."

Mykel glanced once more at the shell of what had been a garrison. He hadn't ever been certain he'd use what his father had taught him about building, but it looked like he was going to wish he'd learned more.

"Fourteenth Company, ready to ride, sir," announced Culeyt before Mykel had even finished reining up.

"Let's go."

Fortunately, the street into the main section of Hyalt was wide enough to ride two abreast, and still leave room for the scattered pedestrians and infrequent carts and wagons. Three lanes farther along, Mykel and the company turned south on the high road, which also served as the main boulevard of the town.

A half vingt south, they came to the town square.

"Company, halt!"

"Sir?"

"That looks like the council building over there." Mykel pointed to a one-story redstone building set between a chandlery and a building without any identifying markings. "If you'd send a scout to inquire . . . we're looking for the head of the town council."

"Yes, sir." Culeyt turned. "Coroden . . ."

While the scout rode toward the building facing onto the square, Mykel studied the area. The square itself was a good hundred yards on a side, centered on a golden marble platform, with a statue of the Duarches set on a pedestal in the middle. Several yards back from the pedestal was a low redstone wall. As in most towns and cities in Corus, the roofs were tiled. The walls of the houses and other buildings were a mixture of stone and masonry, the older structures being of stone, the newer ones of a sandy red brick. The doors and trim were either oiled or painted a dull reddish brown.

He could sense the eyes of several people on the side porch of the inn looking in the direction of the company. A woman with laundry in a basket on her head hurried across the edge of the square, turning away from the riders. Mykel couldn't blame her.

"Sir!" called Coroden. "This is the goldsmith's. The council chamber is off the square that way."

"You head there, and we'll follow," replied Mykel.

The council chamber was only a block away, a redstone building larger than the goldsmith's, with a roof composed of grayish red tiles, and high windows with open shutters rather than glassed panes.

Mykel, Culeyt, and Fourteenth Company waited while Coroden entered the council chamber. He was out of sight only a few moments before returning.

"The clerk says that the head of the council's not here, sir," reported Coroden.

"I imagine that he's not. Find out where he is and how we get there. And his name."

"Yes, sir." Coroden went back into the building, emerging shortly. "The council head is Troral, and he's a wool factor. His place is down two lanes and over a half block, just off the high road." The scout remounted.

That made sense to Mykel. A factor wanted to be close to either a river or a high road.

As the company rode back toward the inn and past the square, heading southward, most of those on the side porch of the inn slipped out of sight. Only a bent old woman carrying a bucket remained. She stared at Mykel.

He met her gaze evenly, and after a moment, she looked away.

Troral's factorage was a modest structure, no more than fifteen yards across the front, and less than that in depth, although Mykel could see a stable down the side lane past a battered loading dock. The factor—a narrow-faced and balding man whose remaining hair was gray and wispy—appeared in the front doorway before Mykel could dispatch Coroden. He wore a wide canvas apron and said nothing.

"You're Troral?"

"Yes." The balding factor's answer was wary.

"I'm Majer Mykel, commanding officer of the Third Battalion. We're here to rebuild the garrison and reestablish Cadmian companies here."

The stocky factor looked up at Mykel, then at the company that filled the side street. "You've got a lot of troopers here, Majer. Hyalt doesn't need that much protection."

"The garrison that was here obviously wasn't enough," Mykel pointed out. "What can you tell me about what happened?"

"There's not much to say, Majer. I'm sure you've been told. One night there was shooting, and the next morning, they were all dead. There were bodies all over. We sent word to the regional alector, and there were Myrmidons here in a few days."

"No one was shooting at anyone else?" Mykel had trouble believing Troral's story. Why would they need Cadmians? Or was it another case where someone was afraid of what *might* happen?

"There hasn't been a shot fired here since then."

What bothered Mykel even more was the feeling he got that Troral was telling the truth, at least as he saw it.

"That's why I wouldn't think you'd need so many troopers. Hyalt's not that well off, but it's peaceable."

"I'm sure it is." Mykel smiled politely. "This is just one company. Third Battalion has five, and there are two Hyalt companies that will remain once we've made sure that none of the irregulars or brigands are left and once the new compound is completed."

"I see. Regional alector sent a message saying someone would be coming to rebuild things. We didn't expect so many troopers. Bad enough that the alector's been buying more provisions in the last season. Drives up prices, and that's hard on folks. What would you be wanting of me?"

"I wanted to let you know why we're here." Mykel paused. "I'd also hope that I'd be seeing the heads of the guilds that handle building early tomorrow."

"I'm not a guildmaster—"

"I understand, but I'm certain you can get the message to them. We will be paying for the construction, once we select the right site."

"You're not rebuilding . . ."

"No. That garrison wasn't defensible, and it's too small. We'll find the site, and then the owner and the council will put in a reimbursement claim with the regional alector."

"They won't pay enough."

Mykel kept smiling. From what he'd seen, the alectors weren't spendthrifts, but they also didn't try to gouge out the last copper the way more than a few merchants and factors he'd seen did.

"I suppose you have to do what you must," grudged Troral. "We all do, and work for less coin than we'd like is better than none." A faint smile crossed his lips. "You might be wanting some blankets and other cloth."

"We might at that," Mykel replied. "Once we're getting close to having the new compound completed." He leaned forward and handed a copy of the proclamation and authorization to Troral. "That copy is for the council."

"It might be hard to build . . ."

"I'm certain we'll find a way, and that you'll be of great assistance." Mykel smiled. "I look forward to seeing the guildmasters. Early tomorrow."

Troral nodded in response. "We'll do what we can, Majer."

Mykel inclined his head, slightly. "A good day to you." He turned the roan back northward, letting Culeyt bring Fourteenth Company behind him. Which would be harder, tracking down insurgents that no one had seen— or would talk about—or building a new compound? He wasn't looking forward to either, and, in a way that he couldn't describe, he was more than a little concerned with the isolated and semifortified structures of the regional alector. With that location and Myrmidons, why had they even needed to call in Cadmians? Or were there more of the ancient soarers around and the Myrmidons didn't want to risk pteridons? Until Dramur, Mykel hadn't even realized that the creatures could be destroyed.

He wanted to brush his fingers across his belt, but he knew that the dagger of the ancients was still there. Was the indestructible dagger somehow a key to the powers that could destroy a Myrmidon or a pteridon—or just a symbol of that power?

Rachyla's warnings seemed far more ominous now that he was in Hyalt than they had in Dramur or even Southgate.

42

On Quattri morning, a good glass and a half before first light, Lystrana stood just inside the door, holding Dainyl tightly. "Be very careful."

"I will, but you're in as much danger as I am."

"Not so long as I'm in the Duarch's Palace." She kissed him on the cheek and stepped back.

Dainyl had his doubts about that, but there was little he could do, and Lystrana was as Talented as he was, if not more so, and certainly more experienced in intrigue. With a brief last smile, he stepped out into the darkness. In moments, he was walking briskly along the boulevard toward the Hall of Justice. The faintest hints of fog swirled off the bay and across the isle of Elcien, although they would vanish with the morning sun. Selena, showing but a crescent, was low in the darkness of the western sky, and while the green disc that was Asterta hung just high enough in the east to be visible over the roofs of Elcien.

Zelyert had effectively ordered Dainyl to confine himself to Myrmidon and Cadmian affairs, and Dainyl intended to do so. He just intended to handle some of those matters in Lysia.

As he had planned, there was only one assistant in the concealed lower chambers of the Hall of Justice, and the young alector nodded politely at the submarshal as Dainyl made his way to the Table chamber.

After carefully replacing the Talent-locks, he stepped onto the Table.

The darkness beneath seemed less black and overpowering, if as chill. Even as he linked to the orange and yellow locator that was Lysia, Dainyl kept his Talent-senses exploring the pure blackness beyond the distinct purpled confines of the translation tube.

The translation tube—or the space in which he traveled—seemed to curve, almost to buck, several times. That was something Dainyl hadn't experienced before, but he concentrated on the locator. Still, within his brief transit, he sensed a half score of the quick green flashes that signified ancients. Why so many?

Then the silvered orange and yellow parted away from him more like mist than shards.

He stood on the Table in Lysia.

As he stepped down, the hidden doorway parted, and Sulerya stepped out. She had deep circles under her bloodshot eyes, and her short black hair was dull and disarranged. "Submarshal . . . it felt like you. I wasn't certain. I'm glad you made it."

"Glad? What happened?" asked Dainyl. "You look exhausted."

"Idiots! Brekylt's recorders . . . I don't know what they did, but yesterday the entire grid nearly collapsed. The word is that Kasyst was killed in the backlash."

Kasyst? Why was the name familiar? Dainyl raised his eyebrows. "Kasyst?"

"The recorder at Norda."

"Oh . . . him."

"You know him?"

"His assistant tried to shoot me as a wild Talent. That was the explanation, anyway. I couldn't very well accuse him of lying." *Especially not then.*

"What exactly did you have to do with it, Submarshal? You're not exactly surprised."

Dainyl shrugged. "They tried to trap me between Tables again when I headed back to Elcien from Lyterna. My shields were adequate."

"Again? They're greater idiots than I thought possible.

They'd destroy—" She broke off her words. "Why are you such a danger to them?"

"I wish I knew. Others must know what I know. You certainly do. So does your father. Sevasya and Khelaryt have to know some of what I know and more besides. Shastylt and Zelyert know a great deal. These days, I don't control anything, not really."

"All that is true." Sulerya's attempt at a smile came out as a tired grimace. "But I don't see Brekylt and his recorders attacking them."

"When did any of them recently translate anywhere except to Ludar? Why do you think that Zelyert and Shastylt are sending me places?"

"Why are you letting them?"

"I could avoid some of the translations," Dainyl admitted, "but I don't see any way out of the difficulties except by discovering exactly what Brekylt and Alcyna have in mind—and being able to prove it."

"They must think that you could. Can you?"

"Not yet, but that's one reason I'm here. I need to talk to Sevasya and some of her senior officers and rankers."

"She's around this morning. I saw her earlier." Sulerya paused. "You won't mind if I don't escort you this time?"

"You're worried about the Table grid?"

"Most of the adjustments and compensations have to be made here or in Dereka. That's the way the system was designed. I think we have it stabilized, but . . ."

"Until you're certain everything is stable, you don't want to be far away," Dainyl finished.

She nodded.

"I can find my way. I hope matters remain calm, though."

"So do I."

Dainyl nodded, turned, and made his way out through the doors, still unguarded, and up the staircase. The courtyard beyond was bathed in hazy morning light, and the heat was like a steamy shower. Even Dainyl blotted his forehead after a score of steps across the paved courtyard toward the small stone building that held Eighth Company headquarters.

"Submarshal, sir! Welcome back to Lysia." The duty officer was on his feet as soon as he saw Dainyl.

"Is the captain in?"

"Yes, sir. That way, sir. Second door."

"Thank you." Dainyl had remembered, but appreciated the directions.

Sevasya was standing beside her desk. A slow smile crossed her wide face. "Submarshal. Two visits in less than a season. What can we do for you?"

Dainyl didn't bother to close the door. Not yet.

"I'm attempting to clarify some matters. You didn't take over here until after Noryan was transferred to Alustre, did you?"

"No. It was a year later." The smile faded.

"Is there anyone still here in the company who was? If there are, I'd like to speak to them."

"I think Undercaptain Juanyl was, but I'd have to check, and maybe Aisenyt. You know that Submarshal Alcyna has tended to require more rotation than in the west?"

"I'm aware of that. I'm also aware that Eighth Company is more stable than the others."

"For the last five years or so, that's true. If you'd like to follow me, sir."

Dainyl followed Sevasya down the corridor two doors to the small file room.

"This will take a moment." She opened the topmost of the second row of file cases, flipping through the jackets inside. "Date of service . . . arrival . . ."

Dainyl smiled and waited.

Less than a quarter glass later, the captain straightened and turned. "I was right. Juanyl was here then. So far as I can see, he's the only one."

"Is he here this morning?"

"Everyone is. We try not to fly on days that are this hot and damp, except very early in the morning, or just be-

fore sunset. His collateral duty is maintenance officer."
She replaced the dossier and closed the file box. "Do you
want to talk to him now?"

"That would be best." Dainyl cleared his throat. "After
Undercaptain Juanyl, I'd also like to talk to Undercaptain
Sledaryk."

"He's only been here a few weeks."

"I know. It's about what happened in Dulka after I visited there. But, if we could see Juanyl first . . ."

"This way." Sevasya turned, and the two walked back
down the corridor, out the rear doorway of the headquarters building, and across the courtyard. They found the
undercaptain in a small room, looking at a set of plans.
Juanyl was a midsized alector, a half head shorter than
Dainyl. His skin wasn't alabaster white, but bore a tinge
of almond, perhaps because of the years of flying service.

"Captain . . . Submarshal, sir. I was checking the drain
plans. With last week's rain, we had some problems . . ."

"Juanyl, the submarshal would like a few words with
you." Sevasya looked to Dainyl.

"There's nothing secret about this, Captain. I'd hoped
you'd stay."

She nodded.

Dainyl turned to the older Myrmidon. "I've been trying to find Myrmidons who knew Majer Noryan before
he went to Alustre. I know that was years ago . . ."

"Twelve years, sir, to the season."

"What can you tell me about his early times in the
Myrmidons?"

"Well, sir . . . I can tell you this. I never thought he'd be
more than a career ranker, sir. Maybe not even that. He
was the company driver for three years. Good with
horses, and shy with people. He was always nervous, and
thin. Never said that much, and looked sort of strange if
anyone told a joke, like he didn't understand. Majer Alcyna, she was the one who said things would change, and
I guess she was right."

"Were those her words?" asked Dainyl.

"That was a long time back, sir, but as I recall, what she said was that times were changing and that even Noryan had a role to play. Sort of smiled when she said that."

Dainyl could imagine Alcyna saying that, especially if he happened to be right about what had happened and was continuing to happen. He could sense Sevasya stiffening inside her relaxed exterior.

"Is there anything else you can remember? Did he have any special abilities?"

"Except with the horses . . . and even the pteridons, I can't say that he did. Often wondered if he felt more comfortable with them. I don't think he ever risked either animal on anything. Don't think he could have, but . . . that was then."

"Did he ever have any close friends here?"

"Not that I know. He was a translation orphan, fostered north of here. Wasn't close to his foster parents, even though they schooled him. Both of them died in an accident of some sort, maybe six months after he went to Alustre. It could have been less."

"How well did he speak?"

Juanyl chuckled. "Who would know? I never heard him say much more than 'Yes, sir' or 'No, sir.' "

Dainyl asked a few more questions, listening carefully to the responses, before saying, "Thank you. I appreciate your spending the time." He turned. "Captain . . . if we could proceed."

"Yes, sir." Sevasya led Dainyl back across the humid courtyard. "For the moment, Undercaptain Sledaryk has been the one drafting flight and schedule rotations for my approval."

Dainyl thought he understood.

The two walked back into headquarters, halting at the first door inside the building.

Sledaryk jumped to his feet. "Submarshal! Captain!"

"The submarshal wanted a few words with you, Undercaptain."

"Yes, sir."

Dainyl took a moment to study Sledaryk, both with eyes and Talent. Two things were clear. First, Sledaryk was relatively young for an undercaptain, and, second, he was strongly Talented, if not particularly well trained.

"How long did you remain in Dulka after Captain Veluara took command?"

"Two days, sir. Just long enough to gather my gear. I was told that Captain Sevasya needed an experienced undercaptain because one of hers had put in for a stipend. I took my pteridon; it's easier that way. I was told that Undercaptain Hasya flew hers to Alustre to be transferred to a new—another Myrmidon."

Sevasya nodded. "Hasya was tired of the damp and the heat and wanted to be in Alustre. She'd found a position with the Highest of the East, with the chief of trade. It was easier just to transfer one pteridon to a new flyer."

"Did you meet Captain Veluara?"

"Yes, sir, but only once or twice. She was pretty busy with the new regional alector. That's Quivaryt. Nothing much got done after . . . after you were there. Not for a while, anyway."

"I imagine," replied Dainyl dryly. "How would you describe Captain Veluara? I've met her, but I'd like your impressions."

"Ah . . . yes, sir." Sledaryk paused. "She looks young, sir, but she's a lot older than she looks, you know, the way Majer Faerylt was. She got right on the business of getting the company moved to the new compound—knew where everything was supposed to be and who was doing what. She knew everyone's name and background, even."

"Would you say that she seemed very experienced?"

"Yes, sir. Very much so, sir."

"Did she say anything about what would happen to the old compound?"

"Undercaptain Lyzetta asked about that. Captain Veluara said that was one of the things she was working out with the RA, and that the Highest of the East had already made plans for the old compound once we'd moved. She didn't say what they were, just that it was up to the Highest."

"Did anyone in Seventh Company know Captain Veluara from an earlier assignment?"

"I don't think so, sir, but I didn't ask anyone. I was getting ready to leave."

"Did Captain Veluara spend much time debriefing you?"

"No, sir. I mean, we spent maybe a glass where she asked about my squad, and the rankers in it, how long they'd been there, if they were local or from places like Alustre, whether any were married, just background information."

"Did any replacement for you arrive, or do you know if the captain intended to promote someone?"

"She said that Submarshal Alcyna would be dispatching an undercaptain from Alustre shortly."

Dainyl nodded slowly. "Thank you, Undercaptain. I think that you'll find you've been extraordinarily fortunate to be transferred to Eighth Company, and I do trust you'll appreciate that." He looked to Sevasya. "Captain . . . I'll need a few moments of your time."

"Of course." Sevasya led the way back to her study.

Neither officer said anything until the captain closed the door.

"How did she think she could get away with it?" asked Sevasya. "Except she did, didn't she?"

"It makes sense. Noryan was a translation orphan. No one knew him, not really. Alcyna picked him when he was still young and then transferred him to Fourth Company."

"How did you figure out that Noryan wasn't Noryan?"

Dainyl shrugged. "I couldn't say. He didn't feel right, and some of the reports—I know one was changed." All of that was true, although it wasn't the whole truth.

"You think Veluara is one, too?"

Dainyl would have wagered that, based on his own earlier observations of the newly promoted captain and on what Sledaryk had said, but he replied, "I don't know. It's clear that she's part of whatever they're planning."

"What are you going to do? If I might ask, sir?"

"For the moment, nothing. One doesn't accuse two distinguished officers without some sort of hard proof."

"And a great deal of support from one's superiors," she added.

"That, too," Dainyl admitted with a laugh. After a moment, he asked, "And what are you going to do, as a Myrmidon captain and daughter of a Duarch?"

"What I can—guard Lysia and do my duty. I'm barred from contacting him, and he's conditioned against listening to anything I might say." Sevasya looked squarely at Dainyl. "You have better access to him than do I."

Dainyl scarcely had any access. He had enough rank to get perhaps a single appointment, and that would have to be through Lystrana. That would put both of them—and their unborn daughter—in even greater danger. What would he say to the Duarch? That he believed the Highest of the East was conspiring, perhaps with the Duarch of Ludar, to do . . . what? Dainyl still had no idea at what end all the conspiring was aimed. To gain power and depose the Archon while bringing the Master Scepter to Acorus? To thwart the possibility that Zelyert *might* want to stop the Master Scepter from coming to Acorus and thus support the Archon? What if Khelaryt happened to be subtly encouraging—or not discouraging—Zelyert's plans, whatever they were? Should the Master Scepter come to Acorus?

The more he saw *what* Brekylt and his allies were doing, the less he seemed able to determine why.

"I have some access, Captain. But without more knowledge, it will not be useful, except to secure my death."

"Then . . . had you best not discover it, Submarshal?"

Dainyl smiled, wryly. "Like all knowledge of value, it is not easy to discover, and once discovered, to understand."

In the end, Dainyl walked briskly back to the Table

chamber, his Talent-senses alert, even as he recognized that Lysia was one of the few places where he was relatively safe.

Sulerya was standing beside the Table as he entered the chamber.

"Are things stable?" he asked.

"For now. Probably for a while. At least until the next time you try a translation somewhere." She tilted her head slightly. "Did you discover what you were looking for?"

"Yes, but it's not anything I can use to prove what's happening."

"You may never be able to *prove* anything, Submarshal. Does that mean you will not act for what you see as the best?"

"That is a good question, Recorder. I don't have an answer for it."

"You'd best find one, then."

Dainyl glanced at the Table. How safe was it? Did he have any choice?

"Submarshal Dainyl?"

"Yes, Sulerya?"

"The Table tracking systems don't seem to be functioning at the moment." The hint of a tired smile crossed her mouth. "That won't affect your translation, of course."

"Thank you." Dainyl stepped onto the Table.

The purpled darkness between Tables was undisturbed. Dainyl did not even sense a single flash of green beyond, and there were no attempts at impeding his progress. The silver-white barrier dissolved away from him.

His uniform was scarcely chill when he stepped off the Table.

Chastyl stood waiting. The recorder inclined his head to Dainyl. "Welcome back, Submarshal. I'm glad to see that you had no trouble with the Tables."

"So am I . . . and thank you." What puzzled Dainyl about the greeting was the genuineness behind the words. Chastyl was clearly pleased to see him, although it was equally clear that the recorder had no special liking for him.

Dainyl arrived at Myrmidon headquarters less than a half glass after morning muster. He was still standing in his study, looking at the reports on the side of his desk, when Shastylt appeared in the study doorway.

"Good morning, sir."

"Where have you been?"

"Is something wrong?" Dainyl reinforced his shields.

"Outside of having a deputy I can't find? No. That's bad enough."

Dainyl wasn't about to argue about half a glass, although Shastylt was often gone for longer periods. "I've been in Lysia—"

"Zelyert told me that he'd strongly suggested you confine your activities to your duties." Shastylt stepped into the study.

"I was there on Myrmidon tasks, sir." Dainyl slipped around his superior and closed the door.

"Such as?"

"I have fairly strong indications that many, if not all, of the officers in three of the four eastern companies are not who we think they are. Noryan is probably a translated Myrmidon from Ifryn."

"He's from Ifryn. He came here as an infant. I checked."

"No, sir. The original Noryan did. He was shorter than I am, rail-thin, and nervous. He had no sense of humor, and didn't want to talk to anyone. He liked horses and pteridons and had no sense of command at all. Alcyna transferred him from Eighth Company just before Captain Sevasya took command. The Noryan who appeared in Alustre is almost as tall as Khelaryt, as muscular as a bull, with shoulders to match, with a low-key sense of humor, and leadership skills. He was an undercaptain in less than two years, a captain in two more . . ."

"That would explain much."

"You don't seem surprised, sir."

"The only thing surprising is that you're still alive."

Shastylt laughed, an edge to his voice that Dainyl had not heard before.

"Why? At this point, I don't have anything that I could bring before the Highest or the Duarch. There might be two alectors left alive anywhere who know firsthand what I just told you, and I doubt either could say absolutely that Noryan is not Noryan. Besides, the Noryan we know has an outstanding record since he was transferred from Eighth Company."

"That wasn't what I meant. The Table grid almost collapsed yesterday, and stability wasn't restored until this morning. You could have been a wild translation by now."

"I was fortunate."

"More than you know, Dainyl." Shastylt stood silent for a moment. "Do you have any idea what Brekylt has in mind?"

"No. Not besides building his own power, that is. It's clear he and Alcyna essentially have control of Third, Fourth, and Seventh Companies, and that they control the Tables in Alustre, Norda, Dulka, and Prosp. They're not pleased with you or with the High Alector of Justice. I was hoping you might be able to tell me why."

Shastylt fingered his squarish chin, then nodded. After several moments, he began to speak, slowly. "Brekylt thought he should have been named High Alector of Justice, and Samist had pressed for that. Khelaryt thought differently, and in a difference of opinion between the Duarches, the final decision rests with the one who has direct supervision. Khelaryt chose Zelyert. As Zelyert has hinted, he has great concerns about how lifeforce growth is managed. Too rapid and too widespread a growth of manufactories will indeed increase indigen lifeforce, but that spike in lifeforce is followed by a rapid decline in overall world lifeforce because the growth is fueled by the destruction of things like the forests, too many fields bearing only one crop, and too much killing of nondomesticated plants and animals. Brekylt and Samist want to increase indigen lifeforce and present that as a reason why Acorus is suited to hold the Master Scepter. Zelyert and Khelaryt believe that a broader-based lifeforce mass is more conducive to supporting the Master Scepter. In effect, the Archon has only said that he will evaluate both Efra and Acorus when the time comes."

All of that might well be true, Dainyl noted, but it was far from a complete explanation. "Are they afraid Zelyert and Khelaryt might be able to prove they are right?"

"I think they fear that they are wrong and that Acorus—and they—will suffer."

"How will they suffer? If the Master Scepter does not come here, will they not remain as they are?"

"No. Khelaryt and Samist will be judged to have failed, and will be replaced by regents of the Archon. All those serving them will be examined. Some may remain. Some certainly will not."

"And if Samist and Brekylt managed to take total control of Acorus, what would the Archon do?"

"If they proved it could best support the Master Scepter . . . nothing. If not, they would be cast into the long translation tunnel without end."

Dainyl felt a cold shiver go down his spine.

"You tell me, Submarshal," said Shastylt. "Are they planning such a revolt?"

"I don't know. I would judge that they are planning for that possibility."

"That is what Zelyert has feared—and planned for."

"Might I ask how?"

"You might, but I cannot say, because he has not answered that very same question for me."

That also was true, Dainyl sensed. It also raised another question. "Can we do anything about Alcyna—and those companies?"

"Can you imagine anything worse than Myrmidon fighting Myrmidon? The drain on lifeforce from any prolonged battles would doom Acorus to being forever subservient—if it didn't plunge the world into immediate chaos and destruction. Your task is much the same as it was in Dramur. We must keep the Myrmidons out of the conflict, not because we do not support the Highest and the Duarch, but because we do."

"Wouldn't it just be simpler for Alcyna or Brekylt to have a mishap of some sort?"

"It would indeed. Do you know anyone who could accomplish that without leaving a trail back to us—and setting Myrmidon against Myrmidon? It's ironic, but they face exactly the same problem."

"So . . . lesser individuals who support them—or us—suffer mishaps . . . until someone can break the stalemate in a decisive way—without ravaging the lifeforce of the world?"

"You have an admirable grasp of the situation, Dainyl. Within those confines, we do what we can and we must. As always. I'll leave you to think about it."

After Shastylt departed, Dainyl walked back to the window. The situation was worse than he had feared, and in more ways than he had expected. He also noted one other interesting point: Shastylt had given him no orders and no directives. They had only been implied.

He also realized something else. Shastylt had never committed to either side, not really. That surprised Dainyl not at all.

43

Mykel was up well before dawn on Quinti, checking with his officers. He hadn't slept all that well, with dreams about the ancient soarers—the first he'd had in some time, but they brought back all too clearly the sense of antiquity and power that he had felt so strongly when he had met the soarer above the mine in Dramur.

The battalion had spent the day before returning some semblance of order to the garrison. Mykel had also made sure that the ammunition wagon had been unloaded and the contents stored in the old armory, underground in the vaults that hadn't been that damaged—just missing whatever ammunition might once have been there. He didn't want Third Battalion's ammunition out in the open. The duty guards had seen no signs of irregulars or brigands, but Mykel hadn't expected they'd appear for a few days, not until word got around, especially since they seemed only to have targeted the Cadmians.

The garrison roof had remained intact in most places. That might have been because the roof tiles were cracked and in poor shape and probably would have come apart if anyone had tried to remove them, but Hyalt wasn't known for heavy rain, and any roof over the troopers was better than none.

Late on Quattri Mykel had visited the chandlery and several other places and gotten the names of some growers. Before long, he'd have to work out provisioning arrangements—along with everything else—because the provisions on the wagons, replenished last in Tempre, would last but another week at best. Then there was the need for fodder for the mounts. Regular furnishings and equipment for the new compound would be sent by wagon from Tempre once it was nearing completion.

Morning muster was barely completed on Quinti when two townsmen appeared, one driving a battered cart pulled by a swaybacked horse, and the other sitting beside him. The cart creaked to a halt outside the gap in the walls that had once held a gate, but even the iron hinges had been pulled out of the brickwork.

Suspecting that the two were the guild heads, Mykel walked toward them. By the time he reached the cart, the driver stood beside the horse, holding the traces loosely.

He was a squarish indigen, with darker skin, strong blunt features, and brown hair showing streaks of gray. His broad hands were callused, with a pinkish welt across the back of his left hand. "Poeldyn, Majer. Building guild. Troral said you'd like to be seeing us."

"Mykel," the majer offered. "I did." He looked to the second man, thinner, perhaps a few years younger, with a full reddish blond beard.

"Styndal—crafters."

"We're going to be relocating and building a larger compound."

"On this hill . . . shoulda been done long time back," muttered Poeldyn.

"What about this hill?"

"Just . . . unlucky . . . always has been." Poeldyn forced a smile. "What you be needing?"

"We'll need stoneworkers, masons, carpenters, tilers . . ."

"You got plans . . . and someone who knows what they mean?" asked Poeldyn.

"I have the plans, and I know something about what they mean." Mykel grinned. "What I don't, I'm sure you two do."

"We don't work for free," added Styndal.

"I have some golds, and a letter of credit for the balance, so much to be drawn every month."

"Credits . . . aren't good for . . ."

"The letter means I can draw golds on it. I assume Troral or one of the factors has arrangements."

Styndal nodded. "He's got arrangements."

"Biggest problem'll be getting quarrymen," offered Poeldyn.

"The quarries haven't been used lately?"

"You might say as so. That was where all the trouble started . . . and for all their blue-flame lances, them Myrmidons weren't all that good at rooting out the strange ones. . . . They'd flame everything, even melt some of the facing stone, and afore long the creatures'd be back."

"Tell me about the strange ones."

Poeldyn glanced at Styndal, then finally spoke. "They were fearsome things. One was half man, from the waist down, and like one of those flying creatures the Myrmidons have on the top. Another one was like a sandox, except with a big triangular horn. There was one big black giant cat with claws sharper'n knives . . ."

"Has anyone seen anything like that lately?"

"No one's wanted to go out to the quarry, not with no one building anything," Poeldyn pointed out. "Not since Borcal . . . anyway."

"Borcal?" The name meant nothing to Mykel, but there was something about the way the crafter had mentioned it.

"He was a squad leader with the Cadmians . . . should have been the undercaptain, from what everyone said. Real good about getting to where trouble was. Funny thing, though. Everyone else got cut up or shot. Looked like he'd been burned. Not much blood, either, not for all the slashes." Poeldyn shrugged. "Since he got killed, no one wants to work the quarry. Never any trouble when his squad was out there. Best shot in Hyalt or anywhere around."

Those words sent a chill down Mykel's back, but he pushed the feeling away. "I'll have a patrol investigate the quarry before anyone returns to work there." He paused. "Who owns the quarry?"

"It belongs to the regional alector, but anyone in the town has the right to quarry there now that they finished their building out west."

"What else should I know?" Mykel kept smiling. "Have the irregulars, the ones who attacked the garrison, been seen lately?"

The two craftmasters exchanged glances once more.

This time, Styndal was the one to reply. "No. Fact is, no one rightly knows who did it. One morning, like Poeldyn said, everyone was dead. Some folks heard screams the night before, and some noise. Some of the bodies were shot, and some were slashed up, like with blades. We never saw anything."

"Not then, and not since," added Poeldyn. "Troral told the alector, and his folks came and took care of things, and they had the flying creatures."

That didn't exactly square with all the reports Mykel had gotten. "What happened to all the ammunition and the supplies, then? And the mounts?"

"Majer . . . sir . . . Maybe the alector's folk took them. If not . . . Hyalt's not the wealthiest of places. Things . . . well . . . who could blame folk if stuff disappeared in the dark."

That was even worse, Mykel reflected, because it meant it was likely that some or all of Cadmian rifles and ammunition were out among the locals—up to fifty rifles, with spares, if all the weapons of the two squads that comprised the garrison had been taken.

"And there's been no shooting since?"

"Well . . . Beznanet got found dead last week. No one minded. He'd been stealing fowl for years. Other'n that . . . nothing."

Mykel waited.

"Will the new place be having spaces for the pteridons?" Styndal asked, almost deferentially.

"All Cadmian compounds have at least a few stages for when the alectors fly in messages. The plans call for two. There won't be any pteridons or Myrmidons here all the time."

"That'll be better. Some of the crafters . . . well, Majer, you know how some folks can be."

Mykel could understand being wary of the pteridons, but not what that had to do with building a compound. "Anything else?"

Poeldyn laughed. "Let us know when you've got the place and when you want us to start, and then we'll look close-like at the plans, see what changes we might have to make."

"I'll do that. Can I leave word with Troral?"

"That you can."

After the two drove off, the cart wheels—or axles—squeaking, Mykel walked back through the battered and crumbling gateposts. He had known there had to have been problems in Hyalt, but he hadn't expected that he'd have to worry about creatures around a quarry in addition to insurgents who didn't sound like any insurgents he'd ever encountered, if they were insurgents at all. But . . . if they weren't, who were they? And the comments about the squad leader who was a crack shot and who'd been burned . . . that sounded like an alector sidearm, and he didn't like the possibility of a rogue alector wandering around Hyalt at all.

44

There are comparatively few alectors, guiding hundreds of thousands of other beings. This has always been so and will continue to be so. What is it, then, that distinguishes an alector from those beings, or from another alector who is no better than the masses? Size and strength are often cited, but bulls are bigger than alectors, and so are sandoxen. Intelligence is also cited, but many among the masses have intelligence close to that of alectors, and in some cases, equal to ours. Nor is Talent enough to claim distinction and leadership.

Those who lead and guide others must possess not only superior physical and mental capabilities, but the personal honor and integrity to assure that their decisions lead to the best possible lives for those they guide. Each individual should have the opportunity to employ his or her abilities to their greatest possible extent in a beneficial, peaceful, and productive manner. To seek power for its own sake, or wealth, or any other excess is but to confirm that the individual who does so lacks the integrity required of an alector who would lead.

All respect a crafter who creates an object of quality and beauty, and all are repulsed by one who would attempt to pass off an inferior product for the same price. Yet all too often respect is granted to the leader or administrator who administers in a fashion that favors one group unfairly over another, but is this not an inferior product of leadership? While equality of ability and accomplishment does not exist in any society, and any society which expects such is doomed, equality of opportunity to excel within one's field must be granted to all. Similarly, respect must be accorded to excellence in every trade and service.

Fostering equality of opportunity and respect for honest accomplishment, and not just for the few who accumulate masses of gold or power over others, those are the virtues of worth for an alector, and only so long as those virtues are held in high esteem will we endure, for personal honor and integrity are the basis of all that we have accomplished. . . .

> *Views of the Highest*
> Illustra
> W.T. 1513

45

In the end, Mykel chose Fifteenth Company to investigate the quarry, partly because he had decided to accompany that force and partly because more than half the company had seen strange creatures in the last battle on Dramur. What with all the other arrangements, including getting directions to the quarry, Mykel and Fifteenth Company didn't get away from their temporary quarters until mid morning on Sexdi.

Mykel and Undercaptain Fabrytal rode side by side, with a pair of scouts ahead by thirty yards, not that they would be much help if someone attempted an attack from a window of a building in Hyalt. Mykel had not seen anything to indicate that was likely, not with the streets and lanes holding women and children, and a handful of men. There had been no reports of any violence in the town, either, and people didn't look fearful, except of him and the Cadmians. Still, he kept looking, and trying to sense if anyone might be targeting them. He didn't feel that, and in Dramur that feeling had been trustworthy.

Ahead, just short of what looked to be a chandlery, he saw a woman, with long blonde tresses plaited into a single braid down her back. She had taken one of the four children with her by the arm. Mykel watched and listened.

"Garytt! I saw that. . . ."

Mykel smiled. He'd heard words like that when his sister Sesalia had addressed one of her brood who'd misbehaved. Before long, she'd be having her fifth. Five children? He hadn't even found any one with whom he'd thought of having children—let alone five.

He gave a wry laugh under his breath. That wasn't entirely true, but Rachyla was about as unobtainable for a Cadmian majer as an ancient might be for an alector. He smiled more broadly as he neared the young mother, but at the sound of the horses, she ushered the four into the chandlery without even looking toward the Cadmians.

Mykel's eyes went back to the structures on each side of the high road. Unlike Southgate or Dramuria, the houses and buildings were of different ages and styles, although all were built of stone or brick or some combination of the two. Some few older houses had split slate roofs, but most had grayish red roof tiles. As Fifteenth

Company rode southward on the main boulevard—the eternastone high road—Mykel observed the side streets and lanes. Roughly every third street was paved with redstone, and had redstone sidewalks, as did the boulevard. The alleys and lanes between the paved streets were of packed reddish sandy soil and had no sidewalks.

Except for a few larger structures clearly belonging to factors, the houses and other buildings were all of one story. The smaller dwellings had few windows, and that made unfortunate sense because wood for shutters was tariffed, and glass was not cheap.

"Hyalt seems like a poor town, doesn't it, sir?" asked Undercaptain Fabrytal.

"I haven't seen many poorer, not of its size," Mykel admitted.

"Makes you wonder why they've got alectors here, I mean, with not that many folks or that much trade."

"There are some mines to the south and west of the quarry. Tin and copper."

Near the south end of Hyalt, the high road turned eastward, but Fifteenth Company continued heading south for another quarter vingt on a older road paved with redstone blocks, many of which were cracked and chipped, and some of which were missing, their space filled with packed dirt or clay. After another half vingt, the road split, the paved section turning west-southwest.

"The one to the left!" Mykel called out.

The quarry road had deep ruts that had been weathered down and filled with fine reddish sand and dirt. There were no recent tracks of either horses or wagons. Before long the road began to rise and did so for close to half a vingt before leveling out onto a stretch of scrubby grassland that ended at the foot of a low hill. From a vingt away, Mykel could see where the hill had been cut away and the redstone layers exposed.

There might not be anything at the quarry, but . . . being prepared made sense, and if there were not, the exercise wouldn't hurt. Mykel turned in the saddle, looking at Fabrytal. "Order a line abreast, by squads, five across. Rifles ready."

The faintest hint of a puzzled frown crossed the undercaptain's face, but he pulled his mount to the side and stood in the stirrups. "Fifteenth Company! Line abreast— by squads. Five across. Third squad centered on me. Rifles ready!"

Fifteenth Company was re-formed within moments, then continued riding across the grasslands.

Less than a hundred yards from where the excavation began, Mykel looked to Fabrytal again. "Have them halt here."

"Company! Halt!"

Mykel surveyed the area to the south. He had only seen one quarry before in his life, and that had been the massive granite quarry to the north of Faitel, where he had grown up. The quarry at Hyalt was far smaller, less than half a vingt from side to side, and extending only fifty or sixty yards into the hillside, with tiers cut out of the stone, like stair steps up the redstone. There was a muddy reddish pool less than ten yards across in the southeastern corner of the lowest level.

"Just a big hole in the ground," said Fabrytal.

"That's what quarries are—holes in the ground where people have taken stone out. This is a small quarry." Mykel surveyed the quarry once more. Something about it bothered him, but he couldn't pinpoint either a specific source or location. Finally, he turned to Fabrytal. "Forward at a walk. Rifles ready."

"Fifteenth Company! Slow walk! Forward! Rifles ready!"

Mykel had his own rifle out as well, disregarding the unspoken adage that a commander should concentrate on tactics, rather than engage in direct combat.

The company had moved forward a good thirty yards toward the unused quarry when a dark shadow appeared just above the base of the quarry, in the western corner where the stonework ended and the hillside remained relatively untouched. Mykel blinked. The shadow looked black, but it *felt* like an ugly pinkish purple. Then it was no longer a shadow, but an enormous catlike creature that raced toward fifth squad, the westernmost troopers of the company.

"Company! Halt! Fifth squad! Fire at will!" Mykel snapped. "Fifth squad, fire at will!"

"Company, halt! Fifth squad . . ." echoed Fabrytal.

Mykel watched intently for a moment, then scanned the rest of the quarry, but he neither saw nor sensed anything else that felt threatening. His eyes went back to the giant cat, its body at least a good two yards in length.

Fifth squad's first shots did little good, and the cat creature accelerated silently toward the troopers. The creature jerked and stumbled as several shots ripped into it, but Mykel could see no wounds, although the cat slowed somewhat. Continual fire poured into the creature as it neared fifth squad. Less than a handful of yards short of the squad, it fell forward, legs twitching.

"Keep firing!" came the command from Vhanyr, the fifth squad's leader.

More shots struck the wounded creature, and it writhed, then slumped onto the ground, but its body still twitched.

"Hold the company, rifles ready," Mykel ordered Fabrytal. "I want to get a good look at that creature."

"Yes, sir. Company hold! Rifles ready!"

Mykel rode along the front of the arrayed company at a fast walk.

Vhanyr had ridden out from his squad several yards, but reined up short of the fallen creature, still twitching on the reddish sandy ground that sported but sparse grass. Mykel reined up beside the squad leader, his own rifle still out and ready.

"Sir." Vhanyr held his rifle in the general direction of the cat. "We must have put fifty bullets into it before it went down."

Mykel would have judged far less than that, but he'd seen over a half score impact the giant black cat. As he watched, it lifted its head and struggled to rise, jaws opening and revealing teeth that seemed half-crystalline, half-yellow. Was it *healing* itself? He lifted his own rifle and fired—once, twice, three times, and again. His shots tore away half the creature's head, and it dropped onto the ground.

The creature had not bled, Mykel realized—unless a purplish blue ichor staining a clump of grass was what the creature had for blood. Nor had it made a sound in the entire span of its attack.

"What is it? Do you know, sir?" asked Vhanyr.

"I've never seen anything like that," Mykel admitted. He'd never read about anything that remotely resembled the black catlike giant.

As he watched, the clumps of grass around the fallen beast shriveled and blackened. The dead creature appeared to lose its shape, disintegrating into a long pile of a greasy-looking purplish black substance. Then, abruptly, bluish red flames burst from the disintegrating corpse, the heat so intense that Mykel eased the roan back away from the pyre.

". . . what the frig!"

". . . never seen anything like that . . ."

Mykel wrenched his attention away from the bluish flames and studied the quarry again. He could see or sense nothing. That didn't mean another of the cat creatures might not appear again at any time.

"Fifth squad, reload! Now!"

Vhanyr's command reminded Mykel to do the same. He did not replace the rifle in its case, but rested it across his thighs, one-handed.

"Sir?" asked Vhanyr.

"We'll be advancing shortly," Mykel told the squad leader, then turned his mount back toward the center of the company. He doubted they would see another of the beasts immediately, but he could definitely understand why the quarrymen were leery of the place. That meant at least two squads on duty all the time the stone was being cut and carted away.

He reined in the roan beside Fabrytal's mount. "Forward at a walk."

"Forward . . ."

Mykel kept studying the quarry, the courses of stone, and the hill that surrounded them. Strange creatures indeed.

46

Dainyl and Lystrana sat in the darkness of their bedchamber, Lystrana reclining on the bed, and Dainyl sitting on the chair beside her.

"The quiet in Elcien is disturbing," Dainyl said. "We know that Ifrits, and it could be scores of them, are coming through the Tables to the east of Corus. Zelyert knows as well. It's fairly certain that the engineers of the east are constructing additional equipment of some sort, probably of a military nature. Three of the four eastern Myrmidon companies are under Brekylt's and Alcyna's control, and I'd wager Second Company in Ludar is aligned as well. If Brekylt can present his position as supporting the Archon, Samist will agree to whatever they have in mind."

"What is your point, dearest?" asked Lystrana.

"Why isn't anything being done from here?"

"It is." She laughed, ironically. "One of the recorders who supported Brekylt is dead. One Myrmidon majer and one RA are also dead. Several engineers are dead. More than a few know that it is dangerous to oppose a submarshal directly."

"Yet all that has changed nothing," Dainyl pointed out.

"Why would it? Khelaryt cannot act unless he has proof that they are subverting the goals set by the Archon. Zelyert and Shastylt will not offer what they know because they cannot prove what is happening. Voicing the uncertain always risks losing power. Neither wishes to do that, if for different reasons."

"What am I supposed to do?"

"What you always do . . . what is right. But you cannot do it until you have an opportunity. I have no doubt that you could go to Alustre and destroy Brekylt and Alcyna. If Zelyert had been wise enough to remove them from power ten years ago, it would have made a difference. How would that change matters now? Except to assure that you would have all those who support them opposed to you, and that you would lose any support from Zelyert and Khelaryt."

"What little support I do have." Dainyl snorted.

"That is better than no support . . . or active opposition."

He knew that she was accurate in that, much as he hated to admit it.

"Where do you think all those alectors from Ifryn are going?" asked Lystrana. "If large numbers of strange alectors appeared in Alustre, would there not be reports, one way or another? You found a number still loyal to Khelaryt there, such as Kaparyk."

The answer was obvious, and Dainyl had felt it all along, even if he had not voiced it. "They're being sent to Dulka, and perhaps Hyalt. They've moved Seventh Company well away from the Table, and there's a perfectly good and empty compound adjacent to the structure that houses the RA and the Table. Alcyna has sent another one of the translated and replacement Myrmidons—that's Veluara—there to keep the Myrmidons in line and away from what's happening. Most of the undercaptains are junior, and the only one who voiced any real insight was transferred to Lysia." He paused. "Some could be going to other centers where the recorders support Brekylt, places like Norda."

"I would suggest isolated centers as well," she suggested. "If the renegade alectors can use the Tables . . ."

"They can hide anywhere," he finished. That suggested Hyalt might be a problem in the future as well, as if he weren't worried enough about Majer Mykel and his Talent.

"What if you conducted an inspection in force there? With Myrmidons from Lysia?"

"I have the feeling that sending Myrmidons from Lysia wouldn't be a good idea. It might be better to send Fifth Company from Dereka. It's much farther, but . . ." Dainyl shook his head. "That's not something I could do without Shastylt's support, or at least not his opposition."

"Not now."

Dainyl understood. He could certainly plan what needed to be done—and how—and suggest to some of the eastern companies that some full-company maneuvers might be necessary later in the year. That would filter eastward, but the vagueness might well keep Alcyna off balance. Then, he reflected, it could also force her to act earlier. Or she could take it as a bluff, and that might be best of all.

47

Mykel looked across the small mesa-like expanse, a vingt across from northwest to southeast, and three-quarters of that in depth from northeast to southwest. It was less than a vingt from the outskirts of Hyalt, and it even had a good spring that fed into the stream running along the southeastern edge of the lower slopes. Farther to the southeast was a flock of sheep, with a single herder and two dogs. The late-morning sun shone out of a clear silver-green sky, and there was but the barest hint of a breeze from the northwest.

The incline to the flattened hilltop was modest, rising only ten yards above the grasslands to the south, and the site was less than half a vingt from the high road north to Tempre. The one drawback was that there was no road or lane connecting the site to the high road, but that could be built since the slope was gentle and the terrain was not that rugged.

Behind Mykel, Seventeenth Company was reined up in formation. Undercaptain Loryalt was to Mykel's left. For the past several days, Mykel had scouted the terrain around Hyalt, assigning different companies to accompany him.

"Take some work, sir, but this site looks a lot better than where the old garrison is," observed Loryalt.

"It's near the high road and not too close to the town. If the town grows, there will still be space." Mykel had his doubts about how much Hyalt would grow, but he wanted to account for that possibility.

"You think it will, sir?"

"You never can tell." Mykel smiled, then added, "We've got some patrolling to do. We'll ride down to the high road and head north to that first lane west. We haven't ridden through that area yet."

"Yes, sir," replied Loryalt.

Mykel took a last look at the site, far superior to the other possibilities he had viewed, before turning the roan down the slope and westward.

"Seventeenth Company! Forward!"

The company rode westward. Less than a quarter of a vingt to the north was another flock of sheep, a small one with less than a score of ewes and half as many lambs. The herder, an angular but short man with dull gray hair and a grizzled beard, watched the company for a moment before turning away.

Once at the high road, Mykel and the company turned north along a stretch that held no wagons or riders except themselves. Nor was there any trace of any recent travel on the lane that Seventeenth Company took westward from the high road. The lane wound between low hills above what might have been a creek in wetter times. Although the hillside on the north side of the road was but lightly wooded, with scattered junipers and low pines, affording relatively good visibility, Mykel had Loryalt send the scouts ahead of the main body of the company a good half vingt.

After another quarter glass, the road climbed over a low ridge. As Mykel rode to the top of the rise, he looked to the south, but could not see the regional alector's complex, although he knew it had to be only a few vingts away. On the other side of the ridge, the lane descended into a wide vale filled with scattered bushes and sparse grass. The tops of the rises on each side of the vale were only three or four yards above the lane itself.

"Send another set of scouts to ride the top of the rises."

"Yes, sir."

While Mykel had not seen anything, and there was little cover, he disliked following a low road without some outriders. In moments, the two scouts were on the rises, riding as easily across the open terrain as were the Cadmians below them.

"There's not much out here, sir," said Loryalt.

"No. Even the grass is sparse." Mykel could see the pair of scouts ahead on a flat stretch of the lane.

The silver-green sky, clear as it was, began to darken, yet the white light of the sun did not dim. Nor were there clouds anywhere. He glanced toward Loryalt.

"Nice day," observed the undercaptain. "Not too hot. Not too cold."

Mykel gave a perfunctory nod, his head turning, and his eyes scanning the low rise to his right, then the dale on the left of the dirt lane, then the rise to the left. He reached for his rifle, taking it from its case and checking once more to make sure it was fully loaded, although he knew it was.

Crack! The very sound shivered through Mykel, yet it was not a sound, loud as it felt to him, that the others experienced. His eyes fixed on a point in midair, a good twenty yards above the road and almost a hundred to the west of where he rode, but well behind the scouts. Blue shapes appeared from nowhere.

"Company halt! Rifles ready!" Mykel snapped. "Now!" Should he spread the company? He glanced to both sides of the road. Spreading the troopers would likely only make them more vulnerable.

"Company halt! Rifles ready!" Loryalt's voice held the slightest trace of surprise.

"Look to the west! Fire on my command!"

At first, Mykel had thought the score or so of creatures that had appeared were ravens, but no ravens were that big—or purpled blue. The flying creatures formed into a wedge that turned eastward, toward Seventeenth Company, and the noonday sun glinted off metallic blue beaks. They were miniature versions of the pteridons flown by the Myrmidons.

The flying wedge of creatures dove toward the Cadmians.

"Fire at will!"

"Fire at will!" echoed Loryalt.

Mykel aimed at the lead creature of the wedge and *willed* his shot home. As the bullet struck, the creature exploded into a ball of blue flame that splattered down on the road some forty yards ahead.

Shots rose up around Mykel.

He forced himself to concentrate on the next flyer. Another ball of flame splattered, this time into the hillside to his right, far closer. By the time he had fired a third and fourth time, the creatures were almost on the company.

A mount screamed, and then a trooper.

The miniature pteridons swept past, and Mykel reloaded. He could feel the heat from where one of the downed creatures burned not ten yards from him. He turned in the saddle, watching as they circled back toward the company, this time coming in from the south, but too far away for the moment for a decent shot.

He raised his rifle, then concentrated, firing once, then

again. Two of the beasts exploded, tumbling from the sky. He fired again . . . and then reloaded, because the creatures had not turned away but were climbing as if to begin another diving attack.

This time three of the creatures all headed toward Mykel. He forced himself to fire deliberately, concentrating on one shot after another, ignoring the shots coming from others in the company.

When the second wave passed, there were only three of the beasts remaining, and they flew steadily northward, passing beyond the rise.

"Stand down! Undercaptain, let me have a report on casualties." Mykel had no doubts that he had lost men and mounts.

"Yes, sir." Loryalt turned his mount.

Mykel reloaded, even though he doubted that the flyers would return immediately, and replaced the rifle in its saddle case. He felt shaky in the saddle, and sweat ran down his face and the back of his neck. He reached for his water bottle and drank.

The creatures that had exploded in flame had burned themselves into blackened piles of ashes, leaving only black greasy splotches on the soil. There were no charred bones or scales . . . only the ashy residue of intense fires. All were scattered in a rough arc around Mykel. He stood in the stirrups and tried to see if there were any other blackened heaps, but the only others he saw were two larger black pyres, large enough to have been men and mounts.

He forced the bile down in his throat as he settled back into the saddle. It took an effort to keep his fingers from touching his belt or the hidden dagger of the ancients.

While he waited for Loryalt to return, he rode forward to the nearest blackened spot on the ground. As with the giant cat, splotches on the grass around where the creature had fallen had turned black, even beyond the burned area. Slowly, he rode back to the head of the company, his eyes and feelings still scanning, trying to see if anything else might appear.

Loryalt reined up short of Mykel. His face was set, slightly pale. "Sir, Seventeenth Company reports six casualties, all dead."

"Thank you, Undercaptain. Their bodies?"

"Ah . . . no, sir. They burned to ashes. There's . . . there's nothing left, sir. Nothing at all."

"Is there anything we can do?"

"No . . . no, sir."

"I wish there were." Mykel turned the roan. "I think it's time we headed back to the garrison. We can let fifth squad lead." He doubted that they would see any more creatures, but continuing the patrol would seem far too callous, and, for the moment, there was little to be gained.

"Seventeenth Company! . . ."

Mykel and Loryalt rode along the shoulder of the road until they reached what had been the rear of the column, where Loryalt ordered the company forward, with the rearguard now the forward scouts, and the former scouts bringing up the rear.

A quarter of a glass passed before Loryalt spoke. "Sir? What were they?"

"I don't know. They look like smaller versions of what the Myrmidons fly. I'd judge that they were the strange creatures that the crafters talked about, but neither one could tell me anything about what the creatures they knew about actually looked like."

"They were hard to bring down. Some of the men said that they hit them three or four times, and nothing happened."

"We killed most of them," Mykel pointed out, "even if it did take the whole company. I'd like to find out what they are, though." Mykel tried to keep the worry out of his voice. His Cadmians could handle the giant cats, but the miniature pteridons? So far as he could tell, only his shots had been effective.

"Yes, sir." Loryalt was silent for a time.

Mykel continued to scan the skies and the terrain, wondering how he could possibly be everywhere, and what would happen if a company ran into the small pteridons when he wasn't around. Did the Marshal of Myrmidons know about the creatures? If he did, why had Cadmians been dispatched, rather than Myrmidons?

He'd need to report about the creatures quickly, even if no more showed up, although that seemed rather unlikely.

48

Mykel shifted his weight on the mounting block, where he sat in the center courtyard of the old garrison in the sunlight of late afternoon, his legs crossed, balancing the oblong of wood that served as a writing desk for the report he needed to submit. At least, he could send it with the sandox coach that served Hyalt on Duadi and Sexdi.

Writing the report was going to be difficult, because he wasn't about to point out, directly, that there were no insurgents or irregulars to speak of, not that he hadn't had enough difficulty in arranging for the purchase of the land and for the beginning of construction on the new Cadmian compound, not to mention the creatures at the quarry. Thankfully, over the preceding week, there had been no more appearances by the miniature pteridons. Not so thankfully, he was still having dreams about the soarers, but he could not remember them with more than a vague sense of events—and a feeling of unease.

Fodder was more expensive than he had hoped, because most animals around Hyalt were grazed—and that was scarcely practical for the mounts of Third Battalion. Mutton and lamb were less expensive, but he suspected that he and the rest of the Cadmians would tire of that before long. He had arranged for a peasant girl to raise chickens for the Cadmians, but even chickens took a while to grow. Another problem had been that, according to the growers, the chandler, and other merchants, the regional alector had been purchasing far more food and supplies over the last season or so.

In between those arrangements, he had to observe and supervise the training of the new Cadmians, as well as extra training for his own "replacement" companies.

He took a deep breath and forced himself to concentrate on writing the dispatch before him, framing each sentence carefully in his mind before writing it out. In a proper compound he would have made a draft, but, for all that Hyalt lay outside the eastern walls of the old garrison, he might as well have been in the field.

Finally, he looked at the key sections and reread them carefully.

... Third Battalion has maintained regular patrols and sent scouts into all areas that might harbor irregulars or insurgents. To date, the battalion has not found any evidence of camps or activity that would clearly suggest recent insurgency. In the course of patrolling, Sixteenth Company was successful in discovering four brigands to the southeast of Hyalt. All but one were killed in attempting to escape, and the survivor was turned over to the town justicer. While Third Battalion will continue to maintain a vigilant stance in the course of its patrolling, training of the Hyalt companies, and rebuilding of the Cadmian compound, thus far it appears as though the Myrmidons were extremely effective in dealing with whatever insurgency previously existed, or in encouraging the insurgents to leave the area for the present time.

The more serious threat to the battalion has resulted from the need to protect the quarrymen. Predators of types unknown locally or in other regions of Corus have attempted to attack both quarry workers and Cadmians on three occasions. Local residents have confirmed that these predators were of the same types dealt with by the Myrmidons earlier. ...

Fortunately, on both times when Mykel had not been present at the quarry, Rhystan or Fabrytal had been, and their companies had been successful in killing the beasts without additional Cadmian casualties.

. . . The most common attacker resembles a large black mountain cougar, but it is far larger, a good two yards in length. It is extremely swift. Concentrated rifle fire was required to bring down the three beasts that have attempted to attack the Cadmians on quarry duty. Once each was killed, within a fraction of a glass, the carcass began to smolder, and then burst into flames. Only ashes were left. The other predators were large birdlike creatures, purple-blue, with long beaks that appeared crystalline. These appeared from nowhere to attack Seventeenth Company as it patrolled northwest of Hyalt. If these creatures, which resemble miniature pteridons, strike a Cadmian, the bird, the Cadmian, and his mount burst into intense flame. In addition some appear to use something like a venom on its beak. One Cadmian was slashed with the beak and died in less than a quarter glass from the poison. . . .

To date, losses to the flying creatures total six Cadmians. There have been no casualties from the attacks of the giant cats. . . .

At the sound of creaking cart wheels and axles, Mykel took a last look at the dispatch before carefully folding it and slipping it into his uniform tunic. Then he set aside his makeshift writing desk and stood to wait for Poeldyn.

The cart creaked to a halt several yards short of Mykel. The swarthy craftmaster swung off the driver's seat of the cart, still holding the leads.

"Good afternoon, Craftmaster." Mykel stepped forward.

"Afternoon, Majer. You know there was another one of those cat creatures at the quarry this morning?"

"I had not heard about this morning. I trust Fourteenth Company took care of it."

"That they did. It was a close thing, though. Makes it hard for the men to concentrate on the work. They say the pay's not enough for that."

"I imagine some would say that, Craftmaster." Mykel found himself both surprised and inwardly amused to hear himself using words his father had said more than once. "Still . . . they're getting close to what is paid in the quarries at Faitel, and I don't know of anyone else needing stones in Hyalt."

"Pay doesn't mean much to a man with a stone bed and a coverlet of earth."

"That's true. We both know that quarrying is hard work. That's why the pay is high already. Several men have had injuries from the work. But I don't believe anyone has died, or even been injured by the cats. You're suggesting additional pay for something that hasn't happened."

"You're a hard man, Majer."

"I'm being fair, Craftmaster. The Cadmians are taking the greater risks, and they get paid far less for a day's work. No one is compelling the quarrymen to work the stone. If we weren't building the new compound and protecting the quarrymen, they'd have no work."

The faintest hint of a hard smile appeared at the corners of Poeldyn's mouth. "Are you sure you weren't the son of a factor, Majer?"

"Eldest son of a crafter. He's a master tiler in Faitel."

"I'll trust to that to make sure all remains fair."

"I'll do my best, Craftmaster." Mykel wasn't promising anything, but he'd probably have to come up with golds or something if anything serious did happen to one of the quarrymen from an attack by a cat or one of the miniature pteridons—and he needed to add that concern to his dispatch report to Colonel Herolt.

"I've the feeling you just might, Majer." Poeldyn nodded. "It's going to be slow for the next few days. The next course of stone has fractures, won't be good for much besides underground bracing of wall foundations. . . ."

Mykel listened intently.

49

Dainyl looked at the stack of reports waiting for him, riffled through them, and set them back down on the desk. After a moment, his eyes fell on the thin volume he had set on the corner of the desk earlier—*Views of the Highest*. He picked it up and paged through it, not quite idly, finally stopping at a section he recalled vaguely. He smiled as he read.

When an alector or an indigen offers a reason for action, or lack of action, or when an administrator acts or sets forth a policy, the discerning alector must always ascertain the structural rationale for such. The structural rationale is the prime and accurate support for a decision or policy, and not usually the reason made public. Anyone who acts, if pressed, will provide a reason for such action, and the reason will invariably support the action, but a rationalization for public attribution and scrutiny is usually not the structural rationale that prompted the action or policy.

His lips curled at the last line. Did anyone above him in the hierarchy ever lay out the true or structural reason for action? Not often. With a snort, he closed the volume and set it aside.

He still needed to go through the reports. He decided to start with the thickest—that of the Cadmian Mounted Rifle regiment. First, he looked at the summaries. Second Battalion was still at Elcien rebuilding and retraining after extensive losses to the grassland nomads. Third Battalion had reached Hyalt and had begun patrols against potential insurgents, continued training the Hyalt Cadmian companies, and had commenced the construction of a new Cadmian compound. Fourth Battalion remained in Iron Stem and was maintaining order and fending off attacks by the icewolves. Fifth Battalion continued operations out of Northport, dealing with fractious Reillies.

There was also a brief section pointing out that, if recruiting and training were begun for replacements before battalions returned from deployments, that policy would bring the various battalions up to full strength earlier and allow for greater retraining before redeploying battalions. Dainyl decided to offer a cautious note to the marshal on that point, suggesting that Colonel Herolt had a valid concern.

Dainyl's more direct and personal concerns lay with Majer Mykel and Third Battalion. The longer before anyone discovered the majer's Talent, the happier—and less likely to be blamed—Dainyl would be. He turned to the section of the report containing greater detail about Third Battalion.

. . . Third Battalion, Majer Mykel commanding, is currently deployed in Hyalt and has commenced building of a new compound there while undertaking patrol actions, in coordination with training the two Hyalt companies, to complete pacification of the Hyalt area, as per the orders of the Marshal of Myrmidons. In addition to dealing with brigands and seeking to prevent attacks by irregulars, Third Battalion has reported several attacks by unidentified creatures. Six fatalities have been incurred as of the latest report from Third Battalion. . . .

Unidentified creatures? Were they wild translations? In Hyalt? Dainyl turned to the pages holding Majer Mykel's more detailed report. His lips tightened as he read about the giant black cats and the small pteridons.

They had to be wild translations, and that confirmed what he had learned about a number of the unreported translations from Ifryn going to Hyalt. But why Hyalt?

After a moment of reflecting on Hyalt, he nodded. Hyalt had been one of the earlier Tables established, and the Table and a number of facilities were actually built into a large hill or small mountain—well away from the town itself.

Dainyl set the report down on his desk and hurried back to the file room. Squad leader Doselt, the administrative clerk, looked up from where he stood before an open file case.

"Sir?"

"I'd like to review all the First Company reports from last summer to date. If you'd gather them immediately."

Doselt looked at the submarshal. "Yes, sir. Right away, sir."

"Thank you." Dainyl walked back to his study and sat down, thinking. Sulerya had indicated that the recorder in Hyalt was sympathetic to Brekylt and, presumably, Duarch Samist, and the presence of wild translations suggested strongly that the same was true of the local regional alector.

Had Shastylt pulled First Company's second squad out of the Hyalt area because he knew that and feared that they would be lost if they remained?

"Sir?" Doselt stood in the study doorway with an armload of reports.

"Put them on the desk. I'll let you know when I'm finished."

"Yes, sir." The Myrmidon placed the reports in two stacks and straightened. "This stack is summer and fall. These here are harvest and winter. There aren't any spring reports in the files yet, sir."

"Thank you. If you'd close the door on the way out?"

"Yes, sir."

Even before the door closed, Dainyl reached for the first report in the summer stack.

A glass later, Dainyl finished the last reports filed by Undercaptain Yuasylt and Captain Ghasylt. There was no mention of strange creatures or wild translations—only accounts of sniping by indigen and lander irregulars and several attempted ambushes by what appeared to be wild Talents, one of which had killed Insorya, the most junior member of second squad, but which had not injured her pteridon. The last report from Captain Ghasylt about the Hyalt mission concluded that the wild Talent had been killed when second squad spotted an ambush from the air and attacked with all five pteridons and skylances.

Dainyl rose. He opened the study door carefully, because he was fuming, but walked carefully down to the duty desk.

Undercaptain Chelysta stood immediately as Dainyl approached. "Submarshal, sir?"

"I'd appreciate it if you would find Captain Ghasylt and have him report to my study immediately. He should be here somewhere. I saw him earlier."

"Yes, sir."

"Thank you." Dainyl turned and marched back to his study.

He had only gone several steps when he overheard the messenger's comment to Chelysta.

". . . wouldn't want to be in the captain's boots . . ."

Dainyl took a deep breath. He needed to calm down. Whatever had happened wasn't likely to have been Ghasylt's doing.

Scarcely had Dainyl reseated himself behind his desk when the captain appeared in the doorway of the study.

"You wanted me, sir."

"Please sit down." Dainyl kept his voice level.

Ghasylt did not meet Dainyl's eyes as he sat in the chair across from the submarshal.

"The latest report from the Third Cadmian Battalion mentions that strange creatures have reappeared, and that according to the locals, they seem similar to the ones previously handled by the Myrmidons."

Ghasylt did not look up, nor speak.

"I didn't recall anything like that," Dainyl said quietly. "There's nothing in your reports, or Yuasylt's, about that."

"No, sir. There's not."

"Might I ask why?"

Ghasylt swallowed, still not meeting Dainyl's eyes. "The marshal told me not to report that. I thought he'd told you."

"It may have been an oversight," Dainyl said, striving once more to keep his voice level, "because I was in Dramur at the time, but since I did not know, discovering that we still have strange creatures in the area around Hyalt took me by surprise."

"Yes, sir. I can see that."

"Tell me about them," Dainyl said more calmly than he felt.

"Well, sir. One was like a huge cat, except faster and all black. Another was sort of like a sandox, except it had a triangular horn, and the last ones—those were the ones that we saw most often—were like small wild pteridons. One of those was what got Insorya."

"I take it that skylances were effective against all of them."

"Yes, sir. Yuasylt said that the hardest part was hitting them. They just went up in blue flame then, though."

"I know there aren't any records, but did Yuasylt say how many they encountered?"

"There were something like thirty of all kinds."

"Were they all there to begin with? Did the numbers lessen after the squad had been there a while?"

"They appeared every few days for a season, and then they seemed to disappear. I mean, no more showed up. That was when the marshal told me to have second squad come back here."

Dainyl nodded, then stood. He'd learned what he needed to know, and probably about as much as Ghasylt actually knew. "Thank you. That's what I needed to know."

"Yes, sir."

Dainyl could sense the captain's relief as he left the study.

While he wanted to talk to Shastylt about it immediately, the marshal did not return to headquarters until late in the afternoon.

Dainyl stepped into the marshal's study and closed the door behind himself.

"Yes?" Shastylt raised his eyebrows.

"We have more wild translations in Hyalt, and from the report from the Third Battalion, Cadmian Mounted Rifles, I'd judge that the number is increasing."

"I don't recall discussing that with you, Dainyl," Shastylt replied mildly.

"I don't believe that you did, sir. That was when I was in Dramur, but it wasn't too hard to figure it out. The Cadmian majer is reporting more strange creatures, one type looking like a giant black cat and the other like a small pteridon. He also notes that the locals say they're the same as the ones the Myrmidons handled. To me, that suggests we have a problem with the recorder and alector in Hyalt. Or that the problem that you resolved before has reemerged." Dainyl smiled pleasantly, shields in place, and waited.

In turn, Shastylt smiled as well. "What do you suggest we do, Submarshal?"

"Before attempting to come up with any plan, I thought it best to consult with you. You have far greater knowledge of what has occurred in the past in Hyalt. For me to proceed without that knowledge would hardly be prudent."

The marshal nodded. "You are always prudent, Dainyl. It is one of your better traits."

Dainyl waited.

Finally, Shastylt continued. "You may not know that Rhelyn is both the Recorder of Deeds and the local regional alector in Hyalt. In such a lightly populated area, it was felt that one alector could handle both duties. His allegiance is to Samist, but he has always been close to Brekylt. You might also recall that one of the Highest's assistants was killed by a wild translation last winter, and the word was that it was on a translation to Dereka. . . ."

Dainyl recalled that Falyna had mentioned something about that, joking that Dainyl might want the position.

". . . That was true enough, but what was not said was that he was translating to Dereka from the Table in Hyalt."

"How many others have had mishaps that way?"

Shastylt shrugged. "I could not say. I do know that very few alectors from Elcien now visit Hyalt." An ironic smile appeared. "There were few enough before, but now there are virtually none."

"No one has done anything?" Dainyl knew the answer, but wanted to judge Shastylt's reaction.

"What would one do? And to what end? Hyalt is viewed as too out-of-the-way, and of little interest to those who do not understand and too dangerous for too little gain by those who do."

"If Rhelyn is building a force of some sort, he could send them through the Table to Ludar or Alustre."

"*If* . . . that is the question, but . . . would you like to take the Table there to verify what might be happening?"

"Not this moment," replied Dainyl. "I would consider it as part of a larger plan—perhaps if a squad of Myrmidons from Dereka were nearby."

"Why Dereka?"

"Because I could go to Dereka and dispatch them from there. If we sent a squad from here, Rhelyn would know long before they arrived."

"You might consider developing a plan along those lines, Submarshal. We may need it." Shastylt stood. "Not now, you understand."

Dainyl was afraid he did.

50

Mykel blotted his forehead as he stood in the late-day shadows of the old garrison's west wall. Summer had indeed come to Hyalt, and with it, cloudless days where the white sun burned down out of the sky with an intensity that reminded Mykel of Dramur, although the air in Hyalt was drier, so dry that unprotected skin exposed to the sun for more than half a glass burned and cracked. At least, Mykel's did, and that was one reason he stood in the shade. He had another report to write, and he needed to inspect the stables, such as they were.

Culeyt stood beside Mykel in the shade. "Hottest day yet."

"They'll get hotter." Two long weeks had passed since Mykel had sent off his last report to the colonel, and he needed to write and dispatch another, but little had happened—except for the continual, if intermittent, attacks by the giant cats at the quarry. So far, none of the Cadmians or quarrymen had been injured, but Seventeenth Company had lost one mount in the last attack. Mykel had observed and supervised, as necessary, various exercises and drills where the three more experienced companies had worked with the Hyalt companies. He had tried to keep the more strenuous drills earlier in the day, when it was generally cooler.

"I can hardly wait, sir."

Both turned as a wagon pulled up outside the garrison gate posts. Mykel read the sign on the side—TRORAL,

FACTOR—and blotted his forehead once more before stepping out of the shade toward the gate.

The council chief stepped down from the bench seat on the wagon, then turned to the driver. "I won't be long."

Mykel walked toward the factor and stopped. "Factor Troral."

"Majer."

"What can I do for you?"

"When you arrived, you talked of insurgents and that sort of thing." Troral looked hard at Mykel.

"We'd had reports, but we haven't found much," replied the majer.

"One of my men . . . his sister and her husband have a stead out to the northwest. He went out there yesterday night. No one was there. Part of the roof beams of one of the goat sheds had burned through and brought down part of the roof, and there were burned patches of ground, but no sign of anyone. Strange thing is that most of the flock was still there, and nothing seemed to be missing from the cellars."

"That is odd." Mykel didn't like that at all. It sounded like the miniature pteridons had attacked the stead, but he'd have to see to make sure. It had been two days since any company had been out northwest. Seven companies sounded like more than enough to patrol at once, especially if he had reduced patrols to individual squads, but after the incidents in the quarries and on the road, he had the feeling that the creatures might well overrun a squad—except for those under Rhystan. Even they would have suffered high losses, and he didn't like the idea of losing some of his more experienced troopers to the various creatures.

"When I heard that, I told him I'd tell you."

"That sounds like more than brigands," offered Mykel. "Where is this stead?"

"If you go north on the high road, you want to take the first lane west past the hilltop with the stone corrals—they're the only ones on the west side of the road. Then you follow the lane west, oh, a good three vingts until it forks. You take the south fork, the one on the left . . .

Mykel concentrated on listening, trying to fix the directions in his memory.

". . . and there are two piles of red rocks on each side of the lane that leads to the house. Gerolt's staying there with his eldest for now."

"We'll head out there in the morning," Mykel promised. "If there's trouble out there, we'd like to stop it before it gets worse."

"I'm sure that Gerolt will appreciate that."

Mykel wasn't so sure about that, especially if whatever company he assigned and accompanied found bodies. "We'll do what we can, and I appreciate the information, councilor."

"Might as well get some use out of you, Majer." Troral nodded, then turned and walked back to the wagon, where he climbed up onto the seat beside the driver.

Mykel turned. He had to get back to work, late as it was, especially if he was going to take a company on patrol in the morning.

"You think it's irregulars or insurgents, sir?" asked Culeyt.

"I hope so." But he had the feeling that what they would find was likely to be anything but insurgents.

In the meantime, he had matters to tend to, although he decided to put off writing a report to the colonel until after the morrow's patrol. That only made sense, he told himself, as he headed for the stables, blotting his brow once more.

51

Early on Tridi morning, Mykel sat astride the roan, surveying the walls of the new compound, so far as they had progressed. Behind him, Fifteenth Company was re-forming, after having watered all the mounts from the new stone troughs outside the foundations of the stables that had yet to be built.

The eastern side wall was complete except for the final capstone course. The western and the rear northern wall had but two or three courses of redstone above the level of the ground, and only the foundations were in place for the southern front wall and main gate. Within the uncompleted compound, the main barracks was the nearest to completion, with roofers setting the reddish gray tiles in place, although none of the interior walls had been completed beyond the main load-bearing beams and supports. He would have liked to have construction ongoing on a paved road to the high road as well, but that would have to wait. There were not enough stoneworkers nor enough stone coming from the quarry.

Still, the compound construction was proceeding in a satisfactory manner, as was the training of the two new Cadmian companies. Both were working under the supervision of Rhystan and Bhoral at the moment, patrolling and drilling along the south high road that ran east to Syan.

Mykel glanced westward. He had not slept all that well, with dreams about the ancient soarers, dreams where they were summoning him toward . . . something, but in those disturbing dreams he never quite got to the point where the soarers were.

He was also not looking forward to investigating what Troral had reported. While he had thought over the possibilities for a better formation for a company under attack by the small pteridons, the problem was simple enough. He was the only one who seemed able to kill the creatures, and that was clearly a result of whatever talent he had. Yet, too tight a formation and any of the beasts would take out more than a single Cadmian if Mykel failed to stop them. Too loose a formation and Mykel would be less effective. It was also apparent that the creatures were not all that intelligent, or they would have determined that he was the only real threat.

He turned his mount. "Undercaptain?"

"Yes, sir. Fifteenth Company stands ready," replied Fabrytal.

"Let's head out."

"Fifteenth Company! Forward!"

Mykel and Fabrytal rode down the gentle slope at the head of the column, with scouts riding out more quickly to take station more than two hundred yards ahead of them. There were no flocks on the grasslands nearby, in part because some of those lands now belonged to the Cadmians—or more properly, to the Marshal of Myrmidons, with oversight by the commanding officer of the First Cadmian Regiment, Mounted Rifles.

"You think we'll find anything out there?" asked Fabrytal a quarter glass or so later, after they had turned north on the high road.

"We'll find something. I hope it's traces of brigands or insurgents."

"Yes, sir. That makes two of us."

There was the slightest haze high in the sky, turning it more silvery, and the sun did not seem quite as intense as it had the past several days. On the other hand, the air was still, without the slightest hint of a breeze.

Close to a glass later, Mykel reined up short of the two piles of red rocks that, if Troral's directions had been correct, marked the stead. The lane beyond the rocks was not long, only a hundred yards. At the end of the lane was a small dwelling, no more than ten yards across the front and a third of that in depth. The roof was a patchwork of tiles of differing sizes and shapes, and the walls were of large mud bricks. The outbuildings were even more crudely constructed, windowless and with sections of roof tiles layered and pieced together along with odd-shaped wedges of roofing slate.

No one was outside, and Mykel could sense nothing untoward, no auras that reminded him of the creatures. He studied the lane itself. There were hoofprints, more than a few, but certainly not a large force. He would have judged ten riders.

"Sir . . ." offered Jasakyt, one of the scouts.

"Yes?"

"Those aren't any hoofprints I've seen. All the shoes are alike, but they're not Cadmian shoes. Ours have the twin diamonds."

Organized irregulars or insurgents? Mykel didn't like that at all. "Anything else?"

"Prints are pretty deep. Deeper 'n ours. Means that they're carrying gear, or they got bigger mounts or heavier riders, or all three. Can't tell much beyond that, except the prints are more 'n a day old."

"No newer prints?"

"Just one or two, and the shoes are different."

"We might as well see if anyone's here."

"Sir . . . best I send a scout in to see," suggested Fabrytal.

Mykel had to agree, if reluctantly. While he felt that Gerolt would not shoot, there was no sense in giving a spooked herder that chance. He nodded.

The undercaptain turned in the saddle. "Dyrsak, Senglat . . . ride in and see if anyone's there. Majer would like to talk to them."

"Yes, sir."

As the two Cadmians rode up the lane, a lean man in brown sauntered out from one of the outbuildings. He stopped and waited for the riders to reach him.

Mykel waited and watched until Senglat raised his hand and waved. "Wait here with the company," he told Fabrytal. "I'll ask about watering the mounts after I talk with him." If need be, Mykel could insist, but he preferred to ask. He eased the roan forward, down the narrow lane toward the two Cadmians and Gerolt.

As Troral had said, four blackened patches had seared the ground and structures, especially just beside the front door to the dwelling and at one corner of an outbuilding.

The patches on the ground were long and thin, more like black streaks or lines. Mykel looked more closely at the outbuilding. In places, the surface of the mud bricks had turned shiny, almost glassy, and above that area the roof beams had burned through. A third of the roof had collapsed into the small building.

Mykel reined up short of the man in brown. "I'm Major Mykel. Troral asked us to come out."

"Gerolt." The man's face was weathered and lined, and streaks of gray ran through his long hair and short, but ragged beard. His heavily scuffed boots bore leather patches of a lighter shade.

"Have you seen any sign of your sister or her husband?" asked Mykel.

"No. Except he was running from something. His boot tracks were far apart. They ended just short of the goat barn there."

"Mind if I look?"

"Help yourself."

Mykel rode slowly toward the building with the blackened corner and partly collapsed roof. As Gerolt had said, there were boot prints—and the prints ended in a larger black spot. Mykel had been afraid of that. He turned to Gerolt. "Troral said that not much was missing."

"Depends on what you mean. Maybe three, four goats and a lamb and ewe don't sound like much to him. They were a lot to Sis."

"Have you seen anyone else?"

"Haven't seen anyone, except you. Did see something glowing over the hills to the southwest afore it got full dark last night," Gerolt said slowly. "Thought it might have been fire. Went away too quick for that. Didn't smell smoke. Wasn't about to go looking."

"You haven't seen any strange tracks?"

"Told you. Haven't seen nothing. . . ."

Mykel asked several more questions, but Gerolt could provide no other information, and Mykel had the strong feeling that the man was telling the truth.

In the end, Mykel secured permission to water the mounts. After all the mounts were watered, Mykel and Fifteenth Company headed back southwest, in the general direction where Gerolt had said he'd seen the glow over the hills.

"What do you think, sir?" asked Fabrytal, riding on Mykel's right. "Could it be those flying things?"

"It's possible." Mykel doubted it. The blackened spots left by the pteridon-like creatures had all been more oval or circular, and the fires hadn't been hot enough to turn particles of sand into glass.

"What could it be?"

Mykel shrugged. He had an idea, and he didn't like it at all. "We'll have to see."

Just past midday, Mykel called for a halt on a flat area to the north of the second line of hills to the southwest of the stead where he had talked to Gerolt. Beyond the first line of hills had only been a swale a vingt or so across filled with the sparse grass that was turning from the green of late spring to the gold of summer—before it dried completely in the arid heat of late summer and harvest. The second line of hills held scattered junipers and bushes and rose higher than the first. Beyond the junipers was another set of hills, rocky and more rugged, and those were close to where the regional alector's compound was located, from what Mykel's memory and maps indicated.

Mykel had halted because men and mounts could use the rest. He would have liked water for the horses, but water wasn't all that plentiful around Hyalt. He had also ordered a stop because he could sense a faint reddish purpleness beyond the juniper-scattered hilltop. That feeling was similar to what he associated with alectors— or at least what he had sensed aboard ship. Whether it was emanating from just over the hilltop or from the more distant regional alector's compound he could not tell, but there was no reason not to look into it.

"Undercaptain."

"Sir?"

"Hold the company here. I'm going up the hill to check something. If you'd detail two men to accompany me."

"Yes, sir." Fabrytal's crisp response disguised his puzzlement. "Jasakyt, Olfyn . . . forward!"

Mykel concealed a smile. Fabrytal had picked Jasakyt because the scout had worked with Mykel before. Olfyn was far more fresh-faced, one of the latest replacements to Fifteenth Company before Third Battalion had left Elcien.

"We're going to ride up the hill. Olfyn, you'll be stationed halfway up, and Jasakyt will take position just short of the top."

"Yes, sir," murmured both rankers.

Mykel eased the roan off the road and started across the grassland. From a distance, the ground appeared to be unbroken tan and green, but when Mykel glanced down, he could see patches of red-sandy soil between the clumps of grass.

After they had covered a hundred yards and started up the gentle slope, Mykel glanced at the older scout, whose face bore a look of fatalistic resignation. "Jasakyt, why the long face?"

"Just thinking, sir."

"Thinking that you don't want this to be like Dramur?"

"I'd hope not, sir."

Just past the midway point on the slope, Mykel turned to the younger Cadmian. "Olfyn, you hold here, right over by that tree." He gestured to a juniper that was little taller than the head of a mounted Cadmian.

"Yes, sir."

Jasakyt and Mykel continued riding up the rise, avoiding the few rocks that protruded from the grass and sandy ground, and turning as necessary to avoid the scattered low brush and infrequent junipers. As they rode, Mykel could sense the growing strength of the purpleness on the far side of the hill.

"Right here." Mykel reined up beside another larger juniper, far enough below the hillcrest that he could not see over it—or that whoever or whatever was on the other side could not see him. He dismounted and handed the roan's reins to Jasakyt, then took his rifle from its case.

"Begging your pardon, sir, but shouldn't I . . ."

"Not this time, Jasakyt. I hope I won't be long."

As Mykel headed up the last part of the hill, he could hear the scout murmur, ". . . worse 'n Dramur, maybe."

As he neared the crest, he realized that he could have ridden farther, because the top was flat and extended another fifty yards before sloping down. While Mykel could see the top of the regional alector's building and upper part of the structure carved out of the redstone cliff behind it, the width of the hill blocked his view of the nearer valley south of him. The feeling of purpleness had grown ever stronger, and he moved more deliberately, changing his approach to take advantage of the scrub and low junipers.

When he finally reached the south side of the ridge, he settled behind the trunk of a juniper. For several moments, he just looked out. From what he could determine, at the base of the ridge was a group of men in shimmering silver uniforms, trimmed in black, with black trousers. They stood behind a cart that held a tripodal framework. Farther to the east, mounts were tethered to a line fastened between two junipers.

A line of light flared from the tripod and struck the side of an embankment carved from the lower part of the hill by a stream in wetter times. Mykel squinted. He wasn't certain if there happened to be a target set before the embankment. Were they firing the device at something or just calibrating it? And who were they?

The feeling of the purpleness was overwhelming, but he needed to know more. If he scuttled away now, what could he say or report? That he thought he'd seen strange troopers with a strange weapon?

He studied the hillside below, mentally charting a path that would bring him to a section of the lower ridge that overlooked the cart and tripod. Then, he slipped from behind the juniper and moved downhill and behind some brush, keeping low the entire time. From what he could tell, none of those below even looked up. From the brush he crept to behind another juniper, and then farther downhill behind more brush, all the time careful to keep his rifle from hitting the scattered clumps of grass or open stretches of sandy soil.

Mykel paused to catch his breath. From where he was, a good hundred yards below where he had started, he had a better view of the troopers below. Both his feelings and his eyes confirmed that the uniformed figures were alectors, and at least one was a woman. There was not just one target, but a line of crude man-shaped figures set up before the sandy embankment with three blackened patches on the embankment behind where previous targets had stood. Purplish energy pulsed around the oblong shape at the top of the tripod, from which protruded a short crystalline barrel.

SSSSS. . . . A line of blue fire seared across the brush above Mykel's head.

He flattened himself, trying to locate the source of the weapon that reminded him of the lightcutter sidearm used by Submarshal Dainyl. In instants, he could see a uniformed alector less than a hundred yards away, downhill and to his right. The alector stood beside a juniper, scarcely bothering to conceal himself.

Another line of blue fire flared, this time almost singeing Mykel's shoulder, so close that he could feel the heat.

"Wild Talent! Or an ancient!"

Mykel wasn't about to have a bunch of strange alector troops after him or his company—not with those weapons. He lifted his rifle, turning and aiming for a head shot. He'd seen what happened when crossbow bolts and bullets struck the uniforms and shimmering clothes of alectors. He squeezed the trigger evenly, firmly, concentrating and *willing* the shot home.

The alector dropped, his weapon tumbling from his hand.

Several of the other uniformed alectors turned. Mykel moved sideways, still on his stomach, and brought his rifle to bear on the tripod, and once more aimed and fired, concentrating and willing the shot home, directing it at the source of the energy.

Soundlessly, brilliant white light flared across the hillside, light so intense that Mykel was blind for several moments, and his eyes burned and watered. As his sight returned, first in sections, with gaps in his vision, he made out an area twenty yards across that had been seared black. The two remaining alector troopers were a pair who had been standing beside the horses, and they clutched at their faces. Of the others there was no sign at all.

Keeping low, Mykel scrambled and scuttled back over the hillcrest. Once he was on the flat top of the ridge, he didn't bother to crouch, but moved at a slow run toward the north side. Just before he reached the point where Jasakyt could see him, he slowed to a swift walk.

"Sir! You all right?" called Jasakyt.

"I'm fine." Mykel's eyes burned, and his vision was blurry, but he counted himself lucky at that. His fingers trembled slightly as he stopped to reload the rifle before he sheathed it, and he had to make an effort to mount.

"Are you sure you're all right, sir? What was that light?"

"One of those strange creatures exploded," Mykel replied. "Then some more did. It was bright enough that it was hard to see for a bit. For the time, though, we won't have to worry about them." What he said wasn't a total lie. There had been strange creatures and an explosion, and they wouldn't have to worry for now. What would happen later was another question, but he wasn't about to explain exactly what happened, not until he had a chance to think things through. He settled himself in the saddle and turned the roan downslope.

"If you don't mind my saying so, sir," said Jasakyt once he had pulled his mount alongside Mykel's, "I'm thinking this could be worse than Dramur."

"It could be, or it might not. We'll still have to see."

"Yes, sir." Jasakyt's polite response carried a tone of great doubt.

Mykel laughed. What else could he do? "You may be right, Jasakyt, but do they ever deploy us for something easy?"

"No, sir. But sometimes you hope."

When they reached Olfyn, the younger scout looked to Jasakyt and then Mykel.

"More of those creatures," Mykel said. "We don't have to worry for now."

The two scouts trailed Mykel, letting him get farther ahead, until Olfyn murmured to Jasakyt, "What . . . did he do?"

"You don't ask, and you don't tell anyone . . . majer's saved more asses by putting his on the line. Good commanders . . . hard to come by . . ."

Mykel smiled ironically. Just how long could he keep that reputation? Especially with alectors in strange uniforms and strange weapons appearing? What was he supposed to do? Should he just ignore it? If he did, and the strange alector engineers or troopers were part of what had been reported as an insurgency, then not warning someone could mean a disastrous attack for which no one would be prepared, with huge losses. If that happened, not only would far too many Cadmians and others be killed, but his own future would be problematical, and that was if he even survived. Yet he couldn't report too much to Colonel Herolt, and by the time the colonel relayed the report to the Marshal of Myrmidons . . .

He snorted, then looked toward the company, still waiting. Fabrytal rode toward him, meeting him a good score of yards away from the head of the column.

"Sir?" The undercaptain's voice was polite, but solicitous. "Were there more creatures over the hill?"

"For a time," Mykel lied, adding more truthfully, "I wish I knew where they came from and how we could handle them better."

"Yes, sir. It seems like only some shots bring them down. They must only be vulnerable in certain small places."

"Something like that," Mykel agreed. "We've done what we can here. We'll ride back to Hyalt along the road that swings westward." That route would carry them westward enough that a line of higher rocky hills would separate them from the regional alector's compound. The company would also cover some roads not patrolled before and reenter Hyalt from the southwest. He hoped that they would not encounter more of the strange creatures, but the more he knew about the terrain, the better.

As he rode, he tried not to think about the report he would have to write—and where and how to send it.

52

Immediately after morning muster on Tridi, Dainyl was headed to the Hall of Justice in the duty coach. He was less than pleased with having to use the Table so comparatively soon after the last attempts to trap him. Still, he needed information, and the only one who could supply it—that he could trust—was Sulerya. Delari was probably trustworthy, but Sulerya knew more, and for the risk involved, he might as well go to the more knowledgeable.

If Hyalt had been designed any other way, Dainyl's efforts to develop a tactical plan to deal with Rhelyn would have been far easier, but then, Hyalt's strengths and isolation were doubtless why Brekylt had made it the initial staging point in the west. One possibility was that Patronyl, the recorder in Tempre, was not fully trusted by Brekylt and the Duarch Samist, since Tempre would have been far more convenient. Another was that forces could not be concealed as easily in Tempre, but that Tempre would follow Hyalt if nothing were done to stop the infiltration.

The coach halted outside the Hall of Justice, and Dainyl stepped out under the hot and hazy day, one without a hint of a breeze.

"Do you want me to wait, sir?"

"No. I don't know how long I'll be."

"As you wish, sir."

Dainyl turned and walked up the wide stone steps and through the columns at the top, crossing the entry foyer, and then the main audience hall, where petitioners were already gathering. He made his way to the concealed entry, screened himself, and opened the hidden doorway to the chambers below. If someone saw him, so much the better, because he would have vanished in plain sight, and that could only reinforce the mystique about the powers of alectors.

At the bottom of the stone-walled staircase, he turned down the corridor toward the Table chamber.

"Cadmian business, Submarshal?" asked Zelyert, stepping out of his study, not quite blocking Dainyl's way.

Dainyl stopped. "Yes, sir. I should be back before too long."

The High Alector of Justice nodded, politely. "You define that rather loosely, Dainyl, but since it's clear there's no duplicity involved, I won't press. Not too much." Zelyert smiled.

"There are some irregularities involving some Cadmians on deployment, sir, and I need to clarify exactly what they may be facing." That was absolutely true, if incomplete.

"You'd prefer not to be more explicit?"

"When I'm gathering information, sir, I hesitate to speculate, because, if I'm wrong, I've given you incorrect information, and I end up looking foolish. I'd be happy to provide you the details of what I know so far."

"In a sentence, if you would."

"The Cadmians in Hyalt have reported some strange occurrences. I need to find out more in order to determine whether we should send back a Myrmidon squad." *If not an entire company, with a few additional measures, if such are even possible.*

"Hyalt?" Zelyert shook his head. "Best be careful there, Submarshal."

"I intend to." *But not quite in the way you think.*

The High Alector stepped back, looking very thoughtful, but said nothing further.

Dainyl would have preferred not to have mentioned Hyalt at all, but there was no avoiding it. While he could have held even tighter shields, that would have alerted Zelyert that his shields were in fact stronger than the High Alector realized and that Dainyl was hiding something. Dainyl just hoped that his reputation for caution would cover his unwillingness to be too specific.

Chastyl stood at one end of the Table chamber as Dainyl entered. "Good morning, Submarshal."

"Good morning, Chastyl." Dainyl gestured toward the Table. "You are not traveling?"

"No. I am just monitoring the Table. There have been more odd energies, but nothing like what happened last week."

Odd energies? Dainyl liked that not at all. Still, he smiled and stepped onto the Table, concentrating on the blackness beneath . . .

Immediately, he dropped into the depths beneath the Table, depths that now seemed more like a blackened purple haze. Simultaneously, he was aware of the purpled confines of the translation tube and that it rested, or seemed to, upon a wider area of blackness.

He pushed that perception away and focused on the orange-yellow of Lysia, linking himself there.

He thought he sensed a green flash and a longer purpled presence, but he slipped through the orange-yellow barrier—more like a curtain of mist than the obstacle it had once been . . .

. . . and found himself once more in Lysia. There was not even a trace of fog rising from his uniform, which only carried the faintest chill.

Sulerya stood in the opening to the hidden chambers, watching him. "I thought it might be you. That was a quick translation. I doubt if any of the recorders, unless they were looking closely, even noticed." She smiled. "What are you here for?"

"I'm sure you know. To talk to you."

"Not Sevasya?"

"Not this time."

"Then, come join me. Close the door behind you." She turned and walked up the hidden passage.

Dainyl found the Talent lock and closed the stone behind him.

Sulerya sat in one of the three chairs. Dainyl took the third chair, leaving one between them, but he turned the chair so that he faced her more directly.

"You look quite serious, Submarshal." The faintest hint of a smile lifted the corners of her narrow mouth, but the incongruous green eyes showed no amusement.

"I am. I'm here for advice and advisement."

"From a mere recorder?"

Dainyl snorted. "You are no mere recorder." He had his suspicions, but there was no point in declaring them. "That is not why I'm here."

"Then why?"

"Can any Table be isolated from the others? From outside the particular Table, that is?" asked Dainyl.

"No." Sulerya frowned. "Not unless enough Tables were shut down to destroy the entire grid, but you'd have nothing then, except perhaps a thin direct link to Ifryn. Each Table was designed to be brought on the grid independently."

"Then, they can be shut down."

"It has happened. Occasionally, a crystal or something has failed. It's not really a problem. The grid will operate with as few as ten Tables, but that risks instability. It initially operated with something like seven, but the translation volumes were far less. Supposedly, it could operate with six, perhaps five, but I wouldn't want to try to translate under those conditions."

"How did they translate in the beginning, then?"

"With great difficulty." Sulerya laughed. "It would have taken more Talent, and probably the help of recorders at each Table. I'm only guessing, though."

"Could you teach me how to shut one down?"

Dainyl could sense the recorder tightening within herself. She did not reply.

"You could, then. The question is whether you can trust me with that knowledge."

"You are asking a great deal, and it is knowledge that is not to be trifled with. It is also supposed to be retained only by the recorders and a few engineers."

Dainyl waited.

"Why do you want it?"

"Because it may be necessary to prevent a greater evil."

"That's a very convenient reply." Her tone was dry.

"Then I will ask of you what you asked of me. Until and unless you can verify independently what I am about to tell you, will you keep the information to yourself?"

"Even if I do not agree to instruct you?"

"Especially if you do not agree to instruct mc."

"I knew you were trouble when you first appeared here."

"Then why did you and your father help me?"

"As many have said throughout history, the alternative was worse. Besides," she added with a harsh but soft chuckle, "you are honorable, and so few are these days. You're also good looking, and I don't see many alectors who are both." After a moment, she said, "You were going to tell me why I should help you."

"We believe that Rhelyn is building some type of force in Hyalt. We believe it is part of Brekylt's plans against Khelaryt."

"There have been a number of translations there," Sulerya affirmed. "Although it is hard to determine for certain, many appear to be coming from Alustre, and some from Dulka."

"The force may well consist of alectors from Ifryn. We may have to isolate Hyalt, but how can we do that if they can send equipment and alectors through the Table?"

"Equipment?"

"Components of road-building equipment configured to act like skylances."

"You *know* this?"

"We know that strange things are happening in Hyalt. We know that significant engineering resources have been diverted in Alustre and Fordall, and that the engineers involved suffered fatal mishaps before they could be questioned by the High Alector of Justice. If we wait to make plans until everything is clear . . ."

"You're not planning something immediate?"

"Not without more evidence," Dainyl admitted. "I can't plan, though, until I know more about Hyalt and Tables. That's why I'd like to know how a Table can be turned off."

"I will teach you on one condition. That you promise *never* to reveal the technique or to discuss it with anyone who does not already know."

"That's recorders and Table engineers?"

"Master Table engineers."

"I agree. I hope I do not have to use it."

She smiled sadly. "That you, of all Myrmidons, have to ask, is a measure of how desperate times indeed are." She stood. "We'll go back to the Table."

Dainyl followed Sulerya, letting her reopen the hidden door. He noted that she added a second Talent-lock to the outer door.

"It won't stop the most Talented—like you—but there's no one around here that Talented."

Dainyl opened his mouth to protest.

"Don't say a word, Submarshal. You're more Talented than most High Alectors."

"I had very little Talent, so little that I was barely accepted into the Myrmidons."

"That's one of the secrets about Talent. The truly great Talents develop late. It's why it's easy for those in control to hold it. Those who might challenge them can be discovered before their abilities are fully mature. You were fortunate to spend so much time in the Myrmidons, where no one looked. You would have been discovered years ago if you'd been an assistant."

Dainyl wondered if his mother had known that—or if she'd just been disappointed that he had showed so little Talent early on.

"The Table looks solid," Sulerya began. "It is not. The surface is mirrorlike, but it is composed of thousands and thousands of identical tiny crystals that hold and store energy. The genius of their design is that they are stable when charged. They draw their energy from the world's very lifeforce. That is why there can never be many . . ."

Dainyl listened, intently.

". . . the controls are within the Table itself and, after the Table is first activated, can only be controlled by Talent . . ."

"Is there a special key or code?" asked Dainyl.

"No. The key is the combination of knowledge and Talent. A recorder also has the advantage of knowing how to operate the Table."

"Your father is effectively a recorder, then."

"Yes. Now . . . follow me with your Talent, carefully please."

Dainyl created the narrowest of Talent-probes to follow the one Sulerya had generated.

"Do you feel the octagonal crystal there? Don't touch it, even with Talent."

"I do."

"There's a brighter octagon, tiny, really, on the underside. If you pulse Talent through that small octagon, the Table will go into an inert state. It will retain power, but it cannot operate until a second, and stronger pulse is sent. Remember, it takes a moment or two before the Table powers down."

"That's it?"

"Would you have known even to look?"

Dainyl laughed. "No."

"Very few alectors have the control you have. Fewer still have the power, and without knowledge, power, and control, nothing would happen."

"What would happen if I pulsed a lot of Talent into that octagon?"

Sulerya was silent.

"I take it that means the crystal would shatter, or something. Is it hard to replace?"

She shrugged, wearily. "It takes time. The Table has to be bled of residual energy, or it will explode. The recorder can do it, or a Table engineer, but it would be several days. Too much energy, and the majority of the crystals would go, and anyone nearby or trying to translate as well."

"In short, don't do it."

"It's a good way for most alectors to commit suicide."

Dainyl understood. "What about using the Table to create Talent-force, either here or in the translation tubes?"

"I don't recall that being a problem for you."

Dainyl waited.

"Look for the paired pink octagons. If you focus your Talent through them, they draw on the power of the tubes themselves. That's why . . ."

"Using them can upset the grid?"

"That's right."

"Would you mind if I try?"

"Gently please."

Dainyl concentrated, thinking about the arms he had seen in Norda. Immediately a pair rose from the center of the Table. He'd pictured an alector's arms, but those rising would have fit on a figure twice the size of the Duarch. Quickly, he imagined a child's arms, and those before him shrank to the size of a full-grown alector. He smiled wryly and disengaged his Talent probe from the paired crystals. Something about the crystals . . . he felt unclean. He shook himself.

"Very effective, Submarshal."

"The crystals feel . . . slimy."

"I've felt that, at times, especially if I've used them for more than a few moments. I don't know why, though. Neither does Father."

"What about using the Table to view events?"

"Try the red diamondlike crystal and visualize a place. Not an alector, because we don't register unless we're near a Table. It was designed not to pick up Talented individuals."

Dainyl had considered trying to locate Majer Mykel, but thought again. Sulerya might catch that. Instead, he focused on Hyalt, the town square, trying to recall what it had looked like in years past when he had overflown it.

The mirror surface of the Table clouded, then filled with a swirled crimson purple mist, before looking down on a golden marble platform set in the middle of low walls, less than a yard high, running a hundred yards on a side, Dainyl judged. Beyond the walls on one side ran an enternastone road, sparkling in the mirror with silver. . . .

"The silver means there's some Talent there, the high road in this case," explained Sulerya.

On the other sides were simple redstone-paved streets. The platform held the usual statue of the two Duarches, side by side on a pedestal. The space between the low red-stone wall surrounding the pedestal and the outer wall flanking the streets was paved as well, but with bricks, rather than stone, and even from the height displayed by the Table, Dainyl could tell that more than a few of those bricks were missing.

He released the image, then decided to try for a view of the outside of Rhelyn's headquarters.

This time, the image showed just buildings, the separate headquarters building of redstone, standing on the flat before a sheer redstone cliff face, from which had been carved an ornate entryway. A single cart of a small and square design stood alone just outside a second doorway carved out of the cliff. On the cart was a tripod and a device that looked somehow incomplete, ending in a silver haze. No alectors were visible, except in two places, where other faint hazes of silver appeared.

"They can't be very Talented," Sulerya observed. "The Table doesn't show anything if they really are. That device on the cart—it's showing Talent . . . or lifeforce."

The equipment looked familiar. Dainyl swallowed. From what he recalled, it was a miniature version of the road-building equipment he had viewed in Alustre.

He eased his Talent from the crystal, and the image vanished, the Table surface returning to its mirror finish.

"You may need to act sooner than you thought, Submarshal."

"It could be," he admitted. "But we don't know for certain what that was, and I don't think that . . ." He shrugged.

Sulerya's brows knit in puzzlement. Then she nodded slowly. "You're going beyond, aren't you?"

"Looking beyond, I'd say. I've been given orders to develop a plan, but not to implement it without the orders of the Marshal."

"You're standing on the edge of the long translation, Submarshal."

Dainyl was well aware of that.

"By the way, you did that well, for a first time."

"I just followed your directions."

"You realize one other thing, don't you?"

Dainyl had no idea what she meant.

"You know as much as most new recorders." She laughed ironically. "My father might coopt you to become recorder in Lyterna, should anything happen to Myenfel."

In spite of himself, Dainyl winced. The thought of spending his life behind and under all that stone was appalling.

Sulerya laughed. "I was afraid you had no fears at all."

Dainyl didn't want to think about it. "Why were you so willing to teach me?"

"Because you have enough Talent to destroy a Table if you went at it wrong, and you're stubborn enough to do whatever you have to. This way . . . there might be a Table left when you're done dealing with Rhelyn."

"That's if we have to, and if I'm successful."

"If you have to, if you're not successful, it won't matter," she replied quietly.

There was definitely more than one meaning to those words.

"I need to get back to Elcien." He stretched.

"You probably do."

Dainyl stepped onto the Table.

The purple-black mist below was all around him, but he focused on the brilliant white of Elcien. He sensed a long green flash, and felt as though he were being observed, somehow, even though the translation felt near-instantaneous. The chill silver-white veil vanished, and . . .

. . . he stood once more in Elcien.

"That *was* quick," observed Chastyl. "I didn't even sense you."

"I'd guess some translations take less time." Dainyl shrugged and stepped off the Table.

"They do vary," replied the recorder.

Dainyl would have liked to have investigated the Table in light of his newfound knowledge, but was not about to with Chastyl standing there.

Instead, he nodded politely and departed. Thankfully,

Zelyert was not in the lower chambers of the Hall of Justice, or, if he happened to be, he did not seek out Dainyl. For that, Dainyl was grateful. He had no intention of revealing what he had learned from Sulerya. But then, except in a general sense, he had yet to determine how he could best apply that knowledge, because, if he merely translated into Hyalt and froze the Table, he would be trapped there amid scores, if not hundreds, of alectors not exactly friendly to him.

Outside, the haze had lifted, and the late midmorning sun beat down on Dainyl. He needed to get back to headquarters and try to figure out some way to neutralize Rhelyn. From what he'd seen, he didn't have that much time.

53

Late on Tridi afternoon, under a sky that had gotten progressively more hazy over the course of the day, Mykel rode into Hyalt, south past the square and then to Troral's factorage, where he reined up, dismounted, and tied the roan to one of the posts in front of the narrow porch.

The factor stepped out of the doorway just as Mykel took the first step onto the porch, wiping his hands on a clean canvas apron.

"What did you find, Majer?"

"There were signs of brigands," Mykel replied, "but someone or something must have scared them off. They left without taking anything, but some of the livestock wandered off. Gerolt wasn't happy about that, but it didn't appear that whoever attacked them went after the goats and sheep. There were also traces of some of the strange creatures."

"Aye. Gerolt said he feared such." Troral paused, then

looked directly at the majer. "Can you do aught about them?"

"We did. We destroyed them, but that won't bring back Gerolt's sister. We stopped on the way back and told him we'd killed them. I can't say that there won't be more, because I don't know where they're coming from."

"That's something none know." The factor shrugged, tiredly. "Folks have decided you're here for the better. There are coins, and you keep your men under control."

Mykel understood what Troral wasn't saying—that all of that could change. "We do what we can. How long Third Battalion will be here isn't up to me. The two Hyalt companies and the compound will stay, and that will mean a few more coins for everyone, what with food and forage." He grinned. "And they will need blankets."

"It will help." The factor's voice was almost glum.

Mykel wondered if the man ever sounded cheerful. But then, would anyone, living in Hyalt? "Were there any of the creatures prowling around before last summer?"

The factor shook his head. "None that anyone talked about. I couldn't say that there might not have been one or two. Every so often someone did disappear, but who could tell whether it was brigands or if they just walked off or took a coach and didn't tell anyone? They weren't the kind to be missed, if you understand what I mean."

Mykel did.

"How long before the compound is finished, do you think, Majer?"

Mykel almost smiled. Troral was really asking how long the town would be getting the coins that flowed in with the building. "I'd judge another three or four weeks to finish the walls. Longer than that for the stables. The crafters are just starting on the inside of the barracks, and nothing's been done on the headquarters building itself." The order of building had been Mykel's choice. "So . . . it could be harvest, or later." He shrugged. "I don't want to rush things so the work's not done right, but I don't want it to drag on, either."

"Till harvest or later . . ." Troral nodded solemnly. "Not too bad." He looked at Mykel with an expression just short of a smile. "You sure that you don't need more than blankets, Majer?"

"I didn't say we did or we didn't." Mykel grinned in response. "I have to see what we can afford on the draw I've been assigned. Building comes first."

"I can see that. Poeldyn says you're a careful man."

"As careful as I can be." Being careful did tilt the odds, but sometimes it wasn't enough, as Mykel well knew.

"All any of us can do." Troral glanced westward along the short street that led to the high road, then back at Mykel.

"There's truth to that. Have you heard anything else? Any other reports of brigands, insurgents or strange creatures?"

"You're asking me? Thought that was your job."

"The more eyes that are looking, the better we can do that job," Mykel pointed out.

"Suppose that's so." Troral shook his head. "No one's told me anything except Gerolt."

"If you do hear anything, I'd appreciate it if you'd let us know."

"Guess I can do that."

Mykel smiled politely. "Thank you. I need to be getting back to the garrison. I just wanted to let you know what we found."

Troral nodded.

After a moment of silence, Mykel stepped down from the porch, untied the roan and remounted. He turned the gelding back north, toward the old garrison.

He still had to write his report about the day's events, and that meant two reports—one to Colonel Herolt and one that would go directly to Submarshal Dainyl. The second report wasn't being careful at all, but Mykel had a definite feeling that being careful wasn't going to be enough, and he'd learned long before not to ignore feelings that strong.

The more he learned, the more worried he was getting. Supposedly, insurgents had killed the local garrison, but the regional alector and his staff had cleaned up the garrison—or covered up what had happened long before Mykel had arrived—and no one had mentioned that one squad leader with talents similar to Mykel's had not been shot, but burned. Had the unfortunate Borcal discovered the alector troops and been able to escape without their being able to identify who he was so that the entire garrison had to be eliminated? Or had he discovered something else?

But if that were the case, why had the marshal of Myrmidons sent the Cadmians back to build a new garrison? And if the alector troops near the regional alector's compound weren't known to the Myrmidons, to whom did they belong?

Mykel could only hope to avoid the local alectors and trust his messages reached Submarshal Dainyl . . . and more important, that the submarshal was not involved with what was happening in Hyalt.

For the moment, what else could he do, except be very careful?

54

Dainyl walked down the corridor in Myrmidon headquarters, glad that he wasn't outside in the early summer downpour that drenched Elcien. Since it was only just past mid-morning, there was a good chance it would pass before he was off duty and could head home to Lystrana. After several days of fretting and plotting, he had a plan for Hyalt. Whether it would work was another question. Whether he would survive it was even more problematical, but even Lystrana had not been able to help him come up with something better.

Ahead of him at the end of the corridor, Shastylt stepped out of the doorway to his study. "Submarshal?"

"Yes, sir?"

"A moment, if you will."

Dainyl followed the marshal into his superior's study, closing the door behind him. He stood and waited, sensing Shastylt's concern, but knowing that it was not directed at him.

The senior Myrmidon remained standing. He tilted his head, then frowned, before clearing his throat and speaking. "The Highest has just received a report that a wild lander Talent has appeared—or reappeared—north of Hyalt. This Talent appears strong enough to have killed one of the junior members of the Table staff there. The alectors there feel that the presence of the Cadmians and their own abilities will suffice, but they did wish to inform us."

Dainyl nodded slowly. Clearly, the recorder did not want Myrmidons in Hyalt. After his view of Hyalt from Sulerya's Table, incomplete as it had been, he had no doubts as to why. "How do they know that it is a lander wild Talent, as opposed to a wild translation?"

"Rhelyn did not bother to convey that information." Shastylt's voice was dry. "Doubtless, he felt we did not need to know that."

"He doesn't want Myrmidons down there. But if he doesn't, why report that at all?"

"Why indeed?"

Dainyl almost swallowed as the thought struck him, but he managed a smile instead. "Because he doesn't want us to actually see what this wild Talent is. Or find out from the Cadmians there exactly how many there have been?"

"Those are the most likely probabilities. He could be trying to delay any reaction on our part. Or he could be trying the exact opposite, drawing us into investigating and setting some sort of trap."

Dainyl could see both as possibilities.

"How is your plan for Hyalt coming?" asked Shastylt.

"I can set it into motion any time. Do you want me—"

"No. Not yet. If Rhelyn and Brekylt are setting a trap, they'll expect an immediate reaction. If they're stalling, we can still give them a little time."

Dainyl had to admit that Shastylt's analysis made sense, but only if they didn't wait too long, and he had no idea just how long too long might be. Then, he might come up with something better, if he had more time—although he had his doubts about that.

"Have you told anyone about it?"

"No, sir. There are a few who might suspect I am planning something, because I needed information, but I have not provided information that would indicate much." Dainyl hoped that was true, and doubted that Sulerya would reveal even what he had found out from her. "The fewer who know, the less risk to the Myrmidons involved."

"You're still a field commander at heart, Dainyl." Shastylt laughed. "Don't let that color your judgment too much. Sometimes, casualties are necessary."

"Yes, sir, but I prefer that they occur to the other side."

"That's fine . . . if we can determine exactly who is the other side."

"It appears that Rhelyn supports Brekylt. That would suggest he's not exactly one to trust, especially now."

"He never has been. His allegiance is to Duarch Samist. Such as his allegiance is."

Dainyl doubted that many of the senior alectors had firm allegiances, not after what he had been learning. Instead of replying, he merely nodded.

"Have you heard about any more appearances of the ancients?"

"No, sir. But . . . I only heard of those I reported when I visited various locales. It's not something that anyone reports."

"There's a great deal that no one reports. That is why we must act with caution."

"Yes, sir."

"I'll let you know when you need to put your plan for Hyalt into action. It won't be for several days, if not longer." The marshal glanced toward the window. "Rain or no rain, the Highest and I have to brief the other high alectors and Duarch Khelaryt."

"The best of fortune, sir."

"That would be useful." Shastylt paused. "Are all the preparations made for the administration of justice on Quinti?"

"The mace and garments are ready, and fourth squad will handle the prisoner."

"Good." Shastylt half-turned, signifying that the meeting was over.

Dainyl stepped out of the study, closing it behind him. He disliked administering justice, even if the condemned alector had murdered an indigen without cause.

As he walked back to his own study, he also considered Shastylt's words about casualties. They made a sort of sense, but there weren't that many alectors on Acorus, not so many that large numbers of casualties were that good an idea, at least not in Dainyl's judgment. And too many casualties among landers and indigens just reduced the total lifeforce of Acorus, which wasn't exactly desirable either, not when the Duarch wanted more lifeforce. More important personally, he really did not wish to be one of those casualties. That was another reason why he'd quietly requisitioned two more lightcutter sidearms—for "operational purposes."

55

Mykel looked up through the darkness at the ancient ceiling. His quarters were a small room in the corner of the garrison from which the doors and windows had vanished, as had all doors and windows, doubtless looted after the slaughter of the garrison. Only the intermittent hint of a night breeze occasionally wafted over him.

Somewhere beyond his vision, somewhere out in the darkness, he could sense shimmering amber-green, and this time he was certain he was not dreaming about the beckoning nature of that sense. He shifted his weight on his bedroll, feeling what seemed to be every grain of sand under the makeshift pallet. The back of his neck and his shoulders were damp, and a thin film of sweat covered his forehead. He wished that he could have sent off the report to the submarshal, but it was still two days before the sandox coach made its next appearance in Hyalt, and the coach would be far faster than any messenger he could send.

He finally sat up on the bedroll and glanced toward his uniform, hung on two makeshift pegs on the wall. A definite glow emanated from his belt—from the concealed slit that held the dagger of the ancients. Yet it was not a glow that any other Cadmian would have seen. That he also knew.

Should he follow the summons?

Slowly, he got to his feet and pulled on his uniform and then his boots. He'd seen enough in Dramur to know that, if the ancients wanted him dead, they didn't have to entice him. Besides, he had the feeling that he wasn't going to get much uninterrupted sleep until he went out to see what was happening. It could be just his imagination.

He checked his rifle, assuring himself that the magazine was full, and then strapped on the extra ammunition belt that he'd carried for years and seldom worn. He'd almost left it behind, trying to persuade himself that majers had no business carrying extra ammunition, but, in the end, he'd brought it.

He moved through the dimness, still surprised at the clarity of his vision in the darkness, but glad to have that acuity. Mykel could see the guard by the gate from well inside the courtyard. There were also two other wall guards, but they were stationed at the rear corners. He struggled to recall the ranker's name before finally coming up with it.

"Vaetyr . . . Majer Mykel here."

"Sir?"

"It's me." Mykel moved slowly forward, his rifle held with the barrel low.

"Ah . . . what can I do for you, sir?"

"I'm going out. I just didn't want to alarm you." Mykel laughed softly. "Or get shot when I return. I don't think I'll be long. I'm going up the hillside to take a look at things when people usually don't." That was true enough, if slightly misleading.

"Yes, sir." Vaetyr sounded more than a little unsure.

"Just keep alert. I shouldn't be that long."

"Yes, sir."

Mykel stepped out through the gate posts. He'd seen no reason to spend time replacing the gates when the old garrison was indefensible against a large force and when an attack by anything else was unlikely. He did circle well to the north because he wanted to stay out of view and earshot of the guard on the northwest rear corner post.

Once he was a good fifty yards north of the north wall, he stopped and looked back at the town. It was dark, without a single lamp or torch lit. Then he turned and studied the hillside to the west. Perhaps two hundred yards up the slope, on the broken redstone that formed an ill-defined hillcrest, was a glow—amber-green.

Mykel took a deep breath and resumed walking, picking his way carefully around the low scrub and the occasional juniper, his eyes, ears, and senses alert for any sounds or indication of brigands or other less than savory possibilities, such as the giant cats. The only sounds were those of insects, the occasional call of a brush owl, and the muted crunching of his own boots on the sandy soil.

As he walked, he wondered why no one had built higher on the hillside. The garrison could have been defended far more easily. There was no sign of any other structure. Hadn't Poeldyn started to say something about it?

He kept moving until he neared the small jumble of rocks that marked the hillcrest. While he neither sensed nor saw nor heard anyone or anything, he didn't like the idea of going farther. He stopped, looking around. The glow had been where he stood—or somewhere close.

Abruptly, he was surrounded by a haze of green.

The soarer was more beautiful—and less human—than he recalled. Hovering there before him, slightly more than half the size of an adult woman, she had green eyes that took him in and looked through him. Her hair was golden green, but he could not tell how long it was because it merged with the halo of power around her. For all the apparent light she created, he could see no shadows, and the air around her was cool, despite the warmth of the night.

She said nothing.

"You summoned me . . . or suggested I should come here," Mykel finally said, his voice low, barely above a murmur. Yet his words seemed to boom out.

You ignored that call almost too long.

"I didn't know what it was. At first, I thought I was just dreaming."

We are not dreams. If you would survive and prosper, you would do well to understand the difference between what you sense and what you imagine.

"Why did you call me?"

Mykel gained an impression of laughter.

Why not? Our interests are the same, although you do not know that. Why that is so we leave to you, but you will not learn that unless you learn more about your talent. There was a pause. *How did you know to come to this spot?*

"I followed the green glow."

You glow far more brightly than do we, for any who would look. You must learn to cloak what you are.

"A dagger of the ancients?"

That is only a name. The invaders, the ones you call alectors, will kill you if they sense what you are. They wish no rivals to their ability. They think of you as wild and untrained, a wild talent.

Mykel started to retort, then swallowed. The last phrase had been the very words used by the alector who had tried to kill him.

"But . . . why?"

You have seen how we and ours must feed. We take but a small portion of what they require. They will bleed the world dry long before its time.

Mykel wanted to protest, but decided against it.

You Cadmians are their herding dogs, to keep order among the steers.

"Why are you telling me this?"

Why not? If you learn to conceal what you are and watch and listen, you will understand. If you do not, you will die at their hands and weapons, as did the other. We would prefer to help those who will preserve the world, rather than destroy it.

"How am I supposed to conceal what I am, and how is one person supposed to do all that?"

Concealment is merely making sure that you do not send forth the energy of your being. One does not have to shout to the world that one exists. Just exist.

"One person?" prompted Mykel.

One person? In time you must find another like yourself. . . . If not, what will be . . . will be. . . .

The glow and the soarer vanished, and Mykel found himself standing alone in the darkness—except he could see that there was another glow. It came from him. Had it always been there? Had he just not recognized it? Or had the soarer done something to make him aware of it?

What could he do? Why did he have to do anything? Because he had no choice. Borcal had done nothing and died—that was the implication of what the soarer had told him. What "other" could there have been? But why did the alectors hate landers like him and Borcal?

They did. That was certain. He still recalled the image of fear and hatred on the face of the alector who had found him.

A grim smile crossed his lips as he began to walk slowly downhill. How could he just *exist*? How could he damp a glow when he didn't even know what caused it?

56

At a quarter past the second glass of the afternoon on Quinti, Dainyl left his study, wearing on his upper left sleeve the crimson armband that signified alector misconduct or blood wrongly shed, or both. The administration of justice was scheduled to begin at the third glass. As often before, the marshal had left Dainyl fully in charge of the proceeding.

Captain Ghasylt was waiting by the duty desk, where he was talking to Undercaptain Yuasylt. He stopped, straightened his crimson armband, and stiffened. "Submarshal, sir."

"At ease, Captain. Is fourth squad ready to escort the prisoner?"

"Yes, sir. They all have their sidearms and armbands. The prisoner was brought in two glasses ago. He's in the holding cell. The duty coach is standing by at the Hall of Justice. One of the Highest's assistants will be standing in for him."

Dainyl didn't like that at all, because the assistants weren't as Talented as the Administrator of Justice, and that would drag out the agony of the proceeding. Still, he nodded to Ghasylt. "Stand-ins all the way around."

"You're taking the marshal's position, sir?"

"Today." With a smile he hoped wasn't too ironic, Dainyl walked down toward the north end of the building to check the holding cell and fourth squad.

Finally, at a quarter before the third glass, Dainyl stepped out into the courtyard behind the headquarters building under high clouds that had kept the summer day from being as hot as usual. The breeze off the bay máde the courtyard almost too cool. Fourth squad would be escorting the prisoner, but the three remaining squads of First Company and their pteridons—less the Myrmidons flying dispatches—had begun to form up south of the flight stage.

Dainyl studied the flight stage, a circular gray stone platform in the center of the courtyard behind headquarters. It stood a yard and a half above the paved courtyard and also doubled, if infrequently, as the site for the administration of justice to alectors. The top of the platform was empty, except for the justice stand—a crossbar affixed atop a single post—set in place for what was to come.

After several moments, Dainyl turned to face south and the three squads of Myrmidons, ranked as closely as possible. Even so, each squad took a square thirty yards on a side, with the five Myrmidons lined up before their pteridons, blue wings folded back.

"First Company stands ready, sir." Ghasylt's eyes met Dainyl's.

"It won't be long." Dainyl took a last survey of First Company. The pteridons of fourth squad were ranked at the back, without their riders, since fourth squad would be undertaking prisoner escort duty. The area on the north side of the landing stage had filled with reluctant alectors from across Elcien, and at one side were three aides to the Duarch, doing their duty of noting all those alectors who were present—or more precisely, those who were not.

Among those present was Lystrana. Dainyl was less than pleased to see her. He worried about the impact on

Kytrana, but Lystrana wasn't far enough along in her pregnancy to be excused. Another four or five weeks, and she wouldn't have to view any administration of justice until Kytrana was a year old.

He looked at his wife, and, from across the courtyard, she returned his look with a smile. He couldn't help smiling as well, if but for a moment.

Finally, Dainyl turned. "Myrmidons, ready!"

"First Company, present and ready!" declaimed Captain Ghasylt.

After receiving the official report, Dainyl turned, standing at attention.

A last group of alectors hurried into the courtyard just before the third glass of the afternoon. All in all, Dainyl judged close to a hundred and thirty alectors—in addition to the Myrmidons—filled the area north of the flight stage, waiting.

Three deep chimes issued from the headquarters building, and the silence dropped across the courtyard.

The senior assistant of the High Alector of Justice stepped from the headquarters building. Acting in place of the High Alector as Administrator of Justice, he wore both purple tunic and trousers, with the black trim required for administration of justice. His upper left sleeve bore a crimson armband identical to the ones worn by the Myrmidons. Across his chest was a black sash. Behind him were two assistants, attired in a similar fashion, except without the sash. The first, an alectress, carried the lash, its black tendrils tipped with razor-sharp barbs. The younger alector who followed held the Mace of Justice.

The Administrator of Justice walked deliberately up the steps and onto the stone stage, setting himself three yards behind the empty justice stand.

"Bring forth the malefactor!" The Administrator's voice, barely a baritone, was nearly lost in the vastness of the courtyard, but the rear doors of the headquarters building opened. Undercaptain Chelysta emerged, two

Myrmidons immediately behind her. A barefooted alector in shapeless dark red trousers and shirt walked behind them, his hands manacled behind his back. Two more Myrmidons followed the malefactor.

Not a single murmur disturbed the courtyard as the Myrmidons escorted the malefactor onto the stage up to the justice form.

The Administrator of Justice watched intently as the Myrmidons unshackled the prisoner. While the Highest's assistant had considerable Talent, it was nowhere near the immense presence of Zelyert himself, but it was doubtless enough to deal with the malefactor, if necessary. The malefactor seemed volitionless as his wrists were clamped to the frame. Then, Chelysta placed the red hood over his head. The Myrmidons stepped back behind the threesome about to administer justice.

The Administrator took three steps forward and to the side, facing the prisoner. "We are here to do justice. You are here to see justice done. So be it." He addressed the alector strapped to the frame: "Sukylt of Elcien, you have abused those who trusted you. You have betrayed the trust placed in you by the Archon and the Duarches. You have deceived, and you have cheated all who live upon Acorus by your acts. For your crimes, you have been sentenced to die."

Almost without pausing, the Administrator turned to accept the lash from the assistant, who then stepped back. The other assistant brought forward the Mace of Justice, raising and then lowering it.

"Justice will be done." The Administrator of Justice raised the lash, and struck.

The barbs on the lash were sharp enough to shred normal cloth and flesh with one stroke. The lash was symbolic as much as physical because, as the lash struck, the Administrator used his Talent and the crystals concealed within the Mace to rip lifeforce from the malefactor, funneling it toward the pteridons formed up in the courtyard.

The direction of that lifeforce was sloppy, Dainyl

sensed, in a fashion that the Highest would not have appreciated, but Dainyl was not about to report that.

The Administrator needed a good ten strokes of the lash—twice what the Highest had ever required—before the figure in the T-frame slumped forward. Blood was splattered not only across his back and over the shredded remnants of the red garments, but across the stones of the stage as well.

Dainyl had stayed himself against the agony radiated across the courtyard, and still found himself close to retching. He could sense Lystrana's discomfort as well, and more than a half score of watching alectors had collapsed.

One last stroke of the lash followed before Dainyl sensed the emptiness that signified death, a relief after the extended flogging.

"Justice has been done." The Administrator nodded to the assistant with the Mace.

The assistant stepped forward and directed the Mace at the figure in the frame. Pinkish purple flowed over the dead alector, who was already turning to dust—another bit of sloppiness. A flash of light followed, and only the empty frame remained.

Immediately, the Administrator walked off the flight stage, followed by the pair of assistants. Chelysta and the Myrmidons waited a long moment before following.

Dainyl turned to face Captain Ghastylt. "First Company, dismissed to quarters."

"Yes, sir. First Company stands dismissed to quarters."

Dainyl turned and walked toward headquarters.

Most of the alectors who had watched the dreadful ceremony had left, but Lystrana remained, standing beside the courtyard doors to the headquarters building. Her face was as pale as it was possible for the face of an alector or alectress. Dainyl moved toward his wife slowly, so that they were nearly alone by the time he reached her. The Myrmidons had all returned to quarters or the pteridon squares with their pteridons.

"Are you all right?" asked Dainyl.

"I will be." She paused, then added, "That . . . was terrible. You could have done a far better job."

"I don't know that I'd ever want to."

"If it has to be done, it should be quicker."

"Maybe the Highest doesn't want it that way," replied Dainyl in a low voice. "He may well want it done in a terrible fashion upon occasion. People don't always understand if things are too easy or painless."

Lystrana nodded slowly. Some of the color had returned to her face. "If he dragged out the administration of justice, he'd seem incompetent or willfully cruel and sadistic."

"I had that thought," admitted Dainyl.

"It still bothers me."

Dainyl's stomach remained knotted, but there was little point in saying so. Lystrana could sense that. "Will you be late tonight?"

"Not that I know. My highest is in Ludar. They all are, even Khelaryt."

Dainyl frowned.

"I know. It doesn't seem wise, but perhaps he feels that it is a way of showing strength."

"Or he's doing it now because it would be more dangerous later. That way, he can request the next meeting of all the High Alectors and Duarches be in Elcien."

"If Samist refuses then . . . it might erode some support."

"It might." As he spoke Dainyl doubted that he would ever be able to calculate such intricacies of position and power—or want to do so.

"I need to go, dearest." Lystrana extended her hand.

Dainyl took it, then offered his arm. They walked around the headquarters building and toward the front gate.

"You'll be all right walking back?" he asked when they reached the gate.

"The walk will do me good." With a smile, she stepped back, but not before squeezing his hand.

He stood and watched her still-lithe form for a time as she walked along the boulevard back toward the Palace of the Duarch. Then he turned. He hoped that the rest of the operations reports had arrived with the latest dispatches, although whether they would tell him anything of value was problematical.

57

Three long days had passed since Mykel had met the soarer in the darkness near the hilltop to the west of the old garrison. The days had been quiet, with no sign of strange creatures in the quarry for nearly a week. The new compound was coming along well enough, with the major work near completion on the barracks. Mykel had even designed and drawn an emblem for the two Hyalt companies, one that both captains did not dislike.

For all that, Mykel remained uneasy.

In thinking over what had happened with the ancient soarer, he had realized just exactly what Poeldyn had not said on the day Mykel had first met the two craftmasters. Poeldyn had said that the hilltop was unlucky. Close as it was to Hyalt, with a view of both the town and the hills farther to the west, and even of the low mountain above and behind the regional alector's compound, Mykel should have realized earlier that more than ill chance was associated with the hill. From what he could tell, the soarers generally appeared in the heights. Although the hilltop behind the old garrison was not all that high, it was the highest point near Hyalt on a gentle ridge that extended in both directions, gently sloping back under the town to the east and into the rolling hills to the west. As he reflected, Mykel realized it was really the only hill or ridge that ran east to west, another fact he should have considered and hadn't, probably because it did not stand out in height or ruggedness.

The other problem Mykel had was what the soarer had suggested—that Mykel had the same interests as the ancients, and that his own interests would not be served by the alectors. How could he trust that? Yet . . . after having been attacked by the strange alectors, and after Rachyla's warnings, and after what he had seen in Dramur about how the alectors manipulated landers and seltyrs, how could he not be wary of alectors, even those in the Myrmidons? Yet . . . it was likely that Submarshal Dainyl had saved him not once, but twice.

In the end, one thing was clear. The soarer had been correct about his talent before he had recognized it for what it was, and her advice about concealment made sense, no matter what else happened. The only problem was that after three nights Mykel had made little progress in discovering how to damp the greenish glow that emanated from him. The night before he had walked back up the hill, but there had been no sign of the soarer—only the faintest hint of her amber-green and all too much of his own deeper and brighter shade of green.

He was more than a little worried, because there was no telling when he might next encounter an alector, and because of the strange creatures, the battalion's companies had to continue their patrols, although he had told his captains to give a wider berth to the area around the regional alector's compound, on the grounds that the RA had the ability to protect his own area and that Third Battalion had been dispatched to protect Hyalt specifically.

Even so, that would only purchase some time.

In the darkness of his temporary quarters, Mykel held the dagger of the ancients in his hand. Perhaps, if he could find a way to damp the glow of the miniature ancient weapon, he could apply that technique in some fashion to himself. The dagger was only metal, and yet it held an amber-green feeling, almost as if it were alive, with an obvious glow emanating from it, if only to his senses.

Except it had not been obvious just to him. Rachyla had been able to feel it as well. Did that mean that she had a talent similar to his? Surely, she should have known that. He shook his head. She might, and she might not. That could wait. With more and more alectors around Hyalt, he needed to concentrate on the task at hand.

First, he concentrated on sensing the dagger, what it was, and what it was not. It felt like steel, in a fashion, and yet it felt partly alive, and the sense of green issued from whatever about it generated the feeling of life. That realization, too, was more of a feeling that anything he could have described.

Next, he closed his eyes and focused his sense of feeling on himself, and what he was.

There was a greater amplitude, far greater, of the green, and no sense of the metallic, confirming his understanding that the green was tied to life. Had the soarers imbued the knife with the force of life itself?

From that, questions cascaded though this mind, and he pushed them aside for the moment, bringing his concentration back to the dagger and to himself. How could one damp out the very force of life itself?

One couldn't, not without damping out life itself. That meant either changing the color he emanated from green to the colors that radiated from most others or finding some way to block—or shield—the energy. Would changing his color limit his talent? If so, he certainly didn't wish that. He was having enough trouble surviving with his abilities. Trying to do so without them was something he wanted to try only as a very last resort.

But how could he create a shield?

What about something that turned back the glow? He tried to visualize such a barrier and then looked down.

The greenish light that he sensed but did not see remained.

Could he combine the green with a darkness, a blackness, that resembled the aura of most men? This time, he attempted to weave together the black and green. He looked down, then chuckled softly. Why was he looking down? He wasn't really "seeing" the glow, but sensing it. Yet his mind was interpreting the sensation as if he were, and what he sensed was more like a sieve of blackness through which streamed rays of green.

What about using the blackness to turn the green back?

That didn't work, either.

For a time he stood in the darkness, once more thinking. The green was far stronger than anything black, and that meant it was the key. What about making the black a framework, but twisting the green back inward and weaving it together?

As he concentrated once more, he tried not to dwell on the manifestly illogical impossibility of what he was doing. After all, it was impossible for men to radiate a greenish glow that only alectors and a few men could sense.

His forehead beaded with pinpoints of sweat, and he felt warm all over, but the greenish glow was gone. He could sense it, but it was contained within himself, not radiating beyond him. He could also tell that it took a certain effort to maintain that shield.

He released the shield with a slow deep breath.

After several deep breaths and a time of resting, he rebuilt it. Doing so was easier the second time, and easier still the third time he did so. On the other hand, he was beginning to feel light-headed. He let go of the shield and sat down on the bedroll, his back against the rough and stained plaster of the wall.

He'd need practice—much more practice—before he felt comfortable with the shield. Still . . . he had figured out a way to keep himself from being noticed for a short period of time—at least from a distance. He had his doubts as to whether his shield would bear scrutiny if an alector were in the same chamber with him.

He felt tired, and sleepy. He had barely stretched out on the bedroll before his eyes closed. His last thought was that he hoped he didn't have to rely on the glow-shield any time soon.

58

Despite his exhaustion from his efforts with the glow-shield, Mykel had slept uneasily and concealed a yawn as he rode beside Rhystan, out toward the new compound. Rhystan and Sixteenth Company would be working for a glass or so with the Hyalt companies in the area to the north of the compound before Rhystan took the Second Hyalt on patrol to the east later in the morning. Mykel would take the First Hyalt on patrol north on the high road. He wasn't about to take them anywhere to the west. Seventeenth Company was on quarry duty, while Thirteenth Company was on patrol duty at the new compound. Fifteenth Company was patrolling the high road to the south and east of Hyalt. Fourteenth Company had light duty—at the old garrison.

"Been quiet lately," observed Rhystan.

"I'd like it to stay that way."

"You're looking too worried for that, sir."

"I probably am," admitted Mykel, wondering once more if he really should be a battalion commander. "There are too many things that no one can explain."

"Suoryt said you sent off two dispatches last week, at the same time, and you gave one of them to the alector on the sandox personally."

"Can't keep secrets among Cadmians." Mykel smiled wryly. "I sent a copy of my report about the missing holders to the Submarshal of Myrmidons. There were some things at that stead that bothered me."

Rhystan waited.

"Some of the burn marks were the same as the ones when the submarshal took out Vaclyn." Mykel kept his voice low. "Those lightcutter sidearms are only issued to colonels and above, I've heard."

"Could they have been pteridon skylances?"

"The angles were wrong."

"I was afraid you'd say something like that, sir. You think the creatures have weapons? Or that we have rogue Myrmidons loose?"

"I don't think it's either," Mykel replied. "That's why I wanted the submarshal to know."

"And why we have four guards on duty in a town that doesn't have a lamp lit much after two glasses past sunset."

"Something killed the last garrison, and I'd prefer not to give whoever or whatever it is another chance. I'll be happier once we have the walls and gates finished in the new compound—and the piping from the spring."

"How long do you think that will be?"

"The water system is done, and so are the walls, except for the capstones. The gates can't go up until the paving stones are in place, and we're waiting for more stone from the quarry for that."

"The mounts will tear up the courtyard if it's not paved."

"Poeldyn says they can pave it by sections, and we won't move in until one section is done. We'll set up tielines and temporary corrals on a paved section."

"That should work. Wouldn't be any worse than what we've got in the old garrison."

"We'll also have more space," Mykel replied. The compound would still be crowded, because it was only designed for four companies—twice the permanent complement—but that was an improvement over an ancient garrison built for two companies.

As he and Rhystan rode up the packed dirt trail that

might someday be the road to the compound, if Poeldyn's quarrymen ever cut enough stone, Mykel surveyed the south walls and the gate area. The heavy iron hinges for the gates had been set in place, and then reinforced and mortared, but it would be at least several days before they could bear the weight of the gates. Still, it would far longer than that before the area around the gates could be paved and the gates installed, but he definitely wanted to be able to close the compound gates.

As he shifted his weight in the saddle, Mykel swallowed another yawn. He did need a better night's sleep—for about a week—but doubted he was going to get it any time soon. He turned to Rhystan. "I'm going to talk to the craftmasters. Go ahead with your training. I'll join you when I'm done."

"Yes, sir. Good luck."

"Thank you." Mykel continued onward. Behind him, Rhystan ordered the three companies westward and around the compound walls.

Thirteenth Company's second squad was deployed on the flat just below the southern walls of the compound.

"Majer, sir!" called Jovanyt, the grizzled squad leader.

"Just headed in to talk to the craftmaster. Where's Undercaptain Dyarth?"

"He's out on the east side, across the stream, with fourth and fifth squads. Herder was trying to graze his flock too close to the walls."

"I'll see him later."

"Yes, sir."

Once he was through the gate-gap in the walls, Mykel rode toward the barracks, then dismounted and tied the roan to the temporary railing where the single cart horse was tethered. He walked across the sandy soil that held deep ruts. Rhystan was definitely right about the need for paving the courtyard, and they'd probably need broken stone and sand packed down as a base under the paving stones. He'd have to explain that in a progress report, because the plans didn't call for anything like that. Even in building a compound, matters didn't turn out exactly as planned.

Styndal stood back from the main doorway to the barracks. He was talking to a crafter, a carpenter from the tool belt. ". . . wall pegs have to be oak . . ."

Mykel waited until the crafter departed before approaching the craftmaster. "Good morning."

"Such as it is, Majer. What can I do for you?"

"Is there a tiler here in Hyalt?"

"A tiler?"

"One who can do decorative mosaics, one that can be set in the wall above the main door to the barracks there."

"Choshyn could do that, so long as it's not too complicated."

Mykel extracted the hand-drawn design from his uniform tunic. "This is the design."

Styndal took it. "Don't see a problem with that, Majer. Another gold, maybe two. Good thing you told me now. Another day or so, and it would be costing more."

"How long before the barracks are ready?"

"The end of next week . . . if your men don't mind sleeping on the floor. Bunks will be another week past that. Could be two."

"They're sleeping on the floor where they are," Mykel pointed out. "What about the stables?"

"Walls are barely past the foundations. It won't take as long as the barracks. There's less finish work. I'd say another month, what with everything else going on. Could be into harvest."

That didn't surprise Mykel. "Remember, there will still be work after that."

Styndal grinned. "You'd not be getting matters done this fast were there not."

"I had that feeling, Craftmaster."

"You still want the stone squares done last? And in the back?"

Mykel noted that the craftmaster had never used the

word "pteridon," or even alluded to the creatures. "Yes. Pteridons don't visit Cadmians often, and I'd rather not have them too close to the barracks or the headquarters building."

"Pretty small for headquarters."

"This is a small outpost for Cadmians."

Styndal just nodded.

After finishing with Styndal, Mykel made a slow and careful inspection of the compound, starting with the new barracks, and winding up with the outside walls. Everything looked—and felt—as it should. He returned to the roan and led the gelding to the water trough and let him drink before he finally mounted.

He'd just ridden out the gap in the walls that would be the smaller north gate when he saw Undercaptain Dyarth riding toward him. He glanced farther north, where Rhystan and the two Hyalt captains were practicing full-company maneuvers, then back to Dyarth, who was turning his mount to ride alongside Mykel.

"Herders!" Dyarth snorted. "Begging your pardon, Majer. He claimed that he'd always grazed here. He didn't see why he couldn't now. We weren't using the grass, and he hated to see good grass go to waste. There's so little of it."

"He's right about that. Around here, anyway," Mykel pointed out. "What did you tell him?"

"Just what you told us. That the land for a half vingt out from the compound walls belongs to the Cadmians and the Marshal of Myrmidons and that the grass is for our mounts. He didn't like it, but he understood the business about the mounts."

"How are your men taking to guard duty here at night?"

"Most of them prefer it. They say that they can get more sleep—those not on duty, I mean, and it's cooler here."

"Good." Mykel nodded. "I'm going to be taking the First Hyalt out on road patrol. You'll be in charge here once Captain Rhystan leaves." That was obvious, but Mykel wanted to reinforce it.

"Yes, sir." Dyarth's head bobbed up and down, before he abruptly caught himself, and grinned sheepishly.

With a smile, Mykel turned the roan back northward toward the flat where the three companies were forming up into road order.

Captain Cismyr rode forward to meet Mykel. The captain had the olive skin that distinguished many of those born and raised in the warmer south of Acorus, along with dark brown hair and eyes. His aura, Mykel noted to himself, was a rich brownish-yellow.

"Majer, First Company stands ready."

Mykel replied with a nod. "We're going to take the high road north for about five vingts, to the farm road that heads eastward . . ." He'd briefed Cismyr earlier, but he'd found that it always helped to reconfirm such details. ". . . the patrol has several purposes. First, it's to establish the Cadmian presence here and to pick up any brigands we might run across. It's also part of making sure you and your men are familiar with all the lanes and roads—or at least as many as we can find before you're on your own . . . and to do it with a large force until we have a better handle on what areas require more men and what require fewer."

"Yes, sir."

"Let's head out."

"First Company! Scouts forward!"

Mykel rode beside Cismyr, observing as the captain ordered the company westward to the high road and then northward.

They had been riding the high road for a quarter glass when a large wagon appeared on the road horizon, more than a vingt ahead of the scouts. One of the scouts rode back toward the company, pulling his mount around to ride beside the captain.

"Spirit wagon, sirs. Wide enough to take more than half the road."

Mykel said nothing, waiting.

Cismyr surveyed the road, then nodded. "We'll pull the company off the road on that low rise ahead. The men won't mind a breather. The mounts won't either." He looked to Mykel. "Unless you have another idea, sir?"

"No. It's usually better not to string a company out in single file, and you won't have much support from the merchants and locals if you force their wagons off the road for routine patrols." Mykel had seen Majer Vaclyn do that a few times, and he'd never seen the reasoning behind it. But then, that was just another example of one of the reasons why Vaclyn was dead.

After the company reached the low rise and drew up in formation, Mykel eased the roan to the higher side of the rise, from where he could get a better view of the surrounding terrain. The captain followed his example.

Despite the high and hazy silver clouds, the morning was already hot, and Mykel was sweating enough that his uniform was sticking to his shoulders and upper back. He blotted his forehead and then took a swallow from one of his two water bottles. Dramur had taught him that one wasn't enough.

Across the high road, to the west, were rolling hills, each line of hills getting higher and drier until they merged with the reddish rocks of the foothills to the east side of the Coast Range. Behind him, to the east, the hills were more like gentle rises, with slightly more grass than those to the west. There were no huts or steads in sight anywhere to the north, suggesting that the regional alector had prohibited them and allowed only seasonal grazing.

He looked back to the high road and the approaching wagon, drawn by four draft horses. As it neared, Mykel noted that the entire high-sided and covered wagon body was painted a rich brown. On the side panel, painted in yellow, were the words *Spyltyr & Sons, Spirits*.

"They can't have that many buyers in Hyalt, can they?" asked the captain.

"Probably not, but they are moving quickly, and the

horses aren't lathered. The wagon's close to empty. They're probably returning to Syan to buy brandy and wine there, and they're carrying just enough to sell to the inns and taverns in Hyalt, I'd guess. They'll travel the other side of the square when they're full, from Syan to Vyan and then Krost, and then either to Tempre or up north to the towns on the Vedra. They might be carrying other goods south as well, maybe spices or shimmersilk, things that are light but valuable."

"Dreamdust?"

Mykel laughed. "Who could pay for that here? Or even in Syan?"

"Filthy stuff, but they must make thousands of golds on it."

Mykel had no idea what the profits on the drug might be, only that people seemed to pay far more for spirits and drugs than for food and clothing. Some people, anyway.

Before long, First Company was back on the road heading north.

They didn't reach the target road until late midmorning. The narrow road, unlike most farm roads, ran along the flat top of the gentle rise that angled east-northeast. The slopes on each side were so gentle and gradual that it was easy to overlook the fact that the rise was really a long ridge that separated the grasslands south of it from the even more arid plains to the north. The irregular surface was barely wide enough for two Cadmians abreast, riding slowly.

While there was one set of recent cart wheel ruts on the road, there were no signs of riders or boots on the sandy soil. The road had been used, but where did it lead? Mykel looked eastward, where, in the distance, there *might* be a hamlet at the base of the ridge to the north, just west of what looked to be a small forest.

Mykel wasn't certain, but, every so often, he thought he felt *something*, a blackness of some kind, but it seemed to be beneath the road. Was he just imagining it? Ever since Dramur, he'd been asking that question of himself more and more, yet all too much of what he would have once called imagination had turned out to be all too real—if in ways he once never could have predicted.

He blinked. Had the day gotten darker? He glanced toward the sun, not looking at it directly, but trying to gauge if the clouds around it had thickened. They had not.

"Rifles ready," Mykel ordered, looking at Captain Cismyr, then unsheathing and checking his own rifle.

"First Company! Rifles ready!" The captain looked at Mykel, not quite quizzically.

Mykel tried to sense from where the attack might come—if it came at all.

Crack! Although the sound/feeling jarred Mykel, he could tell no one else heard or felt a thing.

He glanced back over his shoulder. There, in the western sky, less than a hundred yards behind the last squad of First Company, were three flying creatures. They were unlike anything he had ever seen—even those around the quarries or the miniature pteridons that had attacked Seventeenth Company earlier. Each had the snout of a miniature sandox, except with a silver-purple horn that gleamed in the sunlight, and a long and narrow body like that of a snake, but a snake with two sets of wings similar to those of the miniature pteridons.

"Company! Halt! To the rear! Full turn! Fire at will!" After the briefest hesitation, Mykel added, "In the sky above the road!"

"Company! Halt!" echoed the captain.

The winged snake-oxen dived toward First Company.

Although he hated firing over the company, Mykel aimed at the lead creature, concentrating on it, willing his shot home.

The creature exploded into a blue and purple fireball and tumbled from the sky into one of the thicker patches of grass on the south side of the road. Blush flames flared skyward, along with grayish smoke.

The rankers began to fire, if belatedly. Several shots struck the other creatures, seemingly without effect.

Concentrating on the second creature, Mykel fired, and it, too, dropped from the silver-green sky, striking the road within two or three yards of the rearguard that had become the vanguard with the company's reversal of direction.

Mykel's third shot was true enough, but the creature burst into bluish flame and pinwheeled sideways before bursting into the same bluish flame and slamming into the mount of a Cadmian ranker in fourth squad. Before either Mykel or Cismyr could issue an order, his mate tried to help the ranker from his doomed mount.

The two were far too slow, and both men—and both mounts—flared into intense oily bluish flame.

Mykel stood in the stirrups. "Keep clear of the blue flame! Keep clear of the blue flame."

"Frigging creatures!" Cismyr swore under his breath.

Mykel rode back along the side of the narrow road, knowing there was little he could do, but also knowing that the men needed the gesture. As he rode, he reloaded, although his senses told him that there were no more creatures nearby.

The two officers reined up short of the burning pyre.

Mykel swallowed hard, trying to keep the bile from rising in his throat, forcing himself to get past the reaction from the odor of burning flesh. Several of the troopers had not been able to, and others looked yellowish green.

As before, not even ashes remained when the fires burned out, just black patches of ground where nothing grew—and where nothing would for some time, Mykel suspected.

"Sir?" asked Cismyr.

"There's nothing we can do for them." Should he finish the patrol? He couldn't break off every patrol whenever the strange creatures appeared. In some ways, he regretted that he had with Seventeenth Company after the attack of miniature pteridons. That had been a bad example. "We have a patrol to finish."

"Yes, sir." The captain swallowed. "First Company! To the rear, full turn! Forward!"

The two officers rode on the shoulder past the rankers until they were once more at the head of the column, if behind the scouts. They rode silently for a good half glass. Mykel surveyed the grasslands, and the sky, but saw and sensed nothing—except a few scattered flocks of sheep and the small hamlet ahead.

"It was a good thing there were only three," Cismyr finally said.

"Yes," Mykel agreed. "Seventeenth Company faced something like half a score."

"Half a score?"

Mykel nodded. "You can ask Undercaptain Loryalt about it when you get a chance." He didn't want to say much more, particularly since he had a very uneasy feeling about what had just happened.

The strange creatures at the quarry could be killed by anyone—provided enough bullets struck them. But only Mykel's shots seemed to be able to bring down the flying monsters. Yet the ones that flew had only attacked companies Mykel had accompanied. At least, so far.

59

On Decdi, Mykel had given all the companies, with the exception of the duty squads and companies, a full stand-down day and town leave in Hyalt for those not on duty—and the admonition that anyone who abused that leave or caused trouble would answer to him personally. Outside of three rankers who passed out and missed muster on Londi and then had to be carted back, there were no reports of trouble. Mykel sent all three to the quarry to serve as laborers for the stone-cutters for a week.

Londi turned out much the same as any other day, if slightly cooler, because of heavy low clouds that promised rain . . . and did not provide any. The intermittent breezes swirled dust into the air everywhere, and at times, Mykel could only see a few vingts, even from the knoll-like mesa of the new compound.

Dyarth and Thirteenth Company had quarry duty—and reported no sign of any of the cat creatures, nor did any of the road patrols encounter either brigands or flying creatures. Troral sent a note to Mykel to inform him that the two hundred ten blankets for the Hyalt companies would be arriving on the Sexdi a week hence—well before the bunks and mattresses would be ready.

After returning to the old garrison with Fourteenth Company slightly before sunset, Mykel and his men ate local produce and mutton scarcely better than field rations. After supper, Mykel received evening reports.

Later, after drafting his own daily report, he inspected the garrison and the night guards two glasses after sunset, and then retired to his chamber. There, he pulled off his boots, but did not disrobe. Sitting on his bedroll, he leaned back against the rough-plastered bricks. When would his dispatch with the information about the strange alectors reach the submarshal? More important, what, if anything, would the submarshal do? And if the Myrmidons did nothing, what should Mykel do? What could he do? Just avoid the northwest close to the regional alector's compound? But what if the regional alector requested his presence?

He'd been practicing trying to conceal his aura, but even with what he'd managed, he doubted that concealment would be that effective in close quarters.

A flash of amber-green appeared from somewhere. *Danger . . . danger approaches . . .* After those few words, any sense of the amber-green vanished.

Mykel bolted upright. That had been a clear message from the soarer, or one of them, but he had no sense of a continuing ancient presence, and that was as disturbing as the brief message itself. He pulled on his boots and then took out his rifle. After hesitating a moment, he pulled on the ammunition belt.

Then he slipped out of his doorless space and along the darkened inner wall of the garrison courtyard. The night was quiet, with only the sounds of various insects, and occasional low voices from the far side of the courtyard where several rankers crouched in the corner playing bones—the circle lit by the smallest of lamps. Even though gambling in quarters was technically forbidden, Mykel had allowed small games for low stakes by the simple expedient of showing up any time he sensed large wagers and confiscating the winnings. He'd turned the winnings over to Bhoral, who as battalion senior squad leader was effectively quartermaster as well, with instructions to use them for dried fruit and other items of which the troops seldom got as much as they would have liked.

Mykel paused. Somewhere on the slope to the northwest, he could sense two alectors. The pinkish-purple auras were unmistakable.

He crossed the courtyard, letting his boots sound on the stone. "It's about time to turn in, I think."

The light vanished, amid low mumbles.

"Just get a twin single . . . make the point . . . Majer shows up . . ."

". . . don't complain . . . could have taken the coins . . . sometimes he's so quiet you don't even hear him . . ."

"Yes, sir!" called out one of the Cadmian rankers.

Mykel couldn't help smiling, but that lasted only a moment as he walked toward the small west gate. He needed to get outside the walls. It could be that the pair were only scouting, but he doubted that, not with a warning from the soarer. Still . . . he wanted to see what they had in mind before he acted.

"Sir?" The gate guard was Saluft, from Sixteenth Company, as were all the guards that night, but Saluft was one of the few troopers from Soupat.

"I'm going out. Keep a sharp eye." Mykel did his best

to cloak his aura before he stepped through the brick archway that had once held an iron grate-gate.

"Yes, sir."

As Mykel stood beside the brick wall on the west end of the garrison, from which all too much plaster had peeled away, from what he had earlier seen, the two alectors were still a good hundred yards away, moving slowly, but steadily, toward the garrison from the north. He slipped westward through the darkness.

". . . something out here . . ." Low as they had been murmured, the words carried to Mykel. He couldn't believe that the two were talking, even in whispers.

". . . rather take out the whole garrison . . ."

". . . can't do that . . . just find the one. A few others won't matter . . . but not any more . . ."

Mykel kept moving until he was actually to the southwest of the pair and close to some of the jumbled boulders near the hill crest. Then he released the aura shield.

". . . there he goes! Must have sensed us . . ."

The pair turned back westward, moving up the slope.

Mykel dropped behind a large boulder and rebuilt the shield, such as it was.

"Where did he go?"

"He must be somewhere here, hiding behind something."

Holding his rifle, Mykel held the shields, waiting, wanting them to get a little closer.

". . . know a little something, like the last one, and they get cocky . . . think they're better than they are . . ."

". . . just better steers . . . There!"

Mykel ducked, just before brilliant blue light slammed into the stone above him. His back was sprayed with a rain of fire that burned through his tunic. For a moment, he just froze, before forcing himself into a firing position, aiming, and concentrating, *willing* the two shots home— as head shots.

A flare of blue so quick that it couldn't have been seen

unless he'd been looking was the only response, but the pinkish-purple auras faded . . . and then vanished.

Lines of fire cascaded down Mykel's back as he straightened and began to walk toward where the two alectors had been.

"Majer! Sir? Are you all right?"

"Just hold your post, Saluft," Mykel called back. Even speaking was an effort. He kept walking. Although he was convinced that the pair of strange alectors were dead, he still could sense something remaining.

To cross the fifty yards between the melted rock and the dead alectors felt like it took a good glass, although it was probably only a fraction of that. In the darkness, despite his night vision . . . he could see nothing except two piles of clothes, and a pair of weapons that looked similar to the lightcutter that Submarshal Dainyl had used on Majer Vaclyn.

The uniforms were the source of the faint aura. Mykel squatted. He had the feeling that bending would intensify the pain in his back. A shock ran through his fingers as he picked up the black tunic that shimmered with its own light in the dark. The material was like the dagger of the ancients—imbued with life, although it felt as if it had been dipped or twisted through pinkish-purple. Was *that* why knives and bullets didn't penetrate their uniforms?

His back felt like it had been flayed, but he forced himself to fold the uniforms into a bulky bundle, with the lightcutters inside. He slipped the bundle inside the front of his tunic, wincing as the fabric of his tunic tightened across his back.

That left boots and belts.

"Sir?"

"I'll be back in a moment, Saluft."

Mykel picked up one pair of boots and carried them far enough toward the rocks that he could throw them—underhanded—into the jumble of stones. He repeated the process with the second pair, and then with the belts.

By then his back was an even greater mass of fire.

He turned and trudged toward the west gate.

"Sir," offered the sentry as Mykel approached. "There was a blue flash. What was it?"

"Lightning, I think." Mykel had to force the words out. "It melted some of the rocks and burned me . . . my back." He held the rifle before him to conceal the bulges in the front of his tunic.

Saluft stepped back, and Mykel made his way through the archway.

He was halfway across the courtyard when Rhystan appeared.

"Majer? The sentries alerted me . . ."

"I heard something . . . think I got my back burned with lightning . . . melted some rock there. I'll need someone to dress my back. If you would have them come to my quarters . . ."

"Lightning . . . it *is* cloudy, but I thought I heard shots, not thunder."

"Saluft saw the flash," Mykel said. "The sounds you heard must have been the crack of the lightning."

"I'll get Systryn. He's as good as we've got. I'll be right back."

Mykel forced himself to his small space, where he knelt and managed to get the uniforms and the lightcutters hidden under his bedroll. He managed to get the ammunition belt off, but couldn't lift his arms quite high enough to strip off his tunic. So he lit the small lamp and waited.

The two arrived within moments.

"I'm going to need some help getting the tunic off."

Mykel almost passed out as Rhystan and Systryn peeled off the tunic.

"You'd better sit down, sir," suggested Rhystan.

Mykel knelt on the bedroll. Sitting cross-legged would have just added to his discomfort.

"There are lumps of stone here, sir," offered the ranker. "They're . . . *melted* . . . and part of the uniform is charred. There's only one deep burn, though."

"Just clean things up and dress the wounds," Mykel said dryly.

The cleaning and dressing took more than half a glass, and was one of the less pleasant experiences Mykel had undergone—if not nearly so bad as being shot and nearly dying in Dramur.

Rhystan said nothing until Systryn had left. Then he looked at Mykel. "I thought you weren't going to scout things out by yourself."

"I didn't think getting some air was scouting. I had my rifle."

"Mykel . . . can you tell me what is really going on? Sir?"

Could he? What could he tell Rhystan? Finally, he cleared his throat. "You know the strange creatures?"

"I think we're all familiar with them, sir."

"There are other creatures like them, and some of them look like men from a distance. I haven't wanted to say much because the last thing I want is for the men to be shooting at anything that looks like a man. That's all we'd need here. I have to wonder if something like that was what got the garrison here. That's why I've ordered so many sentries at night."

"What does that have to do with your back?"

"I wish I could tell you. All I know was that I had the feeling that *something* might be outside. I went out to see, and there was a flash of light, as bright as lightning, and the rock beside me melted."

"Is that the official explanation?"

"It's also the only explanation so far," Mykel replied with an ironic laugh.

Rhystan shook his head. "Only you, sir. You start out your career by getting shot in the ass, then get knifed by your own commander, and burned by lightning outside your own garrison. I'm not so certain that it's not safer for you to be in real combat."

"Sometimes I wonder."

"Get some sleep, sir, if you can." Rhystan stepped back, offered a concerned smile, and then departed.

As Mykel lay face down on his bedroll, too tired to move, and in too much pain to sleep, he thought over the situation. He had no illusions about what had happened. Rhystan knew that more was involved, but he'd make sure everyone knew the "official" version. If someone found the boots and belts . . . if it happened to be scroungers from the town, no one would even connect the incidents. If some ranker did, the odds were that he'd try to sell them in town and make a few coppers and keep it quiet. There might be barracks talk, but there was always barracks talk.

That was the least of Mykel's problems. He could only hope that it wouldn't be too long before the submarshal got his message and did something. Then, despite what the soarer had said, Mykel didn't believe that all alectors were out against him and the Cadmians, but most of them might well be out after him if they discovered he had the same kind of talent as the alectors did.

He just didn't know what more he could do not to be discovered, short of deserting, and, if he did that, what protection would his men have if more of the flying creatures appeared? Deserting would also have everyone looking for him, including the Myrmidons, and trying to escape from pteridons wasn't exactly recommended. Still . . . he'd best be ready to leave at a moment's notice if it looked like there was no other option. But he didn't like the idea.

60

Mykel forced himself to get up at his normal time. Getting his undertunic and tunic on was almost impossible, but he managed, although he had to blot his forehead when he finished. He had just about finished his breakfast of too-dry mutton and eggs that were brown from overcooking when Rhystan appeared.

"Majer, sir . . . how are you feeling this morning?"

"Sore and stiff, Rhystan, but better than last night." Actually, Mykel wasn't sure that he was. While his back didn't feel like a fiery mass of pain, it throbbed, and he had not slept well at all.

"I was wondering if you wouldn't mind taking a short walk with me, sir. I was up earlier, and I discovered a few things. . . ."

Mykel managed a polite smile. He had no doubts what Rhystan had discovered. "Then we should take a walk, while it's still early and cool. Up the slope, you think?"

"That might be best, sir." Rhystan's voice was cool, cold even.

The two officers walked across the courtyard and then out through the west gate. The sentry, whose name Mykel didn't recall immediately, stepped back wordlessly. Mykel let Rhystan lead the way up the gentle slope.

Finally, the captain stopped and pointed to the large chunk of sandstone with a glassy surface. "The stone melted on the side. Lightning doesn't strike sideways, from what I know." He gestured toward the larger jumble of stone upslope and west. "I found two pairs of boots in the rocks there."

"That could happen. They might have been left there from when the garrison was taken," Mykel said mildly.

"Those boots weren't Cadmian issue, sir."

"No, they weren't." Mykel half-sat, half-leaned on the edge of one of the irregular chunks of reddish sandstone, glad that the day was hazy enough that the sun wasn't glaring out of the east.

"They looked like alector boots, and that's a different question entirely, Majer." Rhystan's voice was polite, but hard. "And that melted stone looks like the ground looked in Dramur when the submarshal took out Vaclyn."

Mykel could feel the tension in the other officer. He

took a long breath. "It's not what it seems or you think. I've been trying to keep all this quiet. I was hoping that nothing would happen before Submarshal Dainyl got my last dispatch."

Rhystan nodded slowly, but he was still tense. "Was that the report that went on the sandox coach?"

"I sent the regular report to Colonel Herolt and a copy directly to the submarshal. When we go back, you can read the copy I kept. The same kind of burns and melting had happened at that stead to the northwest. Fabrytal took my word that they were from the flying creatures. We followed the traces, and I did go scout alone. You can ask him if you want. I didn't find creatures. What I found was alectors wearing strange uniforms—black and silver—practicing with weapons like the lightcutters, except they were mounted on carts and tripods, and they were more powerful."

"They could be another alector force, one we don't know about."

"They could be, but they weren't. Not one that reports to the Marshal of Myrmidons. If they did, why did they kill the two holders?" Mykel had another question, one he wasn't about to utter, and that was why the Myrmidons, if they did have the vaunted Tables, didn't know about the rebel alectors. "And then there was the squad leader in the garrison here. Poeldyn or Styndal said that he got burned up, but the others got shot or stabbed, but he was the one who had a talent for hitting what he aimed at."

Rhystan stood there silently.

"The other thing is that Troral was telling me that the regional alector has been purchasing a great deal more in the way of supplies in the last season or so. Now . . . if this alector force happens to be on our side, with those kinds of weapons, why are we here?"

"You're suggesting an alector rebellion. That's . . ."

"Unthinkable?" Mykel laughed, harshly. "Then take the other alternative. It's not a rebellion. If it's not a rebellion, why was the garrison slaughtered? And by whom? We haven't found a trace of any force that could have possibly done it."

"I'd rather not consider what you're suggesting, sir."

"I don't care what you'd rather not consider," Mykel struggled to keep from snapping. "The fact is that we've got a strange alector force that probably killed the first garrison, and definitely killed the two holders. If they're friendly, what were two of them doing scouting the garrison here, and firing at me? Have I ever done anything that wasn't in the best interests of the Cadmians?"

After a moment, Rhystan shook his head. "No . . . you've risked more than any officer I know. But why . . . ?"

Mykel would have liked to have shrugged. It would have hurt too much. "I don't know. I wish I did. That's why I sent a special dispatch to the submarshal. I don't want us caught between two groups of alectors."

"Do you think he'll do anything?"

"They don't like to waste things, and they don't want Cadmians shooting at alectors. I've seen enough to know that, especially. Even if we're dispensable, I don't think the marshal would knowingly put us in a situation where we might have to fire at alectors. Given that, I don't think they know."

"That makes the most sense of what you've said. What do we do now?"

"We keep doing what we have been. Keeping the patrols away from where those alectors are practicing, avoiding the regional alector, and trying to get the new compound finished as fast as possible." *And hoping that Submarshal Dainyl will act sooner rather than later . . . before it's too late.*

Mykel rose carefully. "Unless you have anything else, let's walk back. You need to read the dispatch I sent. Right now, I'd prefer that you keep this to yourself. Unless something happens to me, and then tell Culeyt."

"I can see why . . . but the men are talking . . ." Rhystan paused. "They've always talked, though, about one thing and another."

"Poeldyn said that this hill was unlucky, that strange things happened here. Let that get out. Suggest that it's another reason why we're relocating to the new compound."

"That would work, if nothing else happens. Maybe, even if it does."

Mykel glanced southward. "There should have been mounts, or something. I didn't see or hear any last night."

"There were tracks. Four mounts."

"Frig. . . ." Mykel shook his head. "That just proves it."

"My thought as well, sir." Rhystan paused. "Why didn't they send more men?"

"They don't have that many mounts—probably just the ones they stole from the garrison." Mykel wanted to shake his head. Of course. . . . that was why they'd attacked the garrison. In an isolated town like Hyalt, where else would they get horses without it being noticed? Blame it on the strange creatures or local looters. Who would ever suspect the regional alector?

"Makes sense." Rhystan offered a grim chuckle. "How do we get into these situations."

"Easy . . . we're Cadmians."

As they neared the west gate, Rhystan looked at Mykel. "You almost passed out last night, didn't you?"

"Why do you say that?" asked Mykel.

"You would have gotten rid of the boots and belts better, otherwise." Rhystan laughed.

So did Mykel.

61

Dainyl sat on the stone bench in the Duarch's Public Gardens, half-facing Lystrana and half looking westward in the general direction of Myrmidon headquarters. A warm breeze wafted around them, and the scents of summer flowers came and went with the caprices of the light wind. For a moment, he closed his eyes, inhaling the bouquet of fragrances and savoring the warm softness of the air.

"It is a pleasant afternoon," she said. "It's the kind that makes me want to come back every afternoon."

"I thought you sometimes did. It's only a short walk from the palace."

"It's not the same during the midweek. I'm always thinking about what's waiting when I return, and whether Chembryt needs another analysis or briefing."

Dainyl nodded. He understood that.

"Everything is so peaceful on Decdi, more so even than on Novdi afternoons."

"I've always liked the gardens," he replied, "especially in summer, when everything is green and blooming. It's hard to believe so few take advantage of them." Above the trees to his right, the green spire of the Hall of Justice soared into the sky, shimmering in the light, highlighted against one of the few scattered white cumulus clouds.

"I'm glad to see you enjoying the summer. You've been on edge for days."

"It's hard not to be. I feel like I'm waiting for something to happen."

"Is it Brekylt and Alcyna?"

"I'm more worried about Hyalt. I should have seen it earlier. You told me about extra supplies and expenditures for Dulka, Hyalt . . . and Tempre . . . more than a season ago. After going to Dulka and finding out about what happened there, I should have seen that the same thing was possible in Hyalt. But Hyalt is so isolated, without any Myrmidons nearby."

"Dulka is isolated as well, and they moved the Myrmidons. Do you know what's happened there lately?"

"Outside of a new RA who's doubtless more effective than Kelbryt was? Quivaryt is probably just as committed to Brekylt. Let's see. Alcyna transferred Veluara there to command Seventh Company, and she's another one of those sneaked in from Ifyrn." Dainyl snorted. "Shastylt just tells me to leave it alone. That's easy enough for him to say."

"Do you really think matters are that bad in Hyalt?" Lystrana spoke slowly, reluctantly.

Dainyl felt she hadn't really wanted to ask the question, but hoped he would talk about it and then return to appreciating the afternoon.

"They could be. They might even be worse. Or I could be worrying about nothing."

"I don't think you're worrying about nothing."

"Why not?" He chuckled. "You're supposed to be diverting me, cheering me up, telling me not to worry that much."

"Because Samist put through increases in the supply accounts for Dulka, Hyalt, Tempre, and Norda. The engineering sections in Hyalt and Fordall have been increased again—with engineers translated from Ifyrn."

"And your Highest and Khelaryt and Zelyert have done nothing?"

"What could they do? Send you back with two companies of Myrmidons? Do we really want a battle between alectors?"

"The way matters are developing, that may not be a choice. The only choice may be when and where that battle takes place."

"It's all so senseless." Lystrana's words held a hint of bitterness. "It's a wonderful world, and they're all squabbling over who can tell whom what to do. The lowest alector here on Acorus has enough for the best of lives. But it isn't enough. Nothing's never enough. They'll ruin everything. Khelaryt is trying so hard . . . and no one seems to care. I want Kytrana to be born into a world like this garden, and she could be. Why won't they leave well enough alone?"

"Because someone always wants more," Dainyl replied. "Still, for all of his scheming, I think Zelyert feels that way—at least some of the time. From what I can tell, although he's never said a word about it in months, he's afraid that bringing the Master Scepter here will just encourage more of the scheming and plotting."

"He's right. All of the plotting on Ifryn, and the attempted coups, and the infighting—I wouldn't be surprised if they're not one of the reasons why lifeforce declined there faster than anyone had thought."

"Maybe that's why Shastylt and Zelyert don't want me to use the pteridons unless it's absolutely necessary. When we use skylances, we burn lifeforce. A little is all right. It does regenerate, but for battles . . ."

"Can we talk about something else, dearest? Please? It's a beautiful afternoon, and we can't do anything about any of it right now."

Dainyl reached out and took her hand. "I'm sorry. I shouldn't have even brought it up." He offered a smile, only slightly forced. "Do you think Kytrana will have blue eyes or violet eyes?"

"She's an active child, already." Lystrana placed the fingertips of her free hand on her abdomen. "You were very active, your mother says. So she'll have blue eyes."

"Violet, like yours," Dainyl replied.

62

On Duadi morning, after concluding a less than satisfactory meeting with Colonel Dhenyr about the use of operations reports as a means to forecast maintenance requirements, Dainyl had just settled back into his chair for a moment of recovery when the duty messenger appeared in his study door.

"Submarshal . . . this arrived by sandox coach." The duty messenger handed an envelope to Dainyl.

He took it. On the outside was written: *Submarshal of Myrmidons Dainyl, Myrmidon Headquarters, Elcien.*

The handwriting looked familiar, yet he did not recognize it. Abruptly, he looked up. "Thank you."

"Yes, sir." The messenger closed the study door on the way out, although Dainyl had not requested it.

He opened the envelope, took out the sheets inside, and began to read. He read only a few lines before realizing that the report was not only from a Cadmian Battalion commander, but from Majer Mykel. He read quickly through the short report, frowning as he did. When he finished, he went back to the key section, reading it more carefully:

On Tridi . . .

Almost a week ago, Dainyl thought. *But the majer has no faster way to send reports from Hyalt, not that he would dare trust.* He continued.

. . . Fifteenth Company undertook a routine patrol of the roads to the west and northwest of Hyalt after a local factor reported unusual activities and the disappearance of a relative from a stead in the area. Because of the local concerns, I accompanied Undercaptain Fabrytal and Fifteenth Company. We verified that two holders had vanished from their stead. Unusual burn marks appeared on the ground around the stead and upon several buildings. While the locals had vanished, the stead had not been robbed, although some livestock had escaped.

Fifteenth Company made a thorough patrol of the area, but did not find any sign of the missing holder and his wife. In the course of the patrol, while conducting reconnaissance, I observed what appeared to be a squad of troopers. They wore uniforms of brilliant silver and black and were practicing with unfamiliar weapons. Because of the distance, it was not possible to discern the features of the troopers. The weapons they employed in their practice ap-

peared to be similar to the skylances used by Myrmidons, but there were no pteridons in evidence,
and the weapons were mounted on tripods on small
wagons.

These matters may already be known to the Marshal of Myrmidons, and if it is, I apologize for including these details . . .

Dainyl read it again. Why had the majer sent it to him,
rather than the marshal directly? Because he knew Dainyl
would read it, and he was worried about the time it would
take for Colonel Herolt to forward it. That was the obvious
answer, but Dainyl had the feeling that there was far more
there. Majer Mykel had to have known that the "troopers"
were alectors, and the speed of the report suggested
strongly he also knew they were not supposed to be near
Hyalt—and that meant the majer could become an even
bigger problem.

Dainyl shook his head. Once more, the majer could
wait . . . would have to wait, because Brekylt was a far
greater danger. Not only was he building a force, but that
force was using weapons forbidden by the duarches.
And . . . once again, Lystrana had been right.

Report in hand, he walked down the corridor to the
marshal's study.

"Now what?" asked Shastylt, even before Dainyl had
taken more than two steps into his study. "You have that
look, the one that tells me I'm not going to like what
you're about to tell me. What is it?"

"Brekylt is training troops, probably alectors, in the
use of lifeforce weapons at Hyalt." Dainyl left it at that.

"Precisely how did you discover that?"

"A report from the Cadmians." Dainyl held it up. "The
majer didn't claim that. He was very cautious. He only
noted that troopers in shimmering black and silver uniforms were practicing with weapons on tripods that
worked like skylances, and he apologized for reporting it
if it were something of which you were aware. He also

noted that two holders vanished, and strange black marks had burned parts of their holding, but nothing had been taken."

Shastylt's jaw tightened. His left eye twitched, something Dainyl had seen but once or twice in years.

"Sir," Dainyl offered deferentially, "it may also be that Rhelyn can employ those weapons in places or at times where skylances cannot be used."

"You'll have to see that he doesn't."

"I'll will do my best."

Shastylt paused. "I've ordered the weapons artisans at Faitel to develop something for use against the ancients. It was designed to be used where pteridons cannot fly. It won't be ready for some months, but . . ."

Dainyl wasn't quite certain how to read the marshal's words. Were they a veiled suggestion not to be too rash in dealing with Rhelyn, or a veiled threat that the device could be used in place of Dainyl if he failed to be effective?

"If I might read that report . . ."

Dainyl extended it.

The marshal read through it—quickly—and handed it back. "It's written as a copy. The original probably went to Herolt. Worse luck, but we can't blame the majer for that. You make two copies of that personally, and give them to me. Keep the original copy locked away."

"Yes, sir." Dainyl had no doubts that there were at least two more copies—the one that had gone to the colonel and the one for the majer's personal files.

"Forbidden lifeforce weapons, Brekylt's colors, and where steers can observe. That is provocation enough." Shastylt smiled coldly. "Submarshal, you have my leave to implement your plan for Hyalt immediately. I will, of course, forward copies of the report to Zelyert and Khelaryt."

The use of the Duarch's name without a title was another indication that Shastylt was angry, not just concerned.

"There is one other thing you should consider, sir."

Shastylt raised his jet black eyebrows.

"The majer sent that copy of the report directly to me."

"Did he say why?"

"No, sir. As you noted, it was a copy of the report to his colonel. I would judge that he felt we needed to know faster than the normal reporting channels."

"Or that he doesn't trust his colonel." Shastylt frowned. "Why to you?"

"He was one of the company commanders in Dramur. He knows he is going outside channels. I suspect that he wanted a better chance for the report to be read quickly."

"Is he the one that was nearly killed by the battalion commander for trying to carry out his assigned tasks?"

"Yes, sir."

"That makes it even worse. If he's worried enough . . ."

"That's why I thought you should know."

"Can you leave as soon as you make those copies?"

"Yes, sir. I'll stop by my house for my gear, if that's satisfactory."

"Of course."

Dainyl inclined his head, then turned and departed.

Once back in his study, Dainyl began to copy the report immediately. Thankfully, it was short. He made three copies, despite the extra time it cost him, and then handed two of them to the marshal before he took the duty coach home and had it wait for him.

Lystrana was not home, but he left a note on the bed for her, saying very little except that he was on an urgent mission and didn't know when he would be back. Knowing his wife, he had the feeling she might understand where he was headed, and possibly why, but those were not matters he wished to place in writing to anyone. He took one of the spare sidearm holsters, and added it and the weapon to his belt.

The third sidearm went in the small kit bag he packed.

For a long moment, he stood in the bedchamber. He could smell the faint and lingering fragrance of Lystrana, and he recalled what she had said in the Duarch's gardens . . . about Acorus being a wonderful world, if people just wouldn't ruin it. Would what he was about to begin preserve the goodness, or was it a mere reaction that would lead to the same ruinous end?

Finally, he picked up the bag and his flying jacket, and headed back out to the waiting coach. While it was too warm to wear the jacket in Elcien, he had no doubts that he would need it for at least the first part of the flight from Dereka to Hyalt.

Zelyert was not in the Hall of Justice, and the duty assistant barely looked at Dainyl as he walked past her and into the Table chamber. Chastyl remained out of sight, although Dainyl sensed another presence somewhere nearby. Since the recorder was clearly avoiding him, Dainyl donned the flying jacket, then stepped up onto the Table, and concentrated on the darkness beneath. He dropped into the darkness . . .

. . . *a purpled blackness than seemed neither so dark as it once had, although it was certainly not any less chill. He focused on the crimson-gold locator that both represented—and was—Dereka.*

Around him in the darkness that was the translation tube, he not only sensed his destination nearing him, but also that many others had used the tube lately, and all with a deeper purple tinge. Were those remnants an indicator of stepped-up long translations from Ifyrn? Or of wild translations? Both?

Behind and beyond the darkness, he was once more aware of a deeper black, and of traces of greenish gold. Why were the ancients more active? Because of the greater number of long translations? Or because of whatever Brekylt and Samist were implementing in Hyalt?

Before he could speculate further, a faint shower of crimson-gold flew away from him, and . . .

. . . he was standing on the Table in Dereka. Barely the slightest trace of foggy mist wafted away from him as he stepped down onto the stone floor.

"That was a very smooth translation, Submarshal. Only the slightest hint of the cold fog." Recorder Jonyst was waiting in the doorway at the foot of the staircase to the upper level library.

"Good afternoon, Jonyst."

"Good afternoon, Submarshal. I'd hoped I wouldn't be seeing you this soon again."

Dainyl raised his eyebrows as he carried his kit toward the recorder.

"Where you travel, trouble always has followed."

"Mere coincidence." Dainyl laughed, if slightly uneasily.

"Coincidence implies a randomness I have not seen around you."

"What trouble do you foresee this time?"

"If I knew that, Submarshal, I might not be so worried." Jonyst offered an ironic smile. "Most likely, I'd be more worried." His eyes dropped to Dainyl's belt, clearly taking in the two sidearm holsters.

"Is Yadaryst up to something?"

"The honorable regional alector left for Ludar this morning. He has not yet returned, but I expect he will be back shortly. He seldom remains overnight in Ludar."

"He doesn't trust his cousin?"

"Would you?" Jonyst's voice dripped irony.

Dainyl shrugged. The gesture seemed safer. "What else should I know?"

"Little has happened in Dereka since you were last here—except for the collapse of a section of the aqueduct. The city was without water for two days. A stone support in the mountains collapsed. How eternastone could collapse was not made clear to me, but it happened."

The ancients? Or one of Brekylt's weapons? As much as anything made sense, the ancients testing the alectors seemed more likely to Dainyl. Certainly, without water, Dereka would be uninhabitable for long with its current population.

"Might I ask why you are here?"

"To look in on young Captain Fhentyl. As I can, I do try to keep in touch with those company commanders who might need my presence."

"The captain needs it less than many, from what I've heard."

"He may need little supervision, indeed," replied Dainyl, "but submarshals need to feel that their presence is salutatory."

Jonyst laughed. "Guersa is down below. I'm certain she'll be pleased to take you wherever you need to go."

"Thank you."

The recorder only accompanied Dainyl so far as the upper level library, but Dainyl could feel Jonyst's eyes and Talent following him.

Guersa waited with the coach in the covered space just beyond the lower door. She was removing a fodder bag from one of the horses as he stepped out of the archway.

"Submarshal, sir!" The driver smiled warmly and quickly stowed the bag in the space under the driver's bench. "Do you need help with your gear?"

"No, thank you, Guersa." Dainyl had to wonder at her warmth. Landers were usually reserved around alectors. Was that because she had worked closely with Jonyst? The young blonde certainly had no Talent, except for the ability to put people at ease, an ability Dainyl did not have instinctively and often had wished he had. "To the Myrmidons." He paused. "How have things been for you?"

Although Guersa still smiled, Dainyl could sense that his pleasantry had surprised her.

"Except for the time two weeks back when we didn't have water, it's been a good spring and summer, sir."

"Anything happen out of the ordinary?"

"Not having water wasn't ordinary, but it didn't take that long for the engineers to get matters fixed. That could be because there were a lot of them."

A lot of engineers? In Dereka? Dainyl didn't like that. "It's good that they could fix it quickly."

"Yes, sir."

He climbed into the coach and set his kit on the seat across from him, closing the coach door. The small windows were down.

As Guersa turned the coach southward on the main boulevard, Dainyl looked out at the city. The sun hung barely above the peaks of the Upper Spine Mountains, to the west, bearing just a trace of gold against the silver-green sky. Asterta was at its zenith, but Selena had not yet risen.

He surveyed the streets and shops as the coach carried him southward, but he could neither see nor sense anything unusual. That bothered him. Was he too late? But . . . too late for what?

He shook his head and continued to watch the city as he passed through it, but there were no more guards than usual outside the RA's palacelike building.

When Dainyl stepped out of the coach outside the gate to the Myrmidon compound, he turned to the driver. "Thank you."

"Will you be needing a ride back, sir?"

"Not tonight. I can send a messenger if I need you tomorrow, can't I?"

"Yes, sir."

"Good." Dainyl smiled, then lifted his kit, turned, and walked through the gate.

Captain Fhentyl was waiting when Dainyl walked into the Fifth Company headquarters building—although the captain was breathing rapidly.

"Good afternoon, Captain."

"Sir . . . we didn't expect . . ."

"Sometimes, it happens that way." Dainyl smiled. "A moment, if you would, Captain."

"Oh, yes, sir. This way, sir." The tall captain turned and led the way to his study.

Dainyl let Fhentyl enter first, then followed, and closed the study door behind himself.

Fhentyl shifted his weight from boot to boot. "Sir . . . is there . . . a problem?"

After a moment, Dainyl smiled politely. "Not that I

know of. We'll see tomorrow. I'll be conducting a full kit inspection for all of Fifth Company, Captain. First thing tomorrow morning at muster. The entire company, with all deployment weapons and gear."

"Yes, sir." Fhentyl wasn't experienced enough to hide his consternation and curiosity. "Yes, sir." He looked as if he wanted to ask why, but did not dare.

"Every so often, it's necessary. Your Myrmidons need to understand that they must be ready to fly at a moment's notice. By giving you a little warning, I'm hoping that the next time won't be as much of a shock. I expect everything to be ready at morning muster."

"Yes, sir." The captain paused. "There are rumors that something is happening in the east."

"There are always rumors." Dainyl laughed. "Few are anywhere near the truth." *These days, the rumors are less disturbing than the truth is proving to be.*

He would have liked to have said more, but while he trusted Fhentyl, he didn't trust much of anything else in Dereka, except perhaps Jonyst, and surprisingly, his driver. So far as Dainyl could tell, even the walls might report to someone. "After I drop my kit in quarters, I'll be walking through the compound."

"Yes, sir." Fhentyl looked concerned, but Dainyl gathered no sense of guilt.

That in itself was somewhat reassuring to Dainyl, but not enough to change his resolve about keeping his plans to himself until the last possible moment.

63

Wearing his flying jacket and carrying his own gear, Dainyl stepped out into the cool morning air that still filled the Myrmidon compound. Although the sky was a cloudless and bright silver-green, the sun had not yet cleared the higher peaks of the barrier range to the east of the compound, and the courtyard remained shadowed.

He had barely left the senior officers' quarters before Captain Fhentyl approached.

"Good morning, sir." Fhentyl inclined his head. "Is there anything . . . ?"

"There is." Dainyl smiled. "Fit one of the pteridons in first squad with a second saddle."

"Yes, sir." Fhentyl's eyes dropped to the gear bag Dainyl carried. "Would you like that stowed on that pteridon?"

Dainyl couldn't help grinning. "That would be helpful. Has anyone else figured it out?"

"No, sir. Well . . . if they have, no one's saying." Fhentyl took the gear bag.

"Good."

"Sir? Can you tell me . . . ?"

"Not yet. We still have an inspection to carry out. After the inspection, hold everyone in formation, and I'll brief you and the squad leaders. Then we'll lift off."

"Right then?"

Dainyl nodded. "We have a very difficult situation facing us." He paused. "Do you have any trainees who might become riders?"

"Just one, sir, that would be ready for a pteridon."

"Better bring him, too."

"Her. Her name is Brytra."

"I hope we won't need her, but it's possible."

"Let me take care of your gear and the two extra saddles, then, sir." Fhentyl turned toward one of the support alectors and gestured.

Dainyl turned away and walked along the low pteridon squares, taking in the activity as the Myrmidons readied for muster. He listened as well as watched.

". . . full gear inspection . . ."

". . . don't like that . . . means trouble . . . especially with a submarshal . . ."

"Especially this submarshal . . ."

Dainyl forced himself to keep walking.

". . . pteridon he was flying got destroyed and he fell onto a pile of rock and survived . . ."

". . . he got rid of two commanders . . ."

"Careful. That's him over there."

It seemed that no matter how much Dainyl had tried to keep matters quiet, things still filtered out, and usually inaccurately. He turned and walked briskly back to join Fhentyl at the front of the assembled company.

"Stand by for inspection!" Fhentyl's voice carried across the compound, and the few murmurs died away.

The company commander turned to Dainyl. "Submarshal, Fifth Company stands ready for inspection."

"Thank you, Captain." Dainyl nodded and walked toward the first squad.

The inspection took only about a glass. Fhentyl had clearly passed the word, because Dainyl found no discrepancies—and he usually did. He'd been a ranker long enough to know where the fliers might cut corners, but from what he could tell, no one had.

After Dainyl completed surveying the last pteridon in the fourth squad, the two officers walked back to the front of the formation.

"I've seldom seen a company this well prepared on such short notice. What exactly did you tell them?"

Fhentyl smiled faintly. "Well, sir, I just said that I was a relatively new commander, but that you'd spent something like forty years as a ranker and had forgotten more tricks than I ever knew and that you liked to see things done right."

Dainyl didn't doubt Fhentyl's words. He also suspected Fhentyl hadn't told him everything he'd passed on to his squad leaders. "Call up your squad leaders."

"Yes, sir." The captain turned. "Squad leaders, forward!"

Once the officers arrived, Dainyl surveyed the four undercaptains—three men, one woman. He could sense the experience, probably more experience than Fhentyl had, but the captain held a certain charisma, as well as forethought. Dainyl had gathered that from his previous meeting with Fhentyl, and from the captain's reports to headquarters.

After a moment, he spoke. "Captain, Undercaptains, Fifth Company is flying out this very moment. I'll be directing the flight. I will announce our destination at the first rest break. I realize that this is an unusual procedure, but we face unusual circumstances. These will become clear as we near our objective."

Fhentyl swallowed, ever so slightly.

"Any questions? Other than our destination, that is."

"Can you tell us how long we'll be gone?" asked Fhentyl.

"No. What happens in the next few days will determine that. It could be a very short deployment or one far longer. A great deal will be asked of you and your Myrmidons, and I think it's fair to say that you were selected for this because you are the only company that could possibly accomplish what needs to be done."

"Can we let anyone know?"

"Not at present. Surprise is important. Later, yes. I'm not taking you off somewhere, never to be heard from again." Dainyl laughed. "Remember, I'm with you, and I also have a wife who's expecting a child."

He could sense a certain lessening of tension after his last remarks.

"Once you return to your squads, we'll lift off immediately. I'll be flying lead and point for the first leg."

"No one leaves the courtyard," Fhentyl added. He turned to Dainyl. "Is there anything else, sir?"

"Not at the moment."

"Dismissed to squads. Prepare to lift off."

"Yes, sir."

As the squad leaders headed back to their squads, Fhentyl cleared his throat. "Sir, I have you flying with Galya in squad one. She's one of the younger fliers, but very skilled."

Dainyl recalled the Myrmidon, because she had been the only woman in first squad—and petite for an alectress. "And because she's small . . . and less load on the pteridon?"

"Yes, sir."

"That's fine." The other reason was unspoken. Fhentyl understood that whatever Dainyl had in mind was dangerous, and he didn't want two officers on the same pteridon.

Dainyl walked across the courtyard toward first squad. According to the maps, and what he recalled from his own flying, there was a lake on the east side of the Upper Spine Mountains that would make a good restaging and briefing point.

64

Mykel felt better on Tridi—except when he moved suddenly—and riding out from the old garrison was almost a pleasure in the cool breeze from the northeast. The cooler weather was a welcome change from the hot dry air that had blanketed Hyalt for the past week.

He rode beside Culeyt, since Fourteenth Company would be relieving Thirteenth Company at the new compound. He would have preferred to have had all seven companies in one place—the new compound—but it would be weeks at best before that was possible, given the mess inside the walls. He'd hoped to be able to move the battalion sooner, but, as always, everything took longer than planned.

As they rode east from the high road along the dirt track that Third Battalion's mounts had turned into a rough road, Culeyt cleared his throat.

"Sir? Where do you think all the strange creatures are coming from?"

"That's a good question," Mykel replied. "I wish I knew."

"Never seen anything like them, and no one else has, either."

Mykel had the feeling that wasn't quite true. "Unless the alectors have. Maybe that's why they have pteridons."

"If that's so, sir, why aren't they here?"

"Maybe they will be, once the Marshal of Myrmidons gets my reports. In the meantime, Captain, they're our problem."

"Yes, sir." Culeyt was silent for a time, then cleared his throat again. "Doesn't it seem sort of funny, sir? I mean, the Myrmidons have their pteridons and skylances, and all we have is rifles and horses, but we're here, and they're not."

"They were here," Mykel pointed out, although he'd asked himself the same sort of questions more than a few times.

"But they didn't stay."

"No, they didn't. The only thing I can figure is that there aren't that many of them. There's nothing in the organizational charts that says how many Myrmidons there are."

"There isn't?" Culeyt sounded surprised.

"No. I've done some figuring and listening, and I'd be surprised if there are more than ten companies of them. Their companies are much smaller than ours, maybe only twenty-five pteridons to a company. I heard somewhere that they have five to a squad. There's a company in Elcien, and one in Ludar, and a couple in Alustre, and one in Dereka. That's five. I'm sure there are others, but I haven't seen anything on them. Now . . . how many companies do we have just in Elcien?"

"Four battalions . . . twenty companies . . ."

"And there are four battalions out of Alustre alone. We're training two more companies here, and Majer Dohark is building up to a battalion in Dramur."

Culeyt nodded slowly. "You're saying that they only

handle the worst of things because they have so much to cover."

"I'm just guessing, but nothing else makes much sense."

"They travel faster than a mount."

"That's true, but it takes two days for one of their pteridons to fly from Elcien to Dramur. That would mean that it would take a full day to fly here from Elcien and almost that from Ludar. And they use them for urgent dispatches as well."

Culeyt laughed. "So . . . it's the same as always. We get left scraping out the barrel with a short spoon."

"Pretty much," returned Mykel.

"Why did you join the Cadmians, sir, if I might ask?"

"I didn't want to be a tiler or a crafter, and my hands don't work that way. I'm not smart enough to be an engineer, and the idea of grubbing coins in trade didn't appeal much either. I couldn't see spending my whole life in Faitel. What else was there?"

"Think you would have done it different if you knew what you know now?"

Mykel laughed. "That's a fool's question, Captain. We don't get that choice. Anyway, all of us could learn from our mistakes, but who's to say that we just wouldn't make different ones?" There were so many decisions he'd made that had been unwise, yet would he have learned what he had if he'd always made the "prudent" decision? And even when he had made the "prudent" decision, as in the case of finding Rachyla with a rifle in her cart, that prudence had gotten him into more difficulties than imprudence ever would have.

"There is that, sir."

Mykel just nodded. A man—particularly a Cadmian officer—could go crazy second-guessing himself. He looked ahead toward the walls of the new compound, rising from the flat knoll just ahead. As the roan carried him up the gentle south slope to the front gate area—where the gates had yet to be installed—he could see that the stable walls were nearly complete, and that another group of crafters was beginning to hoist the roof timbers into place on the end of the building where the walls had been completed.

"Captain . . . I'm going to check on the crafters. Send a messenger to report to me when you've relieved Thirteenth Company."

"Yes, sir."

Mykel rode through the unfinished gates, surveying the compound. While the building work was progressing, the ground inside the walls was a churned and rutted mess. An area against the western well less than twenty yards square was all that had been paved. Rather than dismount, he had his mount pick his way across and around the piles of building stone and the stacks of timbers that were set, seemingly at random, throughout the unpaved courtyard.

Styndal stood just to the west of the unfinished south doorway to the stables, talking to several men.

Mykel reined up and waited.

Styndal finally finished and then turned. "Morning, Majer. What can I do for you?"

Mykel gestured toward the rutted ground. "How long before you finish the stable? I thought you said you could pave some of the courtyard as you went. I checked with Poeldyn. He said there was enough of the stone for paving . . ."

"There is indeed, Majer." Styndal gestured to his right. "It's stacked there in the northwest corner. What we don't have are the wagons to bring in the gravel and crushed rock to go under it. The ground here was pasture. Seems hard enough, but even a little water and it turns to a squishy clay. Can't set stone on that."

Mykel nodded. It was just as he'd suspected and feared. "You can only do what you can do. How long before you can get gravel and rock?"

"We can get some more in two-three days. The teamsters can haul more of the dressed stone than Poeldyn's stoneworkers can cut and dress. So we've been alternating."

"And the stables?"

"A week, maybe two. That's for the building and roof. Stalls and doors and inside walls, three weeks after that. Could be longer."

From what Mykel could tell, he wasn't about to have the compound anywhere close to being finished until late harvest, maybe even midfall after that—or early winter if things went really wrong. No matter what he had planned, something was missing or overlooked or scarce . . . or took more time.

"Be a lot longer, Majer, except that times aren't that good in Hyalt."

"The flocks and herds look healthy enough," ventured Mykel.

"The herders are losing more animals than they usually do, and it's drier. Doesn't count the ones that get carried off by poachers and . . . other things."

"Strange creatures?"

"Who knows? I'd be thinking it's poachers, myself, but there aren't any signs of brigands, and no more dried mutton and beef is showing up in the markets in the cities of the square, and none here. If more were, prices'd be coming down, and not going up. Can't see where the meat would be going."

Mykel nodded. He had an idea where it was going— the same place where the missing horses had gone. That suggested even more that the regional alector was doing something that wasn't approved by the Marshal of Myrmidons—or by the Duarches. "You can only do what you can, but the sooner the compound is finished, and operating, the happier everyone is likely to be." He grinned. "I know. There won't be as many coins for building, but there will be two companies here, instead of one, and that will help everyone."

"I can see that, Majer." Styndal glanced toward the far end of the stable. "If you don't need me further . . ."

"The stable comes first." Mykel gestured to suggest the craftmaster get on with what had caught his eye.

Styndal turned, took several steps, and bellowed, "Set it down! Now! The far edge is almost off the stone!"

Mykel watched as the triangular frame of timbers was lowered gently back down and as Styndal cornered the crane foreman.

". . . do that again, and you'll be lucky to be gathering gravel in the quarry . . ."

The majer hid a wry smile. It didn't seem to matter. There was always someone cutting corners. He guided the roan toward the small paved area of the compound, then reined up short. From his closer vantage point, he could see where the ground had been dug away at the edges and where a crushed rock base had been placed, filled with sand and finer gravel, and then tamped down.

The sound of a wagon rose above the sounds of construction. Mykel turned his mount and rode toward the south gate. He waited for Troral to reach him.

"Majer," began Troral, once the factor had halted his cart. "I thought I'd find you out here. I got word that your blankets'll be here next week."

"You'll have to hold them until the barracks are ready," Mykel replied.

"I'll have to pay the factors in Dekhron," Troral said, "or send them back."

Mykel refrained from sighing. "I told you that we couldn't use them until the barracks were ready."

"I couldn't guarantee delivery without a firm date before harvest. I told you that."

"Half when they get here, half when the barracks are done."

"You're a hard man, Majer."

"You're a far better factor than I am, Troral." Mykel laughed. "I'm living in a single room without windows or doors, and you've got a far nicer place, I'd say."

"Six parts out of ten," pressed the factor.

"I can only draw so much. You know that. If I can't draw enough to keep construction going, it will be even longer before I'll need the blankets—and you'll lose on that end."

"Then I will have to trust to your good faith, Majer." The factor offered a doleful smile.

"We both do what we can."

"That would be true." Troral stepped away from the cart and extended a heavy parchment envelope to Mykel. "You have acquaintances in high places, it seems."

Mykel tried not to frown as he leaned forward and took the envelope. The heavy paper—or parchment—was stiff in his fingers. The outer envelope bore an ornate seal above the name: Seltyr Elbaryk.

Mykel felt a cold chill, despite the warmth of the morning. Why would the seltyr be sending him a message? Had something happened to Rachyla? Or was she being married off to someone somewhere to get her out of the way?

"Majer . . . are you one . . . ?" Troral broke off the words abruptly.

Mykel understood. At times, the younger sons of those with wealth were sent to the Cadmians—but generally to a company on the far side of Corus from their family. "No. I'm not, but I've had some dealings with the seltyr's family." *Not all of them pleasant.*

Troral eyed Mykel speculatively.

"And not in the matter of coins, Factor Troral."

Troral looked away, but did not move.

The second envelope held his name and assignment: Majer Mykel, Commanding, Third Battalion, Cadmian Mounted Rifles.

The outside of the third envelope was blank. Mykel opened it.

This is to inform you that Rachyla, a favored cousin of the Seltyr Elbaryk, and Herisha, the highly honored sister of her mother, will be serving in Tempre as the seltyr's resident chatelaines for Herisha's nephew Amaryk. Amaryk is the seltyr's factoring

representative in Tempre for the family's new factorage there. . . .

There was no signature, but the handwriting was ele-
gant. It was Rachyla's.

The announcement was a message. There was no doubt
of that, or of the less than veiled sarcasm in the wording.
Mykel wasn't quite sure what that message might be. Was
it merely an announcement? A veiled suggestion that he
might be welcome to call on her in Tempre? The last time
they had talked, in Southgate, her tone had been anything
but encouraging.

"How did this come to you?" Mykel asked.

"With the post and the messages from other factors."

Rachyla doubtless had slipped the missive in with
other announcements—or Herisha had. The impersonal
nature of the words suggested that she was not sure it
would not be found or read by others, although Mykel
had the sense that the seal had not been broken or altered
when he had received it.

"Seltyr Elbaryk is a powerful factor, Majer," Troral
announced.

"I discovered that in Southgate, Troral. His palace is
rather . . . impressive." Mykel offered a smile. "Thank
you for delivering the message. Do I owe you for it?"

"Ah . . ."

"A half silver?"

"That's usual," admitted the factor.

Mykel sensed the reluctant honesty. He fished out the
coin and extended it.

"Thank you." Troral inclined his head. "I need to see
Styndal as well."

Mykel moved the roan into the shadow on the west end
of the newly completed wall. There he read the short announcement again. The words meant little more than they
had the first time. He remained in the saddle, still thinking about why Rachyla had sent such a message.

Less than a tenth of a glass passed before the sound of

hoofs distracted him. A Cadmian in uniform was riding quickly up the slope, moving at a quick trot.

"Majer! Sir!" The rider reined up less than two yards from Mykel.

"What is it?"

"Undercaptain Loryalt, sir, thought you might like to know . . ." The Cadmian paused to cough and clear his throat. "One of the men off-duty, he got into real trouble in Hyalt."

Sacyrt, Mykel thought, but he refrained from asking. "What sort of trouble?"

"He took a fancy to a tavern wench last night and made off with her. Her man discovered it and went after him. He killed him."

"Who killed whom?" asked Mykel.

"Oh, it was Sacyrt, and he killed the local. Took half the duty squad to bring him back. He broke Siliast's arm."

"Wait here for me. I'll be right back."

Mykel found Troral and Styndal next to the north wall. He thought they were arguing, but both stopped and turned as he rode up.

Mykel reined up and addressed Troral. "We have a problem. I wanted to inform you, as head of the council, that one of my rankers apparently murdered a man in Hyalt. I'm returning to find out what happened. We will be conducting a court-martial, probably tomorrow or the next day."

"Majer . . . told you that you brought too many men."

"That wasn't my decision, Factor Troral. I have to follow my orders. If my man is guilty, he will pay, and there will be recompense." Mykel's words came out like ice. "I wanted you to hear it from me, and to know that I do not take this lightly."

"I thank you, Majer." Troral's words were as cold as Mykel's.

Mykel turned the roan.

". . . told him, I did . . ." That was Troral.

"You heard him. Majer has to follow orders. You hear

the way he talked? That fellow's guilty . . . wouldn't want
to be in his boots . . ."

"Maybe not . . . shouldn't have been here. Didn't need
all those Cadmians . . ."

Mykel kept riding toward the north gate. He needed to
tell Culeyt before he headed back to Hyalt. As he rode
toward the captain, Mykel reflected that it was too bad
Sacyrt couldn't have been one of those killed when the
miniature pteridons had attacked Seventeenth Company,
but it seemed like that sort of thing never happened to the
troublemakers. Mykel kept a wry grin to himself—Majer
Vaclyn had doubtless thought the same about Mykel.
Sometimes, it was all a matter of viewpoint.

Early as the day was, he wasn't looking forward to what
he had to do—and he had more than a season left before
the compound would be completed, and who knew what
troubles would come of the strange creatures and alectors?

65

The Fifth Myrmidon Company flew al-
most due west from Dereka following the pass created by
the ancient high road that eventually led to Dekhron.
Dainyl called a halt at midmorning, when he sighted the
small lake in the hills to the west of the more rugged
slopes, an oval of gray-blue, with a long flat stone ridge
on its west side, the natural dam that had created the lake.
Between the ridge and the meadow to the southwest,
there was enough flat space for the full company, although the wildflowers and grass would take some pun-
ishment from so many pteridons and Myrmidons.

Once the company was down, Dainyl drew Fhentyl
aside.

"Captain, Fifth Company has been chosen for a difficult task."

"I had that idea, sir."

"The regional alector in Hyalt has been building a force of renegade alectors, and some are armed with sky-lances powered, not by pteridons, but by special carts."

"There have been rumors . . . but those were about the east . . ."

"There seems to be a connection," Dainyl admitted. "In any event, we'll be setting down tonight about twenty vingts north of Hyalt. There's a way station there. Tomorrow morning, I'll need two pteridons to fly to Hyalt early to meet with the Cadmian majer there. On my return, first squad will accompany me to the regional alector's compound, as if on a normal inspection. The remainder of the company will follow, with a separation of several vingts, flying as low as possible to remain out of sight."

"Then what?"

"We'll have to see. There are several possibilities. First, they could attempt to attack the pteridons. Or they could attempt to invite me in for some treachery. Or they could hole up in their redoubt."

"Redoubt?" questioned the Myrmidon captain.

"Much of the regional alector's space is actually carved into a mountainside. I believe it is one of the earlier Table locations. That may be why the rebels picked this locale."

"You don't expect them to surrender?"

"That is rather unlikely. The kind of weaponry that they have developed is forbidden. The creation of an additional armed force without the permission of the duarches is a crime against them and the Archon. Most likely, they will refuse us entry, or seem to grant it and then attempt some form of treachery. If that is the case, then you and three squads of Fifth Company, as well as part of the Cadmian Battalion, will have to contain them while I undertake other actions."

Fhentyl nodded, less than happily.

"Also, the renegades will likely be wearing uniforms of silver and black."

"Like those in the east?"

"The colors are the same. I don't know about the design. Now . . . if those weapons are brought out, your Myrmidons will need to aim at the carts. That's where the power supplies are. We'll go over all of this tonight, and again tomorrow, after I meet with the Cadmian majer." Dainyl paused, then gestured. "If you'd gather the officers, Fhentyl."

"Yes, sir."

As Fhentyl hurried off, Dainyl considered what he had said. Too little information, and subordinates didn't know enough to act effectively. Too much, and most were confused. Deciding how much was always the problem.

Within moments, Fhentyl returned with the undercaptains.

"Captain . . . Undercaptains," Dainyl began, "we're headed for an operation in Hyalt. We'll be stopping short of Hyalt tonight. There appears to be a group of rebel alectors who have taken over the regional alector's headquarters in Hyalt, and we will have to handle this with both force and delicacy. We don't believe that they're aware that we yet know the situation, but if we appear in force, that will certainly show that. That's why we won't fly all the way to Hyalt today, and why we will have a two-part plan tomorrow." He paused, letting his words sink in. "I'll brief you in more detail tonight, but I wanted to let you know what you're facing." He smiled, wryly. "Especially since I promised to tell you at the first stop after leaving Dereka. As soon as you tell your squads, we'll be lifting off again."

"Yes, sir," replied all five officers in unison.

"Let's go."

Dainyl let Undercaptain Hyksant tell first squad before he headed back to rejoin Galya and her pteridon.

"Submarshal, sir . . ."

"Yes, Galya?" Dainyl stopped short of her and the pteridon.

"These rebels . . . they're really alectors?"

"We don't know if all of them are alectors, but most are. The Marshal of Myrmidons has been aware that something was happening for a time, but until we had firm reports of forbidden weapons, he felt he needed to defer action."

"Sir . . . if I might ask . . ." ventured the petite alectress. "Forbidden weapons?"

"Like your skylance, without a pteridon. They're forbidden because they deplete lifeforce."

The Myrmidon nodded.

"Mount up!" ordered Undercaptain Hyksant.

Dainyl slipped into the saddle, far more stiffly than the lithe Galya. He'd be sore, very sore, by the time they reached Hyalt, yet once he had flown day after day. But being sore was going to be the least of his difficulties. Of that he had no doubt.

66

It took Mykel almost a glass to ride back to the compound. He had barely dismounted and blotted his forehead when he saw Undercaptain Loryalt heading across the courtyard toward him. Despite the cooler air and the breeze, the ride back had been hot, and parts of his back stung where sweat had gotten to the burns, despite the dressings.

"Sir? I'll take your mount." One of the Seventeenth Company rankers—Eisent—appeared.

"Thank you." Mykel handed over the roan's reins.

Undercaptain Loryalt continued to cross the dusty courtyard toward Mykel. The majer waited.

Loryalt stopped. "Sir."

"Undercaptain. What happened?"

"It was Sacyrt, sir. He was off-duty, and he slipped out sometime last night. He met one of the tavern wenches and took her off. He'd even paid for a room in one of the . . . houses."

"What passes for the local brothel? Or one of them?"

"Ah . . . yes, sir."

"Then what?"

"Her man—we don't know if he was actually her husband—he followed them and surprised them. He demanded coins."

Mykel shook his head. "That's an old trick."

"Sacyrt thought so, too. He laughed at the fellow."

"And?"

"The idiot pulled a knife. There was a fight. Not much of one. Sacyrt killed him and then . . . he had his way with the woman. She didn't like that much. He beat her some, and the women in the house called for the patrollers. Sacyrt barred the door. They came down here . . ."

"Wait a moment," Mykel said. "He left last night. I didn't hear anything when I left this morning."

"No, sir. He checked in last night, then slipped back out. He didn't meet her until maybe two-three hours before dawn. They were drinking some in the room. Probably wasn't until close to dawn when all this happened. The patrollers took their time. They decided he was crazy, and they waited. They didn't know, not then, that he'd killed the other man. The body was in the room. The patrollers got to the compound just after you and Fourteenth Company left. I didn't know Sacyrt had killed anyone then."

Mykel nodded. He didn't like it, but the timing made more sense. "I heard there were some injuries in the duty squad."

Loryalt did not quite meet Mykel's eyes. "Yes, sir. They had to break into the room. Sacyrt tried to take Siliast's weapon. Siliast didn't want to shoot. Somehow, Sacyrt broke his arm. The squad leader clubbed Sacyrt, and they tied him up and brought him back. We've got him in the gaol below. It took some doing to get him tied up there. The patrollers took care of the locals."

"Were they sure Sacyrt killed the man?"

"Yes, sir. Dartyl made sure of that. Stabbed right through the eye. The body was cold."

"We'll have to deal with this quickly. We'll hold the

court-martial in the town square tomorrow morning, beginning a glass after muster." Mykel looked squarely at
Loryalt. "You are responsible for making sure all witnesses are there, and that Sacyrt is there as well. Under
no circumstances must he escape. If you have trouble
with the patrollers or anyone, let me know immediately."

"In the town square?"

"I want every person in town to be aware of what happens."

"You sound like you think it's all his fault, sir."

Even knowing what he had felt about Sacyrt, Mykel
wasn't all that certain. He forced a pained smile. "There
are two possibilities, Undercaptain. He is guilty, or he is
not. If he is not guilty, everyone in Hyalt must know that
and must understand why. Do you see why?"

"Yes, sir."

"If we hold a private court-martial here, and he is not
guilty, what do you think will happen? Do you want your
men going into town alone or late?"

"No, sir."

"The same is true if he is guilty. The townspeople must
see that we will punish our own."

"Yes, sir." Loryalt nodded reluctantly. "You'll preside?"

"Yes, but I'd like you to request that the town justicer
sit beside me."

"Yes, sir."

Mykel could sense the undercaptain's confusion. "It's
a gesture of respect. It doesn't change anything. Now . . .
you have a great deal to do."

"Yes, sir." Loryalt nodded, then turned.

Mykel walked slowly toward his quarters. In a way, he
wished that Sacyrt had just knifed someone in the tavern,
but like everything else, neither the court-martial nor the
situation with the locals was going to be simple. But the
sooner he addressed it, the better. Things could only get
uglier and worse.

67

The way station was hardly adequate, but it had a spring, and enough shelter under roof for the twenty-three Myrmidons. Still, Dainyl was stiff when he rose on Quattri. Even stretching and bending didn't help that much. It had been years since he'd slept on a way-station pallet, and he hadn't missed that experience in the slightest. He also did not enjoy the field rations that much, but since the plan was his, he had no one else to blame. Before eating, he studied the maps a last time to refresh his memory of the area.

After eating, he turned to Fhentyl. "I'll be taking Galya and one other flier to pay a call on Majer Mykel."

"Just two pteridons, sir? You think that's safe?"

"Two. We won't be going anywhere near the RA's redoubt. Not until I confer with the majer. There's also a fairly high line of hills just to the north and east of the compound. Directly north, the hills are too rugged. The compound is at least five vingts west of the town."

"Strange, that is."

Dainyl silently agreed, but that was the way it was and had been for hundreds, if not thousands, of years. "When I get back, we'll meet with the undercaptains and go over what comes next." He paused. "If . . . just in case, I don't come back, take the entire company and find Majer Mykel and learn everything you can. Leave the RA alone. Then take the entire company straight to Elcien."

"Not back to Dereka?"

"No. To Elcien, and report directly to the marshal."

"Yes, sir."

"Who else would you suggest accompany Galya and me?"

"Undercaptain Hyksant has suggested Dyrmant, sir. He's quite good with the lance. So is Galya."

Dainyl nodded and went in search of Galya and Dyrmant. Not surprisingly, they were ready, their pteridons away from the others, to the north of the waystation, facing into the light breeze from the west.

"Submarshal, sir."

"Ready to fly?"

"Yes, sir."

"We're heading south to Hyalt. I'd like you to fly fairly low, no more than a hundred yards above the high road. Just follow it to the town, and we'll set down in the old garrison or as close as you can."

Both Myrmidons nodded.

Galya mounted, and Dainyl followed, after cinching his flying jacket closed, taking the silvery saddle behind hers and checking the harness and strapping in.

The pteridon leapt into the light wind, its leathery blue wings spreading. Dainyl could sense the burst of Talent energy required as the pteridon climbed, turning southward in a slow arc before steadying on a course just to the east of and parallel to the high road that led into Hyalt.

Below, the grass appeared greener from the air than it had merely underfoot. A faint haze clouded the southern horizon, suggesting warmer air might soon be approaching. There were few huts or steads on the rolling hills to the north of Hyalt, but almost immediately, they passed over a ridge that held a narrow road that hugged the ridge and headed eastward.

Dainyl followed the road with his eyes and noted that it ended in a small hamlet below a modest wood on the north side of the ridge. After a time, he looked forward again.

Ahead was Hyalt, looking from a distance more like a hodgepodge of reddish and brown buildings clustered randomly around the high road. Below, Dainyl could see clearly the walls and buildings of the new Cadmian compound on a knoll just to the north of the town and east of the high road. Majer Mykel had definitely picked a spot that was designed for defense, and from the stream on the east side, one with water as well. That didn't surprise Dainyl, not where the majer was concerned.

Because of what he had seen in the Table at Lysia, Dainyl could pick out the town square. He frowned. There were a goodly number of Cadmians, mounted and in ranks, on one side of the square, as well as townspeople. Should he land there?

He decided against it. He had no idea where the majer was, and it was probably better to start with the garrison.

"That must be the garrison there, on that rise to the west." Galya gestured. "It'll be tight setting down there."

"Set down in the road outside, then."

"Yes, sir."

Dyrmant continued to circle, skylance out, as Galya brought her pteridon down into a flare. The long wings barely missed the walls of the garrison.

As Dainyl dismounted, he could see that Galya also held her skylance at the ready. "Just wait here."

Galya nodded.

Dainyl took a score of steps toward the gateless entry.

"Sir . . . Marshal?" stuttered the sentry.

"Submarshal Dainyl. Where's Majer Mykel?"

"Sir, he's not here. . . ."

"Submarshal, sir!" called a stronger voice.

Dainyl saw a familiar captain's face, but had to search for the man's name for a moment. "Captain Rhystan."

"Yes, sir." Rhystan came to a halt short of the submarshal and stiffened slightly. "You're looking for Majer Mykel? He is holding a court-martial. One of the rankers killed a local who was trying to get coins from him. The majer felt the locals should see the process."

Dainyl glanced through the gap where the gates had once been into the near-ruined courtyard beyond.

"The court-martial is in the town square, sir," continued Rhystan. "The majer felt that holding the proceeding here would not have been appropriate, for a number of reasons."

"I can see that. I'll ride down there, then. I'll need a mount."

"I'll send a squad with you, sir." The captain gestured to

the sentry. "Tell Wholent to mount second squad and report here with a spare mount for the Submarshal. On the double."

"Yes, sir!"

Dainyl surveyed the captain. Unlike Mykel, he clearly had no Talent, and he seemed slightly older than the majer. "How have matters been going here, Captain?"

"Did you receive the majer's dispatch to you, sir? I wouldn't want to cover what you know."

"His report is one of the reasons I'm here. His wording was cautious, but he seemed to suggest that matters were anything but what might be expected."

"Submarshal, sir, that is a fair statement. The majer has often been known for his directness. When he is not . . . so direct, that is always for a reason."

"What might that reason be, Captain?"

Dainyl could sense Rhystan's discomfort, but he looked down at the Cadmian officer, waiting patiently.

"There have been strange creatures in the quarry," Rhystan finally went on, "and the flying beasts like small pteridons. In addition, at least one member of the former garrison here may have been killed with a weapon resembling your sidearms, sir. With that, and with what the majer saw of the troopers in strange uniforms and weapons similar to the skylances, he was most concerned."

Dainyl nodded slowly. There had been nothing about a death in the garrison with a lightcutter, but his best guess was that someone, perhaps the Cadmian killed with the lightcutter, had observed and recognized the rebel alectors, and enough of the garrison had seen the killing that all had to be silenced. "He and you were right to be concerned. There are rebel forces, and they may have control of the Regional Alector's compound." He looked up at the sound of hoofs on the pavement of the courtyard. The captain must have had a squad on ready standby.

"I'll need to check with the majer." Dainyl walked over to the spare horse and mounted.

"Yes, sir."

As he rode past the pteridon, looming above even the mounted Cadmians, Dainyl looked at the grounded pteridon and its flyer. "Just hold here."

"Yes, sir."

The street down to the high road and the high road itself were nearly empty, although several indigens stared openly at the alector riding with a squad of Cadmians. When they neared the square, Dainyl surveyed the area. Two full Cadmian mounted companies were drawn up— one on the east side of the square, one on the west side.

Dainyl rode slowly up the west side, behind the ranked Cadmians, until he was abreast of the center of the square. There he dismounted and handed the reins to one of the Cadmians. He made his way through a gap in the mounted riders, then stopped.

In the space south of the statue of the duarches was a small table. Behind it sat the majer and a gray-haired local. The local was slightly to one side, in a position suggesting that he was merely advising the majer.

Three benches were set facing the table. On the single bench to the east sat a lone Cadmian, his wrists bound before him, with five Cadmians standing behind the bench, but facing the majer. On one of the other benches on the west side sat a woman with a bandaged and bruised face, and two other women. On the other bench sat two men in patroller's tunics, and a Cadmian with a heavily bound arm in a sling.

Dainyl had to use his Talent to hear the proceedings.

One of the patrollers had just stepped forward. "Cormer, sir."

". . . what you saw on Quattri morning?"

". . . well, at first, wasn't much at all to see. The girls in Wurlua's place, one of 'em came running to the post, said there was a crazy Cadmian in one of the rooms . . ."

Dainyl listened as first one patroller and then the other told his story. Next came the older woman, whose hair should have been white, but was an orangish blonde.

". . . seemed nice enough . . . polite . . . two coppers

for the room for the whole night . . . came in with
Fylena . . . she don't usually go with fellows, but you
don't know . . . Didn't see it, but heard steps later, heavy
ones, and it was Oskart, fellow who's usually with
Fylena. Went upstairs in a hurry. Heard some loud talking. Someone laughed. There was a lot of moving
around, and then everything got real quiet. Didn't hear
nothing, not at all—"

"No cries? No screams?" asked the majer.

"None that I heard. Not until later. Must have been a
glass later. Fylena screamed her head off . . . things like
'Killer!' Other things, too. . . ."

After the older woman—Wurlua, Dainyl gathered—
the next witness was Fylena, the battered woman.

". . . asked me to meet him at Wurlua's for a drink.
Gave me a half silver."

"Why did you go?" asked the majer.

"Tavern closes after midnight . . . he said he had to
check in, but that he'd be back, and that he had a bottle and
a room at Wurlua's . . . seemed nice enough . . . promised
me another half silver . . . anyway, he met me outside Fu-
sot's place, two glasses past midnight, something like
that . . . went up the back way . . . he had some more of the
brandy . . . so did I . . . he started to take off my clothes . . .
told him I wasn't that kind of woman . . . thought he just
wanted company . . ." The woman shuddered, then went
on. "I screamed, but I guess no one heard. . . ."

"How loudly did you scream?" asked the majer.

"Loud, sir. I did. Oskart heard me, and he came
through the door. The trooper there, didn't even give him
a chance, just took his dagger and ran in through his eye.
Then, he barred the door, and gagged me . . . and . . .
he . . . well . . . he did what he wanted . . . more than
once . . . it was." She shuddered again. "When I could get
a hand free . . . got the gag off . . . that was when I really
screamed. . . ."

Dainyl nodded, wondering how the majer would handle the evasions and misstatements.

"Could you explain why no one in the house heard you, but a man who was outside could?"

"He did, sir. He did, and *he* killed him."

The majer asked several more questions, enough that it was clear to Dainyl that he knew the woman was lying.

Then came the Cadmian on trial. Dainyl could sense an ugliness of aura about the man and wondered if Mykel could as well.

". . . wasn't like that at all, sir. . . . Me and the girl were talking at the tavern. I told her that I had to go to the barracks and check in, but I could get back and spend some time with her, if you know what I mean, and she asked what I meant. I gave her half a silver and said I'd like to enjoy her, and that she could have another later. Now, that's as clear as you can get, sir, and she said I could get a room at Wurlua's. . . . When I came back . . . she had the bottle I'd bought, and we went up the stairs. I was in no hurry, figured I had three-four glasses, and she was a pretty thing. . . ."

Dainyl frowned. So far, from what he could tell, the Cadmian had been telling the truth, at least as he saw it.

". . . she starts taking off her apron, and then her skirt, and hangs 'em on the peg on the back of the door . . . must have slipped the bolt on the door . . . well . . . she's not bad-looking, wearing just a shift . . . but the door busts open and this fellow's there with a dagger. He asks what I'm doing with his woman. Frig! I been set up. You expect that in Northa, but not in a sow-town like Hyalt. I just laughed at him, told him to get lost . . . he said he might—if I left first and handed over my purse, seeing as it was his girl. No sheeplover's going to do that to me. Told him that, and he came after me with the knife. . . . Didn't know how to use it . . . I took it away from him . . . woulda just tossed him out, except he kneed me in the balls . . . stabbed him . . . didn't have much choice . . . went into his eye . . ."

Dainyl sensed all was true, except for the Cadmian not having the choice about killing the bravo.

". . . didn't want the woman to scream, and I trussed her up and gagged her." The Cadmian shrugged. "Figured I was done for . . . so I had a drink and . . . got what I'd paid for. Later she got the gag off and started screaming. Patrollers showed up . . ."

Dainyl wanted to shake his head. Why were some indigens so stupid and so ruled by lust? He forced himself to listen to the rest of the witnesses, but their testimony only fleshed out the basic story.

The majer called back several of the witnesses, and asked more questions, mainly, Dainyl suspected, to make certain points to the townspeople who were listening.

A good two glasses later, much later than Dainyl would have preferred, but he didn't see that it mattered that much, since he hadn't actually begun his own operation, the majer summoned the prisoner up before the table.

"Sacyrt . . . the counts against you are as follows. Count one, you were absent from your appointed place of duty. Count two, you killed a man of Hyalt. Count three, you assaulted a woman of Hyalt. Count four, you resisted the lawful authority of the Cadmian forces. Count five, you assaulted and injured a Cadmian in the course of his duties."

Sacyrt looked impassively at the majer, but said nothing.

"This court-martial finds you guilty on charges one, three, four, and five. It finds you not guilty of charge two. When lethal force is used against a man, he has the right to defend himself with whatever means are at hand." The majer paused.

The square was silent.

"You are hereby sentenced to be flogged, five lashes for count one, ten lashes for count three, five lashes for count four, and ten lashes for count five. This sentence will be carried out immediately. Upon completion of the sentence, you are immediately discharged from the Cadmian Mounted Rifles, with loss of all pay and allowances, and any and all privileges arising from previous service."

"Thirty lashes . . . near-on kill a man . . ." muttered one of the locals, loud enough to hear.

"Fair's fair," countered an older woman. "Fylena won't work none for a long time. Never look the same, either. Pretty enough, she was, too."

"Filthy mouth, though . . ."

The murmurs stopped as the majer stood from where he had been seated behind the small table and walked over to the prisoner. He held something in his hands, what looked to be a small dagger. The prisoner's eyes fixed on the dagger, and he turned pale, but the officer merely cut away all the insignia from Sacyrt's uniform. Then he stepped back and made a half turn.

An undercaptain took two steps forward and reported, "Seventeenth Company stands ready, sir!"

"Thank you, Undercaptain. Carry out your duties." Majer Mykel about-faced, so that he looked directly at the statue of the duarches.

"Second squad detail, forward!"

The five-man detail of second squad marched the prisoner over to the stone railing around the statue of the duarches. Dainyl noted that they never untied his hands, even as they forced him to his knees, bound him to the stone railing, and gagged him. Then, the five Cadmian escorts turned as one and marched to the east of the railing, where they about-faced and came to attention.

The majer, wearing the crimson armband of blood wrongfully shed, stepped forward. From somewhere, he had gained a whip, not the execution whip, with razor-sharp barbs, but a standard Cadmian flogging whip.

Majer Mykel stepped forward. His voice was clear. "You have created pain and suffering, and for that you will receive pain and suffering. May each lash remind you of your deeds. With each lash may you regret the evils that you have created." He stepped back and lifted the whip.

The first lash cut lines in the cloth of his tunic; the second cut even deeper lines in both tunic and undertunic. The third drew blood. Sacyrt twisted against his bonds, but the gag muffled any noise he might have made. The majer methodically continued to lash the convicted man, each stroke identical to the one before.

Dainyl could sense what amounted to three separate feelings of agony—yet two came from the majer.

Finally, the majer straightened. "Justice has been done."

Dainyl could sense the strain and the fatigue held inside the Cadmian officer. He frowned. He didn't sense much Talent, not nearly what he had recalled Majer Mykel showing in Dramur.

"Cut him loose, and leave him there," ordered the majer.

The five members of the duty detail stepped forward and cut Sacyrt's bonds, and ungagged him, lowered his unconscious form on the ground before the railing.

"Cadmians. Dismissed to your commander. Return to quarters," Mykel stated flatly, handing the bloody whip to the undercaptain.

"Yes, sir." The undercaptain turned. "Duty detail, break down and return all borrowed equipment. All others, form up."

The majer half-turned, facing toward Dainyl. His face showed no surprise at seeing the Submarshal. He began to walk toward Dainyl, who had remained to the side after the small crowd had dispersed. The Cadmian company on the west side of the square also remained, as did the squad that had accompanied Dainyl.

"Submarshal, sir." Mykel stiffened.

Dainyl studied the majer. He refrained from nodding. From a distance the majer showed no Talent, but upon close inspection his shields were obvious. That was a matter of even greater concern—a lander with shields, but that aspect would have to wait. Dainyl might well need that Talent. "I received your report on Duadi. It was very carefully worded."

"Yes, sir. I only reported what I could absolutely verify."

"Was it your impression that the unknown troopers were alectors?"

"That was my impression, sir. One was, for certain. The others were much farther away, but they looked to be the same size and wore the same uniforms."

The absolute certainty of the majer's words, while expected, still gave Dainyl a chill within.

"What have you done since—about those troopers?"

"I've had all patrols avoid that area. I wasn't certain whether they were a new force or something else. If they are hostile, their weapons would inflict considerable damage on my battalion."

"How considerable, Majer?"

"Considerable enough that a mounted attack would be suicide. From cover, that might be another story. I wouldn't wish to try such an attack unless no alternative is possible."

"I wouldn't, either, not with horses." Dainyl laughed. "Depending on what happens later today, I may need you to ride to Tempre with three companies for a flanking action. Is Captain Rhystan capable of commanding the remaining four companies?"

"Yes, sir. He's very capable. He would make a good overcaptain or majer. At the appropriate time, I would recommend that he be promoted."

"In the meantime, I would like you to take up a position behind the hills immediately to the north and east of the regional alector's compound." Dainyl studied the majer. "Was that from where you observed the rebels?"

"Generally. The ground was rougher to the west. There were several low bluffs there."

"That's the line of hills."

"With how great a force?"

"What would you suggest, Majer?"

"That depends on what you want from us."

"Perhaps nothing. At most, I would need your men to pick off anyone fleeing north and east. It may not come to that today, but if it does, I'd rather not have anyone escaping."

"Six companies," replied Mykel. "Just over the crest of the hill. I'd leave one for existing duties, and to serve as reserves."

"That will do. How long will it take for you to get in position?"

"A glass and a half from now. Two, if you want certainty. We'll ride out the high road and then head west on the first dirt road west past the hilltop with the stone corrals. You should be able to see that from the air."

"Two glasses from when I leave the garrison. I'll ride back with you."

"Yes, sir."

Dainyl sensed that the majer was less than perfectly pleased with the idea, pleasant as his acquiescence had been.

For the first few yards, neither officer spoke, and the only sounds were those of the hoofs of the squad preceding them, and the company following. Dainyl realized something else disturbing—the majer was studying him, observing his shields and Talent. Dainyl wasn't quite certain if Mykel was learning much, but the thought of a lander having that understanding and Talent was chilling. For the first time, he truly understood why Zelyert was concerned about Talented landers. Yet . . . for his own self-preservation, for now, he needed the majer.

"Majer, what haven't you told me?" Dainyl finally asked.

Mykel laughed, ironically. "A great deal, Submarshal, but much of it consists of the rather boring details of attempting to train semi-trained recruits and build a true compound in a town where the principal concern seems to be how many golds the craftmasters can milk from the Marshal of Myrmidons. I've told you most of what has happened, either now or in the reports. The only thing affecting the Cadmians that I haven't mentioned is that one company was attacked by a different set of flying monsters—a cross between miniature sandoxes with horns and small pteridons. There were only three, but we lost men."

"Where did this take place?"

"On the ridge road to the closest hamlet nearby. It heads east off the high road, some ten vingts north of Hyalt."

"Is that the only other attack by flying creatures?"

"Besides those I already reported? Yes."

"Have you had any messages or contact from the regional alector?"

"No, sir. Not a message. Not a word."

"How long before the new compound will be complete?"

Mykel shook his head. "If all goes well, sometime in harvest. If it goes as I expect, by mid-fall."

Dainyl almost laughed at the young majer's realistic attitude, far more like that of a Myrmidon than of a Cadmian. Ahead, he could see the gateless opening to the ruined garrison, and beyond, men and mounts. He still needed to brief the majer on what he expected from the Third Battalion.

68

Although his face held a polite smile, Mykel watched warily as Submarshal Dainyl swung into the second saddle on the pteridon, behind the smaller Myrmidon flyer. What the submarshal had in mind for Third Battalion—even if a full Myrmidon company would be handling any direct attacks—was likely to create more than a few casualties, especially if the rebel alectors had many of the firelance weapons.

He had not wished so close a meeting with any alector, not that he had had any choice at all. Still, he had used the closeness to observe the alector's shields. Had the submarshal noted that? In all likelihood, he had, but how else could Mykel learn? The submarshal already knew what talents Mykel had, and he had a need for Mykel—for now. That need would not last, and Mykel had best be prepared—somehow—before he was no longer necessary.

At the same time, he had been disconcerted by the alector's showing up in the middle of the court-martial. Mykel could only hope he had handled the situation well, but knowing how evil Sacyrt was at heart had made it difficult. The ranker had enjoyed killing the local bravo and assaulting the woman—yet the bravo would have killed Sacyrt. If only the idiot had left it at that, or just taken his pleasure with the woman without hurting her or resisting the patrollers and his own mates . . .

The pteridon spread its wings—then suddenly was in the air, and climbing away to the northeast.

Mykel had sensed a burst of purple from the creature, energy of some sort, as it had launched itself. Was that how the creatures flew? Yet how did they channel that force into flying? Was it something like the way the ancients soared?

"Majer?" Rhystan's voice was low, deferential.

"Oh . . . sorry. I was thinking."

"Can you tell me what the submarshal wants, sir?" asked Rhystan. "I didn't wish to intrude. . . ."

"I appreciate that." Mykel straightened. "We need to get all companies ready, except Seventeenth. We'll ride out immediately, to take a position to the north of the Regional Alector's compound. We're to provide a perimeter guard." He sensed Rhystan's concern and explained, "The submarshal confirmed that there are rebel forces—"

"He told me that while the squad was forming up to escort him down to the square. He didn't say who they were."

"Whoever it is that holds the regional alector's compound is rebelling. The submarshal wouldn't admit they're alectors, either, but we know that they are, and he's brought an entire company of Myrmidons."

"He didn't want to say because it's a matter of pride, you think?" asked Rhystan.

"Probably. Alectors are supposed to be perfect."

Rhystan shook his head slowly. "So they're going to attack?"

"That's how it looks. Now . . . Seventeenth Company will have to take over guard duties at both the compound and the quarry. Culeyt and Fourteenth Company will have to turn quarry duty to two squads of Seventeenth Company and join us as they can. We'll pick up the Hyalt companies and Thirteenth Company on the way. I'll ride with you and brief you on some other possibilities."

"Yes, sir."

Mykel turned his mount into the courtyard. The last thing he wanted to do was provide a picket-line guard against alectors armed with the equivalent of skylances, but he couldn't very well refuse a direct command from the submarshal of Myrmidons. He took a deep breath. *Just get things moving. You can think about the details on the ride.*

"Officers! Forward!"

In less than a quarter glass, Third Battalion—except for Seventeenth Company—had begun to ride out from the old garrison.

Once the column was on the high road, riding northward beyond the outskirts of Hyalt in good order, Mykel and Rhystan rode just behind the vanguard squad. Shortly before, Thirteenth Company and First and Second Hyalt Companies had joined them from the compound.

Mykel had folded the extra ammunition belt into his saddlebags, but had decided against wearing it for now. He hoped he wouldn't need it at all.

After a time, he turned to the captain. "For all that the submarshal told me, there's a lot there that he didn't."

"We discovered that in Dramur, sir."

Mykel frowned. Twinges of pain ran down his back, and he shifted in the saddle, trying to lessen the combination of stiffness and discomfort. Handling the flogging himself had taken more energy than he'd realized. "He was worried. He didn't say a single word about the court-martial."

"Sounds like he is worried. He was interested in the one in Dramur. Why would any alector rebel? They've got everything they need."

"They may be alectors," replied Mykel, "but they're not all equal, and there's always someone who's not satisfied or who wants more power, or who thinks he can do it better. I don't think alectors are any different about things like that. They seem to be more interested in power than golds. So maybe that's another reason."

"They don't need golds."

"I suppose not, but I've seen the seltyrs and factors who have more gold than they'd ever need scrabbling for more."

"Different faults," Rhystan replied dryly. "Neither's admirable."

Mykel had to agree with that.

"Besides providing a covering fire or flank support, or whatever it is, what else does the submarshal want? Did he say?"

Mykel nodded. Ahead he could see the hilltop with the stone corrals. "He's thinking about splitting the battalion. You may have to decide who will take command of Sixteenth Company. If he does, the submarshal will put you in charge of the force remaining here. I suggested you be promoted to overcaptain. He looked like he might agree, but he didn't say."

"There's a lot he isn't saying."

"Is that any different from Dramur?" Mykel's tone was ironic.

"Where are the rest of his pteridons? He can't handle all those alectors with just two."

"He has an entire company somewhere nearby. He didn't want to alert the rebels. We're to take up positions along that road north of where I discovered them. The hill there offers concealment and cover against their weapons. We may not have to do anything immediately, but that's the plan for today."

"Worse than Dramur," affirmed Rhystan glumly.

"It could be." Mykel shrugged—and wished he hadn't as his back protested. "It might not be."

"By the way, sir . . . what happened with the court-martial?"

"Sacyrt was guilty of abandonment of duty, assaulting the woman, resisting authority, and assaulting a Cadmian. Thirty lashes and immediate dismissal."

"Not murder?"

"The man tried to extort coins and then attacked him with a knife."

"Sacyrt will remember. He's not the type to forget."

"When he recovers, and if he lives." Mykel's voice was bleak.

"Where is he?"

"I left him in the dust in the square. Immediate dismissal means immediate."

"The locals will kill him."

Mykel shook his head. "They might take pity on him. Someone might, anyway."

"You can be hard, sir."

"The woman will never look the same, and Siliast may never recover full strength in that arm. The men need to know that sort of behavior isn't acceptable to me." He paused. "Someone always tries the new commander, and even if they don't deliberately, everyone watches to see how he reacts."

"You administered the lashes?"

"Who else?"

Rhystan nodded slowly. "You could."

Mykel thought that an odd comment, but did not pursue it. Was Rhystan saying that Mykel could wield the lash because he had led from the front? Or because he was a new battalion commander? Or both?

"What sort of spacing would you suggest?" he finally asked Rhystan.

"You said that they had weapons like skylances. I'd have them on the ground, just out of sight, over the crest of the hill, until we know whether we're needed. Then put them in prone position, a little less than two yards apart, every other man three yards back. You'd have two lines, then, and one could keep firing, while the other advanced or retreated."

· "That's a thin line, and we'd only be covering about a vingt," mused Mykel. "Still, we're supposed to be picking up stragglers, not facing an attack. There's a bit of a gully below on the southeast side, and that would give us time to reform. They don't have that many mounts and no pteridons." He nodded. "Maybe a little tighter—a yard and a half. That still will give us a front of half a vingt."

"Do you know what the submarshal's going to do?"

"He's going in as if it's a normal visit, or whatever he does. Bait . . . I think."

"Thought Cadmians were the only ones who did that."

"I'm not sure he's a typical alector." *But then, how would I know?* Mykel looked ahead. "Left on the lane heading west, past the corrals! Pass it up!"

"Left ahead! . . ."

As the column turned onto the lane, Mykel glanced back into the sky to the northeast. So far, no sign of the pteridons, but he didn't expect them for another glass. He watched the road, but the sandy soil was heavy enough that what dust there was rose less than a yard, just enough to coat the mounts' fetlocks and lower legs and Cadmians' boots.

Slightly less than two glasses after the battalion had left the old garrison, a glass past midday, the six companies were stationed on the back side of the uneven hills to the north and east of the regional alector's compound. They were gathered in squads, resting in whatever shade there was until ordered into firing positions.

Mykel had dismounted and made his way across the flatter crest of the hill in the center of his line of companies. He lay just beyond the crest on the southern side, stretched behind an irregularly shaped juniper, surveying the hillside below and the terrain between the hill and the Regional Alector's compound. He had left the ammunition belt behind, with the fourth squad of Fifteenth Company, the group that would be flanking him in the center of the line.

The wind had switched, and intermittent hot gusts of dry air out of the south lifted and swirled sand and fragments of dried vegetation, then dropped them randomly. The low haziness that had hugged the southern horizon had climbed steadily toward the zenith as the day had warmed, until the entire southern half of the sky held a faint whitish silver cast. The later afternoon would be hot, a true summer day in Hyalt.

Reddish ground and scattered grass, now mostly summer tan, stretched from the base of the hill to the compound a vingt or so southeast of the base of the hill. Unlike before, there were no signs of any troopers. Mykel couldn't even see any sentries posted outside either the entrance to the freestanding stone building or to the archway carved into the redstone cliff.

Mykel could feel a growing purpleness somewhere behind him. After a moment he turned his head. There, to the northeast, flying in a staggered V formation, with each trailing pteridon higher than the one before it, were five Myrmidons, arrowing toward the regional alector's compound.

Rifle in hand, Mykel made his way back to the waiting squads, using what cover there was, mainly scrub bushes, low junipers and a few small pines.

"Third Battalion! Squads to standby positions! Squads to standby positions."

Dravidyl, the squad leader for fourth squad, appeared and handed Mykel the ammunition belt. "Thought you might want this, Majer."

"Thank you." Mykel nodded and took the belt, draping it over his right shoulder, the one less sore, before turning and heading back to his vantage position to wait and watch what was about to happen between the Myrmidons and those alectors who seemed to hold the compound to the south.

69

Fhentyl was waiting when Dainyl returned to the way station, standing on the flat grassy area to the north of the structures. Dainyl settled the pteridon and then walked toward the captain.

"Sir? I was getting somewhat concerned."

"The majer was in the middle of Hyalt presiding over a court-martial. It would have been worse to interrupt him than to let it play out."

"Yes, sir."

"Extortion, murder, rape, abandonment of duty, and assault on lawful superiors—all in one court-martial and from one bad Cadmian," Dainyl added. "You can see why dragging him away wouldn't have been advisable, not when a glass or two probably won't make that much difference now. Later, yes, but not now."

"Ah . . . what happened?"

"The majer handled it like a Myrmidon officer, fairly and effectively. It was a pleasure to see competence." Dainyl hadn't seen that much exemplary ability among the Cadmians, although he had the definite impression that Mykel was rewarding and building it among his own battalion officers. The late Majer Vaclyn had never recommended officers or commended them, but Majer Mykel clearly had decided on who could replace him and had no hesitation in saying so.

Majer Mykel also had greater control of his Talent than many alectors, and yet Dainyl had the feeling that the majer was truly unaware of the extent of the power he possessed. In a way, Dainyl almost hoped that the majer didn't discover it, because there were so few landers or indigens with the ambition and intelligence the majer possessed. Still, by ordering the Cadmians to provide secondary flanking support and placing the majer where he had, Dainyl hoped that the majer could use his limited Talent against Brekylt's and Rhelyn's forces.

"Now what, sir?"

"As we planned, first squad will escort me. Three will remain circling, while I land with two pteridons. You will follow with the rest of the company, but remain low enough to stay out of view from the compound, but where you can see if any of the circling Myrmidons use their lances or are attacked. In either case, you will immediately join us. If they should attack, our immediate task is to destroy everything in open view and then withdraw, except for a small patrol on a continuing basis to keep them within their walls."

Fhentyl's brow furrowed.

"The single outbuilding is stone. The Table and most of the support structures are carved into the stone of a small mountain. We'll only waste the skylances firing against solid rock. Once they understand that they are confined, we'll keep them there while I undertake the second part of the strategy."

The captain nodded. "Tempre?" After a moment, he added, "You haven't indicated why you wish to take the administrative center there."

"Partly because it's the only place from which they could easily obtain supplies and partly for other reasons. First, let us see how welcoming alector Rhelyn is."

"Sir . . . aren't you exposing yourself unduly?"

Dainyl shook his head. "I don't think so. Whether Rhelyn is behind this or someone else is, a direct attack on a submarshal is a provocation that the duarches are unlikely to take lightly. Resistance by denying access will gain them more time. If they don't know the rest of Fifth Company is nearby, they're less likely to be overtly aggressive, at least if they know word would get back."

"That's why you want the other three circling. But won't they see that?"

"I'm certain that they will. To them, that will convey

weakness and unwillingness and inability to act directly."
Dainyl gestured for Fhentyl to follow him as he crossed
the space between where the two pteridons had set down
and the remainder of first squad.

Undercaptain Hyksant stiffened as Dainyl approached.
"Submarshal."

Dainyl looked to the undercaptain. "As I told you earlier, Galya and Dyrmant will land at the compound with
me. They'll have their skylances at the ready. You and the
other two Myrmidons will circle. You'll also have your
lances out. If you see any sort of cart or any tripodlike device, destroy it instantly—even if there's someone standing beside it. Keep alert for someone pointing one of
them from windows in the buildings or on the roofs."

"What are the tripods?"

"Road-cutting equipment modified to act like a skylance," replied Dainyl. "They don't draw lifeforce from
directly around them, but from crystal storage. That's
why they need carts or something similar."

"Yes, sir."

Dainyl ignored the appalled glances that Fhentyl and
Hyksant exchanged. "That's it. Let's lift off."

As if to punctuate his words, a gust of warm air swept
across the way station, swirling eddies of sandy dust,
then died away. Dainyl walked back to Galya and her
pteridon and climbed into the second saddle.

In moments, first squad was airborne, with Galya's
pteridon leading the formation. Despite the importance
of the flight, Dainyl enjoyed the air on his face, the sun all
around him, and the lands spread out beneath the pteridon's wings. For several moments, he savored flying,
even as a passenger. Then he began to survey the terrain
ahead and below.

As they neared the regional alector's compound, Dainyl
studied the hills, noting that Third Battalion was moving
into position—presumably after observing the pteridons.
He nodded. The majer had kept his men in more comfortable and less exposed positions until necessary.

Dainyl only saw a handful of figures out in the open—between the single stone building and the carved archway to the underground complex. One pointed toward the pteridon squad, and all hurried out of sight into the archway. That strongly suggested guilt and fear.

By the time Galya's pteridon folded its wings and settled onto the flat paved area before the single freestanding stone structure, there was no one left in the open. Dainyl noted that all the windows in the building had been modified into slits, so that the structure resembled a fortress, rather than the regional administrative center it had been originally built to be. He dismounted, one hand on the butt of a sidearm, his shields at full strength.

The main door opened, and a tall alector stepped out into the hot and hazy afternoon sunlight. He stopped less than two steps from the door, which remained ajar.

"Might I ask your reason for being here?"

Dainyl ignored the insolent tone and smiled politely. "Submarshal Dainyl of the Myrmidons, here to pay a courtesy call on Rhelyn."

"The regional alector regrets that he is tied up with some pressing concerns, Submarshal."

Dainyl studied the alector who confronted him, not only with his eyes, but his Talent. The darker purpled aura was an indication that he had translated recently from Ifryn.

"I do hope that the regional alector is in good health," countered Dainyl. "And who might you be? I cannot say that I recognize you."

"I am but a humble assistant to the honored Rhelyn." A wave of Talent extended toward Dainyl, nearly as powerful as that projected by High Alector Zelyert. *You will do as I say . . . do as I say. . . .*

Dainyl's shields held, and he ignored the command. "Then I suggest you humble yourself and allow me a moment with him."

"As I said, he is engaged in more pressing efforts. . . ." *Do as I say . . . .*

Dainyl could sense a concentration of force rising within the structure, and his Talent focused. "Galya! The top slit window on the right! Fire!"

Even before he finished the sentence, Galya's skylance flared.

A soundless flash of white light flared from the slit window, and the narrower redstone blocks more recently added to reinforce and narrow the window exploded outward.

Dainyl's lightcutter was in his hand. The blue beam flared toward the unidentified alector, spraying around his shields. "Dyrmant! The other upper window!"

A welter of lightbeams flashed across the open paved area.

Dainyl pulled the second lightcutter and aimed it—as well as the first— toward the alector, who had stepped back, trying to hold shields and retreat at the same time. Dainyl followed with a Talent-probe.

Galya's skylance arrowed at the insolent alector.

Abruptly, the alector vanished in a purplish haze. Three bluish beams flashed through where he had stood and struck the now-closed wooden door, then sprayed into rainbows. The door was untouched—clearly imbued with lifeforce as a protection.

Dainyl glanced back. Dyrmant's pteridon was riderless, the skylance lying on the sand, and his uniform beside it. The submarshal turned and sprinted to the riderless pteridon, first jamming the lightcutters into their holsters, then grabbing the skylance and half-vaulting, half-climbing into the saddle.

Lift! He sent the command. The pteridon did not even hesitate at his becoming its flier and began to spread its wings.

"Lift off!" Dainyl ordered Galya.

Both pteridons were airborne near-instantly.

Left! Stay low. Dainyl wanted to minimize the chances of the rebels being able to use one of the lightcannon against the pteridons—and their far more vulnerable fliers. As always, the pteridon sensed the thoughts behind the command. Less than fifty yards separated pteridon and flier from the highest of the scrub junipers.

Only when he was a good vingt to the east of the compound did Dainyl begin to climb, followed by the four other Myrmidons of first squad. Just to the north circled the other three squads of Fifth Company. One of the pteridons separated from the company and turned toward the approaching squad.

Shortly, Fhentyl's pteridon drew abreast of Dainyl's, higher and to the left, so that wing-tip vortices did not affect either pteridon. "Sir? What do you require?"

"Dispatch one squad at a time to keep constant surveillance. They're to flame anyone and anything that appears in the open."

"Yes, sir!"

"I'm going to give orders to the Cadmians to leave one company on patrol, both to keep any supplies from nearing the compound and to make sure no one leaves, in case there are tunnels or the like. Don't have any of our pteridons land, no matter what! Once I finish there, I'll return to the waystation and meet you there."

Fhentyl raised a hand in acknowledgment before he banked away from Dainyl.

The submarshal turned north, circling back toward the hills where the Cadmians remained drawn up. He looked over his shoulder. Galya was flying wing, above and to his left.

"Circle while I land!" he called.

"We'll cover you."

Dainyl doubted he'd need that much cover, but it couldn't hurt. The air felt good streaming past his face. He had missed flying, but wouldn't have wanted to return to it because a Myrmidon died carrying out his plans. If he'd had more time, he would have climbed behind Galya and let Dyrmant's pteridon follow, because, sooner or later, he'd have to go through the laborious business of transferring the pteridon to young Brytra, far harder when the previous flier was still alive.

Approaching the Cadmian position from the east, he took a moment to reorient himself, then settled on a point on the ridge just behind the middle of the Cadmian line.

Down . . . on the ridge . . . below the tall juniper.

The pteridon glided in, flared, and settled onto the grassy area on the northern edge of the flatter section of the ridge.

Before long, Majer Mykel hurried toward the pteridon. "Submarshal, sir?"

"Yes, Majer." Dainyl swung down from the pteridon. Belatedly realizing that he still held the skylance, he slipped it into its holder before walking toward the Cadmian officer.

"No rebels or intruders sighted, sir."

"Good."

"We did note skylances and weapons from both the cliff and the structure."

Dainyl hadn't realized someone had fired from the cliff. He'd need to mention that to Fhentyl. "How large a force would you recommend to keep a patrol around this area and to keep anyone from sending supplies into the compound?"

"You're besieging the regional alector's compound?"

"It's no longer his," Dainyl replied. "It is in the hands of those who oppose the Duarch, and they're not to receive supplies."

Mykel frowned.

Dainyl sensed a change in the majer's lifeforce, somehow, behind the shields, but then, Talented or not, the majer was only a lander.

"I'd judge a company in this area," the majer replied, "and two squads from another company to patrol the roads with access to the compound."

"The reason for the patrol of the roads, Majer, is to protect those who might supply the compound. Anyone or anything nearing the compound will be destroyed by those pteridons." Dainyl pointed to the south, where five pteridons circled. "You can also tell your men that those who remain here will not be used in any direct attack. That would be foolish and a waste. Later, they may have to deal with stragglers and survivors, and those could be dangerous. Whatever you and your officers do, do not let any of the rebels approach closer than fifty yards. If you cannot stop them at that distance, pull back. Make sure that Captain Rhystan is clear on that as well. Do you understand?"

"Yes, sir." The majer's eyes never left Dainyl, another trait rare in a lander.

"As I told you earlier, I'll need three companies to ride north to Tempre under your command," Dainyl continued. "There is a possibility that the rebels may have sympathizers in the administrative center there. You're confident in Captain Rhystan's ability to command the remaining companies?"

"Yes, sir." There was the slightest hesitation. "He's very coolheaded and should have been an overcaptain before now."

Dainyl wondered about the hesitation, yet he could sense no equivocation about the majer's endorsement of Rhystan. Something else was at issue. "You still have concerns, Majer?"

"Our rifles have not proved adequate against some of the strange flying creatures, I have to admit."

Dainyl understood that. Some Talent creatures were barely susceptible to skylances. "There will not be many of those. There may not be any, but if there are, the casualties will be light, so long as your men are spread somewhat."

"That's what we did before, but . . . with large numbers . . ."

"They're far more likely to go for the pteridons and Myrmidons," Dainyl added. "They would tend to be drawn to them."

The majer nodded.

How much did Mykel understand? Too much, Dainyl feared, yet he might well need the majer in Tempre—or even later. For that reason alone, it would be better for the majer to undertake the Tempre mission. If he remained in Hyalt, Fhentyl would certainly notice. "Oh . . . if you would tell Captain Rhystan, Myrmidon Captain Fhentyl will be in command of the Myrmidons remaining here."

"Yes, sir."

"How soon can you have your companies on the road to Tempre?"

"In three glasses, sir, but I'd prefer to leave at dawn tomorrow. That will allow men and mounts some rest and better organization of supplies, and duties."

"Dawn tomorrow, Majer. I will be in touch with you before you reach Tempre, with more detailed instructions. If, by some chance, I do not, stop at the last way station outside Tempre on the high road and wait for further orders. Do you have any questions?"

"How long should we plan to be away from sources of supply?"

"The ride to Tempre and four days beyond."

"Ammunition. Should we split what we have evenly between companies? Or will one force require more?"

"An even split." Dainyl suspected he could get resupplies to Tempre far faster than to Hyalt.

"Is there anything out of the ordinary that we should know?"

"I suspect you already know, but any forces in black and silver are not to be trusted, nor allowed to approach."

"I had thought so, sir, but I appreciate the clarification."

After a moment of silence, Dainyl was the one to nod. "Good fortune, Majer." He turned and walked back to the waiting pteridon, mounting quickly.

Lift off . . .

The pteridon was airborne, circling up to rejoin first squad. Dainyl glanced to the southwest. Still five pteridons circling, and no sense of building lifeforce that suggested more lightcannon use.

70

Mykel watched the pteridon rise into the late-midafternoon sky. Two things had caught his attention. First, for the first time since he had known the submarshal, the Myrmidon was riding a pteridon as the flier. Mykel wasn't certain what that meant, but he had the feeling it wasn't good. Second, one phrase used by the submarshal had caught his attention—that the compound was held by rebels who opposed "the Duarch." Duarch—singular. Was there a war between Duarches erupting? With weapons like lightcannon and skylances, he sincerely hoped not, that it was only a minor rebellion, the equivalent of unruly Reillies or Squawts—or, at the worst, like the arrogant seltyrs of Dramur. Unfortunately, he was getting the feeling it was worse than that.

He turned slowly, looking for Bhoral and finally spotting the battalion senior squad leader. "Have all the companies re-form on this side of the ridge and remount, and the officers report to me."

"Yes, sir."

A quarter of a glass passed before Mykel looked across the faces of the officers. Only Loryalt was missing, because Seventeenth Company had taken the quarry and new compound duties. "We've been given new orders, directly from the Submarshal of Myrmidons. Third Battalion and the two Hyalt companies will be re-formed into two forces. I will be in charge of one, and Captain Rhystan the other. . . ." He went on to provide an outline of the situation, concluding with, "Since we will be rotating companies on the picket line, for the remainder of today, and until relieved at Captain Rhystan's discretion, Thirteenth Company will assume the picket and interdiction responsibilities. You will send messengers to report regularly. Are you clear on your duties, Undercaptain Dyarth?"

"Yes, sir."

"The remaining companies of Third Battalion and the two Hyalt companies will form up and return to the garrison. Sixteenth Company will lead. Officers, dismissed to your companies."

"Yes, sir."

While Rhystan mustered Sixteenth Company, Mykel recovered both his mount and the ammunition belt that, he suspected, he would need far more in Tempre than he had thus far in Hyalt.

Less than half a glass later, with the sun well past mid-afternoon, three companies of Third Battalion and the two Hyalt companies rode back toward the high road on their way back to the garrison. Mykel rode beside Rhystan.

"It's a war between alectors, isn't it, sir?" the captain asked after a time.

"The submarshal hasn't said, only that there are rebels, but that's what it looks like."

"We could get squeezed badly if both sides have weapons like those skylances," Rhystan pointed out.

"That's true." Mykel shifted his weight in the saddle. His back remained sore, with occasional jolts of pain through it.

"Do you have any idea which side is to be preferred?" asked the captain.

"Not really. All I know is that the submarshal is in charge of putting down this group and that he's been foursquare and honorable—and that he had had enough sense to put Dohark in charge in Dramur and that he saved my ass when Vaclyn wanted to do me in." *Not to mention saving me from a wound that should have killed me.*

"Funny when an alector is better to you than your own superiors. It makes me wonder what he wants."

"I've asked myself that question more than once, Rhystan. I still don't have a good answer. One thing is clear. The submarshal doesn't suffer fools or deception. He can look right through you and tell if you're leaving something out or deceiving him. Don't even think about trying it."

"I appreciate that word of wisdom." Rhystan's chuckle was close to grim.

"There's something else. The submarshal emphasized that we were not to allow the rebel alectors to approach closer than fifty yards under any circumstances, and that if we could not kill them or drive them off, we were to withdraw. He wanted me to make that point directly to you."

"You've made it. They must have some sort of weapon or power that is deadly that close. Good thing to know, I guess."

"How good, I wonder."

"Do you know what you'll be doing in Tempre? Or how long you'll be there?"

"Not really. He said that he wanted to cut off any possibility of supplies from there."

"We could just block the roads without sending companies up there."

"It's where the closest other regional alector is," Mykel said. "I'm wondering if he's talking more about things like those lightcannon. We couldn't stop those on the road."

"He wants to get control of them before they get into action?" Rhystan frowned. "But if those are around, why haven't we seen them before?"

Mykel was silent for several moments, thinking. The submarshal had been flying a pteridon alone when he had returned from the brief fight or skirmish, and he had been carrying the skylance.

"Sir?"

"I don't think I ever told you, Rhystan," Mykel began slowly, trying to gather his thoughts. "Last harvest, before we got sent to Dramur, I was taking the sandox coach back from Faitel to Northa. One of the ancienteers appeared and fired a crossbow bolt at an alector. The bolt bounced off his clothes—the shiny ones they all wear, at least in public—but he was staggered. In Dramur, the submarshal broke some bones when he fell off the pteridon, but the other two Myrmidons were killed. The other thing was that Dohark told me about an officer he once knew who used a barrel of gunpowder to blow up some Squawts—I think it was Squawts—and he got accidentally flamed by a Myrmidon . . ."

"Accidentally?"

"Dohark didn't think it was an accident, either. Now . . . on quarry duty, it took combined fire to bring down those strange creatures . . ."

"I don't think I see where you're going."

"Why don't we have rifles with larger barrels and bigger shells? Why are the only really powerful weapons on Corus linked to the pteridons?"

"Frig!" The expletive was low and muttered.

"You see? The Myrmidons have the only weapons that can kill an alector—or they did until someone invented or took those lightcannon out of storage."

"They've been hiding that for years."

"And I'd suggest you don't say much about it, or we might suffer the same fate as that Captain Dohark told me about."

"This is getting much worse than Dramur."

"I'm not so sure," countered Mykel. "We haven't lost nearly so many men or officers."

"No yet, but Dramur didn't start out that badly, either." Rhystan was right about that, Mykel had to admit.

"There's one other thing," Mykel ventured.

"Just one?"

"The new compound. You'll have to keep watch on Troral and the mastercrafters. And don't let Troral deliver those blankets. He'll try as soon as I'm gone."

"He's the kind that gives factors a bad name."

"I'd rather deal with him than the seltyrs. So would you."

"That's like deciding between Reillies and Squawts."

Mykel glanced ahead. The high road was still a good vingt ahead to the east.

"Which companies will you take, sir?"

"I'll leave you Fourteenth Company, Thirteenth Company, and First Hyalt. Culeyt and Fourteenth Company and your Sixteenth Company are solid. Bhoral will stay with you as battalion senior squad leader. I'll take Fifteenth, Seventeenth, and the Second Hyalt."

"You're certain?"

"I can do some training on the way," Mykel replied. "If anything happens here, you'll need two solid companies. Cismyr isn't bad, and Dyarth will follow any orders you give. Just make them clear."

Rhystan laughed.

"We'll leave at dawn tomorrow. It will take that long to sort out the provisions and the ammunition. We will take most of the wagons, and you'll have to arrange with Troral for more supplies. I'll have to write up some sort of authorization for you to draw against the letters of credit, and we'll have to go over that later, before I leave."

There were more than a few matters that had to be resolved. Mykel was just glad that he'd made efforts to keep Rhystan informed. At the moment, he wished he'd done more. He also had to wonder about two other nagging matters. Why did the submarshal insist on Mykel's being the one to command the force going to Tempre? Because he knew Mykel was effective against alectors? Or for some reason even less favorable to Mykel?

And why was Rachyla in Tempre? Was that coincidence?

Mykel didn't believe in coincidence, especially since most coincidences he'd encountered turned out for the worse. But he didn't have a better answer . . . not yet.

71

Mykel had tried to lie down and rest once he'd worked out the arrangements for splitting Third Battalion. By then, it was a good three glasses past sunset. For all the strain of the past several days and his own lack of sleep, with the pain in his back, he couldn't even doze. He'd never slept all that well on his stomach, and he couldn't help worrying about the days to come. Just what exactly did the submarshal want from him and the Cadmians? Why was he having them ride away from where the rebels were? Or was there yet another rebel force in Tempre? Finally, he pulled his boots back on and picked up his rifle.

The courtyard was quiet, and Mykel avoided the quiet bones game in the southwest corner, making his way through the darkness to the west gate.

"Sir?"

"I'm going out." Mykel walked out past the sentry stationed in the archway of the west gate of the old garrison and started up the slope to the jumble of redstone and rock. The only sounds were those of his boots and the intermittent sounds of insects. The full green disc of Asterta shone down from almost directly overhead, while Selena showed but the thinnest crescent in the eastern sky, barely above the horizon.

Mykel appreciated the cooler night air—cooler only in comparison to the stifling heat of the late afternoon—but his eyes strayed to the west, although he could see no lights. Still, at sunset a squad of pteridons had still been circling the area around the regional alector's compound.

He came to a halt short of the most rugged section of the hilltop, then half-sat, half-leaned on a redstone boulder that still retained some warmth. He set the rifle across the stone. Letting his thoughts and senses drift, he attempted to gather some feeling as to whether one of the soarers might be nearby. All he could sense was a distant blackness, something that lay beneath the hillside, with apparently less substance than mist, yet which radiated east and west deep beneath the surface of the hill.

There was no sign of one of the ancients.

His fingers dropped to his belt. After a moment, he removed the dagger of the ancients, both from his belt and from its sheath. He considered it, both with his eyes and with his expanded senses. The amber-green "feel" was more golden than the aura he knew he radiated. Could he emulate that feel, use it to call an ancient soarer? Did he want to? More to the point, could he afford not to?

He concentrated on creating a point of light, one that was indeed amber-green.

Nothing happened.

He studied the dagger once more and tried again— with no success.

Could he strengthen the aura around the dagger? Would that work?

This time, he tried to extend his aura to the dagger. That failed as well.

What would work? For a time, he thought. He had been successful in *willing* his shots to strike their targets. What if he merely willed—in the same way—the dagger to glow?

Drawing on the feelings he had when he used a rifle, he willed the dagger to glow, to send a pulse of green.

A momentary, brilliant, flash appeared—one that he sensed, but did not see.

Mykel tried to relax, to capture the sense of what he had done. He tried once more. This time the pulse was slightly longer.

How did one summon an ancient?

The soarer appeared so abruptly that he barely managed not to jump or grab for the rifle. She hovered in the air between him and the garrison, suspended in an amber-green spherical haze, her wings iridescent, and barely moving. Yet bright as that haze seemed to Mykel, he knew the sentry saw nothing.

You do not need the dagger.

"You might not. I seem to."

It is a material . . . talisman. Nothing more. You would do better to work within yourself. The dagger will become . . . a crutch now. What did you intend with your . . . signal?

"To seek information."

The soarer did not reply.

"Do you know what those creatures are that have attacked us? The flying ones?"

They are incomplete and damaged beings fleeing the dying world of the Ifrits. Their being is not strong enough to survive the long journey between worlds. The feeling behind the unspoken words was close to dismissive.

Mykel moistened his lips. "Ifrits? What are Ifrits? Are all the alectors Ifrits?"

There are Ifrits and Ifrits. There are those born here, and those who were not. As they are now, none belong here. They believe they do.

The alectors came from another world? "How did they get here? Why don't they belong?"

Observe them. You will see.

"You said I didn't need a talisman. How can I do what you do?"

You cannot. You can only do what you can. That should suffice. A clear sense of a laugh followed the words.

"But how?" Mykel's sense of frustration filled the two words.

In turn, the soarer conveyed wordless puzzlement.

"How?"

You do not see.

"No! I can only see my own aura, my own being, and the auras of others, if I am close, and I can, I think, place a little of myself in the bullets of my rifle."

That will kill the creatures and the Ifrits. Using too much will kill you. Lifeforce must rebuild unless you draw from the web.

"The web?" Every time he thought he had an answer, or a piece of one, something else came up that he didn't understand.

The soarer extended a delicate hand, not quite touching his shoulder.

Abruptly, Mykel was surrounded by lines of color—thin lines, faint lines, strong lines, all somehow separate and yet tied together. The brightest—thin and golden—ran from the soarer into the hillside itself, to the darkness he had sensed below.

Observe yourself.

From his own body extended a deep but glowing green thread, more like a cord compared to the soarer's thread, that arched into the sky to the northeast.

Your cord could link to the world anywhere, but you have not learned how. That is what you must master. If not, the Ifrits will destroy you.

"You and the alectors—the Ifrits—are enemies, aren't you?"

So are you their enemy. All who would preserve this world are their enemies.

"What did you have to do with Rachyla?"

Another expression of puzzlement.

"The woman who might be like me."

We did nothing. If she is like you, the forces within you will determine what will be.

"What forces?"

Enough. You asked, and we have answered. Do not seek us again until you have mastered yourself and become one linked to the world where you are, and not where you were born.

The night around Mykel was dark again—except for the faint glow from the dagger, and the stronger glow from himself. The threads had all vanished.

The dagger—a talisman. Merely a symbol or a charm?

No, it was more than that. Perhaps a reminder or a hint . . . or a crutch in the beginning, and one he needed to do without according to her. And Rachyla . . . the soarer had no answers there, either.

Where the soarer had been clearer, in a way, was when she "spoke" of the web. That web had to be the web of all living things. He concentrated on what his own lifethread/lifecord had been. This time, he could indeed sense it, arching from him into the distance. Yet the soarer had been linked to the darkness below.

Mykel considered. Should he? He did not want to sever his cord. That was death. Even without any warning from the soarer, he knew that. How could he link to the blackness beneath? An additional thread? He began to visualize a new thread, an additional lifethread, growing from him, seeking nourishment from the darkness beneath.

The stars above spun around him, and Asterta seemed to smile coldly down upon him, mockingly—or was it another soarer? His legs trembled, and he put his head down to keep from passing out. The dizziness passed, and he raised his head.

Was it lighter? Had he been unconscious for glasses, until just before dawn? He glanced up to find Asterta, looking more into the western sky, but the moon of the warrior goddess had not moved from the zenith. He looked toward the garrison, making out the sentry, obviously squinting into the darkness in Mykel's direction.

Good as Mykel's night vision had been before, now, in the deepness of night, he was seeing as if he looked through the earliest of twilight, or even a cloudy afternoon. When he had first begun to uncover his talents, his night vision had improved markedly, but it had still been night vision. He paused. Was he really "seeing" now? It was more a combination of vision and sensing the lifeforces of everything around him.

He almost dared not to look, but he forced himself to sense his own lifethread.

It was a deeper green, and it no longer arced into the sky, but ran to the blackness beneath the hillside.

Mykel shivered, although the night was far from cold. Slowly, he stood. He replaced the dagger of the ancients in its sheath and then the dagger and sheathe in the hidden belt slot. Then he reached out and lifted the rifle off the stone.

For the moment, he did not wish to think too deeply about what had happened, and what he *thought* he had done. Instead, as he walked back toward the compound, he reflected on what else he had learned. Rachyla had been right. The alectors did not belong. But how had she and the seltyrs known? Because her grandsire had learned what Mykel was learning and had given away the dagger—the talisman—when he no longer needed it? Or had he given it away in frustration?

The soarer had been clear enough. The alectors were fleeing and had been fleeing a world that was dying, and they and the soarers were enemies. The soarer had not said that Mykel was the enemy—or friend—of either, but that the alectors would destroy him, and Rachyla had said that as well. Yet Submarshal Dainyl had saved him twice. Why? Because he was a useful tool against the rebels? How long could Mykel trust the submarshal?

What could he do to protect himself?

He had just reached the garrison wall when he realized that his back no longer pained him.

72

Dainyl slept less than well, and not because of the way-station pallets, or the field rations, or even the lack of privacy. Twice during the evening he had sensed flashes of green Talent, but so momentary that he had no idea as to their source. The majer? Or one of the

ancients? In addition to that concern, he worried about
what he had planned. He also worried about what might
be happening with Shastylt and Zelyert in his absence,
neither of whom he trusted fully. Yet he could see no
other real alternatives, not ones without even more dire
repercussions.

He was up at dawn on Quinti, checking the pteridon he
had acquired and getting reports from the individual
members of the squads that had patrolled the area around
the regional alector's compound during the night. None
had seen any visible activity.

Then he gathered Fhentyl and the undercaptains—
except for Undercaptain Jirana, who was flying in command of fourth squad.

"The rebels are going to try to wait us out. For the next
few days, we'll make occasional passes over the building
and the entrance to the cavern tunnels and chambers.
That is only after the squad leader assesses the situation.
When those passes are made, each Myrmidon is to fire at
one of the slits—or openings."

Fhentyl raised his thin black eyebrows.

"First, it will keep them from stationing those lightcannon directly behind the slits. Second, eventually we'll
melt the openings shut."

"But . . . they still have a Table there," Fhentyl observed.

"That's true," Dainyl agreed, "but it limits their ability to
use those lightcannon against us. I'll be here for the next
few days to establish what we need to do, but it's important
that you keep up those efforts while I deal with Tempre."

Fhentyl nodded slowly. "What if . . . others . . . come
from the east?"

"The closest Myrmidon company from the east is in
Dulka. With the terrain, they cannot reach here in less
than three days, and that would be if they lifted off this
morning. I don't see that happening. Those inside the
compound can't do that much, even with a Table. Not that
many alectors can use a Table on a continuing basis."

"Sir . . . alectors against alectors? I had never thought to see this." Fhentyl shut his mouth quickly, as if he'd regretted the words before he had finished uttering them.

"Most of the rebels are dissidents from Ifryn. They've taken Hyalt because it's isolated. How they got here, no one seems to know, but how it occurred isn't our problem. Keeping the situation from getting out of hand is. If we don't stop them, they'll build more of those lightcannon. That will put a greater strain on the world's lifeforce, not that they seem to care, and we'll face a longer and harder struggle." *Not that we won't anyway.*

Dainyl also chose not to mention that at least the main door to the outbuilding had been armored with lifeforce. Were the lightcannon and such defensive measures as the door a symptom of why lifeforce growth was slow on Acorus? More likely it was appearing that lifeforce growth hadn't been that slow, but that some of that growth had been bled off and diverted—and most likely in more places than Hyalt. Who knew or suspected such, and why weren't they saying anything?

"How could they get away with that?" asked Undercaptain Hyksant.

"If someone bribes a corrupt recorder on Ifryn, and an alector vanishes from Illustra, is anyone there going to try a long translation to Acorus to report it or track the malefactor down? Ifryn won't last that many more years." Dainyl could say that, so long as he didn't mention just how critical the lifeforce diminution was on Ifryn. "It's a hope for those who fear that they won't be granted a chance—or those who think they'll have a much better chance by trying a long translation early. They can claim that they want to help somewhere, and if they believe that, seldom will a recorder go beyond that incomplete truth—not given the dangers with making a long translation. We have few enough alectors here that there's always some job to be done."

"But how . . ."

Dainyl didn't see who offered the sotto voce comment.

"From our point of view, that doesn't matter. Our problem is simple. We have a rebel group that is clearly bent on squandering lifeforce. We have to stop them before it gets worse." After the briefest of pauses, he added, "For the next few days, I'll be flying with first squad."

"Sir?" asked Fhentyl, his tone somewhere between quizzical and aghast.

"If I don't, that will put extra work on the others. Besides, I can't do anything up north until the Cadmians reach Tempre. Also, I need to see exactly what's happening. I'd be out there as a passenger if I weren't flying."

"Yes, sir." Fhentyl's voice was glum.

"Try not to worry about it," Dainyl said, although he realized that no company commander could avoid worrying about his superior being exposed to fire. "It's my decision, and you can't do anything about it."

"I'd rather not have to explain that, sir." Fhentyl's tone was almost doleful.

Dainyl laughed, then turned to Hyksant. "I apologize, Undercaptain, but I will take command of first squad for the interim."

"Yes, sir." Hyksant sounded far less unhappy than Fhentyl had.

Less than a glass later, Dainyl led first squad west-southwest toward the regional alector's compound, early enough in the morning that the low-flying pteridons cast long shadows, often against west-facing shaded slopes. As first squad neared the compound, fourth squad turned from its circular patrol pattern and banked back toward the way-station base.

Dainyl made a complete circuit of the area, then reversed his path, heading to fly wing on Hyksant.

"I'm going in closer. Watch and offer cover if anyone fires."

"Yes, sir!" the undercaptain called back.

Dainyl decided on a flight path that would offer minimal exposure. By coming over the low mountains to the northwest, barely above the tops of the scattered junipers, and then turning south, he could get a view of any defenses hidden in the rocks, as well as the back side of the single stone structure. The one clear advantage offered by the skylances over the lightcannon was afforded by the pteridons themselves, who functioned not only as flight platforms, but as lifeforce conduits that recharged the lances almost instantaneously. Since both the skylances and the lightcannon had to be based on the same mechanisms, they both required sunlight for continued operation, although they were probably good for a handful of discharges in darkness.

The difference between the weapons meant, Dainyl hoped, that during the day the lightcannon could not be used as often as the skylances, particularly if the compound remained largely sealed behind stone. For that reason, among others, he wanted to make a flight pass over the area before too much full sunlight fell on the compound.

Down . . . down and right . . . into the turn . . . lower . . . just above the trees. Now! Hard right and due south!

Holding his skylance at the ready, Dainyl drew on what lifeforce he could, and strengthened his personal shields just before he swept over the last of the trees and into the open air just above the cliffs. As he had suspected, a lightcannon had been set up amid the rocks to the north of the complex under the mountain. Two alectors turned, trying to swivel their weapon to bring it to bear on him.

He triggered his lance. The blue-white flame flashed true toward the lightcannon.

A wave of white energy flared skyward, but Dainyl and his pteridon had already passed over where the lightcannon had been.

Suddenly, light blazed around him, so much that he could not see or sense, and his shields barely held.

Up . . . left . . . tight turn . . .

The angle of the turn carried Dainyl and his pteridon far enough west that the higher and rocky sections of the cliffs blocked the second blast from the lightcannon.

Still, he was shaking from the effort of holding lifeforce shields, and he let the pteridon continue a gentle climb westward, releasing his shields and trying to recover some strength. A few moments more under attack, and he and probably the pteridon would have been dust sifting down through the hazy sky.

He glanced back, noting that the remaining circling pteridons of first squad had returned fire. He squinted. One pteridon was circling higher, grasping a skylance in one claw. The pteridon was flyerless.

Dainyl needed to make another attack, for the simple reason that he was one of the few Myrmidons with personal shields strong enough even to get close to the lightcannon near the clifftop. From what he'd sensed, it was far more powerful than the others, and he didn't want any more casualties among the Myrmidons than necessary.

To make another attack run, he needed even less exposure, and to fire his skylance first. From what he could tell, the weapon was mounted directly above the cliffside entrance, concealed somewhere in the redstone boulders. He had concentrated on the first site he had seen, and he should have been looking farther ahead. That had been stupid.

Then again, when had any Myrmidons fought against lightcannon? He shook his head, both at his stupidity, and to clear his eyes.

Right . . . and lower . . .

The pteridon made a descending right-hand turn, and Dainyl straightened on a course fixed directly on the occasional light blasts that flashed skyward from the top of the cliff section of the compound. He edged his course line slightly right, so that he would clear the edge of the cliff just slightly to the south of where the lightcannon was positioned.

Lower . . . barely above the trees . . . just past the edge and hard left.

Dainyl had the skylance ready once more. He triggered it as the pteridon dived clear of the rocky ledge, adjusting his aim toward the concentration of energy that marked the lightcannon hidden behind an aperture a yard wide.

The skylance beam slashed into the half-hidden weapon.

Hard left . . . up . . . just above the trees.

Stones and stone fragments exploded skyward, and more stones and boulders cascaded down from the cliff.

Despite the cool air flowing past him, Dainyl was damp all over. Inside his flying gloves, his hands were wet. He replaced the skylance in its sheath for a moment, and allowed himself a brief moment to stretch slightly while the pteridon began a climbing right-hand turn skyward. Then he lifted one hand and then the other, turning each hand into the wind to let the cool air help dry them. Then he reclaimed the skylance.

As he gained altitude, he could see that a thinning cloud of rock dust rose from where there had been what amounted to a lightcannon port.

As he circled back, Dainyl surveyed the area once more, looking for other possibly hidden weapons. He could sense no other energy concentration, but he didn't doubt that there would be others before too long.

His eyes lifted to the flyerless pteridon. The creature would follow the squad back, indeed, follow the squad until another rider was assigned.

Dainyl frowned. He'd lost two Myrmidons in as many days, and that was more than he'd lost in all the years that he'd been a company commander.

73

Mykel awoke slightly before dawn on Quinti, surprised that he did not feel any pain in his back, only a small amount of stiffness. From what he could tell, whatever else the soarer had done, she had speeded the healing. Or had his linking more directly to the world done that? Or both? Why the soarer might heal him, if she had, was another question, but he wasn't about to turn down such a gift. He dressed quickly, packing his gear and carrying it out to his mount in the half-ruined stable. After checking with the company commanders of his command, the one heading out to Tempre, he made his way to the long room that served as a communal mess, where he had cheese, hard bread, and dried mutton, washed down with the local watered wine, which was weak and close to vinegar. As always, of late, he remained alone.

As Mykel left and headed for the courtyard, Rhystan appeared. "You look better this morning, sir."

"I feel better. A good night's sleep helps." Mykel had to admit that he felt better—physically, at least. Using his improved senses, he studied the captain. Rhystan's aura was darker than that of most people, a deeper brown. Mykel suspected that, in time, he might even be able to tell where people had been born. If he had that time to learn.

"You're about ready to head out?"

"They're forming up now," Mykel replied.

"I wish you well in Tempre, sir."

"The same to you, here." Mykel shook his head, then went on. "If you have to deal with the rebels, there are a few things to keep in mind. First, as I told you last night, those shiny uniforms are a form of armor that stops bullets, but multiple impacts will bruise them, sometimes badly, I'd judge. Still, up close, head shots are more effective. Second, the tripod weapons need power from the carts. I'd try concentrated fire against the carts. If they explode, they'll take out any rebels nearby."

Rhystan cleared his throat, gently. "I don't believe you mentioned how to take out the tripod weapons, sir."

"It could be that I didn't. The carts do explode if enough bullets hit them." Mykel wasn't certain how he knew that, but he felt he was right.

"You didn't mention that to the submarshal, did you?"

"I did mention the weapons. I thought he would know their capabilities."

"For so direct an officer, sir, you . . ." Rhystan broke off and shook his head.

"Now it's your turn, Rhystan. Never tell an untruth. Never conceal what a superior already knows. But choose carefully when and how you let him know what he doesn't know and doesn't want to." Mykel laughed, briefly, and not quite harshly. "As you know, I can speak directly to the dangers of telling senior officers what they don't wish to hear."

Rhystan smiled, faintly.

"You'll do what you think best. We all do. Events decide whether our judgments were accurate, and sometimes, accurate judgments are more fatal than inaccurate ones."

"You're rather cynical this morning."

"It comes with improving health." Mykel smiled. "I need to be riding out. I did recommend you get promoted. I hope it happens. I also hope you have an uneventful picket duty."

"So do I, sir. Good fortune in Tempe."

"Thank you. We'll need it." *We'll need more than that.* Mykel turned and headed back to the courtyard and his mount.

Undercaptain Fabrytal rode up to within a yard of Mykel almost as soon as the majer appeared in the courtyard. "Fifteenth Company stands ready to ride, sir."

"Clear the courtyard, then, and form up outside the gate."

"Yes, sir." The undercaptain turned his mount. "Fifteenth Company, forward. Re-form beyond the gates."

Mykel mounted quickly and rejoined Fabrytal outside the garrison, as he waited for reports from Loryalt and Matorak.

"How long a ride to Tempre, sir?" asked Fabrytal.

"Four days, I'd judge, but it could be more if we ride into bad weather."

"What's Tempre like?"

"I've never been there. I've seen it from the north side of the Vedra. It's a trading city. It's smaller than Elcien or Faitel, but it's got two of the green towers and a river port. There's no Cadmian compound there. We've got two companies in Krost. Those are the closest that I know about."

"Do you know why we're being sent there, when all the action's here?"

Mykel grinned at the undercaptain. "No . . . I don't know exactly why we're being dispatched to Tempre. We'll get orders once we're near there. I have the feeling we won't lack for action, though." *Unfortunately.*

"You think the Squawts have crossed the river . . . or they might?"

"That's unlikely, but we'll find out around Novdi or Decdi."

Loryalt rode up, followed by Matorak.

"Seventeenth Company, ready to ride."

"Second Company, ready to ride. Wagons ready to roll."

"Thank you." Mykel nodded to Fabrytal. "Fifteenth Company, lead the way. You have the scouts."

"Yes, sir." The undercaptain stood in the stirrups. "Scouts out! Fifteenth Company! Forward!"

As his three companies rode along the high road northward out of Hyalt, Mykel kept looking to the west. He could not see the First Hyalt, on picket duty, but he did see five pteridons headed southwest, presumably to relieve those circling around the regional alector's compound.

While he knew in his thoughts that all beings struggled for power and control, he couldn't help but wonder what sort of power was involved with the alectors' rebellion. They certainly controlled the world, and they lived well. His lips quirked, and he shook his head.

He'd have to use the time on the ride north, both to continue training and sharpening the skills of the three companies, but also putting into practice what he'd learned from the ancient soarer and from observing the submarshal—assuming that he could. He pushed the doubts away. If those two could master greater control of the forces that suffused the world, surely he could gain some better control.

Once they were well clear of Hyalt, Mykel dropped back to ride with Undercaptain Matorak. He'd spent less time than he probably should have with the undercaptain and what time he had spent had been largely devoted to training and instruction.

Matorak was one of the darker-skinned Cadmian officers, and a good ten years older than Mykel, a former ranker who had been squad leader, and then a senior squad leader, before being promoted to undercaptain. His lifethread was sandy golden brown and stretched to the southeast.

"Can you tell me any more about this deployment, sir?"

"There's a problem in Tempre. Once we near the city, we'll be joined by some of the Myrmidons and given more detailed orders." Mykel smiled pleasantly. "The submarshal hasn't chosen to provide more information yet."

Matorak nodded slowly, not questioning.

"Why did you join the Cadmians?" asked Mykel.

"As a boy, I decided I did not wish to grow desert nuts and work in the quarries dragging out the golden marble. When I could, I walked to Soupat and waited for the Cadmian recruiter. The Cadmians from Southgate come once a year."

"Is growing the nuts that difficult?"

"One must make sure that nothing grows near the nut tree. Even the slightest sprig of green in the soil will attract the giant crickets, and they will strip the trees. The apprentice growers must sleep in the groves every night in the spring. They must sleep lightly and wake when the crickets hum. My brother killed a hundred crickets one night. He was beaten because he missed two of them, and they ate the flowers on one tree. I thought I would rather work in the quarries until my cousin's leg was crushed between two slabs of marble. My father said that I was ungrateful, and that I would die alone in a far country."

Matorak laughed. "I said nothing, but I thought that was better than dying young in my own land."

"I can see why you became a Cadmian," Mykel said. "What is the desert like near Soupat?"

"In the day, it is like the ovens my mother used to bake bread. Everyone sleeps in the late afternoon. We ate late in the evening, and slept for four glasses so that we could get up and work just before dawn."

"Night watches weren't a problem for you, then?"

"No, sir. I like the night. So do you, do you not?"

"At times." Had Matorak seen Mykel with the soarer?

"They say you are a dagger of the ancients, sir." Matorak's eyes were politely expressionless.

"What is said and what is are often two different things," Mykel replied. "Even when they are the same, the words do not convey the reality." He really didn't want to admit or deny the appellation.

"In the desert, words are a waste of water. In the ocean, speech will drown one."

Mykel laughed.

74

On Decdi morning, like every other morning since arriving in Hyalt, Dainyl was up before dawn. After he had dressed and eaten, he slipped out of the way station, carrying his small bag of personal gear. As the sky lightened from purple-green to green-tinged silver, he looked to the north and the waiting pteridons, and then at the sky. A cooler breeze blew from the northeast, carrying behind it clouds, lower than he would have liked, but high enough for first squad to follow the high road north to Tempre.

The previous days of patrols over the rebel compound had proved far less eventful than the first day, since it had become clear to the besieged rebels that any use of a lightcannon resulted in its destruction. Still, the first day had cost Fifth Company two Myrmidons, in addition to Dyrmant's death. While Dainyl should have anticipated it, the Talent strength of the alector who had met him outside the regional compound had shocked him. Not that someone had that level of Talent, but that an alector of that ability could be so easily spared.

Or had the dead alector just been arrogant, thinking that no mere Myrmidon possessed equal or stronger Talent? Either way, Dainyl reflected, it meant that he would have to deal with either great arrogance among Brekylt's and Rhelyn's rebels or great Talent—if not both.

It was for the best, although he had not planned it that way, that he had not immediately attempted to transfer Dyrmant's pteridon to Brytra, who was now flying with first squad. Definitely a fiery introduction for the young alectress in becoming a flier.

After that first day, the compound had shown little overt activity, except for occasional quick light-blasts, designed more to keep the Myrmidons from venturing too close. In return, Fifth Company had used skylances to seal more of the slit ports, and in response, the rebels created more, if slowly.

Dainyl turned as Fhentyl approached.

"Good morning, Submarshal."

"Good morning. We'll be lifting off shortly."

"Will one squad be enough, sir?" asked Fhentyl. "Things have been more quiet here."

"For now," agreed Dainyl. "That worries me."

"You think that the rebels are planning something."

Dainyl nodded. He was certain of that, but exactly what they might do he had no idea, except that it was likely to be deadly. He just wished he hadn't had to wait so long for the Cadmians to reach Tempre, but he needed ground forces to get into the administrative center—and the Table chamber—in Tempre. From what Lystrana had been able to discover, even more resources had been di-

verted, including some to Tempre. Tempre was a less isolated locale for alectors, and that *might* mean that there
were no lightcannon there—or fewer. That also meant
that Majer Mykel might face more of a locally raised and
trained armed force than Dainyl had originally planned,
which was another reason why Dainyl had finally decided
on sending three companies and the majer, rather than
two under Captain Rhystan, as he had first considered.

"They might try some form of shielded vehicle," he
said slowly to Fhentyl, "like a small sandox coach, for the
lightcannon. Aim for the wheels, that happens. If they do
something like that, have the Cadmians retreat. They
can't stand against those weapons. One way or another,"
Dainyl continued, "the rebels will attempt to break out,
probably tomorrow or the next day. Be ready for it. Don't
accept any surrenders. They have the equivalent of high
alectors in there, and if any of you get close to them,
you'll end up either doing what they want or dead."

"Sir?" Fhentyl stiffened.

"You heard me, Captain. I'm thinking of your health
and survival. They'll do about anything to gain control of
the pteridons, and that includes treachery and murder.
That's why you are not to land there under any circumstances." Dainyl paused. "Why do you think I'm here in
person, and why I had to be the one to attempt to see the
regional alector?"

The captain relaxed slightly, but not all the way.

Dainyl didn't blame him.

"I never thought . . ."

"Neither did any of us," Dainyl replied gently. "But
we're the ones who have to deal with it. Now . . . I need to
be going. Best of fortune, Captain."

"Thank you, sir."

Dainyl offered a smile and lifted the gear bag he carried, then strode across the trampled grass and dirt north
of the way station toward first squad.

Undercaptain Hyksant stood waiting by his pteridon as
Dainyl approached. "First squad, ready to fly, sir."

"Thank you, Undercaptain. Stand by." Dainyl slipped his gear into the harness bag behind the saddle and swung up onto the pteridon.

"Lift off!" *Lift off . . . straight north, gentle climb to two hundred yards . . .*

The pteridon complied, as did the other four, one bearing the newest Myrmidon flier.

75

Mykel and his three companies reached the way station south of Tempre late on Novdi, just after sunset. All along the road, he'd made an effort to replicate the sort of shield that he'd sensed with Submarshal Dainyl. He *thought* he was doing better at it, but how would he know? Still, he had to do something before he outlived his usefulness to the submarshal. That was clear from what both Rachyla and the soarer had told him.

The station was located on the north-south high road a good five vingts north of the intersection between the north-south high road from Hyalt to Tempre and the east-west high road that ran from Hafin on the west coast all the way through the South Pass of the Spine of Corus to Flyr in Lustrea. A low hill behind the station to the east rose less than fifteen yards above the top of the waystation roof. As befitted a major way station, there was a spring, a stable, a corral, and a main building. None were adequate to deal with close to three hundred Cadmians and their mounts, but it was the best to be had.

Because Mykel had felt uneasy about his position, especially without orders from the submarshal, he had posted scouts several vingts away from the waystation along the high road in both directions, with reliefs scheduled as part of the watch rotation.

Well before dawn on Decdi, he was awakened.

"Sir . . ." reported Jasakyt, "There are two, maybe three, companies of troopers riding this way from Tempre. They're not Cadmians." His lips crinkled into a smile. "Hard to tell in the dark, but it looks like fancy uniforms, too."

Mykel was already pulling on his boots and his tunic. "Just troopers? No wagons? Carts? Baggage?"

"No, sir."

"How far were they, and how fast were they riding?"

"Three vingts when I left. They weren't pushing it. I'd say a quarter to a half glass before they get here."

"Battalion! Form up! To horse!" Mykel turned to Jasakyt. "Head back out. No more than half a vingt. Report back when you see them."

Jasakyt nodded and headed off.

"Fabrytal! Here!"

"Sir?" The undercaptain appeared, still pulling on his tunic.

"Form up Fifteenth Company by squads, staggered firing lines, rifles ready. On the flat east of the road, just north of the waystation."

"Sir?" asked Fabrytal.

"How likely is it that three companies of strange troopers would decide to take a leisurely ride before dawn on a Decdi morning?"

"When you put it that way . . ."

"Go! Form up Fifteenth Company as ordered."

Fabrytal left at close to a run.

"Loryalt! Matorak! To me."

Loryalt appeared first, followed by the Hyaltan undercaptain.

"Loryalt, we've got mounted troopers headed this way. I want Seventeenth Company formed up, ready to ride, on the back of the north side of the hill behind the way station. Keep out of sight, but have a scout in position to observe. Once the firing starts, you're to sweep out to the north and cut off any retreat. Give yourself enough space so that you can ride out, stagger the company into a firing line and rake them with at least two volleys before you go after them with sabres. Three volleys or more, if they don't react. Pass the orders to your squad leaders once you form up so they know the plan."

"Yes, sir."

"Head out now. You've got the farthest to go." Mykel turned in the dimness to Matorak. "I want you to set up your company on the south side of the way station. Keep them close together and station them so that no one can be seen by anyone coming south on the high road. Once the firing starts, you're to use the same tactics as Seventeenth Company. Charge out straight, hold the road on the south side. Come to a firing line and rake them. Two volleys. Keep firing at them until they look like they'll charge—or until I order a charge. Or Undercaptain Fabrytal does. And tell your squad leaders."

"Yes, sir."

In the dimness, Mykel could see the unspoken questions in Matorak's face. "They're not Cadmians, and they only think they've been trained. They can't have been in much of a fight, and they have no idea of what our volleys will do to them. They'll break."

Matorak hurried off, and Mykel followed almost at a run. Even so, he was mounted and beside Fabrytal as Fifteenth Company formed up on the flat area on the east side of the road just north of the way station. In the east, the sky was just beginning to lighten.

"Sir? Where are the other companies going?"

"Seventeenth is headed a bit north behind the hill. Second will be concealed behind the waystation. I want them close, but out of sight." What Mykel wasn't saying was that he was counting on the strange troopers to assume that he would not fire first. He wouldn't—not until he had a sign that the troopers were hostile, although he couldn't imagine otherwise on an end-day morning. If the troopers came in firing, that was another question, but Fifteenth Company was drawn up in firing order.

There were other questions as well. Who had created three companies of mounted troopers, and how had they known Mykel was there? Who was sending them against Cadmians and why? Had something happened to the submarshal? Or was the information about Mykel's Cadmians something discovered by the mysterious Tables?

Mykel shook his head. None of that really mattered for the moment. What mattered was how he handled the troopers. Still, as he sat on the roan waiting, he concentrated on trying to strengthen the shield/concealment around himself.

The sky had lightened into a dark greenish gray when the first ranks of the oncoming troopers appeared on the high road, the click of hoofs on stone echoing through the dimness.

Mykel could sense a certain surprise from somewhere.

Then the column halted, still on the road, a good fifty yards to the north of Fifteenth Company.

Mykel smiled, grimly, then called out? "Who goes there?"

"Who are you?" A figure rode out a few yards from the five-man vanguard, all too close to the main body.

"Fifteenth Company, Third Battalion, Cadmian Mounted Rifles," Mykel replied, letting his voice carry. "Who are you?"

"The Alector's Guard of Tempre—charged with maintaining order in and around Tempre."

Mykel waited, studying the officer with both eyes and senses.

"There is no need for a Cadmian presence near Tempre. Regional Alector Fahylt has everything under control."

"Captain," Mykel stated, "that is not what our orders stated."

"Majer, Majer Kersyd. I'm afraid that you must be mistaken, Captain."

Mykel ignored the snub. "I'm a little confused. The Cadmian Mounted Rifles are charged with maintaining order and subduing rebels and insurrections. We have the freedom of the roads as necessary. Exactly what is the Alector's Guard?"

"There are no Cadmians here. There have never been any, and with the growing Squawt threat to the north, the regional alector formed the Guard—"

"Has the Guard ever fought the Squawts?"

"The Guard is here to prevent that necessity."

Mykel sensed the growing unease of the majer. "I see. And what if we insist on proceeding to Tempre?"

"I am afraid we cannot allow that."

"Cannot allow?" questioned Mykel. "You would stop a Cadmian command under the orders of the Marshal of Myrmidons?" With cold certainty, he could sense someone aiming at him.

He jerked aside in the saddle, but even so, something half-twisted him, almost yanking him off the roan. He straightened, and his own rifle came up in a single movement, and he fired, *willing* the shot home. The Guard majer did not even have the chance to look surprised

"Fifteenth Company! Fire at will!" Mykel ordered.

The Cadmians got off three volleys before even scattered rifle shots were offered by the Alector's Guard. From both the north and south, Mykel could sense and hear the hoofbeats of the horses of the other two companies. Following their orders, if slightly later than Mykel would have liked, Seventeenth Company swept up the road from the south, while Second Company swung out and swept down from the north.

Mykel dropped two squad leaders, and an undercaptain. More shots, if scattered, began to fly around him. He kept firing, then reloaded.

"Seventeenth Company! Fire at will!"

"Second Company! Fire at will!"

Shots poured into the tightly massed body of the guard troopers from three sides. Mykel watched, seeing that the rear ranks of the Guard were beginning to turn their mounts.

"Fifteenth Company, rifles away!" ordered Mykel. "Sabres ready! Forward!"

While he began the charge, he let Fabrytal lead Fifteenth Company against the center of the so-called Alector's Guard.

The other two companies followed.

Mykel remained on the road, noting wryly that Fabrytal had ordered five troopers to cover and support him. That was probably for the best, since he felt exhausted—and shouldn't have. He glanced at his shoulder and upper chest, both of which were sore, but there were no holes or marks on his uniform tunic. He wasn't certain he believed it, but the only conclusion he could come to was that his efforts in holding the shields to conceal his abilities had diffused the impact of a bullet. The corollary was that doing so took a great deal of strength, and that meant he still was vulnerable in a firefight, if less so.

He straightened in the saddle, sheathed the sabre, then eased the roan forward to keep abreast of Fifteenth Company, taking his rifle out once more.

In less than a glass, the remnants of the Guard had scattered westward, across the fields of golden wheat, leaving paths of bent and broken grain—and bodies and more bodies. The sun had risen, casting long shadows across the carnage. From what Mykel could see, well close to two hundred Guard troopers lay around the high road and in the nearby sections of the fields.

Another half glass passed before the three companies had returned and re-formed before the way station.

"Report!" ordered Mykel.

"Fifteenth Company. Two dead, five wounded."

"Seventeenth Company. Four dead, eight wounded."

"Second Company. Five dead, four wounded."

Mykel surveyed the company commanders. "This was the easy part. It will get harder. I'm certain that the sub-marshal has something else in mind as well. Now . . . each of you detail a squad to recover rifles and ammunition from the dead and wounded. Disarm the wounded and bring them into the way station. Fabrytal . . . you send scouts north, three vingts. Loryalt to the south. Matorak, your scouts go on the back side of the hill behind us and another set on that ridge to the west beyond the fields. . . . Once everything is set up, stand down, and get the mounts watered and fed and your men rested."

"Sir . . . do we have any orders?"

"We just executed the orders we had. We were to take and hold this way station, and wait for the submarshal to arrive with further orders." That much was essentially true. Mykel just wished he knew for certain what came next, although it was likely to be some sort of attack on Tempre and, based on the fact that there had been an unauthorized mounted force, one on the regional alector's compound was likely. "Dismissed to your companies."

Later, after the companies had completed the body details—for the moment, all two hundred and three were laid out behind the stable—Mykel rode to the top of the hill behind the way station. He reined up in the knee high grass and slowly studied the fields and well-tended woods in all directions. There were close to twenty small steads, but, not surprisingly, no one was out in the fields. He saw no flocks nearby.

He had the sinking feeling that the massacre had been a setup, except he had no idea why, except to undermine the moral authority of the Cadmians. Yet the dead majer had been ready to order an attack. All the Guard troopers had been fully armed, and all rifles—identical to the Cadmian pieces—clearly used or ready for use.

That meant, at least to him, that the outcome didn't matter to whoever had set it up. If he and his companies had been defeated, that would have undermined the Cadmians in one way. By his effectiveness in ruthlessly attacking, he'd undermined the Cadmians in another.

76

As his pteridon swept in toward the way station south of Tempre, in the late afternoon's shadowed sunlight, Dainyl could make out the signs of a battle, even without the sense of lost lifeforce that pervaded the area. The wheat fields to the west of the high road had been trampled, and several locations, even from the air, showed where men and mounts had fallen.

"North of the way station, on the flat!" Dainyl called back to Hyksant. *North . . . to the side of the road . . .*

The pteridon swung west and then descended into the wind, flaring and settling onto the ground already scarred by horses, then folding its long blue leathery wings. In turn, the other four pteridons landed, each farther from the way station.

Majer Mykel had hurried out of the way station even before Dainyl's pteridon touched down, and stood waiting, less than fifteen yards away.

Dainyl dismounted and stretched. His legs ached. He still wasn't used to flying all day, and wondered if he'd ever regain that ability. He doubted it, since, once he finished the Hyalt-Tempre campaign—or it finished him—the pteridon would be taken over by another Myrmidon, and he would go back to headquarters in Elcien. He studied the majer. For better or worse, the lander had tighter shields than before, much tighter. To Dainyl, he almost felt like a diminutive alector, except his shielded Talent was gray-green, rather than grayish purple. Still . . . from a distance, most alectors might not know.

Finally, Dainyl stepped toward the majer, leaving his gear on the pteridon. "You had a battle here."

"Yes, sir. Three companies of something called the Alector's Guard appeared at dawn this morning. They opened fire first."

Dainyl sensed Mykel's grimace as much as he saw the expression.

"It was a slaughter, or close to it. We took out about two-thirds of their men. The others scattered. I've had scouts out as far as seven vingts, just short of the outskirts of Tempre. We haven't seen any sign of other forces. We haven't seen any traffic on the high road south from Tempre. There have been some spirit merchants from Vyan and Krost heading into Tempre, but no others on this section of the high road."

"You said they opened fire first. Did they have rifles?"

"Yes, sir. We collected all the rifles and ammunition from the wounded and the fallen. The rifles are Cadmian issue, but they don't have serial numbers. The ammunition's the same, too."

First Dramur and now Tempre—Dainyl couldn't help asking himself just how many unauthorized rifles had been manufactured and where they all had ended up. "Have you found out anything from the wounded?"

"Not much. The officers were either killed or fled. The rankers were told last night that they would be riding out after Squawts in Cadmian uniforms who had crossed the Vedra and were threatening Tempre. According to the majer in command, this Alector's Guard was formed to offset the threat of the Squawts." Mykel laughed harshly. "That was hard to believe, since the Cadmians pretty much wiped them out in the southern Westerhills. The majer said we had no business entering Tempre. I reminded him that the Cadmians had the freedom of the roads anywhere in Corus. His answer was to start shooting."

"How many men did you lose, Majer?

"Twelve dead, sixteen wounded. Two of the wounded are having a hard time of it. We lost one earlier. We counted something like two hundred six bodies, and we've got thirteen wounded captives left—all rankers."

Dainyl found himself both amazed and appalled.

"Sir . . . this was a setup. We were set to lose either way."

After a moment, Dainyl understood. "Either you Cadmians are ineffective or bloodthirsty tools of the Duarches?"

"That's my guess, sir."

Unfortunately, the majer's assessment made all too much sense. "Then, we might as well be bloodthirsty for a reason. Let me get things settled with the Myrmidons, and then I'll be back, and we'll go over the plans for tomorrow's attack. Our objective is to take total control of the administrative center of Tempre."

"Yes, sir. You want me to wait here?"

Dainyl laughed. "No. Get something to drink. Is there a table in the way station where we can spread out some maps?"

"There are several. One's better."

"Wait for me there."

Mykel nodded and stepped back, then turned and walked briskly toward the way station.

Dainyl watched him. He was fairly certain that the majer had told the truth, but it was getting harder to read the lander, much harder. He shook his head, then started back toward the pteridon for the maps.

As Dainyl neared the pteridons, Hyksant approached. "Sir . . . the majer . . . perhaps I'm mistaken, but I thought I sensed Talent there. With the majer, I mean."

"He has some untrained Talent," Dainyl replied. "Landers occasionally do. While it isn't something that we encourage, or would normally accept, it is to our benefit." He paused. "For now. Only for now. That is another reason why I've been given this mission."

Hyksant nodded slowly. "I had wondered."

"He was the first to discover the rebels. Had he not . . ."

"Ah . . . yes, sir. Landers can be useful."

"In their place, Undercaptain. In their place." *What is their place? What is ours?* As he considered those questions, he realized that less than a year before he would never even have entertained such self-inquiries.

77

Mykel stepped out into the darkness, this time on the south side of the way station, since the Myrmidons and their pteridons had taken the hillside to the north, leaving the way station and stables to Mykel and his Cadmians. In the darkness above, both Selena and Asterta shone brightly, and as close together as he had ever seen them, near the zenith. The night wind from the west was light, still warm, and carried the mixed odors of ripening wheat and death. To the north, he could sense the Myrmidons and their pinkish purple energies, and the gray cloudiness over those energies that represented the submarshal's shields.

The submarshal's plan to take Tempre was straightforward enough. Basically, Mykel's three companies would ride north on the high road, and the five pteridons would use their skylances to clear any large forces or barricades. The Cadmians would have to deal with snipers or individuals hidden where the skylances would not reach. Once the courtyard around the compound was secured the submarshal and one other alector would use the skylances to blast open the main door—assuming that the regional alector did not surrender. Then two alectors and a squad under Mykel's direct command would begin taking the structure, corridor by corridor. The submarshal had been very direct—Mykel *would* lead the force designated to subdue the interior of the complex.

According to the submarshal, there were roughly twenty alectors, half of whom were Myrmidon foot guards. The others, including the regional alector, were functionaries who supervised and directed the tasks of regional administration. The Cadmians were not to approach any alectors closely, but they had leave to fire on any who did not immediately surrender.

Mykel paused. That wasn't quite what the submarshal had said. He'd said that Mykel had leave to fire on them, as did any Cadmian. The implication was clear enough . . . and boded ill for Mykel's future. Yet he still had the feeling that deserting would be far worse . . . so far.

Submarshal Dainyl wanted control of the regional alector's compound. But why? It had something to do with Hyalt. That much was certain, but Mykel didn't believe for a moment that the purpose was merely to interdict supplies to Hyalt—or that such was even the primary reason. Whatever it was, it was clearly vital, because submarshals didn't run company-level operations, even in the Myrmidons—unless a great deal was at stake.

Mykel turned and looked to the northwest, toward Tempre. After receiving the announcement of Rachyla's move to Tempre as the resident chatelaine for young Amaryk, whatever a resident chatelaine might be, Mykel had thought about how he might visit Rachyla, but Cadmian majers just didn't ride close to two hundred vingts for a visit to someone who might well not even wish to see them. Yet when he had asked the soarer about that "coincidence," the ancient had cryptically mentioned "forces within" Mykel and refused to say more.

Were there forces within Rachyla as well?

He shook his head. The more he discovered, the more questions he had.

He'd once believed that, when he attained more rank and responsibility, he would have more latitude and freedom, but from what he'd seen since Dramur, he had less. Or was it that now, as he learned more, he saw how few true choices of any wisdom were open? Or was he just deluding himself, being afraid to step outside the structure of the Cadmians?

After a time, he turned and walked slowly back toward the way station. He needed some sleep—or rest, if he couldn't sleep.

78

Less than a glass after sunrise, Mykel's three companies were already five vingts north of the way station and within two or three vingts of the outskirts of Tempre. The terrain had become slightly more hilly with each vingt they had ridden, and the fields and meadows had given way to orchards. The trees looked to be pears and apples, although Mykel was no grower. In smaller fenced fields between the orchards were occasional flocks of sheep, smaller than those Mykel had seen in the northlands and fatter than those near Hyalt.

For the last two vingts, the high road had risen ever so slightly to climb a large and gradual ridge. At the top of the ridge was an eternastone turnout for wagons, presumably to rest draft horses after the long climb. Beyond the turnout, the high road began an even more gentle descent toward Tempre, spread out before the Cadmians.

"Quiet, this morning," offered Fabrytal, riding beside Mykel. "Especially for a Londi."

"I'm sure the word has gone out that the evil Cadmians are on the march into Tempre, slaughtering all in their path." Mykel readjusted the ammunition belt across his shoulders. If he had to charge through buildings, he wasn't going to be able to go back for shells to reload.

He glanced to his left and then his right, but the wide low ridge that had separated the orchard lands from the smaller steads on the outskirts of Tempre held no structures or dwellings, mainly stands of hardwood and leafy softwood, with almost no evergreens. Despite the heat of summer, the grass beyond the shoulder of the high road was green.

"Looks peaceful ahead," the undercaptain went on.

"It will be for a while. It might even be until we reach the alector's compound."

Ahead, the high road arrowed on its descent directly

toward the River Vedra. Ahead, but appearing to the left of the high road where it cut through the city, were the twin green towers that flanked the river piers. From the maps and the briefing from the submarshal, Mykel knew that the regional alector's complex was at the end of the high road, below another ridge that separated the structures from the River Vedra.

In the distance, across the River Vedra was the southernmost part of the Westerhills, the trees on the distant slopes indistinct in the morning haze. Mykel could only tell that the trees appeared to be mixed softwoods and pine, with near-continuous canopy of foliage.

A shadow fell across the road, followed by another, and then three more, as the pteridons circled above the Cadmians.

Mykel kept studying the high road, and the steads beside the road down toward Tempre. Before long, the steads with smaller patches of land and orchards consisting of only a half score of trees gave way to small dwellings and shops—and all were shuttered.

"They knew we were coming," said Fabrytal.

"It looks that way." Mykel raised his voice. "Scout squads out!"

The undercaptain turned. "Scout squads!"

The two half squads broke off from the main column, one angling east, the other west. They were to scout the two boulevards parallel to the high road. With the pteridons circling, and three companies on the high road, Mykel doubted they'd find much, but it would have been foolish not to look into the possibility of ambushes or flank attacks. Fortunately, the streets and boulevards of Tempre were wide, and none of the buildings, save the towers by the piers, were more than three stories, if that.

Some few houses weren't shuttered, and in places, when he looked down side streets, Mykel could see people here and there. But the high road itself was so quiet that the loudest sound was that of hoofs clicking on the stone. Even the rankers were silent.

Just before the high road ended at the walls before the regional alector's compound, it passed through gardens on both sides, each side bordered with low gray stone walls. Stone paths wound through the grass and under the carefully pruned trees, or alongside the profusion of flowers in their stone-edged beds.

Mykel could feel himself getting edgier as he and Fabrytal followed the vanguard past the gardens and toward the stone complex ahead. Waiting before them were the two sub-squads he had dispatched to survey the side boulevards.

"East side. No forces to report, sir. There's a new compound—gray stone—a half vingt east of here on the cross road. It's got a blue banner."

Mykel nodded. He would have wagered that compound was where the so-called Alector's Guard was based. "Ride back up there to observe. If you see anything, or any more forces, I'll want a report as soon as possible."

"Yes, sir." The acting squad leader nodded, then turned his mount.

"West side. Nothing to report, sir!"

The lack of opposition only made Mykel even more concerned as he rode toward the ungated entryway to the alector's complex. The gray granite walls surrounding the buildings were low, not more than a yard and a third high. The single building comprising the regional alector's compound was modest compared to the palace of the Duarch in Elcien, although the main-front entrance did boast a small pillared entrance above wide stone steps. The building itself was set before the low hills bordering the south bank of the Vedra, hills planted or cultivated in a fashion similar to that of a park. Before the structure was a wide paved plaza.

As his force deployed across the plaza, Mykel ordered, "Companies! Halt! Staggered firing lines! Seventeenth Company, to the rear of the building!"

Even as close as he was to the structure, he could sense no one around. Had the regional alector fled? Had everyone?

The pteridon carrying the submarshal settled on the gray paving stones less than fifty yards from Mykel. The submarshal still held his skylance casually ready as Mykel rode toward the creature and its flier.

"Majer . . . is your squad ready?" asked the submarshal.

"Yes, sir." Mykel paused. "Most of the city is shuttered. We didn't see anyone anywhere near the boulevards or the main roads. There is a new compound to the east. It appears to be where the forces we fought yesterday were based. I have it under observation."

"A wise precaution." The submarshal's tone was dry. "If they are . . . unavailable, it may prove a suitable basing point for you and your forces. We'll discuss that later, if necessary. For now, we need to take the alector's headquarters here. You may not find anyone inside, but we need to make sure. Check the lower levels carefully. Once you've secured each level, send one of your men to report. If you see any alectors, unless they surrender immediately, withdraw and inform me. I'll await your reports here."

"Yes, sir." Mykel rode back to the front of the column. "Third squad forward!" He had picked third squad because the majority of rankers were settled veterans, and he was familiar with them.

He dismounted at the foot of the steps, and handed the roan's reins to one of the Cadmians who would maintain a close watch on the front entry. After the others dismounted, he ordered. "Squad forward."

Mykel held his rifle at the ready, although he let the third squad scout go up the wide stone steps to the arched entry first behind the stone pillars. He and Ryket—the squad leader—followed, flanked by two other rankers.

The circular entry hall, beyond the plain granite arches and the four-yard-high double golden oak doors, bound in brass, soared a full two stories. The edge of the hall was ringed with goldenstone columns, set in pairs, roughly four yards apart. Octagonal green and gold marble tiles comprised the floor, with black diamonds filling the spaces between the larger octagonal tiles. In the middle of the hall was a statue of the Duarches. It might have been a duplicate of the one in the square in Hyalt.

The echo of boots on stone heightened the feeling of emptiness.

From the entry hall, two wide corridors branched. Mykel took half the squad and took the left corridor, sending Ryket and the other ten men down the right side. All the studies and spaces along the corridor that paralleled the front of the structure were empty.

"Spooky, sir," murmured Mergeyt, the ranker following Mykel. "No one here, and it's not even an end-day."

"They didn't have the ability to stand up to us." *And the pteridons, and they knew we were both coming.* The decision to abandon the building and Tempre made sense to Mykel. He just wondered where they'd all gone and how they'd known the Cadmians and Myrmidons were on the way.

There was not a single person in the upper two stories of the structure, and yet it was as if everyone had walked away from their studies and desks and left everything in place, as if they knew they would be back—after an inconvenience.

The other matter was that every door had been left unlocked and unbolted—except one, a slightly larger door set in a stone frame in the northwest corner of the building. It might have been a storage closet, but Mykel didn't think so. He could sense the residue of the purple energies of alectors.

"What do you think, sir?" asked Ryket.

"There might be a staircase behind that. If anyone's left, they'll be down there. Let's see." Mykel studied the lock, protected with some form of energy. "Stand back. Rifles ready."

"Rifles ready."

Mykel decided to try his shields, struggling with the unseen grayness, before he raised his own weapon, concentrating, squeezing the trigger, and *willing* the bullet to the lock.

The lock exploded, and one of the fragments slammed into Mykel. He rocked back, glad he had thought about the shields. Several chunks of bronze lay on the green marble tiles at his feet.

". . . see that?"

"Open it," Mykel ordered quickly, as much to cut off murmurs and rumors as to see what lay behind the door.

Ryket stepped forward, rifle in one hand, then pulled the door lever, stepping back quickly and bringing up his rifle as the door swung open. No one stood behind the door. There was a narrow landing at the top of a narrow circular stone staircase leading downward. So far as Mykel and third squad had been able to determine, the staircase was the first access to the underground sections of the building that they had seen.

Mykel almost nodded. He could sense more strongly the pinkish purpleness that suggested alectors had been here recently. "Ryket, dispatch someone to the submarshal. Have him report that the upper levels are clear and that we're proceeding down to the lower level. Make sure he reports to the submarshal that none of the studies or chambers were locked, except the one to this staircase."

"Yes, sir."

Mykel gestured to the scout. "I'll be right behind you."

He followed the scout down the circular stone staircase, a staircase that extended far more than one level, it seemed to Mykel. At the bottom was another corridor running back eastward, apparently underneath those above. It was lit dimly by a series of lights in brackets affixed to the stone walls. The lights were unfamiliar to Mykel, providing a steady glow, but he saw no oil reservoir beneath them.

The sense of alectors was stronger, but not strong enough to suggest any that close. Mykel took several steps to the first door on the right. Opening it revealed a small storeroom, one in which linens and towels were stacked, presumably for use in the wash chambers on the top level, off the large study presumably used by the regional alector.

Mykel studied the corridor. There were no doors on the left side, at least not for the next twenty yards. The next door revealed a carpentry and cabinetry shop, where the tools were neatly racked. The door after that showed an empty chamber.

Ahead on the left was the only doorway on that side of the corridor, and it was set in stone. The sense of purple was stronger behind that door, and the entire door was encased in the kind of energy that had bound the lock that had exploded.

The scout reached for the handle. "It's locked. The handle . . . it feels funny."

"Leave it." Mykel turned to Ryket. "Send another messenger to the submarshal. Tell him that everything's clear except one room that may have some alectors in it."

"You think so, sir?"

"If they're anywhere, they're here." Mykel smiled faintly. "I don't think I want to try to shoot open another lock."

"Ah . . . no, sir."

"We'll just wait here for the submarshal." Mykel stepped back.

While the door suggested *something* of power lay behind it, Mykel wasn't about to investigate, not after what had happened with the lock on the door to the lower level.

79

As he flew leading the Myrmidons of first squad in observing the majer's advance into the city, Dainyl realized that he had not seen a single rider anywhere on the main roads. The wide boulevards were

empty, something he had never seen in any city in all his
years of flying. Even the great river piers were empty.

When the Cadmian forces were at last drawn up before
the gray granite structure that held the regional alector
and the functionaries who normally administered the
area around Tempre, Dainyl circled the area, barely
above the gray slate tiles of the roof, glancing down at the
open and empty courtyard in the center of the gray granite building. Then he brought his pteridon down onto the
stones of the paved area before the building.

After giving the majer his orders on entering and
checking the building, he dismounted, then stretched his
legs and walked around. Finally, he settled back to wait,
although he kept his eyes and senses checking the area.

A quarter of a glass later or so, he walked toward
Hyksant. "Send someone up, not Galya, to fly recon
around us."

"Yes, sir." Hyksant gestured. "Brytra, for the next
glass, you get to do recon around the city. If you see anything we should know about, get back to us."

Brytra nodded, and in moments, she and her pteridon
were airborne.

Several moments passed before the undercaptain
spoke again. "The RA didn't want to stay around, sir."

"It doesn't look like anyone did."

"He has to have thrown in with the rebels in Hyalt,
then. Why else would he leave?"

Dainyl nodded. Why indeed? Also, the recorder had to
have been involved. How else would Fahylt have known
when and where to send out his Alector's Guard?

More important from a personal standpoint, Hyksant's observations illustrated that all too much of what
Dainyl had felt and assumed for some time was anything
but obvious to all but a handful of people. That meant
that, if matters did not go well, his position would soon
be untenable. The two letter dispatches in his tunic
would help—but only if he succeeded in his plan. If not,
worst of all, his failure could reflect adversely on

Lystrana and Kytrana. Dainyl hadn't forgotten what had happened to Kylana after Zestafyn had gotten involved in matters where the senior alectors around Samist hadn't wanted him.

He walked back to his own pteridon, forcing himself to wait, occasionally looking up into the cloudless silvergreen sky to make sure that Brytra was continuing her surveillance of Tempre. The day was hot and still, and finally, he took off his flying jacket, folded it, and slipped it into the gear bag.

A glass passed before the first Cadmian returned, trotting up, then stiffening and reporting. "Submarshal, sir. The first two floors of the building are empty, sir. There's no one there, and none of the doors were even locked. There was one locked door leading to a lower level. The majer and the squad are checking that out now."

"How did they unlock it? Did they force the door?" Dainyl was more than idly curious.

"The majer shot the lock with his rifle. It . . . it sort of exploded."

"That will be all. You can remain with the other Cadmians." In the event that something else did befall the majer, Dainyl wanted the Cadmian ranker as a witness. He hoped Majer Mykel would hurry in his investigations, because he suspected that Fahylt was already in either Alustre or Ludar claiming that Dainyl had overreached himself and his authority as a Myrmidon submarshal. If he didn't deal quickly with Hyalt, he well might not be a submarshal—or anything—for much longer.

"Yes, sir." The ranker turned and headed back to the squad patrolling the front of the building.

As he waited, Dainyl considered the implications. The tactical retreat made sense, especially since it was clear that Fahylt had not yet developed his local troopers into a truly effective fighting force. The complete and orderly withdrawal indicated that the regional alector believed he would be back in Tempre rather quickly. He couldn't have withdrawn all the landers and indigens—or even the lesser alectors who could not use a Table. They had just been ordered to stay at home until the RA returned. All that, in turn, suggested fairly strong backing from Duarch Samist, since Brekylt was not yet in a position to make such a commitment. Or was he?

Or had all of them worked out something with Shastylt, instead of Brekylt? Dainyl had been ordered to keep his operation secret. If it failed, Shastylt could deny everything and insist that Dainyl had been attempting something unauthorized—or even a coup of some sort. Dainyl was running out of time—and he felt that he'd hardly begun.

Less than a quarter of a glass passed before the second Cadmian appeared, hurrying across the paving stones to Dainyl.

"Submarshal, sir. The majer wanted you to know that there's a locked and sealed door on the underground level. He thinks there might be alectors behind it, and he awaits your orders, sir."

"Thank you. Where is the staircase down to that level?"

"On the back side, in the corner, sir." The Cadmian pointed toward the northwest.

"Remain with your company here." Dainyl turned and crossed the graystone pavement separating him from Hyksant, who stood beside his pteridon. "I'll need Galya—with her lance."

"The lances . . ."

"I know. They're only good for one discharge away from the pteridons. Two at best. But I still might need that." He doubted he would. He needed Galya—or some Myrmidon—for an entirely different purpose, because he didn't want Majer Mykel anywhere near that door and what had to lie behind it.

"Galya! Take your lance and accompany the submarshal."

The two Myrmidons crossed the space between the pteridons and the patrolling Cadmians, who moved aside as Dainyl and Galya neared the stone steps up to the stone columns at the top and the arched entry beyond. Once inside the empty foyer hall, Dainyl lengthened his stride and hurried toward the far corner of the building.

Two Cadmians stood guarding the top of the staircase. Even before he reached the door, Dainyl could sense that the door had been Talent-locked. He nodded. At least, the majer hadn't discovered about Talent-locks and how to undo them. He'd just applied brute force—and that wouldn't work in places like the doors to Tables.

"They're down here, sir," offered the shorter Cadmian.

"Thank you." Dainyl made his way past them and down the circular staircase.

Galya followed, more slowly and farther behind, in order to maneuver her skylance without hitting Dainyl.

The Cadmians had formed a semicircle—all with their weapons aimed at the door. The majer stepped away from his men to meet Dainyl.

"Majer, you and your men have done well. I'd like you and all your men to clear this area. We may need to use the skylance to break through the door. Station two guards at the top of the steps. From now on, until you have further orders, no one—absolutely no one but me and any Myrmidons with me—is to come down here on this level. Is that clear?"

"Yes, sir." The Cadmian officer stiffened.

"What I am doing may take several glasses. It might even take longer. During that time, I'd like you to return to direct command of the Cadmians outside the building. In my absence, Undercaptain Hyksant is in command of the Myrmidons."

"Yes, sir. By your leave, sir?"

"By my leave."

"Third squad, back up the stairs," ordered the majer. "Ryket, lead the way."

Dainyl waited until all the Cadmians had left and were up the staircase.

"Do you want the lance now, sir?" asked Galya.

"I hope you won't need it, yet. I'm going to try a sidearm first. Stand back."

Dainyl triggered just the slightest burst from the weapon, barely a trickle, then released the Talent-locks on the door. He stepped forward and tried the door lever, then turned to Galya. "I'm going in. If anyone but me steps out through this door, whether they're an alector or not, flame them. Don't hesitate. Is that clear?"

"Yes, sir."

Dainyl held one lightcutter ready, checked the other at his belt, and hoped he wouldn't need the one tucked inside his tunic. He opened the door. A quick glance and scan with his Talent indicated that the Table chamber was empty. He stepped inside and closed the door behind him. As with the last time he had visited Tempre, there was nothing in the chamber except for the light-torches mounted on the walls and the Table itself.

The lack of energy around the Table was clear. The Table had been shut down.

Dainyl smiled. He would have been surprised if Patronyl had not inactivated it. Dainyl looked toward the hidden rooms, concealed behind both Talent-illusions and Talent-locks.

He didn't bother with the illusions, but simply unlocked the hidden door and watched, shields at full, sidearm in hand, as the stone slid away to reveal—behind the illusion—the narrow passageway. Patronyl's aura was obvious, but the recorder did not appear.

Dainyl stepped forward, waiting.

A thin alector appeared, standing in the opening, letting the illusion dissolve. His eyes were a pale violet, and he held a lightcutter in his hand. "Ah . . . the formidable Submarshal Dainyl. I should have known you were more than you seemed." He fired the lightcutter even before he finished speaking.

The bluish beam flared around Dainyl and his shields.

Dainyl took three long steps forward, drawing the second lightcutter. He fired both sidearms at Patronyl. At the same time, he forced a Talent-bolt at the recorder.

The lightbeams fragmented, splashing onto the stone, but Patronyl retreated a step.

Dainyl moved forward, two more steps.

The recorder triggered his weapon again, this time following it with a Talent-thrust, but the lightbeam and Talent-blast flared around Dainyl, who took several more steps forward.

Patronyl stepped back once more, and extended a Talent-probe, trying to close the stone entrance on Dainyl. The submarshal deflected the Talent-probe and extended his shields, trapping the recorder against the stone.

Dainyl's forehead was hot, and sweat began to pour down his face as he forced his shields tighter and tighter around the recorder. Patronyl started to lift the lightcutter again, but did not trigger it. Instead, his brows furrowed, and he attempted to create a tunnel through Dainyl's shields.

Dainyl contracted his shields once more, crumpling the half-formed Talent-tunnel designed to funnel the force of the lightcutter at him.

Patronyl's face began to redden as the shields tightened, his own efforts being contracted around him as well.

Abruptly his shields collapsed.

Rather than spend more of his own Talent energy, Dainyl fired the lightcutter in his right hand, retracting his shields from the recorder only in the instant before he fired. The recorder's face turned black, and then ashes filtered to the floor, vanishing as they did, leaving only an empty green tunic and trousers fluttering to the floor.

Keeping his shields in place around him, Dainyl stepped into the passageway and over the heap of shimmersilk garments and boots, trying to sense if any of Patronyl's assistants remained. The first chamber on the right—clearly the recorder's study—held a small desk, a narrow bed, and a black chest. The sole hanging on the wall was a painting of Tempre, showing the twin green towers.

After checking the second chamber—a library of sorts, containing three bookshelves and a small circular table with two chairs drawn up—Dainyl returned to the main table chamber to study the depowered Table. As almost an afterthought, he used his Talent to close the stone slab that served as a door to the hidden chambers.

He holstered both sidearms and sat down on the Table for several moments, resting.

Then he sent a fine Talent-probe into the Table, seeking the main octagonal crystal and the smaller one on the underside. He pulsed a quick Talent-touch to the smaller and still brighter crystal, as Sulerya had taught him. He could feel the Table begin to power up.

While he waited, he walked to the door and opened it. "Galya?"

"Yes, sir?"

"This is a Table chamber. I'm going to use it. I should be back in several glasses. If I'm not, report that to the undercaptain. He's to stand by and maintain control over Tempre and keep this area clear for up to three days. After that, everyone is to return to Hyalt, including the Cadmians. Is that clear?"

"Sir . . . ?"

"I don't have time to go out and explain to Hyksant."

"Yes, sir."

Dainyl closed the door and placed a Talent-lock on it. He still had to wait before the Table was ready to be used.

Should he go out and talk to Hyksant? Retrieve his flying jacket? At that moment, the Table completed its power-up.

Dainyl first made sure he still had the two envelopes that contained the reports he had written earlier, then checked his sidearms, switching the one he had used most with the unused one in his tunic. After that he stepped onto the Table and concentrated on the darkness beneath the Table.

He was in the chill half-light of the translation tube, aware of how it rested upon a deeper blackness, seeking the brilliant white locator wedge that was Elcien. As quickly as he sought that wedge, he was there with the white silver melting before him.

He stood on the Table in Elcien.

Both Chastylt and one of the assistants to the High Alector, who had been talking by the door to the antechamber, turned, their mouths open.

Dainyl remained standing on the Table, looking at the two, even as he extracted the two envelopes.

"Submarshal?"

"I have something for you," Dainyl gestured for the assistant to approach, then handed her the pair of envelopes he took out from his tunic. "One is for the marshal, the other is for High Alector Zelyert. I suggest you not open them, for your own health." He smiled and straightened. "There are others coming from various sources. So I wouldn't delay handing them over."

"Submarshal . . ." stuttered Chastylt. "The grid . . . it is somewhat unstable. The Table in Tempre was off-grid and now is back. I don't know why, but it might be wise not to attempt a translation until it is certain to remain stable."

"I understand. If anything happens, it won't be your fault."

Dainyl unholstered both lightcutters, holding one in each hand, then concentrated on the blackness beneath the Table, ignoring the appalled looks of the two alectors as he dropped into . . .

. . . the chill blackness, a chill that felt momentarily refreshing. This time he had to search momentarily before locating the amber wedge that represented Hyalt. Beyond the translation tube, he could also sense more of the green flashes, but those would have to wait, as if he could do anything about them.

He flashed through the amber mist . . .

. . . and took two quick steps, aiming the lightcutters as he did.

Four alectors turned as one. The tallest, dressed in green, had to be Rhelyn, from his strong aura.

Dainyl fired at the two least Talented alectors. The bluish beams went through their shields and chests. Then he launched a Talent blast and discharged both lightcutters at the alector—alectress—who remained beside Rhelyn. She staggered but remained standing—until Dainyl's second tripartite assault smashed through her shields.

Dainyl took several quick breaths. The Table chamber had no obvious exits, not even a single "formal" entrance. That didn't surprise him.

"You cannot possibly win," observed Rhelyn. "There are a score of alectors within the complex with your level of Talent or better." Rhelyn edged toward a light-torch bracket, clearly not wanting to use Talent energy to open the hidden entrance.

"If you believed that, you wouldn't have crawled behind stone walls and mountains." Dainyl fired one of the lightcutters, but the bolt was only half-intensity and fizzled away as the lightcutter used the last of its stored energy.

Rhelyn's shields shunted the short energy bolt aside.

Dainyl slipped the unpowered weapon into the holster and drew the one from his tunic.

"Three lightcutters. I must say that you come as prepared as you could. It won't be—" Rhelyn broke off his words and threw a Talent bolt at Dainyl.

The submarshal sensed the feint, and, while blocking the recorder's Talent-blast, directed his own Talent-probe toward the pair of crystals within the Table, the ones allowing the user to draw on the power of the translation tubes.

Both probes locked short of the crystals, and that was more than fine with Dainyl, as he stepped off the Table and fired another lightcutter blast at Rhelyn.

"A renegade recorder as well . . . truly evil . . ." grunted the recorder.

Dainyl deflected another Talent-blast and kept moving toward Rhelyn. The recorder drew a long dagger, one whose slender blade shimmered amber-green.

"Talent won't stop this. . . ."

Dainyl sensed that. He stepped back, beyond reach of the long dagger, and clasped his shields around the recorder.

Just before the shields constricted, Rhelyn threw the dagger straight at Dainyl's chest.

Dainyl jumped to one side, but the dagger sliced into his left arm. He still slammed the shields around Rhelyn and fired both lightcutters, but the fingers of his left hand released the lightcutter.

"Too late . . . you're dead . . . too . . ." Rhelyn smiled, then collapsed. In instants, he too was dust.

Dainyl glanced around, then bent and grabbed one of the shimmersilk tunics—it might have been the alectress's—and wadded it inside his own tunic against the slash in his arm. He thought about using another to bind around the outside of his sleeve, but he couldn't do that, not one-handed and in a hurry, and he could tell he didn't have much time. If he'd worn the flying jacket? No . . . whatever the knife had been, it would have sliced through the jacket as well.

He stepped back onto the Table. His timing had to be perfect—or he'd be as dead as Rhelyn. First, he used a quick Talent-probe to find the octagonal crystal. Then, as he fired a full Talent-bolt into the crystal, he concentrated on dropping beneath the Table, into the darkness below.

The world spun, and he felt as though he had been turned on his head and driven through the surface of the Table . . .

. . . into the darkness that was far blacker than he recalled. Could that be because the Table had failed? Or because he was weakening? The shimmering dagger had done more than slice him . . .

He struggled to concentrate on a location for his translation . . . it had to be Elcien. Nowhere else could he get aid quickly. But the white locator wedge kept retreating, as if he could not grasp it with Talent. Why? What was he doing wrong?

Around him the cold intensified, pressing in, possibly because he had been overheated and had used all his Talent reserves. He had to get somewhere, *or he'd end up dead or a mistranslated wild Talent without sentience and short-lived. He thought of Lysia, trying to call up the orange-yellow locator, but that, too, retreated from his Talent-grasp.*

What was *the problem?*

The dagger—it had been amber-green, like the ancients. Was it an ancient weapon designed to be used against alectors? Had it rendered his Talent useless?

Dainyl tried again, this time seeking the crimson-gold of Dereka . . . and felt it too slip from his grasp.

His thoughts were slowing . . . he had to do something.

Green . . . amber-green . . . seek that. Anything would be better than dying in the translation tube.

Using what felt like his last measure of Talent, he reached for the amber-green, for an oval somewhere in the distance . . . that suddenly rushed toward him.

He staggered, but he was out of the darkness, standing in a small chamber, so small that his hair brushed the ceiling. The walls were of a green-tinged amber stone, and the single window was framed in a silvery metal.

Dainyl wasn't anywhere he knew. He glanced down to find that he stood on square silver mirror—like those in the tunnel of the ancient soarers. He glanced at his poorly bound arm. Lifeforce-treated shimmersilk was a poor bandage.

His legs were wobbly, and he looked for somewhere to sit down, to rest. There was a couch, low and small, to one side. Perhaps it was a bed. He turned and . . .

The amber and green and silver vanished behind a different kind of darkness that rose up and engulfed him.

80

Dainyl's eyes opened. Overhead was an amber-green ceiling. He was lying on something hard— very hard. Lines of fire ran up and down his left arm, and his vision of the ceiling blurred, and then cleared, before blurring again.

Where was he? He'd been unable to reach any Table— that much he recalled. Had that been because of the weapon used by Rhelyn—he had the feeling it had been designed to kill alectors—or because of his own failing strength?

His eyes flicked to his right. He was lying on the floor beside a bed far too small for him, and possibly even too tiny for the smallest of adult indigens. Without lifting his head, he glanced the other way, to note a door in the stone wall—made of a golden wood, with a single lever handle of a silvery metal. From where he lay he could only see silver-green sky through the window, bright enough that it had to be day. The window was set in casements of the same metal as that of the door lever—a metal he had not ever seen.

After several moments, his head cleared, and his vision sharpened. With his good arm, he eased himself into a sitting position. With a start, he realized that his left arm had been bound, and that his Myrmidon tunic had been neatly trimmed away just below the shoulder, so evenly that it looked as if it had been sewn that way— until he looked at his right forearm.

Who could cut through that lifeforce-treated fabric that easily?

The light in the room shifted, and he looked up from where he sat on the floor to see one of the ancient soarers, hovering just inside the door he had not heard open.

"Thank you." Whatever else might happen, he owed them his life.

You were dying.

"I had that feeling. Was that because of the weapon?"

Describe the weapon.

"It was a long dagger, and it had an amber-green blade. It went right through my tunic. It shouldn't have."

We thought as much. It was designed for that, long ago. It was a long-bladed sword. It was not an effective weapon. It was our responsibility.

A long-bladed sword? Of course, long-bladed for an ancient. Their responsibility? "It was effective against me."

There was the sense of an ironic laugh.

"Why did you save me?"

For reasons of our own. Does not each act for reasons of her own?

"Do you expect me to do something for you?"

Only if you come to understand the way of all worlds. Only if you understand that it will benefit you.

"What do you want that could benefit me?"

If you do not change . . . when the time comes you will die. You can support lifeforce and live, or draw from it and die.

She was the second soarer who had said the same thing to him, except this one had suggested more.

Before long you must choose—the purple or the green. Now you must rest. Later, you will be strong enough to return . . .

"Just how, exactly, am I supposed to change?"

This time the sense of laughter was far stronger. *That will become clear when the time arrives for your choice.*

"How am I supposed to return?"

The same way in which you arrived. The soarer eased backward and the door closed, with a definite click.

Dainyl blinked. Then he slowly stood. His legs were wobbly, but he took two steps and tried the silver metal lever on the door. It did not budge. The entire door felt as solid as the stones that surrounded the frame in which it was set.

After a moment, he made his way to the window. His fingers were clumsy, but he depressed the flat bracket on one side. He barely started to slide the window open, when frigid air surged through the tiny opening, colder than anything he had experienced.

Dainyl looked out through the closed window, determining that he was in a tower. Well beneath him were other buildings scattered over the space of a vingt or so from the base of the tower. All were enclosed by a circular wall, and everything appeared to have been constructed of the same amber-green stone. Farther beyond the wall was white sand, and beyond that rose a rampart of dark rock, along the top of which ran green-tinted crystal oblongs.

Standing at the window, he felt weak. Was that because of the altitude? He had to be up on the Plateau somewhere. It couldn't be anywhere else, not when he had flown all over the rest of Acorus.

Slowly, he turned and made his way to the small bed, where he sat down. In the end he stretched out on the floor, using the single green quilt of shimmering silk as a pillow.

He closed his eyes.

81

After a glass passed uneventfully, Mykel put half the Cadmians on standby and ordered them into the shade of the gardens to the immediate south of the regional alector's building. He had the mounts of the men standing picket duty, including his own, moved into the shade on the west side of the building and established a rotation of those standing duty, with changes every glass, and orders to make sure that the men drank their water regularly. As the white sun rose in the sky, approaching noon, he summoned Undercaptain Matorak.

The Hyaltan officer rode up from the eastern end of the plaza. "Yes, sir."

"Undercaptain . . . I may be prejudging matters, but it is looking as though we'll be in Tempre for a time. I'd like you to take Second Company and investigate the compound to the east. Secure it, and see how we could occupy it in the event we're posted here for a time." He smiled. "Don't forget to have everyone refill their water bottles."

"Yes, sir." Matorak turned his mount and rode back to Second Company.

Mykel watched for a moment, but the undercaptain had his men and mounts moving before that long, riding eastward along the boulevard that ran east to west in front of the low granite wall before the complex.

Once Second Company was out of sight, he studied the compound again, blotting his forehead. Tempre was not nearly so hot as Hyalt, but it was summer, and he had been in the sun all morning. He thought he heard more movement beyond the gardens to the south. With nothing happening, he imagined that a few more of the braver souls in Tempre might be venturing out. More than three glasses had passed since the submarshal had entered the chamber underneath the building. The other Myrmidon had not returned, either.

From what he had sensed down in the lower depths, Mykel could only surmise that what lay behind the door guarded by purplish power was some alector device of power—possibly one of the mysterious Tables said to be able to view any place in Corus. Another rumor about the Tables was that certain alectors could use them to travel to other Tables. Had the submarshal used the Table to go elsewhere? Where . . . and why? Had the expedition to Tempre been solely to gain access to whatever lay behind that door?

He stiffened. The Myrmidon with the skylance walked quickly down the steps from the main entrance and across the gray paving stones toward the Myrmidon undercaptain. The two talked in low voices for a time. The undercaptain's face bore a frown that remained, even after he looked up.

"Majer! If you would join us?"

Mykel walked quickly toward the two Myrmidons, stopping several yards short of them and the undercaptain's pteridon. "Yes?"

"I don't believe we've formally met. I'm Undercaptain Hyksant." The undercaptain frowned again. "This is a very difficult situation."

Mykel understood. Hyksant was an undercaptain in command of a squad, but a squad that had the power to wipe out an entire battalion under certain circumstances, and Mykel was a majer. Both had been left with definite orders to wait, and neither had the slightest idea where the submarshal was, what he was doing, or when he would be back.

"The submarshal left contingent orders," Hyksant said. "I had hoped we would not have to implement them, but it appears that will be necessary. We're to hold Tempre for the next three days. If he does not return by then, we are to withdraw to Hyalt and regroup there."

"We have done some scouting and discovered that there is a new compound to the east," Mykel said. "It was apparently built to house the troopers we routed yesterday. One of my companies is engaged in investigating and securing it. When we reported it to the submarshal, he suggested that, since the forces that apparently used it would no longer require it, we could use the new compound. I would imagine that there would be space there for you. We should know if it is suitable within the glass."

"If you would inform me, Majer, I would appreciate it."

"I will." Mykel nodded politely.

As he walked back to Undercaptain Fabrytal and the

Cadmians, Mykel reflected that, in a way, Hyksant's use of the word "return" had in fact confirmed that the Table—or something behind that door—was a means of travel. He also confirmed, by what he apparently could not do, that its use was restricted to those of either rank or ability—or both.

Almost another glass passed before one of Matorak's squad leaders rode back into the paved plaza before the building and reined up before Mykel.

"Sir, Undercaptain Matorak reports that the barracks and quarters are secure and will be ready for Third Battalion whenever you require them."

"Thank you, and convey my thanks to the undercaptain. Fifteenth Company will be joining Second Company shortly. At some point, so will the Myrmidons."

"Yes, sir."

After the squad leader departed, Mykel turned to Fabrytal. "Muster Fifteenth Company and head to the compound. Settle them in, and tell them to get some rest. Check the kitchens and see what supplies they have. And the armory, if they have one. I'll be there shortly, after I brief Loryalt and the Myrmidon undercaptain. For the time being, you and Matorak work out a watch schedule for the compound. All men in the barracks are to be in standby status, even if they are resting. I'll want three-man patrols on the streets around here—four patrols for now. Those will rotate among the companies at the compound."

"I'll take care of it, sir."

As Fabrytal began to issue the orders to Fifteenth Company, Mykel walked back to Hyksant. "We have the compound secure. I'm reducing the building guard here to one company. The other two companies will be on standby at the compound, and we'll have mounted patrols on the nearby streets and boulevards."

Hyksant raised his eyebrows.

"If I hold all my men here until the submarshal

returns—or until he doesn't—they won't be able to respond to anything else. The compound is only a fraction of a glass away by horse."

"I see."

Mykel could tell that he didn't. He looked at the Myrmidon officer, his eyes hard on the alector. "I'm certain that the submarshal could explain the necessity of my actions better than I am doing, undercaptain, but having men posted in the sun on granite paving, even with rotations every glass, is extremely wearing. It's also hard on their mounts, even keeping them in the shade as much as possible, because we can't water them enough. I'd like to have both men and mounts rested for the trouble that will come in the next few days. I'm certain that the submarshal will want that also." He was more than certain that there would indeed be trouble, of one kind or another.

This time Hyksant looked away. "As you see fit, Majer."

Mykel smiled pleasantly. "I'm doing my best to carry out the submarshal's orders, as I'm certain you are." He stepped back and turned.

Behind him, he could sense consternation . . . or confusion. He wasn't sure which, only that he'd best be careful in dealing with Hyksant, who seemed far less understanding of what faced either the Myrmidons or the Cadmians than the submarshal did.

Without hesitating, Mykel retrieved his mount and rode to the back of the gray granite building, making his way to Loryalt.

The undercaptain stiffened as Mykel reined up. "Sir?"

"It appears as if we'll be here far longer than the submarshal had thought. I've sent Second Company and Fifteenth Company to that new compound. Split up your company to cover front and back, and have a messenger ready to ride in case you need reinforcement. The companies at the compound will be handling road and street patrols . . ."

When Mykel had finished briefing Loryalt, he turned the mount and began to ride to the compound, wondering just what he might find there—and how long indeed they would be in Tempre.

82

The compound was close to luxurious by Cadmian standards and so recently completed that Mykel could smell the varnish and oils. In places along the entry archway, freshly cut sawdust had drifted into corners.

Mykel had taken one of the senior officers' quarters, reserving the largest for the Myrmidon submarshal—although the bed was far too short and he doubted that Dainyl would wish to remain there long when he returned, if he returned—and one of the others for the undercaptain. There were adequate junior officer spaces for Mykel's three undercaptains and for the other Myrmidons. In fact, there was enough space for a full battalion and more. That suggested to Mykel that the Myrmidons were facing more than a few rebels. Some chambers in the officer's area had never been used, and one whole wing of the barracks had never been occupied, although there were bunks with mattresses and blankets.

While he was glad to have decent quarters for his men, Mykel was worried—more than worried. Three companies and a squad of Myrmidons were scarcely enough to hold a city, even a small city. Enough to take it, but holding it was another question. He also still had no idea exactly what the submarshal wanted.

There was also something else about the compound nagging at him, something that should have been obvious, so obvious that when he realized it, he would reproach himself for stupidity. But, as he looked around the quarters in which he stood, taking in the large bed, the wardrobe, and the well-crafted writing desk, he could not identify the source of his misgivings.

After leaving his gear in the quarters he had taken, ignoring the dress uniforms of the majer who presumably had been the one Mykel had killed in the dawn massacre, Mykel stepped out onto the covered balcony and then hurried down the stone steps to find Fabrytal.

His eyes took in the dressed granite stones of the compound buildings, and the well-fitted windows . . . and he stopped . . . dead.

"You're an idiot, Mykel . . ." he murmured. Spontaneous rebellions did not have the time to design, construct, and complete well-planned stone-walled compounds. Nor did they have the time to produce hundreds of uniforms, or obtain hundreds of weapons. Whatever had been going on had been planned for some time. But why hadn't the alectors seen it?

He shook his head. Because some alectors were indeed behind it, doubtless powerful ones, and that indicated that a great deal was at stake. A very great deal, and he and his Cadmians were caught right in the middle.

For the moment, he had no choices . . . but he needed to keep alert to all the implications.

He glanced from where he stood in the main inner courtyard to the southeast corner where Fabrytal was talking with Undercaptain Matorak, then resumed his progress toward the two. Both officers turned as Mykel approached.

"Sir."

"Did you find any stragglers here?"

"No, sir. Even the cooks had gone," Matorak replied.

"What about supplies?"

"They left pretty much everything. There's plenty of staples—flour, lard, even a bunch of cheese wheels, and close to ten barrels of ale and lager."

"Good. What about gear left behind? Have you put all their gear in the empty storeroom?"

"Yes, sir." Fabrytal paused. "If I might ask, sir . . ."

"Some of them lived. They might like it back, once we depart. I'd prefer we not be thieves or pillagers."

"I thought that, but some of the men . . . they were rebelling . . ."

"We don't know how long we'll be here." Mykel paused, then added, "Or if we'll have to stay here or get sent back here in the future." *As for rebelling, it's only a rebellion if they're not successful.* "What about fodder for the mounts? Is there any grain?"

"Not so much as we'd like, but there's enough for a week, I'd guess," replied Matorak.

"I shouldn't have to say this, but no one leaves the compound, except on duty or patrol. We don't know what's happened to all the people in that building, or if there were more troopers sent somewhere else."

"Any more word on how long we'll be here?" asked Fabrytal.

"If we don't get any new orders, three more days. If we do, we could ride out tomorrow, or two seasons from now." Mykel smiled. "That's being a Cadmian."

"Yes, sir."

"I'll be here in the compound, inspecting what we have to work with. If any messages come in, find me at once."

Both undercaptains nodded.

Mykel turned. He needed to inspect the compound quickly. Perhaps it would tell him something more, although he had his doubts about that.

83

Dainyl woke up sometime in the night, dark enough in the small chamber that it was dim even for his night sight. He was cold, although several thin and filmy blankets had been placed over him, and he now lay on a thin pad that seemed to provide some warmth, enough that he was not shivering. He sat up slowly, fighting dizziness, and discovering that on the tiny bed was a tray holding a large apple, a bunch of grapes, a wedge of yellow cheese, and a small loaf of dark bread. There was also a solid cylindrical glass filled with something that looked and smelled like ale. In the corner of the room, almost under the window was what looked to be a chamber pot. He did not recall it being there earlier.

Without hesitation, he took a sip of the unfamiliar ale first, then sampled a piece of the bread. Then he alternated eating bites of the other items on the tray. He left not even crumbs, and by the time he had drained the last of the ale, the dizziness had largely vanished.

He stood, slowly and carefully, and walked to the window. Chill radiated from it. Looking out into the darkness at the stars, he saw more stars than he had ever observed, each an unvarying point of light. Not a one twinkled the way the stars did anywhere else he had been in Acorus, but then, he'd never been up on the Aerlal Plateau before. So far as he knew, no alector had been.

How did the ancients live in such cold, let alone build cities? What sort of tools did they use? Did they even use tools?

The questions that inundated him vanished as the door opened and an ancient appeared in a glow of amber and green that provided light but no warmth. This soarer did not display any marked difference from the others he had encountered, but the essence of her being radiated great age.

You asked why we had saved you. We did not save you. You reached us unaided. We have kept you from dying.

"Why?"

Allowing you to die would serve no useful purpose. While you live, you may yet see.

"See what?" Dainyl was all too conscious of unspoken assumptions behind the "words" of the ancient.

How the world lifeforces tie together. How all worlds have such ties.

"Why is seeing this so important?"

A sense of a shrug came to Dainyl. *To the world, it is not important. What will be, will be. To you, it will be far more vital.*

Vital? "What if I do not see? What if I do not act? What then?"

Like all of your kind, you will die, for you will have no ties to any world. Any being must be part of a world.

Dainyl understood that. "Why is it important enough to you that I change and live?"

Because you are not so different from those you term steers as you believe. Because you and they must share . . . ????. . . .

Dainyl could not understand the phrase she used, although he felt it meant some sort of energy linkage.

Without that, they will perish, for not enough of them possess it. Without them, you will perish.

"Why do you care?" Dainyl doubted that the ancients were acting altruistically. No beings ever did. Every thinking creature acted in what it perceived as its own interest.

No world should die before its time. It is not necessary.

He wanted to snort at that. "I would think that you would like to see us gone?"

No. This world would have died before its time without you. For that, we owe you. For our restraint, you owe us. You will not acknowledge that restraint. That is why you must change, so that you will not be like the others.

"I don't know how to change." More important, he wasn't certain he wanted to, either.

You have been shown. Enough. The cold finality behind those words declared the futility of pursuing more questions there.

"How long have I been here? When can I leave?"

You have been here two days. Sleep tonight, and you will leave tomorrow. If you rest well.

Two days? He glanced down at his arm, realizing that the dressing had been changed.

You are strong. The lifespear seldom fails to kill any who are not of the world. Even so, you are not strong enough to survive what will be unless you change. A sense of regret, or sadness, followed her words.

Without another word—or thought—she slipped away from him, and the door closed.

This time, he did sense the tightly focused green Talent. The force of that Talent was modest, but the control precise.

Two days? But he could leave tomorrow.

The ancient's words conveyed a certainty about the destruction, not of the world, but of all alectors who would not "change," as she and the other soarer had conveyed it. Was it simply finding a way to link himself directly to Acorus, rather than through the Master Scepter? What would that do to an alector? From what he knew, it would certainly reduce his strength, perhaps a great deal more.

He tried to push those thoughts away. He was an alector, an Ifrit out of Ifryn, for all that he had been born on Acorus.

He doubted that he could ever get back to sleep, but he had to try. Slowly, he walked back to the pad and blankets and lowered himself onto the pad and arranged the blankets.

Surprisingly, his eyes closed immediately.

84

With the sun came wakefulness for Dainyl, but no ancient arrived, nor did any more food. It must have been a good two glasses after that before the door opened, and an ancient hovered outside. Although all of the ancient soarers shared the same appearance, at least to Dainyl, she was far younger than the one who had met with him the day previous.

The . . . portal is in the next chamber.

He followed her out into a foyer. There were no steps up or down, just circular openings in both the stone floor and ceiling. There was also a door, open to a second chamber. Dainyl entered the room. The ancient trailed him. The room was almost identical to the one in which he had been confined, except that set into the amber green stone floor was one of the silver mirrors.

It is linked temporarily to your parasitic tube. Once you leave here, the link will vanish.

Dainyl forbore mentioning that he had managed to reach the tower without such a link.

The lifespear wound you suffered allowed you to seek us.

Just how much could they discover from his thoughts? He pushed that thought aside and stood on the silver mirror, concentrating on the blackness, on the blue locator wedge that was Tempre . . .

. . . and he was in dark chill. The locator was distant . . . close to the limit of his Talent reach . . . and yet, when he extended a Talent-probe, it suddenly was upon him, and silvered-blue shards flew past him.

Dainyl found his legs shaking as he stood on the Table in the unadorned chamber in Tempre. Carefully, he stepped down. Then he sat on the edge of the Table, trying to regain his strength. He was weaker than he had realized, but glad to be back in the world he knew. Or did he only think he knew his world?

Thoughts along those lines would have to wait. He needed to find out what had happened in his absence. He rose and stepped to the door of the chamber. It took a moment for him to release the Talent-lock, and then to replace it after he stepped outside into the empty corridor beyond.

His boots clicked on the stone floor of the corridor, and then on the steps leading up to the main level of the building. Both Cadmians had stepped away from the door and had rifles ready when Dainyl emerged.

"Submarshal, sir. Sorry, sir."

"That's all right. Do you know where the majer is?"

"If he's not outside, sir, he's been staying close to the compound, sir."

"Thank you."

As he walked along the corridor toward the front of the building, he used his Talent to pick up the murmured conversation between the two.

"Wonder what he tangled with . . ."

"Wouldn't want to be it . . . alectors are tough. He fell a hundred yards onto solid rock and only had a broken arm and leg . . ."

"Majer's tough, too."

"Not that tough."

At least the Cadmians had a healthy respect for alectors. Dainyl kept walking.

Once he was outside, in the early-midmorning sunlight, if under a hazy sky, he went down the steps looking for Hyksant. The mounted Cadmians on patrol duty eased away from him, but he saw only a single Myrmidon—Galya—and two pteridons. One was his, waiting.

Once he neared her and the pteridons, she smiled. "Submarshal . . . the undercaptain is at the compound. We've been alternating here."

"A short flight is in order. I'd appreciate your remaining on watch here."

"Yes, sir."

Dainyl climbed onto the pteridon, trying not to show any weakness. The pteridon rose quickly, and descended even more quickly, but Dainyl was happy when the pteridon set down in the open space before the compound, not that far from the three other pteridons. After he dismounted and started toward the compound, carrying his gear in his good hand, his eyes took in the solid walls and the well-dressed stone.

Hyksant appeared from somewhere and hurried toward Dainyl. He frowned as the submarshal approached, and his eyes dropped to the submarshal's bound left arm.

"I know." Dainyl shook his head. "I was sidetracked

along the way. The Tables malfunctioned. I shut down the Table in Hyalt, but Rhelyn used one of the weapons of the ancients on me, and I got coated with some . . . well, you can sense what it's like. It should vanish once I heal."

"Rhelyn . . . ?" Hyksant appeared as though he didn't know what to ask.

"Oh . . . he's dead, and all the rebels are trapped inside Hyalt with no way out. I hope that Captain Fhentyl is taking advantage of that. We'll need to fly back there once we settle matters here. We'll plan to leave first thing in the morning."

"What about Tempre, sir?"

"We'll leave the majer in charge until the RA returns. Once that happens, he can turn over control to the RA and ride back to Hyalt."

Hyksant nodded knowingly.

Dainyl let him think what he would. The majer just might surprise Fahylt when he returned. One way or the other, one problem should be resolved, either that of Fahylt or that of the majer. In a perverse way, at least for an alector, Dainyl almost hoped that the majer came out on top. "If you would show me where we're quartered?"

"Oh . . . yes, sir." Hyksant turned. "This way."

"Was the majer correct about this compound?" He gestured at the main gate, guarded by a pair of armed Cadmians.

"Yes, sir." After a moment with Dainyl's eyes on him, Hyksant went on. "He's been quite proper. He reserved the largest quarters for you and the next largest for me, and the other officers' quarters for my squad and his undercaptains. They found supplies and fed us. The compound is new, you know?"

"I've thought about that. Fahylt has been preparing for this for quite some time. An independent force of uniformed and mounted indigen rifles, a stone compound . . ."

"You think we should still leave tomorrow, sir?"

"I definitely do," replied Dainyl. "The majer has reduced, if not destroyed, his guard. His recorder is dead—"

"He is?"

"Oh . . . I don't believe I told Galya that. Yes, he was waiting in the Table chamber. He didn't expect three sidearms. Even if Fahylt returns, without a recorder, he'll find it harder to get information." Dainyl broke off his explanation as they drew closer to the pair of guards. He did not resume speaking until they were walking across the inner courtyard, away from any Cadmians. "I did make a detour and deliver a report to the marshal and the High Alector of Justice."

"We haven't seen anyone from Elcien . . . or any other Myrmidons. Or Cadmians."

"I am certain we will not. They will wait until the outcome is certain. Fahylt doubtless fled . . . where he has support." Dainyl barely stopped himself from suggesting that the RA had fled to Ludar, but revealing the possible split between the Duarches would not be wise. "We need to clean up Hyalt, and then get Fifth Company back to Dereka."

"Yes, sir."

Dainyl didn't respond to the skepticism behind the undercaptain's acquiescence. He'd already figured out how to handle Hyalt, now that the Table was inoperative. It would be deliberate, but very certain. He might even have to wait several days after returning to Hyalt, because he would need his full ability with shields, but he had the feeling his strength was already returning. He frowned. Was there something about the ancient city that weakened alectors?

"Sir?"

"I was just thinking about all we have to do."

Hyksant started up a set of stone steps. "Your quarters are up here."

Dainyl followed. Hyksant opened the end doorway, revealing a single chamber, quite large for a lander, and at least not cramped for an alector, although the ceiling was lower than Dainyl would have preferred, but he didn't have to stoop. Typical quarters, but the lander-sized bed was triple width.

Once inside, he turned to the undercaptain. "If you would take care of preparing for our departure tomorrow? And in about a glass, have someone bring me something to eat. Ale and whatever there is."

"Yes, sir."

"Also, if you would find Majer Mykel and have him attend me here."

"Yes, sir."

After Hyksant departed, closing the door behind him, Dainyl stretched out at an angle on the bed. Overlarge it might be for a lander, but his boots stuck out off the end. Still, he'd slept on a hard floor for too many nights. His eyes closed.

Less than a quarter glass later, there was a knock on the door. "Majer Mykel, sir."

"Come in, Majer." Dainyl didn't bother to get off the bed, although he eased himself into a sitting position, propped up against the plain headboard. The majer had enough Talent to see through any charade Dainyl might put on.

Mykel stepped into the quarters, easing the door shut behind him.

"Pull up a chair and tell me what you and your men have been doing since I left."

"Yes, sir." The majer took the straight-backed desk chair that would have been both uncomfortable and too small for Dainyl and set it to one side of the bed, then seated himself. He cleared his throat. "After you left, and it seemed likely that you might not return immediately, I ordered the Cadmians into a rotation, with one company guarding the building, and the other two here at the compound on standby, except for four mounted patrols of the streets and boulevards . . ."

Dainyl listened, not just to what the majer said, but to the manner in which he conveyed the information. So far as Dainyl could determine, Mykel shaded nothing, reporting honestly and directly. ". . . we've seen no signs of any more troopers, or anyone wanting to enter the building. People in the city seem to be going back to what they usually do, except no one is using the gardens, or the streets and boulevards around here. We have bought some goods, mutton and some beef, to supplement the supplies here. I had to draw on the line of credit. . . ."

"That's to be expected."

After Mykel finished, he sat and looked at Dainyl, waiting.

"Majer?"

"Yes, sir?"

Dainyl could sense the lander's wariness behind his formality.

"In the morning, first squad and I will be returning to Hyalt to deal with what remains of the rebels there. Until the regional administrator or other proper authorities return, you are to assume control over the regional administration building and this compound. I suggest that you continue with very light control over this area, and not over the city proper, except as necessary for your safety and that of your men. Once an administrator is in place, you are to return to Hyalt."

"If an alector returns, how am I to determine whether he is the proper authority? Do I assume any alector who claims to be the administrator is the administrator?"

"I am certain you, of all Cadmians, Majer, will know."

"Do I have your authority to question an alector about that?"

"I doubt it will come to that, but . . . yes, if it is necessary. Order and the rule of the proper Duarches must be maintained. Without that, all would be chaos."

The majer nodded, soberly.

Dainyl could sense that the lander was anything but pleased—and that he well understood what Dainyl was doing.

Abruptly, the majer looked squarely at Dainyl. "Sir, might I ask how you were wounded?"

Dainyl laughed. "Even alectors are not immune to all weapons. It was only a glancing slash, but I was fighting several alectors at once." He paused. "That will be all for now."

"Yes, sir." The majer rose immediately and replaced the chair before the writing desk.

"I may have some additional duties for the Cadmians later."

Mykel nodded, then made his way out.

Once the door closed, Dainyl fingered his chin. The majer had not been at all surprised at being left in Tempre to sort out matters, and his question about Dainyl's wound had been anything but idle. The last thing Dainyl needed was a Talented Cadmian majer—except the way matters were developing, that was in fact exactly what he needed.

And Hyksant *might* not say much to Fhentyl until later, but if Mykel prevailed, Dainyl could not count on silence for long. So what sort of accident or mishap would be necessary? Was there another alternative?

Dainyl stretched out and waited for his food to arrive.

85

Less than a glass past dawn on Quattri, Mykel stood outside the gray stone compound, less than two yards from Submarshal Dainyl. To the southeast of the two officers, the Myrmidon squad was readying for liftoff into a silver-green sky dotted with white clouds. The air was already warm, and the day promised to be hot, not unexpectedly for late summer.

The submarshal looked straight at Mykel with his deep blue eyes, so unlike the violet of most alectors, Mykel had begun to realize. "You are in command of this area, but only so long as no regional alector is present. I have conveyed the situation to the High Alector of Justice, but the Myrmidons cannot remain here while Hyalt has still not been returned to the control of the Duarches. How soon the Duarches will send an administrator, I cannot say. I doubt that Regional Alector Fahylt will return, but, if he does, you are to turn the area over to him. If not, then to his designee or legitimate successor as named by the Duarches." The submarshal laughed. "How you determine that legitimacy is a matter of judgment."

"I doubt that I am in any position to argue with an alector claiming such a position," Mykel pointed out.

"It is unlikely that any rebels will attempt to claim such. They would know you would report their assumption of power. Therefore, any who attack you first are more likely to be unauthorized to assume administrative control."

Mykel nodded politely. That was a set of rules he could accept. Exactly how successful he might be in dealing with rebel alectors remained to be seen, although he suspected that his success would rest on just how many alectors were involved.

"Once you are relieved here, Majer, you are to return to Hyalt. If you are not relieved within two weeks, you are to send weekly reports directly to me, one copy to Hyalt, and one to Elcien, by sandox coach."

"Yes, sir." As close as he stood to the alector, Mykel sensed several things. First, while the submarshal's wound was healing, the alector had been clearly weakened by what appeared to be a superficial slash. Given what Mykel had seen of Dainyl's recuperative powers in Dramur, Mykel had to believe that the single slash had come close to killing the Myrmidon officer. Second, around the wound area, the alector's aura was tinged with amber-green—and Mykel had never sensed anything but pinkish purple from any alector. What sort of weapon could have done that damage? Something like his dagger of the ancients? At that moment, Mykel almost could feel the heat of the miniature weapon beating through the leather of his heavy belt, illusory as he knew the feeling to be.

"Finally, you are to make sure that the lower level of the compound remains guarded and off-limits to everyone. Everyone. Is that clear?"

"Yes, sir."

The submarshal nodded brusquely. "That is all. I hope to see you and your Cadmians in Hyalt before too long." Without another word, the Myrmidon turned and moved quickly toward the last pteridon. The other Myrmidons had already mounted.

Mykel watched as the pteridons rose into the silver-green sky, one after the other, seemingly on the ground one moment, and then in the air the next, their long blue wings spread. With each beat of the wings, they rose upward, heading south.

Mykel turned and walked back toward the compound, thinking. Why had the submarshal left him in such a seemingly impossible situation? Why wasn't someone being dispatched immediately from Elcien or Ludar to take over running the city and the area? It was as if he wanted Mykel dead, but didn't want to act himself.

Dead? Rachyla had told him that the alectors would seek to kill all those who carried the dagger of the ancients and who learned what it represented. In point of fact, everything that Rachyla had told him about the alectors—angrily, as he recalled—was seemingly being revealed as truth. He wished he'd had the sense to listen more, and to draw her out. Abruptly, he smiled. There was no reason he couldn't visit her now, or at least try. She might be able to tell him more, and he could use all the information she might have.

He headed back through the compound gates, nodding to the two guards, and into the inner courtyard, seeking Fabrytal. He found the undercaptain outside the west wing of the stables, talking with his senior squad leader Chyndylt.

"Majer, sir," offered Chyndylt. "The undercaptain and I were just about finished . . ."

"You can stay." Mykel grinned. "I need a little recon and local information—in order to get some information."

"Yes, sir?" Fabrytal looked puzzled.

"There is a factor here in Tempre who has recently arrived from Southgate. His chatelaine has some information we may need very badly, based on what the submarshal informed me just before he left." Mykel smiled faintly. "I need to know where the villa of the factor Amaryk is in Tempre, and later, or tomorrow, I'll need an escort of a full squad to ride there."

Chyndylt repressed a smile.

Mykel looked at the senior squad leader. "She turned out to be right about a number of things, concerning the submarshal. I'd prefer to see if she knows more. It might save us some troopers in the next week." He looked back at Fabrytal. "We're in charge until the alectors return— the *proper* alectors, that is, and I have to decide who is the proper alector."

Fabrytal swallowed. Chyndylt's incipient smile vanished.

"You can see why any information might be useful."

"Yes, sir."

"While you're finding that out, I'll be down at the regional alector's headquarters. I think a little investigation into who was running the region besides the regional alector might prove useful." *At the very least, they might prove useful in justifying whatever actions may be necessary.*

"Yes, sir."

With a smile and a nod, Mykel left the two and made his way to the stable, where he saddled the roan, and then rode out, heading west along the boulevard toward the alector's complex.

As he neared the gray granite building, a slight breeze picked up, out of the south, bringing the scent of the flowers in the gardens on the south side of the boulevard. From what he'd seen, Tempre was a pleasant city. So why had the regional alector thrown in with the rebel alectors? Mykel had to shrug. It had to do with power. Everything did, but how, he had no real idea. He just wanted to do his duty and get out of the situation with the least damage possible.

If he left without a successor regional alector, that would be dereliction of duty—and he didn't want even to think about what happened to commanding officers who were found guilty of that. At the very least, he had to turn matters over to an alector with some semblance of authority, and to do that he needed to know more. He also knew that his time was getting short, because once others knew that the Myrmidons had left, it was likely that someone would appear to claim power.

Seventeenth Company had the duty dealing with the empty building, and Mykel rode around the east side until he located Loryalt, still mounted and discussing something with his fourth squad leader.

The undercaptain immediately turned his mount and waited for Mykel.

"Yes, sir? Any word? We saw the Myrmidons leave."

"We're in charge until the proper authorities return. I'm going inside and conduct an inspection of sorts up in the RA's study. That's so I have some idea who the proper authority might be. I don't know how long that's likely to take."

"Yes, sir."

"If anyone who looks like an alector appears, send someone for me immediately. I don't think that will happen soon, but you never know. When you're relieved, pass that on to Undercaptain Matorak as well." Mykel paused. "How are things going?"

"Quiet, sir. It's like everyone is avoiding the place."

"Let's hope it stays that way for a bit."

"Yes, sir."

After leaving Loryalt, Mykel rode farther around the

building, finding a brass-ringed hitching post in the shade near the small rear entry. There he dismounted and tied the roan, before making his way up the stone steps into the building, conscious that the fourth squad was watching him. He carried a blank order book and a marker for the notes he hoped to take.

Once inside, he had to walk to the front of the building, taking the marble-floored corridor back around to the wide staircase—also of green marble—that led to the second level.

The study of the regional alector was set on the southwest corner, as part of a suite that extended from double doors, each with an etched glass panel set in the golden oak. The scene was that of the twin towers flanking the river piers. Immediately behind those doors was a foyer, set with chairs, and a single table desk positioned at an angle such that whoever sat behind it could view both the double doors and the single door to the regional alector's private study.

There was only a single file box in the outer foyer, placed against the paneled wall behind the desk. Mykel opened it, to find it largely emptied. What remained were individual sheets of paper, with seemingly cryptic notes. He scanned them, but after leafing through them, decided that they all referred to various appointments and engagements in some fashion—but there were no names at all. At the back of those notes, he did find one folded paper with a list of names.

Fahylt	Regional Alector
Adaral	Deputy RA
Shesala	Appointment Clerk

There were close to twenty names with titles on the list. Mykel folded the paper and slipped it into his tunic. From the way it had been folded, he suspected that some of the names were possibly outdated, but it was a start.

He paused outside the closed inner door. There had

been no one inside when he had first searched the building. Still . . .

He could hear nothing, sense nothing. He opened the
door, but no one was in the inner study, an oblong chamber a good ten yards in depth and fifteen in length. The
longer side was on the south, with wide floor to ceiling
windows, each two yards in width, separated from the
next by granite edged in oak. Because the building had
been built slightly up the hillside, the windows afforded a
sweeping view of Tempre. The west windows offered an
equally sweeping vista of the towers and the pier, although the base of the northern tower was blocked by
part of the hill.

The inner north wall was composed of bookshelves
rising from waist height, with built-in file cases below,
the kind where the front dropped down and the case could
be slid partway out. Only a relative handful of books
rested on the shelves, spaced between small sculptures of
various sizes. The alector's desk was angled across the
corner of the room facing outward. Behind it was a
comfortable-looking wooden armchair. On the floor was
a thick dark green carpet, and in the center was woven in
gold the twin scepters of the Duarchy.

Toward the east end of the chamber was a circular dark
wooden conference table, around which were set five
wooden armchairs. All the furniture was large, sized for
alectors, Mykel noted.

Mykel set the order book on a vacant space on a shelf
and opened the top file case on the west end and began to
leaf through the sheaves of papers. The first sheaf dealt
with something about logging on the south side of the
River Vedra somewhere to the west of Tempre. The second sheaf had also to do with logging. Everything in the
first case was related to logging and timber. So was the
second case. The third case dealt with maintaining
swamps and bogs, and cited instances where individuals
had been fined—or in one case, executed—for attempting

to drain swamps. The fourth held papers about alternation of field crops . . .

Was this what regional alectors dealt with?

As he went from file case to file case, Mykel made certain that he left everything in the same apparent order. Even hurrying as fast as he could, it took him more than a glass to glance through all the file boxes. There was nothing about the Alector's Guard, nothing about rifles, and nothing about Hyalt.

Standing there, he frowned. That wasn't quite right. He'd gone through the papers so quickly that he couldn't conclude that. There certainly wasn't anything obvious there about those subjects, and he had the feeling that there wouldn't be.

With a last glance around, and after slipping the order book into his tunic, he made his way from the private study back into the main upper-level corridor and then down the main staircase to the main level. From there he turned right—west—and followed the corridor to the northwest corner.

The two Cadmian guards looked up as Mykel walked toward them.

"Majer, sir. All's quiet here, sir."

"Good. I'm going down to inspect the area."

After the slightest hesitation, the taller guard—Beilyt, Mykel recalled belatedly—replied, "Yes, sir."

"I shouldn't be too long, but you never know."

"Yes, sir."

Mykel stepped up and opened the door, still missing its lock, then closed it and took several steps before pausing, trying to extend his hearing, listening.

". . . wouldn't go down there . . ."

". . . think he ought to be there?"

"It's his head. That's why majers get more coins."

". . . hope he's not down there long . . ."

Mykel continued to make his way down the circular stone staircase. At the bottom he turned and walked quickly down the empty corridor, dimly lighted by the light-torches in their infrequent bronze wall brackets. When he came to the narrow square arch, in which a solid oak door was set, he stopped and studied it.

As before, a sheen of the unseen purple power covered all the wood. Given the amount of power and the violent reaction that had occurred when he had used a rifle in his own way on the lock of the upper level door, Mykel wasn't about to try any form of force.

Thinking about the submarshal's wound, he took out the tiny dagger of the ancients from its hidden belt slot and touched the lock with it. A flare-point of light appeared—the kind he could sense but not see and the purpleness receded for a span or so from the point of the dagger.

Somehow, Mykel didn't think that was the answer. He replaced the dagger in its belt slot and continued to ponder the puzzle. The submarshal had entered the chamber, without explosions, and he had returned the same way. That meant there *had* to be a way to release the purple energy.

Mykel stood before the closed door, letting his senses accept what was there. After several moments, he began to discern a pattern. A heavier line of purple ran from the lock and door handle to a node on the inside of the door frame. That node was like a knot, energy tied within energy.

How could he untie that knot? He had the feeling that if he "cut" it, the energy would explode—and probably rebound against him.

Slowly, he tried to trace the patterns of energy, seeking a beginning, or an end, to the knot or lock. The effort to mentally follow the energy threads was wearing, and despite the coolness of the corridor, he could feel himself beginning to sweat. After a time, he located the end of the thread. He used his own ability to tug on it.

Nothing happened.

He tugged and twisted, but the lock remained in place.

He attempted to let the knot retrace itself and unwind. That didn't work, either. Next he tried linking the ends of the coiled and twisted energy, but the two repelled each other.

It had to be something relatively simple, he told himself. It *had* to be.

What if he turned the one end inside out, and let it recoil? He wasn't certain if that was how to describe what he had in mind, but it was worth a try.

No sooner had he started the process than, with a faint purple flash, the lock vanished.

He extended his hand to the door lever, gingerly, and still holding what he thought of as his shields in place.

His fingers touched the lever. He depressed it and opened the door. Since he could not see or feel anyone in the chamber, he stepped forward, closing the door behind himself. In the exact center of the room was a black oblong of shimmering stone, not quite the height of a dining table—one of the rumored Tables. He could sense the purpleness that enshrouded it, perhaps powered it, so strong that he found his guts tightening. He forced himself to step forward, and as he did, he saw that the surface was like a silver mirror. He looked more closely and saw his own face, dark-circled green eyes under a frowning forehead and short blond hair.

He looked up from the Table and around the chamber. There was not a single hanging on the fitted stone walls and not a single furnishing in the chamber. Nor were there any alcoves or windows, or any other door except the one he had used to enter. Just the chamber and the Table, nothing more.

Although it seemed impossible, Mykel could sense, in the stone beneath the Table, what seemed like a misty purple-blackness that extended immeasurably into the distance. And beneath that . . . the greenish blackness that he had sensed on the hillcrest to the west of the old garrison in Hyalt.

Should he try to find out more about the Table?

How could he not try? Except he wasn't about to attempt to travel anywhere.

He let his perceptions travel across the Table, but he could only sense the purpleness that welled up from it, linked to the blackish purple mist beneath the stone, as if that unseen conduit powered the Table.

He looked at the Table closely once more, trying to call up something—a vision of his parents. There was no response. As in the case of the lock on the chamber door, Mykel suspected that, if he only knew more, operating the Table would not be impossible. Difficult, perhaps, but not impossible.

After nearly half a glass of attempting various uses of his abilities, he decided that he was wasting his time, and there was always the possibility that some alector might appear and find him there. Finally, he turned, walked to the chamber door, which he opened, and stepped back out into the stone-walled hall. After a last look at the Table, he closed the door.

Should he try to replace the energy lock?

He shook his head. If he did so, the lock would be greenish, not pinkish purple, and that would tell the submarshal—or anyone who talked to him—that Mykel was definitely involved and had the ability to recognize and undo such a lock. As matters stood now, they might guess, but they would not know.

He walked briskly toward the stone staircase. Now, more than ever, he needed to find out what else Rachyla might know. She might not care for him, but she would never betray him to the alectors. That much, at least, he *knew*.

86

Midafternoon arrived on Quattri before
Fabrytal's scouts returned with the information on
Rachyla's location, but Mykel had already decided
against waiting any longer than necessary—and against
subtlety. He had no idea when alectors might appear, or
even if the submarshal might send other orders.

Escorted by the full fifth squad from Fifteenth Company, he rode south from the compound and then west,
into the hillside area where the wealthy lander factors
lived. From what his scouts had determined, the villa of
young Amaryk was but a block off the Silk Boulevard.
While the villas were large, not all bore the white walls
of Southgate, and most had roofs of split slate tiles,
rather than the red fired-clay tiles of the south. The roads
and boulevards were also narrower, although that posed
little problem because those few out and about immediately removed themselves upon seeing the Cadmian
squad.

"That's the place, sir," announced Vhanyr, the squad
leader, gesturing at the gate ahead.

Mykel and the squad reined up short of the iron
gates—composed of plain bars with a few iron leaves,
stark compared to the gates of the villa of Seltyr Elbaryk
in Southgate.

The guards stationed just inside the gates glanced at
Mykel, then at the twenty armed Cadmians.

"Majer Mykel to see the chatelaine Rachyla," Mykel
announced politely.

"Ah . . ."

"Is she here?"

"No . . ." stuttered the shorter guard, dressed in the
light gray of a Southgate retainer.

"You're lying. I *will* see her."

The other guard whispered, "Open the gates . . . he must be the Cadmian officer the alectors left in charge of Tempre."

The gates swung open.

Mykel turned to Vhanyr. "Post a few men here to keep watch."

"Yes, sir." The squad leader gestured. "Yulert, Buant, Juntyr, and Gheryl—you've got the gate duty. Report to me if you see anything strange." He raised his voice. "Fifth squad! Rifles ready!"

Mykel eased the roan forward through the gates and past the three-yard-high walls and onto the stone drive.

Compared to Seltyr Elbaryk's palace in Southgate or even Rachyla's estate in Dramur, the villa was small indeed—a mere two stories fronting perhaps thirty yards. The split slate roof had been recently replaced, as shown by the darker slate than that on nearby structures, and the outer white plaster walls recently painted in gleaming white that reflected the sun.

The doorman bolted erect at the sound of hoofs coming down the narrow lane and into the small circular drive before a rotunda barely large enough for a single coach.

"The honored Amaryk is at the factorage, sir."

"I'm here to see the chatelaine Rachyla." Mykel's voice was cold.

The doorman, despite the twin daggers at his belt, stepped back.

"Now."

The retainer froze for a moment, his eyes taking in the Cadmians and their rifles, before he slowly tugged on the bell-pull.

Within moments, Rachyla stood in the doorway before the open door, clad in light green trousers, a darker green short-sleeved tunic, and boots of a green so dark they were almost black. The fabric of both tunic and trousers was shimmersilk, but she wore no jewelry. Her smile was mirthless. "Majer Mykel. I might have guessed that you would call, now that you hold Tempre."

Beside her, the doorman paled.

"Only until alectors arrive from Elcien," Mykel replied. "Might I come in for a moment?"

"Of course. How could we deny you?"

"Sir?" questioned Vhanyr.

"I'll be all right for now. Out here is where you might be needed." Mykel dismounted and handed the roan's reins to Feranot—the ranker behind the squad leader. Then he walked up the two steps to the low entry.

He bowed slightly to Rachyla. "I appreciate your being here to see me."

"Where else would I be, Majer? Would you come in?"

"Thank you." Mykel stepped through the archway, his senses alert, but he could detect no one nearby except for Rachyla—and the doorman, who remained outside as the chatelaine closed the heavy iron-bound door of dark wood.

The entry foyer was in keeping with the rest of the villa—larger than most merchants' dwellings, and far smaller than anywhere Rachyla had lived before, Mykel surmised. The interior walls had been replastered in white, which lightened the windowless space. Three archways led from the entry area.

Rachyla turned to the left, gesturing to the chamber beyond. "This is the front sitting room. It is one of the few chambers fit for visitors."

Mykel let her lead the way and followed her into a room that was almost square. The only windows were set high on the south wall, more than two yards up from the dark brown tiled floor, and all were closed against the summer heat, kept at bay by the thick masonry walls. The walls had been replastered white. At the far end was a hearth, on which rested a blue-black porcelain heating stove. Under the windows was a narrow table, less than a yard in length, empty except for a vase filled with pale yellow roses. Flanking the table were two bookcases. Two comfortable armchairs, upholstered in a smooth beige fabric, flanked a settee similarly covered.

Mykel gestured for Rachyla to seat herself.

"For an enemy, Majer, you have always been honorable." She took the armchair closest to the archway.

He wanted to protest that he had never been her enemy. The opponent of her father, but never her enemy. There was little point in saying so.

"All the walls were shades of brown. It was worse than that prison cell where you placed me." Rachyla's voice was close to expressionless. "Amaryk saw nothing wrong with the colors."

"Colors are important." He tied to keep his own voice equally calm.

"I understand that you slaughtered more helpless troops. That seems to be a habit with you."

"They attacked us before dawn on Decdi. That's scarcely the act of troops either helpless or innocent."

Rachyla opened her mouth, then closed it. "I apologize, Majer. Like me, you must do what you can to survive in a dangerous situation. Whatever else you may do or you may be, you do not lie."

Mykel couldn't believe what he heard—or sensed. From Rachyla, those words were a great concession. Yet . . . the concession had been impartial and with little warmth. He inclined his head slightly. "I came to apologize and to request a favor. The two are related." He smiled wryly.

She laughed softly, but, again, without warmth. "You do not like to apologize. For that alone, I will accept an apology. The favor . . . what you wish I must hear."

"The apology is for not listening more closely to what you had to say about the alectors. The favor is to request that you tell me all that you know about them."

Her laugh was close to boisterous, if still melodic in the way that he always wished he could recall, and yet never seemed to be able to do once he had left her presence. He waited.

Her deep green eyes focused on him. "You are a dangerous man, Majer. You are dangerous to yourself, and to us, but you are dangerous to the evil ones. Unlike most landers, even seltyrs, you have the power to kill those who call themselves alectors, even when they are protected."

Mykel wondered how she had come to that conclusion, but he merely nodded for her to continue.

"My grandsire said that we were like cattle to them. We were to be fed and kept content as possible. Then, one day, perhaps before I was as old as he was then, thousands of them would appear, and the world would change. Even the seltyrs of Dramur would be dispossessed of what they had . . ." Rachyla shrugged. "I cannot say, but it would appear that those days are fast approaching."

"The alectors are beginning to fight among themselves," he volunteered.

"What do you think that means?"

"People fight when they seek the golds of others or when they believe others are trying to wrest golds from them. The alectors fight over power. That they are fighting now when they have not before suggests a time of change." He offered a smile. "What else do you know of them?"

"They are never to be trusted. They live in our world, but they are not of our world." She leaned forward. "One can sense what people are. Some feel good, some evil, and some . . . they are neither, seeking only what they wish. The evil ones feel different. They feel removed."

"You haven't seen that many, have you?"

"Only one, closely, but my grandsire saw many in his time. I do not think they have changed." Her eyes challenged his. "Do you, Majer?"

"I was not around in your grandsire's time, Rachyla, but . . . I believe you are right."

"You are so kind, to grant me that I might be correct."

Mykel concealed a wince. "What else can you tell me?"

"You are a patient man, Majer. Why are you so concerned that you would seek out a mere woman?"

"I am concerned, and you are no mere woman. You know that." He paused, then added, "The submarshal left me in charge of the alector's buildings and told me only to turn them over to the proper alector, and that I was to decide who was proper."

She shook her head. "That is a sentence of death. You must presume to be equal to one of them, and none of them can accept that. Is the submarshal the same one as in Dramur?"

"Yes."

"I said he had a use for you, and that he did not preserve your life out of goodness, but for a purpose."

"You did." He laughed softly. "I recall your words well."

"He will play you off against his enemies. To survive, you will have to kill them, and that will prove that you are a danger to all of them."

He nodded. "I had considered that."

For the briefest moment, an expression he could not define crossed her face.

"Then you must kill them all, so that none can say how they perished." She smiled coldly. "When they die, they turn to dust at that moment. That should also tell you that they are not of this world."

If they are not of this world, how did they come here? He almost asked that question, but did not. He knew the answer; he just hadn't realized that he did.

"You see? You understand."

"What else?"

"Majer, you know far more than do I."

Mykel laughed again. "That, Chatelaine Rachyla, is flattery. Beyond the work of weapons and arms, you know far more."

"Beyond those and the ancient ones . . ." She paused. "You have encountered them, have you not? Even spoken with them."

"Why would you say that?"

"Your eyes. Your whole being, it is like the dagger you carry. It was not so when . . . when you came to Dramur . . . and that feeling is stronger now. You are more rooted to the world where you are."

His lips curled. There was little point in trying to deceive Rachyla. He looked at her. Had she changed in the way she declared he had? Her aura still seemed predominantly black, but perhaps it was more shot with green. Had his once been like that? "Yes."

The fierceness in her eyes softened—but only for a moment. "Then you know what you must do."

Mykel was afraid he did.

She rose from the armchair. "I do not think I can tell you much you do not already know, Majer."

"You have told me much." He stood, reluctant to depart, yet knowing her words were true.

"I have only confirmed what you feared."

"You are a dangerous woman, Rachyla."

"Herisha's nephew does not think so."

"The more fool he."

She did not answer, but turned toward the entry foyer. Mykel followed.

Once in the foyer, she stepped aside and nodded toward the heavy door.

He opened it, then inclined his head. "Thank you."

"You are welcome, Majer." Her words were cool, dismissive.

He stepped out onto the outer landing. The doorman shied away, pressing himself back against the wall.

Feranot led the roan forward and handed the reins to Mykel, who mounted quickly, then looked back to Rachyla, who had remained standing in the doorway. Their eyes locked.

She stepped back and closed the door. But her eyes remained on him until the door separated them.

"Sir?" asked Vhanyr.

"We need to head back. We have a few matters to take care of." *Such as figuring out how to deal with the returning alectors without disobeying orders and without getting killed.*

And he had to figure out why Rachyla had sent him an announcement that she was in Tempre, when it was clear she still regarded him as an enemy. Did she seek to play him off against the alectors?

He smiled sardonically. That he would not put past her in the slightest.

87

Fhentyl stood waiting as Dainyl's pteridon set down north of the way station late on Quattri afternoon. The flight had tired Dainyl, but not so much as he had feared it might, although he was stiff.

Rather than hasten toward the captain, Dainyl stretched and glanced around. Summer thunderclouds had massed in the west, over the eastern slopes of the Coast Range in the distance, but they often did in late summer. Seldom did much rain fall east of those slopes, though, and that was why grazing around Hyalt had to be controlled—one of the ostensible reasons for a regional alector, although the simple and truthful reason was that it was where a Table was necessary to balance the grid.

How many ostensible truths concealed deeper reasons?

More than he'd believed possible, Dainyl suspected as he finally picked up his gear and walked toward Fhentyl.

The junior captain stiffened slightly as Dainyl approached. "I admit, sir, I've been concerned." His nose wrinkled, as if the submarshal emitted a noxious odor.

"So have I. You can sense the presence of the ancients, I take it?"

"Ah . . . yes, sir."

"That was one of the reasons I was delayed. I inactivated the Table here in Hyalt. I also killed Rhelyn and several of his assistants. The problem was that he wounded me with a weapon of the ancients that drains lifeforce. It also . . . well, you can sense it if you look at my left arm. It should vanish in time." Dainyl snorted. "It wasn't my doing."

"How did you . . . ?"

"That's something I can't reveal, except that I learned a trick or two in Lyterna and elsewhere. The Table can't be reactivated except with certain equipment and supplies that I'm fairly sure Hyalt doesn't have. Have they made any attempts to leave? What have your patrols discovered?"

"Things haven't changed much since you left. Not until this morning, anyway. That was when they wheeled out two of those lightcannon behind Talent barriers. They took out Huerlyn in second squad. The blast was strong enough that it destroyed his skylance as well. The pteridon was singed a bit, but looks all right now. The rest of the squad came in low and out of the northwest, the way you did, sir." Fhentyl smiled grimly. "There's a large hole in front of the cavern entryway."

"Have they increased their use of the lightcannon?"

"No, sir. That's dropped off."

"What about the Cadmians? Have they reported any action?"

"They've reported some night scouting. They lost several troopers the night before last, but they claimed that they killed both rebels. I don't know if others may have escaped."

"Claimed?"

"Captain Rhystan sent a package sealed up. His note stated that he had retrieved the enclosed material and thought the submarshal would like to see it. He also said that only one trustworthy scout and he had been privy to the material."

Dainyl couldn't help wincing, even though it could have been worse.

"My thoughts also, sir, but at least their officers are being thoughtful and loyal."

"That's true." *More so than some of ours.* "Tomorrow,

we'll take the compound, starting with the building first."

Fhentyl looked puzzled.

"You're wondering why we didn't start that way? Because they could have used the Table to bring more crystals and components for the lightcannon. They could also have brought in more rebel alectors. Now that they're cut off . . ."

"That's why you went to Tempre."

"We had problems there, too, as Hyksant can tell you. Fahylt threw in with them, or he was trying to build his own power base. He actually formed his own mounted rifles like Cadmians. Majer Mykel wiped them out. He's holding the RA's building until the Duarches decide who to send to replace Fahylt. Or, the Archon forbid, send Fahylt back."

"You think they would?"

Dainyl knew all too well that was possible if he weren't successful quickly, but he just shrugged. "That's not our problem. Ours is the rebels remaining in Hyalt." He glanced to the southeast. He was slightly surprised that Alcyna or Majer Noryan hadn't shown up with a pteridon company, but it could be that his own efforts at secrecy had delayed Alcyna's ability to react. He hoped so.

"I'm glad you're back, sir. You're certain the arm . . . ?"

"I'm almost at full strength. Let's get something to eat, and then we'll go over the plans for tomorrow." Field rations or local produce, whatever it might be, he was hungry enough to eat it.

He started toward the way station. Despite what he'd told Fhentyl, he was tired, and he had the definite feeling that his troubles were only beginning.

88

Fhentyl and Dainyl stood to the south of the way station, in the cool sunlight just past dawn on Quinti morning. The haze in the eastern sky was more pronounced and promised an even hotter and drier late summer day. In the time Dainyl had been in Tempre, almost all the grasses on the hillsides and rolling plains had turned gold, a harbinger of harvest season, less than two weeks away.

"We need barrels of oils that will burn, even tallow, fats, whatever we can get," Dainyl said. "We'll need all the sulfur and pitch that you can find. If you can find arsenic or other poisons, that would be even better."

Fhentyl presented the quizzical expression that Dainyl was beginning to dislike.

"We need to get them out of there," Dainyl went on. "That means making the place uninhabitable for them, or for most of them."

"Yes, sir."

"There are openings on the top where they had those lightcannon firing out through slits. Liquids can flow down through openings."

Fhentyl nodded.

"Once the liquids are there, what happens if we use a skylance to turn them into flame? And if we keep pouring liquids down there? Remember, they've had to keep things sealed up somewhat. Fifth Company will use skylances to help seal anywhere that smoke is seeping out. After a time, it should get hard to breathe in there."

The junior captain swallowed. "They're alectors . . . and you're going to treat them . . . like vermin?"

"They are vermin. They've fired on the Myrmidons of the Duarchy, and they've killed part of your company. Do you have a better idea, Captain?"

"No, sir."

Dainyl could tell that Fhentyl was less than happy, but then, before the rebellion was crushed, more than a few alectors weren't going to be happy. "Would you like to lead the first assault into those caverns on foot—without doing something like this?"

"No, sir."

"Do you have any better ideas about dealing with them? We've had them holed up in there for a week, and more than half that time has been without a Table." *Which means they think someone is going to rescue them.*

Fhentyl's eyes shifted away from Dainyl, but he did not reply.

In short, you don't like what I'm planning, but you don't have any other ideas except wait and hope, and that isn't going to work. Waiting would only magnify the problems Dainyl and Fhentyl faced, something that Fhentyl clearly didn't understand.

"What would you do if another Myrmidon company attacked us?" Dainyl asked.

"Myrmidons shouldn't be fighting Myrmidons, sir."

"That's true. But regional alectors shouldn't be attacking Myrmidons, either."

The other problem was that Fhentyl had become a captain so recently that, while he could conceive theoretically of rebellion and subversion, accepting either as a reality was proving extremely difficult for the junior officer.

"Yes, sir."

Dainyl forced a concerned expression onto his face. "I understand. It's a difficult situation, but we just have to make the best of it, and we need to get on with matters. It's going to take all of today, and probably tomorrow to set this up." That was optimistic, but Dainyl knew he was running out of time. Yet trying a direct assault, even with skylances and pteridons, would create horrible casualties, and might create exactly what the rebels wanted— riderless pteridons that they could coopt, one way or another. "Go ahead and start trying to gather the materials. Have the local factors and merchants use their own wagons to transport the barrels and amphorae to a staging point east of the complex. I'll contact Captain Rhystan and have the Cadmians set up to receive all of that. We'll also need nets and some strong canvas so the pteridons can lift them to the clifftop above the cave area."

Fhentyl nodded reluctantly.

Dainyl refrained from mentioning that the rebels had no incentive to surrender. Fhentyl was having enough difficulties in accepting the situation.

89

Less than a glass after dawn, Fifth Company was formed up north of the Hyalt way station, each Myrmidon beside a pteridon, except for Fhentyl and Dainyl, who stood a distance apart. While Sexdi and Septi had been hot, the haze and still heat that surrounded the alectors indicated that Octdi would be even hotter. For all that it had taken three days to organize the attack, Dainyl was glad in one respect, because he felt almost recovered from the lifeforce-draining wound inflicted by Rhelyn.

"Fifth Company, ready to fly, sir. Third squad is already in position, guarding the barrels and kegs." Fhentyl's voice conveyed a notable lack of enthusiasm.

Dainyl had to wonder if a friend or relative of the captain might be trapped in Hyalt. It didn't matter, not now. "I'll take first squad to the flat above the caverns, and we'll replace third squad. Third squad will take the first passes at sealing off vents that we haven't already sealed. Second squad is to have its pteridons drop heavy boulders on the roof of the outbuilding until there's a hole big enough for the brimstone. Fourth squad needs to keep the rebels from bringing out any of the lightcannon."

"Yes, sir."

"We're not taking any prisoners until after we've captured both areas. We don't have any way to restrain them. We don't have enough Myrmidons to watch them, and they'll escape from the Cadmians." *The ones here under Captain Rhystan, anyway.*

"I understand, sir. No prisoners until we hold the area." Fhentyl sounded even less happy than he had a few moments before.

Dainyl was glad he had a rationale for his action, because, after what he'd already experienced, he had no intention of letting any of the rebels live, not if he could help it. They'd destroy everything that the Duarches had built, and they'd do it in years, rather than generations.

"Let's lift off." He gave a quick nod before turning and striding across the open space to his pteridon.

He mounted quickly, then looked to Hyksant and raised his arm. *Lift off . . . straight ahead.*

The pteridon was airborne, wide blue wings beating strongly, climbing steadily to the southwest. Before long, below and to his left, Dainyl could make out the Cadmian company set up on the ridge, standing by in case there might be any stragglers or escapees from the forthcoming attack. The men and their mounts cast long shadows in the early sunlight.

Ahead lay the regional alector's complex, seemingly deserted, although Dainyl could sense lifeforce within, even from more than a vingt away. *Lower . . . to the clifftop . . . from the north . . .*

"First squad! Follow the submarshal!" Hyksant's voice carried through the stillness of the morning air. "Hold off landing until third squad lifts off the cliffs."

Dainyl's pteridon settled onto a narrow rocky ridge directly to the north of the assembled array of barrels and kegs. He dismounted and, after climbing over a small jumble of rocks, walked around two scrubby junipers and toward third squad.

"Undercaptain . . . thank you for standing by here."

"Yes, sir."

"You understand your next assignment?"

"We're to circle and wait for you to start creating smoke. Then we make passes across the cavern area, using the hills as cover until the last moment, and employ our lances to seal whatever places where the smoke comes out."

Dainyl nodded acknowledgment. "You may lift off."

"Yes, sir."

The submarshal watched the five pteridons rise. Then he turned and made his way back to his own pteridon, where he retrieved the skylance and began to make his way down the rocky incline, staying in sight of the vitreous channel crudely carved and formed by Talent and skylance over the previous two days. It led to the mostly blocked highest slits where a lightcannon had been used earlier by the rebels. At the top of the channel, two Myrmidon rankers from first squad waited with the kegs, barrels, and the three barrels filled with brimstone, a thick gooey mass of pitch, heavy oil, and sulfur.

It took Dainyl a quarter glass in climbing down the slope before he stood a mere three yards from the target slit, but behind a chunk of redstone.

"Ready?" Dainyl called.

"Yes, sir," Hyksant called back.

"Start with a barrel of oil! A bit at a time."

"Coming, sir."

Although his pteridon was on the cliff above, it was close enough to recharge the skylance he held. He lifted the weapon and waited.

His eyes went skyward, where third and fourth squads circled. Third squad waited to begin sealing vents, fourth squad to attack any sign of rebel activity.

A stream of oil began to flow down the channel. Within the first few barrels of oil was some of the sulfur Hyksant had been able to discover and retrieve from Hyalt, although most was in the brimstone that would come later. Dainyl forced himself to wait, just to allow the oils to keep flowing, while he let his Talent monitor their progress down into the large central chamber that lay below the staircase and landing on which the one lightcannon had been mounted.

A quick flash of light flared from somewhere below Dainyl, and a pteridon wheeled and swooped, its flier triggering bursts from his skylance in returning fire. The pteridon rose and passed directly over Dainyl before climbing farther skyward.

Dainyl checked the oil flow with his Talent, then turned back up toward first squad. "The liquid brimstone! Now!"

The shadow of one of the second squad pteridons crossed Dainyl, and he watched as the pteridon, a large boulder in its crystalline talons, flew out from the cliff and released the boulder. Dainyl could hear the impact easily as the boulder crashed onto the slightly slanted roof of the stone building that stood a good hundred yards to the east of the cliffs and the cavern complex.

Another pteridon followed the first. This time, the Myrmidon ordered a release too early, and the chunk of redstone slammed into the side of the second and highest level.

Dainyl turned his attention back to the vitreous channel and the gooey sludgy ooze that crept past him to the battered slit that afforded access to the tunnels and chambers below.

After a quarter of a glass, when close to a barrel of brimstone was oozing downward inside the complex, Dainyl triggered the lance, aimed directly at the point where the oil dripped from the overhang and into the space in the slit. Yellowish flame flared, and black oily smoke. Dainyl extended his shields, with just enough force so that the smoke and flame triggered by the lance had no place to go but down, following the mixture of oils into the caverns below.

He held the shields so that the flames did not creep back up the channel and so that the smoke was forced downward and into the alector's spaces.

Dainyl had calculated that the oils and brimstone used so far might burn for as long as half a glass. Then they would have to begin the process again. After that, he would have to start using the skylance to heat the channel and melt tallow and fats to burn, and he would still have to hold the shields.

What he planned was long, hard, and tedious. It also might result in far fewer Myrmidon casualties.

Above him, the second squad pteridons continued their circling bombardment, picking up boulders where they easily could to the north and west of Dainyl, then swooping down on the freestanding building, and releasing their loads.

He glanced at the building. Already a good third of the tile roof was smashed, and he could see several of the roof timbers already where the tiles had been battered away or crushed.

Dainyl kept working on firing the oils and brimstone and forcing them into the caverns. Even from where he was working, the stench was close to unbearable.

Abruptly, one of the circling pteridons of fourth squad swooped, lance flaring, then another. One pteridon did not follow the others, but merely circled. Without a Myrmidon, it would follow the squad until Fifth Company returned to Dereka. Then it would not rise into the sky until a new Myrmidon became its flier.

A thin line of smoke issued from the cliffside to the south of Dainyl, and within moments, the third squad Myrmidons began to make passes over the area. It took two passes by the entire squad before the plume of smoke dwindled away to the faintest haze.

Another bombardment run by second squad, and even more of the roof timbers of the outbuilding had been revealed, and in several places, there were gaping holes in the roof.

Dainyl turned and called up the slope. "Hyksant! Take the keg of brimstone and hit the timbers on the outbuilding!"

"Galya! Stand by!" Hyksant relayed the order.

The petite Myrmidon slipped into the silver saddle.

Her pteridon grasped a keg, then burst skyward, before gliding eastward away from the cliff.

Dainyl watched. The keg struck one of the exposed timbers, close to the ridgeline, and brimstone oozed across the timbers and began to drip below. Dainyl lifted his lance and concentrated. It took two bursts before a section of the roof burst into flame.

Galya continued to circle the building, her skylance at the ready.

In moments, the entire upper section of the building was in flames. The Myrmidons of second squad had stopped their bombardment and took over the patrol above the building, while Galya returned and landed her pteridon on the cliff above Dainyl, rejoining the rest of first squad.

Dainyl forced himself to shift his attention back to the vitreous channel. "Another load of brimstone!"

"Yes, sir."

As he waited for the black and gooey mess to slide and ooze down to him, Dainyl studied the situation. Before long the rebels would have to leave the outbuilding, assuming that any remained there. Once that was resolved, he could devote his full energies to the tunnel complex below.

Despite the mounting heat, both from the sun and from the fires below and behind his shields, the brimstone coming down the channel was sluggish. Dainyl triggered the lance briefly, targeting the section of the channel below the brimstone, and the heated stone seemed to help, but it seemed to take forever before the first of the black mass reached the lip of the channel.

Dainyl had to swallow hard not to choke on the smoke that escaped as he shifted his shields to allow all the brimstone past them and to fall, flaming, into the slit that had widened under the impact of flame and shields. He still found himself coughing, and close to choking, wishing for the slightest breeze to blow the noxious smoke that had escaped his shields away from him.

There was no breeze, and even the wingbeats of the pteridons of third squad, passing overhead on their continuing efforts to seal the vents and slots of the complex, did not generate enough movement of air to reach Dainyl.

With a rumbling crunch, part of the roof on the flaming building collapsed.

Within moments, two figures in black and silver ran from the building. The first made it a good hundred yards before being flamed by one of the Myrmidons from squad four—the second less than fifty.

A lightflame flared from the building, narrowly missing the second fourth squad pteridon as it recovered from the attack on the fleeing rebels. The three circling fourth squad Myrmidons all fired at the building. Because the main entry was on the east side, blocked from Dainyl's view, he couldn't see exactly what happened. He just heard the explosion and watched part of the east side of the redstone building sag away from him.

He forced his concentration back to the brimstone he was flaming and forcing downward into the tunnel complex. He thought he sensed more deaths from the burning building, but he continued his efforts to force the smoke and gases downward.

The stones of the southwest corner of the redstone building crumbled, and then the rest of the structure began to settle in upon itself. Three more rebel alectors ran from the structure and were flamed down. Dainyl had the sense that there would not be any more rebels emerging from the ruins.

He turned his full attention back to forcing fire and brimstone into the tunnels. Before long, black and gray smoke began to seep, then pour out of the main front entrance to the cavern complex. Dainyl could not see the recessed archway directly, but the increase in smoke suggested that someone had opened the main doors.

One of the squad four pteridons swooped down, and the Myrmidon fired her lance into the entrance. The amount of smoke decreased, but not entirely.

A line of light flashed up from the entrance to the cavern section of the complex, but by the time one of the Myrmidons from fourth squad reacted, the weapon had been retracted well inside the stone archway.

"What's in the channel is all that there is, sir!" called Galya from the clifftop.

"Thank you."

Dainyl waited until the last of the tallows and oils flowed past him, and he eased them through his shields and let them drop, flaming, into the holocaust he sensed building in the rock-walled tunnels below.

Then he finally released his shields, thankful he had not been required to use all his abilities and strength there, took his lance, and began to climb back up the rocky incline to where his pteridon waited.

Galya greeted him as he paused at the top.

"You look hot, sir."

"It is hot down there." He glanced to Hyksant. "We're going down. Now!"

"Yes, sir!"

Dainyl mounted the pteridon, checked everything, then raised his arm. "Lift off."

"First squad, lift off. Follow the submarshal!"

Dainyl concentrated. *Down . . . as close to the cliff as possible . . . north of the entrance . . .* The pteridon banked and then swept down, heading southward, then flaring, and coming to a halt less than twenty yards north of the entrance from where smoke seeped into the noon sky.

Dainyl vaulted down to the sandy ground, skylance in hand, and hurried forward to the corner of the cliff, just short of the recessed archway cut into the stone. There he waited for the remainder of first squad to rejoin him.

Galya appeared next, then Hyksant, and the other two.

"You need to use the lances sparingly, and against anyone you can." He added quickly, "Without hitting me."

Skylance in hand, he rushed around the corner, triggering the lance at the doorway at the end of the short tunnel.

A blast of Talent energy sheeted around him, blocked by his shields. He triggered the skylance for a second brief burst, and then a third, moving forward toward the Talent-shielded doorway that was half-ajar and from behind which gouts of brimstone smoke intermittently puffed and then died away, before streaming out again.

Another burst of Talent energy, not quite so strong as the previous blast, smashed at him, the impact on his shields slowing him. He fired again, trying to use his Talent to bend the energy around the corner. He sensed another death and fired again, this time with his sidearm, using the same technique.

A figure jumped to one side, holding a silvery dagger that Dainyl recognized too well. Two skylance blasts flared past Dainyl and converged on the rebel. The ancient sword-lance fell to the stones.

Dainyl crashed into the door full-strength, forcing it back.

More lightbeams flared back and forth, and Dainyl felt a Myrmidon behind him die.

He fired his sidearm again, and for a moment, there was stillness. He could sense no one nearby and slipped past the open door in to the entry hall, not more than five yards square behind the door. It was empty. Several separate piles of silver and black alector's uniforms and boots lay scattered across the stones.

The stench of brimstone was almost unbearable.

Dainyl smiled coldly, then used a set of partial screens to press the smoke and gas back down the corridor. Behind his shields, he moved forward, but he no longer sensed anyone nearby.

The huge hall or meeting room to his right was empty, filled with the remnants of brimstone and smoke. Silver and black tunics, boots and clothes lay everywhere.

Dainyl halted, then turned to Hyksant. "I don't think there's anyone left, but take the rest of the squad and check. Be careful."

"Yes, sir." The faintest smile crossed the undercaptain's lips.

"Don't say it," Dainyl said, knowing what Hyksant was doubtless thinking about a submarshal who led a charge against a half-fortified entrance. The only problem was that only Dainyl had shields strong enough to do it. Still, if someone hadn't flamed the rebel with the sword-lance . . .

He turned quickly and headed back to the entry area. The ancient weapon lay against the stones on one side of the outer entry tunnel. He picked it up carefully, sensing the cruel power in it, a hunger for . . . what? The lifeforce of alectors?

Should he keep it? He shook his head. Every alector who had tried to use it was dead. Dainyl didn't care for those odds.

"What is it?"

Galya's words roused him from his consideration.

"A deadly ancient weapon. Find somewhere to tuck it away for now. Better yet, bury it, and don't tell anyone where. Even the slightest cut can be fatal to an alector, including whoever carries it." He set the weapon on the waist-high narrow stone ledge, a stone wainscoting. "Wrap it in something, too." He paused. "I thought . . ."

"The undercaptain detailed me to you, sir."

Dainyl started to nod, then caught sight of an alcove just inside and partly hidden by the door he had earlier forced. He stepped forward and eased the door away from the stone. Just inside the alcove were two of the lightcannon, sitting on small handcarts.

"Let's get them out into the sunlight," Dainyl said, "out in the open." He wheeled one, heavy as it was, down the stone corridor and out into the hazy and smoky heat of early afternoon. With greater effort, Galya wheeled the other one after him.

Kneeling beside the one, he inspected it quickly, but minutely, with his Talent as well as his eyes. One aspect caught his eye immediately. The power level was only set halfway up. That confirmed his suspicion that the rebels had been trying to destroy Myrmidons and not pteridons. It also confirmed his suspicions about the lack of truth in what Zelyert and Asulet had told him about the destruction of pteridons.

Fhentyl and two other pteridons touched down in the open space directly to the east of the entry to the cavern spaces. Fhentyl hurried to meet Dainyl, who stood.

"Is there anyone . . . ?" began the captain.

"Hyksant is checking, but I don't think so. There wasn't as much resistance as I'd expected. There aren't any supplies left either, not to speak of."

At the sound of boots, both officers turned.

Hyksant stepped into the sunlight. His face was pale and drawn. "There . . . there must have been hundreds of them. Hundreds."

"Are there any survivors?" asked Fhentyl.

The undercaptain shook his head. "I don't think we killed them all, though. Most of those in the back corridors—there was dust and smoke on the tunics and boots. They'd been there for a while."

For a while? Dainyl shook his head. "I don't see how we could have killed so many by anything we did before today."

Even Fhentyl looked puzzled. "There isn't much in the way of supplies, but there is some food—or was until the fire got to it. And they wouldn't have killed their own."

"I don't think so." After a moment, Dainyl looked directly at Fhentyl. "Have someone count the dead—the tunics and boots. Then collect them and stack them in the main chamber of the front archway. I need to check out a few things, as quickly as I can. Just leave these lightcannon here for a moment, but don't touch them."

"Yes, sir."

As he walked back through the curved corridor that he felt led to the Table chamber, Dainyl kept puzzling over what Hyksant had discovered. What could have killed so many? Certainly, the first attacks hadn't sealed the complex enough to suffocate hundreds. The only other thing he had done had been to shut down the Table. Had the suddenness of that . . . ?

He almost stopped walking. The ancient soarer had talked about the need for ties directly to Acorus, about changing if he wanted to survive. That one time, for an instant, she had shown him lifethreads stretching to . . . where? Back to Ifryn? Even Lystrana had pointed out that alectors were linked to the world only indirectly and through the dual scepters and the Master Scepter. Could it be that the links for more recent alectors arriving on Acorus were more susceptible to disruption and that, if they had translated directly from Ifryn to Hyalt, he had inadvertently severed those links by his violent shutdown of the Hyalt Table?

He forced himself to keep walking, disturbed by the potential implications, until he reached the normally hidden doorway that led to the Table chamber. The odor of smoke and sulfur remained strong as he stepped inside.

The Table remained inert, looking and feeling like a black stone oblong. Even the normally mirrored surface was black. He released the low-level shields he'd been holding and continued to survey the chamber. Three sets of boots and clothing remained, in discrete piles around the Table. He kept searching, but found no papers, and no documents, nothing to indicate where the rebels had come from or who might have supported them. He doubted that, one way or the other, there would be any evidence in the ruins of the redstone building.

"Submarshal! Submarshal! There are pteridons coming!" Galya stood in the doorway.

Dainyl turned and ran for the front entrance.

Fhentyl was standing just outside. "You can't see them from here, but Arylra reported them. They're just above the horizon to the southwest, a full company."

"I'm not surprised," Dainyl replied. Not pleased, but hardly surprised.

"What company are they?" asked Fhentyl. "You're acting like they're with the rebels."

"I'd judge that they are, and I'd wager that it's Seventh Company out of Dulka. Captain Veluara has some ties to the rebels."

"Is the entire east of Corus rebelling?" Fhentyl looked appalled.

"No. The Myrmidons at Lysia are loyal, and Third and Fourth Company are too far away to have flown here. I've already had trouble with Dulka." Everything Dainyl said was true, but he hoped Fhentyl didn't analyze his words too closely.

"But . . ."

"Get your squads airborne. Circle over the cliff top and to the west, so that they have to come over the entrance to the tunnels here. I'll join you later, but I want to try something with those lightcannon."

"Are you certain you don't want anyone here, sir?"

"Absolutely." Dainyl paused, then added, "Keep the pteridons fairly low as long as you can."

"You're really going to try the lightcannon?"

"Try is the appropriate word," Dainyl replied. "I don't think they'll expect it, and if I can hit their captain, that might disorganize them a bit."

"You think they'll surrender?"

"No. I think they've all been told that we're the rebels, and seeing the mess we made of the complex here, they won't be inclined to think otherwise, no matter what we say."

Fhentyl frowned. "Hate to see Myrmidon against Myrmidon."

"You think I like it?" countered Dainyl. "I warned the marshal about what was happening in Dulka and Hyalt months ago. Until two weeks ago, he seemed to feel matters would work out. You need to get the company airborne. We can talk about how this happened later."

"Yes, sir."

Dainyl waited until Fifth Company had all departed,

rising into the afternoon sky, then stepped farther out. *Over here . . . close to the cliff.* The pteridon obediently used wings and Talent to place itself less than ten yards from the cliff entrance.

Dainyl positioned the pair of lightcannon just inside the stone archway and angled the discharge formulators upward to where he thought the oncoming pteridons might appear on their course toward Fifth Company. Then he turned the power lever all the way up. From what he'd observed and what he sensed, he'd only have one or two shots with each lightcannon before it exhausted its stored energy. Then, he settled back to wait for the oncoming Seventh Company.

By all rights, Veluara should be the lead flier, or one of the two at the point of the wedge. He might be able to tell, if the pteridons approached low enough. If not, he'd take out the leaders and then try to finish the job with his own pteridon and skylance.

Less than a quarter glass passed before he saw the wide wedge of Seventh Company. He glanced back to the west, but the cliff blocked any view of Fifth Company, and that meant that Fhentyl was hanging back far enough to give Dainyl a good shot—he hoped.

Dainyl forced himself to wait until the lead pteridon was just short of directly overhead before he pressed the firing stud, extending his Talent to guide the light-bolt.

The flare was brighter, far brighter, than he'd thought, and his eyes watered. Even before he could see again, he had felt the double flash of the dissipation of purpled life-force. Both flier and pteridon had vanished—near instantly.

Dainyl moved to the second lightcannon, aiming it at the pteridon that had been flying wing on the leader. The second flare was equally bright, and the results the same.

The Seventh Company formation broke, peeling back away from the cliff.

Dainyl checked the lightcannon, but neither showed

any power remaining, and he wasted no time in running to his pteridon and scrambling into the silver saddle and harness.

Up . . . fast pursuit!

The pteridon flashed skyward. Dainyl could sense the lifeforce drain, the very squandering of resources that Shastylt had warned against, but Dainyl didn't see any alternatives at the moment.

A pair of the Seventh Company pteridons converged on him, trying to swoop down on him from their higher altitude.

Dainyl waited until the last moment before throwing up his strongest shields, then triggering his lance, boosting and directing the blast at the Myrmidon he recognized—Undercaptain Klynd.

While Klynd's lightbolt sheeted around Dainyl, the submarshal's fire slammed through the undercaptain's far weaker shields. In moments, Klynd's uniform fluttered downward through the sky, and his pteridon grasped the skylance before climbing and circling away.

Keep climbing . . .

The pteridon responded, and with lance-blasts flying around and past him—few actually even glancing off his shields—Dainyl was above Seventh Company. To the west, he could see Fifth Company regrouping into an attack wedge and moving eastward.

Dainyl wanted to end that battle before it began, and he circled, trying to pick out one of the squad leaders, amid the conflicting orders as Seventh Company realized that Fifth Company was also forming for an attack.

After a second swooping pass and a pull-up, in which he had to fend off more skylance bolts, Dainyl recognized the uniform and vaguely familiar face of an undercaptain. He banked and then looped, coming down almost on top of Weltak, before flying formation to the left of the undercaptain.

"Weltak! Bring them down, or I'll destroy every one of you, one at a time!"

The undercaptain's eyes widened as he turned his head and recognized Dainyl. "No, sir! Got orders!"

Dainyl lowered his lance and fired—using Talent to blast through the undercaptain's comparatively nonexistent screens. Another set of boots and a uniform fluttered downward through the skies, and another pteridon wheeled away from the company, climbing skyward to wait out the battle.

Lyzetta! Would she listen to reason?

Dainyl made two more passes before he located the once-junior undercaptain. Then he had to follow her through a series of dives, loops, and banks. His guts were tight, and his head was throbbing, before he managed to get close enough to her to shout out, "Undercaptain Lyzetta! This is Submarshal Dainyl. I've taken out all your seniors. You don't land your company now, and I'll take out you and everyone else."

The undercaptain's head jerked upward, and she fired her skylance.

Dainyl let the blast sheet around him. He couldn't hold the shields much longer.

"You fire again, and you're dead! Just like Veluara, Klynd, and Weltak!"

She lowered the lance, helplessly.

"You've got a tenth of a glass. Put them down in formation in front of the burned-out building."

Dainyl banked away, climbing westward, before anyone else tried to fire at him.

In moments, he was flying alongside Fhentyl.

"They're going to set down. I'm going down after they're in formation. Keep circling. If anyone tries to lift off, flame them."

"Yes, sir."

Dainyl banked back to the south to make sure Lyzetta ordered Seventh Company to ground.

More like a quarter of a glass passed before Dainyl's pteridon touched down before the remnants of Seventh Company. He held his shields, although the effort was getting exhausting, and his fingers trembled, so much so that he laid the skylance across his thighs, his hands only resting on the weapon. He couldn't do much more.

"Lyzetta! Any other squad leaders forward!"

Two undercaptains appeared—what Dainyl expected, since he'd killed Weltak, Klynd, and Veluara. Dainyl looked over the two.

"Whether you know it or not, you've just been part of a rebellion against the Duarch and against the Marshal of Myrmidons. Regional Alector Rhelyn—he was the RA here in Hyalt—had been gathering translated alectors from Ifryn as part of a force to take over Acorus. Before we go any further, I'd like each of you undercaptains, one at a time, to walk inside the entrance there and look at all the alectors' shimmersilk uniforms stacked in the large chamber to the left. Lyzetta, you go first."

The alectress did not look at Dainyl, but she did turn and follow his directions. She came back quickly, her expression frozen.

"Now you." Dainyl did not know—or couldn't recall—the other undercaptain's name.

When both undercaptains stood before Dainyl once more, he surveyed them silently before speaking.

"You and your pteridons will not return to Dulka. You will accompany me and Fifth Company to Tempre and then to Dereka."

"Might we ask why, sir?" asked Lyzetta.

"Captain Veluara was part of the rebel group. So is RA Quivaryt. Your old compound is being used as a base for the rebel alectors. Marshal Shastylt has said that there could be little as bad as Myrmidons fighting Myrmidons. That will occur again if you return to Dulka—unless each of you is killed and your place taken by a rebel. That has already occurred a number of times."

Lyzetta and the other squad leader exchanged glances.

"That's why you're coming to Dereka. It's for your protection as well."

"That's all?" Lyzetta finally asked.

"You may have to fight against other rebels. I hope not, but I can't promise that." Dainyl was exhausted. He hoped he could make the flight back to the way station. "You're to lift off and follow me to the way station we're using a base. We'll leave tomorrow for Tempre."

"Sir?"

"There's nothing left here," Dainyl added. "We've had the compound under siege for more than a week, and we ended up flaming it from the inside."

He could sense the dismay from the Myrmidons.

"The Duarches do not take rebellion lightly, especially from alectors," Dainyl said, using what little Talent-force he had left to project coldness and authority. "Neither do I. It's a waste of resources and lifeforce." After a moment, he added, "If you would mount, Undercaptains, and follow me."

Dainyl concentrated. *Lift off . . . northeast . . . to the way station.* As the tireless pteridon burst skyward, his legs were trembling, and his vision tended to blur, but he couldn't afford to show weakness. Not yet.

90

Mykel rose before dawn on Octdi. He hadn't slept well, and he was worried. He'd heard nothing from the submarshal, and no alectors had appeared, not that he'd expected them immediately. Quinti and Sexdi had been slightly cooler than the previous days, but a warm wind had begun to blow out of the south late on Septi, and that promised a far warmer Octdi.

Beginning on Quinti, Mykel's scouts had noted riders in blue, especially on the hilltops to the north and west of the regional alector's compound—and some were physically large enough to be alectors—but they rode off before the scouts could get close enough to find out more. The fact that they vanished suggested that they were indeed alectors.

Mykel sought out Undercaptain Matorak even before he headed to the mess to eat, because, as duty company on Octdi, Second Hyalt also provided the inside guards for the still-vacant regional alector's gray granite building. He found the undercaptain outside the stables.

"Yes, sir?"

"Marorak, we're going to change the way we guard those doors. The ones inside the building. If anyone should come up the doors from below in force, the guards are in a poor position. There's nowhere to go and no cover."

"That's true, sir. What do you have in mind?"

"Post one of them at the southwest corner where the corridors intersect. From there, he can see if anyone comes up the steps from below. Post the second on the west side of the entry foyer. That way, the one observing the doorway can relay what he sees to the one in the entry foyer, and the second guard can immediately inform you or the squad leader right outside. If those who arrive are alectors, tell the guards to withdraw to the outside without informing the alectors. If you get that word, have your men mounted and ready to ride here so that we can turn over the complex quickly. Make sure you pull the squad from the rear, the north side, immediately. If there's trouble, there won't be enough cover back there."

"If they're not alectors?"

"Then tell them that the building is off-limits until an alector representing the regional alector arrives. If anyone starts shooting, then take positions and defend yourselves. Those stone walls in front might provide good cover."

"You're expecting trouble, sir?"

"I hope not, but if there is, you need to be prepared. If, and I hope it doesn't happen, you have to defend yourself against rebel alectors, remember that those clothes of theirs stop bullets, but they don't totally stop the impact. If they get hit enough, they will go down."

Matorak nodded slowly.

"I know," Mykel said softly. "It isn't the best position, but that's part of being a Cadmian."

Matorak offered a twisted smile. "It still beats growing nuts or quarrying marble."

"Or laying tiles," returned Mykel.

They both laughed—briefly.

Uneasy as he felt, after leaving Matorak, Mykel decided to saddle the roan, then eat. On his way back from the stable to the mess, he glanced at the sky to the south, already hazy. Although the sun was barely up, the air was as warm as it usually had been in midmorning.

Breakfast was overdone mutton strips with egg toast, and some apricots. There was lukewarm cider, a welcome change from ale, and Mykel drank two mugs, as he sat there by himself, thinking. He just hoped he could turn the buildings back over to an alector and move his companies out of Tempre as quickly as possible. The less he had to do with alectors, the better. That still left the problems with the submarshal, but, for whatever reason, he'd left Mykel alone so far.

So far. Rachyla might well be right, that Dainyl had a use for Mykel that wasn't in Mykel's interest, and that use was probably why he was still in Tempre. He shook his head. He just wanted to get out of the city in a way where he wouldn't be actually directly disobeying orders.

Finally, he stood, getting ready to leave when Fabrytal walked in, followed by a ranker, who, as soon as he saw Mykel, hurried toward the majer.

"There's an alector in blue at the place, sir, and he wants to see the head Cadmian. Undercaptain said he looks mean, sir."

Mykel looked to Fabrytal, who had moved toward Mykel when he had heard the message. "You and Loryalt form up everyone, out front, rifles ready. As soon as you're formed up, ride to join me and Second Hyalt." He looked to the ranker. "You head back and tell Undercaptain Matorak I'm on my way."

"Yes, sir."

"Come with me for a moment," Mykel ordered Fabrytal, as he hurried out of the mess, back toward the stables. "When you and Loryalt join us, you set up more on the west, and Loryalt on the east. I don't want someone sneaking out the back, not with their weapons, and outflanking us. I told Matorak to pull his men from the rear directly behind the building, because there's no cover there, but you two can rake it from cover on the sides. The last thing—I told Matorak this already—about firing at rebel alectors. Did he pass it on?"

"Yes, sir. Their clothes stop the bullets, but not the impact."

"Make sure Loryalt and your men know it, too." Mykel was almost running as he crossed the center courtyard.

"Yes, sir." Fabrytal cleared his throat. "Begging your pardon, sir, but . . ."

"How do I know this? Part of it's experience. I saw an alector take a crossbow bolt last year, and it knocked him down, and I could tell he was hurt. Part of it I learned from others."

"Was that why . . . ? Sorry, sir." Fabrytal flushed. "I need to get the men ready."

"The lady Rachyla? Yes." Mykel turned toward the stable without looking back.

Fabrytal bellowed out his orders. "Fifteenth Company! Mount up! On the double! Loryalt! Same for Seventeenth Company!"

"Seventeenth Company! Mount up! . . ."

Mykel hurried into the stable. Once there, he led out the roan, checked his rifle, then unpacked the ammunition belt and slung it place. Only then did he mount.

As he rode out through the granite gates, turning westward on the boulevard, heading toward the complex, he looked to his right at the granite building, still amazed that the regional alector had constructed such a compound without the knowledge and approval of the Myrmidon Submarshal. Or had Dainyl known and had he just waited to act for reasons of his own? With alectors, it was clear, often one could not tell.

The hot south wind whipped the Cadmian banner that Mykel had ordered placed on the flag staff in the center of the south wall. He'd had the Alector's Guard banner folded for delivery to the submarshal when—and if—he returned.

Despite the gusts of hot wind, or because of it, the gardens on Mykel's left seemed limp and wilted as he rode past them.

He nodded to himself as he neared the compound. Most of Second Company, while mounted, had moved out of the plaza immediately before the alector's headquarters and stood ranked behind the front stone walls. Matorak remained waiting, standing beside his mount, less than fifteen yards from the front entry to the building. Three Cadmians flanked him. Mykel eased his rifle from its holder, but rested it across his legs, as he rode toward Matorak.

The undercaptain turned his head momentarily, as if to make sure it was Mykel.

"Undercaptain," Mykel said loudly. "I'll handle this. Return to your company."

Matorak looked up and back at Mykel, surprised at the harshness in the majer's voice.

"Get everyone out of here, back behind the wall." Mykel mouthed the words, not even daring to speak them. He knew how acute the hearing of some alectors could be.

A hint of an understanding glint appeared in the undercaptain's eyes, but his voice was as cold as Mykel's had been. "Yes, sir."

Matorak had barely vaulted into the saddle and begun to ride away when an alector stepped out from behind one of the four columns at the top of the steps up to the building. While the color of his tunic was the same blue and gold as the Alector's Guard had worn, the fabric was the treated shimmersilk that all alectors apparently wore.

"Who are you?"

"Majer Mykel, commanding, Third Battalion, Cadmian Mounted Rifles."

"Why are you here?" The alector's voice carried contempt and anger.

"The Submarshal of Myrmidons ordered us to guard the area until the regional alector or a designated representative returned," replied Mykel politely.

"There was no need of that. Alector Fahylt had his own forces. What happened to them?"

Mykel tensed. How was he supposed to answer that? "I was not aware that any regional forces were authorized to any regional alector." He could sense more alectors moving out from the building and behind the pillars at the top of the steps. "Are you the designated representative of the regional alector?"

"You don't ask questions, steer. You obey without question."

Besides his unbelievable arrogance, there was something else different about this alector, although Mykel couldn't immediately place it. What he did understand was that the alector would take offense at anything he uttered and that Mykel wasn't getting out of Tempre without a fight. Rather than say anything, he waited, his rifle across his knees. He also tried to strengthen what shields he had, yet keep them hidden. Matorak and his men needed more time.

"Answer me, steer."

"What would you like me to say? I wasn't aware that you asked me anything. I had only asked if you were designated by the Duarches to resume administration."

"What happened to the Alector's Guard—if you happen to know?"

Mykel didn't care for the continued evasion of his question about the alector's authority, but he replied, "They rode away after we arrived in Tempre." That was true enough in its own way.

Mykel could sense that there were ten alectors behind the pillars.

The one who had been speaking lifted a hand weapon, one Mykel recognized as similar, if not identical, to the submarshal's sidearm. "Do you know what this is, steer? Do you know what it will do?"

"It appears to be a Myrmidon officer's sidearm. I wasn't aware that those were given to administrative alectors."

"You are too insolent to remain alive—"

Before the alector finished his words, Mykel's rifle was up and aimed. He squeezed the trigger and *willed* the bullet home.

The bluish lightbeam from the sidearm slashed into the stone as the arrogant alector's body toppled forward.

"Take cover!" Mykel ordered. "Rifles ready!" He turned his mount, urging the gelding across the plaza, and trying to hold what shields he had, hoping that the surprise of his attack would gain him a few moments.

"Talent steer! Kill him!"

One lightbeam flashed by Mykel, so close he could feel the heat, but only one, as he turned the roan sharply behind the stone wall and vaulted from the saddle.

"Fire at will!" he ordered, lifting his own rifle again.

For several moments, lightbeams flashed from the stone pillars as alectors ducked out and aimed their sidearms.

What could Mykel do now? The alectors behind the pillars had as much as admitted that they were rebels. He could hear the hoofs of the other two companies, headed down the boulevard toward them. He turned, looking for Matorak, not seeing him, but locating a squad leader. "Squad leader! Here!"

The darker-skinned and wiry subofficer hurried toward Mykel, careful to keep his head below the top of the wall. "Sir?"

"Send someone out to meet the other two companies. He can go on foot and use cover. They need to carry out their orders without exposing themselves to direct fire from the front of the building."

"Yes, sir. Fylankar! Front! Orders from the majer . . ."

Mykel turned his concentration back to the building, easing up just enough to aim the rifle over the top of the wall, concentrating on where he *knew* one of the rebel alectors was. He squeezed the trigger.

Another body sprawled out onto the stone steps.

Knowing that the rebel alectors would return fire immediately, Mykel shouted, "Second Company, heads down!" Still, he was ready for the next head to peer out from behind a pillar. He fired, twice, before the second bullet hit, then dropped completely below the wall, where he reloaded, watching as the blue lightbeams coruscated above. With each lightblast came the odor of melting and burning stone.

The screams of a badly burned mount shrilled through the morning air. Mykel should have ordered the mounts farther back, but he hadn't thought that so many of the alectors would have had such sidearms. Until today, the submarshal was the only alector he'd ever seen with one.

When the flurry of lightbeams died way, Mykel eased westward along the wall, still out of sight, past nearly a half squad of Second Hyalt, before he peered just above the wall. He thought he could sense six or seven alectors behind the pillars.

Slowly, he eased his rifle up, and fired twice more, then ducked back down.

"Heads down!"

Yet another set of lightbeams flared, but Mykel had the sense that the flashes were fewer, and the discharges weaker.

He slipped up and fired again, seeking yet another of the rebels, then ducked back down. He felt he'd missed, because he had not concentrated enough.

Only a few flashes of light followed his shot.

Jasakyt appeared, running along behind the wall, then slipping into place beside Mykel. "Sir, Fifteenth Company's on the west side. We got the wall, but there were about five of them with those weapons to the northwest. We lost near-on a squad, but they're all dead. Chyndylt ran one down with his mount. We've got the rest pinned inside. Undercaptain wants to know if you have any orders, sir."

"Keep them pinned. If you hit them enough times, they die, just like we do. We're getting rid of the ones guarding this door. Once it's clear, we'll move in." Mykel hadn't realized that would be his strategy, but it was clear that he had few choices—as Rachyla had predicted. He could either take the building and somehow seal off the door to the Table, or he could withdraw and leave Tempre. Anything else would kill Cadmians for no result. But then, retaking the building might do the same. Except . . . somehow, he knew that taking the building was what needed to be done.

"Yes, sir. I'll tell the undercaptain." With that, the scout turned and hurried back along the wall, keeping low.

Mykel reloaded, and then concentrated on the building. One of the windows on the main level was open. It had not been before. He watched, waited, then aimed, concentrated, and fired.

He saw nothing, but he *felt* that an alector had died.

He ducked just before another barrage of lightbeams raked the wall. The odor of more molten stone rose in the hot and damp air.

As the beams passed and died away, Mykel eased back up and fired twice, dropping back behind the wall, and reloading while he waited for another reaction. There wasn't one.

Keeping his head down, he moved back to the eastern end of the wall, moving behind the crouching Cadmians of Second Company. He came to a halt just short of the granite post that marked one side of the ungated entry to the paved plaza. He eased himself up behind the post, trying to get a feel for how many alectors remained.

As he stood, blocked from attack by the granite, he heard firing begin in the rear of the building, coming from both east and west. He could only see a scattering of bluish lightbeams, and those died away. Mykel smiled grimly. The rear exit hadn't proved effective for the alectors, either.

He studied the front columns. From what he could sense, three alectors remained.

Once more, he lifted his rifle, aiming and *willing*.

After two shots, the third alector scrambled into the building. If Mykel had had just a little more time . . . but the deliberated, Talent-aided shots took longer.

"Matorak!" Mykel reloaded again, glad he'd worn the ammunition belt.

Within moments, the undercaptain was by Mykel's side.

"They've withdrawn inside. Right now, they don't have a defense. Designate a squad to follow me in."

"Yes, sir. Second squad." Matorak turned his head. "Jorust! Second squad! Over here!"

As the squad gathered, Mykel studied the building, watching for a window to open. As he'd suspected, one did, on the upper level. He raised his rifle and fired.

This time a body twisted forward, falling out the floor-to-ceiling window and hitting the pavement with a dull thud.

Mykel took a moment to reload. He wanted a full magazine going back into the building.

"They're ready, sir."

Mykel turned. The squad crouched in a line behind the wall. He raised his voice. "We're headed to the building. As soon as we clear the wall, spread out. Don't get close to another Cadmian until we get inside the front pillars. We'll regroup there."

He looked back to the building. He'd probably lose some men, but now was better than waiting. The rebels could get reinforcements, from wherever they did, anytime. He wondered if they had come through the Table, but pushed the thought aside. "Matorak, send messengers to Fifteenth and Seventeenth Company. Tell them we're assaulting the building, and not to fire into it, just at any rebel who tries to leave."

"Yes, sir."

"Second squad! Forward!"

Mykel sprinted from behind the granite gate post, trying to see and sense if anyone fired at them. Only a handful of lightbeams flashed toward the scattered Cadmians, but one, possibly more, took their toll. Mykel knew that stopping and trying to shoot would only make him a greater target.

He was panting hard when he scrambled up the granite steps and behind the first line of pillars, rifle ready. The space between the columns and the archway was empty, except for tunics and trousers and boots. He half-shook his head. It took getting used to—that when alectors died, they turned to ashes and dust within moments.

"That rebel . . . he fell out of the window . . . nothing left but his uniform. Saw him hit . . ."

"We'll worry about that later," Mykel stated. "However they die, they've got those lightguns, and they can kill, and we need to get rid of them before they can call in reinforcements. I need two flankers. If anyone pops up, shoot them in the chest. That'll knock them around enough that they'll have trouble aiming." He moved toward the double doors, one of which had been left ajar.

The rebels weren't used to fighting, not grind-it-out fighting, and that would help. Standing so that the door shielded him, Mykel eased it open.

The entry hall was empty, but he could sense someone behind the archway on the right.

Mykel smiled, then reached back, and motioned. "Hand me one of those boots."

A ranker passed it forward. "Feels slimy, somehow."

Mykel tossed the boot into the hall, then raised his rifle in one motion.

With the *clunk* of the boot on the marble floor, the rebel peered out. Mykel concentrated and fired.

The alector in blue pitched forward, and the lightcutter skittered across the marble tiles.

"Frig . . ."

Mykel ignored the muttered expletive, trying to locate

any other alectors. Then he slipped inside and kept to the left wall, moving quickly, then stopping short of the archway to the right, on the east side.

From the outside, on the north side, came another barrage of rifle fire.

Mykel dropped to his knees and took a quick look down the corridor. He caught a glimpse of blue at the corner, and raised his rifle and fired.

The rebel spun out and sprawled on the floor, then scrambled to his feet. He almost made it back to cover when Mykel's next shot took him down.

The sound of boots on stone, and the diminishing purple aura, indicated a retreat.

Mykel turned. "Jorust. Take half the squad. Stay here, and be ready to sweep the corridors in both directions. The other half comes with me." He hurried through the archway and moved quickly down the corridor, past doors closed when he had last checked the building, sensing no one in the studies.

When he reached the corner, he stopped, then took a quick glance. The next corridor heading to the rear of the building was also empty, but he could still hear the sound of distant boots. Were they heading for the lower level, and the Table? Trying to retreat while they could?

Mykel forced himself to move methodically, checking the studies on each side of the corridor, using his men to cover his rear, but, in less than a half glass, it was clear that there was no one on either the upper floor or the main level, and the shooting from outside had died away some time back.

With some trepidation, he moved to the open doorway that led below. Absently, he noted that the lock remained missing. He smiled, briefly. Exactly who would have repaired it? Somehow, he doubted that the rebel alectors would have. They seemed far too arrogant to stoop to that.

"You wait here, until I get to the bottom." Mykel did not sense anyone on the stairs. Still, he moved slowly down the dimly lit steps.

Just as he stepped onto the main floor, the slightest rustle came from his right. He jumped back toward the cover of the archway, trying to strengthen what he thought of as shields, but too late. Bluish-flame angled past his left shoulder, clipping his tunic and part of his upper arm, with pain so intense that he nearly dropped the rifle.

"Frig . . . frig . . ." His eyes watered, but he was at least out of the line of fire.

He hadn't sensed a thing. Not a thing.

The same frigging thing had happened in Dramur. He should have learned.

"Sir? You all right?"

"I'll be fine. There are some rebels down here. Hold a moment." Mykel lowered himself to his knees, then eased forward to the edge of the stone casement of the archway, waiting.

Another blast of light flared past him well over his head.

He kept waiting.

It seemed like a quarter of a glass before a third—and weaker—blast struck the wall beyond the foot of the stone stairs, but it was doubtless far less than that. Even before that, Mykel forced himself to peer aim, aim, and fire.

The alector's lightcutter beam etched a line in the ceiling before the rebel alector crashed to the stone floor. There was no one else in the lower corridor.

"All right," he said quietly. "Half of you come down. The others guard the top."

He continued to wait behind the stone, watching the corridor, while the four rankers slipped down the stairs. Still, no rebels appeared. Had the one been the only rebel who could hide his aura? Why hadn't he remembered? He'd gotten so used to employing his extended senses that he'd forgotten that they didn't pick up absolutely everyone.

"That's a bad burn, sir."

"We're almost done. One of you go tell the undercaptain that, and have him send word to Undercaptain Fabrytal."

"Ah . . ."

Mykel inclined his head toward the ranker who stood on the last step. "You. They need to know."

"Yes, sir."

Mykel eased out into the corridor, rifle ready, even though he sensed nothing. With the three rankers flanking him, they moved down the corridor. No one appeared.

The door to the Table chamber was open.

Mykel moved slowly to the edge, then took a quick look. The chamber was empty except for some uniforms scattered across the floor. For a time, he stood in the doorway. His left arm burned, so much that he could barely move it. But he *had* to do something about the frigging Table. But what?

The Table pulsed purple. He'd seen enough to know that the purple force—was that what they called Talent?—carried tremendous energy.

Finally, he turned. "You three. Move back ten yards."

"Sir."

"I'm not going anywhere." He didn't try to smile before he turned and reloaded the rifle. Then he tried to sense from where the energy came—from what amounted to a node on the far side, and the node was close to the side of the stone base of the Table.

He couldn't fire a bullet through solid stone. But was it solid stone? It couldn't be, not if it transported alectors, not if it displayed images.

If . . . if he aimed at the south wall, and *willed* the bullets to ricochet back into the guts of the Table, willing with all his effort, he could direct them to strike that nexus of energy. That way, if the Table exploded . . . when the Table exploded, he corrected himself, he'd be shielded by the heavy stone wall.

Slowly, he raised the rifle, ignoring the blistering and agonizing stabbing pain in his left arm, and concentrated, squeezing the trigger, *willing* and trying to add some of the green energy that flowed around him. One shot, then a second . . .

He didn't squeeze the trigger a third time. The building shook and the heavy stones flexed and threw him across the corridor. He felt himself flying . . . trying to hold his inadequate shields, and then . . . blackness . . .

91

Mykel woke with a start, and that sudden jolt sent spasms through his entire body. His left arm was hot and painful, but he was almost surprised to be alive. On the wall to his left was a lamp, but each eye saw a separate image of the polished brass and etched glass fixture. He closed his eyes and then opened them. There were still two images.

He was propped up in a large bed, with a shimmersilk sheet across him. His forehead was damp, and he was sweating. His left shoulder was loosely covered with thin gauze and an ointment had been applied under it to his blistered skin. He had been undressed, except for underdrawers . . . No, he wore underdrawers but they felt silky.

"So, you're finally awake. That took long enough, for just a few bruises and a burn."

The voice was feminine, cold, and reminded him of someone. He turned his head, slowly, carefully. Rachyla sat in a carved chair less than a yard away from the bed. She wore a pale green vest and trousers, and a darker green vest. Her dark hair was slightly disarrayed, only the second time he had ever seen anything about her less than perfect.

"What . . . ?" His mouth was so dry he could not say another word.

"What are you doing here?" She laughed, in low but harsh tones. "Amaryk is furious. That would be reason enough." The cool smile faded. "Your undercaptain brought you here with some secrecy. He sees more than he says. I told Amaryk that I felt it unwise to displease the acting commander of Cadmians who had routed the evil ones and who held the city. I also told him that if anything happened to you, he would suffer. That made him even less happy." She offered him a beaker, guiding it to his right hand.

His fingers trembled, but he managed to turn more and drink. The ale felt both harsh and cooling as he swallowed. "Thank you."

"It is the least I could do, Majer. You fed me when I was ill . . . as well as you could." Her tone was matter-of-fact, cold.

"How long have I been here?"

"Just since this afternoon. It is near midnight now. I had thought you might wake." She stood and peered into his eyes. "I thought as much. Did you strike your head?"

"I struck . . ." He tried not to cough, but couldn't stop. It felt as though his entire back was bruised. When the coughing subsided, he took the smallest sip of the ale, hoping it would calm his throat. He waited, then spoke again. "I hit everything. The explosion threw me into a stone wall."

"You have a concussion. It will pass. What about your shoulder?"

"One of the rebel alectors shot me with one of their weapons."

"The ones that burn with light?"

Mykel nodded, trying to keep from coughing.

"You should not be alive." After a moment Rachyla went on. "You will need a new sabre and scabbard. Your belt buckle snapped into three pieces. I know of no one who has been wounded with the burning weapons and who has lived."

He would have shrugged, but he knew that would have sent shooting pains everywhere.

"I cannot say I am fond of you, Majer, but I am not at all fond of the evil ones, and for your killing of so many, I am appreciative."

"How did you know . . . ?" Mykel stifled a yawn. How could she possibly have known?

"I asked your undercaptain why he brought you here. He said that you had killed more than a score of the evil ones—he called them rebel alectors—but whatever name they have, they are evil. He felt you would be safer with someone who knew something about them. He did not want you helpless in the compound."

As he lay there, taking another sip of ale, looking at Rachyla, exhausted as he was, he had sensed something strange about her words, especially at first, but his head throbbed, and he could not identify why he felt that way. He could not sense much about how she felt, unlike most people, from whom he could gain a sense of feeling and sometimes more. He frowned. She was like the seltyr trooper in Dramur and the alector who had shot him— one of those few he could not feel or sense.

"For many reasons, I could not deny him. Not when the evil ones have done so much to us." She laughed, once, harshly. "It is so ironic that you, who serve them, have done more to avenge my family than anyone."

"You planned it that way. Or hoped . . ." He tried to stop the coughing, but he doubled up in pain anyway. After a moment he lay back, his head swimming.

"Me, Majer? I could not plan my own course, let alone yours."

Mykel felt differently, but the coldness of her voice and his own exhaustion told him he should not pursue those thoughts. He should not have said as much as he had. He should have said something about Fabrytal and nothing about Rachyla. He definitely owed Fabrytal— and it was clear the undercaptain was more perceptive than Mykel had realized. He managed another swallow of the ale, realizing that he had emptied the beaker— between drinking and spilling it.

Rachyla took it from him. "That is enough for now. You should not eat or drink any more until your eyes are better."

Until his eyes were better? He could see, if in double images, or was that what she meant?

She said something, but he could not make it out.

". . . sorry . . ." he mumbled.

"Why do you persist?" she asked. "Even when you cannot move, you arrive at my door."

"The ancient said we were tied, somehow," he said tiredly. Was that what the ancient soarer had said, or was that how he had interpreted it?

"You must have imagined it." Her voice was chill once more. "The ancients do not tie men to women. Nor do they advise men—not those who wish to live."

"Believe what you will, Rachyla." His eyes were heavy again, and he struggled to stay awake, to keep looking at her. His eyes closed anyway.

92

On Novdi morning, Dainyl could barely move. His legs were stiff and sore. His head throbbed, and occasional shooting pains stabbed down the arm that had been sliced earlier with the ancient sword. Had Galya taken care of that? He'd forgotten that in the welter of follow-up details. Several of the pteridons of fallen Myrmidons had been loaded with items Dainyl had not wished to leave—mainly all the lightcutters. In the end, he'd destroyed the two working lightcannon, because they were too heavy to carry by pteridon and too dangerous to leave in any custody but that of the Myrmidons.

Slowly he forced himself off the too-short pallet bunk and into a sitting position. Then he stood and pulled on the rest of his uniform. After gathering himself together and taking care of various necessities, he returned to the way station proper, and to the corner where rations were laid out. At least there was some ale. He poured some from the pitcher into one of the tin mugs and took a long swallow. He didn't see Fhentyl, but Galya was standing to one side.

"Galya?"

"Yes, sir?"

"Did you bury that . . . weapon?"

The Myrmidon nodded. "Yes, sir." She shook her head. "Could tell that wasn't something anyone needed to use."

"Don't tell me where. Don't tell anyone else about it."

"No, sir."

"You're to accompany me on a quick flight—after I have something more to eat. I need to convey some orders to the Cadmians before we leave."

"I'll get my gear and wait for you outside, sir."

Dainyl nodded, his mouth full.

When he did leave the way station, heading for his own pteridon, he saw Fhentyl.

The captain was standing beside his pteridon, checking his gear. "We'll be ready in less than a glass, sir."

"That's fine. I'm flying over to the Cadmians, with some last orders. I won't be gone long. Galya will accompany me."

"We'll be waiting, sir." Fhentyl's tone remained *very* formal.

Dainyl could sense the underlying fear and concern, and a deeper puzzlement, possibly a questioning of why anyone would pit one company of Myrmidons against another. He offered a smile. "We won't be long," he repeated, turning toward his own pteridon.

Although he was stiff, in moments he was in the saddle and harness and airborne, with Galya flying wing to his left. Farther to the southwest, he could make out faint wisps of smoke still rising from the burned out building.

After he landed on the slight slope to the west of the old garrison—he didn't feel like trying to squeeze the pteridon into the narrow space east·of the walls—Dainyl dismounted, but he wasn't about to seek out Captain Rhystan. He was far too sore, and he still had a day's flying ahead of him. Fortunately, he did not have to send Galya for the captain, or even to wait long.

The senior captain walked briskly from the old garrison out to the pteridons and their fliers. He headed directly to Dainyl.

"Submarshal, sir?"

"Captain, the Myrmidons will be leaving shortly. You are to continue with your primary duties of completing the Cadmian compound and readying the two companies to take over once the compound is completed. In the meantime, you are to mount a patrol of the area around the regional alector's compound. Your principal task is to keep all locals and foragers out·of the burned-out building and tunnels. Do you understand?"

"Yes, sir." Rhystan's voice was pleasant, but formal.

"I cannot say when a regional alector will return, or when the complex will be rebuilt. You will doubtless be notified, if Third Battalion is still deployed here. Majer Mykel may be tied up in Tempre for a while longer, or he may return within the week. We'll be heading there next. You'll remain in command here until he returns."

"Yes, sir."

"Do you have any questions, Captain?"

Rhystan paused, then frowned. "Are there . . . were there any survivors who escaped? Third Battalion did not see any, but it would be good to know . . ."

"Not so far as we know. If there are any, they cannot number more than a handful, if that. I do not think they will bother you."

"Yes, sir." Rhystan stepped back, respectfully watching, as Dainyl mounted his pteridon.

Lift off . . . to the northeast . . . The pteridon burst into the air.

As he climbed, Dainyl surveyed the grasslands, now universally golden, and then the high road, with only a handful of wagons and riders, far fewer than would be the case to the north and west, especially on the high roads bordering the Bay of Ludel. From the air, the new Cadmian compound looked nearly finished, except for the piles of stone both within and outside the walls, and the dirt road that led down to the high road.

After landing the pteridon north of the way station, he immediately dismounted, concealing the wince he felt at the soreness in overstrained muscles.

Fhentyl appeared immediately. "We're still headed to Tempre, sir?"

"Yes. We'll overnight there. There is space for both companies." Dainyl glanced past the captain to see Lyzetta standing back a distance, waiting to talk to him.

Fhentyl turned. "The undercaptain wanted a word with you." With a nod, he stepped away. "We're ready whenever you give the word, sir."

"It won't be long." Dainyl gestured for Lyzetta to join him. "You wanted to speak to me, Undercaptain?"

"Yes, sir. Will you be assigning an officer to command Seventh Company?"

"Not at the moment. You will remain in command."

"Captain Veluara had placed Asyrk as senior, junior only to Klynd." Lyzetta's voice was even, but there was tension behind it.

"I'd like to see him. I'll talk to you both."

"Yes, sir. Just a moment, sir."

Dainyl had the feeling he knew what was coming. With Veluara having been appointed to command by Alcyna, how could it have been otherwise?

When, moments later, Lyzetta returned with an angular alector, Dainyl barely managed to refrain from nodding. He could sense the slightly darker purple of an Ifryt translated, not recently, but within the past few years, and shields stronger than those of any normal undercaptain.

"Submarshal, sir?" Asyrk inclined his head politely. "You wished to see me?"

"I wanted to see you both."

Lyzetta looked intently at the other undercaptain, and

Dainyl understood immediately why she had raised the question. It also confirmed his decision to have her hear Asyrk's story. She already suspected his origin, and as Asyrk's commander, which she would be, if Dainyl allowed Asyrk to live, she should know his background details.

"Yes, sir." Asyrk's eyes met Dainyl's.

Behind the level gaze, Dainyl could sense apprehension, if not outright fear. "Asyrk. How is Illustra these days? Or recently, should I ask?"

"You knew about Veluara, didn't you, sir?" When Dainyl did not reply, the undercaptain went on, "Will you destroy me, too, Submarshal?"

"I might. Tell me why I shouldn't."

Asyrk squared his broad shoulders. "Illustra will not last long, sir. It might not be another year. When I departed two years ago, there had been three attempts to overthrow the Archon. In the last one, he destroyed more than a score of pteridons. Each effort and the Archon's reactions to each have destroyed lifeforce more swiftly. Alectresses who gave birth without permission were being secretly executed, along with their husbands and children. Their relatives were told that they had been translated to Acorus or Efra. . . ."

Lyzetta's eyes widened at the last. Dainyl could not honestly admit he was surprised. Shocked at the coldness of the Archon's actions, but not surprised. He continued to listen.

". . . my company was ordered west to Elunin. When we returned, my wife had vanished. No one would say— or could say—where she had gone or why, except that she had been there on a Tridi and the house was empty on Quattri. She would not have left like that. When I could, I searched for her, for over a year. All I found out was from an old indigen who swept the floors of the Hall of Justice. He said that all the relatives of Majer Ilusyrn had disappeared. She was the daughter of his cousin. A daughter of a distant cousin!"

"I take it Ilusyrn displeased someone?" asked Dainyl.

"He led the second Myrmidon revolt. He claimed that the marshal and the Archon had been removing all the officials who opposed their plans for the diaspora to Acorus and Efra. He offered proof that many of the families of those around the Archon were already on Efra—those who survived the translation, I suppose."

"How did you manage to get to Acorus?"

"My cousin was a recorder. He told me a few things, but he was afraid to help me. I bided my time, and brought him some of the best Laeso red wine—twenty golds a bottle, but what did I care? I drugged it, of course, but with fheln. It's not toxic, so that you can't sense it. It just combines with alcohol to put people to sleep. The fheln cost three times what the wine did, and it took me months to obtain. When he and his assistant went to sleep, I got onto the Table." Asyrk shrugged. "If Caela had been translated, I had one chance in two to end up on the right world. If she'd been killed, what did it matter which world I ended up on?"

"Didn't you know the risks? Only one in three or four survive a long translation."

"Remaining on Ifryn was certain death, and no one was going to let a mere Myrmidon undercaptain make a translation to a better world." Asyrk stopped, waiting.

"Where did you end up here, and how did anyone let you become a Myrmidon?"

"I got to Norda—I suppose it could have been anywhere—and I told the recorder there that I was a Myrmidon undercaptain who'd been forced to make the long translation." A half smile crossed Asyrk's lips. "That was mostly true.. He didn't know whether to believe me or not. So he turned me over to Majer Noryan. He didn't know me, but he'd heard of me . . ."

Lyzetta frowned.

Dainyl almost nodded. Another confirmation of his suspicions about Noryan.

". . . and he put me in his company, where he could

watch me. I was an assistant armorer for a while, until he lost someone to the ancients. Then I started flying again."

"Why did he send you to Seventh Company?"

"He told me to obey Captain Veluara, and I'd do fine. I didn't, and he said he'd make sure that the submarshal in Elcien would find out who I was, and I'd end up like Majer Faerylt. So . . . now you know anyway, sir."

Despite the undercaptain's shields, Dainyl could tell every word, or close to every word, had been the truth. He had the feeling that getting to the Table had not been quite so easy or clean as Asyrk had indicated, but the feelings about his wife, and particularly about the state of affairs on Ifyn, rang all too true. So did the part about obeying Veluara. By threatening to reveal the identity of unauthorized translations, Alcyna and Noryan could build personal allegiance without revealing any of their plans.

Dainyl let the silence continue for a moment before clearing his throat gently. "Seventh Company has been through enough change, undercaptains." He smiled grimly. "Here is my decision. Captain Lyzetta will command Seventh Company. Asyrk, you will be the senior undercaptain, but only so long as Lyzetta remains hale and healthy. Should anything happen to her, you will no longer be a Myrmidon. If I'm terribly displeased, you may not be anything at all. Is that clear?"

Asyrk inclined his head, then raised it. His eyes contained relief. "Yes, sir. Anything the captain needs, all she need do is ask."

Dainyl looked to Lyzetta. "Captain, prepare Seventh Company for departure."

"Yes, sir."

Dainyl turned and walked back toward his pteridon.

He thought he had read the situation correctly. He hoped so. With all the deaths over the past week, he didn't want to add more. He also wanted to convey absolutely that he judged on an individual basis. What

Asyrk had said about the Archon's entourage suggested that the Archon had already planned to transfer the Master Scepter to Efra. Did Zelyert and Shastylt already know that? If so, why were they going on with the charade? Did that mean that both the Duarches were doomed to be replaced?

Dainyl had felt matters were less than good, but hearing what Asyrk had said had chilled him to his core.

He checked his gear, and then climbed into the saddle and harness deliberately. On the flight north, he needed to reconsider his plans.

93

The white sun was less than a glass from setting, hanging over the River Vedra and the hills to the northwest of Tempre, when Dainyl brought his pteridon down in a gentle circle around the complex of the regional alector. As he descended, he could see a Cadmian patrol stationed in the now-shadowed plaza before the building. After another pass, he could make out the telltale marks of lightcutter sidearms on the pavement. Yet the Cadmians were guarding the plaza. That meant the majer had repulsed armed alectors. If he had tried and failed, the Cadmians would have withdrawn.

Back to the east . . . down in front of the compound . . . on the flat. The pteridon complied, as always, flaring and setting down with scarcely a jolt. Stiff and sore as he was, Dainyl dismounted quickly.

The other pteridons landed, then moved into formation to conserve space, before a Cadmian undercaptain hurried from the compound toward the submarshal.

He halted several yards short of Dainyl. "Submarshal, Undercaptain Fabrytal, sir."

"Undercaptain? Where is Majer Mykel?"

"He was wounded, Submarshal, sir. It looks like he'll recover." Before Dainyl could ask more, the undercaptain plunged on. "Some of the rebels came back. I don't know where they came from. We were patrolling as you ordered, sir. All of a sudden, someone was claiming he was in charge. When the major asked if he was appointed by the Duarches, they started using those weapons—like the one you have. The major organized an attack, and we finished them off. They killed two squads of our men. The major got us behind the stone walls and kept us shooting. Took most of the day, but we finally pushed them inside the building, and the major led second squad in after them."

"When did all this happen?"

"Yesterday, sir. It started early in the morning."

That was better than it could have been. At least, he could use the Table and get back to Elcien before too many rumors circulated.

"How did the major get wounded?"

"I don't know, sir. That is, he and the squad with him pushed the few rebels left down to the lower level, and then there was an explosion. One of the major's arms was burned, not too badly, but he got thrown into the stones when part of the wall exploded."

An explosion near the Table? Dainyl didn't like that at all. "What sort of explosion?"

"That room we couldn't enter. It was in there. We had to lift some stones off the major. Not many, but it blew out the door and the casement."

Worse yet. Dainyl forced himself to ask another question. "Have you seen any more of the rebels?"

"The scouts have seen one or two in that blue uniform, from a vingt or so away, but they're keeping their distance. They might be stragglers from the Alector's Guard. They've been too far away to tell for sure."

"Do you have men in the regional administrative building?"

"Just two, to make sure no one tries to sneak in and

take anything. We stacked all the boots and uniforms in that entry hall. I wasn't sure where the majer wanted them. Those sidearms, I've got those locked in the armory here."

"I think I'd better take a look at the building first. I'll fly over there and be back shortly. Wait for me."

"Yes, sir."

Dainyl hated getting on the pteridon again, but it was quicker than riding a horse, and certainly wouldn't get him any sorer. Galya accompanied him.

They left their pteridons right in front of the steps up to the entrance.

One of the Cadmians rankers ran ahead, calling out, "Submarshal's coming in."

Dainyl appreciated that. He didn't need Cadmians—or anyone—taking shots at him, although he did hold his shields. Once inside the entry hall, he saw the rebel alectors' uniforms—all shimmersilk blue and lifeforce-treated—and boots. The boots were easier to count—thirty-seven pair.

He shook his head.

So did Galya. "Sir . . . ? Did the Cadmians . . . did they?"

"They did. The majer can be quite resourceful."

"Too bad he's not a Myrmidon."

Dainyl chuckled. "That would solve more than a few problems." *But then, it just might create even more.*

Dainyl sensed no one else in the building as he made his way along the corridors and then walked down to the lower level. Galya followed, carrying her skylance.

Once he left the stairs to the lowest level and looked along the corridor, he could see and sense the devastation.

"Looks like something exploded, sir," offered Galya.

Dainyl nodded. "Wait right here."

"Yes, sir."

He made his way to where the entry to the Table chamber had been, now an oblong opening in the stone wall, and peered inside. The top of the Table looked the same as ever, but one section of the base had blown away, with enough force that what remained of the edges of the stone entryway had been pushed a yard into the corridor, and the door lay broken in three sections, despite the heavy iron straps. How the majer had even survived, Dainyl had no idea.

Picking his way among the rubble, Dainyl surveyed the Table chamber. He found four sets of blue shimmersilk uniforms and boots, as well as four lightcutters, all fully discharged.

What had happened?

Had the majer trapped them and somehow had someone fired a lightcutter into the Table? Or had they had someone who'd been trained as a recorder and who had tried to do too much with the Table?

For all of the majer's abilities, Dainyl doubted that the Cadmian could have done anything to cause a Table to explode. Although . . .

Dainyl frowned. Perhaps he'd never know. Not for certain.

One thing was sure. More than thirty alectors, all with lightcutters, had been in the building. Had they all translated in? From where? Dulka was the most likely source, but perhaps some had been local alectors. Even so, it was clear that there were far more alectors on Acorus than the Duarches knew—or that they acknowledged. No wonder lifeforce growth was slower than projected.

Dainyl turned and walked back toward Galya. "I've seen what I needed to see."

The petite Myrmidon nodded, but said nothing, taking her skylance and following him back through the building and out to the pteridons.

Undercaptain Fabrytal was waiting, as ordered, although a Cadmian squad leader hurried off as Dainyl dismounted.

"I was just making sure that your Myrmidons have quarters and food, sir."

"They'll appreciate that, Undercaptain, and so do I. I do have a few more questions."

"Yes, sir."

"Did all the rebels have sidearms?"

"So far as we could tell. We're two short of matching with the uniforms, but we couldn't find any more."

"I appreciate your efforts, Undercaptain. I'll take those off your hands, once we're ready to depart." Not only had the rebels used unauthorized weapons, but there was a chance some might even get into the hands of landers and indigens. Hadn't Fahylt and his people thought at all? Or had he really thought he'd be able to set up some sort of independent state? Was that so infeasible if the Master Scepter was headed to Efra? "I need to see the majer. Is he at the compound?"

"No, sir. We didn't have anyone who could help."

"Where is he?"

"He's being cared for by a chatelaine of one of the factors, sir."

Dainyl could sense both fear and nervousness in the undercaptain, but not deception. There was also concern. Dainyl wanted to shake his head. He doubted many of his officers would risk themselves that much to protect him. "I'm not about to hurt him, Undercaptain." *Not now, not the way matters are going.* "You and he have accomplished more than anyone could possibly have expected."

"Yes, sir."

"If you would escort me, Undercaptain."

"I'll bring down a squad and some mounts, sir. How many do you need?"

"Just one." Dainyl supposed he would have to ride, after all.

After the Cadmian hurried off, Dainyl turned and sought out the two Myrmidon captains, who had just finished organizing the pteridons by squad for the night.

"Fhentyl, Lyzetta. Make what arrangements you need for spaces and food with the Cadmians in the compound. I'll be back in a while. The Cadmian majer was wounded, and I need to talk to him to find out some things."

"We'll be fine, sir. Do you want an escort?"

"The Cadmians have proved to be quite adequate," Dainyl replied dryly.

Less than a half glass later, Dainyl was riding through a set of plain iron gates in the southwest of Tempre, accompanied by a full squad of armed Cadmians.

By the time he and Fabrytal had dismounted, two people stood under the small rotunda portico, and a functionary in gray stood to one side, radiating both fear and disapproval.

Of the two directly before the open doorway, one was a young man radiating the arrogance of privileged landers, dressed in the white of a seltyr factor. He appeared like a child in comparison to the woman, who, although young, carried herself with a certain maturity that reminded him of Lystrana.

The woman looked at Dainyl, ignoring Fabrytal. The submarshal recognized her—the Talent-resistant seltyr's daughter. Her aura still showed resistance, but no actual Talent. What in the world was she doing in Tempre?

"What do you wish?" asked the young man. While his voice was polite, he reeked of self-centeredness.

"We're here to speak to Majer Mykel."

The man inclined his head to the woman. "That is the chatelaine's affair. You are welcome as you please." He stepped back and vanished into the small villa, as if glad to avoid dealing with Dainyl.

Another time, another place, Dainyl might have made an issue of it, but the lander was the type who would destroy himself soon enough, and Dainyl had greater concerns.

"Chatelaine?"

"He's weak. No thanks to you."

"I'd like to speak to him."

"This way." She turned.

Dainyl followed her through the modest-sized white-plastered entry hall and up a wide curved stairway to the second level. Fabrytal brought up the rear. The first door on the right was open, and she stepped through it.

"Someone to see you, Majer." She stepped to one side, but did not leave the chamber.

Once more, Dainyl decided not to make an issue of her presence. He doubted anything that might be said would be new to her. He studied the majer, who was pale, but alert, sitting in a wide bed, bare-chested, with a sheet drawn partly over him. A light dressing covered his upper left arm.

"I received a report from Undercaptain Fabrytal." Dainyl inclined his head to the junior officer. "About your handling of the rebels who tried to take over the regional administrative building."

Mykel nodded, but did not speak.

"How did you know the . . . they were rebels?"

"That wasn't hard. The one who talked to me called me a steer and said we had no authority to ask anything of him. He was also wearing the blue and gold, and they all had the same kind of sidearm you carry." The majer closed his eyes for a moment.

Dainyl sensed he was as much exhausted as wounded, so exhausted Dainyl could barely detect any Talent at all.

"How did . . . hostilities start?"

"I asked if he was designated by the Duarch to take over the duties of the regional alector. He didn't answer and threatened me with his sidearm. I asked where he had gotten it, since it was a Myrmidon weapon. He tried to shoot me. Things went from bad to worse, then."

Dainyl could well imagine, and he didn't need the detailed description. He knew more than enough. He smiled. "Once you recover, Majer, you are to withdraw to Hyalt and consolidate Third Battalion and complete your duties there. Until you depart Tempre, your forces are to withdraw from the administrative complex, but hold the compound. The Seventh Myrmidon company will be sharing the compound with you until you depart. They will take over guarding the administrative building. Both you and the Myrmidons are not to seek out any rebels, but should they appear, they should be destroyed." Dainyl offered a smile. "I doubt that anyone will attack."

"Yes, sir."

"I wish you a speedy recovery, Majer. You have done more than anyone would believe possible."

Dainyl stepped back and let Fabrytal lead the way down to the entry hall. The chatelaine followed. When he reached the front entry, Dainyl turned to her. "Thank you for your care of the majer, and for your courtesy in allowing us to see him."

"It wasn't courtesy. It was common sense. You have power. I do not."

Although the words were far different from Lystrana's, both in tone and style, there was still something about her that reminded Dainyl of his wife. "Good day, Chatelaine, and thank you."

As he rode back to the compound, Dainyl considered the situation. The majer and his Cadmians had killed more than thirty-five alectors, perhaps as many as fifty, all armed with lightcutters. The details of the deaths would have to be kept quiet for many reasons. Dainyl would just report that more than thirty rebel alectors had been disposed of by forces under his command, and that in the conflict, the rebels had sabotaged the Table. That would need repair and replacement as soon as possible, as would the Table in Hyalt.

Dainyl had hoped to use the Tempre Table to return to Elcien, but now he would need to return to Dereka with Fifth Company and take the Table from there.

He'd also hoped to leave Cadmians to guard the complex, but that was out of the question now. They'd either get massacred, or they'd kill more alectors. The first alternative didn't set well with Dainyl, and the second wouldn't set well with either the High Alector of Justice or the Duarches. Dainyl doubted it would matter to Shastylt. As for Hyksant and Fhentyl knowing that the majer had Talent, he'd just tell them that the majer's

wounds had reduced his Talent, that he might not even recover, but that if it became a problem, he'd take care of it.

Leaving Seventh Company wasn't all disadvantageous.
It would provide a logical reason for keeping the company in the west and out from any direct control by Alcyna. In fact, it would probably be days before she even
discovered where the company was. Tables didn't show
pteridons and alectors.

Dainyl smiled at that—briefly. He had little enough to
smile at these days.

94

Mykel had dreamed. That he knew when
he struggled awake on Decdi. He also knew that the
dreams had been anything but pleasant. He just didn't recall exactly what they had been and was just as glad he
didn't. His back did not hurt him so much, but he felt far
stiffer overall, and while he could move his left arm, any
motion sent sharp pains from shoulder to fingertips.

The shutters to the wide window had been cracked,
enough for him to tell that it was still early, not much after dawn, but not for him to see what he thought might be
a small interior courtyard. The bronze wall lamp had
been snuffed, and the room was dim.

He was slow in getting out of bed and making it to the
adjoining bath chamber and facilities, tiled, and with running water, if only lukewarm, but a definite luxury he particularly appreciated, stiff and sore as he was. By the time
he relieved himself, washed up some, and returned to
bed, he felt exhausted, but he did manage to adjust the
pillows to prop himself up. For a time, he just rested
against the pillows, his eyes closed.

Sometime later, at the click of the door lever, he
opened his eyes.

A young woman, scarcely more than a girl, dressed in the light gray smock of a retainer, over darker gray trousers stepped through the half-open door of the bed-chamber. She carried a tray, but did not speak as she approached the bed. Her eyes avoided Mykel's as she placed the tray on the side table. A second, older woman in gray appeared with a wooden bedtable that she placed over Mykel's legs. Then the younger woman placed her tray on the bedtable. Both departed without a word.

Mykel looked at the meal on the tray—egg toast, perfectly golden, with breakfast browned potato strips, a fresh peach, sliced into crescents in a light clear syrup, three strips of beef in a cream gravy, a pitcher of steaming hot cider, and another one of ale, with two mugs. At the side was a small pitcher of berry syrup for the egg toast.

He ate slowly, and discovered he could not quite finish the beef. Usually, he would have preferred the hot cider, but good as it was, he found the ale settled more easily.

He wondered where Rachyla was. He recalled talking to her on Decdi afternoon—he thought that was the right day—but he found he did not remember what he had said. Why couldn't he remember? He let himself rest on the pillows, trying to recall.

He must have dozed off, because he jerked awake at the sound of boots on the tile floor. The bedtable and tray had been removed, and he had not even noticed.

Rachyla stepped into the chamber and seated herself in the side chair, an image of perfection in dark green shimmersilk shirt and trousers, with a light green vest.

Mykel found himself smiling. "This is far better fare than I was ever able to provide for you. Thank you."

"I am glad you recognize that, Majer." As always, it seemed, her voice was cool. "How are you feeling this morning?"

"Better."

"That is good."

"We talked yesterday, did we not?"

"We did."

"I find I cannot remember."

"That happens with head injuries, Majer. You have quite a lump on the side of your skull. You are fortunate it is so hard."

"What did we talk about?"

"I asked you about how you became a Cadmian. I learned a great deal about your family. Then you fell asleep."

Mykel wished he could recall the conversation.

"Sleep helps heal. You do look better. You could not have looked much worse."

"I do feel better. It might be best if I did not remain longer."

"Majer. Ruela reported that it took all your effort to walk to the washroom and back. Amaryk and I could not afford to have you leave in such weakened condition. Neither your officers nor the submarshal would look kindly upon that. You will be here at least two more days. Longer if you do not regain your strength."

"I did not wish to impose any more than I have."

"Any damage you have done has already been incurred. Do not compound it by leaving before you are strong enough to do what you must."

There was, unhappily, all too much wisdom in what she said, Mykel realized. He *was* weak. "I defer to your wisdom, chatelaine."

"Would that others did." Rachyla closed her mouth, as if she had said too much.

Mykel wasn't sure how to reply in a way that did not appear either condescending or naïve about her situation. Finally, he asked, "What did you think about Submarshal Dainyl? Besides the fact that he's one of the evil ones?"

"You should not mock one who offers you hospitality, Majer."

"I apologize." He paused. "I'd like your thoughts, but all you've ever said is that he's evil."

"All the alectors are. Their presence on our world is

evil." Rachyla shifted her weight in the side chair slightly, turning to face Mykel directly. "Some are evil merely by their presence, and do not add to that evil. Others would be evil upon whatever world from which they come. Some few, although evil by their presence, strive to do their duties without creating more unfairness and unhappiness. The submarshal is more powerful now than he was in Dramur. He will create even more evil by attempting to do what he sees as good. Few of the other alectors will appreciate what he does, but will fear to oppose him directly. That makes matters exceedingly dangerous for those who must do his bidding or be near him—as you have twice discovered."

Mykel nodded. "That is true."

"My words, Majer, are but those of a mere woman."

"As I have told you, Rachyla, more than once, you never have been nor ever will be a 'mere' woman."

"You waste words on flattery, Majer."

"Truth is not flattery," he replied. "My words may be unwelcome, but they are neither wasted nor untrue."

"Such gallantry. So wasted."

Not upon you, not that it will make any difference. "Gallantry is all that I can offer at the moment."

He thought he caught the hint of a smile in Rachyla's eyes, but if it had been there, it vanished immediately as she stood. "I am glad that you are improving. You need to rest, Majer."

"I fear I have little choice."

"You do not. I will check the dressing on your arm this afternoon." With a quick nod, she turned.

Mykel listened to her boots on the tile, fading away.

He closed his eyes.

95

Although Fifth Company had lifted off from Tempre less than a glass past dawn, the last pteridon did not set down at the Myrmidon compound in Dereka until little more than a glass before sunset on Decdi. Dainyl was stiff, sore, and tired, and decided that making a Table translation to Elcien that evening, much as he wanted to see Lystrana, would be unwise. He needed to go into whatever awaited him relatively fresh and rested. Even on an end-day evening, there might be less than pleasant surprises awaiting him.

While he slept relatively well, he awoke just before dawn, and was at the recorder's goldenstone building little more than a glass later. He wore his flying jacket, and under it, not obviously, two fully charged sidearms.

Unsurprisingly, Jonyst waited for Dainyl in the recorder's library just above the steps that led down to the Table chamber.

The recorder rose from the armchair where he had been perusing a sheaf of papers. "Good morning, Submarshal."

"Good morning, Recorder."

"I've been watching events through the Table—as I could." Jonyst paused. "Before I forget, you should know. Yadaryst came in and used the Table last evening. It was, I'd say, less than a glass after you and Fifth Company returned. He was in a hurry. He hasn't returned." Jonyst's black eyes held a humorous glint.

"I don't imagine he told you where he was translating?"

"No, but the only Table on the grid that showed activity after he left was the one at Ludar." Jonyst grinned. "I did tell him that the Tables at Hyalt and Tempre weren't functioning."

"They both need substantial repairs."

Jonyst's grin vanished.

"From the mess they left, it looks like Fahylt's personal forces did something they shouldn't have in Tempre. A section of the Table exploded. The Table in Hyalt . . . the power crystal was shattered. Other than that . . . it looked to be fine."

"I know you're in a hurry, Submarshal, but would you mind explaining?"

Dainyl did, although his explanation dealt with the two regional alectors and their forces, and the actions of the Myrmidons and Cadmians—and, of course, the apparent support of Rhelyn and his rebels by Veluara and Quivaryt. Dainyl did not say more about the damage to the Tables, or the ancients. When he finished, he waited for Jonyst to speak.

"You've forced a number of people to act before they were ready, and others to decide whom they will support before the outcome is clear." The elderly recorder cleared his throat. "You will not be popular with many of the High Alectors or with the Duarch Samist. Khelaryt will be pleased, but he can do little to support you directly."

"How do you read the east?"

"Brekylt and Alcyna will disavow any support of Rhelyn, and they will claim Captain Veluara acted without orders. Quivaryt will continue to build forces for them in Dulka. Sulerya and Captain Sevasya will become more isolated, and Sevasya will have trouble getting certain supplies unless you ship them directly from the west. Shortly, Alcyna will request that Seventh Company be returned to Dulka."

Dainyl nodded, thinking that it might be wisest simply to post Seventh Company to Tempre for a time, or even permanently. That would cause hardship for some of the Myrmidons, at least temporarily, but he could probably find ways to get the immediate families of those few who had them to Tempre. That would also put a check on Fahylt as well, particularly if Dainyl kept in close touch with Captain Lyzetta. "What else? You have seen far more over the years . . ."

Jonyst cocked his head, just slightly. "There will be

more 'unauthorized' translations, primarily to the east, and the recorders there will deny them. They will claim that Sulerya and I are either misrepresenting what is happening or lying in order to turn the Duarches against those living east of the Spine of Corus."

"There were more than two hundred rebel alectors in Hyalt."

"I'm scarcely surprised, Submarshal. I would imagine they represented less than a third of the successful undocumented translations from Ifryn."

"Do the Duarches know this?"

"I'm certain that they do. What would you have them do? Send your Myrmidons out to kill them? Station Myrmidons at every Table and carry every one off to a locked chamber in Lyterna?"

"Matters must be terrible in Ifryn." Dainyl already knew they were bad, but he wanted Jonyst's reaction.

"Far worse than you can believe from what I have learned in the last week or so. The Archon's guards and the remaining Myrmidons guard the Tables. Illustra has become a fortress. All of influence and position who can have translated to Efra."

"Then it's been decided that the Master Scepter will go there?"

"That was decided some years ago. No one told me or announced it, but that is the only conclusion to be drawn."

"Why didn't you mention this to me earlier?"

"About the Master Scepter? Would you have believed me?" countered Jonyst. "I have no proof, only suppositions, and until Ilerya and Wasen translated here . . ." He shrugged.

"They're from Ifryn?"

"My new assistants." The recorder's smile was weary. "She was an assistant to the recorder in Ruveen. Her husband was a transport clerk. I didn't ask how they managed access to the Table. What point would there be to it?"

"None." Dainyl had known that problems were mounting, but even in his most pessimistic moments, he hadn't realized that the situation had gotten so bad so quickly.

"Now that you know, Submarshal, what are you going to do?"

Dainyl returned the smile of the recorder with one that was doubtless equally weary. "Whatever I can, however I can." He glanced toward the steps down to the Table. "I'd better start."

"Just remember. Trust those closest to you least, except, in your case, for your wife." Jonyst gestured toward the staircase, then started down the steps.

Dainyl followed.

Once in the Table chamber, he noted that the hidden door was closed. "I take it that Yadaryst doesn't know?"

"He barely has enough Talent to know where the Table is. He hates translating. He doesn't often. How he makes it between Tables has mystified people for years."

Dainyl had to wonder if the RA were merely adept at concealing his Talent. He'd have to keep that in mind. With a nod, he stepped up onto the Table. He concentrated, focusing on the brilliant white locator that was Elcien almost before he was through the Table . . .

. . . and into the translation tube. Although he thought he sensed another flash of deeper purple, before he could even try to perceive more, he was flashing through the silver-white mist . . .

. . . and standing on the Table in Elcien.

Chastyl looked up from the end of the Table. "Submarshal."

"Recorder. Is the Highest in?"

"I do not believe so. The Duarch summoned him . . . something about the Myrmidons overreaching their authority in Hyalt and Tempre, I believe. I don't believe the marshal was asked. Not yet." Chastyl offered a guileless smile

Dainyl returned the smile as he stepped off the Table. "I appreciate the information. If you would inform the High Alector that I am back, and that matters may not be what they seem? I will be in touch with him shortly."

"I will be happy to do that, Submarshal. Do you happen to know, by the way, what happened to the Tables in Tempre and Hyalt?"

"I'm under the impression that rebel alectors supporting RA Fahylt had something to do with the partial destruction of the Table in Tempre, and that matters got out of hand with Recorder Rhelyn in Hyalt. That can happen when you have two hundred unauthorized translations from Ifryn armed with lightcutter sidearms."

Chastyl's eyes widened.

"There was more going on in Hyalt than met the eye. Rhelyn was thinking bigger than his abilities." Dainyl opened the door to the anteroom. "Until later."

He hurried up the hidden steps and out through the south door from the Hall of Justice. He was sweating slightly, despite the late summer fog off the bay, by the time he had hailed a hacker and was on his way to Myrmidon headquarters. He opened the flying jacket, but did not remove it.

When the carriage stopped outside the Myrmidon gates, Dainyl quickly handed the driver half a silver and walked swiftly through the gates toward the headquarters building.

"Submarshal, sir! We didn't expect you," offered Undercaptain Chelysta, clearly the day's duty officer.

"Is the marshal in? Alone?"

"Yes, sir. He came in very early."

"Good." Dainyl turned and headed for Shastylt's study. He opened the door, stepped in, and closed it behind him.

The marshal turned from the window, his pleasant smile covering cold determination. "I'm surprised that you even bothered to return, Dainyl."

Dainyl couldn't say he was even faintly surprised at Shastylt's attitude—or the full shields he held.

"And it's obvious you've even been consorting with the ancients. Shameful . . ."

"Consorting?" For an instant, Dainyl was puzzled.

Then he laughed. "That's the Talent residue of the weapon Rhelyn used to try to kill me. It was a sword created by the ancients to kill alectors. Where he found it, I have no idea."

Shastylt had been about to speak, but paused, as if stunned by Dainyl's words, the only time Dainyl could recall the marshal being speechless, even momentarily.

"In any event, I thought it might be easier this way."

"Easier? You delude yourself, just as Tyanylt did."

"To find out what you had in mind, I meant. I always knew you would only do what benefited you. The only question was how my disposing of Rhelyn and Patronyl would further your plans."

"My plans? I am supporting the Duarches. You're the one who has been the rebel. Going off and co-opting innocent Myrmidons in an effort to wipe out or discredit a rival. You really didn't think you could get away with that, did you?"

"Zelyert won't accept that, you know."

"He won't have any choice, not when Brekylt reports that you and Alcyna were planning a coup. If she deposes him, of course, you will have been in league with Brekylt."

"It doesn't matter in the slightest to you, does it? Whether Ifryn is falling apart, or alectors are scheming to create their own lands here on Acorus, no matter what the costs?"

"They'll all fail. They don't understand. It's too bad that you're one of the few that does."

Dainyl nodded and stepped toward Shastylt. "What about the ancients?"

"They're not a problem, not really. They were useful to encourage the production of the special weapons."

"I see. All hail the Duarches Brekylt and Shastylt."

"Why not? Khelaryt and Samist won't ever see that Acorus can't take an influx of worthless Ifrits. Besides, the Archon has already made his decision to transfer the

Master Scepter to Efra, and that means Khelaryt and Samist will have to be replaced, sooner or later."

"What do you propose to do with all those who will be sent here before—and after—the Master Scepter is transferred to Efra?"

"We will make it clear that life here is difficult except for those with skills. Those who have them will be willing to attempt the long translation."

Dainyl could see the logic behind the approach, as well as Shastylt's unspoken willingness to do away with those who offered little . . . or those who might get in his way.

He took another step forward, reinforcing his own shields.

"You think too highly of yourself, Dainyl." Pure Talent blasted from the marshal.

Dainyl let it sheet around his shields, as he drew both lightcutters.

"You poor fool. All shields and no offense. You could never be marshal or anything else, were I not behind you."

The next Talent-blast was enough to rock Dainyl, but not breach his shields. "Besides, how would you explain lightcutter burns on my tunic? That would suggest very foul play, Dainyl." Another Talent-flare slammed Dainyl's shields.

Dainyl felt himself smiling. "You wanted Myrmidon to fight Myrmidon, didn't you? You wanted factions within the Myrmidons. You even picked me, so that when you revealed I had committed treachery, it would destroy the ideals and the spirit of the Myrmidons."

A third Talent-blast showed no diminution of Shastylt's abilities.

"You always saw more than others . . . but not . . . enough."

Dainyl was more than ready for the pulsed blasts of Talent, designed to vibrate shields enough that the holder lost control. He merely angled his shields slightly and let the vibrations reverberate back at the study walls and windows. The half-open window behind the marshal rattled in its casement.

Shastylt changed tactics, gathering a massive concentration of Talent-force.

In that instant, Dainyl channeled most of his shield energy into a lance that jabbed a minute aperture in the marshal's shield. At that moment, he fired both sidearms and funneled the energy into a needle, aimed straight through the aperture at Shastylt's forehead.

The marshal's eyes barely widened before he fell forward onto the circular blue and gray rug that bore the Myrmidon colors.

Dainyl holstered the sidearms, then blotted his forehead. He stood waiting until the marshal's body vanished into fine ashes and dust, and, in turn, until they, too, vanished. There were no lightcutter marks on tunic, trousers, or boots.

After several moments, he heard bootsteps heading toward the door. He turned. "You can come in, Colonel."

Dhenyr stepped into the study. His eyes flicked from the empty Myrmidon uniform on the carpet to Dainyl and back to the carpet.

"The marshal's heart stopped. I think the surprise of my return was too much for him." Dainyl looked at the colonel. "I'm requesting your immediate resignation. I assume you'd prefer that to a court-martial for treason."

"Treason?" Dhenyr laughed.

Dainyl sensed the hollowness of the laughter and waited.

"Treason? For what?"

"Altering reports. Passing information to those who shouldn't have it. I'm sure I'll find more now that I've been away for a month."

The colonel's lightcutter was in his hand.

Dainyl barely broke a sweat in crushing the breath out of Dhenyr with his shields.

Once more he waited until the colonel's physical body vanished. The process took longer because the colonel was far younger than Shastylt had been. Then Dainyl went to the study door and stepped into the corridor.

"Duty officer!"

Chelysta hurried down the hallway.

Dainyl stepped back and gestured to the study. "Undercaptain . . . we have a problem. I was discussing the rebels with the marshal. I had discovered that Colonel Dhenyr had been offering them information and that he had altered records. The marshal asked me to summon the colonel. When he was confronted with the evidence, the colonel went wild with his sidearm and tried to attack us both. When it was all over . . ." Dainyl gestured to the uniforms on the floor.

"I'm sorry about the marshal, sir. The colonel left us cold, but the marshal, he was a Myrmidon. I am so sorry. . . ."

"So am I." And Dainyl was, for many reasons.

After a time, he looked at Chelysta. "You're the duty officer. If you would draft a report on this . . . unfortunate . . . deplorable . . . situation, I'll go over it and review it with you when I return. I need to inform the High Alector of what happened immediately and in person."

"Yes, sir."

"He should know." Dainyl shook his head slowly. "I don't think this could have come at a worse time."

"No, sir. But at least the colonel didn't get you both."

"I was fortunate. I just wish we'd seen all this coming. I wish the marshal had." That, too, Dainyl did wish, but Shastylt had not seen that the results of his plotting could only have had one end—even if he had been successful in removing Dainyl.

For all his desire to report to Zelyert before matters got even worse, it was close to a half glass later before Dainyl took the duty coach to the Hall of Justice.

As if he had been expecting Dainyl, Zelyert stood outside his small study.

The High Alector of Justice beckoned for Dainyl to enter. Dainyl did, closing the door behind him.

Zelyert did not seat himself, but offered a cautious smile. "I wasn't certain who I would see, you or Shastylt. How is the marshal?"

"Colonel Dhenyr attacked us. I was fortunate enough to survive. The marshal wasn't, perhaps because of the shock at my return."

"I wouldn't have foreseen matters turning out so, but I can't say that I'm surprised," mused Zelyert.

"How much do you know?"

"My dear Dainyl—or Marshal, now, I suppose—whatever do you mean?"

Dainyl snorted. "Shastylt had this idea that he and Brekylt would claim that Alcyna and I were attempting a coup. They are or were positioning themselves to be the next Duarches after it became clear that the Master Scepter was destined for Efra."

"I was aware that he had some such in mind. So did Khelaryt. It was better to see how far he got. And who might stop him."

"What do you have in mind now?"

"Nothing." Zelyert smiled. "Of course, you might be interested to know that Submarshal Alcyna and Majer Noryan have sent a message expressing their concern about the instability of Marshal Shastylt and requesting that I look into his dispatch of you to discipline a regional alector and his staff."

"Two regional alectors. Fahylt fled to Ludar."

"Yes, I heard that he attempted a translation. Most unfortunate. He arrived as a wild translation and was flamed down. The Tables can be quite unstable at times. Did you know that both the Tables in Hyalt and Tempre are not functioning?"

"Rhelyn was responsible for the failure of his Table. That I knew. One of the reasons it took me longer to return was that the rebel alectors in Tempre destroyed a section of the Table when they were attempting to flee the Myrmidons and Cadmians."

"You dispatched Cadmians against alectors?"

"No, sir. While I was dealing with Hyalt, I discovered that Fahylt had thrown in with Rhelyn. I split my forces and went to Tempre, along with half the Cadmians. Fahylt had created an Alector's Guard with landers and indigens. He also had a force of alectors, although I did not discover that until later. He even built a stone compound for the Alector's Guard. They tried a dawn ambush of the Cadmians. . . ." Dainyl went on to provide a summary of what had happened after that, omitting all references to the ancients and concluding with ". . . and when the rebel alectors returned, they attacked the Cadmians with contraband lightcutters. I collected those, and they're being sent to you under seal from Dereka. The Cadmians suffered significant losses, but managed to hold their own until the rebels ran out of power for their weapons. The Cadmians killed some, and some were killed by whatever they did to the Table."

"So . . . Rhelyn had more than two hundred alectors, and Fahylt had more than thirty."

"Yes, sir."

Zelyert shook his head. "You are resourceful, Dainyl. Now that you are marshal, what do you have in mind?"

"I wasn't aware that I was, sir."

"Who else would I appoint? You wouldn't be anyone's first choice, but you've proved to be too tenacious for anyone to suggest anyone else. You're a shade too honorable, Dainyl, and stronger than most would prefer." Zelyert reached back and picked up something from the desk. "You might as well put these on. They're marshal's stars. The Myrmidons cannot be without a commander, not for a moment."

"You had those ready."

"I suspected. I also felt that Shastylt would not be able to bear the thought that you could resolve problems he didn't want resolved."

"I know. He picked me because he was looking for someone to whom few would object and who could not possibly block his plans."

Zelyert laughed. It was not a pleasant sound, cheerful and hearty as it seemed. "And what do you think of me?"

Dainyl had already thought that inquiry might be coming. "You always knew that the Master Scepter would not come here. So did Khelaryt and Samist. The question became how to deal with the situation. Samist and Brekylt wanted to encourage long translations from Ifryn to certain alectors who would support them in building their power. Translated alectors draw more lifeforce than those born here. You must know that. So you're behind whatever measures I undertook that reduced those numbers, but it's not something that you or Khelaryt can acknowledge." Dainyl cleared his throat, not because it was dry, but because he was missing something and needed a moment to think. He had it! "You let Alcyna and Brekylt build those forces because, that way, you knew where all those alectors were, and . . ." Dainyl let the words trail off, watching the High Alector.

"You didn't answer the question, I don't believe."

"You have grave doubts that a peaceful or successful transition of the Master Scepter to Efra will be possible, and you realized that a secondary status for Acorus would create further unrest, plotting, and instability, and you will do whatever is necessary to minimize the chaos. Absolutely whatever," Dainyl added.

"Every transition of the Master Scepter has been brutal and bloody. How could it not be? Half of the alectors on Ifryn don't have enough Talent to survive a long translation, and most of those who do won't be terribly useful and will be a drain on whatever world where they arrive. No one wants to leave the comforts of Ifryn until it becomes obvious the world is guttering out. Then everyone who sees it wants to leave, and the Myrmidons become guards of the Tables and executioners of those who try to invade them, and that use of skylances and pteridons draws down lifeforce even more quickly, hastening the end." Zelyert's lips curled. "Acorus is poor and rough, and cold and miserable, and we have made certain everyone knows that. Did you know that on Efra there are three Myrmidons stationed at every Table, and anyone translating from Ifryn who cannot demonstrate a skill or a pass from the Archon or a High Alector is killed on the spot? Last year three hundred were killed. This year the number will be double that."

"Acorus has received what . . . five hundred over the past three or four years?" Dainyl was fishing, but he wanted to know.

"Six hundred. You have kindly removed close to half of them. The more arrogant and aggressive ones. It was planned that way. More important, you removed the lightcutters. In that, Samist and Brekylt went too far."

"And most of the others who fled to Acorus are in Dulka."

"About half. We may need them. I would appreciate your not reducing Dulka to rubble without first consulting me."

"I will certainly do so." That was an easy enough promise to make. Dainyl could certainly consult.

"Now that you have everything figured out, Marshal Dainyl, what do you plan?"

"In a day or so, how about a translation to Alustre to offer Alcyna the position of Submarshal in Elcien, and another courtesy call upon the eastern regional alector?"

"That is rather . . . chancy, is it not?"

"I think not. I've undertaken no great actions east of the Spine." Dainyl smiled. "I do plan to relocate Seventh Company to Tempre, though. Also, I'd rather have Alcyna in the west."

"Those are good political moves, but you're still a Myrmidon field commander at heart, Dainyl."

"Not totally. I haven't seen my wife in weeks, and I'm headed home to see her."

"Give her my best."

"She deserves that, and more."

Zelyert stiffened, momentarily, then laughed. "I'm surprised Shastylt didn't see that."

Dainyl knew exactly what the High Alector meant. "He didn't want to. The Duarches would be far better served by some alectresses than by many of their male RAs."

"Such as your wife?"

"She's certainly one, but there are others."

"You don't want to mention their names?"

"There's little point, and in these times, it could only endanger them."

"You have gotten cynical, Dainyl. Perhaps not cynical enough, but it's a start. We'll talk more after I brief Khelaryt. Say, on Tridi. In the meantime, you can make whatever changes you need at headquarters."

"I intend to." Dainyl inclined his head, then turned. He held his full shields until he was out of the Hall of Justice and in the duty coach, headed back to Myrmidon headquarters. He wished he were headed home, but Lystrana wouldn't be there, not until evening, and he had more than a few loose ends to resolve.

Marshal of Myrmidons. Lystrana would be both pleased and appalled at how matters had turned out, and his mother would be delighted. He'd let Alyra find out from others. She'd always valued their reaction more than her son's.

Who could fill Dhenyr's billet? And what of Majer Mykel? Those were just the first of his problems. . . .

96

By Londi midafternoon, Mykel had managed to get himself shaved, bathed, and dressed in a uniform Fabrytal had sent, except for his outer tunic. He sat in a shaded corner of the small inner courtyard by himself, watching the finches and the lazulis in the dwarf pear trees that flanked the small herb garden. The blistered and dying skin was peeling off his burned arm, and at times, the combination of pain and itching made him want to claw it. He did not, not when even brushing the area hurt.

The cushioned rattan chair was comfortable, and the silent serving girl Ruela kept the mug of ale filled. In his lap was a geography book that he had found on the bed-side table, presumably placed there by Rachyla, or at her direction. He had read close to fifty pages, although he had been forced to close his eyes at times to rest. He had found the section about the ancient aqueducts to Dereka fascinating, as well as the description of the sheer six-thousand-yard-high cliffs that bordered the Aerlal Plateau on all sides.

He looked up at the silver-green sky, catching sight of Asterta, washed out by the brilliance of the sun. The moon of the warrior goddess—yet it reminded him of Rachyla, a warrior goddess in her own way. He had not seen her all day, except very briefly when she had stepped into his bedchamber and noted that Fabrytal had dis-patched some personal items to facilitate his recovery, in-cluding a new Cadmian belt buckle and a replacement sabre. She'd placed them on the side table and left before he could even ask her to stay.

He started to pick up the book once more when he glimpsed a figure across the herb garden—Rachyla. He set the book down and watched as she neared. Today, she wore trousers and a shirt of a pale tan, with a black vest, trimmed in a deep green that matched and brought out the intensity of her eyes.

"Majer, you are recovering."

"Good food, good care, and good surroundings." He smiled. "Would you sit, please, at least for a moment?"

"For a moment." She settled into the chair set in the shade at an angle to the one where Mykel sat. "Herisha is at the market, now that matters are returning to a less un-certain state, and Amaryk is at Gheort's. He is the heir-second to Seltyr Asadyl, and his sister is said to be quite beautiful."

"I am perceived as unsuitable company for a chatelaine, then."

"Most unsuitable." Her voice remained cool, although Mykel still heard musicality within it. "A Cadmian majer, the son of a master tiler? Totally unsuitable."

"Even for a chatelaine who is otherwise unmarriageable?"

"Majer . . . you presume." She started to rise from the chair.

"I apologize. Please do not go."

After a moment, her hands released their hold on the arms of the chair, and she let herself settle once more.

"I can see that I am most unsuitable for you in any permanent way," Mykel said carefully. "I do not see why that precludes your talking to me."

"Women may be swayed by the words of a handsome man, especially one who is as dashing and as unprincipled as, shall I say, a Cadmian officer." A faint smile appeared and vanished. "Many of the young women in Southgate with whom you danced, Majer, would have wished more than a dance. This was not lost on Elbaryk. I was sent here because Amaryk requires two chatelaines, because Elbaryk judged you might be more likely to return to Southgate than come to Tempre, and because he could do no less and retain his honor."

"And he would certainly do no more?"

"Majer."

"I apologize." Mykel had never apologized so often and so quickly. He took refuge in a sip from the mug of ale. "The geography book you left or had left for me is interesting."

"How much have you read?"

"Fifty pages, a little more. I couldn't help wondering about the ancient aqueducts in Dereka. They must be very old. I'd like to see them, I think."

"Perhaps you will. They might send you there."

"I doubt it. The regiment in Elcien—it's in Northa, re-

ally, but it sounds better to say our headquarters is in
Elcien—we're deployed where there's trouble. Then we
come back to headquarters for replacements and retraining, and after that they send us out again. We might go to
Dereka, but they've never had any trouble. There usually
isn't in places where Myrmidons are stationed."

"With their weapons, I imagine not. How long do you
think the Myrmidon company will remain here?"

"Until the trouble is over. Have any alectors returned to
the administration building?" Mykel felt isolated and out
of touch.

"Some. Amaryk said that there is an acting regional
administrator appointed by the Duarches. Your Cadmians
do not guard the building now."

"I'm not surprised." How much should he say? How
much had he said that he didn't recall? "We ended up
shooting a few of the alectors who rebelled."

"You are fortunate they did not turn the pteridons
upon you."

"We had re-taken the building long before they returned, and no one knew what we had done except for
those in the battalion. Since the alectors' bodies turn to
dust soon after they die, there was no evidence of how
they died."

"Does that not tell you they are not of this world?"

"It does, and you were right about that. I should have listened more closely when you suggested that in Dramur."

Rachyla laughed, mirthlessly. "You should be
wounded more often, Majer."

*To hear you laugh, even coolly, it would almost be
worth that.* "That is a high price to pay for a compliment
from you. Still . . ."

"You can be so gallant when you are not killing people."
Her voice was not quite so hard as it might have been.

"I wouldn't have thought you disapproved of my
killing alectors."

"I do not, but they are not people. They are arrogant
beasts."

"I think, Lady Rachyla, that arrogance comes with un-bridled power. I have seen many who are not alectors who are arrogant. I have not seen enough alectors to know if any of them are not arrogant."

"You reproach me . . . after we have cared for you."

"I do not believe I ever said anything about your being arrogant," Mykel replied.

For a time, Rachyla was silent. "You did not."

"Perhaps I should go. I have intruded upon your hospitality more than I intended. I would not wish to impose more."

"Majer. You need at least one more night of undisturbed sleep. I would not have you leave and suffer injury because you departed too soon." Rachyla rose and stood beside the chair, her long and graceful fingers resting on the rattan of the back. "Besides, the carriage will not be available until the morning."

Mykel inclined his head to her. "I defer to your judgment, Lady."

"I am not a Lady. Nor will I ever be one, and I would suggest that you not refer to me in that fashion."

"Then I will not, Chatelaine. Again, I must thank you for your kindness and care." Mykel meant the words, and not with any sarcasm. He had his doubts about whether he would be recovering at all, particularly given the submarshal's concerns and Mykel's own growing Talent, had he not been under Rachyla's protection.

Rachyla looked at him, then shook her head. "You grant me too much, Majer." Abruptly, she turned and walked away.

Mykel watched her. He could not sense what she felt, but he had to wonder how much sadness she held within. But there was nothing he could do, for all too many reasons.

97

Dainyl had hoped to leave headquarters and return home relatively early to be there when Lystrana arrived, but drafting the dispatches and all the administrative details concerned with his becoming marshal took far longer than he expected. But then, he reminded himself, as he signed the last dispatch, he had neither a submarshal nor an operations chief to assist him.

He didn't like making it a habit, but he had decided to take the duty coach home.

When he walked out of headquarters, into a light rain that had followed the earlier fog, he carried his flying jacket over his arm. Rain or no rain, the afternoon was too warm and muggy to wear it. Wyalt, the junior Myrmidon in First Company, and duty driver until a pteridon became available, jumped up from where he had been sitting on the sheltered stone entryway. "Marshal, sir?"

"You can take me home, if you would, Wyalt."

"Yes, sir."

Dainyl climbed into the coach and settled onto the hard seat. It had been a long day, but he was looking forward to seeing Lystrana. He just hoped she wasn't off somewhere.

As the coach traveled eastward on the boulevard, Dainyl looked to the south, at the Palace of the Duarch. How did Khelaryt feel, knowing that the decision to move the Master Scepter to Efra had in effect already been made? Was that part of the conflict Dainyl had sensed when he had met with the Duarch—that he was being required to carry out acts and policies that were unrealistic because decisions had already been made that invalidated those policies?

Questions swirled through his thoughts, so much so that he did not even move for several moments after Wyalt brought the coach to a halt outside his house. Then he scrambled out, turning to the driver. "I appreciate the ride, Wyalt."

"My duty, sir, and my pleasure. It was an awful thing about Marshal Shastylt, sir, but it's good to see that you're marshal now, sir."

"Thank you." With a smile, Dainyl inclined his head to the driver, then turned and started up the steps to the front door. He had just put his hand out to the door lever when it opened.

Lystrana stood there, and a broad and relieved smile crossed her face. Immediately, she said, "You were hurt. I could sense it. You're still—"

"I'm fine."

"Not completely."

"I will be." He stepped forward.

Only then did her eyes go to Dainyl's collar and the new green-edged gold stars there. Her mouth opened, but she said nothing for a long moment. Finally, she asked, "You're Marshal of Myrmidons?"

"Stranger events have occurred." Dainyl found himself grinning.

She smiled quizzically. "That was your urgent mission?"

"No, that just happened this morning. As a result of the urgent mission." He stepped forward and put his arms around her, dropping the flying jacket as he did. He could feel the swell of her body against him, and sense the growing presence that was their daughter.

Their lips met.

Much later, they settled across the table from each other, wearing dressing robes. Dainyl just looked into her perfect violet eyes, without speaking.

Zistele set the serving dish on the trivet, along with the basket of bread, while Sentya placed the goblets to one side, with a pitcher of cider and a bottle of wine. Both serving girls retired to the kitchen.

"It's a simple fowl casserole. I hadn't planned on your being here for supper," Lystrana pointed out.

"This is fine. I'm just glad I'm here. I didn't have a chance to let you know in advance, and . . ."

"It wouldn't have been wise," she concluded. "I still don't know what you've been doing for the past month." She smiled. "Except that it was urgent and secret enough that you couldn't say and no one else would."

"Where should I—"

"Wherever you think makes the most sense," she replied. "I know some of what happened, but not all." She offered a sardonic laugh. "I am certain that what has been reported in Elcien is far from all of what happened." She took the serving spoon and ladled a healthy helping of the casserole and noodles onto his plate, and then an equally generous serving onto her own.

"Cider?" asked Dainyl.

"I'll have that with the meal. I might have a sip of the wine later."

Dainyl poured her cider and wine for himself, then lifted his goblet. "To us, and to Kytrana."

Lystrana lifted hers as well. "I'm glad you're home safely."

"As am I."

"I worry about that greenness around your shoulder."

"I thought it would be gone by now, but it doesn't hurt, and I feel as strong as ever."

Lystrana flushed.

After a moment, so did he. "That's not what I meant," he finally protested.

"I love to see you blush. You so seldom do."

Dainyl shook his head. What else could he do?

"You haven't told me what your urgent mission was," she prompted. "There were Myrmidons in Hyalt and Tempre, and both Rhelyn and Fahylt have suffered fatal mishaps of one sort or another."

"It all began when Majer Mykel sent a dispatch to me personally."

"The lander who might have Talent? The same one?"

"The very same one. He noted that there were alectors in the black and silver of the east in Hyalt, using lightcannon . . ." Dainyl went on to tell Lystrana everything, even about his time with the ancients, concluding with ". . . and Zelyert said that no one else could be marshal, and that everyone would deny that what had happened was anything but a local problem with Rhelyn and Fahylt."

"The Master Scepter . . . going to Efra." Lystrana tilted her head, then looked at Dainyl. "That explains so much. I was going to tell you, but you doubtless have deduced much of this already. Samist and Khelaryt meet but infrequently. My Highest says that when they do, little is said, and they cannot agree on the distribution of resources between the east and the west."

"The shadowmatches keep them from being overtly hostile to each other, or from acting directly against each other."

"They do not keep those around them from being hostile—as you have discovered," Lystrana pointed out. "What do you think will happen?"

"What do you think?" he countered.

"Things are just going to get worse here in Elcien and in Ludar. If the Duarches are not removed by the Archon, those like Zelyert and Brekylt will scheme to replace them, and they will rule without the constraints of the shadowmatches."

"It's too bad you can't be a regional administrator. There are a few vacancies," he said with a laugh.

"I'm not ruthless enough, dearest. That is what it will take to maintain order in the seasons and years immediately ahead."

"And I am?" Dainyl had his doubts about Lystrana's self-assessment. She would do what was necessary.

"You're not ruthless to everyone. You can be hard to those who are cruel and oppressive to others, and to those who scheme and plot, but you exercise judgment, and you do look for solutions that are fair to everyone. You worried about the Cadmians, and you protected them and their majer."

"How could I not? They followed my orders, and without the majer's observations and understanding and their sacrifices in stopping Fahylt's rebels, we would be in the midst of an all-out rebellion, with Myrmidons fighting Myrmidons, and the Duarches helpless to do anything. The Duarches can do little enough, it's clear, but their image restrains many. And I still worry about the majer. He knows more than he should, and he has gained more Talent. I told Fhentyl that he might not survive, but that I would deal with the majer later if he did live."

"He has been helpful to you."

"I can't help thinking about what the ancient said. Somehow, it seemed . . . unwise to follow the policy."

"Trust your feelings," Lystrana said softly.

"I have, but I worry." He paused. "I have to say that I'm also worried about the ancients. I can still recall the one, the ancient one, telling me that I or we needed to change to survive, that we could not survive without the landers and indigens and that they could not survive without us."

"We already know that."

"This was different," Dainyl said slowly. "She was saying that unless we had ties directly to this world we *would* die. It wasn't a boast, and there was an absolute sad certainty behind it. I've never felt such sadness and certainty together in anyone."

"She could be mistaken."

"She could."

"You don't believe she was, do you?"

"No, and that troubles me."

"Do you think they have that much power that they could do now what they would not when we were weak and few?"

"The weapon that Rhelyn used against me? She said that it was not an effective weapon, and that it was their responsibility. She said almost no one wounded even slightly by it survived, and yet that all my strength would not suffice to save me if I did not change."

"How are you supposed to change?"

"Somehow, I think, to break the ties to the dual scepters and the Master Scepter and tie myself directly to Acorus."

"Did she tell you how you were supposed to do this?"

"She said I knew . . . and she refused to say more." Dainyl looked down at the empty wine goblet. He hadn't remembered drinking it all.

"That troubles you more than all the unrest, and all the plotting, doesn't it?"

He nodded. "Whatever happens with all the plotting, it's something we have a chance to address. I don't get that feeling after meeting with the last ancient. They are planning something. Whenever I've mentioned the ancients to Shastylt or Zelyert, they've made some statement about how we can deal with the ancients. I told them both about the ancient sword, and it made no impression at all. None."

The two sat across the table from each other in the darkness, saying nothing.

Finally, Lystrana rose, gracefully. "We can do little more tonight, dearest. Tomorrow will bring what it will, and we will face it."

Dainyl stood, then took her hand. He squeezed it gently.

With Lystrana . . . he could face whatever lay ahead. With her.

98

Mykel studied himself in the mirror. He had to admit he still looked pale, but he couldn't stay at Amaryk's villa any longer, for all too many reasons. He'd slept well enough, although he'd awakened several times, but he hadn't seen or sensed anyone, not that he would have sensed Rachyla. Then, he had probably awakened hoping that he would see her, unlikely as that ever would have been.

Outside, two glasses past dawn, the sky was overcast, with thickening dark clouds that hinted at a storm to come. He hoped that the rain would end before the next day, so that he could begin the long ride back to Hyalt with the three companies. That might be pushing matters, given his condition, but even if he waited several days, he wouldn't think about Rachyla quite so much in the compound, not so much as when he knew she might be around any corner.

What could he do? It seemed as though she would always consider him her enemy—or the enemy of her dead father, at the very least, and he hadn't even been the one to kill the seltyr. He'd done his best to save Rachyla, and that had gained him only contempt, or so it sometimes seemed.

His fingers dropped to his belt, not quite touching the dagger of the ancients. Perhaps . . . perhaps . . .

He nodded. It was a wager of the greatest odds, but the only one left for him to play. As a mere Cadmian majer, he had few enough options, and fewer still in the future, he suspected. *Do you want to risk it?*

What risk was there, given what had already happened?

He took a deep but slow breath and looked once more at the uniformed Cadmian in the mirror, a blond and green-eyed officer with dark circles under his eyes, healing bruises splotched across his face. He tried a smile. It looked more like a grimace. Without looking at his reflection again, he turned and walked back into the bedchamber, where he clipped his scabbard to his belt.

After checking the chamber to make sure that he had not left anything, he picked up the cloth bag that Fabrytal had used to deliver his personal items and stepped out into the upper hallway. It was empty. He walked down the wide steps to the entry hallway, also empty.

Would Rachyla just let him walk out? He could not let that happen. One way or another he had to force the issue, to see her a last time. What else could he do besides what he had planned? Courtesy, kindness, interest—they had made no impression on her.

He chuckled mirthlessly, silently. She never showed whether anything made an impression on her, and because he could not sense what she felt, unlike others, he had no idea what lay behind her reserve, her measured antagonism. Yet, somehow . . . he could not just walk away. *The more fool you, then.*

From the half-open front door, the gray-clad retainer looked at him. "The carriage, it is ready, Majer."

"Thank you. I'll be there in a moment." He handed the retainer the bag, then turned and walked back along the main floor corridor away from the front sitting room. Rachyla had a study off a short hallway to the right. She might be there. If not, he would try the courtyard.

The door was ajar, and he could see her sitting at the writing desk. She was not writing, but looking down at the polished wood before her that held nothing, not a book, not a sheet of paper. He knocked gently, then eased the door open and took but a single step inside.

Rachyla looked up, not at all startled. "Why are you here, Majer? I thought you were leaving this morning."

"I am. I wanted to thank you again, personally, before we left for Hyalt. Might I come in?"

"I believe you already have."

"Thank you." Mykel tried to keep the irony out of his tone, but suspected he had failed.

"Why do you seek me out? You know how I feel about you."

"Because I owe you for saving my life."

"Majer, you certainly would have recovered without me."

"I might have survived the explosion and the wounds. I have some doubt as to whether I might have survived other aspects of recovering."

"What could I have done against an alector, Majer? A chatelaine? A mere woman?"

Mykel shrugged, ignoring the twinge down his left arm. "At times, I trust my feelings far more than reason. This was one of those times. Thank you."

"I will accept your thanks, Majer, nothing more. I believe the carriage is waiting." Rachyla stood and looked pointedly past Mykel in the direction of the front entry.

Mykel managed to keep from frowning or tightening his lips. He had no other options, no other choices, but to go through with it. He took one step forward. "I would prefer it were not this way—"

"Majer . . . I asked you before, and you did not answer. Why do you persist in finding ways to see me? Do you not understand that I cannot consider you a friend? That such is not possible?" Rachyla squared her shoulders, facing him head-on.

For all of her directness, Mykel felt that she was not exactly meeting his eyes—or addressing what he had to say.

"Then . . . would you consider me an enemy?" he asked.

"Perhaps as a gallant and honorable one." Her tone verged on bantering. "On a day when I am feeling charitable."

Mykel withdrew the dagger of the ancients from his belt. "Then I can return this to you, on behalf of your family."

Rachyla stiffened, but did not step back. "You would not."

"I would. You will not see what is. Neither did I. Daughter of a seltyr, would you refuse such a gift?"

She straightened, extending her left hand. "I will not. You have been my enemy since you destroyed Stylan Estate as it was."

Mykel eased the dagger and the sheath he had fashioned into her hand, careful not to directly touch her fingers. Then he stepped back. "You have accepted this dagger of your own free will, Rachyla of Stylan and of Tempre. It is yours." He inclined his head for a moment. "To good-hearted and noble enemies, Lady Rachyla."

Then he turned, walking quickly, but not too quickly, to the entry foyer. He did not look back, but kept his eyes on the half-open door that would all too soon close behind him.

If Rachyla had made her choice, then he had made his, the only one he as a Cadmian could—a Cadmian's choice.